Instructor's Manual

Fiction 100
An Anthology of Short Stories
Ninth Edition

James H. Pickering
University of Houston

Prentice Hall
Upper Saddle River, New Jersey 07458

© 2001 by PRENTICE-HALL, INC.
PEARSON EDUCATION
Upper Saddle River, New Jersey 07458

ISBN 0-13-032652-6
Printed in the United States of America

Contents

V.   Bibliography of Short Fiction Criticism   217

Preface to the Ninth Edition

We have never found one way to completely and satisfactorily teach literature and probably never will. Literature itself is too explosive. Our critical and pedagogical techniques are too susceptible to the vagaries of taste. The times continually develop new needs and make new requirements upon us. It would be naive, therefore, to suppose that we shall ever reach complete and lasting agreement on how we should proceed.[1]

John Gerber of the University of Iowa was an outstanding teacher-scholar, who well understood the dynamic nature of literature and the boundless creativity of the men and women who teach it. I came across Gerber's wise comments way back in 1971 at the time I was preparing the first edition of this manual. A quarter century and nine editions later, there is more reason than ever to believe in the correctness of Professor Gerber's observations. And I believe now as I believed then that what is true about studying and teaching literature is equally true of manuals accompanying literature textbooks. The most helpful are the least directive and intrusive: those that deemphasise answers, however tentatively delivered, in favor of questions, strategies, and resources that instructors can use, adapt, or simply disregard as they see fit. It is this philosophy that has guided the putting together of this manual over the years. I feel much the same, by the way, about the *Reader's Guide to the Short Story* which has for several editions come shrink-wrapped with the text. Use it as you will, though I would note that the section "Writing on the Short Story" has with the current iteration been brought into the age of the Internet.

The *Instructor's Manual* for *Fiction 100* is divided into five sections. Section I explores the three most frequently used approaches to short fiction, the analytical, the thematic, and the historical; discusses the relative merits and weaknesses of each approach; and offers a series of alternative tables of contents. Section II explores student responses to literature—both cognitive and affective—and sets forth a number of activities that have proven effective for encouraging such responses in the classroom. Section III acknowledges what is now obvious: the electronic age has invaded our lives and our classrooms. In this section I have tried to indicate some of the current resources that are out there on the Internet that instructors can make use of in teaching *Fiction 100*. Section IV is far more traditional. It consists of a series of brief critical commentaries on the stories themselves. These discussions can perhaps best be used in connection with Section V, a bibliography of short fiction criticism. In updating the bibliographical entries for successive editions of *Fiction 100*, I have been consistently amazed by how the body of short fiction criticism has grown. The manual for the first edition of 1974 contained 627 separate bibliographical entries. That number has now grown to over 4,000 in the current edition, a certain sign that the study of short fiction is most certainly alive and well in our colleges and universities.

I should also like to thank the many colleagues from across the country and abroad who have written or, in recent years, e-mailed me about *Fiction 100* and its *Instructor's Manual*

---

[1]John C. Gerber, "Literature—Our Untamable Discipline," *College English*, XXVIII (February 1967), 350.

and made suggestions towards their improvement. Editing and writing are solitary, often lonely, occupations and your help and advice has been greatly appreciated. Many of you, including a number of former students, have long-since become friends.

James H. Pickering
Houston, Texas

I
Approaches to the Short Story

A. The Elements of Fiction: The Analytical Approach to the Short Story

Perhaps the most frequently used method for teaching a college course in the short story is the analytical one, which attempts to increase appreciation and understanding inductively by introducing the student to the basic elements of fiction. The great popularity of this approach among college teachers dates from about 1943, the year that Cleanth Brooks and Robert Penn Warren published the first edition of their now-classic textbook anthology *Understanding Fiction*. In the open "Letter to the Teacher" which prefaced the book, the two authors stated their rationale quite clearly: "It seems to us that the student may best come to understand a given piece of fiction by understanding the functions of the various elements which go to make up fiction and by understanding their relationships to each other in the whole construct."[1]

The claims of such an approach are, of course, no longer revolutionary, nor have they gone, especially in recent years, unchallenged, at least in their strictest applications. Nonetheless the analytical approach, with its clear emphasis upon the integrity of the literary work, continues to have much to recommend it. To begin with, it does provide what all college English teachers would probably agree is absolutely essential for the formal study of literature: a method of analysis and a basic set of conceptual tools in the form of a critical vocabulary, tools that once mastered can be transferred from one text to another. Second, by insisting upon close, careful reading the analytical approach encourages the student to sharpen and clarify his or her own subjective response to literature and equips the student with a language to articulate that response. Third, the analytical approach presents the teacher with a workable, if not always easy, method for organizing and structuring a beginning course in the short story.

No one but the most hardened formalist would argue today that dividing the study of fiction into such components as plot, setting, character, point of view, etc., is entirely satisfactory. The definitions of such terms themselves, however well formulated in the abstract, often present difficulties in their application to a given story. They remain, after all, generalizations, which require constant retesting and refinement, a fact that students frequently forget or do not see. Then, too, when applied too schematically, as in the heyday of the New Criticism, the analytical approach sometimes has the unhappy effect of making literary criticism and not literature the actual subject of study. (Critical analysis, we must always remember, is a means to an end—not an end in itself.) And finally, the analytical approach, by positing the authority of literature within the work itself, does have the ten-

---

[1] *Understanding Fiction*, of course, was an attempt to do for fiction what I. A. Richards and his associates had previously done for the study of poetry. It is also well to remember, as Monroe Spears notes, that "In historical terms, the New Criticism is related to larger cultural developments: to the increase of literacy and the spread of education in general, and specifically to the rise of English literature as a university subject and the consequent need to devise effective ways of teaching it. These phenomena called for a pedagogy that would concentrate on reading." Monroe K. Spears, *Dionysus and the City: Modernism in Twentieth Century Poetry* (New York, 1970), pp. 197-198.

dency to ignore or minimize other areas proper to literary study and discussion, especially the relationship of literature to human experience in general and to the student's own experience in particular. Fortunately, such dangers, though real enough, are not necessarily fatal, and, once recognized, can be counteracted in the classroom by an alert teacher. On balance, the analytical approach remains an attractive and effective method for guiding the student into and through a first college course in the short story.

Fortunately, too, most instructors come out of graduate school well equipped to handle such an approach. What they need is not further grounding in the basic method and terminology of critical analysis, but rather concrete suggestions for making this approach "work" in the classroom setting. For such suggestions I refer the reader to the section of this manual entitled "Literature and Student Response: Activities for the Classroom."

In pursuing the analytical approach, the instructor will invariably have to meet (and perhaps should go out of his or her way to meet, if the occasion does not naturally arise early in the course) the reluctance of some college-age readers to submit to the rigors of formal literary analysis—"tearing the story apart" is the way it is usually put—in preference to simply *reading and enjoying* literature. Handling this question with tact and good humor are admittedly difficult, and there are no surefire ways to meet it when it does arise. Nevertheless, such a challenge must be respected, no matter how infuriating it may be to those who have committed their professional lives to the assumption that literature can, in fact, be studied in a formal, systematic way. The challenge must be respected even when the teacher has every reason to suspect that it arises out of the questioner's intellectual laziness, because it often mirrors exactly the inarticulated doubts and perplexities of students whose commitment to literature is serious and real. By the end of the course, hopefully well before, most students can be made to see that pleasure and enjoyment are not antithethical to critical appreciation and understanding but rather dependent upon them, and that both are actually heightened by the process of careful reading, disciplined understanding, and the capacity to render discriminating judgments.

The suggested table of contents, which follows this discussion, divides the stories in *Fiction 100* into eight categories: Plot, Character, and Setting (the three elements that create a fictional story) followed by Point of View, Theme, Symbol and Allegory, Style and Tone (those that govern an author's handling of the story), and an omnibus category that I have chosen to call Humor, Satire, and Popular Fiction. The last category, of course, differs in kind from the preceding eight. It is included here to provide the explicit occasion for studying the kinds of stories that seem to have great appeal for the current generation of college-age readers, the kinds of stories that my experience tells me they are most likely to pick up and read on their own. The first seven categories, those focusing on technique, each contain between twelve and forty-eight stories; the eighth contains twenty-three. Within each category I have attempted to arrange the stories according to their approximate degree of difficulty.

Some teachers, especially the more experienced ones, may well take issue with my categorization. Flannery O'Connor's "A Good Man Is Hard to Find," included here under Theme, might just as easily and defensibly be studied under the rubric of Plot, Setting, Character, Point of View, or Symbol. In the same way, Joseph Conrad's "The Secret Sharer," which I have listed under Plot, might also be listed under Character, Theme, Point of View, and Symbol. The same kind of thing, I hasten to add, is true to a greater or lesser extent with many of the stories in *Fiction 100*. My response is to urge instructors to construct their own categories and establish their own syllabuses to suit the needs of their students and the predilections of their taste.

The first and most important task that the instructor who chooses the analytical approach will have in putting *Fiction 100* into actual classroom use is to develop in his or her students the critical vocabulary that is essential if productive dialogue and communication are to take place. This requires, above all, patience, time, energy, and plain hard work. Fortunately, most teachers will discover that their students bring with them from their high school English courses at least a rudimentary knowledge of such terms as plot, character, theme, and point of view. Very often, in fact, today's beginning college course in fiction differs from its high school counterparts not so much in kind as in level of sophistication. Students possess a good deal of basic information about fiction, even if imperfectly grasped and understood, upon which the college teacher can erect the superstructure of his or her own course.

In order to help students develop a working knowledge of the metalanguage of fiction and the principles of the short story, I have with this edition expanded the glossary of literary terms into a handbook on the short story.

One final point. When the analytical approach flounders, when classroom discussion becomes stale and academic, it is very often because we teachers allow our students to regard the elements of fiction as "things" with an objective existence of their own. What students need to see, indeed what we must make them see, is that these elements of fiction are labels, convenient abstractions arising out of our needs as critics to grasp and describe our experience with a given literary text. They are, in this sense, no more "real" than atoms and protons are. Physicist Werner Heisenberg puts the case well in describing what has happened to science in our own century.

> We can no longer speak of the behavior of the particle independently of the process of observation....When we speak of the picture of nature in the exact science of our age, we do not mean a picture of nature so much as a *picture of our relationships with nature*.[2]

So too with the student of literature embarking on the task of critical analysis. Symbols, for example, are not ingredients put into the work by the author, but the name we give to the activity we choose to engage in while reading and studying his or her work. We do not "find" symbols; we read symbolically. We do so partly, to be sure, because of the nature of the work itself, but partly—and this is the important thing—because of certain notions we hold as students and teachers about the way in which literature can be profitably approached and studied. The concept of the elements of fiction, like the Periodic Table of Chemical Elements, offers a more or less constant system of classification. To classify, to regard fiction as an object that can be taken apart and then put back together, is one way to approach and participate in the work of literature; but it is not the only way. Once students grasp this truth, literature at once becomes dynamic, alive, and "available," and students are ready to respond to literature through the kinds of activities suggested in Section II.

Teaching the Elements of Fiction:
Questions to Ask and Answer

PLOT

1. What is the conflict (or conflicts) on which the plot turns? Is it external, internal, or some combination of the two?
2. What are the chief episodes or incidents that make up the plot? Is its development strictly chronological, or is the chronology rearranged in some way?
3. Compare the plot's beginning and end. What essential changes have taken place?
4. Describe the plot in terms of its exposition, complication, crisis, falling action, and resolution.

---

[2]Werner Heisenberg, "Non-Objective Science and Uncertainty," in *The Modern Tradition: Backgrounds of Modern Literature*, Richard Ellmann and Charles Feidelson, Jr., eds. (New York, 1965), p. 446.

5. Is the plot unified? Do the individual episodes logically relate to one another?
6. Is the ending appropriate to and consistent with the rest of the plot?

CHARACTER

1. Who is the protagonist of the story and who (or what) is the antagonist? Describe the major traits and qualities of each.
2. What is the function of the story's minor characters?
3. Identify the characters in terms of whether they are flat or round, dynamic or static.
4. What methods does the author employ to establish and reveal the characters? Are the methods primarily of showing or of telling?
5. Are the actions of the characters properly motivated and consistent?
6. Are the characters finally credible and interesting?

SETTING

1. What is the story's setting in space and time?
2. How does the author go about establishing setting? Does the author want the reader to see or feel the setting; or does the author want the reader both to see and feel it? What details of the setting does the author isolate and describe?
3. Is the setting important? If so what is its function? Is it used to reveal, reinforce, or influence character, plot, or theme?
4. Is the setting an appropriate one?

POINT OF VIEW

1. What is the point of view? Is the point of view consistent throughout the story or does it shift in some way?
2. Where does the narrator stand in relation to the work? Where does the reader stand?
3. To what sources of knowledge or information does the point of view give the reader access? What sources of knowledge or information does it serve to conceal?
4. If the story is told from the point of view of one of the characters, is the narrator reliable? Does his or her personality, character, or intellect affect an ability to interpret the events or the other characters correctly?
5. Given the author's purposes, is the chosen point of view an appropriate and effective one?
6. How would the story be different if told from another point of view?

THEME

1. Does the story have a theme? Is it stated or implied?
2. What generalization(s) or statement(s) about life or human experience does the story make?
3. What elements of the story contribute most heavily to the formulation of the theme?
4. Does the theme emerge organically and naturally, or does the author seem to force the theme upon the work?
5. What is the value or significance of the story's theme? Is it topical or universal in its application?

SYMBOL AND ALLEGORY

1. What symbols or patterns of symbolism (or allegory) are present in the story? Are the symbols traditional, original, or private?
2. What aspects of the story (e.g., theme, setting, plot, characterization) does the symbolism (allegory) serve to explain, clarify, or reinforce?
3. Does the author's use of symbolism (allegory) seem contrived or forced in any way, or does it arise naturally out of the interplay of the story's major elements?

STYLE AND TONE

1. Describe the author's diction. Is the language concrete or abstract, formal or informal, literal or figurative? What parts of speech occur most often?
2. What use does the author make of imagery; figurative devices (simile, metaphor, personification); patterns of rhythm and sound (alliteration, assonance, consonance, onomatopoeia); repetition; allusion?
3. Are the sentences predominantly long or short; simple, compound, or complex; loose, periodic, or balanced?
4. Describe the author's tone. Is it, for example, sympathetic, detached, condescending, serious, humorous, or ironic? How is the tone established and revealed?
5. What kind(s) of irony does the author use: verbal irony, irony of situation, dramatic irony? What purpose(s) does the irony serve?
6. What are the distinctive characteristics of the author's style? In what ways is the style appropriate to the work's subject and theme?

HUMOR, SATIRE, AND POPULAR FICTION

Humor

1. What kind of humor does the author employ? (Is it gentle and sympathetic, witty and sophisticated, or cruel and derisive?)
2. How does the author go about achieving humor? Is it primarily through subject matter, plot, characterization, style, or tone, or through some combination of the preceding?
3. Is the evocation of humor central to the author's purpose, or is it a natural by-product of the story itself?

Satire

4. What does the author set out to satirize?
5. What is the implied standard of behavior or set of values that lie behind the satire?
6. Is the satire incidental or is it central to the authors purpose?
7. Is the satire effective?

Fantasy (including Science Fiction)

8. What aspects of or assumptions about the conventional (real) world does the story set aside or extend? What kinds of concessions does the author ask the reader to make?
9. Is its purpose simply harmless escape or enjoyment, or is fantasy employed to make a purposeful statement of some kind?

Detective Fiction

10. According to John Cawelti, the pattern of action of the detective story has "six main phases" though they do not always "appear in sequence and are sometimes collapsed into each other: (a) introduction of the detective; (b) crime and clues; (c) investigation; (d) announcement of the solution; (e) explanation of the solution; (f) dénouement." The "classical detective story," Cawelti also notes, "requires four main roles: (a) the victim; (b) the criminal; (c) the detective; and (d) those threatened by the crime but incapable of solving it."[3] To what extent and in what ways do the stories in the text adhere to Cawelti's formulas?

---

[3]See Chapter 4, "The Formula of the Classical Detective Story," in John G. Cawelti, *Adventure, Mystery, and Romance: Formula Stories as Art and Popular Culture* (Chicago, 1976), pp. 80–105. See also, Dennis Porter *The Pursuit of Crime: Art and Ideology in Detective Fiction* (New Haven, 1981).

11. What traditional elements of short fiction does the detective story seem to emphasize the most? Which elements does it tend to deemphasize? Why?
12. What kind of individual is the detective hero? What are his defining characteristics? What kind of moral and social values does he seem to represent and affirm?

Western Fiction[4]

13. What is the role or function of the story's setting in time and space? What influence does it have on character and action?
14. What characteristics define the hero and the villain? What traditional American values and attitudes does each represent, affirm, or deny?
15. What traditional elements of short fiction does the western story seem to emphasize most? Which elements does it tend to deemphasize? Why?

Teaching the Elements of Fiction: Suggested Table of Contents

PLOT

1. Washington Irving, "Rip Van Winkle"
2. Richard Wright, "The Man Who was Almost a Man"
3. Art Coelho, "My First Kill"
4. Agatha Christie, "The Witness for the Prosecution"
5. Bret Harte, "Tennessee's Partner"
6. Guy de Maupassant, "The Necklace"
7. Henry James, "Four Summers"
8. Irwin Shaw, "The Girls in Their Summer Dresses"
9. Joyce Carol Oates, "Four Summers"
10. Susan Minot, "Lust"
11. Thomas Hardy, "The Three Strangers"
12. Nathaniel Hawthorne, "My Kinsman, Major Molineux"
13. James Baldwin, "Sonny's Blues"
14. Richard Ford, "Rock Springs"

CHARACTER

1. Guy de Maupassant, "Rust"
2. Kate Chopin, "Athénaïse: A Story of a Temperament"
3. Anton Chekhov, "The Darling"
4. Dorothy Parker, "Big Blonde"
5. Katherine Mansfield, "Miss Brill"
6. Bret Harte, "Tennessee's Partner"
7. Mary Wilkins Freeman, "A New England Nun"
8. Anton Chekhov, "The Lady with the Dog"
9. John Cheever, "The Country Husband"
10. Robert Phillips, "Surprise!"
11. Daniel Stern, "Brooksmith"
12. Amy Tan, "Young Girl's Wish"

---

[4]Important studies of the key elements and defining characteristics of the American western story are found in John G. Cawelti's *The Six-Gun Mystique* (Bowling Green, Ohio, 1970) and in Chapter 8, "The Western: A Look at the Evolution of a Formula," of his *Adventure, Mystery, and Romance: Formula Stories as Art and Popular Culture* (Chicago, 1976), pp. 192–259.

13. Dorothy Johnson, "The Man Who Shot Liberty Valance"
14. Elizabeth Bowen, "The Demon Lover"
15. Alice Munro, "A Real Life"
16. Bel Kaufman, "Sunday in the Park"
17. F. Scott Fitzgerald, "Winter Dreams"
18. Laurie Colwin, "A Country Wedding"
19. Alice Adams, "His Women"
20. Elizabeth Strout, "A Little Burst"
21. John Updike, "Here Come the Maples"
22. Zora Neale Hurston, "Spunk"
23. Kathryn Chetkovich, "Appetites"
24. Raymond Carver, "I Could See the Smallest Things"
25. Susan Glaspell, "A Jury of Her Peers"
26. Alice Walker, "To Hell With Dying"
27. William Faulkner, "Barn Burning"
28. Elizabeth Tallent, "No One's a Mystery"
29. Bernard Malamud, "The Magic Barrel"
30. Judy Troy, "Ten Miles West of Venus"
31. Rick Bass, "Antlers"
32. Alice Munro, "Menseteung"
33. Ivan Turgenev, "The Country Doctor"
34. William Kittredge, "We Are Not in this Together"
35. Mary Robison, "Coach"
36. Doris Lessing, "Wine"
37. Charlotte Perkins Gilman, "The Yellow Wall-Paper"
38. Tobias Wolff, "Say Yes"
39. Pam Houston, "How to Talk to a Hunter"
40. Patricia Zelver, "Love Letters"
41. Bobbie Ann Mason, "Shiloh"
42. Susan Minot, "Lust"
43. Leo Tolstoy, "The Death of Ivan Ilych"
44. Louise Erdrich, "Mauser"
45. John Steinbeck, "The Chrysanthemums"
46. Leslie Silko, "Yellow Woman"
47. Raymond Carver, "Cathedral"
48. Raymond Carver, "What We Talk About When We Talk About Love"
49. Joyce Carol Oates, "Where Are You Going, Where Have You Been?"
50. Thomas Mann, "Death in Venice"

SETTING

1. Washington Irving, "The Legend of Sleepy Hollow"
2. Edgar Allan Poe, "The Cask of Amontillado"
3. Washington Irving, "Rip Van Winkle"
4. Bret Harte, "Tennessee's Partner"
5. Kate Chopin, "The Storm"
6. Mary Wilkins Freeman, "A New England Nun"
7. Alice Munro, "Wild Swans"
8. Judy Troy, "Ten Miles West of Venus"
9. Albert Camus, "The Guest"
10. Stephen Crane, "The Blue Hotel"
11. James Baldwin, "Sonny's Blues"
12. Tobias Wolff, "Nightingale"
13. W. D. Wetherell, "Wherever That Great Heart May Be"

14. Ursula Le Guin, "Horse Camp"
15. John Irving, "Trying to Save Piggy Sneed"
16. Nadine Gordimer, "Home"
17. Joseph Conrad, "Heart of Darkness"

POINT OF VIEW

1. Sherwood Anderson, "I Want to Know Why"
2. Ambrose Bierce, "An Occurrence at Owl Creek Bridge"
3. Joyce Carol Oates, "Four Summers"
4. Ring Lardner, "Haircut"
5. Joseph Conrad, "Youth"
6. Gail Godwin, "Dream Children"
7. Anton Chekhov, "The Lady with the Dog"
8. John Irving, "Trying to Save Piggy Sneed"
9. Irwin Shaw, "The Girls in Their Summer Dresses"
10. Sandra Cisneros, "The House on Mango Street"
11. Jo Sapp, "Nadine at 35: A Synopsis"
12. Alice Adams, "His Women"
13. Henry James, "Four Meetings"
14. Daniel Stern, "Brooksmith"
15. Henry James, "The Real Thing"
16. John Updike, "Separating"
17. John Updike, "Here Come the Maples"
18. William Carlos Williams, "The Use of Force"
19. Ernest Hemingway, "Indian Camp"
20. Liza Wieland, "The Columbus School for Girls"
21. William Faulkner, "A Rose for Emily"
22. Eudora Welty, "Why I Live at the P.O."
23. Raymond Carver, "I Could See the Smallest Things"
24. Nikolai Gogol, "The Overcoat"
25. Herman Melville, "Bartleby the Scrivener"
26. Elizabeth Tallent, "No One's a Mystery"
27. Tillie Olsen, "I Stand Here Ironing"
28. Toni Cade Bambara, "The Lesson"
29. W. D. Wetherell, "Wherever That Great Heart May Be"
26. Thomas Mann, "Death in Venice"

THEME

1. Kay Boyle, "Astronomer's Wife"
2. Joseph Conrad, "Youth"
3. Sarah Orne Jewett, "A White Heron"
4. Edgar Allan Poe, "The Cask of Amontillado"
5. Samuel L. Clemens, "The Man That Corrupted Hadleyburg"
6. Charlotte Perkins Gilman, "If I Were a Man"
7. Art Coelho, "My First Kill"
8. John Updike, "Separating"
9. Frank O'Connor, "Guests of the Nation"
10. Jo Sapp, "Nadine at 35: A Synopsis"
11. Garrison Keillor, "The Tip-Top Club"
12. W. P. Kinsella, "Shoeless Joe Jackson Comes to Iowa"
13. Mary Grimm, "We"
14. Ralph Ellison, "King of the Bingo Game"
15. Flannery O'Connor, "A Good Man Is Hard to Find"

16. Isaac Bashevis Singer, "Gimpel the Fool"
17. Elizabeth Winthrop, "The Golden Darters"
18. Saul Bellow, "Looking for Mr. Green"
19. Rick Bass, "Antlers"
20. Tillie Olsen, "I Stand Here Ironing"
21. Joy Williams, "Taking Care"
22. Thomas Mann, "Death in Venice"

SYMBOL AND ALLEGORY

1. Herman Melville, "The Lightning-rod Man"
2. Ann Beattie, "Janus"
3. Nathaniel Hawthorne, "Young Goodman Brown"
4. Katherine Mansfield, "Miss Brill"
5. Katherine Anne Porter, "The Grave"
6. Shirley Jackson, "The Lottery"
7. William Kittredge, "We Are Not in This Together"
8. Gabriel García Márquez, "A Very Old Man with Enormous Wings"
9. William Carlos Williams, "The Use of Force"
10. W. P. Kinsella, "Shoeless Joe Jackson Comes to Iowa"
11. Donald Barthelme, "Cortés and Montezuma"
12. James Joyce, "The Dead"
13. Joseph Conrad, "Heart of Darkness"
14. Thomas Mann, "Death in Venice"

STYLE AND TONE

1. Samuel L. Clemens, "The Celebrated Jumping Frog of Calaveras County"
2. Edgar Allan Poe, "The Fall of the House of Usher"
3. Washington Irving, "The Legend of Sleepy Hollow"
4. Kate Chopin, "The Story of an Hour"
5. James Joyce, "Araby"
6. Joy Williams, "Taking Care"
7. Katherine Mansfield, "Her First Ball"
8. William Faulkner, "Dry September"
9. Donald Barthelme, "Cortés and Montezuma"
10. Ring Lardner, "Haircut"
11. Henry James, "The Real Thing"
12. Sandra Cisneros, "The House on Mango Street"
13. Garrison Keillor, "The Tip-Top Club"
14. Ernest Hemingway, "Hills Like White Elephants"
15. Ernest Hemingway, "Indian Camp"
16. Joyce Carol Oates, "Where Are You Going, Where Have You Been?"
17. Zora Neale Hurston, "Spunk"
18. Pam Houston, "How to Talk to a Hunter"
19. Toni Cade Bambara, "The Lesson"
20. Raymond Carver, "What We Talk About When We Talk About Love"
21. Raymond Carver, "I Could See the Smallest Things"

HUMOR, SATIRE, AND POPULAR FICTION

1. Donald Barthelme, "Cortés and Montezuma"
2. Ray Bradbury, "August 2002: Night Meeting"
3. Elizabeth Bowen, "The Demon Lover"
4. Agatha Christie, "The Witness for the Prosecution"
5. Samuel L. Clemens, "The Celebrated Jumping Frog of Calaveras County,"

6. Samuel L. Clemens, "The Man That Corrupted Hadleyburg"
7. Stephen Crane, "The Bride Comes to Yellow Sky"
8. Arthur Conan Doyle, "A Scandal in Bohemia"
9. Carlos Fuentes, "Aura"
10. Gabriel García Márquez, "A Very Old Man with Enormous Wings"
11. Washington Irving, "The Legend of Sleepy Hollow"
12. Washington Irving, "Rip Van Winkle"
13. Dorothy Johnson, "The Man Who Shot Liberty Valance"
14. Garrison Keillor, "The Tip-Top Club"
15. Garrison Keillor, "What Did We Do Wrong?"
16. Stephen King, "The Man in the Black Suit"
17. Rudyard Kipling, "They"
18. Ring Lardner, "Haircut"
19. Herman Melville, "The Lightning-rod Man"
20. Robert Phillips, "Surprise!"
21. John Updike, "A&P"
22. Eudora Welty, "Why I Live at the P.O."
23. Tobias Wolff, "Nightingale"

B. The Thematic Approach to the Short Story

The thematic approach to short fiction begins with the question, "What is the story about?" It begins, that is, by asking the reader to focus his or her attention on the human experience evidenced in and explored by the story itself and on the ideas and values that the story raises, affirms, or calls into question. The thematic approach is an admission that literature, whatever else it may be, is a way of knowing about life. It asserts that literature exists not in a vacuum but in a relationship to the larger world of shared human experience, which it seeks to reflect and illuminate, though its presentation need not be realistic or literal in the transcription.

For the traditional college-age reader, the appeal of shared experience is an especially compelling one. Perhaps at no other time during his or her adult life will the interest in human values and ideas and the way in which such values and ideas connect with his or her own widening experience be quite so great. As yet without a firmly vested set of interests to defend—a career, a family, a fixed life-style—the student may never again be quite so free, and willing, to explore the endless varieties of human experience that fiction reveals. To allow the student to study literature thematically is to encourage him or her in that exploration and quest. It is also a way to allow literature itself to exercise the humanistic function that we have long claimed for it.

The thematic approach recommends itself on at least four grounds: (1) It builds upon what the student already knows and understands by the very fact of his or her humanity, and it builds upon and appeals to interests that are already developed or are developing; (2) It lends itself to kinds of comparison and contrast not possible with other approaches; (3) It generates exciting class discussions and a wide variety of potential writing assignments; and (4) It has immediate appeal for students who have no prior deep commitment to literature as a form of art.

There are limitations and dangers, of course, the chief of which is its tendency to divert attention away from the individual literary work by focusing solely on the ideas or features that can be extracted from it. Teachers must take considerable pains to point out that the thematic approach does not lessen the need to understand the inner construction of a given story and the author's special mastery of the fictional techniques at his or her disposal. Students must come to see that while all works of art exist in a collateral relationship with the larger world of universal human experience, they also, somewhat paradoxically, are unique and have a self-contained, independent existence of their own that has an equally important claim on the reader's attention and understanding. In the final analysis, it is this inner coherence alone that tells us just how different two stories, apparently so alike in theme and idea, really are.

The establishment of thematic categories is not as simple a task as it might appear. Like all methods of categorization it is far from foolproof, especially when dealing with as heterogeneous a collection of short stories as those in *Fiction 100*. Thematic labeling is in many respects an a priori exercise in interpretation. As much, it risks the setting up of expectations and assumptions about a given story, which may in the end prove incorrect. It may also encourage simplistic response. Further, since stories very frequently have more than one theme, such labeling may well do the story under consideration an inherent injustice by violating the complexity of the author's original vision and the story's final achievement. To simplify is not always to enlighten, which is another way of saying that the best stories have a most mischievous way of eluding our best attempts to pin them down.

Fiction 100 contains a multiplicity of themes, some capable of fairly easy statement, some not. As a collection, it can be broken down into a wide variety of thematic categories. Those that follow—and they are, I think, largely self-explanatory—are, therefore, suggestive only. Other, perhaps better, categories will doubtless suggest themselves to those who use this book. For my own part, I have attempted to delineate only the larger, more obvious divisions into which the bulk of the stories seem naturally to fall.

One suggestion I would make to the teacher choosing the thematic approach is that he or she deliberately arrange the syllabus so as to juxtapose older and more recent stories. Students, quite understandably, tend to react most strongly to modern and contemporary stories that present a world whose experiences, to some extent at least, they already share. Juxtaposition can do much, therefore, to introduce students to what is timeless in the human experience and by so doing help free them from the kind of parochialism of which all of us are too often guilty.

The Thematic Approach
Suggested Table of Contents

AGGRESSION AND VIOLENCE

ALIENATION AND INVOLVEMENT

1. James Baldwin, "Sonny's Blues"
2. Raymond Carver, "Cathedral"
3. Ralph Ellison, "King of the Bingo Game"
4. Nathaniel Hawthorne, "Young Goodman Brown"
5. Robert Hever, "Mr. Stanfield's Memo"
6. D. H. Lawrence "The Horse-Dealer's Daughter"
7. Thomas Mann, "Death in Venice"
8. Herman Melville, "Bartleby the Scrivener"
9. Tillie Olsen, "I Stand Here Ironing"
10. Robert Phillips, "Surprise!"

ART AND THE ARTIST

1. James Baldwin, "Sonny's Blues"
2. Raymond Carver, "Cathedral"
3. Samuel L. Clemens, "The Celebrated Jumping Frog of Calaveras County
4. John Irving, "Trying to Save Piggy Sneed"
5. Henry James, "Four Meetings"
6. Henry James, "The Real Thing"
7. Thomas Mann, "Death in Venice"
8. Alice Munro, "Meneseteung"
9. Liza Wieland, "The Columbus School for Girls"

BETWEEN MAN AND WOMAN

1. Alice Adams, "His Women"
2. Rick Bass, "Antlers"
3. Elizabeth Bowen, "The Demon Lover"
4. Kay Boyle, "Astronomer's Wife"
5. Raymond Carver, "What We Talk About When We Talk About Love"
6. Anton Chekhov, "The Darling"
7. Anton Chekhov, "The Lady with the Dog"
8. Kate Chopin, "Athénaïse: A Story of a Temperament"
9. Kate Chopin, "The Storm"
10. Kate Chopin, "The Story of an Hour"
11. Laurie Colwin, "A Country Wedding"
12. Arthur Conan Doyle, "A Scandal in Bohemia"
13. Louise Erdrich, "Mauser"
14. William Faulkner, "A Rose for Emily"
15. F. Scott Fitzgerald, "Winter Dreams"
16. Mary Wilkins Freeman, "A New England Nun"
17. Carlos Fuentes, "Aura"
18. Susan Glaspell, "A Jury of Her Peers"
19. Charlotte Perkins Gilman, "If I Were a Man"
20. Charlotte Perkins Gilman, "The Yellow Wall-Paper"
21. Nadine Gordimer, "Home"
22. Mary Grimm, "We"
23. Ernest Hemingway, "Hills Like White Elephants"
24. Pam Houston, "How to Talk to a Hunter"
25. Zora Neale Hurston, "Spunk"
26. Washington Irving, "The Legend of Sleepy Hollow"
27. Washington Irving, "Rip Van Winkle"
28. Henry James, "Four Meetings"

29. Bel Kaufman, "Sunday in the Park"
30. Garrison Keillor, "What Did We Do Wrong?"
31. D. H. Lawrence, "The Horse Dealer's Daughter"
32. Doris Lessing, "Wine"
33. Bernard Malamud, "The Magic Barrel"
34. Katherine Mansfield, "Her First Ball"
35. Bobbie Ann Mason, "Shiloh"
36. Susan Minot, "Lust"
37. Alice Munro, "Meneseteung"
38. Joyce Carol Oates, "Four Summers"
39. Joyce Carol Oates, "Where Are You Going, Where Have You Been?"
40. Dorothy Parker, "Big Blonde"
41. Jo Sapp, "Nadine at 35: A Synopsis"
42. Elizabeth Strout, "A Little Burst"
43. Leslie Silko, "Yellow Woman"
44. John Steinbeck, "The Chrysanthemums"
45. Elizabeth Tallent, "No One's a Mystery"
46. Judy Troy, "Ten Miles West of Venus"
47. Ivan Turgenev, "The Country Doctor"
48. John Updike, "Here Come the Maples"
49. John Updike, "Separating"
50. Liz Wieland, "The Columbus School for Girls"
51. Joy Williams, "Taking Care"
52. William Carlos Williams, "The Use of Force"
53. Tobias Wolff, "Say Yes"

BROTHERHOOD AND RESPONSIBILITY

1. James Baldwin, "Sonny's Blues"
2. Donald Bartholme, "Cortés and Montezuma"
3. Ray Bradbury, "August 2002: Night Meeting"
4. Albert Camus, "The Guest"
5. Joseph Conrad, "The Secret Sharer"
6. Stephen Crane, "The Blue Hotel"
7. William Faulkner, "Dry September"
8. Bret Harte, "Tennessee's Partner"
9. Dorothy Johnson "The Man Who Shot Liberty Valance"
10. Herman Melville, "Bartleby the Scrivener"
11. Frank O'Connor, "Guests of the Nation"
12. Daniel Stern, "Brooksmith"
13. W. D. Wetherell, "Wherever That Great Heart May Be"

INITIATION AND DISCOVERY

1. Sherwood Anderson, "I Want to Know Why"
2. Toni Cade Bambara, "The Lesson"
3. Kathryn Chetkovich, "Appetites"
4. Art Coelho, "My First Kill"
5. Raymond Carver, "Cathedral"
6. Joseph Conrad, "Heart of Darkness"
7. Joseph Conrad, "The Secret Sharer"
8. Joseph Conrad, "Youth"
9. William Faulkner, "Barn Burning"
10. F. Scott Fitzgerald, "Winter Dreams"
11. Mary Grimm, "We"

12. Nathaniel Hawthorne, "My Kinsman, Major Molineux"
13. Nathaniel Hawthorne, "Young Goodman Brown"
14. Ernest Hemingway, "Indian Camp"
15. Washington Irving, "The Legend of Sleepy Hollow"
16. Henry James, "Four Meetings"
17. Sarah Orne Jewett, "A White Heron"
18. James Joyce "Araby"
19. James Joyce, "The Dead"
20. Stephen King, "The Man in the Black Suit"
21. W. P. Kinsella, "Shoeless Joe Jackson Comes to Iowa"
22. Ursula Le Guin, "Horse Camp"
23. Bernard Malamud, "The Magic Barrel"
24. Katherine Mansfield, "Her First Ball"
25. Katherine Mansfield, "Miss Brill"
26. Susan Minot, "Lust"
27. Joyce Carol Oates, "Four Summers"
28. Joyce Carol Oates, "Where Are You Going, Where Have You Been?"
29. Frank O'Connor, "Guests of the Nation"
30. Katherine Anne Porter, "The Grave"
31. Leslie Silko, "Yellow Woman"
32. Daniel Stern, "Brooksmith"
33. Elizabeth Tallent, "No One's a Mystery"
34. Amy Tan, "Young Girl's Wish"
35. John Updike "A&P"
36. W. D. Wetherell, "Wherever That Great Heart May Be"
37. Liza Wieland, "The Columbus School for Girls"
38. Elizabeth Winthrop, "The Golden Darters"
39. Tobias Wolff, "Nightingale"
40. Richard Wright, "The Man Who Was Almost a Man"

THE NATURE OF MAN

1. Raymond Carver, "I Could See the Smallest Things"
2. Samuel L. Clemens, "The Celebrated Jumping Frog of Calaveras County"
3. Samuel L. Clemens, "The Man That Corrupted Hadleyburg"
4. Joseph Conrad, "Heart of Darkness"
5. William Faulkner, "Barn Burning"
6. Thomas Mann, "Death in Venice"
7. Gabriel García Márquez, "A Very Old Man with Enormous Wings"
8. Bret Harte, "Tennessee's Partner"
9. Nathaniel Hawthorne, "Young Goodman Brown"
10. Shirley Jackson, "The Lottery"
11. Dorothy Johnson, "The Man Who Shot Liberty Valance"
12. Garrison Keillor, "The Tip-Top Club"
13. Ring Lardner, "Haircut"
14. Jack London, "To Build a Fire"
15. Bernard Malamud, "The Magic Barrel"
16. Herman Melville, "Bartleby the Scrivener"
17. Herman Melville, "The Lightning-rod Man"
18. Flannery O'Connor, "A Good Man Is Hard to Find"
19. Edgar Allan Poe, "The Cask of Amontillado"
20. Isaac Bashevis Singer, "Gimpel the Fool"
21. W. D. Wetherell, "Wherever That Great Heart May Be"
22. Patricia Zelver, "Love Letters"

THE REALITY OF DEATH

1. Rick Bass, "Antlers"
2. Ambrose Bierce, "An Occurrence at Owl Creek Bridge"
3. Elizabeth Bowen, "The Demon Lover"
4. Kate Chopin, "The Story of an Hour"
5. Art Coelho, "My First Kill"
6. William Faulkner, "Dry September"
7. Ernest Hemingway, "Indian Camp"
8. Zora Neale Hurston, "Spunk"
9. James Joyce, "The Dead"
10. Stephen King, "The Man in the Black Suit"
11. Rudyard Kipling, "They"
12. William Kittredge, "We Are Not in This Together"
13. Thomas Mann, "Death in Venice"
14. Flannery O'Connor, "A Good Man Is Hard to Find"
15. Frank O'Connor, "Guests of the Nation"
16. Edgar Allan Poe, "The Fall of the House of Usher"
17. Katherine Anne Porter, "The Grave"
18. Leo Tolstoy, "The Death of Ivan Ilych"
19. Alice Walker, "To Hell with Dying"
20. Joy Williams, "Taking Care"

SOCIETY AND THE INDIVIDUAL

1. Samuel L. Clemens, "The Man That Corrupted Hadleyburg"
2. Stephen Crane, "The Blue Hotel"
3. William Faulkner, "Barn Burning"
4. William Faulkner, "Dry September"
5. Gabriel García Márquez, "A Very Old Man with Enormous Wings"
6. Nikolai Gogol, "The Overcoat"
7. Nadine Gordimer, "Home"
8. Thomas Hardy, "The Three Strangers"
9. Washington Irving, "The Legend of Sleepy Hollow"
10. Washington Irving, "Rip Van Winkle"
11. Shirley Jackson, "The Lottery"
12. Thomas Mann "Death in Venice"
13. Katherine Mansfield, "Miss Brill"
14. Herman Melville, "Bartleby the Scrivener"
15. Herman Melville, "The Lightning-rod Man"

C. The Historical Approach to the Short Story

I

The short story as we know it today—that is, the short story as a consciously organized, highly unified piece of literary craftsmanship—is of comparatively recent origin. There have always been "stories" of course, examples of short fiction—simple, straightforward narratives in prose or verse—are to be found in the folktales, ballads, fables, myths, and legends of all nations and all cultures. At first they were circulated and passed on as part of oral tradition; later they were written down, and with the advent of printing, published and sold. Stories constitute an important part of our cultural heritage. They have served our need to share knowledge and experience, to teach, to amuse and delight, and have been told and written down with a greater or lesser degree of sophistication depending on the maturity of the audience and, of course, the maturity of the storyteller. Such stories go by many names—tales, sketches, legends, parables, or simply anecdotes—but all provide recognizable antecedents for the modern short story.

The short story and the novel as independent and self-conscious literary genres trace their beginnings to eighteenth-century England and to a number of identifiable and far-reaching changes taking place within English society itself. During the first decades of the eighteenth century the forces unleashed by capitalism and the rise of commerce and manufacturing had created new and ever-widening pockets of urban, middle-class society, hungry for culture and possessed with just enough money, leisure, and education to pursue and enjoy it. Theirs was a demand, however, that neither drama nor poetry could fully satisfy, for both of these traditional forms required a developed sense of art and culture, which the untutored middle class rarely shared. Moreover, drama and poetry, especially the latter, had become identified in the common mind with the world of court and country, a world of privilege and tradition that these urban dwellers did now know and with which they could not identify. When the opportunity arose, therefore, it was almost inevitable that the sons and daughters of the middle class should turn instead to prose fiction, first to the novel and somewhat later to the short story—two forms of literary art that existed for the most part quite independent of the established literary standards of the day. That this new reading public should in turn come to influence, if not dictate, fiction's choice of subject matter, theme, and point of view followed almost as a matter of course.

The popular literature of any period tends to capture and reflect the dominant social, economic, political, religious, and scientific climate of the age in which it is written. This was particularly true of eighteenth-century England, where the new scientific rationalism of Newton and Locke conspired with an increasingly fluid and open social and economic order, and a more democratic political system, to attach new importance to the ability of the individual Englishman to make his own choices respecting the affairs of everyday life and thus in a measure control his own destiny. As Ian Watt has observed, "For those fully exposed to the new economic order, the effective entity on which social arrangements were now based was no longer the family, nor the church, nor the guild, nor the township, nor the collective unit, but the individual: he alone was primarily responsible for determining his own economic, social, political, and religious roles."[5]

The eighteenth-century novel, by realistically portraying a world with which ordinary readers could at once identify, clearly reflects this growing spirit of individualization and secularization. Beginning in 1719 with the publication of Daniel Defoe's *Robinson Crusoe*, authors like Samuel Richardson, Henry Fielding, Tobias Smollett, and Laurence Sterne brought forth a series of novels explicitly addressed to the needs and interests of the urban, middle-class readership for which they wrote. Writing for the most part in a plain, unembellished style in keeping with the education of their audience, these authors sought to create convincing characters caught up in a series of misadventures whose solutions served to illustrate the fundamental importance of prudent and proper behavior in an increasingly complicated world. Their successes not only called forth hundreds of imitators but in a relatively short period of time secured for the novel a dominance it has yet to relinquish.

The development of the short story, on the other hand, took a somewhat different course. Although recognizable antecedents of what we now call the short story are to be found occasionally in British newspapers and magazines throughout the eighteenth century, it was not the English authors but their nineteenth-century American counterparts who played the leading role in creating and perfecting the short story as a literary form. Until relatively late

---

[5] Ian Watt, *The Rise of the Novel: Studies in Defoe, Richardson, and Fielding* (Berkeley: U California P, 1957) 61.

in the nineteenth century and the appearance of Rudyard Kipling and Thomas Hardy, the best-known Victorian writers of fiction consistently demonstrated a preference for the novel and left the fate of the short story to others, though they were quick enough to capitalize on the immediate financial advantages afforded by serializing their novels for the magazines before publishing them in book form. When they did attempt short stories, the results were often undistinguished and crude. In Charles Dickens's case for example, his short pieces, with very few exceptions, were little more than sketches or highly impressionistic essays— clever evocations of the mood and atmosphere of London life—as opposed to symmetrical, unified short stories with carefully developed patterns of plot and action.

The strong preference for the novel was attributable in large measure to the literary tradition in which the Victorian novelists worked. Having been raised and educated within the great tradition of the English novel—the tradition that by 1830 had produced not only Fielding, Richardson, and their contemporaries but Jane Austen and Sir Walter Scott as well—it was perhaps only natural that their methods and techniques (not to mention their temperaments) should become those of the novelist. Novels were what their readers and publishers expected and demanded of them, and readers and publishers were then, as now, powerful taskmasters. Part of this preference for the novel was probably also the result of the peculiar vision or outlook that so characterizes Victorian fiction and sets it at once apart from most American fiction of the same period. The Victorian vision was a broad social one, embracing whole sections of life and society, and predominantly interested in delineating character in its relationship to society its a whole. Such a vision seems, in fact, to have been virtually incapable of rendering a mere slice of life. Rather, it had to serve up "the whole plum pudding," and as a result almost necessitated the expansiveness that only the novel, a three-volume novel at that, could provide. Short fiction was not wholly neglected in nineteenth-century England—the ghost story, the humorous-satirical story, and the retold legend did find their way into such magazines as *Blackwood's*, *Fraser's*, *Bentley's Miscellany*, and Dickens's own *Household Words*—but it was the sprawling, panoramic novel, not the compact and cohesive short story, that comprised the best of Victorian prose fiction.

In America

In America, on the other hand, a different set of conditions prevailed, which tended to move the would-be author in the direction of the short story. As a result, virtually every important nineteenth-century writer of fiction—Washington Irving, Edgar Allan Poe, Nathaniel Hawthorne, Herman Melville, Mark Twain, Kate Chopin, and Henry James among them—either began as a writer of short fiction or produced at least one noteworthy story during his or her lifetime. At the beginning of the century, as American writers set out on the important task of creating a native literary culture independent from England and the "old world," they found themselves confronted by an obstacle unknown to their British contemporaries. While the American copyright law of 1790 adequately protected the works of home authors, the absence of an international agreement on copyright meant that American publishers were free to pirate and reprint foreign novels without the payment of customary royalties. It was not uncommon, in fact, for American publishers to station agents in London whose sole assignment was to rush copies of new British works aboard ship for transit to America so that those books could be reprinted as quickly as possible. The results were predictable where would-be American authors were concerned. Even in a day in which Americans were loudly proclaiming the need for a literature constructed out of native subject matter and set on native soil, there were comparatively few American publishers with the audacity or vision to underwrite an unknown American novelist, however promising, when they had at their disposal, and for free, a wealth of established English talent upon which to draw.

The appearance of the popular miscellany known as the "gift book" or "annual" in the 1820s and 1830s, and the appearance of such famous American magazines as the *Knickerbocker*, *Godey's*, and *Graham's* in the 1820s and 1840s, thus provided a badly needed outlet for the young unestablished American writer who aspired to literary greatness. The periodicals paid cash—about five dollars a page in Melville's time—for fiction that could be published complete in a single issue. The compensation was adequate, if not spectacular, and as a result the magazine came to play an increasingly important role in the development of American literature throughout the nineteenth century and, of course, on into the twentieth. While the artistic quality of the vast bulk of nineteenth-century magazine fiction was probably no higher in America than in England, it is quite clear that almost from the very beginning the short story won an acceptance among writers of unmistakable ability that it was long denied in England. The role played by magazines in the development of the American short story was critical. As Eugene Current-Garcia has observed, "Without the magazine for an outlet, it is doubtful whether the short story would have emerged at all in the United States; lacking this outlet, it certainly could not have prospered."[6]

One is also tempted to attribute something of America's inclination toward short fiction, especially in the present century, to the accelerated, swiftly changing, pragmatic quality of American life itself. In the course of settling a continent, solving the vast political and social problems of a new democratic nation, and building and rebuilding a modern industrialized civilization, Americans have always been a people "on the go" who regard reading as rather a luxury. The emphasis in America has been, and is, on getting things done and getting them done quickly; and this preoccupation with speed and efficiency has been carried over to the national taste in literature as well. The chief advantage of the short story is that it can be read quickly—Poe in his famous 1842 review of Hawthorne's *Twice-Told Tales* insisted, in fact, that a short story should occupy no more than an hour of the reader's time. The development of the short story in American thus seems, in retrospect, to have been almost inevitable, precisely because in many ways it mirrors the character and personality of the nation itself. The short story is an art form that allows the American to indulge his or her need for literature and then to get on with the pressing business of day-to-day living.

In both America and England the shifting literary and intellectual climate of the nineteenth century inevitably left its mark on the development of both the novel and short story. This development can be seen not only in the changing assumptions of individual authors about the aims and purposes of fiction itself, but in the conscious choice of subject matter and its manner of treatment as well. As the century unfolds one can trace a general movement away from the subjective romanticism and gothicism of Irving, Poe, Hawthorne, and Sir Walter Scott (including their highly idealized rendering of setting and character) toward the more objective treatment of the realist and naturalist with their deliberate concentration on the commonplace and representative issues of daily life. Plots cease being loose, episodic, and melodramatic, and become close-knit and frequently subordinate to such other concerns as character. One notes as well the changing role of the narrator and the increasingly sophisticated use of point of view. The narrator in many cases ceases to be a disembodied authorial voice standing outside the story; instead the narrator moves inside to become immersed and lost in the personality of one or more of the characters. Style changes too. Where once it was discursive, formal, and often highly "literary," style becomes increasingly rooted in the speech patterns of ordinary, everyday men and women. Style itself becomes a means of creating and sustaining the desired verisimilitude.

---

[6]Eugene Current Garcia, *The American Short Story Before 1850: A Critical History* (Boston: Twayne, 1985) 1.

In France and Russia

In France and Russia, the two other major western centers of nineteenth-century literary activity, the historical pattern of development—despite obvious national differences—was much the same. In France as in England the appearance and success of the novel can be traced directly to the rapid advances made in the technology of printing and to the values and tastes of a growing middle-class readership. Despite the fact that the realistic novel, with its close and often critical rendering of society, quickly became the dominant mode of nineteenth-century French fiction, the short story was not neglected, thanks to the proliferation of newspapers supported by advertising revenues and the rise of the monthly periodical. The French short story as a self-conscious art form dates from about 1830 (Prosper Merimee published his first short story, "Mateo Falcone," in 1829), the year in which the great French novelists of the century began to make their appearance. Public acceptance came almost immediately, and within the space of a single decade the short story had established itself as recognized genre to which many of the most gifted writers of the century were willing to turn their talents. Honore de Balzac, Stendhal, Gustave Flaubert, and Emile Zola, the four great novelists of the century, all tried their hands at the short story, and their example was inevitably copied by others. As in America (but not in England) the quality of French nineteenth-century short fiction was high, culminating in the disarming, close-knit tales of Guy de Maupassant as the century drew to a close.

In Imperial Russia the bulky monthly reviews—the so-called "fat journals," headquartered in Moscow and St. Petersburg—provided the major outlet for the country's nineteenth-century fiction. Although a conservative and feudal aristocracy, bureaucratic governmental interference, and political censorship were facts of life in Czarist Russia, the "fat journals," perhaps because they were few in number and select in readership, managed to survive, and by the 1880s at least a dozen reviews could boast a circulation of nine to ten thousand copies per issue. *The Contemporary*, founded by Alexander Pushkin, published most of Ivan Turgenev's influential *Sportsman's Sketches* and serialized his first two novels; *Notes of the Fatherland* (1839–1884) serialized two early novels by Feodor Dostoevsky; *The Russian Herald* (1856–1887) published Dostoevsky's *Crime and Punishment* and *The Brothers Karamozov*, several of Turgenev's novels, and parts of Leo Tolstoy's *War and Peace* and *Anna Karenina*; and *The Russian Idea* (1889–1918) published most of Anton Chekov's better known short stories. The importance of fiction to the cause of cultivating and sustaining independent, progressive thinking within Czarist Russia far transcended its relatively small audience. As Walter Allen notes, with particular reference to authors like Dostoevsky and Turgenev, "since fiction was often the only place in which dangerous thoughts could be discussed, not always with perfect safety to the novelist, the novel became the main vehicle of criticism—of society, of morals, of the Russian attitude to the West, of man's relation to God and to his fellows, indeed of Russian man in relation to the whole world, visible and invisible, in which he lived.[7]

Some of the reasons that the short story should make considerable headway in nineteenth-century America, France, and Russia while languishing, relatively speaking, in England have been explored above. Irish author Frank O'Connor (1903–1966), in his perceptive and challenging short volume *The Lonely Voice* (1963), offers still another possible explanation, perhaps the most intriguing of all. For O'Connor, himself one of the great storytellers of the twentieth century, the emergence of the short story in different countries is to be traced to "a difference in the national attitude toward society." "I am strongly suggesting," O'Connor writes

---

[7] Walter Allen, *The English Novel: A Short Critical History* (New York: Dutton, 1954) 155.
[8] Frank O'Connor, *The Lonely Voice: A Study of the Short Story* (Cleveland: World, 1963) xiv.

that we can see in it [the short story] an attitude of mind that is attracted by submerged population groups, whatever these may be at any given time—tramps, artists, lonely idealists, dreamers, and spoiled priests. The novel can still adhere to the classical concept of civilized society, of man as an animal who lives in a community, as in Jane Austen and Trollope it obviously does; but the short story remains by its very nature remote from the community—romantic, individualistic, and intransigent.[8]

Such a theory would, of course, account for why the American short story has become "a national art form." America has traditionally been, and in many crucial ways still is, a land of heterogeneous population groupings—"submerged population groups" to use O'Connor's phrase—whose very pluralism and diversity has had a decided impact on its artistic and intellectual development. Although O'Connor unfortunately did not live long enough to develop his theory in any but the most sketchy way, it remains an intriguing hypotheses that merits further elaboration and discussion.

The Short Story in the Twentieth Century

Thus, by the end of the nineteenth century narrative prose fiction had become firmly established in both Europe and America as the dominant form of literary art, at least as far as most readers and literary consumers were concerned. The twentieth century has shown no sign of reversing that trend. Although the achievement of twentieth-century drama and poetry has been significant, and in many instances profound, the fact remains that for the average reader the easiest, most direct, and most convincing access to the "felt life" of the age is through the short story and the novel. That modern readers continue to respond to fiction takes nothing away from the inherent power of either drama or poetry; it may, in fact, only confirm what we know to be true, that in variety and quality, as well as in sheer quantity, the accomplishment of twentieth-century fiction has been impressive.

The development of fiction in the twentieth century can perhaps best be understood in relation to the changed and changing intellectual climate of the century itself—to what man has come to learn about himself, about the world in which he lives, and about the increasingly uncertain connection between the two. Confronted by new scientific discoveries, the maturation of modern industrial technology, and the disillusionment and widespread economic and social dislocation that accompanied and followed World War I, many of the old comforting verities and assurances that constituted the Victorian outlook have slowly given away. Discoveries in physics served to cast doubt on many of the long-accepted postulates of science, including the concept of physical reality itself. Discoveries in biology and psychology seemed to confirm a deterministic and behavioristic view of human nature, directly challenging older beliefs about the relationship between mind and body; while the work of Sigmund Freud and his student Carl Jung suggested that the key to human behavior lay beneath the surface of character and personality in the hidden recesses of the subconscious. Such discoveries, taken together, raised among other things serious question, about where reality itself could finally be located; and while it is perfectly true that such ideas never touched the popular mind in any deep or permanent way, their impact in intellectual circles, including literary men and women, was profound. For the twentieth-century writer the lesson was plain enough: the realistic surface of life could not be trusted or taken for granted. To find "reality" and to participate in the real drama of human events one must continually probe beneath the surface in an attempt to capture, if only for a moment, the fleeting reality of things.

The most characteristic and representative twentieth-century fiction fully reflects this impulse to probe and analyze. In terms of literary technique, this impetus is most apparent in the emphasis on plot and character. Older, more traditional authors tended to direct the reader's attention to plot—that is, to a series of events put together in chronological, linear fashion "to tell a good story"—and to present their characters in terms of how they responded or reacted to those events. Modern authors, on the other hand, tend to reverse this emphasis: Their interest is less on "what happens *to* character" than "what happens *in* character." That is, the author, from the beginning, focuses the attention of the reader on the characters, and is interested in the events of plot to the extent that a character's emotional, intellectual, or physical response serves to reveal or develop his or her values, personality, or psychological state.

This analysis of character is apparent as well in the subject matter of twentieth-century fiction. Although many modern and contemporary writers have turned the attention of their fiction to examining the social and political fabric of twentieth-century life, they characteristically do so in order to illustrate, document, or explore the progress of individuals who are being asked to cope with a world where fixed and permanent values are often suspect or found to be wanting altogether. Such words as "isolation," "aloneness," and "alienation" frequently recur in reference to modern literature in response to a vision of life in which, cut off from the certainties of the past, forces man to live in a chronic state of unease and self-examination. At times, particularly in the years following World War II, such a vision of the human predicament has encouraged authors to experiment with new and radical literary techniques. Writing against a backdrop of fragmented experience and discontinuity (if not outright unmeaning) such authors as Jorge Luis Borges, Flannery O'Connor, Donald Barthelme, Joyce Carol Oates, and Gabriel García Márquez have set before us a fiction of wild unpredictability, in which action and event (plot) are hard to follow or nonexistent, characters are barely present if at all, and the other traditional narrative techniques and conventions of the realistic story so transformed or distorted as to confuse and perplex even the most sophisticated readers. Gone is the whole middle range of experience in which most of us live. In its place the reader encounters the bizarre and grotesque, a highly subjective world of fantasy, neurosis, and madness in which nothing is reassuring and familiar and where "reality" is almost incomprehensible. In its most extreme form such experimentation has produced the contemporary "anti-novel" or "anti-story" in which the author virtually abandons his or her concerns with "subject," form, "meaning," and "form," as those terms have been traditionally defined. As might be expected, the "success" of such experiments has become the subject of intense critical debate.

Generalizations such as those described above are, of course, inherently dangerous, for they tell only part of the truth about twentieth-century novels and short stories, most of which continue to do, in a fairly traditional manner, what fiction has always done so well: tell a story in an interesting way. It is true as well that here we have been largely discussing "elite" fiction—the kind of fiction that experienced readers and critics predict will have lasting merit—at the expense of popular fiction—the spy and detective story, the western, the gothic romance, science and all speculative fiction, and fantasy—which, as any reader knows full well, competes with and indeed dominates the kind of fiction reviewed by the *New York Review of Books* and the *New York Times*. Such a state of affairs is by no means new or unexpected, since popular and elite fiction have existed comfortably side by side, particularly in magazines, since the eighteenth century. Nor is the distinction, which is usually made on the grounds of intrinsic quality or merit, necessarily an invidious one, for many educated readers (and authors) including professors of English enjoy works of both kinds and manage to shift their attention from one to the other without excessive guilt or apparent loss of literary sophistication. The very quantity of today's mass-produced, mass-marketed fiction does, however, pose an additional challenge for any reader who is seriously interested in improving his or her critical ability—the challenge to demonstrate how and why one work is better or more satisfactory than another.

The history of the short story in the twentieth century has been an interesting and exciting one. The influence of French and Russian authors has, on the whole, been relatively slight, and the credit for the excellence the short story has achieved belongs once again to America and to a lesser but still important extent to Great Britain and Ireland. To be sure, Russia, despite the burden long imposed on the literary artist by Communist ideology, can boast such skillful story writers as Isaac Babel, Maxim Corky, Boris Pasternak, and Alexander Solzhenitsyn; and twentieth-century France has produced Albert Camus, Jean Paul Sartre, Alain Robbe-Crillet, and others. Argentina has Jorge Luis Borges; Columbia, Gabriel García Márquez; Mexico, Carlos Fuentes, and Juan Rulfo; Spain, Miguel de Unamuno; Germany, Thomas Mann and Franz Kafka; Japan, Yukio Mishima; Canada, Morley Callaghan, Margaret Atwood, and Alice Munro. Still, in numbers and in quality, the advantage in the present century clearly lies with American, British, and Irish authors—with Sherwood Anderson, Kay Boyle, John Cheever, William Faulkner, F. Scott Fitzgerald, Ernest Hemingway, Henry James, James Joyce, Rudyard Kipling, D. H. Lawrence, Doris Lessing, Bernard Malamud, Katherine Mansfield, Flannery O'Connor, Frank O'Connor, Katherine Anne Porter, John Updike, and Eudora Welty, to cite only a few of the writers represented in the current edition of *Fiction 100*.

Although twentieth-century American publishers, aided by the "paperback revolution," have to some extent overcome the reluctance of their nineteenth-century counterparts to publish volumes of collected stories, the success of short fiction in the present century has once again been tied to the existence of the periodical. Yet, paradoxically, the last half century—which may quite properly be regarded as the high water mark of the short story— has also been a period in which the big-circulation American magazine has been in rapid decline. Gone are such large-circulation, well-paying magazines of the late 1940s and 1950s as *Saturday Evening Post* (which once sold for a nickel), *Collier's*, *Red Book*, and *This Week*, whose combined audience at one point reportedly reached sixty million readers. To be sure, the stock in trade of such editorially conservative magazines was the "slick" story, facile in situation, plot, and characterization, of a type that could be counted on to please (and certainly not offend) their vast middle-class clientele. Occasionally, however, they published quality stories as well. Stories by William Faulkner, Ernest Hemingway, and F. Scott Fitzgerald, for example, appeared frequently in the *Saturday Evening Post*. (The *Post*, over the years, in fact, published almost seventy stories by Fitzgerald alone.)[9]

The field of large-circulation magazines regularly offering quality stories has today narrowed down to the likes of *The New Yorker*, *The Atlantic Monthly*, *Harper's Magazine*, *Esquire*, and *Playboy*, magazines that are designed to appeal to rather select and specialized audiences. Though the stories carried in *The New Yorker* have sometimes been criticized for the similarity of their subject matter, tone, technique, and audience, its list of authors reads over the years like a literary "Who's Who": Alice Adams, Sherwood Anderson, Donald Barthelme, Jorge Luis Borges, John Cheever, Alice Munro, Isaac Bashevis Singer, James Thurber, and John Updike, to name only a few. William Peden is certainly correct when he observes that "Over the long haul, issue in and issue out, it has published more good fiction than any other magazine in America."[10]

Much of the burden for publishing short fiction in the present century, and particularly in recent years, has fallen upon the "little magazines," once mainly the refuge of impecunious poets, many of them university-affiliated or sponsored: for example, the *Yale Review*, *Tri-Quarterly*, *Sewanee Review*, *Chicago Review*, *Georgia Review*, *Iowa Review Kenyon Review*, *Antioch Review*, *Virginia Quarterly Review*, *Paris Review*, *South Atlantic Quarterly*, *Massa-

---

[9] Not surprisingly, as Philip Stevick notes, "there was a price to be paid. Joseph Blotner, in his life of Faulkner, recorded episodes in which Faulkner revised a rejected story, modifying the baroque intricacies of his prose and muting his idiosyncratic voice." Philip Stevick, *The American Short Story, 1900–1945: A Critical History* (Boston: Twayne, 1984) 8.

[10] William Peden, *The American Short Story: Front Line in the National Defense of Literature* (Boston: Houghton Mifflin, 1964) 22.

chusetts Review, Colorado Review, and *Prairie Schooner*. Limited severely by their small advertising revenue, rising printing, production, and mailing costs, small staffs, small circulations, and their inability to pay their authors any but the most modest of honoraria, many of these "little" magazines live continually on the brink of financial disaster.

Happily for the contemporary short story most of the better ones continue to survive. That they are able to do so is attributable in large measure to the willingness of their contributors to forego immediate financial reward, though of course all authors hope that with sufficient exposure (and the creation of an audience) a trade house will agree to pick up and publish their stories in collected book form. Not surprisingly, many of these authors are themselves academics, making their homes on college and university campuses where they earn their livelihood as writers in residence or professors of English. Of the writers represented in *Fiction 100*, Donald Barthelme, Ann Beattie, Saul Bellow, Kay Boyle, Raymond Carver, William Faulkner, Louise Erdrich, Mary Grimm, Dorothy Johnson, Pam Houston, Bernard Malamud, Joyce Carol Oates, Frank O'Connor, Robert Phillips, Mary Robison, Daniel Stern, Judy Troy, Alice Walker, Liza Wieland, Joy Williams, and Tobias Wolff have at one time or another taken up residence on the college campus.

Although periodically there are doomsayers who predict its decline, the short story continues to flourish, and, for the present at least, the optimists seem to have the better of the argument. For William Peden, the continuing success of short fiction, especially in America, is attributable to its ability to capture and communicate a world in flux: "The short story in America has always been a thing of individuality, freedom, and variety. Flexibility is its hallmark, and no other literary form is so close to the rapidly changing pulse of the times in which it is written and which in turn it reflects with vigor, variety, and verve."[11]

II

Many of the short stories included in *Fiction 100* (those by Turgenev, Gogol, Irving, Poe, Hawthorne, Maupassant, Hardy, Chekov, James, and Joyce, to cite only the most obvious examples) were chosen, in part at least, because of the important places they occupy in the historical evolution of short fiction. Their inclusion makes it possible for an instructor to organize his or her course chronologically in order to illustrate the development of the short story as an independent literary genre. The values of such an approach are several. It teaches us that all literature exists in time—is "implicated in time," if you will—and such bears the unmistakable imprint of the period and culture in which it was written. It teaches us that many of the methods and techniques that we now take so much for granted in the modern short story are actually the result of a process of slow, irregular experimentation and innovation. It teaches us that each successive age has its own reigning mode of literary sensibility—be it romanticism, realism, or naturalism—which shapes, however subtly, the author's vision of the world and the way he or she arranges and gives emphasis to the materials at his or her disposal.

A chronologically organized course has the inherent advantage of being neat, tidy, and eminently logical. Students at all times know where they are, where they have been, and in some rough, imprecise way, where they are going. For this reason, such an arrangement will serve equally well the purposes of the instructor who wishes to emphasize the formal, analytic approach or the instructor who wishes to emphasize the thematic approach. The three approaches which we have discussed need not and should not be considered mutually exclusive. In fact, the historical approach, if it is to be fruitful, demands that the student understand fully the elements of fiction and how they work together to establish a formal literary construct. The instructor will want to lay heavy emphasis upon the all-important fact that though a literary work of art inevitably partakes of the age in which it was written, it nonetheless at any given moment in time has an independent, timeless existence uniquely its own.

---

[11]Ibid., 6.

Chronological Table of Contents

	"The Yellow Wall-Paper"	Charlotte Perkins Gilman (1860–1935)
1894	"The Story of an Hour"	Kate Chopin (1851–1904)
1896	"Athénaïse: A Story of a Temperament"	Kate Chopin (1851–1904)
1898	"The Blue Hotel"	Stephen Crane (1871–1900)
	"The Bride Comes to Yellow Sky"	Stephen Crane (1871–1900)
	"The Storm"	Kate Chopin (1851–1904)
	"Youth"	Joseph Conrad (1857–1924)
1899	"The Darling"	Anton Chekhov (1860–1904)
	"Heart of Darkness"	Joseph Conrad (1857–1924)
	"The Lady with the Dog"	Anton Chekhov (1860–1904)
	"The Man That Corrupted Hadleyburg"	Samuel L. Clemens (1835–1910)
	"The Story of an Hour"	Kate Chopin (1851–1904)
1904	"They"	Rudyard Kipling (1865–1936)
1910	"The Secret Sharer"	Joseph Conrad (1857–1924)
1912	"Death In Venice"	Thomas Mann (1875–1955)
1914	"Araby"	James Joyce (1882–1941)
	"The Dead"	James Joyce (1882–1941)
	"If I Were a Man"	Charlotte Perkins Gilman (1860–1935)
1917	"A Jury of Her Peers"	Susan Glaspell (1876–1948)
1921	"I Want to Know Why"	Sherwood Anderson (1876–1941)
1922	"Her First Ball"	Katherine Mansfield (1888–1923)
	"The Horse Dealer's Daughter"	D. H. Lawrence (1885–1930)
	"A Hunger Artist"	Franz Kafka (1883–1924)
	"Miss Brill"	Katherine Mansfield (1888–1923)

	"Winter Dreams"	F. Scott Fitzgerald (1896–1940)
1924	"Indian Camp"	Ernest Hemingway (1898–1961)
	"Witness for the Prosecution"	Agatha Christie (1890–1976)
1925	"Haircut"	Ring Lardner (1885–1933)
	"Spunk"	Zora Neale Hurston (1901–1960)
1927	"Hills Like White Elephants"	Ernest Hemingway (1898–1961)
1929	"Big Blonde"	Dorothy Parker (1893–1967)
1930	"A Rose for Emily"	William Faulkner (1897–1962)
1931	"Guests of the Nation"	Frank O'Connor (1903–1966)
	"Dry September"	William Faulkner (1897–1962)
1936	"Astronomer's Wife"	Kay Boyle (1903–)
1937	"The Chrysanthemums"	John Steinbeck (1902–1968)
1938	"The Use of Force"	William Carlos Williams (1883–1963)
1939	"Barn Burning"	William Faulkner (1897–1962)
	"The Girls in Their Summer Dresses"	Irwin Shaw (1913–1984)
1940	"The Man Who Was Almost a Man"	Richard Wright (1908–1960)
1941	"Why I Live at the P.O."	Eudora Welty (1909–)
1944	"The Grave"	Katherine Anne Porter (1890–1980)
	"King of the Bingo Game"	Ralph Ellison (1914–)
1945	"The Demon Lover"	Elizabeth Bowen (1899–1973)
1948	"The Lottery"	Shirley Jackson (1919–1965)
1949	"The Man Who Shot Liberty Valance"	Dorothy Johnson (1905–1984)
1950	"August 2002: Night Meeting"	Ray Bradbury (1920–)
1951	"Looking for Mr. Green"	Saul Bellow (1915–)

1953	"Gimpel the Fool"	Issac Bashevis Singer (1904–1991)
	"A Good Man Is Hard to Find"	Flannery O'Connor (1925–1964)
1954	"The Country Husband"	John Cheever (1912–1982)
	"The Magic Barrel"	Bernard Malamud (1914–1986)
1957	"The Guest"	Albert Camus (1913–1960)
	"Sonny's Blues"	James Baldwin (1924–1987)
	"Wine"	Doris Lessing (1919–)
1961	"I Stand Here Ironing"	Tillie Olsen (1913–)
1962	"A&P"	John Updike (1932–)
	"Aura"	Carlos Fuentes (1929–)
1966	"Where Are You Going, Where Have You Been?"	Joyce Carol Oates (1938–)
1967	"Four Summers"	Joyce Carol Oates (1938–)
	"To Hell with Dying"	Alice Walker (1944–)
1968	"A Very Old Man with Enormous Wings"	Gabriel García Márquez (1928–)
1972	"The Lesson"	Toni Cade Bambara (1939–1995)
	"Taking Care"	Joy Williams (1944–)
1974	"Yellow Woman"	Leslie Silko (1948–)
1975	"Separating"	John Updike (1932–)
1976	"Dream Children"	Gail Godwin (1937–)
	"Here Come the Maples"	John Updike (1932–)
1977	"Cortés and Montezuma"	Donald Barthelme (1931–1989)
1979	"My First Kill"	Art Coelho (1943–)
	"Shoeless Joe Jackson Comes to Iowa"	W. P. Kinsella (1932–)
	"We Are Not in This Together"	William Kittredge (1932–)

1980	"Love Letters"	Patricia Zelver (1923–)
1981	"Cathedral"	Raymond Carver (1939–1988)
	"Coach"	Mary Robison (1949–)
	"I Could See the Smallest Things"	Raymond Carver (1939–1988)
	"Nadine at 35: A Synopsis"	Jo Sapp (1944–)
	"The Tip-Top Club"	Garrison Keillor (1942–)
	"What We Talk About When We Talk About Love"	Raymond Carver (1939–1988)
1982	"Rock Springs"	Richard Ford (1944–)
	"Shiloh"	Bobbie Ann Mason (1940–)
1983	"Sunday in the Park"	Bel Kaufman (–)
1984	"A Country Wedding"	Laurie Colwin (1944–1992)
	"Lust"	Susan Minot (1956–)
1985	"Janus"	Ann Beattie (1947–)
	"No One's A Mystery"	Elizabeth Tallent (1954–)
	"Say Yes"	Tobias Wolff (1945–)
	"What Did We Do Wrong?"	Garrison Keillor (1942–)
1986	"Horse Camp"	Ursula Le Guin (1929–)
1988	"Brooksmith by Henry James"	Daniel Stern (1928–)
	"Home"	Nadine Gordimer (1923–)
	"Meneseteung"	Alice Munro (1931–)
	"We"	Mary Grimm (–)
1989	"The House on Mango Street"	Sandra Cisneros (1954–)
	"How to Talk to a Hunter"	Pam Houston (1962–)
1991	"Antlers"	Rick Bass (1958–)

	"The Columbus School for Girls"	Liza Wieland (1960–)
	"The Golden Darters"	Elizabeth Winthrop (1948–)
	"Mauser"	Louise Erdrich (1954–)
	"Wherever That Great Heart May Be"	W. D. Wetherell (1948–)
1992	"A Real Life"	Alice Munro (1930–)
	"Surprise!"	Robert Phillips (1938–)
1994	"The Man in the Black Suit"	Stephen King (1947–)
	"Ten Miles West of Venus"	Judy Troy (1951–)
1995	"Young Girl's Wish"	Amy Tan (1952–)
	"His Women"	Alice Adams (1926–1999)
1997	"Nightingale"	Tobias Wolff (1946–)
1998	"A Little Burst"	Elizabeth Strout (1956–)

Short Story History and Criticism

Aldrich, Earl M. *The Modern Short Story in Peru* (University of Wisconsin Press, Madison, 1966).
———. "Recent Trends in the Peruvian Short Story," *Studies in Short Fiction*, VIII (Winter 1971), 20–31.
Allen, Walter. *The Short Story in English* (Oxford University Press, New York, 1980).
Averill, Deborah. *The Irish Short Story from George Moore to Frank O'Connor* (University Press of America, Washington D.C., 1982 .
Aycock, Wendell M., ed. *The Teller and the Tale* (Texas Tech University Press, Lubbock,1982).
Backus, Joseph M. "'He Came Into Her Line of Vision Walking Backward': Nonsequential Sequence-Signals in Short Story Openings," *Language Learning*, XV (1965), 67–83.
Bader, A.L. "The Structure of the Modern Short Story," *College English*, VII (November 1945), 86–92.
Baker, Howard. "The Contemporary Short Story," *Southern Review*, III (Winter 1938), 576–596.
Baldeshwiler, Eileen. "The Lyric Short Story: The Sketch of a History," *Studies in Short Fiction*, VI (Summer 1969), 443–453.
Baldwin, Dean. "The Tardy Evolution of the British Short Story," *Studies in Short Fiction*, XXX (Winter 1993). 23–33.
Bates, H. E. *The Modern Short Story: A Critical Survey* (T. Nelson and Sons, London, 1941).
Bayley, John. *The Short Story: Henry James to Elizabeth Bowen* (St. Martin's Press, New York, 1988).
Beachcroft, Thomas Owen. *The English Short Story* (Longman's Green, London, 1964).

————. *The Modest Art: A Survey of the Short Story in English* (Oxford University Press, London, 1968).

Beck, Warren. "Art and Formula in the Short Story," *College English*, V (November 1943), 55–62.

Beebe Maurice. "A Survey of Short Story Textbooks," *College English*, XVIII (January 1957) 237–243.

Bell, Madison. "Less is Less: The Dwindling American Short Story," *Harper's* (April 1986), 64–69.

Bennett, E. K. *A History of the German Novelle: From Goeth to Thomas Mann* (Cambridge University Press, Cambridge, Eng., 1934).

Berces, Francis. "Poe and the Imagination: An Aesthetic for the Short Story Form," *Journal of the Short Story in English*, No. 2 (1984), 105–113.

Beyerl, Jan. *The Style of the Modern Arabic Short Story* (Charles University Prague, 1971).

Bleifus, William. "The Short Story in Text and Intact," *College English*, XXIII (February 1962), 402–408.

Bone, Robert. *Down Home: A History of Afro-American Short Fiction from Its Beginnings to the End of the Harlem Renaissance* (Columbia University Press, New York, 1988).

Bonheim, Helmut. *The Narrative Modes: Techniques of the Short Story* (D.S. Brewster, Cambridge, Eng., 1982).

Boulanger, Daniel. "On the Short-Story," *Michigan Quarterly Review*, XXVI (1987), 510–514.

Boyce, Benjamin. "English Short Fiction in the Eighteenth Century: A Preliminary View," *Studies in Short Fiction*, V (Winter 1968), 95–112.

Boynton, Percy H. "American Authors of Today: The Short Story," *English Journal*, XII (May 1923), 325–333.

Brickell, Herschel. "The Contemporary Short Story," *University of Kansas City Review*, XV (Summer 1949), 267–270.

Brombert, Victor. "Opening Signals in Narrative," *New Literary History*, XI (1980), 489–502.

Brown, Julie. *American Women Short Story Writers: A Collection of Critical Essays* (Garland Publishers, New York, 1995).

Brown, Julie and William Cain, eds. *Ethnicity and the American Short Story* (New York, 1997).

Burgess, Anthony. "On the Short Story," *Journal of the Short Story in English*, No. 2 (1984), 31–47.

Burke, Daniel. *Beyond Interpretation: Studies in the Modern Short Story* (Troy, N.Y., 1991).

Burnett, Whit, and Hollie Burnett. *The Modern Short Story in the Making* (Hawthorn Books, New York, 1964).

Campbell, Ian. "The Scottish Short Story: Three Practitioners," *Journal of the Short Story in English*, X (1988), 17–44.

Canby, Henry S. *The Short Story in English* (Holt, Rinehart and Winston, New York, 1909).

Carter, Susanne. *Mothers and Daughters in American Short Fiction: An Annotated Bibliography of Twentieth-Century Women's Literature* (Greenwood Press, Westport, Conn., 1993).

Chapman, Michael. "The Fiction Maker: The Short Story in Literary Education," *CRUX, A Journal of Teaching English*, XVIII (1984), 3–20.

Clarke, John H. "Transition in the American Negro Short Story," *Phylon*, XXI (Winter 1960), 360–366.

Cortazar, Julio. "Some Aspects of the Short Story," *Review of Contemporary Fiction*, III (1983), 24–33

Crant, Philip A., ed. *The French Short Story* (University of South Carolina Press, Columbia, S.C., 1975).

Current-Garcia, Eugene. *The American Short Story Before 1850* (Twayne Publishers, Boston, 1985).

Current-Garcia, Eugene, and Walton Patrick, eds. *What Is the Short Story?* Rev. ed. (Scott, Foresman and Co., New York, 1974).

Curnutt, Kirk. *Wise Economies: Brevity and Storytelling in American Short Stories* (Moscow, Ida., 1997).

Dawson, W.J. "The Modern Short Story," *North American Review*, CXC (December 1909), 799–810.

Dollerup, Cay. "The Concepts of 'Tension', 'Intensity', and 'Suspense' in Short-Story Theory," *Orbis Litterarum*, XXV (1970), 314–337.

Duncan, Edgar Hill. "Short Fiction in Medieval English: A Survey," *Studies in Short Fiction*, IX (Winter 1972), 1–28.

———. "Short Fiction in Medieval English: II. The Middle English Period," *Studies in Short Fiction*, XI (Summer 1974), 227–241.

Ellis, Robert P. "Short Fiction in Antiquity," *Critical Survey of Short Fiction*, Revised Edition, Frank N. MaGill, ed. (Salem Press, Pasadena, Ca., 1993), pp. 2565–2575.

Engstrom, Alfred G. "The Formal Short Story in France and Its Development Before 1850" *Studies in Philology*, XLII (July 1945), 627–639.

Evans, Walter. "Nineteenth-Century American Theory of the Short Story: The Dual Tradition," *Orbis Litterarum*, XXXIV (I 979), 314–330.

———. "Short Fiction: 1800–1840," *Critical Survey of Short Fiction*, Revised Edition, Frank N. MaGill, ed. (Salem Press, Pasadena, Ca., 1993), pp. 2650–2668.

Farrell, James I. "Nonsense and the Short Story," *The League of Frightened Philistines and Other Papers* (Vanguard Press, Inc., New York, 1945), pp. 72–81.

Ferguson, Suzanne. "Defining the Short Story: Impressionism and Form," *Modern Fiction Studies*, XXVIII (1982), 13–24.

Firchow, Peter E. "The Americaness of the American Short Story," *Journal of the Short Story in English*, X (1988), 45–66.

FitzGerald, Gregory. "Introduction," *Modern Satiric Stories: The Impropriety Principle* (Scott, Foresman and Co., Glenview, Ill., 1971), pp. 2–47.

———. "The Satiric Short Story: A Definition," *Studies in Short Fiction*, V (Summer 1968), 349–354.

Flora, Joseph M., ed. *The English Short Story, 1880–1945: A Critical History* (Twayne Publishers, Boston, 1985).

Foster, David William. *Studies in the Contemporary Spanish-American Short Story* (University of Missouri Press, Columbia, Mo., 1979).

Friedman, Norman. "What Makes a Short Story Short?" *Modern Fiction Studies*, IV (Summer 1958), 103–117.

Fusco, Richard. *Maupassant and the American Short Story: The Influence of Form at the Turn of the Century* (Pennsylvania State University Press, University Park, 1994).

Gadpaille, Michelle. *The Canadian Short Story* (Oxford University Press, New York, 1988).

Garrett, George. "American Short Fiction and the Literary Marketplace," *Sewanee Review*, XCI (Winter 1983), 112–120.

Geismar, Maxwell. "The American Short Story Today," *Studies on the Left*, IV (Spring 1964), 21–27.

Gereben, Agnes. "The Syntactics of Cycles of Short Stories," *Essays in Poetics*, XI (1986), 44–75.

———. "The Writer's 'Ego' in the Composition of Cycles of Short Stories," *Essays in Poetics*, IX (1984), 38–77.

Gerlach, John. *Toward the End: Closure and Structure in the American Short Story* (University of Alabama Press, University, Ala., 1985).

George, Albert J. *Short Fiction in France, 1800–1850* (Syracuse University Press, Syracuse, N.Y., 1964).

Gerould, Katherine Fullerton. "The American Short Story," *Yale Review*, XIII (July 1924), 642–663.

Grabo, Carl H. *The Art of the Short Story* (Charles Scribner's Sons, New York, 1913).

Gullason, Thomas A. "The Short Story: Revision and Renewal," *Studies in Short Fiction*, XIX (Summer 1982), 221–230.

———. "Revelation and Evolution: A Neglected Dimension of the Short Story," *Studies in Short Fiction*, X (Fall 1973), 347–356.

———. "What Makes a 'Great' Short Story Great?" *Studies in Short Fiction*, XXVI (Summer 1989), 267–277.

Hanson, Clare. *Short Stories and Short Fictions, 1880-1980* (St. Martin's Press, New York 1985).

Harris, Wendell V. "Beginnings of the True Short Story in England," *English Literature in Transition*, XV (1972), 269–276.

———. *British Short Fiction in the Nineteenth Century* (Wayne State University Press, Detroit, 1979).

———. "English Short Fiction in the 19th Century," *Studies in Short Fiction*, VI (Fall 1968), 1–93.

Harte, Bret. "The Rise of the Short Story," *Cornhill Magazine*, VII (July 1899), 1–8.

Head, Dominic. *The Modernist Short Story: A Study of Theory and Practice* (Cambridge University Press, New York, 1992).

Hedberg, Johannes. "What is a 'Short Story'? And What is an 'Essay'?" *Moderna Sprak*, LXXIV (1980), 113–120.

Hemmererechts, Kristien. "The Modern Short Story, Continued," *Modern Fiction Studies*, XXIX (1983), 253–255.

Hibbard, Allen. "Short Fiction Since 1960," *Critical Survey of Short Fiction*, Revised Edition, Frank N. MaGill, ed. (Salem Press, Pasadena, Ca., 1993), pp. 2750–2763.

Hornby, Nick. "The *New Yorker* Short Story," *Contemporary American Fiction* (St. Martin's Press, New York, 1992), 7–29.

Howe, Irving. "Tone in the Short Story," *Sewanee Review*, LVII (Winter 1949), 141-152.

Howells, William Dean. "Some Anomalies of the Short Story," *North American Review*, CVXXIII (September 1901), 422–432.

Huntington, John. *Rationalizing Genius: Ideological Strategies in the Classic American Science Fiction Short Story* (Rutgers University Press, New Brunswick, N.J., 1989).

Ingram, Forrest L. "The Dynamics of Short Story Cycles," *Northwest Ohio Quarterly*, II (1979), 7–12.

Kempton, Kenneth Payson. *The Short Story* (Harvard University Press, Cambridge, 1947).

Kennedy, J. Gerald. "Toward a Poetics of the Short Story Cycle," *Journal of the Short Story in English*, XI (1988), 9–25.

Kilroy, James, ed. *The Irish Short Story: A Critical History* (Twayne Publishers, Boston, 1984).

Kimbel, Bobby Ellen, ed. *American Short Story Writers, 1910–1945* (Gale Research, Inc., Detroit, 1991).

Kostelanetz, Richard. "Notes on the American Short Story Today," *Minnesota Review*, V (1966), 214–221.

Laszlo, Janos. "Readers' Historical-Social Knowledge and Their Interpretation and Evaluation of a Short Story," *Poetics*, XVII (1988), 461–481.

Lawrence, James Cooper. "A Theory of the Short Story," *North American Review*, CCV (February 1917), 274–286.

Leal, Luis. "The New Mexican Short Story," *Studies in Short Fiction*, VIII (Winter 1971), 9–19.

Levy, Andrew. *The Culture and Commerce of the American Short Story* (Cambridge University Press, New York, 1993).

Liberman, M.M. "Stasis, Story, and Anti-Story," *Georgia Review*, XXXIX (1985), 527–533.

Lieberman, Elias. *The American Short Story: A Study of the Influence of Locality and its Development* (The Editor, Ridgewood, N.J., 1912).

Lohafer, Susan. *Coming to Terms with the Short Story* (Louisiana State University Press, Baton Rouge, 1985).

————, and Jo Ellyn Clarey, eds. *Short Story Theory at a Crossroads* (Louisiana State University Press, Baton Rouge, 1989).

Logsdon, Loren and Charles W. Mayer, eds. *Since Flannery O'Connor:* Essays on the Contemporary American Short Story (Yeast Printing Company, Macomb, Ill., 1987)

Lund, Michael. *America's Continuing Story: An Introduction to Serial Fiction, 1850-1900* (Wayne State University Press, Detroit, 1993).

Magill, Frank N., ed. *Critical Survey of Short Fiction* (Salem Press, Englewood, N.J.,1981), 2 vols.

————. ed. *Critical Survey of Short Fiction,* Revised Edition (Salem Press, Pasadena, Ca., 1993).

Mann, Susan Garland. *The Short Story: A Genre Companion and Reference Guide* (Scarecrow Press, Westport, Conn., 1988).

Marcus, Mordecai. "What Is an Initiation Story!" *The Journal of Aesthetics and Art Criticism,* XIV (Winter 1960), 221–227.

Marler, Robert F. "From Tale to Short Story: The Emergence of a New Genre in the 1850s," *American Literature,* XLVI (May 1974), 153–169.

Martin, Peter A. "The Short Story in England: 1930s Fiction Magazines," *Studies in Short Fiction,* XIV (Summer 1977), 233–240.

Matthews, Brander. *The Philosophy of the Short Story* (Longmans, Green and Company, New York, 1901).

Maugham, W. Somerset. "The Short Story," *Points of View: Five Essays* (Doubleday & Co., Inc., New York, 1958), pp. 163–212.

May, Charles E. "From Small Beginnings: Why Did Detective Fiction Make Its Debut in the Short Story Format," *Armchair Detective,* XX (1987), 77–81.

————. "The Nature of Knowledge in Short Fiction," *Studies in Short Fiction,* XXI (Fall 1984), 327–338.

————. "Short Fiction: 1840–1880, *Critical Survey of Short Fiction,* Revised Edition, Frank N. MaGill, ed. (Salem Press, Pasadena, Ca., 1993), pp. 2669–2709.

————. "Short Fiction: 1880–1920," *Critical Survey of Short Fiction,* Revised Edition, Frank N. MaGill, ed. (Salem Press, Pasadena, Ca., 1993), pp. 2710–2728.

————. "The Short Story in the College Classroom: A Survey of Textbooks Published in the Sixties," *College English,* XXXIII (January 1972), 488–512.

————., ed. *Short Story Theories* (Ohio State University Press, Columbus, 1976).

Millet, F.B. "The Short Story." *Contemporary American Authors" A Critical Survey* (Harcourt, Brace and Co., 1940), pp. 85-97.

Mirrielies, Edith R. "The American Short Story," *Atlantic Monthly,* CLXVII *(June 1941),* 714–722.

Mish, Charles C. "English Short Fiction in the Seventeenth Century," *Studies in Short Fiction,* VI (Spring 1969), 223–330.

Moffett, James. "Telling Stories: Methods of Abstraction in Fiction," *ETC.,* XXI (December 1964), 425–450.

New, W. H. *Dreams of speech and Violence: The Art of the Short Story in Canada and New Zealand* (University of Toronto Press, Toronto, 1987).

Newman, Frances. "The American Short Story in the First Twenty-Five Years of the Twentieth Century," *Bookman,* LXIII (April 1926), 186–193.

————. *The Short Story's Mutation: From Petronius to Paul Menard* (B. W. Huebsch, New York, 1925).

O'Brien, Edward J. *The Advance of the American Short Story* Rev. ed. (Dodd, Mead and Co., New York, 1931).

O'Connor, Flannery. "Writing Short Stories," *Mystery and Manners,* Sally and Robert Fitzgerald, eds. (Farrar, Straus & Giroux, New York, 1969), pp. 87–106.

O'Connor, Frank. *The Lonely Voice: A Study of the Short Story* (World Publishing Company, Cleveland, 1963).

O'Faolain, Sean. *The Short Story* (Devin-Adair Company, Old Greenwich, Conn., 1951).

Orel, Harold. *The Victorian Short Story: Development and Triumph of a Literary Genre* (Cambridge University Press, New York, 1986).

O'Toole, L. Michael. *Structure, Style and Interpretation in the Russian Short Story* (Yale University Press, New Haven, 1982).

Pasco, Allan H. "On Defining Short Stories," *New Literary History*, XXII (Spring 1991), 407–422.

Patrick, Walton R. "Poetic Style in the Contemporary Short Story," *College Composition and Communication*, XVIII (May 1957), 77–84.

Pattee, Fred Lewis. *The Development of the American Short Story: An Historical Survey* (Harper and Brothers, New York, 1923).

———. "The Present Stage of the Short Story," *English Journal*, XII (September 1923), 439–449.

Peden, Margaret Sayers, ed. *The Latin American Short Story: A Critical History* (Twayne Publishers, Boston, 1983).

Peden, William. *The American Short Story: Continuity and Change, 1940-1975* (Houghton Mifflin Company, Boston, 1975).

———. "The American Short Story During the Twenties," *Studies in Short Fiction*, X (Fall 1973), 367–371.

———. *The American Short Story: Front Line in the National Defense of Literature* (Houghton Mifflin Company, Boston, 1964).

———. "Publishers, Publishing and the Recent American Short Story," *Studies in Short Fiction*, I (Fall 1964), 33–44.

Penn, W. S. "The Tale as Genre in Short Fiction," *Southern Humanities Review*. XV (1981), 231–241.

Perry, Bliss. "The Short Story," *A Study of Prose Fiction* (Houghton Mifflin Co., New York, 1902), pp. 300–334.

Pickering, Sam. "The Cheap Repository Tract and the Short Story," *Studies in Short Fiction*, XXI (Winter 1975), 15–21.

Pitcher, Edward W. R. *Fiction in American Magazines Before 1900* (University of Kentucky Press, Lexington, Kty., 1993).

Pochman, Henry A. "Germanic Materials and Motifs in the Short Story," *German Culture in America: Philosophic and Literary Influences: 1600-1900* (University of Wisconsin Press, Madison, 1957), pp. 367–408.

Polsgrove, Carol. "They Made It Pay: British Short Fiction Writers, 1820-1840," *Studies in Short Fiction*, XI (Fall 1974), 417–421.

Pratt, Mary Louise. "The Short Story: The Long and the Short of It," *Poetics*, X (1981), 175–194.

Pugh, Edwin. "The Decay of the Short Story," *Living Age*, CCLIX (November 14, 1908), 387–395.

Rafroidi, Patrick and Terence Brown, eds. *The Irish Short Story* (Humanities Press, Atlantic Highlands, N.J., 1979).

Regan, Stephen. "'If The Presence of the Past': Modernism and Postmodernism in Canadian Short Fiction," *Narrative Strategies in Canadian Literature: Feminism and Postcolonialism*, Corol Ann Howells, ed. (Open University Press, Philadelphia, 1991), pp. 108–133.

Reid, Ian. *The Short Story* (Methuen, London, 1977).

Reynolds, Clay. "Wither the Great American Short Story," *Texas Review* XI (Spring/Summer 1990), 40–-44.

Rhode, Robert D. *Setting in the American Short Story of Local Color, 1865-1900* (Mouton, The Hague, 1975).

Rochette-Crawley, Susan. "Recent Short Story Theory," *Contemporary Literature*, XXXII (Spring 1991), 133–138.

Rohrberger, Mary. *Hawthorne and the Modern Short Story* (Mouton, The Hague, 1966)

Rohrberger, Mary, and Dan E. Bums. "Short Fiction and the Numinous Realm: Another Attempt at Definition," *Modern Fiction Studies*, XXVIII (1982), 5–12.

Ross, Danforth, *The American Short Story* (University of Minnesota Press, Minneapolis, 1961).

Rutledge, Amelia A. "Forms of Fiction in the Early Middle Ages" *Critical Survey of Short Fiction*, Revised Edition, Frank N. MaGill, ed. (Salem Press, Pasadena, Ca., 1993), pp. 2597–2607.

Schlauch, Margaret. "English Short Fiction in the 15th and 16th Centuries," *Studies in Short Fiction*, III (Summer 1966), 393–434.

Schultz, Marilyn. "Short Fiction in the Eighteenth Century," *Critical Survey of Short Fiction*, Revised Edition, Frank MaGill, ed. (Salem Press, Pasadena, Ca., 1993), pp. 2640–2649.

Shattock,Jonne and Michael Wolff. *The Victorian Periodical Press: Samplings and Soundings* (Leicester, Eng., 1982).

Shaw, Valerie, *The Short Story: A Critical Introduction* (Longman, London, 1983).

Smith, C. Alphonso. *The American Short Story* (Berlin, 1910).

Smith, Horatio E. "The Development of Brief Narrative in Modern French Literature: A Statement of the Problem," *PMLA*, XXXII (1971), 583–597.

Stanford, Derek. "A Larger Latitude: Three Themes in the Nineties Short Story," *Contemporary Review*, CCX (February 1967). 96–104.

Stephens, Michael. *The Dramaturgy of Style: Voice in Short Fiction* (Southern Illinois University Press, Carbondale, 1986).

Stevick, Philip, ed. *The American Short Story, 1900-1945: A Critical History* (Twayne Publishers, Boston, 1984).

Stroud, Theodore A. "A Critical Approach to the Short Story," *The Journal of General Education*, IX (January 1956), 91–100.

Sullivan, Walter. "Revelation in the Short Story: A Note on Methodology," *Vanderbilt Studies in Humanities*, I, John Philip Hyatt and Monroe K. Spears, eds. (Vanderbilt University Press, Nashville, 1951), pp. 106–112.

Summers, Hollis, ed. *Discussions of the Short Story* (D. C. Heath & Co., Boston, 1963).

Tallack, Douglas. "American Short Fiction: A Bibliographical Essay," *American Studies International*, XXIII (October 1985), 3–59.

———. *The Nineteenth-Century American Short Story: Language, Form and Ideology* (Routledge, London, 1993).

Thomas, Deborah. *Dickens and the Short Story* (Philadelphia, 1982).

Thompson, Richard L. *Everlasting Voices: Aspects of the Modern Irish Short Story* (Troy, N.Y., 1989).

Thurston, Jarvis, et al. eds. *Short Fiction Criticism: A Checklist of Interpretation Since 1925 of Stories and Novelettes* (Alan Swallow, Denver, 1960).

Vannata, Dennis. *The English Short Story, 1945-1980: A Critical History* (Twayne Publishers, Boston, 1985).

Voss, Arthur. *The American Short Story: A Critical Survey* (University of Oklahoma Press, Norman, 1973).

Walker, Warren, ed. Twentieth-Century Short Story Explication, 3rd ed. (Shoe String Press, Hamden, Conn., 1977. Supplement I, 1980; Supplement II, 1984).

Waller, Gary F. "Short Fiction in the Sixteenth and Seventeenth Centuries," *Critical Survey of Short Fiction*, Revised Edition, Frank N. MaGill, ed. (Salem Press, Pasadena, Ca., 1993), pp. 2620–2639.

Ward, Alfred C. *Aspects of the Modern Short Story: English and American* (University of London Press, London, 1924).

Watson, Noelle, ed. *Reference Guide to Short Fiction* (St. James Press, Detroit, 1994).

Weaver, Gordon. *The American Short Story, 1945-1980: A Critical History* (Twayne Publishers, Boston, 1983).

Weixlmann, Joe. *American Short-Fiction Criticism and Scholarship, 1959-1977: A Checklist* (Ohio University Press, Athens, Ohio, 1982).

West, Ray B. "The Modern Short Story and the Highest Form of Art," *English Journal*, XLVI (December 1957), 531–539.

———. *The Short Story in America, 1900-1945* (Henry Regnery Company, Chicago, 1952).

Wevers, Lydia. "The Short Story," *The Oxford History of New Zealand Literature in English* (Oxford University Press, New York, 1991), pp. 203–268.

Wharton, Edith. "Telling a Short Story," *The Writing of Fiction* (Charles Scribner's Sons, New York, 1925), pp. 33–58.

Wright, Austin McGiffert. *The American Short Story in the Twenties* (University of Chicago Press, Chicago, 1961).

II
Literature and Student Response: Activities for the Classroom

A. Introduction

As one reads one has the feeling one is moving into and through something and that there is movement within oneself—a succession of varied, complex, and rich mental and emotional states usually involving expectancy, tensions and releases, sensations of anxiety, fear, and discovery, sadness, sudden excitements, spurts of hope, warmth, or affection, feelings of distance and closeness, and a multitude of motor and sensory responses to the movement, rhythm, and imagery of the work as well as a variety of activities and responses—recognition, comparison, classification, judgment association, reflection—usually spoken of as intellectual. Very few experiences encourage one's consciousness in so many ways and give one such a sense that something is going on within oneself.[12]

The critic must both begin and end with...the complex of thought and feeling which the work elicits in him and which is formed *in* the work. This, of course, admits a degree of subjectivity into critical procedure and discourse, but this subjectivity is inescapable and is always present—though it may be masked by an objective-sounding terminology or by a rhetorical strategy by "by-passing" the stage of direct response. This does not mean that the critic lets himself go, that he engages in unbridled impressionism. He is always obliged to check his response against its cause, to analyze the work in order to verify or correct his response.[13]

Practically everything discernible in fiction has this two-sidedness: it is verbal and affective. The verbal aspect guides the reaction and prevents it from being arbitrary; the affective aspect is the fulfillment of that which has been prestructured by the language of the text. Any description of the interaction between the two must therefore incorporate both the structure of effects (the text) and that of response (the reader).[14]

Literature is not at its best when presented as achieved knowledge. The temptation is to instruct, but that violates what literature offers....At its best literature provides an occasion for exploring and professing.[15]

---

[12]Walter J. Slatoff, *With Respect to Readers: Dimensions of Literary Response* (Ithaca, N.Y., 1970), pp. 6–7.
[13]Elias Schwartz, *The Forms of Feeling: Toward a Mimetic Theory of Literature* (Port Washington, N.Y., 1972), p. 39.
[14]Wolfgang Iser, *The Act of Reading: A Theory of Aesthetic Response* (Baltimore, 1978), p. 21.
[15]William Stafford, *Friends to This Ground* (Champaign, Ill., 1967), p. 27.

Whatever organizational method the instructor chooses to follow, his or her major concern and challenge in the classroom will be to help students develop their abilities to respond to literature. As this section of the manual will attempt to indicate, student response to literature can take many forms, some familiar and more or less traditional, others new and somewhat experimental. In the main, those offered here rest on two key assumptions about the nature of literary study: (1) That there is both an affective and a cognitive content to what we call the "literary experience"; and (2) That the effective and creative teacher, recognizing the fact, will, at certain moments of his or her course, deliberately use the one to stimulate, illuminate, and reinforce the other.

One has only to read through recent issues of *College English, English Journal,* or *the CEA Forum,* or scan the publication lists of NCTE, to sense the many exciting changes now going on in English. Originally inspired, in part, by the now-historic Dartmouth Seminar of 1966, whose fifty participants openly called into question the prevailing cognitive emphasis of current literary study, the "New English" and its proponents have inspired a sweeping reevaluation of the entire English curriculum and the way in which English was being taught and studied not only in the elementary and secondary school but on into college as well. As might be expected, formal literary study received its share of attention. Here a major complaint was the tendency of many teachers to treat the literary work solely as an *objective reality* whose final meaning and significance exists quite apart from the *subjective reality* of the reader.

Those that argue the debilitating effect of such a view upon high school and college students leave much empirical evidence to support their case. As D. H. Harding observed some thirty years ago, "At the present time, there is too much learning about literature in place of discriminating enjoyment, and many students arrive at and leave universities with an unprofitable distrust of their personal responses to literature."[16] Though such charges will hardly come as much of a surprise with the teacher who has followed the past three decades of growing disenchantment with the claims of the New Criticism, what is new (and exciting for its possibilities and opportunities) is the remedy that has evolved in the form of a "response-centered" approach to literature. It is from the context of such an approach (which, as we shall see, is by no means antithetical to the three approaches discussed earlier) that the activities and teaching suggestions in this section are put forward.

The term "literary response," as it is used here, "encompasses the cognitive, affective, perceptual, and psychomotor activities that the reader of a poem, a story, or a novel performs as he reads or after he has read."[17] Responses may be intellectual or emotional, verbal or nonverbal, particularized or general, overt and immediate or postponed beyond the act of initial engagement only to occur later in the form of subsequent feelings or ideas. A response-centered approach to literary study begins by reasserting what literature teachers have always known, or at least sensed, namely that each reader comes to a literary work preequipped with his or her own separate identity and personality—a unique range and depth of human experience—and that reading is primarily an attempt to effect some kind of meaningful synthesis or "transaction"—to use Louise Rosenblatt's term—between the external reality of the work and the internal, subjective reality of the reader.

A response-centered approach does not deny a work its objective reality and its range of possible and acceptable meanings; neither does it succumb to the kind of critical anarchy feared by Wellek and Warren—that "a poem is the experience of the reader." Instead it asks students to respond honestly and naturally, intellectually as well as emotionally, to the work at hand, and then, having done so, to set out to discover why they respond the way they do—an act which inevitably leads students back out of their inner life and the matrix of their

---

[16]D. W. Harding, "Response to Literature: The Report of the Study Group," in *Response to Literature*, James R. Squire, ed. (Champaign, Ill., 1968), p. 16.
[17]Alan C. Purves, *Elements of Writing about a Literary Work: A Study of Response to Literature* (Champaign, Ill., 1968), p. xiii.

own experience toward the linguistic construct of the text. By so doing, students become aware of how their own experience, values, and sensibility color and influence their literary response. Students learn to clarify what they are in fact responding to in the subject matter, structure, technique, and language of the work. And, finally, as their responses become sharpened by contact with the verifiable, empirical data available in the text, they are encouraged to form interpretive and evaluative judgments about the work itself.

The implications of a response-centered approach are clear. Once we recognize that the experience of literature legitimately includes the active and authentic experience of the student-reader, we automatically extend the possibilities of literary study and the range of activities that take place in the classroom. Once we take seriously the idea that literature is the touchstone of human experience which reaches out to embrace the dynamic personal experience of the student, the classroom becomes a place where we can more fully challenge and foster intellectual curiosity and creativity, promote genuine discovery and personal growth, and deepen human awareness through raising, clarifying, and analyzing emotional and intellectual responses to the "felt life" of literature. By building upon a foundation of what students know best—namely themselves—we restore to literature much of the authentic pleasure we have for so long insisted is part of its unique experience and help to assimilate literature into the lives of our students.

Of course, there will be debate and honest disagreement, culminating at times in the recognition that no final consensus about a given story seems possible. (As teachers, indeed, we should be surprised, even disappointed, if such were not the case; after all, it is upon such differences of opinion that the professional reputations of literary critics arc founded.) If consensus is possible, fine. But let us always ask (and make sure that students understand) "why?" And if it is not, let us use the forum of the classroom to explore and discover "why not?" remembering always that experiential differences among individuals are very real and that they shape the way in which we internalize, analyze, and conceptualize that outer reality we call the world. Above all, let us remember that there is a danger lurking within the democratic impulse for consensus. Pushed too far it becomes, stripped of its good intentions, an impulse for authoritarianism and a subtle form of censorship.

The activities that follow are intended to provide a series of meaningful contexts in which literature can be discussed and explored in a positive and humanistic classroom environment. They are intended to suggest to new and experienced teachers alike some of the opportunities and possibilities that exist either within or without the framework of the analytic, thematic, and historical approaches discussed earlier. As conceived here, such activities can in fact do much to inform and illustrate matters of form, structure, and technique. As we think about and talk about our encounter with the total experience of a literary work (its attitudes, ideas, and the feelings, perceptions, and ideas it engenders in the reader), our sense of underlying patterns and techniques invariably grows. We discover, in short, that a knowledge of the formal aspects of fiction and a knowledge of the language of objective criticism are indispensable if we are to experience and understand the literary work and that such knowledge inevitably serves to sharpen and instruct (not retard) our personal response.

Quite obviously, not all of the following activities and suggestions will be appropriate for every course and every instructor. Literature courses emphasizing the short story will vary widely, according to the temperament of the instructor, the level of sophistication of the students, and their stated aims and goals. I conceive this section of the manual, indeed the whole of the manual, as providing a body of potential resources which the teacher can draw upon or leave alone as he or she wishes. Rightly used, however, I have found that these activities lend interesting variety to a curriculum often characterized by a day-to-day sameness of approach and help to overcome some of the passivity, silence, and regimentation which at times besets even the best of classes and the best of students. Further, I see them as extending the possibilities of literary study by encouraging students to participate more actively and more fully in the literature they are reading and as a way to help students to conceptualize, articulate, explain, and defend their feelings and ideas about their total experience with a work of literary art. The activities described in the following pages are not offered as vacations from the hard work of learning. What they do achieve is to reintroduce into the literature class an element of play and fun that, given the pressures and preoccupations of our lives and the lives of our students, we as teachers sometimes tend to neglect and overlook.

B. Group Study (Collaborative Learning)

Because so many of the activities outlined in this section suggest the desirability of breaking the larger class unit into smaller, semiautonomous groups for the purposes of discussing, writing, studying, dramatizing, and preparing materials for presentation to the entire class, a few words on the subject are in order. Group study, or "collaborative learning" as many prefer to call it, has proved for many English teachers an attractive, educationally sound, and productive alternative to the customary instructional format that places a strict emphasis on "doing your own work" and places the teacher at the front of the room facing neatly arranged rows of students.

Group study has a number of advantages, three of which come at once to mind. First and foremost, it increases student involvement and participation with the subject matter of the course by multiplying the opportunities in which that involvement can take place. Many good students, we all know, are reluctant to participate freely in a large class setting, creating by default a vacuum in which their more vocal and aggressive classmates are allowed to dominate and monopolize discussion. Faced with such a situation, the teacher has two alternatives, neither of which is satisfactory. He or she can call on silent students, hoping to draw them into discussion (at the risk of embarrassing and intimidating them), or continue to reward the aggressive with attention. Any occasion that facilitates the flow of questions facilitates the learning process—especially when students themselves ask the questions. The questions *they* ask are better than our own, define what they know, what they do not know, and where their particular interests lie. Second, group study provides the occasion for exercises in self-directed learning, a skill traditionally much neglected in undergraduate education. If one of the goals of a college education is to create students who are capable of learning without the constant aid and intervention of a teacher, then group learning provides a valuable means to such an end. And finally, when constituted as writing workshops in which assigned papers are planned, read, and discussed, small groups provide the kind of positive environment in which students can learn a great deal about what constitutes effective writing. Of this I shall have more to say in the section on student writing.

Group study or collaborative learning has attracted considerable attention and intellectual support in recent years through the efforts of English teachers like Kenneth A. Bruffee. Those interested in theory as well as practice might well start with Bruffee's highly-readable 1993 book, *Collaborative Learning: Higher Education, Interdependence, and the Authority of Knowledge*, in which the author argues convincingly that when students are encouraged to depend upon one another and not on the teacher they are able to form genuine learning communities. When this happens, the English classroom becomes very much like the "real world" where collaboration, teamwork, and interdependence are increasingly the norm and students come to understand that knowledge is finally a "consensus among the members of a community of peer something people construct by talking together and reaching an agreement."[18] A most valuable lesson indeed. For instructors interested in exploring this subject more fully I have included the list of suggested readings (below).

---

[18]Kenneth A. Bruffee, *Collaborative Learning: Higher Education, Interdependence, and the Authority of Knowledge* (Baltimore, 1993), p. 3.

Like most good ideas that teachers conjure up for the benefit of their colleagues, group study is often easier to describe than to put into effective operation. Many students, in fact, have little or no familiarity with such a form of cooperative enterprise. Traditional American education, as many of our students have known it, emphasizes individual activity and competition (with grades as prizes) rather than cooperation and collaboration, and tends to disapprove of students who look to others for help or reinforcement. For this reason, the success of group study greatly depends upon the leadership role of the teacher. In the end, though he or she must remain unobtrusive, it is the teacher who makes things go. The teacher is stimulator, clarifier, facilitator, and resource person. He or she must manage to keep up with the activities of each group, listening but not intruding, so as to be able to identify problems important enough to bring to the attention of the class as a whole. What this suggests, of course, is that group study, like other parts of the course curriculum, requires careful forethought and planning. When group study works, it is almost always because the teacher has made a major investment of time and effort.

The most familiar and common group activity is discussion in which the students enter into a dialogue among themselves about a story they have read. Group discussions can be either structured (perhaps at first they should be) with the teacher posing a question or topic to each group or unstructured and free form. They can be used to explore aspects of a story not previously discussed in the larger class setting or to expand upon areas of interest already identified. One way to insure that such an activity will ultimately have a focus is to appoint a recorder or secretary for each group whose responsibility is to summarize the group's discussions and conclusions (if any) for later presentation to the class as a whole, with the teacher reserving the final minutes of the hour for his or her own summation.

For Further Reading:

Adams, Dennis M., and Mary Hamm. *Cooperative Learning: Critical Thinking on Collaboration Across the Curriculum* (Charles C. Thomas Publisher, Springfield, Ill., 1996).

Astin, Alexander W. *Four Critical Years: Effects of College on Beliefs, Attitudes and Knowledge* (Jossey-Bass, San Francisco, 1978).

————. *What Matters in College? Four Critical Years Revisited* (Jossey-Bass, San Francisco, 1993).

Belenky, Mary, et. al. *Women's Ways of Knowing: Development of Self, Voice, and Mind* (Basic Books, New York, 1986).

Bennis, Warren G., and Herbert A. Shepard, "A Theory of Group Development," *Human Relations*, IX (1956), 415–437.

Bizzell, Patricia. *Academic Discourse and Critical Consciousness* (University of Pittsburgh Press, Pittsburgh, 1992).

Bouton, Clark, and Russell Y. Garth, eds. *Learning in Groups* (Jossey-Bass, San Francisco, 1983).

Bruffee, Kenneth A. "Collaborative Learning and the 'Conversation of Mankind,'" *College English*, XLVI (1984), 635–652.

————. *Collaborative Learning: Higher Education, Interdependence, and the Authority of Knowledge* (Johns Hopkins University Press, Baltimore, 1993).

Chickering, Arthur. *Commuting Versus Resident Students: Overcoming the Educational Inequities of Living Off Campus* (Jossey-Bass, San Francisco, 1974).

Dewey, John. *Experience and Education* (Collier, New York, 1963). (Originally published in 1938.)

Elbow, Peter. *Writing without Teachers* (Oxford University Press, New York, 1973).

Forman, Janis, ed. *New Lessons of Collaborative Writing* (Boynton/Cook, Portsmouth, N.H., 1991).

Foyle, Harvey C. *Interactive Learning in the Higher Education Classroom: Cooperative, Col-

laborative, and Active Learning Strategies (National Education Association, Washington, 1995).

Gere, Anne Ruggles. *Writing Groups: History, Theory, and Implications* (Southern Illinois University Press, Carbondale, 1987).

Goodsell, Anne S., Michelle R. Maher, and Vicent Tinto. *Collaborative Learning: A Sourcebook for Higher Education* (National Center on Postsecondary Teaching, Learning, and Assessment, University Park, Pa., 1992).

Haring-Smith, Tori. *Learning Together: An Introduction to Collaborative Learning* (Addison-Wesley, New York, 1993).

Hawkes, Peter. "Collaborative Learning and American Literature," *College Teaching* XXXIX (1991), 140–144.

Jacob, Evelyn. *Cooperative Learning in Context* (State University of New York Press, Albany, 1999).

Johnson, David W., et. al. *Circles of Learning: Cooperation in the Classroom* (Association for Supervision and Curriculum Development, Alexandria, Va., 1984).

Johnson, David W., Roger T. Johnson, and Karl A. Smith. *Cooperative Learning. Increasing College Faculty Instructional Productivity* (ASHE-ERIC Higher Education Report No. 4, George Washington University, School of Education and Human Development, Washington, D. C., 1991).

Lewin, Kurt, and Paul Grabbe. "Conduct, Knowledge, and the Acceptance of New Knowledge," *Journal of Social Issues*, I (1945), 53–64.

Mason, Edward. *Collaborative Learning* (Agathon, New York, 1972).

Mills, Barbara J., and Philip G. Cottell. *Cooperative Learning for Higher Education Faculty* (Oryx Press, Phoenix, 1997).

Newcomb, Theodore M., and Everett K. Wilson, eds. *College Peer Groups: Problems and Prospects for Research* (Aldine, Chicago, 1966).

O'Donnell, Angela M., and Alison King, eds. *Cognitive Perspectives on Peer Learning* (Lawrence Erdbaum Assoc., Mahwah, N.J., 1999).

Rau, William, and Barbara Sherman Heyl. "Humanizing the College Classroom: Collaborative Learning and Social Organization Among Students," *Teaching Sociology*, XVIII (1990), 141–155.

Reither, James A., and Douglas Vipond. "Writing as Collaboration," *College English*, LI (1989), 855–867.

Schwartz, William. "Group Work and the Social Scene," *Issues in American Social Work*, Robert W. Klenk and Robert M. Ryan, eds. (Wadsworth, Belmont, Ca., 1974).

Sharan, Shlomo. "Cooperative Learning in Small Groups: Recent Methods and Effects on Achievement, Attitudes, and Ethnic Relations," *Review of Educational Research*, L (1980), 241–271.

Sharan, Shlomo, and Hana Sachar. *Languages and Learning in the Cooperative Classroom* (Praeger, New York, 1990).

Slavin, Robert E. *Cooperative Learning: Theory, Research, and Practice* (Prentice-Hall, Englewood Cliffs, N.J., 1995).

Trimbur, John. "Consensus and Difference in Collaborative Learning," *College English*, LI (1989), 602–616.

Weiner, Harvey S. "Collaborative Learning in the Classroom: A Guide to Evaluation," *College English*, XLVIII (1986), 52–61.

A Word about Grading

It is often difficult in any group situation for the teacher to assign a grade to a given activity or project and be certain that he or she is doing full justice to all members of the group. Human nature and human aptitude being what they are, some students will take a more active interest and work harder toward the success of a group activity than others. For this reason, the teacher may decide not to grade such activities at all, and choose to rely instead on examinations and papers, the two traditional standards of measurement. If, on the other hand, the teacher does decide to grade group activities, he or she may wish to give a normative grade to the group as a whole and then let group members grade each other on the basis of their individual contributions. The teacher may also choose to provide a written evaluation to be filed with the rest of the student's work. Remember, however, not to confuse evaluation with grading (though grading is, of course, one means of providing evaluation). While students do not need to be graded on a day-to-day basis, they do require a constant flow of evaluation, from teacher and peers alike.

C. The Journal

The keeping of a journal, a technique used successfully by many teachers in composition classes, can also be used as a way of getting students to record their first, spontaneous responses to short stories they read on their own before coming to class. Such an activity not only encourages students to respond immediately and honestly to what they read, but provides a method of getting those impressions (thoughts, feelings, questions, comments) down on paper before they slip away and are forgotten. Because the impressions and ideas recorded in a journal are the student's own, journal-keeping aids the student in his or her personal quest for self-definition and self-identity. It helps to build self-confidence and a capacity for self-directed work. It gives students a real sense, very often for the first time, of their own unique values, tastes, and biases. It makes them see that language is not a neutral process, but is itself a mode of perceiving, a way of establishing order and meaning, and a method of discovery.

Students usually take to the keeping of a journal without much difficulty, though a minimal amount of instruction and direction is probably necessary. It might be a good idea for the instructor to read a few samples from journals kept in a previous course (if he or she has them) or to read a few appropriate passages from the journals of Emerson or Thoreau. (The opportunity for teachers themselves to keep—and occasionally share—a journal of their own should not be overlooked.) Entries should probably be kept reasonably short, and, of course, should be recorded in the student's own prose. As a distillation of a student's reactions to literature, these entries need only be candid and immediate; we are not concerned with great thoughts, only honest ones. The main thing, students should be told, is to get an idea down, without too much attention as to how complete and polished the sentences and paragraphs are (we think in fragments anyway). Many students come to take considerable pride and pleasure in journal writing, and will report back months later that their journal-keeping habit has persisted, albeit for new and widened purposes.

Besides its obvious use as a means of getting students into the habit of writing about literature, the journal has a number of other potential uses.

1. A journal provides students with a permanent record of their experience with literature. It is hoped that at the end of the course students will be able to look back in their journals and see just how far they have progressed in their abilities to appreciate and understand the way in which fiction works.
2. A journal can be used as the basis for small or large group discussions. Students can be asked to bring their journals to class and the instructor, upon occasion, can ask a few students to read aloud their previous evening's entries as a prelude to the day's discussion. When students bring their journals to class, they come, in a very real sense, prepared.
3. A journal may be used as a source for theme topics, especially those topics that ask the student to explore in some detail his or her own personal responses to a story.

4. A journal can be used to record in-class writing assignments. (Many teachers regularly introduce writing into the last fifteen to twenty minutes of a weekly class period as a means of supplementing formal out-of-class essays. The focus of such assignments can vary greatly: students can be asked to respond to a question about the work as a whole or to one of the editor's "Questions for Study," or to engage in a free-writing exercise on an aspect of the work of their own choosing.)
5. A journal can be used as a place to store up materials for first ventures into creative writing; see the section on creative writing.

Journals, by definition, are essentially private records, and the teacher will have to decide just how much use he or she wishes to make of them in the classroom. If the teacher has reasons to believe that open use will tend to compromise student spontaneity, public use of journals will be minimal. Journals can be collected and read by the instructor (perhaps even commented on in writing), though they probably should not be graded. Some sort of review, however, is usually necessary in order to make sure that students have grasped (are grasping) the essential details upon which their public written discussions and analyses will be dependent.

One additional activity in connection with the journal also suggests itself. It can be used as a place where students are asked to set down a plot summary of what happens in a given story. Whether this is done in the journal (and there is a danger that such a use will subvert its major function), the plot summary is a useful way or encouraging students in the close reading of a text. No matter how sophisticated a college class is, it is surprising how much sloppy reading (and actual misreading) of stories goes on. Plot summaries are nothing more than a record of the narrative level of the story, the "what happens." Once the class is agreed on the "what happens," it becomes much easier for the instructor to ask questions which focus on the "how?" and "why?"

For Further Reading:

Belenky, Mary Field, et. al. *Women's Ways of Knowing: The Development of Voice, Self, and Mind* (Basic Books, New York, 1986).

Burnham, Christopher. "Crumbling Metaphors: Integrating Heart and Brain Through Structured Journals," *College Composition and Communication*, XLIII (1993), 508–515.

Fulwiler, Toby, ed. *The Journal Book* (Boynton/Cook, Portsmouth, N.H., 1987).

Gannett, Cinthia. *Gender and the Journal: Diaries and Academic Discourse* (State University Press of New York, Albany, 1992).

Mallon, Thomas. *A Book of One's Own: People and Their Diaries* (Penguin, New York, 1984).

Progoff, Ira. *At a Journal Workshop* (Dialogue, New York, 1975).

D. Student Writing

Writing is, of course, a major activity for the literature class and in the experience of many teachers works best as a learning experience when papers are read and discussed by students themselves in a small-group, workshop setting. The logistics of such an activity are simple: they require only that student papers be *reproduced* and *distributed* to the members of each group in advance. The advantages of the workshop method are several. To begin with, it breaks students of the deadly (and often stultifying) habit of writing only for the teacher and reminds students that they are *real* writers writing for a *real* audience that they must constantly keep in mind if their writing is to be clear and effective. By so doing, students thus imitate the way in which literary criticism is in fact written by professionals and become critics themselves in the very best sense of the word. Immediate peer-group feedback serves to make student-writers aware (as no amount of formal instruction can) of the true variety of writing strategies, styles, and approaches available in formally discussing literature. And finally, as a strategy for sharing insights and ideas as well as for offering advice about writing effectiveness, the workshop approach is a way of truly integrating writing into a course in literature. As students discuss each others' papers, they will find themselves not only responding to the paper at hand but through that paper responding to the literary work itself. They will discover for themselves the truth of the old adage that writing about a subject is indeed a way of possessing it.

At the end of such workshop sessions, students can be asked to provide a brief written critique of one or more of the papers they have been discussing before sending those papers on to the teacher for comments and evaluation. The instructor may, of course, wish to provide a day or two of additional time for final revision before the papers arc submitted.

Critical Writing

Critical writing about literature is terribly difficult. Its very difficulty explains, in part at least, why many college professors do not write very much, if at all, a fact that teachers would do well to keep in mind when dealing with undergraduates, many of whom will probably have had little or no previous experience with this kind of formal writing. The value of the critical essay is nonetheless very real. Not only does it encourage (and in fact demand) a close and careful reading of the literary text, but it provides students with invaluable training and practice in such important rhetorical skills as marshaling evidence, formulating generalizations, and making interpretive judgments. Though most students, left to their own devices, would probably not choose to organize their response to literature through a formal critical or interpretive essay, most will indeed come to see that the critical essay is a logical (and in its way an even necessary) activity in the process of exploring and sharing one's response to a literary text.

As in any new leading activity, students must be given careful and adequate preparation. The teacher may wish to set aside a period or two to talk about and explain how to go about the task of writing a formal critical analysis, possibly using student papers from an earlier class as models. The greatest initial mistake that a teacher can make, it seems to me, is to ask students early in the course to write a critical analysis about an entire story. This is an invitation to disaster. Not only are the results likely to be unsatisfactory to student and teacher alike, but the failure will frustrate, perhaps even paralyze, the student. It is absolutely necessary to assign the novice writer a topic that is manageable. My own practice with first papers is to assign a topic dealing with characterization, the aspect of fiction with which students seem to have the least trouble, in a story already discussed in class, preferably one that has had the advantage of small group discussion. As a second step, I like to break the class down once again in small groups, this time for the purpose of letting the students talk together about the topic (each group can be assigned a different one for the sake of variety), possible ways of approaching and handling it, the kind of evidence needed, and the problem involved. Such a prewriting activity pays dividends. A student sitting down to write his or her own paper the following evening comes to the task with a fair degree of self-confidence and a sense of being prepared and adequate to the task. My other early topics are much the same: I attempt in each instance to isolate a different aspect of fiction, point of view, theme, style, setting, plot, etc., depending, of course, on the story at hand. Each topic is limited enough in scope that it can be dealt with fairly thoroughly in three to four pages.

From here, depending on the progress of the class, I usually move to topics of the kind raised directly or indirectly by the "Questions for Study" appended to the stories in *Fiction 100*:

1. Which event or episode in the story is the most significant and why? (A topic that helps students relate particular episodes to the theme of the whole story.)
2. Who is the story's protagonist? (A particularly good topic for stories like Melville's "Bartleby" where a real critical issue is at stake.)
3. What is the importance of a preselected passage (or passages) and how does it (do they) relate to the story as a whole? (This topic encourages students to reread the story carefully.)
4. Why did the author choose to tell the story from a particular point of view? Or, how might the story be different if narrated from character X's point of view? (A topic which asks students to weigh alternatives carefully.)

Many topics of comparison and contrast will also suggest themselves through perusing the thematic table of contents above. I also think that it is a good idea, on occasion, to let students choose their own topics. Our best writing—our most immediate and honest writing—is invariably done in response to subjects that we care about, that interest us, and, though I sometimes require advanced approval (lest a certain topic prove unwieldy), I see nothing wrong in extending this possibility to students.

One thing, however, is certain. Effective critical papers are seldom written in a vacuum, unless the students are both very experienced and very talented. Rather, they emerge out of our actual teaching of the course, out of our patient efforts to apprise students in advance of the problems and opportunities they will surely encounter along the way. This means we must allow time in class to respond to student questions, even as we attempt to anticipate them. If possible, try to encapsulate your assignment in a written hand-out that also contains the protocols for format, length, deadline, etc., as well as a careful summary of the standards by which the finished paper will be judged. All of these "prewriting" activities will pay rich dividends for students and teacher alike. For the students, the dividend is some measure of the kind of self-confidence that we all need in approaching a new and difficult undertaking. For the teacher, it is a leg up on the evaluation process that inevitably will follow. When assignments are carefully and fully given, the teacher has established in advance a more helpful context in which to point out where and how a given paper has failed to realize the assignment. Richard Larson makes the point well when he writes that

> students learn little from simply trying to outguess the teacher, from striving to write a theme in response to an assignment that seems pointless or confused. And they can hardly be expected to write a good theme if the assignment requires activities of mind that they have not practiced and do not know how to perform. They may, to be sure, learn from failures, but how frustrating it is to be told one has failed when one had no idea of how to seek success.[19]

Two final comments about the writing of formal analyses addressed to newer, less-experienced teachers—both of which return to the very difficulty of the undertaking itself. First, good writing, as every professional knows, requires the appropriate investment of time and energy, and we serve ourselves and our students best when we attempt to establish for them the same kinds of writing conditions and circumstances that we claim as absolutely essential in pursuing our own writing. Obviously there are restrictions such as course-imposed deadlines that must be respected and met. But even so, we need to establish procedures that encourage students to spend time in engaging and exploring their topics before they write through a variety of prewriting and brainstorming strategies. We need to make clear the need to come to grips with the all-important questions of audience and purpose, and the variety of available rhetorical strategies that follow from those decisions. And we need to make

---

[19]Richard L. Larson, "Teaching Before We Judge: Planning Assignments in Composition," *The Writing Teacher's* Sourcebook, ed. by Gary Tate and Edward P. J. Corbett (New York, 1981), p. 219.

certain that students understand the importance of, and as far as possible consciously engage in, each stage of the writing-composing process: prewriting, writing, revision, editing, proofreading, and evaluation. Second, a teacher will do well to make his or her written comments on a paper as positive as possible so as not to discourage the apprentice writer unduly. There may be more advantage to a few rather detailed comments on specific matters than in trying to point out flaws and errors in schoolmarm fashion wherever they occur.

In establishing the writing context of the course, experience has taught me to make certain that students have a functional working definition of *plagiarism*. One need not be preachy or overly legalistic on the subject, but it never ceases to amaze me how many students arrive on campus each fall (and in my office or the office of the associate dean in the subsequent course of the year) with what appears to be—and no doubt probably is—only the sketchiest notion of where legitimate "research" ends and plagiarism begins.

Evaluating Critical Writing: A Few Notes

No teacher particularly enjoys reading, evaluating, and grading papers—at least beyond a certain point. That much I take as one of the givens of the profession. Thus the only justification for the time and energy expended in such an exercise is that it provides a significant learning experience for the student-writer. The following brief notes are offered as a way of furthering that process.

1. Make your evaluative comments personal and authentic, those of a concerned *reader* rather than simply those of an objective and thoroughly impersonal *grader*. If your comments are directed simply at justifying a final grade, the student is likely to look only at that grade, file the paper away, and forget about it. Do not be afraid of sharing your gut-level emotional reactions (both positive and negative) as a way of responding and as a way of reminding the student that he or she has written for a real live audience.
2. Ask yourself (and then the student) whether the writing is "honest." Or is it, in part or in whole, formulistic, academic, cliché-ridden, insincere, and given to rhetorical flourishes that all but obscure the student's own authentic voice?
3. Offer praise wherever possible. Often the simple four-letter notation "good" will do more to encourage student writing than a whole paragraph filled with proofreaders marks. When a sentence (or a paragraph) is well written and makes its point effectively, by all means let the student know (and, if at all possible, try to indicate why). Your comments should encourage the student to go back to the paper in order to learn from what he or she has done (or neglected to do).
4. Direct attention by way of comments to those parts of the paper that do not "work," where writing breaks down and confusion sets in. Is the difficulty grammatical, structural, or logical? Again, try to help the student to see why his or her writing fails to be effective and offer some suggestions and strategies on how it might be revised. And try to deal in specifics rather than in generalizations.
5. Critical essays often fail to be effective because certain key critical questions are never addressed, let alone answered. When this occurs, you do the student a real service by raising the issue at that point in the paper where the student should have raised it himself or herself.
6. Critical essays often fail to fulfill their own possibilities because the student failed to see and develop them. Utilize your comments to point out this lack of development and to indicate briefly some of the missed opportunities. On the other hand, some essays will fail because the topic chosen is too large or too ambitious to be treated in the designated format. This fact too should be duly noted and commented on, so that the tactical error can be avoided next time.
7. Try to make your comments supportive even when you are irritated by the suspicion

(often well founded) that the student "completed" his or her paper ten minutes before class. Comments that can be interpreted or construed as attacking the writer's personality or character may satisfy your own outraged sense of being put upon but are unlikely to encourage the student to mend his or her ways. Try to remember that while standards of excellence and decorum are important, you are, in part at least, being paid to be imposed upon by students.

8. Be sure to end with a final summarizing comment (not simply a grade) which both praises, if possible, and makes specific suggestions for improvement. Try to key that improvement to work on a specific problem or problems in a way that helps the student reach for and locate a solution.

9. I find it appropriate to utilize both holistic ("of the whole") and analytic ("of the parts") evaluations of writing assignments in the literature class, as long as one recognizes that (a) certain kinds of assignments demand certain kinds of evaluative strategies and that (b) while holistic assessment can yield—and relatively quickly in terms of the expenditure of time and effort—overall judgments about quality, students still need the kinds of suggestions for improvement and feedback that more time-consuming analytical assessments alone can provide.

10. Create an occasion to discuss papers in class (whether or not formal revisions are to be required) by using mimeographed examples or an overhead projector. Encourage discussion among students of the strong and weak points of a given paragraph or essay, or how and why some papers achieved their purposes and others did not. Share with them candidly your own reactions, what you liked, what you didn't like, and why.

11. Keep a file of critical essays of various kinds written by students in earlier classes and invite students to consult them between papers. This kind of postwriting/prewriting activity (like those suggested above) can be helpful.

Creative Writing

The literature-based course in creative writing is hardly a new idea, but very often courses in literature offer little or no chance for students to try their hand at creating the very kind of literature that they have been studying. Such a state of affairs, on the face of it, is hard to explain, let alone justify. It occurs in the English classroom largely, I suspect, because of the tendency to honor, and build into the curriculum, the unfortunate assumption that teaching literature and teaching writing are mutually exclusive functions of English teachers. Courses in short fiction do, nonetheless, afford an excellent opportunity to introduce students to creative writing by allowing them to create their own "fictions" in response to the fictions they have read and studied. The writing of literature is itself, of course, a valuable language activity, and when undertaken within the context of a literature class allows students not only to explore their own linguistic resources and their accumulated experiences as maturing individuals, but to make use of what they have learned about the way that professional story tellers manipulate the elements of fiction (particularly the crucial issue of point of view).

Here again a small-group, workshop approach, offering immediate and spontaneous feedback, seems advisable. As student-writers discuss each other's stories, the ability or inability of a given writer to grasp the basic elements of fiction and integrate them into his or her story will naturally and inevitably become the center of the group's discussion and just as inevitably members of the group will find themselves drawing upon what they have understood about the stories by professional writers previously studied in class. Adequate time should be allowed for revisions and polishing after the student-authors have had the benefit of their "editors'" opinions. Each group might then recommend a story or two to the class as a whole, and the activity concluded by publication of these "best stories" in mimeographed booklet form.

To overcome the familiar problem of the novice fiction writer ("What do I write about?"), the teacher may want to provide a "germ" (to use Henry James' word) in the form of a newspaper article containing a human interest story. Or the teacher might write a brief synopsis of a story that he or she has read but which is likely to be unfamiliar to most students (the latest issue of *The New Yorker* is a convenient source) and then allow the students to "recreate" the story in any way that they choose. The advantage here, of course, is that student stories can later be compared to the professional original and discussed in relationship to it. A third possibility (for a shorter assignment) is to direct students to a story they have already read and ask them to write an alternative ending (or a sequel), being careful not to violate the established integrity of the characters themselves.

The use of newspaper articles as germs for short stories is particularly useful as a way for students to demonstrate their own understanding of the differences between the "real" events of everyday life and the "felt life" of literature as well as the actual working dynamics of such key fictional elements as plot (particularly conflict), point of view, and character.

In offering comments and suggestions on students' stories, one device is to call attention to specific authors in the text who have handled similar stylistic, technical, or thematic problems in the same or in a different way. Such a strategy, of course, turns students' attention back upon the very course of study that provided the occasion for this particular writing exercise.

What follows below is one such student assignment which I received in my sophomore-level introduction to fiction class during the Spring 1999 Semester. I am grateful to Farah Meerza for allowing me to reprint it here. The assignment—one she chose—was to re-write Bel Kaufman's "Sunday in the Park" from the point of view of the father. Not only is her story "creative" in every sense of that word, but it also demonstrates fine critical insight into the tensions and nuances of Kaufman's original.

Joseph Sr. watched happily as little Joe Jr. ran off on his sturdy three-year-old legs to find adventure in the park sandbox. He wore a satisfied grin as he thought of how his son was going to grow up to look just like his father. Joe had the family's cunning green eyes, he was energetic, playfully aggressive, stubborn, and wouldn't you know it, Joe was going to be a big boy just like his dad.

Joe Sr. loved bringing his son to this park every Sunday, it was quiet at this time, all the ooh-ing and aah-ing fussy mamas with their perfect little babies in dainty new clothes had gone home to perfect houses to cook perfect banquets for their shirt and tie clad husbands. He picked his newspaper off the bench and with a derisive snort threw the main page, editorial, and financial section aside in favor of the Sunday comics. *Now this is great stuff*, he thought.

Occasionally he gave a glance in Joe Jr.'s direction and chuckled heartily at the intense concentration on his son's face. There was nothing in the world comparable to watching Joe Jr. discover potential uses for sand. He laughed again and returned to the comics.

A little more time went by and he checked on Joe again. Now he was making little mounds in the sand and then pulverizing them one by one with his clenched fists. *Maybe I'll start him on boxing*. As his admiring father was about to go back to the funnies, he spotted a couple with a little boy Joe's age walking towards the bench right next to the sandbox. He'd never seen them before and watched them warily as the mother sat down in her pretty dress and the father sat next to her, looking for the *Times Magazine* section. The woman in the long flowing pastel dress smiled lovingly at her skinny little boy as he hesitantly made his way to the sandbox. *Now she's a beauty*, Joe Sr. thought as he half looked at her and half looked at his paper so as not to appear obvious. He felt her look up and quickly buried his nose in the paper again. Realizing she was only looking at her son in the sandbox with Joe, he shifted his gaze to the man sitting beside her. He immediately felt his insides clench in anger and at the same time felt like laughing at the sight.

The man sitting beside her had an intelligent and arrogant face. His too formal shirt and tie and trousers gave away his position, and fine fingers told of a man who knew no manual labor. He obviously never spent much time in the sun either. Joe didn't trust men like that, snobs who took advantage of and looked down upon hard-working men like himself in front of their fancy office buildings. The man was working on a crossword puzzle as if it held some great secret that would unlock all the knowledge of the universe. The fool was paying no attention to his wife or his child.

The couple's little boy sat in one corner of the sandbox, careful not to get too close to Joe Jr. He was hesitant to play with Joe at all. *Even the kid's a snob!* Joe's father thought, taking an instant dislike to the unsure little boy.

As if sensing his father's feelings from afar, Joe scooped up a fistful of sand and in a flash aimed it at the boy in the corner to get his attention. The sand missed the boy but he did not even look up. *Look at that, he's still ignoring my son!* Joe Sr. pretended to concentrate on the paper while the boy's mother looked up alarmed. Her strong admonishing voice carried across the playground while she shook a finger at Joe. *The nerve of the woman! How dare she lecture my son! That little snotty kid of hers is the one who needs some manners!* Joe voiced his opinion by spitting out of the corner of his mouth. *Let's see what Miss Manners thinks of that!* Joe peered over his paper to see her reaction. *Good, she's nervous. She should be! Such a pretty woman, ha!*

In defiance, little Joe threw another pile of sand at the scrawny kid, landing squarely in on his forehead. The rest of the sand fell in his hair and all over his clothes. *That was a good one Joe!* he thought in supreme satisfaction. He held his breath waiting for the other boy to get up and react. But nothing. Not a peep out of him, the little boy in his dirtied new clothes just looked towards his parents in helplessness while Joe Jr. stood in a steady fighting stance ready to defend himself at the first sign of trouble. *That's my boy, never back down!*

This time when the mother scolded Joe, her jaw was clenched tightly and her face was filled with tension. Joe couldn't believe she had the gall to use that sharp tone in her "mustn't do this and mustn't do that" speech to little Joe. But then she was just one of *them* after all. Joe's father looked directly at his son, letting all who were present know he was there and very aware of the situation, he said clearly and authoritatively, "You go right ahead Joe. Throw all you want. This here is a public sandbox." *They don't own it, they don't own us. Your son is not better than mine, how dare you tell him mustn't? You and your fancy shmancy words trying to make my kid feel bad! Your husband doesn't ever care, you stupid woman, look at him just sitting there Mr. High and Mighty!*

The woman turned toward her husband who was just now becoming aware of what had been going on. Joe heard an arrogant voice telling him, "You're quite right, but just because this is a public place." Joe felt his blood boil as he focused on the man's fancy look-down-on-everyone glasses, imagining how good it would feel to shove them down the man's slender woman-like throat. Then he looked the thin man over from head to toe wanting desperately to put the man in his place and knock him off the pedestal he obviously thought he was on. "Yeah? My kid's got just as good right here as yours, and if he feels like throwing sand, he'll throw it, and if you don't like it, you can take your kid the hell out of here," Joe countered. *What do you think of that, little man?!!*

"Now just a minute, you must realize . . ." the man began as he straightened his glasses.

"Aw, shut up!"

The man grew pale as Joe towered over him. But he still continued to talk, "This is ridiculous" he started in a shaky voice. He wore the same look of helplessness his son had earlier. "I must ask you . . ."

"Oh yeah?" The man's snotty "must's" were grinding harder on Joe's nerves. *Don't try to push me around, I'm gonna put you in your place!* Joe stepped forward menacingly until he was eye to eye (well eye to chest since the other man was shorter) and toe to toe.

"You and who else?" *Gonna get the little wifey to stand up for you you little snobby spineless weasel?*

The man seemed to shrink before his eyes and looked as if he would wet himself any minute. Grinning inwardly Joe watched as Mr. High and Mighty hurried to grab his kid out of the sandbox. He fought hard not to laugh when the kid began to wail in protest. The man looked as helpless dealing with his own kid as he had with Joe. His wife just followed with a worried expression, she had said nothing more. Joe watched them as they rushed out of the park like two scared rabbits. He could still hear their kid wailing as they walked out of the gate and headed down the street.

He turned and walked over to little Joe who was now sitting in the sandbox and sobbing quietly.

"Daddy, why didn't that boy want to play with me?"

Joe did not know what to say. How could he explain? He scooped little Joe up in his arms and started out the gate. It wasn't really that nervous little boy's fault. Then whose fault was it really? No matter how much he tried to think of something else, anything else, he kept running over what had happened in his mind. It shouldn't bother him should it? Why? Why? He had no answer. The thrill of chasing the man and his family off now felt like lead in his stomach. He held his son's little hand and walked home still wondering.

E. Oral Interpretation

Just when the short story finally severed itself from its long oral tradition is a matter of some doubt, though the advent of cheap newspapers and books and the rise of monthly periodicals during the late eighteenth and early nineteenth centuries undoubtedly played a major role. Surely by the time of Charles Dickens, as the immense popularity of his public renditions of "The Death of Little Nell" and other excerpts from his writings attest, fiction had, for the average person at least, all but disassociated itself from the spoken word. In our own times, the very fact that actor Hal Holbrook could build a successful career reading and "being" Mark Twain suggests how unaccustomed we have become to "hearing" our literature.

There is no reason to belabor the point, other than to suggest that a valuable activity of the English classroom is an attempt to restore the author's "voice" to literature. Reading stories out loud, or hearing them read out loud, is a much more valuable adjunct to the interpretive process than many teachers themselves recognize. The sounds of Hemingway's "Hills Like White Elephants," for example, provide an invaluable clue to the story's meaning. The individual choice of words with their monosyllabic sameness and the short, choppy sentences with their unmodulated rhythms, to cite just two aspects of the famous Hemingway style, tell us much about the kind of existential world in which his characters live and move. In much the same way, the identification through the sound of the characters' "voices" indicates a good deal about their underlying attitudes in the face of a world whose predominant quality seems to be despair. Students can come to understand and appreciate much better the distinctiveness of literary style when they hear as well as read the words. This is particularly true of the unfamiliar style of nineteenth-century authors: the quiet discursiveness of Washington Irving, the heightened, often stilted, language of Edgar Allan Poe, or the rhythmical, stately prose of Nathaniel Hawthorne.

The most obvious "oral" classroom activity is, of course, playing the recordings of stories read by professional actors and readers. Recordings provide an easy and fairly inexpensive way to train the ear and to sensitize students to the various devices of language that characterize an author's prose style. A number of the stories in *Fiction 100* currently available on cassette are listed at the end of this section.

Other activities, requiring the active rather than the passive participation of students, also suggest themselves. The aim in every case is to draw attention to words and the sound of words, which otherwise remain inert and go "unheard," and to emphasize the author's own sensitivity to the possibilities of language and the way it is used to reinforce meaning. The simplest activity is to let two or more students read preselected parts of a story aloud before the class. This will undoubtedly call for some prior rehearsal and the blocking out of parts or roles. In so doing, the author's stage directions should receive proper attention, for stage directions too are one of the authentic "voices" of a story and provide insight into such crucial technical matters as point of view. Students will usually be surprised to discover just how many voices an author actually does employ in telling his or her story (the active verb "tells" in fact presupposes an oral voice) and how many different voices a given story contains. Careful listening will also reveal where shifts of tone occur, where intended emphasis falls, and just how much of a character's personality is revealed by the sound of his or her voice. One good way of getting students to appreciate the rhythmical and syntactical differences between the styles of two authors is to prerecord passages from different authors (say Hemingway and Henry James or James Joyce and Nathaniel Hawthorne) on a cassette recorder and then play them back several times.

Short Stories on Cassette and CD-Rom

AUTHOR AND STORY	READ BY	DISTRIBUTOR
Ambrose Bierce—"An Occurrence at Owl Creek Bridge"	N/A N/A Richard Pyatt	Audio Editions Jimcin Recordings Listening Library
Ray Bradbury—"August 2002: Night Meeting	Ray Bradbury Ray Bradbury	Audio Prose Listening Library
Raymond Carver—"Cathedral"	Raymond Carver	Audio Prose
Kate Chopin—"The Story of an Hour"	N/A	Jimcin Recordings
Agatha Christie—"Witness for the Prosecution"	Anthony Quayle	Audio Editions
Samuel L. Clemens—"The Celebrated Jumping Frog of Calaveras County"	N/A Thomas Becker Jack Whitaker	Audio Editions Commuters Library Listening Library Jimcin Recordings
Samuel L. Clemens—"The Man That Corrupted Hadleyburg"	Walter Zimmerman/ Jim Killavey	Jimcin Recordings
Joseph Conrad—"Heart of Darkness"	Jim Roberts Jim Killavey Norman Barris	Jimcin Recordings Jimcin Recordings Listening Library Audio Books on Compact Disc
Joseph Conrad—"The Secret Sharer"	Norman Barris	Listening Library Audio Books on Compact Disc
Joseph Conrad—"Youth"	Jim Roberts N/A Norman Barris	Jimcin Recordings Jimcin Recordings Listening Library
Stephen Crane—"The Blue Hotel"	N/A N/A N/A	Audio Editions Jimcin Recordings Listening Library

Stephen Crane—"The Bride Comes to Yellow Sky"	N/A	Audio Editions
	N/A	Jimcin Recordings
	Jack Dahlby	Listening Library
Arthur Conan Doyle— "A Scandal in Bohemia"	John Gielgud	Audio Editions
	Ben Kingsley	Audio Editions
	Basil Rathbone/ Nigel Bruce	Audio Editions
	Walter Covell	Jimcin Recordings
	John Brewster	Listening Library
William Faulkner—"Barn Burning"	Barrett Clark	Listening Library
William Faulkner—"A Rose for Emily"	Tammy Grimes	Audio Prose
	Barrett Clark	Listening Library
Richard Ford—"Rock Springs"	Richard Ford	Audio Prose
Mary Wilkins Freeman—"A New England Nun"	N/A	Jimcin Recordings
Charlotte Perkins Gilman—"The Yellow Wall-Paper"	Claudette Sutherland	Commuters Library
Gail Godwin—"Dream Children"	Gail Godwin	Audio Prose
Nikolai Gogol—"The Overcoat"	N/A	Jimcin Recordings
	Martin Donegan	Listening Library
Thomas Hardy—"The Three Strangers"	N/A	Jimcin Recordings
Nathaniel Hawthorne—"My Kinsman, Major Molineux"	N/A	Jimcin Recordings
Nathaniel Hawthorne—"Young Goodman Brown"	N/A	Jimcin Recordings
	George Backman	Listening Library
Pam Houston—"How to Talk to a Hunter"	Pam Houston	Audio Editions
Washington Irving—"The Legend of Sleepy Hollow"	N/A	Jimcin Recordings
	Hurd Hatfield	Listening Library
	Hurd Hatfield	Spoken Arts
	Elliott Gould	Audio Editions
	Jim Beach	Blackstone Audio Books
Shirley Jackson—"The Lottery"	Shirley Jackson	Listening Library
James Joyce—"Araby"	Richard Setlok	Commuters Library
	Frederick Davidson	Blackstone Audio Books
		Audio Books on Compact Disc
James Joyce—"The Dead"	Danny Hurston and	Audio Editions
	Kate Mulgrew	Audio Prose
	Richard Setlok	Commuters Library
	Jim Killavey	Jimcin Recordings
	Frederick Davidson	Blackstone Audio Books
		Audio Books on Compact Disc

Sarah Orne Jewett—"A White Heron"	N/A	Jimcin Recordings
Rudyard Kipling—"They"	N/A	Jimcin Recordings
W. P. Kinsella—"Shoeless Joe Jackson Comes to Iowa"	N/A Grover Gardner	Audio Editions Blackstone Audio Books
Ring Lardner—"Haircut"	Henry Morgan	Listening Library
Bernard Malamud—"The Magic Barrel"	Eli Wallach	Listening Library
Guy de Maupassant—"The Necklace"	N/A Edward Blake	Jimcin Recordings Listening Library
Herman Melville—"Bartleby the Scrivener"	N/A James Mason	Jimcin Recordings Listening Library
Joyce Carol Oates—"Where Are You Going, Where Have You Been?"	Joyce Carol Oates	Audio Prose
Dorothy Parker—"Big Blonde"	Lauren Becall Lauren Becall	Audio Prose Listening Library
Edgar Allan Poe—"The Cask of Amontillado"	Christopher Lee Lloyd Battista Ralph Cosham N/A Edward Blake	Audio Editions Commuters Library Commuters Library Jimcin Recordings Listening Library
Edgar Allan Poe—"The Fall of the House of Usher"	Christopher Lee N/A Edward Blake	Audio Editions Jimcin Recordings Listening Library
Edgar Allan Poe—"The Purloined Letter"	Edward Blake	Listening Library
Katherine Anne Porter—"The Grave"	Siobhan McKenna Siobhan McKenna	Audio Editions Audio Prose
Isaac Bashevis Singer—"Gimpel the Fool"	Theodore Bikel Theodore Bikel	Audio Editions Audio Prose
Leo Tolstoy—"The Death of Ivan Ilych"	Walter Zimmerman	Jimcin Recordings
John Updike—"A&P"	John Updike	Audio Prose
John Updike—"Separating"	John Updike	Audio Prose
Eudora Welty—"Why I Live at the P.O."	Eudora Welty	Audio Prose

Addresses of Distributors

Audio Books on Compact Disc, Inc.
5161 Staverly Lane
Norcross, Georgia 30092
1-888-749-6342
Fax 770-417-1242
www.abcdinc.com

Audio Editions
P.O. Box 6930
Auburn, California 95604
1-800/231-4261
Fax 800/882-1840
www.audio-editions.com

Audio Prose
The American Audio Prose Library, Inc.
P.O. Box 842
Columbia, Missouri 65205-9916
1-800/447-2275 (Missouri 314/443-0361)
Fax 573/499-0579
www.americanaudioprose.com

Blackstone Audio Books
P.O. Box 969
Ashland, Oregon 97520
1-800-729-2665

Commuters Library
7334 Knapp Ct.
Falls Church, Virginia 22043
703/847-6355
Fax 703/827-8937

Jimcin Recordings
P.O. Box 536
Portsmouth, Rhode Island 02871
1-800/538-3034
FAX 1-401/849-0610
www.jimcin.com

Listening Library, Inc.
One Park Avenue
Old Greenwich, Connecticut 06870-9990
1-800/243-4504
www.listeninglib.com

F. Role Playing

Role playing (it is also referred to as improvisation or creative dramatics) provides an excellent way of intensifying the experience of literature and of getting at and exploring such technical aspects of fiction as characterization and point of view. Role playing can be spontaneous and wholly improvised (triggered, for example, by the teacher passing out slips of paper with the names of various characters and the narrator) or prepared in advance by preselected groups of students working from a set script. In the latter instance, direction is provided by such devices as asking students to isolate at least one of the character's major traits as they address themselves to acting out their assumed character's reactions to an idea or situation in the story itself or to some external situation.

Insofar as it requires students to return to the text to gather and sort out evidence and to find validation for their ideas, role playing demands, as a precondition, disciplined understanding of the text at hand. Most students come to see, in fact, and rather quickly, that how they choose to play their assigned role in itself constitutes an act of interpretation and analysis. Students must ask themselves many questions about how a character experiences life, how that character views himself or herself, and how he or she views and interacts with the other characters. Students must weigh the importance (or lack of importance) to be attached to nonverbal gestures and to the other little pieces of an author's stage directions embedded within the linguistic text, which often go unnoticed. Students must, that is, explore the whole range of artistic techniques that constitutes the art of characterization. By so doing, of course, they also bring into focus the crucial relationship between characters and narrator and thus gain insight into the controlling function and fundamental importance of point of view. Role playing is a particularly good way of focusing attention on dialogue, its stress and tone, and its relationship to characterization, a dynamic that students often tend to underemphasize in the reading process.

While role playing by a small group requires the attention and tolerance of the rest of the class, their participation should by no means be wholly passive. At the appropriate time the class, as audience, should be encouraged to enter in by asking questions and making comments. They should feel free to probe the character-actors with questions such as "Why did you do that?" "Why do you think so?" and "Why do you feel that way?" Such questions will send both questioner and respondent back to the literary text, the place where such activities should both begin and end. Some teachers have enjoyed considerable success by having several groups of students work up the same scene in order to demonstrate the variety of interpretations possible with a given story and the very real influence that actors and director exert upon the adaptation of a work of literary art. In addition, role playing can be employed as a prewriting activity, particularly for those assignments having to do with characterization and the problems of characterization.

Since it is very hard for some students to perform before an audience of their peers, a class must be a fairly cohesive unit if role playing is to be successful. For this reason, it might be a good idea for the teacher to participate actively in the early sessions.

G. Literature, Film, and Other Media

My task which I am trying to achieve is, by the power of the written word to make you hear, to make you feel—it is, before all, to make you *see*. That—and no more, and it is everything. If I succeed, you shall find there, according to your deserts, encouragement, consolation, fear, charm—all you demand—and, perhaps, also that glimpse of truth for which you have forgotten to ask.

—Joseph Conrad

The short story—in its use of action is nearer to the drama than to the novel. The cinema, itself busy with a technique, is of the same generation: in the last thirty years the two arts have been accelerating together. They have affinities—neither is sponsored by a tradition; both are, accordingly, free; both, still are self-conscious, show a self-imposed discipline and regard for form; both have, to work on, immense matter—the disoriented romanticism of the age.

—Elizabeth Bowen

Both literature and film are liberating arts...(they) present to us an artist's ordering of the chaos of human experience—Literature and film are similar also in that both tend to be content oriented—Both require cognitive participation in order to have the reader or viewer understand them. Finally, both film and literature frequently offer some form of entertainment.

—John Stuart Katz

The fact that a number of film adaptations of the stories in Fiction 100 are currently available suggests still another valuable and intrinsically interesting way of promoting student response to literature. Like it or not, the motion picture and other forms of nonprint media are an ineradicable part of today's student culture. By the time the average adolescent finishes high school, he or she has watched more than 500 movies (not to mention some 15,000 hours of television). Such exposure continues, of course, throughout the college years by means of film series, film societies, film festivals, television, the local movie house, and at home by means of the ubiquitous VCR, so that by the time of graduation this same mythical student, consciously or not, often has acquired a knowledge of the "grammar of film" that would put many older adults to shame. Though Marshall McLuhan was certainly correct enough in his initial charge that most modern adults have generally failed to understand the impact of media on our cognitive and perceptual capacities and the extent of its influence upon our lives, the situation is, fortunately for all concerned, changing. Relatively few English teachers, I suspect, would now argue with the NCTE's insistence that "visual literacy" is an absolute necessity in a media-oriented world or that film study per se (its aesthetics and technology) has a rightful place of its own somewhere in the high school and college curriculum. Indeed, once we come to see that film is in fact a kind of "literature," whose rhetoric, method, and techniques are in many ways analogous to the print literature we have always claimed as our domain, and that the experience of film can do much to illuminate, clarify, and extend the experience of print literature, the argument for including film within the English curriculum itself becomes a compelling one.

Though a detailed knowledge of the grammar of film, the techniques of filmmaking, and film criticism are valuable in their own right, many teachers of English simply have not yet had time to acquire this expertise. Such a handicap is not fatal, and as the growing body of writing on the subject of literature and film suggests (see the bibliography following this discussion), a little reading and practical experience can do much to offset what ever deficiencies may exist. Here again, as in so many areas of our educational lives, student and teacher can learn together, and without mutual embarrassment. What is important to recognize is the fact that film and fiction are both narrative modes that attempt to order experience by presenting a sequential series of events, that both involve such common elements as theme, plot, setting, point of view, characterization, mood, tone, imagery, and symbol, and that both accord their subject a treatment which can be characterized as romantic, realistic, or experimental. To be sure, there are differences of method and technique enforced by the very nature of the medium that encapsulates them, but an exploration of such differences goes far toward answering that all-important question of what happens when literature is translated into film and in telling us a good deal about the relative strengths and weaknesses of the respective genres and tire options available to the practitioners of each.

The use of film adaptations in a course on the short story has much to recommend it logistically. In the first place, most such films are short enough to be viewed twice within a given class hour, a prerequisite to understanding which most film experts see as absolutely essential. In the second place, rental fees for short films are correspondingly reduced, a consideration of no mean importance in this budget-conscious day and age. In addition, thanks to the videocassette revolution, film adaptations of many short stories (including those in the highly regarded PBS "American Short Story" series) are now available locally in video stores (in either VHS or BETA format) at a fraction of the cost of renting or purchasing standard 16mm films by mail. If you decide to rent a videocassette for classroom use, be certain that your rental contract legally permits such showings.

The kind of discussions, the kind and range of questions, and the kind of additional activities that can be generated by a comparison of film adaptations and their originals will, of course, vary. For this reason, the questions listed below are of a most generalized nature and are intended as suggestive only. The only stricture I would offer (and it is, admittedly, a personal one) is that because the film is shown within the context of a literature course, the weight and focus of such questions and discussions should finally come to rest upon the literary work and upon how the study of an alternative form of media experience (the film) can lead us to a deeper, fuller understanding and appreciation of the literary text. As in other response-related activities, student response to film should be encouraged to range widely over the cognitive and affective components of the film experience. It should, nonetheless, if the activity is to be most rewarding (and here the teacher must play a major role), finally direct the student back to the verbal construct of the literary work itself.

Literature/Film: Ten Questions

1. What devices are used by the author and filmmaker to provide narrative structure?
2. How do author and filmmaker go about suggesting time and the passage of time—both actual (horological) time and psychological time?
3. What techniques do the two mediums employ to establish characterization?
4. How does the filmmaker reveal what is taking place in the mind of the protagonist and the minds of the other characters?
5. What is the point of view of the story? Where is the point of view—the eye of the camera—located on the screen? What effect does the location of the camera's eye have upon the other elements in the film?
6. How do the two media go about establishing setting, mood, and tone? What imagery and symbols do each employ?
7. How is theme presented and revealed to reader and viewer?
8. What specific cinematic techniques does the filmmaker employ—close-up, middle-distance, and long-range shots, sound effects, flashbacks, and lighting?
9. How faithful has the filmmaker been to the original story? What liberties has he or she taken? What has been added and what has been left out? And why?
10. Which experience (the film or the printed story) is the more satisfying? Why?

Adaptations of Short Stories in Fiction 100 on Film and Video

AUTHOR AND STORY	FILM TITLE/SHOWING TIME	DISTRIBUTOR
Ambrose Bierce—"An Occurrence at Owl Creek Bridge"	a. Same (1962) (b&w, 27 min.) Robert Enrico, dir.	Viewfinders, Inc. Indiana University Kit Parker Films
	b. Same Classic Literary Stories, Vol. 3	Media Basics Video
	c. Same (29 min.)	Teacher's Video
Kate Chopin—"The Story of an Hour"	Same (5 versions) (color, 26 min.)	Films for the Humanities

	"The Joy that Kills" (color, 56 min.)	Films for the Humanities
Agatha Christie— "The Witness for the Prosecution"	Same (1957) (b&w, 114 min.)	United Artist film with Charles Laughton, Tyrone Power, Marlene Dietrich, Elsa Lanchester; Billy Wilder, dir.
Samuel L. Clemens—"The Man That Corrupted Hadleyburg"	Same American Short Story Collection	Teacher's Video

Joseph Conrad—"The
Secret Sharer"
	a. "Face to Face" (1952)
	   (b&w, 45 min)
	b. Same (1973)
	   (color, 30 min.)
		Kit Parker Films
		
		Britannica
		Indiana University

Joseph Conrad—"Heart of Darkness"	Same (color, 105 min.) John Malkovich & Tim Roth	Media Basics Video Viewfinders, Inc.
Stephen Crane—"The Blue Hotel"	Same (1974) (color, 54 min.) David Warner and James Keach	Indiana University Media Basics Video Teacher's Video
Stephen Crane—"The Bride Comes to Yellow Sky"	"Face to Face" (1952) (b&w, 45 min.)	Kit Parker Films
Arthur Conan Doyle— "A Scandal in Bohemia"	Same (color, 53 min.) PBS Mystery Series Jeremy Brett as Holmes	Viewfinders, Inc. Media Basics Video

William Faulkner—
"Barn Burning"
	a. Same (1977)
	   (color, 41 min.)
	   Tommy Lee Jones
	
	b. "The Long, Hot
	   Summer" (1958)
	   (color, 117 min.)
	   Paul Newman, Joanne
	   Woodward, Orson Welles
		Indiana University
		Media Basics Video
		Viewfinders, Inc.
		Teacher's Video
		
		Kit Parker Films

William Faulkner— "A Rose for Emily"	Same (1983) (color, 27 min.) Angelica Houston & John Houseman	Media Basics Video Pyramid Film & Video Viewfinders, Inc.
Charlotte Perkins Gilman—"The Yellow Wall-Paper"	Same (1978) (color, 15 min.) Same (BBC drama) (color, 76 min.)	Indiana University Films for the Humanities
Susan Glaspell—"A Jury of Her Peers"	Same (1980) (color, 30 min.)	Indiana University Films Incorporated

Nikolai Gogol—"The
Overcoat"
	a. "The Cloak"
	   (1926 Russian version)
	   (b&w, 70 min., silent)
		Museum of Modern Art
		Corinth Films

	b. Same (1959 Russian version) (b&w, 73 min.) A. Batalov, dir.	Contemporary Films
	c. Same (1960 Russian version) (b&w, 78 min.)	Corinth Films
	d. "Bespoke Overcoat" (color, 30 min.) (British adaptation)	Univ. of Cal.
	e. Same (70 min.)	Media Basics Video
Bret Harte—"Tennessee's Partner"	Same (1978) (color, 15 min.)	Indiana University
Nathaniel Hawthorne— "Young Goodman Brown"	Same (1972) (color, 30 min.) Donald Fox, dir.	Pyramid Film & Video Indiana University
Shirley Jackson—"The Lottery"	Same (1969) (color, 18 min.)	Britannica Indiana University Media Basics Video Educational Frontiers
Henry James—"The Real Thing"	Same (1978) (color, 15 min.)	Indiana University
Sarah Orne Jewett— "A White Heron"	Same (1978) (color, 26 min.)	Media Basics Video
Dorothy Johnson—"The Man Who Shot Liberty Valance"	Same (1962) (b&w, 122 min.)	Baker & Taylor
James Joyce—"Araby"	Same Michael O'Kelly, prod. Set on location on North Richmond Street	Not yet commercially available
James Joyce—"The Dead"	Same (color, 98 min.) Anjelica Houston & David McCann John Houston, dir.	Media Basics Video
	Same Michael O'Kelly, prod. Set on location on Usher's Island	Not yet commercially available
W. P. Kinsella—"Shoeless Joe Jackson Comes to Iowa"	"Field of Dreams" (1989) (color, 106 min.) Kevin Costner, James Earl Jones, and Burt Lancaster	Deep discounted everywhere
D.H. Lawrence—"The Horse Dealer's Daughter"	Same (30 min., color)	Media Basics Video Teacher's Video

	Katherine Cannon & Philip Anglim	
Thomas Mann—"Death in Venice"	Same (1971) (color, 130 min.) Luchino Visconti, dir.	Viewfinders, Inc.
Guy de Maupassant—"The Necklace"	a. Same (1980) (color, 20 min.)	Britannica Educational Frontiers
	b. Same Classic Literary Stories, Vol. 2	Media Basics Video
Herman Melville—"Bartleby the Scrivener"	a. Same (color, 59 min.)	Films for the Humanities & Sciences
	b. Same (1969) (color, 28 min.)	Britannica Indiana University Educational Frontiers
	c. Same (1972) (color, 73 min.) Anthony Friedman, dir.	Viewfinders, Inc. Media Basics Video Teacher's Video
Joyce Carol Oates—"Where Are You Going, Where Have You Been?"	"Smooth Talk" (1985) (color, 92 min.) Joyce Chopra, dir. Tom Cole, screen play	PBS American Playhouse Series
Edgar Allan Poe—"The Cask of Amontillado"	a. Same (color, 10 min.)	Films for the Humanities & Sciences
	b. Same Classic Literary Stories, Vol. 2	Media Basics Video
	c. Same (1979) (18 min.) Bernard Wilets, dir.	Britannica Educational Frontiers
Edgar Allan Poe—"The Fall of the House of Usher"	a. Same (1928) (b&w, 45 min., silent) Jean Epstein, dir.	Museum of Modern Art
	b. Same (1969) (color, 30 min.)	Britannica Educational Frontiers
	c. Same (85 min.) Vincent Price & Mark Damon	Media Basics Video
John Steinbeck—"The Chrysanthemums"	Same (22 min.)	Pyramid Film & Video
Leo Tolstoy—"The Death of Ivan Ilych"	Same (1978) (color, 28 min.)	Mass Media Ministries
Richard Wright—"The Man Who Was Almost a Man"	"Almos' a Man" (1977) (color, 39 min.) LaVar Burton and Madge Sinclair	Indiana University Inc. Media Basics Video Viewfinders, Inc.

Baker & Taylor Entertainment
8140 North Lehigh Avenue
Morton Grove, Illinois 60053
847-965-8060
www.baker-taylor.com

Britannica
Encyclopedia Britannica Educational Corporation
310 South Michigan Avenue
Chicago, Illinois 60604
1-800/554-9862
Fax 1-312/347-7966

Corinth Films
34 Gansevoort Street
New York, New York 10014
www.awa.com

Educational Frontiers
132 West 21st Street
New York, New York 10011
1-800-753-6488

Films for the Humanities & Sciences
P.O. Box 2053
Princeton, New Jersey 08543-2053
609/275-2400
1-800/257-5126
FAX 609/275-3767
www.films.com

Films Incorporated Video
5547 North Ravenswood Avenue
Chicago, Illinois 60640-1199
1-800/323-4312 (Ill. 312/878-2600)
Fax 312/878-0416

Indiana University
Center for Media and Teaching Resources
Bloomington, Indiana 47405-5901
812/855-2103
1-800/552-8620
Fax 812/855-8404

Kit Parker Films
P. 0. Box 16022
Monterey, California 93942-6022
1-800/ 538-5838 (Cal., Alaska, Hawaii 1-408/649-5573)
Fax 408/393-0304
www.kitparker.com

Mass Media Ministries Films and Video
2116 N. Charles Street
Baltimore, Maryland 21218
1-800/828-8825

Media Basics Video
1200 Post Road
Guilford, Connecticut 06437
1-800/542-2505
FAX 203/458/9816
www.mediabasicsvideo.com

Museum of Modern Art
11 West 53rd Street
New York, New York 10019
212/708-9530
Fax 212/708-9531

Pyramid Film & Video
Box 1048
Santa Monica, California 90406
1-800/421-2304
FAX 310/453-9083
www.pyramidmedia.com

Teacher's Video Company
P.O. Box ENJ-4455
Scottsdale, Arizona 85261
1-800-262-8837
FAX 602-860-8650

Viewfinders, Incorporated
P.O. Box 1665
Evanston, Illinois 60204-1665
1-800/342-3342
FAX 1-847/869-1710

Literature and Film: Selected Bibliography

Aycock, Wendell, and Michael Schoenecke. *Film and Literature: A Comparative Approach to Adaptation* (Texas Tech University Press, Lubbock, Tx., 1989).

Barrett, Gerald R.,and Thomas L. Erskine, eds. *From Fiction to Film: "An Occurrence at Owl Creek Bridge"* (Dickinson Publishing Company, Encino, Cal., 1973).

———. *From Fiction to Film: "The Rocking-Horse Winner"* (Dickinson Publishing Company, Encino, Cal., 1974).

Beja, Morris. *Film and Literature* (Longman, New York, 1979).

Bluestone, George. *Novels into Film* (University of California Press, Berkeley and Los Angeles, 1957).

Branigan, Edward. *Point of View in the Cinema: A Theory of Narration and Subjectivity in Classical Film* (Mouton Publishers, Berlin, 1984)

Bryan, Margaret B., and Boyde H. David. *Writing About Literature and Film* (Harcourt Brace Jovanovich, Inc., New York, 1975).

Cancalon, Elaine D., et. al. *Intertextuality in Literature and Film: Selected Papers from the Thirteenth Annual Florida State University Conference on Literature and Film* (University of Florida Press, Gainesville, Fla., 1994).

Charney, Maurice, and Joseph Reppen. *Psychoanalytic Approaches to Literature and Film* (Farleigh Dickinson University Press, Rutherford, N.J., 1987).

Chatman, Seymour. *Coming to Terms: The Rhetoric of Narrative and Film* (Cornell University Press, Ithaca, N.Y., 1990).

———. *Story and Discourse: Narrative Structure in Fiction and Film* (Cornell University Press, Ithaca, N.Y., 1978).

Cohen, Keith. *Film and Fiction: The Dynamics of Exchange* (Yale University Press, New Haven, 1979).

Donelson, Ken. "Getting at Literary Terms Through Short Films," *Film Literature Quarterly*, XI, i(1983), 56–65.

Emmens, Carol A. *Short Stories on Film* (Libraries Unlimited, Littleton, Cal., 1978).

Fell, John L. *Film and Narrative Tradition* (University of Oklahoma Press, Norman, 1974).

Geduld, Harry M., ed. *Authors on Film* (Indiana University Press, Bloomington, Indiana, 1972).

Harrington, John. *The Rhetoric of Film* (Holt, Rinehart, and Winston, New York, 1973).

Huss, Roy, and Norman Silverstein. *The Film Experience: Elements of Motion Picture Art* (Dell Publishing Company, New York, 1968).

Jinks, William. *The Celluloid Literature* (Glencoe Press, Beverly Hills, Cal., 1971).

Kawin, Bruce F. *Telling It Again and Again: Repetition in Literature and Film* (Cornell University Press, Ithaca, N.Y,, 1972).

Lawson, John Howard. *Film: The Creative Process* (Hill and Wang, New York, 1964).

Lupack, Barbara Tepa. *Take Two: Adapting the Contemporary Novel to Film* (Bowling Green State University Press, Bowling Green, Ohio, 1994).

———. *Vision/Re-Vision: Adapting Contemporary American Fiction by Women to Film* (Bowling Green State University Press, Bowling Green, Ohio, 1996).

McDougal, Stuart Y. *Made into Movies: From Literature to Film* (Henry Holt Company, New York, 1985).

Maddux, Rachel, Stirling Silliphant, and Neil D. Isaacs. *Fiction into Film* (Dell Publishing Company, New York, 1970).

Marcus, Fred H., ed. *Film and Literature: Contrasts in Media* (Chandler Publishing Company, Scranton, Pa., 1971)

———. *Short Story/Short Film* (Englewood Cliffs, N.J., Prentice Hall, 1977)

Maynard, Richard A. *The Celluloid Curriculum: How to Use Movies in the Classroom* (Hayden Book Company, Rochelle Park, N.J., 1971)

Orr, John, and Colin Nicholson. *Cinema and Fiction: New Modes Of Adapting, 1950-1990* (Edinburgh University Press, Edinburgh, 1992).

Peavler, Terry J. "Teaching Film and Literature: A Few Principles," *Journal of General Education* XXIII (Spring 1980), 64–72.

Phillips, Gene D. *Conrad and Cinema: The Art of Adaptation* (Peter Lang Publishing, New York, 1995)

Poteet, G. Howard, ed., *The Compleat Guide to Film Study* (National Council of Teachers of English, Urbana, Ill., 1972)

Richardson Robert, *Literature and Film* (Indiana University Press, Bloomington, 1969).

Rollins, Peter C. "Film and American Studies: Questions, Activities, Guides," *American Quarterly*, XXXVI (August 1974), 245–265.

Seger, Linda. *The Art of Adaptation: Turning Fact and Fiction into Film* (Henry Holt Company, New York, 1992).

Selby, Keith, et. al. *Screening the Novel: The Theory and Practice of Literary Dramatization* (St. Martin's Press, New York, 1990).

Sheridan, Marion C., et al. *The Motion Picture and the Teaching of English* (Appleton-Century-Crofts, New York, 1965).

Simons, John D. *Literature and Film in the Historical Dimension: Selected Papers from the Fifteenth Annual Florida State University Conference on Literature and Film* (University of Florida Press, Gainesville, Fla., 1994).

Smith, Julian. "Short Fiction on Film: A Selected Filmography," *Studies in Short Fiction*, X (Fall 1973), 397–409.

Sojka, Gregory S. "The American Short Story into Film," *Studies in Short Fiction*, XV (Spring 1978), 203–204.

Trembly, Elizabeth, and William Reynolds. *It's a Print!: Detective Fiction from Page to Screen* (Bowling Green State University Press, Bowling Green, Ohio, 1994).

Literature, Film, and Student Writing

The use of film adaptations in the short story course suggests a number of possibilities for writing. The most obvious, of course, is a formal critical analysis growing out of the kind of discussion about the relationship between literature and film suggested in the preceding bibliography. Another type of writing project, perhaps less obvious, is a detailed scenario or shooting script based upon stories whose authors employ visual and representational techniques that can be described as cinematic. The table of contents of *Fiction 100* offers many such examples: Crane's "The Blue Hotel," Hawthorne's "My Kinsman, Major Molineux," Joyce's "The Dead," and Steinbeck's "The Chrysanthemums," to name just a few of the more obvious ones. The principle value of such an activity lies precisely in the extent that it encourages students to involve themselves intimately with the details and language of the short story they have chosen and that its completion necessitates a creative act of literary interpretation in the best and most basic sense or that term.

Here again, small-group work recommends itself, though the class as a whole might well be asked to undertake the initial, all-important task of breaking the larger story unit down into manageable and meaningful segments for individual groups to work upon. Having done so, the assignment can then proceed on an individual or group basis. I recommend the small-group format because of the number of significant decisions that must be made before an actual script is begun: e.g., what additions, deletions, and changes will have to be made in coming to grips with point of view, plot and structure, characterization, and dialogue. How is the problem of interior monologue (the character's own thoughts) to be handled? What kind of actors are to be employed, and what are they to look like? Where is the camera's focus to be placed, and what kinds of shots are to be used and when? Do we wish to shoot in black and white or in color? And what of sound effects? Is there to be musical accompaniment, and if so what kind? Is there to be a narrator? If so, how is his or her voice to be introduced? What kind of lighting and set designs seem most appropriate? Once these technical decisions have been reached (and students should be reminded to consult and reconsult the text for their authority), the actual writing exercise can begin, be completed, be reproduced, and then be passed out for discussion by the class as a whole.

Visual Statements

Visual statements, responding to one form of symbolic representation by creating another, provide still another way in which nonprint media can be utilized in the English classroom to organize and present feelings and perceptions about short fiction. Literature, we all agree, if it is to be truly meaningful must be grasped and held by the imagination of the reader. Visual statements provide a concrete way of dramatizing that engagement. As exercises in creative self-expression, visual statements in the form of collages, montages, and picture essays are a means of exploring and illustrating our responses to such aspects of fiction as characterization, theme, setting, atmosphere, and tone, as well as our total response to an entire literary work. Such statements help students to appreciate better why authors go to such lengths to create a "sense" of characterization, place, mood, and so forth, and the ways in which these verbal effects are in fact achieved. The requirements are simple: construction paper, pictures from magazines and newspapers, crayons, pen and ink, colored chalk, scissors, paste, string, ice cream sticks, swatches of material, and, for that matter, any kind of construction material readily available.

In the hands of students, even those without much prior experience, the results are frequently fascinating. The most obvious choice of stories are those, once again, where the visual element is most pronounced. Almost any story, however, will "work," and, in fact, it is often a good idea to ask students to respond visually to stories whose imagery is not predominantly visual. Visual statements can be used either to reinforce or counterpoint the text, or to provide it with a new metaphoric or symbolic dimension. For Flannery O'Connor's "Everything That Rises Must Converge," for example, collages might be created that juxtapose the world of the Old South to which Julian and his mother are so strongly tied and the confusing and frightening world of the New South with which they have so much difficulty in coping. Such assignments culminate, of course, in a form of "show and tell" in which students are asked to verbalize, explain, and defend their responses by going back to the story to authenticate and validate the representation they have created.

Where cassette recorders are available, students can be asked to create a multimedia presentation. They can be asked, for example, to find and record classical, modern, or popular music appropriate to the story's atmosphere or to a given character; they can experiment with a number of different recordings played back at different speeds to create a montage effect (here two recorders can be effectively employed to facilitate editing); or they can blend music with a narrative voice reading the story or with voices dramatizing a scene from the story. The possibilities indeed are endless, bounded only by the limitations of the student's or the teacher's imagination.

III
Resources on the Internet

It has been estimated that some nine million Americans use the Internet each day and that Internet traffic is increasing by thirty percent a month. And as many of us have learned, or are learning, there is lots of good stuff out there on the Internet including resources for teachers of literature. They include:

- On-line catalogs of some of the great libraries of the world, including the Harvard University Library and the Library of Congress. What a joy to be able to do basic bibliographic work from the comfort of one's study.
- On-line and down-loadable texts of an increasingly large number of novels and short stories, including the complete works of William Shakespeare. Carnegie Mellon University has been making electronic texts available since 1990. For those texts included in the current edition of *Fiction 100*, see below.
- Web sites dedicated to individual authors which often include biographical and bibliographical information, reviews, texts, photographs, and lists of criticism. For those authors included in the current edition of *Fiction 100*, see below.
- The Electronic Demonstration Center maintained by the Modern Language Association (MLA), where, among other things, you can down-load MLA's style sheet for citing electronic sources.
- On-line writing laboratories (OWLs) located at colleges and universities. Most of these sites understandably restrict their services to their own students, but some, like the one at Purdue University, offer down-loadable handouts and services to Internet browsers. At Purdue's Web site you can access some one hundred handouts on writing and writing-related issues including a handout on the citation of electronic sources in both MLA and APA formats.
- Commercial publisher's and university press Web sites. At Prentice Hall's Web site, you can download a copy of this book's table of contents. Many of these publishers provide on-line catalogs.
- Virtual bookstores, where you can search and buy. These include Amazon, which advertises itself as the "World's Greatest Bookstore," where you can browse a catalog containing a million titles or take a look at the "Daily Spotlight" and lists of featured books and books in the news. A more recent edition to the Net and just as formidable is Barnes & Noble, whose range of features fully rivals those of its better known predecessor. These two giants are not alone.
- Reference books: encyclopedias, bibliographies, thesauruses, dictionaries, etc.
- The home pages of English departments and individual English instructors. Instructors often make available their resumes, syllabi of courses they are teaching, and, sometimes, examples of their students' papers.

The list quite literally goes on and on. Internet sites, to be sure, vary greatly both in usefulness and quality. They also change daily, and are subject to idiosyncrasies of those who establish and maintain them . Web sites that are not maintained, like any other information source, quickly become outdated and simply add to the clutter of the Internet. The main point here, however, is that ready or not (and once again many of our students are far ahead of us), the electronic age has hit the English classroom with a vengeance.

Gaining access is fairly easy. Any of the established search engines will do (Yahoo!, Excite, Infoseek, Magellan, Webcrawler, Lycos, Fast, etc.). The main problem is that most of us simply have difficulty finding the time to get on the Internet and to keep up. Our students, on the other hand, can and do, and so it behooves all of us to be aware, if only in an occasional way, of what is out there in cyberspace that touches on the domain of literature.

As an aid to that search, I have included two lists. The first is a list of the texts in the current edition of *Fiction 100* for which there are electronic texts on the Internet. The second is a list of authors on whom information of various kinds can be obtained electronically.

Given the very nature and complexity of the electronic medium, and the difficulty of finding time to access it, the collaborative approach to learning once again suggests itself. Students can be encouraged to surf the Net in connection with their literature course and then to share their finds with fellow students (and with their teacher). These findings can either be shared in class or jotted down in student journals.

Authors on the Internet

Alice Adams	Susan Glaspell
Sherwood Anderson	F. Scott Fitzgerald
Toni Cade Bambara	Richard Ford
Donald Barthelme	Carlos Fuentes
Rick Bass	Gail Godwin
Ann Beattie	Nadine Gordimer
Saul Bellow	Thomas Hardy
Ambrose Bierce	Bret Harte
Elizabeth Bowen	Nathaniel Hawthorne
Kay Boyle	Ernest Hemingway
Ray Bradbury	Pam Houston
Albert Camus	Zora Neale Hurston
Raymond Carver	John Irving
John Cheever	Washington Irving
Anton Chekhov	Shirley Jackson
Kate Chopin	Henry James
Agatha Christie	Sarah Orne Jewett
Sandra Cisneros	James Joyce
Samuel Clemens	Bel Kaufman
Laurie Colwin	Garrison Keillor
Joseph Conrad	Stephen King
Stephen Crane	W. P. Kinsella
Arthur Conan Doyle	Rudyard Kipling
Ralph Ellison	Ring Lardner
Louise Erdrich	D. H. Lawrence
Mary Wilkins Freeman	Ursula Leguin
Gabriel García Márquez	Doris Lessing
Charlotte Perkins Gilman	Jack London

Bernard Malamud
Thomas Mann
Katherine Mansfield
Bobbie Ann Mason
Guy de Maupassant
Herman Melville
Susan Minot
Alice Munro
Iris Murdoch
Joyce Carol Oates
Flannery O'Connor
Frank O'Connor
Tillie Olson
Dorothy Parker
Edgar Allan Poe
Katherine Anne Porter

Leslie Marmon Silko
Isaac Bashevis Singer
John Steinbeck
Elizabeth Tallent
Amy Tan
Leo Tolstoi
Ivan Turgenev
John Updike
Alice Walker
Eudora Welty
W. D. Wetherell
William Carlos Williams
Elizabeth Winthrop
Tobias Wolf
Richard Wright

Texts on the Internet

Ambrose Bierce, "An Occurrence at Owl Creek Bridge"
Anton Chekov, "The Darling"
Anton Chekov, "The Lady with the Dog"
Kate Chopin, "Athénaïse: A Story of a Temperament"
Kate Chopin, "The Storm"
Kate Chopin, "The Story of an Hour"
Joseph Conrad, "Heart of Darkness"
Joseph Conrad, "The Secret Sharer"
Joseph Conrad, "Youth"
Arthur Conan Doyle, "A Scandal in Bohemia"
Charlotte Perkins Gilman, "The Yellow Wall-Paper"
Susan Glaspell, "A Jury of Her Peers"
Nathaniel Hawthorne, "My Kinsman, Major Molineux"
Nathaniel Hawthorne, "Young Goodman Brown"
Washington Irving, "The Legend of Sleepy Hollow"
Washington Irving, "Rip Van Winkle"
Henry James, "The Real Thing"
Sarah Orne Jewett, "A White Heron"
James Joyce, "Araby"
James Joyce, "The Dead"
Herman Melville, "Bartleby the Scrivener"
Herman Melville, "The Lightning-Rod Man"
Joyce Carol Oates, "Where Are You Going, Where Have You Been?"
Edgar Allan Poe, "The Fall of the House of Usher"

I have found that communicating with students by e-mail is infinitely preferable to communicating by either phone or fax because it is far less intrusive. My students know that my computer is not always on, and I encourage them to contact me whenever they need to. They know that when they write to me electronically I will respond. Another advantage of e-mail is that their communications and my own can be shared simultaneously with other class members—with the whole class if necessary. Teaching as I do at an urban university where most of my students are commuters, I have found that e-mail is also a way of building and sustaining a sense of community among teachers and students but in a way that protects my privacy and theirs. There are dangers with this as with any non-direct face-to-face form of communication. Without facial expression and tone as a guide it is sometimes possible to mistake the sender's intention. And with this as with any form of communication there are rules and etiquette which you would be wise to establish in advance.

IV
Short Story Commentaries

ALICE ADAMS, "His Women"

I suspect that many students will find this story confusing, not to their liking, or both. The problem is, of course, that the protagonist, Carter, is not a very likeable person. We are not told much about him. We know that during the 1970s—at the time of his marriage to the "truthfully beautiful and chronically unfaithful" Isabel—he was a teaching assistant in business administration. Whatever he is, and is not, is defined by his relationships with the three women of the story.

His marriage to Isabel, we are told, is a marriage for which the masculine world of The Citadel had left him unprepared. "Drinking was what they did best together; making love was not." Drinking makes Isabel "amorous." Drink leaves Carter, on the other hand, "turned off" and "far too often" "incapacitated." Carter is "devastated" by Isabel's departure.

If Isabel is beautiful, Meredith, the professor of music to whom Isabel introduces Carter, is not. Meredith is "Big, tall, dark, sexy," with a face "not pretty but memorable." (Isabel initially, and unkindly, described her to Carter as "big and fat" and "built like a cow.") Isabel and Carter's relationship belongs to the 1970s—to Carter's graduate student days. His relationship with Meredith belongs to the 1980s, though just what Carter does for a living (presumably, since he is still in Chapel Hill, he is teaching in the business school) is never made clear. We do know that he has made money in the stock market, and that he used the money to purchase the house in which he and Meredith have lived (the house whose sale has become the sticking point in their impending divorce). We also know that Carter has lost money in the market, and that this his principal wealth is now tied up in the house that he and Meredith jointly own. We know little about Meredith as well, other than that her past life has been filled with affairs and boyfriends. Soon after his divorce with Isabel is final, Carter and Meredith are married. For a time at least, life is good: "Sex with Meredith was sweet and pleasant and friendly...."

But Meredith proves as unfaithful as Isabel. We know about Adam, with whom she drifts in and out of love. Presumably there are others. Rejected, Carter seeks a divorce, only to discover in the process the "somewhat abrasive" New Yorker, Chase Landau, who "fell in love with him." Chase assuages his grief. She also is able to plumb his inner life. Chase makes him "safe," and "appreciated." Though Chase admits him into her bed (with her belief in "safe sex" she is clearly a selective mistress), it is a relationship to which Carter is unable to commit himself because he is unable or unwilling to detach himself from Meredith. When she announces her willingness to take him back, he returns.

Chase is deeply hurt. "I just want you to know a couple of things," Chase tells Carter on the phone:

> One, I was really in love with you. God, if I needed further proof that I'm seriously deranged. I always fall in love with the most unavailable man anywhere around.

In the end, Carter is left with Meredith—the "unlovely, untrustworthy, but deeply familiar Meredith." Is he wiser for it all? Probably not, for "despite himself" Carter thinks of Chase. "Is it now too late? Suppose he went back to her and said he was through with Meredith, would she take him back? Would she ask him to come and live with her?" The answer, Carter decides, is "no." Carter's fate seems fairly clear: a "lovely house" and the continuation of a life that has been, and is, unfulfilling. Though Alice Adams' story is not a pretty tale, it is, perhaps, a cautionary one. A tale for our times.

SHERWOOD ANDERSON, "I Want to Know Why"

"I Want to Know Why" is certainly one of the best of Anderson's initiation stories. As an initiation story it can be paired and discussed with a number of other stories in *Fiction 100*.

The story is carefully and artfully structured in two interrelated parts. The first part consists of the long expository section in which the narrator tells us in a rambling and discursive (though wholly credible) way what happened when he and his friends stole away from Beckersville to Saratoga. It climaxes with the race in which the stallion Sunstreak easily beats the gelding Middlestride. In the process the narrator builds up an idyllic relationship of the empathy between man and horse, as symbolized by the "shine" in Jerry Tillford's eyes just before the race. The second part of the story (which builds upon—and then undercuts and destroys—the values and expectations already established) concerns the events that take place the night after the race at "the rummy-looking farm house."

A sample of critical commentary on the story should prove helpful in getting at the issues which Anderson's story raises and explores:

> Critics of Sherwood Anderson's "I Want to Know Why" are agreed that this is the story of an adolescent boy whose development toward maturity is influenced by the shock he receives near the end of the story in seeing his idol, Jerry Tillford, in a house of ill-repute. Simon O. Lesser reads the story in Freudian terms with the boy's idealization of Jerry as a father substitute shaken in the farmhouse scene, while Cleanth Brooks and Robert Penn Warren see the crux of the story the boy's dismay at seeing Jerry, a creature possessing free will and a knowledge of right and wrong, making an evil choice. But although these interpretations have much to recommend them, both fall short of arriving at the full meaning of the story. Each properly stresses the event that leads to the boy's disillusion, but neither takes sufficiently into account the elements in his character which make his problem particularly acute, for neither treats the point of view of the story with the attention that the first person type of narration demands.
>
> —Donald A. Ringe (1959)

> The story is narrated by a boy who loves racehorses and the track life, and who has discovered to his disgust and bewilderment that one of the horse-trainers whom he greatly admires can feel the same toward a hard-mouthed prostitute as toward a clean-limbed and magnificent thoroughbred racehorse. The boy, nearly sixteen now, looks back almost a year to the occurrence about which he has been puzzling ever since. "I am getting to be a man and want to think straight and be O.K., and there's something I saw at the race meeting at the eastern track I can't figure out." The boy's wish to "think straight and be O.K." contrasts sharply with his earlier behavior, which is an innocent celebration of the subrational life of his senses. He is, at the time of the earlier incident, child enough to belong quite wholly to the primitive realm of the race track, the horses and the swipes, the trainers, the sights and sounds, the feelings and smells of the racing world, his keen enjoyment of it recalling Huck's adoration of the Mississippi.... In this primitive milieu of sensory impressions, of trainers and "niggers," of "aching" admiration for the hard and lovely thoroughbreds, the boy moves as naturally as a fish in a stream.
>
> —Glen A. Love (1976)

72

The story seems another instance of the initiation motif that is so characteristic of the period's fiction; indeed, one recognizes a number of conventions in its movement from the narrator's expressions of his unwitting wish to remain a child, to a climactic event that simultaneously confirms his innocent intuition and prefigures its inevitable loss, to his bewilderment on discovering his surrogate father's "rottenness." Even so, Anderson departs from the usual pattern: the narrator does not actually become an initiate…, nor is this adolescent's attainment of sexual sophistication quite the point. Almost by definition, the initiation story proceeds from ignorance to knowledge; here, in contrast, the narrator begins with an account of his sure moral judgment and ends with a confession of his uncertainty. A critical approach to "I Want to Know Why" virtually requires consideration of the reasons for this inversion.

The implications of the conclusion appear self-evident: in kissing the prostitute, Jerry Tillford has shown himself to be just another adult, thereby betraying the narrator's trust in his mentor's moral superiority; furthermore, since Jerry also functions as an older alterego, his fall from grace anticipates the narrator's encounter with his own "rottenness" as he advances into manhood. (Thus, it is not only Jerry but also life that betrays the adolescent's innocent faith.) Nothing in the ending violates the readers expectations; in fact, Anderson has specifically foreshadowed it by having the narrator, early in the story, complain about a trick played on him. An adult had said that eating half a cigar would stunt his growth, but the foul-tasting remedy "did no good. I kept right on growing. It was a joke." The same elements—anger at the treachery of adults, despair over the inability to halt biological change, and fear of not fitting into a mysterious scheme of life—recur in the ending; in effect, it is the joke's complement.

—Frank Gado (1983)

"I Want to Know Why" reverberates with the shivers of recognition of the presexual adolescent mind. The story throbs with often confused, often unidentified sexuality, but it definitely draws a direct connection between horses, men, women, and sexuality. Each of three horses—Middlestride, Sunstreak, and Strident—comes to represent a key personality trait and sexual profile of the narrator and other characters. Middlestride and Sunstreak are both the kind of horse that makes the narrator's "throat hurt to see." Middlestride is a gelding, Sunstreak a stallion. Middlestride is "long and looks awkward"; Sunstreak is "nervous and belongs on the biggest farm we've got in our country." Though Sunstreak is a stallion, he is compared to "a girl you think about sometime but never see"; he is also "hard all over and lovely too." Such ambisexuality is a significant theme in the story. Sunstreak's name implies that he is fast, clear, bright, and hot; Middlestride's name suggests a slow, muddled, lumbering, tepid horse. One of the prostitutes at the farmhouse is "like the gelding Middlestride, but not clean like him, but with a hard ugly mouth.…

The narrator is trying to find his position between Middlestride and Sunstreak, between being a gelding and being a stallion. He is trying to find out how he is going to run in life once he gets his chance. Early in the story he observes that "any thoroughbred, that is sired right and out of a good mare and trained by a man that knows how, can run." At that point the boy cannot run like a thoroughbred. By the end of the story, however, the boy is like Strident, "a new colt (that]… will lay them all out".…This is, in fact, his future destiny—to "lay them all out" once he sorts out the confusing information about sex.

—Robert Allen Papinchak (1992)

JAMES BALDWIN, "Sonny's Blues"

"Sonny's Blues," which appears with Baldwin's other major stories in the 1965 collection *Going to Meet the Man*, has been generally singled out as the best of the author's attempts at short fiction. "Sonny's Blues," Harry L. Jones writes,

> is the most perfectly realized story in the collection, that is, if one is operating in a scheme that insists on a cyclical structure and a fitness of the formal elements to the whole. There is nothing wasted in the story; even the flashback is structural. Albeit leisurely paced, the story does move from situation, complication, climax, to denouement. While there is some problem with the realization of the character of the narrator, even he is more fully presented than many of the other characters in the short works, and since he serves as a foil to Sonny, the narrator functions well largely because Sonny is so fully developed.

"Sonny's Blues" is the narrator's story. Its focus is on his slow and painful process toward awareness, self-discovery, and involvement. The younger brother, Sonny, is both the object and the means of that quest. By understanding the meaning and significance which Sonny attaches to his music, and the reconciliation which the process of understanding makes possible, the narrator is able to come to grips with and discover himself.

The narrator, a college graduate with a respectable teaching career, has adopted a way of life, and a set of values, expectations, and attitudes, which isolate and distance him from the realities (the "darkness") of both his own racial heritage and the human condition in general. Sensitive and articulate as well as educated, the narrator, in his attempt to live a quiet, ordered, insulated life in the midst of an environment from which he has tried to disassociate himself, has compromised and lost his identity. Opting for security, he has forgotten his father's admonition that there "Ain't no place safe for kids, nor nobody." In the process he has also psychologically and physically distanced himself from his musician brother who has chosen another path—another way to cope. The two brothers *are* very different.

> I simply couldn't see why on earth he'd want to spend his time hanging around nightclubs, clowning around on bandstands, while people pushed each other around on the dance floor. It seemed—beneath him, somehow....

Just how different the two are is neatly summarized in Sonny's response to the narrator's conventional and prudential observation that "you know people can't always do exactly what they *want* to do—"; "No, I don't know that.... I think people *ought* to do what they want to do, what else are they alive for?"

The movement toward understanding begins with the discovery of Sonny's arrest in the black-and-white pages of a newspaper, The newspaper account gives Sonny and his problem a reality that the narrator can no longer deny: "I couldn't believe it: but what I mean by that is that I couldn't find any room for it anywhere inside me. I had kept it outside me for a long time. I hadn't wanted to know." The emerging desire to know—to seek "that part of ourselves which had been left behind"—is reinforced and hastened by the death of the narrator's own small daughter (a child, significantly enough, named Grace). The tragedy of her death teaches him about human pain and suffering. "My trouble made his real." The concept of suffering—or, rather, of redemption and reconciliation through suffering—is central to the story. It is a lesson that Sonny has already learned. As he tells his brother,

> No, there's no way not to suffer. But you try all kinds of ways to keep from drowning in it, to keep on top of it and to make it seem—well, like *you*...there's no way of getting it out—that storm inside. You can't talk to it and you can't

74

make love with it, and when you finally try to get with it you realize *nobody's* listening. So you've got to listen. You got to find a way to listen.

A series of past events, whose recollection allows the narrator to better understand the complex feelings and attitudes of the present, comprise the central section of the story. It yields to the climactic scene in the jazz nightclub and to the organizing metaphor of the blues. Through his appreciation of the blues, the narrator discovers the significance which music has for Sonny and for others like him and the relationship of that meaning to the possibilities of self.

> They were not about anything very new. He [Creole] and his boys up there were keeping it new, at the risk of ruin, destruction, sadness, and death, in order to make us listen. For while the tale of how we suffer and how we are delighted, and how we may triumph is never new, it always must be heard. There isn't any other tale to tell, it's the only light we've got in all this darkness.

> I seemed to hear with what burning he [Sonny] has made it his, and with what burning we had yet to make it ours, how we could cease lamenting. Freedom lurked around us and I understood at last, that he could help us to be free if we would listen, that he would never be free until we did.

As Donald C. Murray notes, "The final point of the story is that the narrator, through his own suffering and the example of Sonny, is at last able to find himself in the brotherhood of man. Such an identification is an act of communion and 'Sonny's Blues' ends, significantly, with the image of the homely Scotch-and-milk glass transformed into 'the very cup of trembling,' the Grail, and the goal of the guest and the emblem of initiation." "Sonny's Blues" is a powerful and compelling story. Not the least of its virtues is the fact that in the process of becoming sympathetically engaged with the narrator we learn, as John M. Reilly observes, a good deal about "the human motives of the youths, whose lives are reported to others only by their inclusion as statistics of school dropout rates, drug usage, and unemployment."

TONI CADE BAMBARA, "The Lesson"

There is much to appreciate in Bambara's deceptively simple story of a trip by a bunch of inner-city-black kids to New York's famous upscale Fifth Avenue toy store F.A.O. Schwartz. One probably needs to begin discussion with the narrator Sylvia herself, for this clearly is Sylvia's story; and the way in which Bambara handles point of view is certainly one of the most effective parts of the story. Note, for example, how much the author accomplishes in the story's first paragraph. The very first sentence locates us in time: "Back in the days when everyone was old and stupid or young and foolish and me and Sugar were the only ones just right, this lady moved on our block with nappy hair and proper speech and no makeup." The voice that begins the sentence is the older Sylvia looking backwards on the events she is about to narrate. The voice that concludes the sentence, by contrast, is the voice of the younger Sylvia describing her nemesis Miss Moore from an earlier, adolescent point of view. Though the voice that narrates the rest of the paragraph talks to the reader from the same kind of dual perspective, that dualism soon vanishes and by the beginning of the second paragraph the voice that talks to the reader is the voice of the earlier Sylvia. How Bambara makes that voice a credible one is in large measure a tribute to her ability to reproduce language that rings true to our memories as adult readers of how things once were (or seemed to be) among the street-smart young.

Particularly praiseworthy is Bambara's ability to capture succinctly the extraordinary energy and raucous, irreverent behavior of Sylvia and her friends. Their very names are those out of our own childhood experience (Sugar, Junior, Flyboy, Fat Butt, Junebug, Q. T., Rosie Giraffe, Mercedes) and so is their behavior as they are rounded up at the mailbox by Miss Moore before setting out from their neighborhood to visit Fifth Avenue:

> So me and Sugar leaning on the mailbox being surly, which is a Miss Moore word. And Flyboy checking out what everybody brought for lunch. And Fat Butt already wasting his peanut-butter-and-jelly sandwich like the pig he is. And Junebug punchin on Q.T.'s arm for potato chips. And Rosie Giraffe shifting from one hip to the other waiting for somebody to step on her foot or ask her if she from Georgia so she can kick ass, preferably Mercedes'.

The "lesson" of the story is quite clear. It is stated succinctly by Sugar: "You know, Miss Moore, I don't think all of us here put together eat in a year what that sailboat costs....I think...that this is not much of a democracy if you ask me. Equal chance to pursue happiness means an equal crack at the dough, don't it?" Sylvia resists this lesson just as she resists Miss Moore. That resistance—though Sylvia fails to grasp its origin—has much to do with the assumptive world that it calls into question. The college-educated Miss Moore has taken it upon herself to educate the children of the neighborhood. Sylvia doesn't want to be educated. Her response, predictably, is one of anger and non-cooperation.

Part of Sylvia's resistance also has to do with her youth. Sylvia is simply not as smart or as knowing as she would have us believe. For example, while she is able to repeat Miss Moore's lesson about poor people needing to wake up and demand their "share of the pie," her rejoinder is an admission of ignorance: "Don't none of us know what kind of pie she talking about in the first damn place."

What, however, are we to make of the story's ending? Sylvia is clearly angry at Sugar's willingness to enter into and play Miss Moore's question-and-answer game. But she may be angry as well by her intimidation of the fact that if Sugar (and by extension Miss Moore) are right, then her own assumptive world is wrong. And if she is wrong, and there is inequality in the distribution of wealth, then she herself as an adult will have an obligation to do something about it. Her final remark—"Ain't nobody going beat me at nuthin"—seems to refer to Sugar. But does it? Or is it, in fact, an admission that Miss Moore has in fact gotten through to her and that Sylvia herself now knows, however partially and incompletely, that she will have to compete in the world for her own "share of the pie"? Bambara prepares us for the ending by having Sylvia confess the strange feeling of shame that overtakes her as she enters into the toy store:

> Not that I'm scared, what's there to be afraid of, just a toy store. But I feel funny, shame. But what I got to be shamed about? Got as much right to go in as anybody.

Sylvia may consciously resist the lesson that Miss Moore has brought them there to teach, but she herself intuitively knows that the world of F.A.O. Schwartz is not a world to which she and her friends, however cocky and smart they pretend to be, belong.

It is, finally, interesting to note that there is no judgment rendered by the older Sylvia upon the behavior or attitudes of her younger self. In this respect, compare her forbearance with the harsh judgment which the narrator of James Joyce's "Araby" renders upon his younger self as "a creature driven and derided by vanity." In the case of Bambara's story just what the older Sylvia finally thinks of the person she once was must be inferred from the text itself.

DONALD BARTHELME, "Cortés and Montezuma"

The short fiction of Donald Barthelme belongs to the cutting edge of contemporary avant-garde literature. His stories, like avant-garde fiction in general, are characterized by a rejection or reordering of the traditional elements of realistic fiction—plot, character, setting, theme, dialogue, etc.—in favor of a rendering of life that emphasizes the fragmented and fragmenting nature of the contemporary human experience. Barthelme's particular gift is his language, his ability to capture the clichés, jargon, and other forms of verbal banality which characterize so much of the speaking and writing of our time. As Lois Gordon notes, "Barthelme exaggerates the mass anesthetization of contemporary life through his bombardment of similarly inventive phrases, as well as juxtapositions, manipulations, and plays on odd, related, and seemingly unrelated materials. His extraordinary ear for the sounds of language and his parodic mastery of its spoken and written forms, elicits from his reader enormous laughter (and insight)." Helpful introductions to Barthelme's work can be found in Lois Gordon's *Donald Barthelme* (Twayne: Boston, 1981) and Maurice Couturier and Regis Durand's *Donald Barthelme* (Methuen: London: 1982).

Barthelme's "Cortés and Montezuma" is a story about the sixteenth-century conquest of the Aztec nation. As the footnotes make clear, the major narrative events of the story actually took place, and can be located in the pages of Bernal Diaz del Castillo's *The True History of the Conquest of New Spain* (1632), which the author cites, as well as in other chronicles of the conquest, which Barthelme has evidently read, but does not mention by name. Moreover, Barthelme has deliberately patterned his narrative style in imitation of the cadences of anachronisms as photographs, home movies, caviar, and the sudden entrance upon the scene of Charles V, Emperor of Spain, serve to remind us, Barthelme is not writing history though he most certainly is challenging some of our notions about the "events" of history and about the lives of those who are caught up in the historical process. His is a story about finite historical events as seen in the context of the human relationships they encompass and order.

The emphasis of the story is on friendship—the incipient friendship between Cortés and Montezuma, the conqueror and the conquered—as it might have been in another time and place. Their friendship is introduced at the very beginning of the story. Montezuma accepts Cortés because he believes him to be the "great god" Quetzalcoatl. They exchange gifts, and are soon portrayed, "walking, down by the docks...holding hands," talking theology (a refrain that is echoed throughout the story). Cortés is bitten by a green insect—Montezuma "sucks the poison from the wound." But, encapsulated as they are within their historic roles, their friendship, however genuine, is an uneasy one. Montezuma burns the messages he receives from the hills, "so that Cortés will not learn their contents"; Cortés employs a detective to follow Montezuma; Montezuma employs a detective to follow Father Sanchez; Juan de Escalante and five others are slain and impaled with their horses; the friendship of Montezuma and Cortés "is denounced as contrary to the best interests of the people of Mexico, born and yet unborn."

The tragedy of their *personal* relationship is, of course, that both men are caught up in the inexorable drama of *impersonal* history whose "facts," events, and pattern they can neither control nor alter. Indeed, they behave like actors in a play of someone else's construction. They lack the ability (or is it the will) to act as free agents. Form reinforces content. The paragraphs are short. They portray events in the present tense as they are set down by an omniscient narrator who records both action and response. The style itself, much like the style of the Spanish chronicles it parodies, suggests the relentless press of preordained events: "Because Cortés lands on a day specified in the ancient writings, because he is dressed in black, because his armor is silver in color, a certain *ugliness* of the strangers, taken as a group—for these reasons: Montezuma considers Cortés to be Quetzalcoatl, the great god who left Mexico many years before, on a raft of snakes, vowing to return."

Montezuma, in his role of absolute ruler, far more than Cortés, is aware of the drama of which he ought to be in charge. "'The ruler prepares dramas for the people,' Montezuma says. 'If the drama is not of my authorship, if events are not controllable by me— .... Therefore it is incumbent upon you, dear brother, to disclose to me the ending or at least what you know of the drama's probable course so that I may attempt to manipulate it in a favorable direction with the application of what magic is left to me.'" Note that twice "Cortés has no reply." Cortés' mission, as he himself defines it, is an impossible one: "I cannot leave until all the gold in Mexico, past, present and future, is stacked in the holds." Moreover, the lethargic Cortés, who seems largely resigned to the role he must play, deliberately seeks to deny and destroy his ability to control events: when confronted with "reports, documents, photographs," "Cortés orders that all of the detectives in the city be arrested, that the profession of detective be abolished forever...." At the end of the story, Charles V, improbably but quite appropriately, enters to ask: "'Was there no alternative?'" to which Cortés lamely responds, "'I did what I thought best.'" And in some later, fictionalized, afterlife, Montezuma's ghost "rebukes the ghost of Cortés. 'Why did you not throw up your hands, and catch the stone?'" The question is, of course, a poignant and pointed one, for the alert reader will recall that earlier in the story Doña Marina had shared her vision of "Montezuma...struck in the forehead by a large stone," to which Cortés had responded "'Don't worry....Trust me.'" The implication is that had either man acted differently, the texts of history, including del Castillo's, might have been changed, but that such acts would have required that either or both be willing and able to break out of the historical pattern that gives them their identities and defines their roles as soldier and king.

RICK BASS, "Antlers"

Bass's story, significantly, begins with the annual Halloween party, an event, following the close of the tourist season, that brings the three dozen permanent residents of their remote rural valley together for an evening of hard drinking and dancing. The party obviously assumes deeper psychological and anthropological overtones with the donning of antlers and butting of heads which speaks to some kind of primordial ritual which unites these damaged souls, the hunters and the hunted, with the primordial force which animates all of life. Bass's story, in a very real sense, explores the ability of his characters to understand the meaning and significance of this event for their own lives.

And a damaged lot these "hardy of heart" people are. They come to the valley, some seventy miles from the nearest town, and then stay there, for many reasons: "Some are on the run, and others are looking for something; some are incapable of living in a city, among people, while others simply love the wildness of new untouched country." The Halloween party over, they return to their "dark cabins" to wrestle with whatever demons have brought them to this "small place" to begin with. "Many of us have come here from other places and have been running all our lives from other things," notes the nameless narrator, "and I think that everyone who is up here has decided not to run anymore." Choosing not to run, on the other hand, brings on its own set of problems.

Among those who have decided "not to run anymore" are Suzie, the bar waitress, Randy, the bowhunter, and the narrator himself. It is the relationships between and among these three, the emotions and feelings that they brings forth, and the illumination and new understanding which they ultimately produce, that stand at the center of Bass's story.

Suzie "has moved through the valley with a regularity, a rhythm, that is all her own and has nothing to do with our—the men's—pleading or desires." Interestingly enough, we learn very little directly about what attracts the men of the valley to Suzie. While the relationships she establishes with these men presumably have their sexual component, Suzie is never described by the narrator in sexual terms. Indeed, we are told quite the opposite about her liaisons: "There wasn't a lot of heat in it for most of them—not the dizzying, lost feeling kind you get sometimes when you meet someone for the first time...." The word that defines a relationship with Suzie is not "heat," but rather "comfort." In the case of the narrator it is the kind of comfort that comes from their ability to share—and enjoy—simple things. "Our dates were simple enough," the narrator explains, "we'd go for long drives to the tops of snowy mountains and watch the valley. We'd drive into town, too, seventy miles away down a one-lane, rutted, cliff-hanging road, just for a dinner and movie." Later, the image of the two of them, sitting in a single chair, enjoying the sights and sounds of nature as darkness falls, suggests a kind of sensitivity to life and to each other which ultimately brings them back together and cements their relationship. When Suzie decides to leave the narrator—as she has left every man in the valley—he is deeply affected: "It felt like my heart had been torn from my chest, like my lungs were on fire...." The depth of these emotions set the narrator apart.

The narrator then hopes that Suzie will date Randy, the single male in the valley with whom she will have nothing to do. Her rejection of Randy, the men of the valley and the narrator believe, is caused by Suzie's attitude toward Randy's bowhunting—a sport that the narrator graphically describes. In a measure, of course, this is true. But Randy's bowhunting is only symptomatic. As the story progresses—and we learn more about Randy and his obsession (note the image of him practicing "in the middle of the day, shirtless, perspiring, his cheeks flushed")—the reader comes to sense that Suzie's rejection and fear result most fundamentally from her awareness of demons that define and drive Randy's deeper being. Suzie's ability to empathize with the hunted (as her participation in the ritualistic butting of antlers at the Halloween party suggests) allows her to sense in a way the narrator initially does not Randy's underlying anger and hatred, a cold-blooded anger and hatred which finds its public (and largely socially acceptable) outlet in bowhunting.

Only gradually does the narrator come to understand the fear which Suzie feels for Randy, an understanding which is clearly reinforced by the momentary look of cold-blooded "fury, terrible fury" which Randy turns on him in the story's final paragraph before "the polite mask" comes "back down over him." Though the narrator does not approve of bowhunting, his initial impulse is to defend Randy and his sport as "just something he did, something he couldn't help." Illumination, he admits, comes slowly: "All this time," the narrator notes when Suzie's relationship with Davey ends, and shortly before he tells the reader "that Suzie went home with me" to resume their relationship,

> I'd been uncertain whether it was right or wrong to hunt if you used the meat and said those prayers. And I'm still not entirely convinced one way or the other. But I do have a better picture of what it's like now to be the elk or deer. And I understand Suzie a little better, too; I no longer think of her as cruel for hurting Randy's proud heart, for singling out, among all the other men in the valley, only Randy to shun, to avoid.
>
> She wasn't cruel. She was just frightened. Fright—sometimes plain fright, even more than terror—is every bit as bad as pain, and maybe worse....
>
> If Randy can have such white-hot passion for a thing—bowhunting, he can, I understand full well, have just as much heat in his hate. It spooks me the way he doesn't bring Suzie presents anymore in the old, hopeful way. The flat looks he gives me could mean anything: they rattle me.
>
> It's like I can't see him.
>
> Sometimes I'm afraid to go into the woods.

Though the narrator himself is only partially able to articulate the fact, it is his very capacity for sensitivity and understanding (a sensitivity and understanding that his musings suggest) that has brought Suzie back to him. Suzie clearly senses in the narrator the kind of human qualities that have eluded her in all the others.

ANN BEATTIE, "Janus"

One of the most fascinating things about this small gem of a story is its structure. It manages to hold our attention for more than three-quarters of its length with nothing more than an account of the growing relationship between the central character and a *bowl*! In this, Beattie seems to leave paralleled the techniques of a certain kind of gothic tale in which an object casually purchased in some strange little shop (often oriental) turns out to have magical or supernatural properties. But as we are told over and over by the narrator in this story, there really is nothing remarkable about this bowl aside from the regard the owner has for the particular quality she believes it to possess. She believes that the bowl is responsible for her success as a realtor, either through the "luck" it confers, or through its ability to impart a special aura to any house in which it is placed. On second thought, perhaps one cannot entirely rule out even magic, for its owner goes to considerable lengths to suggest that it does have properties that are strangely magnetic.

The story works upon us through a curious kind of misdirection. While we are keeping our eye upon the strange phenomenon of a woman beginning to feel guilty about her relationship to a bowl, *almost as though it were a lover*, suddenly the fact is casually dropped upon us that indeed the woman *has* a lover, or had one, anyway, and that is where she got the bowl in the first place—as a gift from him. He is no longer about, though. She has refused his ultimatum that they stop living a "two-faced" life and take steps to regularize their relationship:

> When she would not decide in his favor, would not change her life and come to him, he asked her what made her think she could have it both ways. And then he made the last move and left. It was a decision meant to break her will, to shatter her intransigent ideas about honoring previous commitments.

What *is* this bowl, then? And why does she feel guilt over it when she felt none over a love affair of apparently considerable depth and duration? Has she merely projected this lost lover who gave her the bowl *onto* the bowl? Or is the bowl, credited by Andrea for her "luck" in business, really an emblem of her growing awareness of her own power and competence, as she looks with one face toward her old commitment to being a wife and with another toward the realization of her own identity? As Andrea contemplates the bowl at the end of the story, a "world cut in half, deep and smoothly empty," one is tempted to identify it conventionally as a symbol of brittle and sterile femininity. But we cannot ignore the assertion that "in its way it [is] perfect." Andrea has obviously moved away from her husband in taking a lover. Her resisting that lover's ploy intended to "break her will" and force her to move into his world, is to take one further step toward realizing her own existence.

SAUL BELLOW, "Looking for Mr. Green"

This story is rather thickly interlarded with philosophical allusions that may at first intimidate student readers; but Bellow's most important concern is right there on the surface—how do people make themselves real or unreal to one another? The setting is depression Chicago, in the late twenties or early thirties. Employment is very scarce, so these little clerical jobs for the city are plums, and attract people like Raynor and Grebe, who would be considered "overqualified" these days—i.e., much better educated than their jobs demand. Grebe and his boss Raynor are able to engage in a bit of learned horseplay, exchanging Latin phrases, alluding to classical problems of philosophy, notably the question of "ultimate reality" and "the fallen world of appearances."

There is a great deal of gritty detail in the story: gutted filling stations, wrecked and crumbling factories, junkyards, cold, ugly tenements. Incongruous with the urban setting, a hunting metaphor runs through the story. Grebe (which is, incidentally, a species of fishing bird) talks about himself as "stalking prey" that takes on protective coloration and becomes invisible to anyone from the outside. The irony is that Grebe has come to *give*, rather than to take or to threaten, and this fact encourages a tenacity in him that he begins to enjoy exercising.

Part of the speculation about reality in the story takes the form of Grebe's recognition that what makes things real is a "common sense," that is, social agreement about them. If enough mutual desire is directed toward a goal, whatever it is can come into being—like the Chicago transit system, thoroughly dreamlike in the first stages of its conception, but not palpably present. Grebe's whole day has been involved with vastly differing perceptions of what is real or important. Staika, the "bleeding mother," shows up at the welfare offices and makes an immediate impact upon the system because she refuses to leave until the people in authority are fully aware of her presence and her problem.

Mr. Green becomes a kind of test case for Grebe. He has been so elusive, almost like a rumor, that the search begins to take on the dimensions of a philosophical issue: whether there can ever be a shared reality (or humanity) between such divergent backgrounds as the one from which the college-educated, Latin-quoting Grebe comes and that of the clients for whom he is searching, who have (with the contrasting exception of Mr. Fields) almost totally divested themselves of any official identity. Of course, one thing ties them together: Grebe and his clients alike are living on the same welfare system, and as Mr. Fields remarks, "money is the only sunbeams." But the clincher for Grebe is the large, drunken, naked black woman he meets at the bottom of the stairs of the house that says "Green" on its doorplate. What has Grebe assumed about the "cripple" that he believes his quarry to be? Whatever Mr. Green is, at this moment he seems to be upstairs getting drunk and making love, just like any human being. Even though he is nowhere to be seen, he is so solidly implicit in the undeniable presence of the woman that Grebe hands her the check.

Raynor stands at one end of the welfare system talking about the "fallen world of appearances," and Mr. Green at the other, with Grebe as an intermediary between the two. At the extreme of pessimism, the idea of "man" or "woman" is lost; individuals of each culture become mere representative abstractions to one another ("That's the way *they* are"). It becomes problematic whether any single person can ever be fully present to someone of another race or class. Yet Grebe is on a hunt for the Truth, and he seems to find it in those large, naked breasts that come charging at him from out of the dark. There's the common bond: sex, motherhood. The large, abstract category of "the human," is here made quite concrete and particular.

AMBROSE BIERCE, "An Occurrence at Owl Creek Bridge"

Students are usually sharply divided on their response to this story, and their reasons for liking or disliking it are often precisely the same—that it has a "surprise" ending, that the narrative plays a trick on them. For those who dislike it, the feeling usually has something to do with the "honesty" of the piece, that it gets its response "cheaply" by a simple, unannounced shift in the story's center of consciousness. Certainly there is something to this criticism, but the discussion provides a perfect opportunity to point out that not all literature operates by the same rules, and although one may prefer this to football, it is illogical to condemn a football game for not being a tennis match.

Such a discussion also opens the opportunity to demonstrate that indeed Bierce *has* paid his dues—that he has prepared the ground *very* carefully for his effects. One can begin by pointing out the static formality of the scene that goes with an execution, a "framing" that makes this death very different from all those combat mortalities with which the men are said to be so familiar, hardly anyone or anything moves as the "camera" pans over the spectacle, pausing momentarily upon the details of the appearance of each sentry and each formation of troops. What possible difference can it make how civil war rifles were held or stacked in certain formal military postures? Bierce is slowing the action, hushing all sound in preparation for another literary effect that is both very old and very new: the idea of the subjectivity of time. But this is no quasi-supernatural tale like "Sleeping Beauty" or "Rip Van Winkle," nor a futuristic fiction in which time travel is simply taken for granted. Rather, this is quite consciously a "realistic" fiction in which Bierce tries to keep to the rules of scientific probability. The implicit explanation of the whole hallucination sequence is that Farquahar's thought processes have speeded up to such a degree in the face of impending extinction that normal time lapses seem to him more and more retarded. The river crawls beneath him as though it were chilled syrup, and the slow, measured, anvil-like percussions that he hears are the ticks of his watch. His senses have become dilated, presumably so as to take in one last profound gulp of experience before the end.

Suddenly the narrative is shifted to a previous moment in the sequence of events. We are given the background and explanation of why this gentleman of noble and handsome demeanor, who is obviously (as the narrator informs us) "no vulgar assassin," happens to be standing at the business end of the hangman's noose. The man is a planter of no mean fortune and would be serving the "great cause" (i.e., the Confederacy) were it not for some unspecified, overriding circumstance. The diction of this whole section is quite different from the first part of the story. In effect, here Bierce is "faking" a direction quite opposite to that he intends to run. Farquahar is a member not only of another social class from that of his captors, but of another *literary* class as well. The Old South from which this "nobleman" comes is that seen through the traditions of the chivalric romance, in which the hero is constantly facing overwhelming odds and making hairbreadth escapes. The whole effect is heightened by our knowledge that the handsome young planter has been cold-bloodedly entrapped by the Union scoundrels.

Thus the audience has been set up by misdirection for the kind of world in which such last-minute escapes are quite unexceptional. The relief and exuberance of the feeling of escape are heightened by the particularity of the description of nature, and it is not until Farquahar begins to notice the odd, alien-looking appearance of the night sky that there is any clue to the "real" ending—which suddenly jerks us up short as the romantic phase of the fiction runs out and we are back in the realm of bleak probability.

ELIZABETH BOWEN, "The Demon Lover"

"The Demon Lover," the centerpiece story in Bowen's 1945 collection *The Demon Lover and Other Stories*—is often considered her finest story. It is perhaps also her best known. Though one can read "The Demon Lover" as a conventional ghost story (certainly all the elements are there including the demon lover of the traditional folk ballad), the best approach is the one suggested by Douglas A. Hughes in his 1973 essay "Cracks in the Psyche: Elizabeth Bowen's 'The Demon Lover'" Hughes and most recent critics read the story as the deft psychological portrait of a middle-age woman who has managed to suppress for years her real self (as represented by her dead fiance). The house (stuffy, dark and long-closed) in which she finds the letter announcing the promised assignation with her dead lover thus becomes the analogue to her emotional life. Allan Austin is certainly correct when he points to Bowen's careful use of imagery by means of which she builds "the link between the house and her subconscious. If it is haunted," Austin concludes, "it is because she is."

Short as the story is most of the information we need to come to an understanding of Mrs. Drover's hidden inner life is all there, at least by intimation: the flashback to 1916, and her final leave-taking as a nineteen-year-old girl from a soldier who, in the dimness of memory at least, is both cold and cruel; the empty years that subsequently intervene until her marriage at age thirty-two to Mr. Drover; the unspecified illness attendant to the birth of her third child which has left her with a tic. For Phyllis Lassner (1991), the letter itself is the key to how the story is to be read and interpreted, particularly in terms of the hold the dead soldier exerts upon the living woman. It

> binds Kathleen Drover to a promise she has no way of fulfilling. "Presumed killed" in action for 25 years, her fiance nevertheless expects her to drop whatever she has made of her life to fulfill his need to see her. The letter assumes betrayal because it allows for no other reality than his. Despite its polite language, his right of retribution is contained in his expectation that she be there regardless of her needs. And indeed, his appearance in a form symbolizing the infinite depths of his rage creates the story's terror. Kathleen Drover's everlasting terror is...clearly predetermined..., for it is clear that she would always be compelled to build her life around her promise to him to "need [to] do nothing but wait." Ultimately, Mrs. Drover is driven by a male fantasy of her total devotion and by the rage that presumes she is doomed to fail. What is therefore so terrible is the sense of a setup— that she is damned to a lonely hell if she waits for her fiance and doomed to be with him if she does not.

Lassner finds the letter's signature the final sign of just how completely his consciousness has overtaken hers:

> This process is so complete that, as the "K" of his signature shows, Kathleen is haunted by becoming his reflection. Like his hidden face at their earlier parting, the letter represents him only as she responds to it. Like her memories, the letter is a ghostly artifact, a sign that as a survivor of two wars she has internalized their terrors and guilt.

No matter how one wants to reconstruct the inner life of the woman that is Kathleen Drover, the story's final scene, again one of enclosure, is skillfully wrought, and the story's final paragraph—which will well repay close line by line analysis—captures completely Kathleen Drover's terror as she is carried off into the night.

KAY BOYLE, "Astronomer's Wife"

The following essay was written by Anne Brown, a former student at Michigan State University, in response to the assignment "Characterization in Kay Boyle's 'Astronomer's Wife.'" I am grateful to Anne for letting me use it in *Fiction 100* as an example of student writing:

"Kay Boyle's story 'Astronomer's Wife' deals with the polarity of two approaches to life, one intellectual, the other physical. At the beginning of the story Mrs. Ames, the protagonist, perceives this contrast in terms of the difference between man and woman. Later when she meets the plumber she is bewildered by the fact that he deals *as a woman* with matters under hand, and then speaks of action and object as simply *as women do*. She realizes then that there are two types of men, as embodied in her astronomer husband and the plumber. 'Her husband was the mind, this other the meat, of all mankind.' Faced with a choice between the two, she chooses to go 'down' with the plumber. That this choice is the natural one is apparent from the beginning of the story.

"When Mrs. Ames first wakes, she sets the day in motion by a series of actions, while her husband lies in bed sleeping, or feigning sleep. He dreams while she acts. Her rhythmic exercises and her projected chore of thrashing the mayonnaise for lunch underscore the way in which her day proceeds, beat by beat, without reflection. Her husband, as an astronomer, is above all this.

"The contrast is felt painfully by Mrs. Ames. Her husband's silence tells her that 'man might be each time the new arching wave and woman the undertow that sucked him back.' She feels awkward and unfit; she wrestles with the uncouth forces inside her. As a result of this suppression she has forgotten that she is young: the light has been extinguished from her eyes. Even her voice is hushed in the presence of her husband's silence.

"Mrs. Ames accepts the situation and her husband's scorn because she doesn't know of any other way. When the plumber comes and speaks to her of matters under hand, she is perplexed at first because she thinks all men deal with 'nameless things that can't pass between thumb and finger.' It is at this moment that she realizes that there are two kinds of men, represented in the extremes by the plumber and the astronomer.

"The difference in the two men is implicit in their occupations. The astronomer is oriented towards the sky. He likes to go up, on the roof or on the mountains. The plumber is a man of the earth. He goes down: down into the drains. The contrast between the men revolves around the idea of up and down. The astronomer keeps himself aloof from everyday life and aloof from his wife. He concerns himself with lofty ideas. While the astronomer lies upstairs in bed, the plumber is down in the yard, dealing with the lower, baser realities of life.

"The difference between the two men is underscored by the way in which they are described. In describing the astronomer metaphors are used. We know much about how his mind works, but nothing about his appearance. In contrast, the plumber is described in terms of his physical appearance and his actions. Passages in which Mrs. Ames reflects upon her husband in abstract terms alternate with her here-and-now awareness of the plumber's presence. The contrast is especially apparent in this passage:

> The mind of man, she knew, made steep and sprightly flights, pursued illusion, took foothold in the nameless things that cannot pass between thumb and finger. But whenever the astronomer gave voice to the thoughts that soared within him, she returned in gratitude to the long expanses of his silence. Desert-like they stretched behind and before the articulation of his scorn.

> Life, life is an open sea, she sought to explain it in sorrow, and to survive women cling to the floating debris on the tide. But the plumber had suddenly fallen upon his knees in the grass and had crooked his fingers through the ring of the drains' trapdoor. When she looked down she saw that he was looking up into her face, and she saw too that his hair was as light as gold.

"The change from abstract to concrete description coincides with the shift in her thoughts about life with her husband to the plumber. This technique is effective in showing the difference between these two men. Passages in which Mrs. Ames is described in physical terms show how she too, like the plumber, deals in the concrete.

"Because of their similarities Mrs. Ames is drawn to the plumber. Whereas 'the mystery and silence of her husband's mind lay like a chiding finger on her lips,' the plumber's down-to-earth manner puts her at her ease. He speaks of things that are comprehensible to her. His fingers, she notes, are blunt but comprehensible. The painful difference she feels with her husband is not present with the plumber. And the plumber's story about making his cow a new cud out of flowers and things and what-not is a promise to Mrs. Ames that he can restore to her what she has lost in her association with her husband. Mrs. Ames, knowing what he says to be true, opts to go down with him into the drains. The symbolism in the end is obvious. She steps 'into the heart of the earth,' which represents the concreteness of the plumber's approach to life, cutting herself off from the sky which is her husband's domain."

RAY BRADBURY, "August 2002: Night Meeting"

Bradbury's *The Martian Chronicles* (1950) remains after more than forty years one of the classics of American science fiction. Consisting of twenty-six separate stories, some of which were published before the work as a whole was conceived, *The Martian Chronicles* survives, in part at least, because of the artistic integrity and excellence of many of its individual parts. "August 2002: Night Meeting" is a case in point.

The opening exchange between Tomas and the old man Pop should be studied closely, for it serves to establish the mood, setting, and theme of Bradbury's story. We learn about Mars, its terrain, climate, and history, about its mood of isolation, desolation, and loneliness, and about the "crazy" sense of time that hangs over the apparently lifeless planet. We also learn "how *different* it is." For Pop, who has deliberately sought to remove himself from the culture in which he was born and to "forget Earth and how things were," this "difference" is a quality to be savored. "Enjoy it," he tells Tomas. "Don't ask it to be nothing else but what it is." It is Pop's view of things—his vision of life and its new, unexpected, and varied possibilities (like the kaleidoscope he received "for Christmas seventy years ago")—that prepares Tomas for his encounter with Muhe Ca, the Martian.

The lesson takes. Tomas proceeds on his journey "laughing quietly," sensing "a smell of time in the air tonight…you could almost *touch* time," and turning over the subject in his mind in a series of fanciful similes. It is at this moment that two dimensions of time momentarily interact with one another. "Like the steps in a prescribed ritual," Edward J. Gallagher observes, "this exercise in imagination calls forth a being from another time, 'a strange thing,' a Martian with melted gold for eyes and a mechanical mantis for a vehicle."

The relationship between Tomas and Muhe Ca passes through a series of stages. At first, they cannot understand one another, a barrier which is overcome by a form of mental telepathy born of a mutual desire to communicate and share. Next there is the protracted and heated debate over reality. Each character understandably enters the discussion firmly encapsulated within the truth and reality of his own time dimension. They can see and hear each other, but cannot "touch" or "see" what the other touches or sees. The moment is psychologically threatening: to acknowledge and accept the possibility of someone else's reality is, simultaneously, to cast doubt upon one's own. At stake is the issue of identity.

Finally, agreeing to disagree, they accept and affirm each other's differences and thereby for a brief moment achieve communion and comradeship. To quote Gallagher again:

> They "shake" hands and exchange wishes to join in the exciting pleasure of each other's present.

Bradbury doesn't give either culture the last reality; nor does he return the story to a human perspective. Instead he preserves the balance struck between the two cultures by holding the narrative point of view neutrally at the scene after both beings disappear with parallel reflections of their experience.

ALBERT CAMUS, "The Guest"

"The Guest" takes place in Algeria following the end of World War II on the eve of the 1954 civil war between Algerian nationalists and French colonists, who would ultimately be reinforced by half a million French soldiers. Despite Charles de Gaulle's attempt in 1958 to settle the rebellion with a new constitution calling for reform and granting more political autonomy to the Algerians, the guerrilla war went on for another three years. By the time that Algeria finally gained its independence in 1962, almost 200,000 people had been killed. These facts are mentioned as background for Camus' story.

"The Guest," as Laurence Perrine correctly suggests.

> is about the difficulty, the agony, the complexity, the necessity, the worth, and the thanklessness of moral choice. It tells us that moral choice may be difficult and complex with no clear distinction between good and evil, and with both rational and irrational, selfish and unselfish claims justifying each course of conduct. It tells us that moral choice is a burden which man would willingly avoid if he could, but also that it is part of the human condition which man cannot evade and remain man. It shows us that man defines himself by moral choice...and establishes his moral worth thereby. But the story also shows that moral decision has no ulterior meaning, for the universe does not reward it.

Though such a thematic statement may seem simplistic, and might well be in the hands of a lesser writer, in "The Guest" Camus has constructed an extremely complex and provocative story. Daru, the French Algerian schoolmaster, is obviously a man of compassion and goodwill. A servant of the French colonial bureaucracy, he has established a comfortable life for himself on a "high, deserted plateau" where he discovered that, in contrast to the poverty and political unrest around him, living "almost like a monk" makes him feel "like a lord." For all its "solitude and...silence" his isolated school has become a congenial way of life.

Into this isolation the "real" political world intrudes in the persons of Balducci and the Arab. It is interesting to note that despite the fact that a kind of fellowship does gradually develop between Daru and the Arab—"a sort of brotherhood he knew well but refused to accept in the present circumstances"—Daru's refusal to accept the obligation or duty thrust upon him by the French authorities is an immediate response. He signs Balducci's paper with great reluctance, and then only after he has insulted a man who regards him as a son. The conscious motive for his decision is clearly stated: though Daru is "revolted" by "that man's stupid crime," "to hand him over was contrary to honor."

Initially, of course, Daru hopes that the issue of moral choice will resolve itself: that given the opportunity the Arab will escape. He assumes falsely, that is, that given the opportunity for freedom a man will choose to exercise it (even though such an assumption *also* assumes that the Arab, who has grown up in a colonial society defined by French authority and law, understands, without having been taught, what freedom in fact means). Daru may also fail to take into account that as the murderer of his own cousin the Arab has in some measure isolated himself from his own people. But, whatever the reason, the Arab does not exercise that choice, and so the burden remains Daru's. And Daru chooses: he chooses to let the Arab make the decision for himself. Whether that decision really constitutes a choice at all, or whether, as some critics have argued, Daru is really guilty of having avoided the responsibility of moral choice, is but one of the vexing questions that the story legitimately raises. Once the Arab chooses prison, Daru is left isolated and alone to face the judgment on the blackboard for a decision that he not only did not choose but had decided was not even his to make.

Since we see the events of the story only from Daru's point of view, the Arab remains an ambiguous figure. Is he guilty or innocent of the crime of which he is accused? Why does he act so passively in the face of a situation in which he obviously has so much at stake? Is he a member of the rebel party, as the message on Daru's blackboard possibly suggests? What does he mean when he says "Come with us"? Is he referring to Balducci and the road to prison, or is he referring to his fellow revolutionaries? And, finally, when given the option, why does he voluntarily choose prison? The story clearly raises these questions, but only provides hints of possible answers, a technique which seems to underscore the awesome difficulty of making judgments and decisions in an existential universe.

RAYMOND CARVER, "Cathedral"

James W. Grinnell, reviewing the stories in Raymond Carver's third volume of short stories, *Cathedral* (1993), in the Winter 1984 issue of *Studies in Short Fiction*, offers the following comments:

> They are still hard little gems of fiction but they are a few carats heavier than those of the earlier books. Six of the twelve are first person narrations; all are restricted to their characters' stunted perspectives, which is to say, to Carver's tight control. He does not mock his people nor does he suggest that their lives would be improved if they examined them, if they were to expect, inspect and introspect more. A kind of literary minimalist, Carver simply presents his people and their stark lives as if there were nothing richer out there, no American milieu of affluence, of new horizons, of hope. We readers have to carry our own emotional baggage to and from these stories because Carver will not porter for us.

Carver's "Cathedral" is a story culminating in an event that provides its protagonist-narrator with a moment of heightened self-awareness and perception. It is also a story about human compassion and understanding and the ability to communicate.

The two men upon whose relationship the story turns are, quite obviously, very different. The narrator is essentially an introverted and uncommunicative human being, rigid and closed to new experience. The "cool," cynical, conversational tone he adopts to tell the story serves to mask his inner doubts and anxieties. A man without friends (according to his wife), inept at small talk, and thus prone to say foolish things, the narrator is plainly uneasy at the prospect of Robert's visit and later in his presence. Not surprisingly, he resents Robert's arrival as an unwanted intrusion upon his privacy, and acts out his irritation by making him an object of sardonic humor: "Maybe I could take him bowling." The narrator is also plainly worried about Robert's influence upon his wife's inner life, a reality which, like her poetry, they apparently do not share. In his relationship with the larger world, the narrator sees himself as a victim—as a man who dislikes his job but feels that he has no other options, nowhere else to go. His response is deliberately to narrow the focus of his experience to a manageable, comfortable, and thoroughly predictable routine consisting of television, alcohol ("It's one of our pastimes"), and marijuana. Still there remain demons that cannot be totally exorcised. Though the narrator confesses that "Every night I smoked dope and stayed up as long as I could before I fell asleep," he is plagued by recurring nightmares.

Robert is in many respects his opposite. Unlike the narrator, Robert is a man with many friends, who, despite his blindness, relishes his experiences (like riding on the train) and is relaxed and "comfortable" in human situations. His is a life of change and growth, not stagnation. He wants to know and to learn. "Robert had done a little of everything, it seemed," the narrator observes, "a regular blind jack-of-ail trades." In short, if the narrator seems to have become trapped by his experience, Robert appears liberated by his. Robert's great personal gift is his human sensitivity, his ability to reach out to others with compassion and understanding (to the narrator's wife in her time of loneliness and depression; to Beulah, his own wife, who dies slowly of cancer; and finally to the reluctant narrator himself). In return, he seems able to touch and liberate qualities and qualities that otherwise remain latent and neglected.

The plot of "Cathedral" is not so much determined by incident or event as it is by the changes in attitude that take place in the narrator, culminating in his surprising willingness to participate with Robert in drawing the cathedral. At the beginning of the story, these attitudes are almost totally closed and negative. In part, it is a matter of Robert's blindness ("His being blind bothered me...my ideas of blindness came from the movies."), but it is also a matter of the fear and insecurity that define his view of the world.

The cathedral of the story's conclusion suggests a range of possible symbolic meanings, but as usual with such matters it is best not to attempt to be overly specific in the attribution. Though cathedrals traditionally represent man's spiritual aspiration for human fulfillment and inner reconciliation, such an aspiration is never overtly expressed by Carver's narrator. Whatever the cathedral and the shared act of drawing it mean to the narrator must be inferred from his sparse and oblique remarks: "It was like nothing else in my life up to now....But I didn't feel like I was inside anything." What is clear from those comments is that a moment of transcendence has taken place. Such moments of illumination and insight in literature as in life are rare, unpredictable, fleeting, and ambiguous. Joyce refers to them as "epiphanies." Psychologist Abraham Maslow calls them "peak experiences." Whatever their name, their importance ultimately derives from their ability to stimulate changes that last. Will the changes in the narrator last? The answer to that question lies, of course, in a dimension beyond Carver's story, which ends simply: "'It's really something,' I said."

RAYMOND CARVER, "I Could See the Smallest Things"

This story is quintessential Carver. That is, it is fully representative of what we have come to expect of so-called minimalist fiction; what John Barth has described as "terse, oblique, realistic . . . , slightly plotted, extrospective, [and] cool-surfaced." Moreover, it makes use of one of Carver's recurring subjects, or themes: insomnia. For Carver, Ernest Fontana notes, "insomnia is a sickness of the mind that brings one to epiphanies, moments of painful revelation." In the early Carver stories such as "I Could See the Smallest Things," he continues, "this revelation is granted to women, and what is revealed to them is the irremediable separateness of their husbands and their own fundamental aloneness."

In Carver, however, insomnia is also something more. Increasingly, Fontana writes, insomnia

> provides the model for Carver's fictional technique—specifically, his increased use of present tense interior and dramatic monologue rather than third-person discursive narrative. . . .

With these comments by way of background, we can turn briefly to the story.

Nancy, Carver's protagonist, is narrating an experience from her past. "I was in bed when I heard the gate." Getting up, she goes to the window and surveys the moon-swept lawn:

> There was light enough so that I could see everything in the yard—lawn chairs, the willow tree, clothesline strung between the poles, the petunias, the fences, gate standing wide open. . . . Eveything lay in moonlight, and I could see the smallest things.

The only jarring note is that she sees the moon as "covered with scars." Those "scars" we soon come to suspect are her own.

Sam Lawton, who Nancy soon encounters on the lawn below searching out and killing garden slugs, is one of Carver's damaged males. A reformed alcoholic, still going through withdrawal, Sam has become fixated on the slugs. "They're taking over. . . ," Sam tells her. "I put bait out, and then every chance I get I come out here with this stuff. Bastards are all over."

Sam Lawton is a clearly lonely, frightened man. And it seems safe to say that whatever the roots of his own insomnia and fears may be, they are objectified by the slugs he feels compelled to find and destroy. Sometime in the past, after the death of his wife Millie of heart failure at 45, Sam, has quarreled with the narrator's husband, Clifford. They had both been drinking heavily. In the aftermath, the men have built fences between their houses, a fact that Sam at least now regrets. "I wish me and Cliff was friends again," Sam tells Nancy.

But the story is not about Sam Lawton. Rather, it is about Nancy and her relationship with Clifford, a relationship that we infer from the usual Carver-type clues is less than satisfactory. Nancy finds Cliff's breathing "awful to listen to." She characterizes him not as asleep but "passed out," with his "mouth gaped open" and his arms hugging "his pale chest." Part of this dissatisfaction seems to be sexual. Adam Meyer is surely correct when he comments that Nancy's "conversation with Sam seems rife with sexual tension; as she reminds us on many occasions, she is walking around in her robe."

Her conversation with Sam over, Nancy returns to her bed. She is still an insomniac, unable to fall asleep. But now her thoughts focus upon the sleeping Clifford:

> I gave Cliff a little shake. He cleared his throat. He swallowed. Something caught and dribbled in his chest.
>
> I don't know. It made me think of those things that Sam Lawton was dumping powder on.

The implications of the final paragraph, of course, are puzzling, and it is here that much classroom discussion will surely focus. For Adam Meyer, the ending is one of avoidance:

> Having perceived this new image of Cliff as slug, Nancy seems ready to break with him entirely. Nevertheless, she cannot bring herself to take decisive action. . . .
> She senses the abyss at hand, as is so often the case in Carver Country, but she decides to pretend it doesn't exist. "She seeks to obliterate her insight" (Stull, "BH" 1985, 6), to become like a slug herself. Her only thought is the oblivion of thoughtlessness.

This may seem, to some, rather extreme. Ernest Fontana seems a bit more convincing about the nature of Nancy's revelation, the "small thing" that she has seen:

> Nancy is awakened, against her will, to the painful realization that she is alone like her fenced-in neighbor in a world of sleeping slugs, one of whom is her husband.

RAYMOND CARVER, "What We Talk About When We Talk About Love"

The comments of fellow writer Geoffrey Wolff about the story suggest a good beginning point:

> "What We Talk About When We Talk About Love" I admire so much because, first of all, I don't think there has ever been anything even approximately as good written about drinking. I've done enough drinking in my life to know how

it feels, what happens to syntax, what happens to diction, as the light begins to come down in the room and the stuff goes further down in the bottle. The room darkens, and you see your whole life darken too. The only other writer who can do that kind of story is Cheever. Cheever stories do have that kind of quality.

Wolff, of course, is correct. This is a drinking story, at least in the sense that the occasion of drinking provides—as it so often does for people—the opportunity to talk and communicate, with alcohol acting as a stimulant. Students should be able to follow the changes in the story's syntax and diction (including the increasing profanity) which indicates the process of drink, as well as the changes in he images of light and shadow. They will also understand—if for no other reason than the title tells them—that the story is about love. What they will doubtless have more trouble with is deciding just what the story, finally, means.

"What We Talk About When We Talk About Love" was published in 1981 as the title story in a volume that concluded some twenty years of relative obscurity. It brought Carver to the attention of reviewers and critics and ushered in the major phase of his tragically short career. The plot of this minimalist story is simple, and deceptively so: two couples, Mel and Terri McGinnis and Nick and Laura sit around a kitchen table as the sunlight of afternoon fades, drink cheap gin and tonic water. They also talk. "Somehow," Nick, the narrator notes, we "got on the subject of love." The discussion turns on two separate anecdotes: Terri's experience with her former lover, Ed, "who loved her so much he tried to kill her" and finally kills himself with a gun; and her cardiologist husband's, Mel's, anecdote about the old man, badly injured in an automobile accident who becomes deeply depressed because he can't see his wife's face. Nick and Laura, who are somewhat younger and have only "been together" a year and a half, assume roles that are largely those of passive listeners.

What is clear from Terri's anecdote about Ed, in which Mel willingly intrudes, and from the anecdote that Mel then offers up, is that they are both willing to ponder the subject and meaning of love, in part at least because though married for four years each is still drawn to (and indeed is obsessed by) his and her former partner. For Terri, still trying to comprehend, Ed's violence is indeed an act of love, his bungled suicide attempt and suicide a sign that he cannot live without her. Mel, the cardiologist (Carver's choice of professional role is hardly accidental), not surprisingly, disagrees. As Ewing Campbell notes, it is psychically advantageous for him to do so: "If he sees that Ed's passion hardly qualifies as love, he need not feel quite as emotionally threatened by the dead lover...." What Mel does not see is "the parallel between Ed's violence toward Terri and his violent feelings toward his former wife." "At the same time," Campbell continues,

> Mel may sense his own sentimentality (in his desire to be a knight), immediate gratification (in eating, drinking, and getting high), and compulsiveness, features of arrested emotional development shared with Ed, for he says about himself, "I like food....If I had to do it all over again, I'd be a chef, you know?" Mel's alcoholism and attraction to pills also testify to this self-gratifying impulse. Spiritual love, the idealized state of chivalric love, and the devotion of the elderly couple, having made a strong impression on him, may represent antidotes to or, at least, havens from his emotional immaturity. Or, as is more likely, extensions of that immaturity, for such imaginary escapes are further proof of underdevelopment.

Mel may "talk about love," but we as readers may find ourselves wondering what love for him is finally all about. We should also consider just how blind the conversation suggests he is to the truth about himself?

One also needs to consider the roles (and functions) of Nick and Laura. Nick is, of course, the story's narrator, and as such one needs to attempt to measure the impact of the events upon him and the extent to which they touch his depths as a human being. Nick, it is clear, is made somewhat uncomfortable by the course of the conversation. As a result, he attempts to keep himself at the periphery of things. He enters into the conversation enough to keep it going, but offers little in the way of an analysis of validation, let alone introspection. Whether Nick deliberately chooses not to be introspective, chooses not to attempt to understand his own experience or the experience of others (or whether he is actually incapable of doing so) is not clear. What he says, however, may be less important than his actions, for in taking Laura's hand and, later, putting his hand on her "warm" thigh, he is offering her a statement of reassurance if not of love. Nick's (and Laura's) reluctance to engage are, at one level, hardly surprising. Married for such a short time, and clearly still infatuated with one another, why have that infatuation marred by troublesome thoughts?

Just how affected Nick finally is by what he hears depends as well on just how one comes to read and interpret the story's final paragraph: "I could hear my heart beating. I could hear everyone's heart. I could hear the human noise we sat there making, not one of us moving, not even when the room went dark." Perhaps Nick's consciousness of "the human noise" and the common beating of hearts suggests a new awareness of his own vulnerability and the vulnerability of his relationship with Laura. The ending is, to be sure, finally ambiguous. What we are left with is the constant refrain of Carver's fiction: the sense of the limitations of human communication, the inability of people (even people in love) to listen and to understand.

JOHN CHEEVER, "The Country Husband"

As the story opens, the husband of the title, Francis Weed, has just been through a somewhat frightening experience on his return flight from a business trip, and demands a bit of extra attention from his family and the quality of the relationship between the husband and wife: "She paints with lightning strokes that panorama of drudgery in which her youth, her beauty, and her wit have been lost. Francis says that he must be understood; he was nearly killed in an airplane crash, and he doesn't like to come home every night to a battlefield." No mystery here; the marriage is a cliché (if not an archetype). The wife is depleted by repetitious, unrewarding work while the husband sulks at not getting the attention he feels he deserves for his heroism in facing the outside world.

Because the center of consciousness of this story lies with the husband, we are inclined to accept his view of most of the things and people in his life. He commutes by train to his work in New York and comes home to sleep in (perhaps) Connecticut. His wife takes care of the domestic end of the commute and seems rather superficial, concerning herself with the house, the children, and the social calendar. The husband briefly indulges an erotic fantasy which in turn triggers an impulse to be boyishly rude to one of the town matrons, leading to the exclusion of his family from one of the "key" social events in the community, which precipitates Mrs. Weed's decision to leave her husband. Francis Weed then swears to change if she'll stay, takes his problem to a psychiatrist in the city, and thereafter vents his surplus erotic energy through woodworking in his basement. It all seems very slight and mildly funny. His libido has temporarily slipped its leash and like the neighborhood's perpetually loose dog, has disturbed some of the community's shrubbery.

But there is rather more to Cheever's story than that. The author is attempting a practical illustration of something that would draw sneers if stated outright: that a community is like a family. And further, that a community may be a very delicate organism but can strike back rather violently if it feels itself too much abused. (It is intimated that the perpetually loose pup may soon come upon a lethal piece of steak.)

When we reevaluate Francis's little jaunt off the main path of his life, we begin to notice certain rather more serious shortcomings in his nature; for example, that the girl, Anne, is

91

vulnerable to his attentions because her own father had abdicated his responsibility. The girl needs an adult male to be parental toward her, but Mr. Weed's mind is on obscure parking spots. He is committing the equivalent of incest, or would be given the opportunity. And further, because of his adolescent jealousy, he strikes a gratuitous blow at the fortunes of a fatherless young man who needs his help in getting a start in life. These acts alone are rather serious violations of familial trust, but there is more: Weed's abuses of his most immediate family. He has not been aware enough of the network of associations his wife has been at pains to establish to know that his childish assault upon the feelings of an old lady on the train platform could have repercussions for his own children. The most telling shock to his self-absorption, however, comes from his wife, who points out to him that the carelessness with which he scatters his dirty clothing throughout the house is an unconscious signal of his hostility toward the person upon whom he is most dependent for the comforts of everyday life. His wife's accusation of such insensitivity on his part, together with his sudden realization the next morning on the train that his vague erotic longings cannot even distinguish between the object of his infatuation and any other young woman, draws Weed to the conclusion that he is a tare in the fields of his community and is in dire need of help. That he is thrown against the wall and frisked by the police as he comes into the psychiatrist's office is a double-edged irony. After all, he is not some kind of dangerous character. Is he?

ANTON CHEKHOV, "The Darling"

Chekhov's story belies its apparent simplicity. Part of the problem may be the fact that, as Renato Poggioli, echoing the earlier view of Leo Tolstoy, observes, the story's conclusion "transcends the original intent": what begins as a satiric attempt to exploit a "stock comic situation"—for all the men in Olenka's life are indeed "slightly ridiculous characters"—unexpectedly "develops into a vision of beauty and truth." Read in this way, Olenka becomes the embodiment of a pure, unselfish, and uncritical love and, therefore, to quote Tolstoy, a being "wonderful and Holy." The opinions which Olenka so easily adopts and then mouths testify to the completeness of her commitment, the sublimation of self. What begins as a gentle satire thus ends as a sympathetic treatment of, and tribute to, feminine devotion. But, if so, what are we to make of Sasha's tormented cry ("I'll give it you! Get away! Shut up!") and of the fact that Smirnin, the veterinary surgeon, having been offered Olenka's devotion, returns to his wife and later apparently all but disappears? And what are we to make of the fact that Smirnin is annoyed rather than pleased by Olenka's opinions? Karl Kramer, citing these facts, argues that Olenka's love is in reality a dominating and destructive force, that she "emotionally feeds" on the three men in her life and later on the boy Sasha, and that, unlike Kukin and Pustovalov, both Smirnin and Sasha recognize and resent the fact and seek to repel her "love." Students will find much to discuss here, including the portrait of a woman whose male-dominated society denies her self-expressions and individuality apart from the men who happen into her life.

ANTON CHEKHOV, "The Lady with the Dog"

"The Lady with the Dog" is generally regarded not only as one of Anton Chekhov's most famous short stories but as among the best introductions to Chekhov himself. As Virginia Llewellyn Smith writes,

No other single work of Chekhov's fiction constitutes a more meaningful comment on Chekhov's attitude to women and to love than does 'The Lady with the

Dog.' So many threads of Chekhov's thought and experience appear to have been woven together into this succinct story that it may be regarded as something in the nature of a summary of the entire topic.

Despite its title, "The Lady with the Dog" is obviously Gurov's story. Chekhov allows the reader to see the world and the events of the story only from his point of view. This third person limited omniscient focus is so persistent and narrow that the attentive reader finds himself an increasingly understanding, and perhaps even sympathetic, participant in Gurov's world.

Gurov is 39, balding, and decidedly entering middle age. Though he takes pride in his sexual encounters and conquests, his experiences with women have been far from satisfactory. As the narrator explains,

> He could remember carefree, good-natured women who were exhilarated by love-making and grateful to him for the happiness he gave them, however short-lived; and there had been others—his wife among them—whose caresses were insincere, affected, hysterical, mixed up with a great deal of quite unnecessary talk, and whose expression seemed to say that all this was not just love-making or passion, but something much more significant; then there had been two or three beautiful, cold women, over whose features flitted a predatory expression, betraying a determination to wring from life more than it could give, women no longer in their first youth; capricious, irrational, despotic, brainless, and when Gurov had cooled to these, their beauty aroused in him nothing but repulsion, and the lace trimming on their underclothes reminded him of fish-scales.

Gurov, as critic Donald Rayfield notes, casually and callously "divides women into sensualists, intellectuals and predators. Each category repels him as easily as it attracts him: the first by its gratitude, the second by its conceit, and the last by its coldness so that, in Chekhov's unforgettable image, 'the lace of their underwear seemed like fish-scales.'"

Through all his aimless philandering, Gurov has never been in love. Though he has apparently wakened sincere passion, even love, in some of the women with whom he has consorted, Gurov's own legacy is one of anger, hatred, and bitterness.

A good case can be made, I think, that Gurov's real problem is that he is afraid of women, afraid of genuine intimacy, and afraid of a relationship which demands that he give of his essential self. The "lessons he has received" from women, we are told early in the story, have been "bitter." In response, he masks his disappointment (and fear of inadequacy) by cynically holding all women in contempt as "inferior." The seaside resort city of Yalta, with its unreal vacation-like atmosphere, is an ideal place for casual, somewhat sordid, love affairs. Knowing this, Gurov takes full advantage of the opportunities that come his way. Then he meets the unpretentious and unremarkable woman with the dog.

The center of Chekhov's story is, of course, Gurov's evolving relationship with Anna. From the outset she is plainly different from the other women Gurov has known. Though other women have played games and toyed with Gurov, Anna does not. Gradually we discover that the situations of these two are remarkably similar. Each has married young. Each is the victim of a loveless marriage which the social conventions of the day prohibit them from leaving. Each is bored and lonely. If they are to find happiness, it must be outside the bonds of married life.

What begins for Gurov as just another pleasurable liaison without emotional involvement, quickly evolves into something far deeper and far more meaningful. To the extent that the new love that Gurov and Anna come to share is powerful and true (as we are led to believe is), the road they travel together will of necessity, as the final lines of the story suggest, be "complicated" and "hard." Moreover, as both realize, "the end [of that road] was still far, far away." The very fact that they feel the weight of the burden, however, serves as a validation of a love now shared.

Students should be able to trace without too much difficulty the successive stages of Gurov's and Anna's relationship, and come to see how far the lovers have removed themselves from their former lives, lives of regularity and routine where the defining reality is boredom and ultimately death. They have now entered the world of the unknown. This world is anything but safe and secure; it is also anything but boring. By embracing the unknown, and only by embracing the unknown, Chekhov seems to imply, is it possible that true love can be found.

The story has three separate and distinctive settings (from Yalta to Moscow, and from Moscow to Anna's home town of Petersburg). Each setting and the events that take place there aid in developing the plot of the story and in revealing the characters of Gurov and Anna. It is important to note that it is only when Gurov is back in Moscow, in the shallow, pointless, hypocritical, yet thoroughly "civilized," world he unhappily shares with his wife—that Gurov begins to understand the significance of his relationship with Anna. Gurov's decision to turn his back on Moscow and to follow Anna to Petersburg, where he engages her in the remarkable episode at the theater, marks his first step into the unknown and onto the hard and difficult road where Anna has agreed to join him.

KATHRYN CHETKOVICH, "Appetites"

Chetkovich's story, originally published in ZYZZYVA, was chosen by Garrison Keillor for inclusion in *The Best American Short Stories 1998*. In his "Introduction" to that volume Keillor speaks of his preference for stories that say "something true about somebody's life" and of his immediate distrust of any "that carries its lesson under its arm." Such comments provide ample reason for including the story in his volume, for on both grounds "Appetites" would seem fully to qualify.

Kathryn Chetkovich offers the following contributor's note about the story:

> I wrote the first version of this story fifteen years ago, when I was halfway through a creative writing program and my critical understanding of what constitutes a story had begun to interfere with my capacity to actually write one. My doubts, by this time well informed and well articulated, were looming large, and in an effort to get something, anything, down on paper, I began this story, with no real idea of where it was going. A couple of years before, I had lived for a while in a house with two other women, some mice, and a baby grand piano that was never played, and I started there.

> I worked on the story off and on for the next several years, periodically sending it out, getting it back, and then—a little compulsively, maybe—rewriting it, often with the unnerving suspicion that I was making it different but not necessarily better. I enjoyed fooling around with the various elements, but at some point the story itself always seemed to slip away from me—I couldn't figure out what it was "about." But the last time I went to work on it, a couple of things seemed to have worked their way to the surface. I knew the narrator had to have a secret, and the story picked up some energy when I figured out what that secret was. And then I realized that the mice, who had been recklessly killed, maimed, and poisoned in various earlier drafts, should be spared. When I wrote my way to that new ending, the story, although still a mystery to me in some ways, seemed to work.

Such comments, with all their clear honesty, are helpful. They remind us, and through us our students, that writing fiction remains for many of its most successful practitioners a decidedly mysterious craft—that the author is often not quite sure about what he or she is trying to say or what the story itself is really all "about." Chetkovich's statement, in short, is an excellent antidote to those who would have us believe that writing is a highly premeditated and conscious process with the writer in control, first, last, and always.

"Appetites" might well be titled "Secrets." Amanda, Faith, and Carla each bring to their shared apartment a past which is kept more or less hidden. For Amanda, the narrator, that past has to do with Billy. Their relationship has been, and continues to be even in his absence, a complex one. It includes lies, recriminations, and an episode, perhaps a pattern, of physical abuse. It is a relationship that has left Amanda adrift, with the feeling that she has been in a "leaky lifeboat."

Amanda's attraction to Faith is an immediate one. "I knew that life near this woman if I could arrange it," she admits as they first meet, "would be different and better. I was prepared to give up whatever was asked of me to make that happen." Faith is stunningly beautiful. "She looked like someone whose job, once you're dead, is to introduce you to God." This surely is one of the story's triumphant lines.

What is there about Faith, who has obviously had her way with men, that makes her the way she is? She seems to Amanda rather bigger than life, a woman whose very gestures are filled with meaning. As Faith takes Wayne's arm, Amanda thinks: "I recognized the gesture when I saw it: how to touch a man who has not touched you first." Faith coolly, casually and carelessly glides through the world. Yet she openly warns Amanda that physical beauty is not always an asset. "You think being pretty is everything. Believe me it's not."

Then there is the talented and athletic Carla, who Amanda discovers, to her discomfort, is "becoming the big sister I was always glad I never had." Carla admits she has made compromises. From the age of five, Amanda learns, Carla was "supposed" to be a concert pianist. Now she owns a baby grand piano, reads sheet music in bed, and muses, apparently ruefully, that "When something's that big a part of your life, it's hard to know who you are without it. . . ." At the end of the story, with fingers "trembling," she plays for the first time. "It struck me then," Amanda notes, "that Carla had a gift that had brought her pain simply because it was not a bigger gift. . . ."

And what of Amanda herself and her "Billy thing"? What does she seem to learn in the course of the story? What intelligent and informed guesses can we make about what is likely to follow for her? At the end of the story, listening to Carla play, Amanda feels she has "found a key," but then quickly adds, "a key I have found again and lost, found and lost, a hundred times since."

I think students will enjoy reading and discussing this story. It does contain, in Keillor's words, "something true about somebody's life." And it most certainly does not carry "its lesson under its arm."

KATE CHOPIN, "Athénaïse: A Story of a Temperament"

It is often very tempting for some students to supply as a moral to this tale the folk-wisdom that what women really need to make their lives "natural" or "complete" is to bear a child. And indeed, there is something of that in the story. But the real center of the action is an initiation, and Kate Chopin knows, either through her reading or through her observations of life, that rituals are not magical; they cannot create maturity or an acceptance of change, but are only formal recognitions of something that is already supposedly a fact. Athénaïse (note the suggestion of parthenogenesis in her name) is married but she does not *feel* married. We do not know precisely why, nor does she. Certainly her husband, Cazeau, is older than she, and he seems to be a rather gruff man from the first descriptions we have of him, but nothing is ever mentioned that will allow us to convict him of brutality, despite our initial suspicions.

We learn very soon that Cazeau's foul mood is due to the extended absence of his young wife. We wait for him to explode—to break furniture, beat a horse or a servant—but nothing of this kind occurs. We are certain that something ugly and violent is bound to happen, however, as he rides up to the home of his in-laws where his wife has taken refuge from him, especially when we see Athénaïse's brother Montéclin sulking about, and learn that there is bad blood between him and Cazeau. But Cazeau simply saddles Athénaïse's horse and points her in the direction of his plantation.

Not long after Athénaïse's first attempt at running away from Cazeau, we see her plotting a new escape with Montéclin. It is his idea that she should leave her husband this time for good, and he has secured and paid for a room in New Orleans where Cazeau will not be able to find her. Again, it is as though the narrator is oblivious to the expectations she is setting up. Montéclin's is the kind of plot we expect for the exploitations of the young woman's innocence, and again we await the melodramatic climax to this situation which, again, never transpires. Chopin's whole strategy up to this point has been to lead us to expect some violent irrationality on the part of one or another of the men to explode. But we are shown no violent confrontation between Athénaïse and Cazeau, nor between Cazeau and his brother-in-law, nor anything so sensational as an incestuous relationship between Montéclin and his sister or the selling of the innocent Athénaïse into sexual servitude. What kind of story *is* this, anyway?

But there is still the possibility of an adulterous affair as the friendship between Athénaïse and her fellow lodger, Gouvernail, ripens. This would be a likely time for the husband to find where she has been lodging and come into the city to slay both his wife and her lover. But in fact all that happens is that Athénaïse has made a very good friend of a man our narrator is at great pains to describe as a "progressive," and who therefore has no scruples whatsoever about taking up an intimacy with a married woman. Athénaïse on her part finds that she enjoys the company of Gouvernail enormously, a feeling which he recognizes and appreciates. But he also recognizes that this young woman deeply loves her brother (with no hint of perversity), and that without being aware of it herself, she is deeply in love with her husband as well. So, while Gouvernail may have little regard for the "official" boundaries of marriage, he is extremely cautious in not abusing the affections of the young woman.

The innocent Athénaïse learns of her pregnancy, and as if suddenly awakened from her girlhood, she feels herself to be the true and loving wife of Cazeau, even though we learn that Cazeau has written a letter granting her complete freedom if she cannot be happy in their marriage. What strikes one about this narrative is not only what we are led to expect from the lurid, sensational tale we keep waiting for this to become, but what we are led to expect from *life*. This is "A Tale of Temperament," and one expects the word "temperament" to apply only to Athénaïse. But it reveals instead our expectations of the *masculine* temperament. There are simply too many challenges to traditional male values in the story for things to end so benignly, especially given the time and culture about which Chopin is writing. What is so outrageous about the story is that we find men being *reasonable* in their concern for a young woman. Is this, then, some new kind of utopian fiction?

KATE CHOPIN, "The Storm"

The story is a product of Kate Chopin's life-long concern over the role of women within the confines of marriage, a concern that in many ways locates her closer to our day than to her own. Students who have at least a passing understanding of Victorian morality both in literature and in life are likely to be surprised by the explicit sexuality of the story. Given those mores and what usually passed for "female fiction" at the turn of the century, it is understandable that Chopin would choose not to publish the story during her own lifetime. "The Storm" is unusual (perhaps even revolutionary) in at least two other respects as well: Its subject is sexual fulfillment outside of marriage. No moral judgments are rendered.

Some other notes and comments:

- As parts 3, 4, and 5 make clear, the passionate liaison between Alcee and Calixta of part 2 has no adverse consequences for either party or for the continuity or stability of their separate marital or familial lives. Chopin apparently means it quite literally when she concludes her story with the statement "So the storm passed and everyone was happy." This indeed is the point of the obvious *discontinuity* between part 2 of the story and the other four parts. The physical storm of Chopin's story provides a perfect parallel or metaphor for the sexual passion that overcomes Alcee and Calixta, but their passion, unlike the storm's, is tumultuous without being destructive.

- Barbara C. Ewell is certainly correct (*Kate Chopin* [New York, 1986]) when she writes that much of the impact of part 2,

> despite occasionally stilted diction—derives from its imagery. Religion and nature, the two realms that Chopin consistently associated with human sexuality, mingle here. The religious imagery is hinted at earlier in the story, after Alcee is driven in from the gallery to the sitting room. The increasing sexual tension is introduced by his glimpse of the adjacent bedroom, "dim and mysterious" with its "white, monumental bed," intimating an inner sanctum, a holy place. And later, as Calixta and Alcee's desires intensify, the Song of Songs is evoked, while the lovers' discovery of new dimensions of sensuous self-knowledge is rendered precisely in terms of hidden, sacred truths.... Chopin adroitly matches the storm's irresistible development with the effects of passion on the two...lovers—from the lightning bolt that occasions their first physical contact, to the convenient veil of the heavy rain as they lie in bed, to their ultimate consonance with the storm's climax and gently, exhausted retreat. By the storm's end, both the literal two-year drought and the metaphorical one of the lovers' estrangement have ended. Just as the storm has released its pent-up energies, so have Alcee and Calixta vented the repressed sexuality of their physically unsatisfying marriages.

- Sections 4 and 5, which focus on Alcee and Clarisse, may even be read to suggest that Alcee's love for Clarisse and his commitment to their marriage have been somehow strengthened by his affair with Calixta. Are we then to understand that extramarital affairs are being recommended as a good thing?

- Students may wish to consider the ways in which the story challenges traditional beliefs about women and their sexuality. Clarisse, is should be noted, would seem to embody a more traditional (and unexpected) attitude towards sex. "Devoted as she was to her husband," we are told, "their intimate conjugal life was something which she was more than willing to forgo for a while." The implication, perhaps, is that Clarisse, for her part, finds marriage a bit confining. There is also the implication here that pure sexual pleasure and marriage are ultimately incompatible.

- We are given few details about Bobinot, but those we are given suggest that he is a good father (he physically comforts Bibi during the storm) and a considerate husband (he buys a can of shrimp for Calixta). Apparently, however, his lovemaking with Calixta has never reached the same kind of passionate intensity that she reaches with Alcee. In this connection, the adverb "stolidly" which is applied to Bobinot in part I may well provide an important clue. According to the OED the word "stolid" is defined as follows: "Dull and impassive; having little of no sensibility; incapable of being excited or moved."

KATE CHOPIN, "The Story of an Hour"

This ironic little gem has much in common with Kate Chopin's other writings. It is, of course, a psychological exploration of the way in which the institution of marriage, and by extension society at large, represses and limits women from reaching and enjoying freedom and the full range of life's possibilities.

The central episode of the story is the psychological rebirth which Louise Mallard undergoes in the upstairs room where she has retreated and taken refuge after news arrives of her husband's presumed death. It is important that students pay particularly close attention to the successive stages of the physiological and psychological process that she undergoes, for it is Kate Chopin's ability to present these stages economically, and in a way that seems natural and uncontrived, that demonstrates her uncommon ability as a short story writer.

After the first "storm of grief has spent itself" (the public emotional outburst which she has shared with her sister, Josephine, on first hearing the news), Louise "sinks" down in the "comfortable, roomy armchair," and is overcome by "a physical exhaustion that haunted her body and seemed to reach into her soul." Hers is at that moment "a dull stare," "a suspension of intelligent thought." In both a physiological and psychological sense, Chopin's description rings true.

The chair in which she sits faces an open window, beyond which is a world that is teeming with human and natural life. That world is clearly ignorant and disregardful of the tragedy which has just overtaken Louise. Note, however, that Louise is still capable of responding to life. Part of this life, which she simultaneously sees, smells, hears, and feels, significantly enough takes the form of "notes of a distant song which someone was singing." Those notes Louise at first hears only "faintly." The song, we soon come to understand, symbolizes the new life and its possibilities that are now to be hers. Its notes will become louder and clearer as the episode in the bedroom unfolds. Slowly the song and the other forces of life crowd out and push aside the life-negating forces grief, however real and powerful they at first have seemed.

The experience that Louise Mallard now undergoes, as several commentators have pointed out, is clearly sexual in the way it overtakes, overpowers, and then transforms her:

> Now her bosom rose and fell tumultuously. She was beginning to recognize this thing that was approaching to possess her, and she was striving to beat it back with her will—as powerless as her two white slender hands would have been.

It is important to note that Louise at first psychologically fights the new recognition. She has been so shaped and controlled by the male-dominated social and economic conventions that define the world of marriage that the "joy" which she now feels at first seems "monstrous."

Louise's face, we are told, "bespoke repression and even a certain strength." In the end, however, it is her inner strength, presumably strength which has never before been called upon or tested, which allows her to break through the "repression" which would limit and contain her.

Yet, even as she becomes aware of the new life that beckons, she is aware that she will still have to go through with her husband's funeral and the forms and conventions that go with putting the old life away. Before she can permanently shed that life she will have to wear one of its masks (the mask of the bereaved wife) one more time. For a time, the new life and the old will have to co-exist. By now, however, she has come to realize that for her the future holds out something far different than conventional widowhood. Hers is to be a life which she herself can now control: Louise will be finally able to "live for herself."

The story is not, I think, an indictment of marriage per se, though I suspect that students will be interested in trying to establish from the text the kind of marriage that Louise and Brently Mallard have experienced. Rather, Chopin would have us focus on what there is about Louise Mallard that has been psychologically repressed and thwarted by the marriage in which she has found herself. The extent to which she has allowed herself to become caught up and shaped by the conventional attitudes and beliefs of her world is wonderfully suggested by the assumptions that those around Louise make about how she will respond to the news of her husband's death.

There should be plenty of lively discussion about the story's ending. Some students may find it manipulative and contrived, in the way many "slick" O. Henryesque stories are. Others will see that Louise's reaction to her husband's return is psychologically valid given the experience of rebirth and transformation which she has successfully passed through. Note that it is precisely at that moment that Louise decides to leave her room and re-enter the world, a world whose new defining premises are far different from those to which she has previously given her allegiance, that Brently Mallard makes his dramatic reappearance, "composedly carrying his grip sack and umbrella."

In terms of elements of fiction, the story, of course, offers a marvelous opportunity to discuss the use of irony, which begins in sentence one with the flat assertion by the narrator that "Mrs. Mallard was afflicted with heart trouble." It is, of course, the author's effective and consistent use of irony throughout the story that finally rescues it from the realm of melodrama.

AGATHA CHRISTIE, "Witness for the Prosecution"

This is a story that I have wanted to anthologize for a long time. The chief impediment, until recently, was the Christie estate, which, for reasons which were never really made clear to me, would not grant permission to reprint. The reasons, it turns out, had less to do with the royalties (or agreements) governing the very successful stage production of 1953 (for which Agatha Christie herself provided the script) or the equally successful 1957 motion picture version (for which United Artists paid 116,000 pounds) featuring Charles Laughton, Tyrone Power, and Marlene Dietrich. Rather it had to do with the simple fact that the original story of 1948 had been greatly altered in both its stage and film versions, and that the author, consequently, was apparently unwilling to have comparisons made. Christie's inclination to deny reprintings was only reinforced by the fact that when the play was transported from London to Broadway in December, 1954, it became an instant hit and critical success. Not only did *Witness for the Prosecution* enjoy an almost two-year run of 646 performances (outstripping its 468 performances at the Winter Garden Theatre in London), but it was chosen by the New York Drama Critics Circle as the best foreign play of 1954.

The long prohibition is now over. That it did not end sooner is, of course, too bad for several generations of students, who no doubt would have found the story not only interesting in its own right as an example of first-rate mystery fiction, but would have found it instructive and insightful to have been a allowed to compare it with either the play or film versions. One thing they would have found through such comparison is that the author's sense of poetic justice surfaced in the stage and film scripts. In the 1948 short story, the murder (apparently) goes scot free. In the play, on the other hand, Leonard Vole's escape from legal justice is blunted by an act of private retribution. Despite the fact that many counseled Dame Christie to leave the ending alone, she was persistent. "I stuck out over the end," she said, "I don't often stick out for things, I don't always have sufficient conviction, but I had here. I wanted that end. I wanted it so much that I wouldn't agree to have the play put on without it."

Adequate ending or not, "The Witness for the Prosecution" continues to wear well. No small part of its success is the author's ability to draw the reader (like the well-meaning solicitor Mr. Mayherne) into the story and set the reader up for an ending which reverses our expectations. Just how the author accomplishes this feat (and how she plays upon the psychology of the reader) should form the basis for very interesting classroom discussion as should a consideration of the extent to which Dame Agatha in fact "plays fair" with us in bringing off the story's surprise ending. If so, what clue does she provide along the way that, in retrospect, justify and explain that ending?

SANDRA CISNEROS, "The House on Mango Street"

As the first Question for Study suggests, an understanding of Cisneros' brief but finely crafted story depends on our ability to understand the story's narrator and the narrator's emerging understanding of the world. The narrator is, of course, a child—son or daughter we do not know, though given the author's gender and interests it is probably safe to conclude that the narrator is a she. The simplicity of style and tone are very much in keeping with what we expect of a child, but the direction of her comments tell us that she is nonetheless a child coming-of-age. She is not only old enough to remember the past, but old enough to have an emerging set of values and attitudes from which to observe and question the world around her. She remembers that before Mango Street "we lived on Loomis on the third floor, and before that we lived on Keeler. Before Keeler it was Paulina, and before that I can't remember." Now the family has arrived at the house on Mango Street, which it owns rather than rents, where it no longer shares the yard with another family downstairs, and where "there isn't a landlord banging on the ceiling with a broom."

Nevertheless, what gives the story its emotional power and poignancy is the narrator's growing suspicion that the no matter how much the lot of the family has been improved by this latest remove to a house "far away, on the other side of town," that her parents have yet to realize their dreams: "it's not the house we'd thought we'd get." The daughter clearly identifies the fact of having a house (and the kind of house one has) with the realization of one's socioeconomic aspirations and dreams. "They always told us that one day we would move into a house, a real house that would be ours for always so we wouldn't have to move each year."

As her descriptions of the successive houses in which they have lived make clear, the daughter has become painfully conscious of the face and fact of poverty. And, as her reaction to the nun's questions suggests, she has now old enough to be embarrassed by it. But what is most painful of all, is the emerging realization that the family may never have "a real house" and that her father's rationalization ("Temporary, says Papa. But I know how those things go") is simply that, rationalization.

The story does seem to end, however, on a note of optimism and affirmation. The narrator understands that the house on Mango Street is not a "real house." But she herself has not yet given up on her own dream, a dream transferred (as dreams so often are in America) from parent to child: "I knew then I had to have a house. A real house. One I could point to." What she wants is a house she can point to with pride—not a house (like the one on Loomis) to which the nun has pointed with such incredulity and scorn.

SAMUEL L. CLEMENS, "The Celebrated Jumping Frog of Calaveras County"

The story of Jim Smiley and his celebrated jumping frog made Sam Clemens famous as Mark Twain following its publication in 1865. What is interesting, however, is not that

Mark Twain invented it, for he did not—the jumping frog story had been circulating orally in western mining camps for a number of years and had appeared, at least twice, in newspaper versions—but rather what the story became in the hands of a master storyteller. Mark Twain himself throws considerable light on the technique employed in his essay "How to Tell a Story" (1895):

> The humorous story depends for its effect upon the *manner* of the telling; the comic story and the witty story upon the matter....The humorous story bubbles gently along, the others burst....The humorous story is told gravely; the teller does best to conceal the fact that he even dimly suspects that there is anything funny about it....

Mark Twain's contribution to the jumping frog story is precisely in the *manner* of the telling, in the way he establishes the external narrative frame with its immediate contrast between the outside narrator (the literary man, Mark Twain, who is at once both naive and pompous) and the inner narrator (the garrulous and taciturn Simon Wheeler), who tells the story of Jim Smiley with "earnestness and sincerity," without smiling or frowning, and without betraying "the slightest suspicion and enthusiasm."

The narrative structure of the story is surprisingly complex; there are, in fact, as Sidney J. Krause perceptively notes:

> at least eight levels of story interest, each of which has several sides to it, so that the design better resembles a nest of boxes than it does a frame. There is 1) the story of the narrator's spoken and unspoken attitudes toward a) the friend who wrote him from the East and lured him into a trap, toward b) Simon Wheeler whom he regards as a garrulous simpleton, toward c) Jim Smiley, the fabulous gambler, toward d) the animals that Wheeler personalizes, and toward e) the stranger who pulled a western trick on a Westerner and got away with it. Then there is 2) the story of Simon Wheeler's attitudes toward a) the narrator and through him and his friend, toward b) Easterners at large, toward c) Jim Smiley, toward d) the animals and toward e) the stranger. Wheeler, moreover, represents 3) the western community at large that is continuously entertained by Smiley's antics. Also there are the attitudes of 4) the stranger, and of 5) Sam Clemens toward the various parties in his tale. Finally, we have the more restricted attitudes of 6) Smiley himself, which are confined to his animals and such persons as he can get to bet on them; and not the least significant attitudes are those of the animals themselves, particularly 7) the bull-pup and 8) the jumping frog.

Also to be noted is the careful arrangement of the episodes of the "plot" (focusing on "the fifteen-minute nag"; the "little small bull-pup" Andrew Jackson; and the celebrated jumping frog Dan'l Webster), each of which is described with increasing detail and complexity in a vernacular filled with humorous simile and comparison. Finally, there is the level of moral satire. To quote Krause again:

> Wheeler is to some extent the West getting its revenge for the trick of an Easterner, at the same time he plays an instructive joke on the fastidious Mark Twain... His pretensions can be immediately ascertained from his looking down upon Wheeler, from the difference between his language and Wheeler's and from his failure to see Wheeler's story as anything but long, tedious and useless. The fictive Twain thus stands somewhat in the relation to Wheeler that Smiley does to the stranger.

SAMUEL L. CLEMENS, "The Man That Corrupted Hadleyburg"

The content and tone of "The Celebrated Jumping Frog" and "The Man That Corrupted Hadleyburg" differ markedly. The former, one of the great comic tales in all American literature, belongs to the days that Mark Twain spent on the American frontier; the latter to the late 1890s, a period that saw the failure of the Paige typesetting machine in which he had heavily invested and the celebrated author's subsequent forced bankruptcy in 1895. A year later the death of his daughter Susy left him further distraught. These events established the pessimistic and despairing outlook which plagued the author's final years and left him railing at the "damned human race" and the cosmic injustice wrought by an uncaring God.

Twain's much-praised tale is a clear and open attack on moral hypocrisy and materialism as it exists beneath the smug facade of American small town life. It is also, in the words of Maxwell Geismar (1970) "a story of a terrible moral conformity, a fear of generous or bold human action, a show of public virtue as a mask for private gain, an overwhelming social hypocrisy which covers the contortions of small, if not evil souls." But as James D. Wilson (1987) argues, "The philosophical bases and moral didacticism of the fable . . . suggest that Mark Twain was less concerned with provincial sociological analysis of a specifically American condition than with probing and dramatizing the more universal problems of human nature, guilt, free will, and conscience." Hadleyburg, for all its pride in its own integrity, is not a very pleasant place. It is, in the words of the story, "a mean town, a hard stingy town, and hasn't a virtue in the world but this honesty it is so celebrated for and so conceited about." Cases in point are the town's ostracizism of men like Jack Halliday ("loafing, good-natured, no account) and the Reverend Burgess ("the best-hated man among us"). For all its vanity and smugness (or perhaps because of it) Hadleyburg proves an easy mark for the strange visitor it has wronged. The hoax he places in motion easily corrupts its nineteen leading citizens and leaves Hadleyburg an object of ridicule for the nation.

Some other critical comments on the story:

- "It is the acquisitive instinct, the greed for wealth, that is involved in this probing of humanity's frailty. The stranger controls the action of the characters by building up a certain set of circumstances to which he knows they will respond as one man: they have no interior motivation, no wills of their own, to save them from the trap which the stranger sets for them, baited by his own knowledge of human greed.

    Nevertheless, in spite of his strongly marked deterministic pattern, Mark Twain is unable to eliminate moral judgements from his solution. The characters, thieves and hypocrites as they are, are all held responsible for their acts by way of the derisive condemnation of the audience; and the two old people, the only ones who win the reader's sympathy, likewise hold themselves morally responsible and are so conscience-stricken that they actually die of broken hearts."

    —Gladys Bellamy (1950)

- "On the surface, the story is an attack on human greed, but at its deeper levels it reflects Twain's return to the unresolved problems which had perplexed him in Huck Finn's moral conflict and an exploration of the possibility that experience can unify man's moral perceptions and his motivating emotions. In this context, Twain's concept of determinism, especially environmental determinism, or training, does not conflict with his moralism; on the contrary, his moralism functions here in terms of his determinism. Moreover, his view of conscience in this story is not, as Miss Bellamy implies, that of the conventional religious moralist; it is far more complicated than this, synthesizing as it does the principal elements in his earlier concepts of conscience."

—Clinton S. Burhans, Jr. (1962)

- A good deal of critical attention has focussed on the ethical and philosophical import of 'Hadleyburg,' but little on its allegorical ingenuity, and to miss this aspect of the story is to miss much of its satirical and moral force. The purpose of this essay is to examine "Hadleyburg" as another example of the Eden myth that, as R. W. B. Lewis in his *The American Adam* has demonstrated, is so prominent in the American literary tradition. When one recognizes that "the mysterious stranger" in the story is Satan, then Hadleyburg becomes an ironic Eden that is diseased by hypocrisy and money-lust—an Eden that is symbolic of the fallen hopes of the American forefathers for a new paradise on Earth where mankind could begin afresh in peace and brotherhood and Godliness. In Twain's treatment of the Eden myth, Satan plays the role of saviour rather than corrupter. The Eden of Hadleyburg, microcosm of America, is already corrupted by greed and deceit before Satan arrives on the scene. Although his initial motivation may have been revenge, the result of Satan's machinations is to lead Hadleyburg, perhaps without his volition, to some degree of moral reformation."

—Henry B. Rule (1969)

- "Satan-Stephenson, as in the traditional Christian view, wins only to lose, since at the end he is duped into thinking Richards was in fact incorruptible. At the same time, the ending of the story in which we find the citizens of Hadleyburg willing to confront temptation and not be caught "napping" again, does not necessarily suggest any real *moral* change in them that would justify reading the conclusion of the *felix culpa*. We can see this by examining the complex and ironic relationships Stephenson triggers, but which entrap him too."

—Stanley Brodwin (1973)

- As a number of commentators have pointed out, the tightly plotted story succeeds in no small measure because of the effectiveness of its chosen point of view: a third person narrator who reports the action objectively while resisting the temptation to moralize.

ART COELHO, "My First Kill"

Coelho's story of a young boy's first hunt and kill is a simple, yet utterly convincing, narrative. It is, on the other hand, rich and complex in its psychological implications and as such should make for interesting classroom discussion. The story's authenticity results in the author's ability to establish the credibility, candor, and honesty of his introspective twelve-year-old narrator so that the climax of the story when it comes (the death of the two pheasants, and the boy's attempt to cover up his lack of genuine hunting prowess) seems natural and unforced. The effective use of setting provides an appropriate background and frame.

This is, of course, an initiation story. It is a story about guns and hunting and all the traditional associations about manhood and manliness that the act of premeditated hunting evokes. "The theme of this story," Coelho has written the present editor, "evolves around this one truth: 'If you reach for too much glory in life, you will end up without any at all; and then pay a price that will haunt you forever.'"

On the day after his twelfth birthday the narrator takes his brand new rifle (significantly enough a gift from his father) into the field to hunt on his own for the very first time. The father's ("the boss's") expectations and admonitions are very much on his mind. "And more important," the boy notes at the end of the first paragraph, "my dad would want to know exactly how the morning went. Later I'd have to look straight into his eyes and measure up to everything that happened during the hunt." Coelho's story, in fact, is about "measuring up" to adult authority: about making sure that whatever you shoot is "good enough" to put on the supper table; about understanding that the shooting of predators like owls and species like sandhill cranes are a "no-no"; about remembering that "Speed is not the most important thing....It's the calculated reflex that counts" and that "it's not good to waste shells."

The battle between the two cocks and its aftermath provides the story's climax. The boy is old enough to understand tie "drama of the fight" which takes place before him and how the younger cock fakes "the extent of his injury to make the older one more sure of himself." It is at the moment of the young cock's triumph (as he stands on his legs, flapping his wings, and cries out to his harem of hens) that the boy deliberately and yet spontaneously kills him with a single shot. The taking of life—the drawing of blood—not surprisingly brings with it momentary exhilaration: "I was jumping up and down with excitement. The quarter of a mile walk to get around to the opposite slough bank where the game birds were seemed like forever to me."

The boy's admission that he has made a serious mistake is reported as simply and honestly as the act of killing itself:

> When I got up close and saw the bloody spurs above their feet I realized I had done something wrong. I began to see how the younger cock fought so bravely against the stronger one. It reminded me of Howard Davis, the school bully, who tried to take my girlfriend away. I, too, had to fight against great odds to win the love of Maria. For almost a week I had worn the shiner on my right eye like a badge of honor.

Significantly the boy's understanding of the meaning of what has taken place is prompted by a memory from the human world in which he himself has been an actor. And the very fact that he is able to draw the comparison in the first place signals maturity and growth and as such constitutes the moral center of Coelho's narrative. The remainder of the story—the decision to shoot the older cock in order not "to make dad suspicious of my hunting ability"—is anticlimactic. Yet it also compounds the legacy of guilt (a legacy objectified by the blood stain on the rifle's new stock) that the boy carries away from the experience: "what made me hurt inside more than anything else was having to fake the thrill of the hunt for dad." The price paid is a considerable one. By not "measuring up," and, more importantly, not admitting it, Coelho has written, the boy fails on three "separate fronts":

> one, he fouled the natural beauty of the wild by not giving the pheasants a fair chance; two, he fouled his own self-image of committing a cowardly act; and worst of all he never allowed himself to be human, to show he could make a mistake in his father's eyes. He never gave his father a chance to forgive him. Of course the intensity of the story hinges on this strongly felt guilt and shame, this weight upon his shoulders that he dare not confess. His fear of losing any of his father's love by his indecent act with his birthday rifle. Making this traditional gift from father to son, into something sad and agonizing.

LAURIE COLWIN, "A Country Wedding"

Laurie Colwin's "A Country Wedding" typifies much of contemporary short fiction in the sense that it appears to be an artless and unforced glimpse into the private life of a character, who like you and me, is struggling to make sense of it all. Most of the interpretation is left up to the intelligence of the reader, who must decide, from minimal evidence, the issue or conflict that Freddie is trying to face and resolve. To this extent Colwin's story imitates the flow of daily life itself, a life which, as Freddie herself muses, consists mostly of things like "Standing on a road kissing your husband, taking the car to be serviced, letters, meals, telephone calls, arrangements, and errands." In other words, hers (like ours) is a life that offers few, if any, epiphanies.

Freddie and Grey seem, by background and interests, an ideally-matched couple. An urbanite, she has learned much from him about the out-of-doors, lessons she clearly seems to have enjoyed. They are leading the lives of upper-middle class professionals—he a lawyer, she an economist—and financial worries seem non-existent. Their relationship is one defined by affection rather than passion. There are, perhaps significantly, no children.

Though she ought to be content with her lot, Freddie is bored by its routine and sameness. How else to explain her prolonged affair with the dilettantish ex-banker, James Clemens? He appears cynical, world-weary, and as such inclined to the kind of cutting remarks he directs towards Freddie's new dress. Their affair seems mechanical and totally sexual—we are told, in fact, that sex on the "ratty couch in Freddie's bare little study" is at the center of their relationship. It is interesting to note that she admits him to her "bare little study," where she practices being an economist, rather than to the bed which she shares with Grey. If her relationship with Grey is one of affection without passion, with James just the reverse seems to be true.

Freddie's decision to call off their protracted affair seems to have coincided with Penny Stern's wedding, and her trip with Grey back into the idyllic, pastoral world of her childhood. The dress, which she has picked out, also seems to have something to do with it. Once back in the world of New Brecon, in the country world along the Hudson north of Manhattan, Freddie's relationship with her husband is rekindled.

Penny Stern, the new bride, throws additional light upon Freddie and her problems. Penny on her wedding seems dispirited and unenthused. The marriage ceremony (and perhaps married life itself) seems something she feels she must simply endure. Is her marriage to David simply one of convenience—the act of two adults no longer young? Perhaps. Certainly Penny's conversation with Freddie suggests as much. In Penny's attitudes we may well see beginnings of the kind of ennui that leads to trysts with the James Clemenses of this world.

And what of Freddie? What next? Her conversation with Penny is illuminating. Consider, for example, the implications of her statement that

> When I look back over the last two years, I can't believe the person who lived that life is me. I never had interesting romances like you. *That* was my interesting romance. I thought if I gave it up I would be my same old self, but I seem to be some other old self.

"You'll get over it," is Penny's response. To which Freddie adds, with conviction, "Actually, I don't think I will." Freddie's is an interesting, if cryptic, response, coming, as it does, just lines before her statement that "I was a nervous wreck and felt horrible all the time." Her comment seems strange to the extent that as affairs go, hers has seemingly had little or no dire consequence.

The final scene is important for the two women, in different, yet strangely complementary ways. For Penny this escape to their former haunts, where the two women for a moment play the girls they once were, seems a way of avoiding, however briefly, the beginning of her new married state. For Freddie, too, it is a time out, though as she gazes back across the pond at Grey talking with Penny's father, her "heart beat faster to see him."

Clearly, the final understanding that Laurie Colwin would leave us with is focused by the concluding exchange that takes place between the two childhood friends, now married women:

"I guess we've had it," Penny said. "I mean we ought to paddle home." She sighed, "Doesn't everything feel *unknown* to you"?

"It's as plain as the nose on your face," Freddie said.

"I feel as if life is all spread out in front of me but I don't know what's there," said Penny.

"That's what life is like," Freddie said.

JOSEPH CONRAD, "Heart of Darkness"

"Heart of Darkness" is another of Conrad's fictions narrated by that wise old sea-dog, Marlow, and it is wonderful to watch this captain of crafts ply his other craft, the art of storytelling. At one point he likens the hazards of the journey upstream to "rescue" Kurtz to the trials suffered by fairy-tale knights-at-arms, "as though he [Kurtz] had been an enchanted princess sleeping in a fabulous castle." And again, as he tells of arriving at the company's downriver station, he alludes to the "Inferno" of the gully in which the sick and injured African workers have gone to die, and we realize that besides a quest for romance, this is also an epic descent into the underworld, the gates of which are back in Brussels, guarded by the two crones in black. Further, the method and symbolism of the story parallel (sometimes strikingly) certain time-travel fictions like Mark Twain's *Connecticut Yankee* and H. G. Wells' *The Time Machine*. Marlow is taking us upriver, further into the belly of the Great Serpent, but he also claims to be taking us backward in time, toward the dawn of human history.

Of course, Marlow's conception of native African cultures as "living fossils" or as representative of earlier stages of human development (and therefore a window upon what Europeans were like thousands of years ago), is anthropological nonsense. His Africa is a bizarre, phantasmagoric place, where the banks of the river are peopled by frenetic, incomprehensible beings who seem to have little better to do than to cavort gruesomely before the European adventurers. But such was the popular view of the "dark continent" (as it was known at least through the 1950s) and Marlow, like Othello before the Venetian senate, hypnotizes his audience with tales of "the anthropophagi," if not of Othello's "men whose heads do grow beneath their shoulders." Conrad trots out this minstrel show for much the same reason Hawthorne sometimes uses Native Americans, to represent "the children of darkness" whose lurid, passionate rites might be an enticement to Europeans out of reach of their churches and bosses and police (provided, notes Marlow significantly, the Europeans have enough imagination to be attracted).

At the heart of the "Heart of Darkness" resides the Faustian hero Kurtz, this enormously gifted man who has made a bargain With The Darkness, trading his Christian salvation for the pleasure of exploring the whole uncharted territory beyond the "lawful" limits of civilized inhibition. Marlow is like those students of the other Marlowe's Dr. Faustus who beg their master to give up his dabbling in The Black Arts before it is too late. But this Marlow is merely in sympathy with Kurtz and is by no means his disciple.

Because Conrad-Marlow has committed his narrative to the Dantean model, he must turn up the volume of his atmospherics full blast, pumping the idea of "the nameless" and "the unspeakable" for all they're worth in order to make Kurtz's activities seem both more damnable and more tragic (in the classical sense) than the crimes occurring downstream—with the coastal station as purgatory and so on into the more profound darkness of the inner circles. Nevertheless, Kurtz's damnation (like that of Faustus) is a brilliant one, infinitely preferable to the "flabby, pretending, weak-eyed devil of a rapacious and pitiless folly" who reigns wherever the "pilgrims" and their like are to be found.

The trick for Marlow is to be able to travel to the center of "the mystery" and to be able to see into it without being drawn in by it; and the mystery may have little to do, except incidentally, with headhunting or "unspeakable" rites. It may, in fact, be quite as simple as a gift for oratory and a fascination with being able to move others by it to carry out virtually any act one wills them to do. There is nothing specifically "African" about the phenomenon. Certainly, Marlow Conrad sees the appeal in becoming a kind of Hitlerian spellbinder. But the *restraint* that he keeps mentioning is a restraint upon his own "voice"; that is, a constant attention to his "craft," meaning both the reluctant steamboat and the resisting language that the narrator uses as a vessel to carry himself and his audience safely into the darkness of the human heart *and back*. The implication is that he is too concerned with the nuts and bolts of his art to get carried away with his ability to move people through language. That is why this spinner of yarns says he *hates a lie*, hates telling people merely what they most want to hear, which is the political (and religious) spellbinder's special talent.

"The Horror," then, may well be Kurtz's inability to curb his appetite for manipulating innocents like the natives and the eclectic Russian. The reason that Marlow feels that same horror back in Brussels in the apartment of The Intended is because the idolatry she feels toward Kurtz reveals again the man's fatal and irresistible ability to charm. Here, even Marlow feels himself compelled to lie, and he ends the interview by telling The Intended what he knows she longs to hear. Kurtz had something of an advantage in representing himself as a miracle-worker in the jungle because those people had never seen firearms before; but it is clear Marlow feels that Europe, all such "whited sepulchers" as the city of Brussels, is ready after so many years under the influence of that "flabby, weak-eyed devil" to follow willingly such a blood-stirring dictator as Kurtz has the power (and weakness) to become. Marlow exempts the British, however, presumably on the grounds that they (with himself as a prime example) are kept too busy by their work ethic to be running off after messiahs or perhaps, even, *the* Messiah.

JOSEPH CONRAD, "The Secret Sharer"

The essential action of this story turns upon the initiation of a young officer attempting to assume his first command. This effort mainly involves gaining the respect of his crew of veterans and avoiding the very real possibility that his authority will degenerate into a joke. Conrad concerns this initiation with a *doppelganger* that the young captain pulls naked out of the sea one night while the ship is still riding at anchor. These two are so much alike, share so many of the same class assumptions, that the young captain immediately accepts the explanation of the fugitive, Leggat, as to why his murder of a fellow crewman aboard the *Sephora* was justified, if not laudable.

Thus it is that the captain acquires the "secret self" who almost exactly resembles him, and whom he keeps hidden away below decks in his private cabin. Of course, this other self happens to be wanted for murder, and the captain is willing for some reason to become an accomplice in the crime, despite his penchant for correctness in virtually all other matters. That Leggat is pulled up "headless" out of the deep and kept contained below to be released at some critical future moment seems very suggestive in the context of the full story.

Evidently, some part of the captain's initiation has to do with an adjustment in his relationship to the law. Like his counterparts in Susan Glaspell's "A Jury of Her Peers," the narrator considers himself an especially sensitive member of the criminal's own class, and therefore feels justified in shielding the murderer from those whose understanding of the motive would be too crude to render a "proper" judgment. In Conrad's story, however, the elitism is that of the traditional ruling classes and is therefore rather more disturbing than in Glaspell's work. In any case, when the captain of the *Sephora* comes aboard to ask if there has been any sighting of the fugitive, the narrator can tell at a glance he is not the "right sort" to judge the actions of such a refined spirit as Leggat's. He therefore takes it upon himself to obstruct the law that, under other circumstances, would be his particular duty as a captain to see carried out.

The mechanism of the narrators' initiation has to do with a recognition that as a leader of men, his judgment must come from deep within himself, regardless of how ridiculous his mysterious behavior is making him look in the eyes of the crew, and in spite of what the laws of nations dictate. Somehow keeping his own values intact, even at the risk of appearing either criminal or crazy, is precisely what his fidelity to his "secret sharer" is about. Leggat is part of the captain himself, the criminal, wandering, outcast self, the acceptance of which Conrad takes to be (for better or worse) a mark of the true leader. At the same time, the hat which the narrator has given Leggat, a mark upon his head like the mark of Cain, also becomes a mark to steer by, as he takes the ship perilously close to that dark island (which is another "heart of darkness"). So the knowledge of his own outlaw nature is a navigational aid in journeys into the abyss. The narrator knows what he is capable of, and has taken the calibration of his own nature and therefore needs no outside standards or measures to guide him. The assertion of his willingness to risk the whole ship for this principle is politically very scary. But within the bounds of this fiction, it is merely the prelude to a Happy Ending, which even takes the form of a kind of wedding celebration between the captain, his ship, and the crew, who all become one body because they have accepted him as their head. He has stuck to his own judgment in the face of all their experience and expectations, and with the help not of bread, but of a hat cast upon the waters, is able to pull it off.

JOSEPH CONRAD, "Youth"

The narrator of the "inner" story (for there is another narrator telling us about the storyteller) is once again Marlow, the wise old salt who shares his African adventures with the same group of colleagues in "Heart of Darkness." But this is a considerably lighter tale, a collection of episodes (each punctuated with a "pass the bottle") concerning one jinxed old sailing scow trying to make it to Bangkok with a load of coal. The succession of failures is in many ways very serious. A great deal of money is being lost by the interested parties, as the ship must be taken back to port time after time to have its leaks repaired. The poor little bandy-legged captain cannot get this first command of his lifetime afloat; and most importantly, when they finally do get under way, they are headed for a disaster from which they are just barely lucky enough to salvage their own lives.

Throughout the narrative, however, the point that is constantly celebrated is the pure, dumb optimism of the young. Each of these discouragements is simply another adventure to the twenty-year-old Marlow. He has nothing invested and is absolutely free of any burden of ownership or responsibility for others. Even when matters are most life-threatening, all that occurs to him are the hilarious incongruities of the situation. When they are "blown up," the captain rushes out of his cabin and demands to know what the crew have done with his table. The crew assembles and they look more like characters in an animated cartoon who have survived an explosion: their clothes are in tatters, their faces blackened, their hair and beards singed off. And when Marlow climbs back aboard the burning ship to see why the crew have not joined him in the lifeboats, he sees them all gathered on the poopdeck eating cheese and crackers as though they were throwing a farewell picnic. But whatever happens to young Marlow, if he stays alive (as there is never any doubt in his own mind he will), there is still the great mystery of The East awaiting him. Ironically, by the time they have been through their ordeals, this group of scorched, hairless British merchantmen present a far more exotic spectacle to the Asians than the Asians to the British.

However, the tone of the story does not remain quite so hilarious throughout the narration. By the end, Marlow is feeling somewhat philosophical (or at least sentimental) and laments the passing of that time in his life when setbacks and disappointments were merely different kinds of adventure on the way to another fascinating destination. The old coal-scow suddenly begins to take on a vague symbolic function, as if it were an emblem of meditation for Shakespeare's sonnet number 73 which begins, "That time of year thou mayst in me behold . . ." and goes on,

> In me thou see'st the glowing of such fire
> That on the ashes of his youth dost lie,
> As the deathbed whereon it must expire,
> Consumed by that which it was nourished by.

STEPHEN CRANE, "The Blue Hotel"

Although almost all those who have written about Stephen Crane acknowledge the achievement of "The Blue Hotel," there has been surprising and vigorous disagreement on just how the story should finally be read and interpreted. This fact virtually guarantees lively classroom discussion, as long as the teacher is careful to develop the major lines of inquiry. The chief point of critical contention, of course, is the precise meaning of the final section, section IX, and its relationship to the rest of the story. The speech of the taciturn little Easterner (some have argued that he serves as authorial spokesman) taken at its face value introduces a moral and humanistic reading of events—"Every sin is the result of a collaboration. We, five of us, have collaborated in the murder of this Swede."—that would seem to prevent the story from being interpreted in purely naturalistic terms. Other commentators (R. W. Stallman prominent among them) challenge such a view. They see the final section as an unfortunate "tacked on" appendage, and see the Easterner's statement as little more than an attempt to rationalize away with the "fog of mysterious theory" a sequence of events which demonstrate only that in a chaotic, cruel, and indifferent universe man is victim of inexplicable forces quite beyond his own control. To decide which of these two obviously mutually exclusive interpretations is correct, we must study closely the preceding eight sections in an attempt to discover the extent to which character and event confirm or refute the Easterner's judgment.

Though all the characters in the story (Scully, Johnnie, the cowboy, the Easterner, the gambler) deserve close scrutiny, Crane's focus is clearly on the "shaky and quick-eyed" Swede whose idiosyncratic personality, egocentrism, and distorted, fearful view of the world quickly identify him as a man apart, as an individual with whom positive human communication is difficult, if not impossible. At the outset of the story, Scully, the seducer of men, dominates and controls the scene within his hotel. But once, in an ill-fated gesture of comradeship, he offers the Swede whiskey, his control is broken and the "demonic" Swede, having substituted false bravado and aggressive behavior for his initial fear, takes over. What happens next is logical and almost predictable. By attempting to dominate and manipulate his environment by means of crude intimidation, the Swede fully arouses hostility and overt anger in all but the silent Easterner, thus further isolating himself from human community. First comes the new card game, with the Swede himself as boardwhacker; then the accusation of cheating; then the fight with Johnnie; and, finally, intoxicated with victory and identifying himself with the fury of the storm, the Swede successfully manages to transform a garish Fort Romper saloon into precisely the kind of violent dime-novel world of which he has been so fearful. The "dreadful legend atop the cash-machine" thus records a character-fulfilling prophecy: "This registers the amount of your purchase." The fact that the Swede, in the fullness of his conceit, is guilty of reprehensible behavior—that he has, thereby, initiated the very events that cost him his life, though it may confirm the Cowboy's complaint ("Well, I didn't do anything, did I?") by no means contradicts the verdict of the Easterner. To quote Joseph Satterwhite, "The Easterner fails to make clear to the Cowboy that 'the human movement' is the complete breakdown of communication, understanding and sympathy between the social organization and the Swede." Read in this way, a case can be made that the judgment of the Easterner, however little he may really in fact understand the Swede and the precise nature of his delusions, is indeed the appropriate one.

"The Blue Hotel," it goes almost without saying, provides a particularly good vehicle for discussing the elements of Plot, Character, Setting, Theme, and Symbol.

STEPHEN CRANE, "The Bride Comes to Yellow Sky"

As George Monteiro notes at the conclusion of his fine essay about Crane's story, "'The Bride Comes to Yellow Sky'" has been described in various ways: it is an 'ironic comedy of fear,' a 'funny parody of necromantic lamentations over The Passing of the West,'the 'tale of a childlike man confronting anew, and more complex, situation than his simple code allows for,' and—most often—a 'Wild West story' crossed with the 'anti-climactic Western—humor tradition.'" And so, of course, it is. Most of all, of course, "The Bride Comes to Yellow Sky" is a story about change: about the domestication, taming, and ordering of the Old West—the Old West as represented by the lawless, demonic, and impulsive behavior of Scratchy Wilson. Put another way, Crane's story is about the inevitable historical conflict along the American frontier between the forces of nature and the forces of civilization.

Change is apparent everywhere. From the opening paragraph of the story on, there are signs that the historic West is passing before the encroachments of the East. This is seen not only in the "whirling" motion of the train (which "seemed simply to prove that the plains of Texas were pouring eastward"), but in such apparently small details as Scratchy Wilson's shirt ("which had been purchased for purposes of decoration and made, principally, by some Jewish women on the east side of New York") and boots (whose red tops are adorned with "gilded imprints" "of the kind beloved in winter by little sledding boys on the hillsides of New England").

The principal symbol of change and domestication taking place in Yellow Sky is, of course, Jack Potter's marriage with a woman whose most obvious quality is her commonplaceness. (Note that Crane refers to marriage as "this foreign condition.") Ironically, as Ray B. West points out, by entering into a quick and unexpected marriage, Potter is as guilty as Scratchy Wilson of behaving on impulse. Potter can get away with such behavior in the anonymity of San Antonio. There, as Crane notes, "he was like a man hidden in the dark." But in the light of Yellow Sky, Potter has obligations which proceed from his role as town marshal and it is the awareness of his role—of what his fellow townspeople will think—that is at the root of his anxieties. Until the very end of the story the extent of Potter's own domestication hangs in the balance, and Crane makes the point emphatically clear during the climactic meeting between Potter and Scratchy Wilson in the main street of Yellow Sky. For a moment Potter wavers, for a moment he is tempted to fall back into his earlier and traditional role as gun-toting lawman. But then, as Crane tells us, "somewhere at the back of his mind a vision of the Pullman floated, the sea-green figured velvet, the shining brass, silver, and glass, the wood that gleamed as darkly brilliant as the surface of a pool of oil—all the glory of the marriage, the environment of the new estate."

Potter's marriage (as he himself so painfully senses in the opening section of the story) implies changes both for himself and for the community of which he is in charge. For

Scratchy Wilson these periodic drunken sprees ending in armed confrontation have been part of a ritualistic game. But now the game is over. The rules have changed. Marriage has domesticated the West. With changes such as this, and all they portend, Scratchy Wilson cannot compete. And so, in the arresting tableau which ends the story, Wilson, "a simple child of the earlier plains," simply shuffles off into the proverbial sunset: "His feet made funnel-shaped tracks in the heavy sand." Crane carefully prepares us for this final scene by details throughout which emphasize human organization and man's capacity to change his environment. Note, for example, Crane's description of the bride's dress in the opening section and, later, his description of the buildings which line the streets (and frame the action) in Yellow Sky.

A key element of the story is, of course, parody. As Chester L. Wolford notes, Crane uses "classical myth and conventions to extend and deepen the story. "Such myth and convention"

> play a vital part in a mock-epic debunking of the myth of the American West. One of the standard techniques of the mock-epic is to describe realistic, mundane actions in epic language, or to build expectations with epic language in order to deflate the realistic performance which follows. Section 11 of "The Bride," for instance, provides an epic build-up for Scratchy Wilson who "is drunk and has turned loose with both hands." The reader and the newcomer in the saloon are assured that "there'll be some shootin'—some good shootin'," for Scratchy is "a wonder with a gun." We are told that in his efforts to entice someone into battle, Scratchy will often shoot at a door, dog, a window, a house, or any other symbol of domesticity. Section III describes Scratchy's more realistic performance; Scratchy fails to live up to the expectations provided by Section II. He misses the dog. He misses the piece of paper nailed to the barroom door. He even commits two cardinal sins among mythic antagonists: he has to reload periodically, and he fumbles and drops his revolver when facing his opponent. A gunfighter may be many dastardly things—mean, cruel, beady-eyed, and unwashed—but he may not be clumsy. And few mythical gunfighters reload their guns. It is all too mundane.

Among the best critical discussions of the story to date are those by George Monteiro, James Overton, Ben Vorpahl, Ray B. West, and Chester Wolford.

ARTHUR CONAN DOYLE, "A Scandal in Bohemia"

Though "A Scandal in Bohemia" is unique because of the appearance of Irene Adler ("that woman"), the only antagonist ever to outwit the great Victorian detective-hero, the story in most of its other essentials is vintage Sherlock Holmes. It is also part of the tradition of popular mystery or detective story whose basic (and most successful) formula has remained surprisingly constant since it sprang forth practically full blown in three stories published by Edgar Allan Poe in the 1840s ("The Murders in the Rue Morgue," "The Mystery of Marie Roget," and "The Purloined Letter"). According to John Cawelti, *Adventure, Mystery, and Romance: Formula Stories as Art and Popular Culture*, Chicago, 1976), the pattern of action of the detective story has "six main phases" though they do not always "appear in sequence and are sometimes collapsed into each other…(a) introduction of the detective; (b) crime and clues; (c) investigation; (d) announcement of the solution; (e) explanation of the solution; (f) denouement." The "classical detective story," Cawelti also notes, "requires four main roles: (a) the victim; (b) the criminal; (c) the detective; and (d) those threatened by the crime but incapable of solving it."

"A Scandal in Bohemia" not only clearly falls within the formulaic pattern that Cawelti sketches, but, perhaps with the exception of its opening (which lacks Doyle's usual conciseness), virtually all of those special qualities which identify a Sherlock Holmes story are in place: the tight, highly focused, fast-paced plot, dialogue which is compressed and kept to a minimum), the lack of extraneous digressions. Holmes is on top of his game with his faith in the rationally explained causal relationship between apparently unrelated events and the plodding, humorless, yet good-hearted, Dr. John Watson, the embodiment of middle-class values is just as we expect him to be, dependable in all things.

"A Scandal in Bohemia" displays the human side of Sherlock Holmes in his attitude towards Irene Adler, who is perhaps the strongest and most interesting female character in the entire Holmes canon. The story also reveals Holmes's middle-class bias against aristocrats. When the King of Bohemia expostulates "Did I not tell you how quick and resolute she was? Would she not have made an admirable queen? Is it not a pity that she was not on my level?" Holmes responds "coldly": "From what I have seen of the lady she seems indeed to be on a very different level from your majesty...."

Devotees of Sherlock Holmes have been particularly intrigued with the "real life" identity of Irene Adler and the King of Bohemia. Favorite candidates for Irene include the well-known Victorian actress Lillie Langtry (1852–1929), for the King, Edward, Prince of Wales (1841–1914), the future King Edward VII, and Archduke Franz Ferdinand (1863–1914), the heir to the Austro-Hungarian Empire, whose assassination ignited World War I. According to William S. Baring-Gould (*The Annotated Sherlock Holmes*, New York, 1967, I, 354): "Many Sherlockians... would still prefer to believe that 'Irene Adler' was the professional name taken by the late Clara Stephens of Trenton, New Jersey, the aunt of the late James Montgomery...":

> We never mention Aunt Clara,
> Her picture is turned to the wall,
> Though she lives on the French Riviera
> Mother says that she's dead to us all.

Alison and J. Randolph Cox put the allure of Irene Adler into proper focus with the observation that "The mysterious woman of the stage, with her shrouded past and dubious present, was a popular character of the period. She was a social phenomenon reflected in news reports and on society pages. Doyle did not invent her, but his immortalized Irene encompasses elements from ladies of the *demimonde* who were as immediately apparent to his readers as are the charms of our own generation's heroes." Of the King they note: "The British middle classes were obsessed with information about the life of the royals; whole magazines were devoted to describing, explaining, and predicting their dress and movement throughout society. Scandal dogged their every act. It is against this background that the sly digs at the King of Bohemia would have first been read."

One additional point about the story has astounded and confounded Sherlockians: the unexplained substitution of Mrs. Turner for Mrs. Hudson as the landlady of 221B Baker Street. Mrs. Hudson appears in every Sherlock Holmes story save this one. Why? Was Watson a careless proofreader? Was Mrs. Turner a hired temporary? Or was she "a friend of Mrs. Hudson who was acting as *locum tenens* while she was on holiday or ill"?

Finally, it should be noted that "A Scandal in Bohemia" turns on a Holmsian premise of dubious validity: "When a woman thinks that her house is on fire, her instinct is at once to rush to the thing which she values most. It is a perfectly overwhelming impulse, and I have more than once taken advantage of it." An interesting opportunity for class discussion lurks in that assertion.

The appeal of the Sherlock Holmes stories are of course timeless as the number of modern sequels (new and long-lost Holmes stories seem to be "discovered" virtually every year) makes perfectly clear. As Julian Symons observes in his study of the genre (*Bloody Murder. From the Detective Story to the Crime Novel: A History*, Viking, 1972), "Sherlock Holmes became a myth so potent that even in his own lifetime Doyle was almost swamped by it, and the myth is not less potent today." "A Scandal in Bohemia" offers a good opportunity to discuss the reasons for this appeal as well as the quintessential qualities that Holmes shares with other heroes of popular detective fiction. As a point of departure, one might well begin with the appeal Holmes exerted in his own time: his power in Stephen Knight's words (*Form and Ideology in Crime Fiction*, Indiana, 1980) "to assuage the anxieties of a respectable, London-based. middle-class audience." In Victorian England, Knight continues,

> Great emotional value was found in an individual who seemed to stand against the growing collective forces of mass politics, social determinism, and scientific, super-individual explanation of the world, all of which appeared as mechanistic threats to the free individual. A figure like Holmes, who treated all problems individualistically and who founded his power on the very rational systems which had inhumane implications was a particularly welcome reversal of disturbing currents. Aloofness, self-assertion, irritation with everyday mediocrity were not merely forgivable—they were necessary parts of a credible comforting hero.

In some respects, it may be said, conditions have changed but little in the century which intervenes between Doyle's time and our own.

RALPH ELLISON, "King of the Bingo Game"

The nameless black protagonist of the story is another of Ralph Ellison's invisible men, powerless and helpless in a world in which, without a birth certificate, he is unable to establish the fact of his own existence and identity. By employing a limited omniscient point of view, Ellison is able to dramatize and render credible and convincing, the narrator's consciousness as it records the successive events of the story. It also allows him to provide the reader with key bits of information that explain the protagonist's motivation and help to define his world. The information contained in the story's first paragraphs also prepares us to understand the full psychological and symbolic significance of the protagonist's encounter with the bingo wheel. We learn, among other things, that the protagonist is from the South, poor, and without birth certificate or job; that "up here [in the North] it was different. Ask somebody for something, and they'd think you were crazy"; that the man is hungry (a hunger which has spiritual as well as physical dimensions); that he has seen this particular motion picture, with its fantasy of heroism and sex, three times and that he is comforted by the knowledge that, unlike the events of his own life, he knows how things will turn out; that Laura (presumably his wife or lover) is dying and that he hopes to win the jackpot in order to provide her with a doctor; that he is tormented by a traumatic nightmare of persecution out of his boyhood which concludes with "white people laughing." The fact that the action takes place in the isolating, womb-like darkness of a cheap movie theater with its fixed beam of white light is also significant. These facts together underscore the helplessness and defenselessness of the protagonist's situation and his belief that "Everything was fixed," and explain his willingness to accept humiliation and ridicule in order to become "king of the bingo game."

The crisis of climax of the drama occurs, again significantly, "on stage," where the protagonist is given his chance at the wheel. The wheel, of course, symbolizes chance, fate, destiny—the chance to control the wheel, the opportunity to seize control, take charge of, and determine his own life. (In its larger context the bingo wheel may represent the "system" which operates in white America.) Note how the moment the wire is in his hands his feeling of powerlessness gives way. In that moment he feels "reborn" with an almost godlike strength; he has "a sense of himself that he had never known before." Fate's hapless scapegoat has, in effect, become its king. Note too the tenacity of his hold: to let go is to once more surrender the control of his life to others. We need also to consider the irony of the conclusion. Ellison's protagonist both wins and loses: the bingo wheel comes to rest on double-zero, not unlike the cash machine in Crane's "The Blue Hotel," even as the descending curtain, set in motion by a white man's "slow wink," crushes him to death.

LOUISE ERDRICH, "Mauser"

Louise Erdrich's "Mauser" in its subject, setting, theme, and approach seems very typical of what we have come to expect of the contemporary short story. In this case we are offered a brief glimpse (a glimpse that is at once both comic and sad) into the lives of three ordinary and vulnerable people.

Not surprisingly we identify from the outset with Erdrich's unnamed narrator—the voice which speaks to the reader and tells the story. At the beginning she seems to possess a good humored and balanced sense of who and what she is. She prides herself on being clear-sighted and emotionally even-tempered, and is very much tuned in to Travis Houpart and his "bullshit" when he makes his play in the bar. She deftly puts him on notice with the comment "I'm not going to do anything stupid either." Then, when she comes to realize that she has gained the upper hand (at the moment when Travis finally mentions his wife's name), she follows up with the pointed, yet devastating questions: "What's new with you? With Mauser?"

For all her apparent self-confidence and equanimity, the narrator, we soon come to understand, is a vulnerable human being. She is coming off a broken love affair in which she has been ditched in favor of another female employee at the construction company. In its aftermath she tells us that what she looks for in people is character. Presumably depth of "character" is what her previous lover lacked, and so, of course, does Travis Houpart with whom she is about to become involved.

For reasons which she can scarcely articulate, the narrator finds herself thinking about Travis Houpart. She then begins to protect him by altering his invoices. Such protection, of course, is unnecessary. Mauser is clearly willing to overlook his brother-in-law's performance on the job and Travis's career at the construction company is anything but insecure. Such protectiveness makes sense only as part of the mindless fascination for Travis that overcomes the narrator.

Just why she falls for so obviously a "characterless" man as Travis Houpart (particularly when she knows precisely who and what he is) is not to be easily explained. All she can say is that "Somehow I'd got it into my head that I meant something to this guy. Because it can happen. Clichés in love songs. Roses, violets, little tin birds. Sometimes you can't think fast enough to keep them from getting to you."

Travis Houpart appears to all the world as a pleasant and pleasing fellow. "A laid-back good-time boy with high-school basketball trophies rusting on top of the TV," Travis looks like "a man worth meeting." He is, the narrator makes clear, extremely "attractive on the outside": "trim," "reassuring," "regular-featured," and "even-toned." He sports clean white shirts in a blue collar town. In his case, as in the case of other men like him (for Travis is a recognizable type), looks are deceiving. For all his looks, Travis Houpart is "pure liability." He is a vain and "empty" man, who feeds on "female admiration" and makes his "living off his wife's brother's good will."

Mauser, the brother-in-law and boss, clearly defines the boundaries of Travis's world. The narrator compares him to "a dad" and a "brick wall"—and both comparisons ring true in psychological terms. Of the two male characters in the story, Mauser is clearly the more interesting, largely, I think, because unlike Travis we feel his complexity and are less able to take his measure. As the successful owner of the construction firm, Jack Mauser prides himself on being in control. No little part of that control resides in the fear he instills in his employees through the exercise of his "explosive and foul anger" which combines "the drama of a Richard Burton delivery with raw Teutonic rage."

For all his ferocity in the work place, Mauser also has his weaknesses. One "streak of irrational vulnerability" results from his adoration of his sister Rhonda, Travis Houpart's wife. The other is his "dangerous" rage itself. Both weaknesses can potentially result in a loss of control, and loss of control is what overtakes Mauser in the story's climactic scene.

What brings these three characters together and momentarily entwines their lives is the scene in the trailer-office in which the hither-to amorous Travis holds the narrator so that Mauser will catch them together as lovers. It is a moment of betrayal and revelation. (What makes that betrayal particularly poignant is that it comes in the context of the narrator's confession to Travis: "I'm not the kind of person who can afford to get hurt. Don't hurt me.") Enlightenment comes instantaneously: "That was when I saw he had decided on the spur of the moment to use me to get to Mauser. I was a prop, a plastic blow-up companion, a partner easily disposed of. His real relationship was not with me, or maybe with any woman, but with Mauser."

The narrator is summarily fired, ostensibly because she has falsified Travis's reports. (Mauser is, of course, protecting Rhonda by removing her rival.) Vulnerable the narrator may be; but she has her limits and her dignity. "I'm not so different from Mauser," she tells us. "When I love someone, that's it. You can drive me past a limit too." Deciding that "Travis had things too easy in life so far," she sets out in her compact car to get revenge. And she gets it, too, running Travis's truck into a ditch with a full load of gravel. (Interestingly enough, it is she who "ditches" him.)

Ironically, Travis gets his own particular kind of revenge when he squashes Mauser's candy-apple-red Cadillac ("beside Rhonda, the only thing in the world that Mauser truly loved"). This revenge, however, is the result not of Travis's cleverness or premeditation, but rather of his own mindless, "desperate" attempt to free his dump truck from the ruts and thereby escape Mauser's equally mindless rage. The scene that ensues is one of pure comedy.

The story's final scene in which Mauser and the narrator, emotionally drained and exhausted, return to town together should make for interesting classroom discussion. What, for example, has the narrator decided when she says of Mauser, just before she leaves him behind at the seafood quick-stop: "He was a man of solid worth and deep attachments, Mauser. He had a temper, but I didn't have to fear it anymore"? What kind of conclusion *does* such a scene offer the story and in what ways is it appropriate given what has gone on before?

WILLIAM FAULKNER, "Barn Burning"

"Barn Burning" is the story of Sarty Snopes' inner psychological struggle, culminating in his conscious decision to repudiate his father's demonic will and lawless, amoral code. Instead, Sarty chooses another, higher vision which, though imperfectly understood, acknowledges the claims of law, society, justice, and human commitments that transcend the natural ties of kin and family ("the old fierce pull of the blood"). Such a formulation of theme is, of course, much too simple. Sarty's growing moral awareness is never formulated in such easy intellectual terms. Rather, it is to be traced through the series of nine episodes, taking place over a six-day period, which comprise the story's tightly knit narrative structure and which serve, as Edmond L. Volpe has pointed out, as "objectifications, as in a nightmare, of the boy's psychological and emotional tensions."

The dramatic interplay between *external* events and *internal* consciousness is made possible by the story's point of view. Though "Barn Burning" is Sarty's story, the narrative voice is not Sarty's own. (Students might well be asked to discuss the serious limitations that a first-person point of view would impose.) The choice of a third-person narrator, an older, more mature adult who empathetically identifies with Sarty and is able to understand and dramatize his inner turmoil and anxiety, makes possible an enlarged perspective which both explains and makes possible the story's heightened rhetoric and prose style. The advantage of a third-person narrator becomes immediately clear in the synesthesia of the opening scene which joins the smell of food with the sense of fear. As Joseph Reed notes, "The continuously sliding perception and run-on style give us not just an intense introduction to Sarty but instant identification and empathy with him: he senses things with the wrong organs because of his intensity and he transfers this intensity directly to us. We quickly discover that it is not just the product of hunger or deprivation but of an attempt to distract himself—he is taking his mind off the serious proceedings of the justice of the peace to escape a process he does not want to be involved in...." Sarty knows that if asked he will have to lie to protect his father. The third-person point of view also makes possible the moments of flashback and foreshadowing which are so essential to our full understanding of the story.

As the events of the opening scene make clear, Sarty enters the story with an already-developed moral sensitivity to right and wrong. That moral sensitivity brings about a slow and painful process of emancipation that culminates in his decision to warn Major de Spain and then to flee. Understanding how Faulkner's point of view functions, and to what end, allows the reader to trace this process of moral growth in the episodes that follow.

The galvanizing figure of the story is, of course, Ab Snopes, whose cold, ruthless, and self-righteous penchant for barn burning—a major crime in a rural, agricultural society—speaks "to some deep mainspring of his...being." To Sarty, he is a man "without face or depth—a shape black, flat, and bloodless as though cut from tin in the iron folds of the frockcoat which had not been made for him, the voice harsh like tin and without heat like tin." He is a figure with clear demonic characteristics: note Ab's pride, his "stiff and ruthless limp," his identification with fire, and the fact that, like the devil, he is a man who casts no shadow. The imagery which surrounds Ab, together with his cold, mechanical, lawless behavior, serve to suggest and to summarize his inner moral nature.

In opposition stands Major de Spain. For Sarty, the de Spain house ("big as a courthouse") symbolically embodies the idea of truth and the concept of a peaceful, secure, and ordered society capable of checking his father's lawlessness. The boy's emotional response is summarized by the narrator (because Sarty himself "could not have [put the thought] into words, being too young for that"): "They are safe from him. People whose lives are a part of this peace and dignity are beyond his touch, he means no more to them than a buzzing wasp: capable of stinging for a little moment but that's all; the spell of this peace and dignity rendering even the barns and stable and cribs which belong to it impervious to the puny flames he might contrive...." So powerful is the "spell" that Sarty even dares hope that "Maybe he will feel it too. Maybe it will even change him now from what maybe he couldn't help but be."

Also worthy of class discussion is the story's final scene. "Sitting on the crest of a hill," before entering the "dark woods below," and without knowing "how far he had come," Sarty's "terror and fear" are gone. But the "grief and despair" remain; and in response, in order to salvage something redemptive to hold on to, Sarty's mind harkens back to the Civil War when his father was a member of "Colonel Sartoris' cav'ry!"—a final illusion that the narrator immediately destroys. Sarty's future is, of course, ambiguous and unclear, but the images which conclude the story are those of promise: the promise of sunrise and a spring morning and "the liquid silver voices of the birds" which call unceasingly. Significantly enough, "He did not look back."

116

WILLIAM FAULKNER, "Dry September"

The connection made in this story between racism and sexism has by now become pretty much a commonplace; but at the time of its writing, such an analysis demanded of Faulkner a fairly radical detachment from his own background. One of the major concerns of the story is to explore the interpenetration of "real life" and "literary reality," as certain cultural myths are seen to control human behavior almost as powerfully as instincts control the behavior of other animals.

In the opening scene of the barbershop, we are not surprised that the youngest man present is the one most attracted to the enactment of these pitiful ragged remnants of the chivalric code, the "protection" of the women of his own class (which in this situation means race) from the attentions of any "lesser" male. It also makes sense that the travelling salesman (the barber's "client") might be interested in precipitating some sensational incident in a community toward which he feels no lasting commitment. The barber himself, however, is hesitant to make any rash judgments about the incident. He says he knows the man being accused and does not believe it lies within his nature to commit the act attributed to him. "And besides . . ." he says, and goes into his own version of the "well known peculiarities" of unmarried women of a certain age. What he gives of human sympathy with one hand he takes back with the other. In any case, all rationality of any kind is swept away when the man of action, the war veteran McLendon, steps in the door and quells all dissent through the force of his thirst for violence.

The narrative provides nothing whatsoever from the point of view of the primary victim of the lynching. In fact, we do not know if the murdered man had anything to do with the rumored offense, or whether any such offense even took place. However, we are given considerably more insight into the life of the *other* victim of the lynching: "Aunt" Minnie. As Minnie walks out in public for the first time since the "incident," she is keenly aware of her fellow citizens' prurient interest in what (if anything) was "done" to her. She is also aware that the knowledge of her affair with the bank teller makes her only marginally "worthy" of any such vengeance as was taken in the name of her smudged honor, and that in any case, the vengeance was not enacted for her sake, but for the "crime" of an alleged breach of the society's racial barriers. This combination of assaults upon her human dignity places Minnie on such a rack of torment that she is literally driven mad.

The final impressionistic scene at the McLendon home gathers together nearly all the symbolism of the title's late summer drought. Perhaps "Aunt" Minnie's life has been pointless and sterile, but the McLendons' marriage seems much the same, as McLendon walks into his home late at night and tongue-lashes his wife for staying up (as he believes) to check upon his comings and goings. The enactment of his "defense" of feminine innocence has left him angry and unfulfilled because the myth is without any nourishing moral content. It is a mere pretense for the venting of rage against "otherness," whether of gender or of race.

WILLIAM FAULKNER, "A Rose for Emily"

CHRONOLOGY:

Date	Event	Reference in the Text
1854	Emily born.	II
1884	Emily's father dies.	II
1885	Homer Barron appears and begins his courtship.	III

1886	Emily purchases poison; Homer Barron disappears; the smell appears; the upstairs room is closed.	II, III, IV
1894	Colonel Sartoris remits Emily's taxes.	I
1906	Colonel Sartoris dies.	I
1906–1908	Emily gives up her lessons.	I
1916	Aldermen seek to collect taxes.	I
1928	Emily dies at 74.	I, IV, V
1930	Faulkner publishes the story.	

"Faulkner's well read 'A Rose for Emily,'" as Ruth Sullivan observes, "has been variously interpreted as a mere horror story about necrophilia and madness, as a story about the Old South contending with the New Order of the Post-Civil War era, as a tragic tale of a woman's noble but doomed effort to resist the forces of time, change, and death, and as a tale of the catastrophe that can result when someone allows illusion to become confused with reality." All of these elements are clearly embedded in the story, and all are worth pursuing in the course of classroom discussion.

The chronology of events suggested above is included to help clarify the plot insofar as it can be recovered and reconstructed from a narrative in which only one specific historical date (1894) is provided. Since our ability as readers to understand, appreciate, and correctly interpret the meaning of the story ultimately depends on our ability to understand its events and the causal relationship between them, a chart such as the one suggested—and instructors are encouraged to check their reconstructions against my own would seem to provide an appropriate departure for the purposes of analysis.

Having arrived at some general agreement about the correct chronological sequence of events, we are prepared to ask ourselves why Faulkner deliberately rearranges the narrative structure and what light this sheds on the story's meaning. Three reasons come at once to mind. First of all, such a rearrangement allows the narrator, whose identity and motives are themselves worthy of consideration, to prevent our discovery of the causal relationships existing between certain events, relationships of which the narrator himself is at least partially aware, since the events of the story are complete: Emily is dead and buried and her house has at last been made to yield its macabre secrets. For example, though we learn about the mysterious smell as early as part II, we do not learn about Homer Barron's final disappearance until part IV. Secondly, the narrative structure which Faulkner provides serves to create and reinforce the story's atmosphere and its mood of unreality, suspense, and mystery, a mystery which, it should be added, is never really totally solved. Though we do come to learn a good deal about Emily Grierson, much about the spinster, her motives, and the events of her lifetime remains obscure, thus inviting a variety of interpretations about the story's final meaning and intent. Thirdly, the structure forces us as readers to suspend and postpone our own judgments about Emily herself. We are allowed—if we will—to adopt a sympathetic stance toward her *before* becoming fully aware that she is a murderess who has engaged in acts smacking of necrophilia.

A close study of the five sections of the story also reveals a clear underlying structure. As Floyd Watkins has pointed out, "The contrast between Emily and the townspeople and between her home and its surroundings is carried out by the invasion of her home by the adherents of the new order of the town. Each visit by the antagonists is a movement in the overall plot, a contributing element to the excellent suspense in the story, and a crisis in its own particular division of the story." Episodes I and V frame the story: they take placed in the narrative present. Episodes II, III, and IV, with their shifting chronology, take place in the past. In episode I, Emily's house and privacy are invaded by the Board of Aldermen who attempt to collect her taxes. In episode II, her house is invaded twice, once by the men who sprinkle lime to stop the smell and once by those who come to force her to give up her father's body. Episode IV contains invasions by the Baptist minister and by Emily's relatives from Alabama; and episode V focuses on the final assault of the townspeople, who, following Emily's funeral, swarm into the house to penetrate its secret. Each of these invasions is more or less successful; only in episode III do Emily's house and privacy remain inviolate. Since, as the symbolism of the story makes clear, the Grierson house (which lifts "its stubborn and coquettish decay above the cotton wagons and the gasoline pumps") is a symbolic extension of Emily herself, each of these invasions, intrusions, and forced entrances is clearly an attempt by the curious to penetrate and "know" Emily herself. Moreover, it can be argued, as William V. Davis and others do, that the town's reaction to Emily after each of these successive episodes is summarized by the five adjectives offered by the narrator at the end of episode IV—"dear, inescapable, impervious, tranquil, and perverse"—"each becoming as it were a sort of metaphorical characterization of each of the differing states through which the townspeople of Jefferson (and the readers) pass in their evaluation of Miss Emily." The analysis of plot thus is crucial to our understanding of the story, for it is upon the basis of what the town learns, and what we as readers learn in the process, that we can begin to formulate a thematic statement or series of thematic statements about Faulkner's classic story.

F. SCOTT FITZGERALD, "Winter Dreams"

It is difficult to believe that Fitzgerald produced this story only three years previous to his masterful *The Great Gatsby*. Many of the same themes dealt with in "Gatsby" are present here as well, but the springs of their essential sentimentality are so nakedly apparent that one is tempted to make a case for a totally ironic reading of the narrative.

The story starts in a rather stale way: the young hero, a nobody, catches a glimpse of the pampered daughter of one of the wealthiest families in town. Of course, this little girl is going to become his Woman of Destiny. In order for this to be possible, it is necessary to transform the not-quite-poor little golf caddie into "the young and already fabulously successful Dexter Green," This transformation is accomplished within less than a paragraph, for it is necessary that the inaccessible Judy Jones become accessible so that she can become once more inaccessible. Though the young man is now able to afford virtually anything he desires, occasionally, says the narrator, "He [runs] up against the mysterious denials and prohibitions in which life indulges. It is with one of these denials…that this story deals."

Judy Jones is in some respects a literary relative of Henry James's Daisy Miller. She possesses enormous charm, beauty, and energy, and is magnetic in the frankness with which she asserts her own vitality. But more complexity is attributed to Daisy by James than Fitzgerald allows Judy Jones, and more honesty, as it turns out. All we can perceive of Fitzgerald's character is a short attention span, a giddiness at finding herself so young and beautiful and popular. There seems little room left over for any real depth of personality. At one point, she is made to cry and to remark to Dexter how tired she is of everything: "I'm more beautiful than anyone else…why can't I be happy?" This is also the moment she asks Dexter to marry her, though Dexter believes later that her proposal of marriage was simply to demonstrate her power over him—to cheer herself up by showing that she could make him break his engagement to another young woman. If we are to take this analysis of motive seriously, we are being told that in almost every respect aside from the physical, Judy Jones is a rather ugly person, and that Dexter even knows this and is driven compulsively to possess her as another of those "glittering things" desirable only for its inaccessibility. Add to this Dexter's notion that the First World War is a good place to go for relief from emotional disappointments, and it is a toss-up which character is less appealing.

In the final analysis, however, Judy Jones is a cipher. What she stands for in the hero's life is merely his youth, the time and place of his greater erotic intoxication. It has virtually nothing to do with her personally, for it is clear that even if Dexter could have Judy Jones, it would not be for herself, but as a souvenir of the season of his romantic illusion. "The dream was gone," he says upon hearing that Judy has aged and is not the icon he has etched in his imagination. He has lost her "just as surely as if he had married Judy Jones and seen her fade away before his eyes." Tears of self-pity stream down his face, "For he had gone away and could never go back any more." Judy has let him down again by not remaining eternally inaccessible to everyone and everything, but especially to time.

RICHARD FORD, "Rock Springs"

Richard Ford has graciously provided the editor (November, 1989) with the following comments about the writing of short stories including "Rock Springs":

> To me, it is not very interesting to divulge or to learn precisely how the raw matter of a story originates in life: to know, for instance, what *actually* happened to the author in Rock Springs; who actually said a line that later reappears in a story; what parts were made up, what parts put down verbatim. Everything in a story—at least in my stories—originates in life of some sort; life remembered, life altered by being committed into language—life made up. To stress actuality threatens to devalue the up-to-now unknown yet indispensable truth literature would bring into existence.

> "Rock Springs" originated and developed the same way every story I've ever written has—from a few pages of notes transcribed out of my notebooks after I'd decided I wanted to write a story. These notes comprise lines I was interested in and that seemed possibly usable as dialog; or the name of a place or a character, or some statement of inclination about how a story is to be written; an important incident described in a tone that is attractive to me. All these notes I simply mull over and annotate until the trajectory of a story occurs to me, or else until I can write a first line from which the story somewhat haphazardly follows. Always I go back to my notes when I'm stuck. Always I reconsider everything—the story, all the notes, anything I can think of that seems important—before I write the ending.

However elliptical Ford's remarks, "Rock Springs" does have the quality of "life remembered and misremembered." And life for Earl, the narrator-protagonist of the story, is out of control. Troubles haunt him. Things have not gone well for Earl, in fact, since "the old glory days," he finds himself searching for answers and for meaning among the confusions of the present. By retelling the events of a story that, presumably, has taken place, Earl is simultaneously exploring them, and by doing so he measures and defines himself for the reader. The answers he thinks he has discovered all are tinged by a kind of sadness and melancholy:

> I thought...how I never planned things well enough. There was always a gap between my plan and what happened, and I only responded to things as they came along and hoped I wouldn't get in trouble. I was an offender in the law's eyes. But I always *thought* differently, as if I weren't an offender and had no intention of being one, which was the truth. But as I read on a napkin once, between the idea and the act a whole kingdom lies.

The story he tells finds Earl once again on the road, following another "scrape with the law," this time "in Kalispell over several bad checks." The Mercedes, stolen from an ophthalmologists' parking lot, momentarily raises his spirits and hopes: "I felt like a whole new beginning for us, bad memories left behind and new horizons to build on…everything seemed like the end of the rainbow."

But this takes place before Rock Springs, before the Mercedes breaks down and gives out and before Edna decides to leave him. In the story's concluding scene we see Earl out in the Ramada Inn parking lot looking for a new car to steal. Alone with his responsibilities toward Cheryl and Little Duke ("no one to see about them but me alone"), Earl is left to ponder the character of his life and the nature of the success which seems to elude him. The "difference between a successful life and an unsuccessful one," he decides, is "how many troubles like this one you had to face in a lifetime….And that's what I wanted for me. Fewer troubles, fewer memories of trouble." The story ends as Earl comes across a Pontiac with Ohio plates, whose backseat is filled with "kid's toys and some pillows and a cat box with a cat sitting in it staring up at me like I was the face of the moon." The car looks "familiar." It contains "the very same things I would have in my car if I had a car." Suppose. he thinks, the owner was watching. Would that owner be able to identify with him?

Richard Ford's characters, like those of so many contemporary writers, are clearly defined by their moral dimensions—by their attitudes, their behavior, and by the nature of their commitments. In Earl's case there is much that is admirable. To the world at large, Earl appears to be the consummate "loser." But, as the reader learns, he is something better than that. Earl is genuinely concerned about the welfare of his daughter Cheryl—that she have "a better shake in things"; he is thoughtful and considerate of Edna (a woman who clearly has had "troubles" of her own); he is a man who can appreciate the beauty of a western sunset. As we learn from the episode with the woman in the mobile-home community, Earl is readily able to identify and commiserate with others. "She was good nature's picture," Earl decides, "and I was glad she could be, with the little brain-damaged boy, living in a place where no one in his right mind would want to live in a minute." He can identify with others. Can anyone identify with him?

And it is precisely these qualities that illuminate Earl and the question he poses in the story's final lines. As Ronald L. Johnson notes, "That question indicates that the narrator is searching for some act of compassion which will enable him to endure his present trouble. This story ends with that question, forcing the reader to wonder how similar men are in their desires for security and a meaningful life." The implied answer is, of course, that men are similar indeed.

MARY WILKINS FREEMAN, "A New England Nun"

"What can we say that will express our sense of the beauty of Miss M. E. Wilkins' A New England Nun and Other Stories?" begins a reviewer for the Critic in May 1891:

> So true in their insight into human nature, so brief and salient in construction, so deep in feeling, so choice in expression, these stories rank even with the works of Mrs. Stowe and Miss Jewett. It is the marvelous repression of passion and feeling in the New England character that Miss Wilkins has drawn with such technique. Beneath the icy surface of demeanor she has looked into the heart of this strong self-contained people and has seen boiling and bubbling wells of fervency. It is chiefly from New England women that she has made her studies, and there is nothing narrow, sad, colorless life that has escaped her observation.

Such a view captures well the high regard that Mary Wilkins Freeman was held in her own day when she formed one of the schools of regional writers known as the Local Colorists.

Of all her attempts to capture and convey a vision of New England village life none has been judged more successful than "A New England Nun." The story has always ranked high in the Freeman canon. Though it is a relatively simple story, easily accessible to beginning students of literature, it is nonetheless a story whose depth and subtleties belie its surface simplicity. As a result it has begun to attract, particularly in recent years, increased critical attention.

Several modern studies are particularly interesting to the extent that they suggest strategies for classroom exploration. For example, David H. Hirsch (1965) suggests that we study closely the scene when Joe Dagget enters Louisa's house and the two engage in a brief discussion (and concludes Joe's remark, "Yes, it's pretty hot work in the sun"). Hirsch notes that

> the scene pulsates with tightly controlled dramatic tension. Though Louisa and Joe are plain, inarticulate people who cannot reveal themselves to each other, nevertheless, their relationship is charged with an undercurrent of significance which reveals them to the reader in spite of their own silence and reserve.

Hirsch then goes on to describe the story as "almost a case study of an obsessive neurosis, that is, a 'neurotic disorder in which there are repetitive impulses to perform certain acts.'" He then describes in detail "Louisa's neurotic compulsiveness" which "becomes especially prominent after her meager store of conversation has been exhausted": her need to set the books in order, her sewing, her disposal of the currants, her examination of the rug after Joe leaves, etc. "To Louisa and her domain at least," Hirsch writes, "Joe represents a constant threat of potential chaos. He does not, indeed, cannot, belong in the established order of Louisa's home life and his intrusion into that life brings inevitable discord."

Marjorie Pryse (1983) feels very differently. She views Louisa Ellis as "an uncloistered" nun. "When Louisa Ellis reconsiders marriage to Joe Dagget," she writes,

> she aligns herself against the values he represents. Her resulting unconventionality makes it understandably difficult for historians, themselves the intellectual and emotional products of a society which has long enshrined these values, to view her either perceptively or sympathetically. For Louisa Ellis rejects the concept of manifest destiny and her own mission within it; she establishes her own home as the limits of her world, embracing rather than fleeing domesticity, discovering in the process that she can retain her autonomy; and she expands her vision by preserving her virginity, an action which can only appear if not "foolish" at least threatening to her biographers and critics, most of whom have been men.
>
> In analyzing "A New England Nun" without bias against solitary women, the reader discovers that within the world Louisa inhabits, she becomes heroic, active, wise, ambitious, and even transcendent.

Though Ms. Pryse's view may still be in the minority, there has clearly been a new willingness to view Louisa Ellis and her situation with sympathy. As Perry D. Westbrook reminds us (1988), "it would be wrong...to dismiss Louisa's way of life as entirely trivial and unfulfilling, though her fellow villagers and contemporary readers would doubtless have considered them so. Instead of marriage she has deliberately chosen an alternative in which her sewing and her meticulous housekeeping—themselves forms of artistic expression—provide her very real satisfaction."

CARLOS FUENTES, "Aura"

Within the past two decades, there has been a tremendous growth in the popularity of fantasy literature in this country among readers under thirty. Some academics have speculated that this shift in taste is largely due to a desire in this generation of students to escape the sphere of politics. Be that as it may, Carlos Fuentes' "Aura," despite first impressions, probably has little in common with this latest North American gothic revival. Rather, writers such as Fuentes, Borges, and Marquez approach their odd, dream-like worlds from the opposite direction: from the political programs of Realism and Modernism, which aimed at sweeping away the vestiges of the Romance and the literary imitation of idealized aristocratic manners. It may simply be that the political regimes under which these writers have spent their lives have become so bizarre and so out of touch with the norms of any common reality that their stories and novels have had to strain the limits even of Surrealism to render the literary equivalent of the political "facts."

Of course, your students will undoubtedly want to keep the discussion centered upon the wonderful effects of the tale, and there is certainly enough to construe at that level to make the plot entirely satisfying. Mysteriously, a young scholar is very particularly solicited in a newspaper ad to come into the home of one Consuela Llorente to prepare for publication the memoirs of her late husband. The narrator, Felipe Montero (who designates himself "you" throughout the narration), soon finds himself implicated in a web of witchcraft. The incredibly old widow, through some sort of magic that seems to involve exotic plants and the sacrifice of cats, is able to produce a golem or simulacrum of herself as she was in the freshness of her own young womanhood. The action climaxes with Montero in the arms of the withered Consuela, himself having been transformed into an aged General Llorente, the old woman's dead husband.

But Fuentes is a social critic as well as a fiction writer, and like Marquez, he is an incurable political fabulist. It is not incidental that the narrator is a scholar whose chief ambition is to connect the most influential ideas of Spain's Golden Age (during the European Renaissance) with her conquest of the New World. But he cannot quite do that yet, and his need of money has him instead revising the second-rate French of a dead general. The general himself is a parody of the history "you" would write. He left his native Mexico to become educated in Europe, and through friendship with "the intimates of Napoleon III" returned to his homeland on the staff of the ill-fated Hapsburgian "Emperor," Maximillian.

How does an idealistic young scholar end up rewriting the words of a man, General Llorente, who took his sense of significance from such late, loony schemes of European empire? And who is this Consuela who keeps one end of her dark bedroom ablaze with votive candies before a rat-infested altar? How is the hero's lust for the beautiful aura connected with that other incarnation and communion (as she holds in her naked lap a thin bread-wafer which they share in their second tryst)? Whatever Consuela represents, our glimpse of her waltzing with the general's glittering tunic seems to sum up a great deal of what has seduced the young writer-scholar. The heroic dream of the quest, linked with religious idealism and the thirst for empire, is a potent combination. The New World writer may believe that he has a mission to liberate Aura from the tyranny of the hag, but the very impulse is already "the old story" reasserting itself. The history our young hero finds himself rewriting and reliving is what one would expect from someone who (in the political sense as well) finds himself in bed with the aged mistress of the house and all of the Old World dreams she represents.

GABRIEL GARCÍA MÁRQUEZ, "A Very Old Man with Enormous Wings"

Like all speculative fiction, "A Very Old Man with Enormous Wings" is a "what if" story. What would happen, García Márquez asks, if a "flesh-and-blood angel," in the form of a decrepit, sick old man, were forced to take refuge among the inhabitants of a poor, backward, "sad" society?

George R. McMurray, in his 1977 study of García Márquez, offers a number of suggestions toward the story's interpretation:

> "A Very Old Man with Enormous Wings" is particularly intriguing because it can be read on several different levels. First of all it is a delightful fantasy for children. For the adult reader, however, the protagonist reinforces themes pervading many of García Márquez's works: the angel's decrepitude is another example of physical decay; man's loss of innocence is suggested by the angel's fall from his heavenly abode to an unhappy earthly existence; the failure of the church is conveyed by preposterous ecclesiastical investigation of the angel; and the theme of solitude emerges from the angel's uncommunicative nature and isolation from all men. The absurd attempts to explain the angel's appearance logically and to discover his *raison d'être* demonstrates the limits of human reason, whereas his reduction to the status of a sideshow freak for the monetary gain of others implies a condemnation of capitalistic exploitation. On the mythical level, the angel recalls the youthful Greek hero Icarus who defied the gods by flying too close to the sun, melting the wax by which his wings were attached and causing him to plummet into the sea. The old man, however, suggests an ironic reversal of the Greek myth, a symbol of modern alienation and decadence, that contrasts sharply with a more poetic and heroic past.

Whatever the story's meaning and interpretation, García Márquez is particularly skillful in the way he blends together realistic detail and a flat, prosaic style—with its understated humor—in order to allow the reader to accept an otherwise implausible and preposterous situation and series of events more or less at face value.

Because angels and artists both embody special abilities and talents that are precious because they are rare, "A Very Old Man with Enormous Wings" can be profitably compared to Franz Kafka's "A Hunger Artist" in the sense that both deal with the mistreatment and rejection of those who, however talented, are misunderstood. Certainly, both García Márquez's angel and Kafka's artist are exploited for private gain by their keepers and are made objects of curiosity by their provincial societies. And both are eclipsed and replaced in public favor by other, more exotic, attractions: by "a woman who had been changed into a spider for having disobeyed her parents" in one story, and by "a young panther" in the other. The relationship between these two stories should make for interesting classroom discussion.

CHARLOTTE PERKINS GILMAN, "If I Were a Man"

This is a marvelous tour de force, one that is sometimes curiously overlooked by Gilman scholars and critics and those who anthologize Gilman's works. For example, in Denise Knight's recent *Charlotte Perkins Gilman: A Study of the Short Stories* (1977)—published as part of the Twayne Studies in Short Stories series, which prides itself on providing a comprehensive, if brief, overview of the body on an author's work—this story is mentioned not at all. The omission seems strange, particularly because the story, as art, has much to recommend it. The story is also a natural for interesting and even provocative classroom discussion.

Shelley Fisher Fishkin sees "If I Were a Man" as a fictional expression of one of the "highly imaginative" issues that Gilman raised in her journalism. Fishkin mentions specifically an article titled "The Dress of Women" in which Gilman "probes the iconography of male and female dress in painstaking detail, giving special attention to the roots of 'a totally different costume for men and women.'" Gilman wrote:

> This clothing of women is most modified by psychic conditions. As they were restricted to a very limited field of activity, and as their personal comfort was of no importance to anyone, it was possible to maintain in their dress the influence of primitive conditions long outgrown by men. And as, while men have varied widely in the manifold relations of our latest economic and political growth, women have remained for the most part all in one relation—that of sex; we see at once why the dress of men has developed along lines of practical efficiency and general human distinction, while the dress of women is still most modified by the various phases of sex distinction.

Such a statement, which radiates the strength of Gilman's voice and feelings, provides a good springboard for discussion of the story, in which the young, dutiful wife, Mollie Matthewson, suddenly finds herself quite literally in her husband's shoes, having been transformed in body if not quite yet in mind. Gilman uses her double-consciousness, as she explores her new role and re-experiences the not so everyday world around her, to generate the story.

It is important to note how Mollie is "set up" by the author. We are told in paragraph three that Mollie is "true to type": "Whimsical, capricious, charming, changeable, devoted to pretty clothes, and always 'wearing them well,' as the esoteric phrase has it." She is "also a loving wife and devoted mother possessed of 'the social gift,'"—"If ever there was a true woman it was Mollie Matthewson." Then comes her sudden transformation. (Perhaps it is only accidental, but at the risk of making too much out of such things, I would point out that in Mollie's last name already lurks two masculine elements, a "he" and a "son.")

If students have difficulty with the story, it may lie with Mollie's wish to be a man. If she is, as Gilman suggests, "a true woman," then why does she wish "heart and soul she was a man"? Is Gilman suggesting that such a desire lurks in the hearts of some, or all, women? That Mollie is resentful of her husband this morning, and having been angered by Gerald's "superior pride," sees herself as "acquiescing," "little," and very much at a disadvantage is clear.

At first Mollie simply feels "funny" and different. But this soon gives way to feelings of "delight," "of being *the right size*," and of "comfort." What Mollie Matthewson discovers, what she does and what she says as she sets out to complete her husband's day makes up the balance of the story. There is a great deal of irony here, which students should have little difficulty in identifying. If your students are like my own, be prepared for a response (from some) of anger and a sense of betrayal. One thing seems certain, whether or not in the end students feel that the story is too contrived, and that they have somehow been put upon, classroom discussion will not be dull.

Shelley Fisher Fishkin finishes her brief discussion of the story by offering the following comment and suggestion:

> If Gilman's story "If I Were a Man" should strike a reader today as outdated or antiquarian, the results of the "pocket census" I conduct every time I teach the story will prove instructive. The men in the class add up the total number of pockets on the clothing they are wearing, and take the average; the women do the same. Despite all the proverbial unisex dressing of the nineties, the men always end up substantially ahead. I then ask how many women have had their purses snatched and how many men have had *their* pockets picked. The results add up to what one might call a gender-based index of vulnerability.

Try it.

CHARLOTTE PERKINS GILMAN, "The Yellow Wall-Paper"

Since its "rediscovery" by feminist critics more than a decade ago, Charlotte Perkins Gilman's story of a young wife's nervous breakdown has become something of a classic. Though the root causes of the narrator's illness are only hinted at, the husband's role in creating conditions which foster Jane's fantasies, hallucinations, and progressive withdrawal from reality is clear enough. John is a doctor, "practical in the extreme" who "has no patience with faith, an intense horror of superstition, and…scoffs openly at any talk of things not to be felt and seen and put down in figures." Denying the reality of his wife's illness ("a slight hysterical tendency"), he treats her with impatience and condescension, takes away her responsibilities as wife and mother and the possibility of "congenial work, with excitement and change," encourages her to repress her emotions, discourages the journal writing which gives those emotions an outlet, and reduces her to a child isolated for her own good in a barred room which has once been a nursery. By the time the story begins, meaningful communication between the two (if it ever in fact existed) has become an impossibility, and only in her journal—which becomes the reader's access to the story—can Jane "say what I feel and think in some way—it is such a relief!"

Denied a creative, healthy, and emotionally meaningful relationship with her human environment, Jane becomes increasingly fixated by the ugly yellow wall-paper of the nursery, which intrigues and fascinates even as it confuses and repels. By skillfully manipulating the first-person point of view, Gilman succeeds in creating in the wall-paper the mirror image of the protagonist herself. At first, the wall-paper is only "impertinent," "irritating," "unreliable," and "infuriating," as vague, ill-defined and confusing as the illness itself. Gradually, however, she begins to identify with, and project herself onto and then behind, the wall-paper, until she is no longer able to maintain the separateness of her own identity. Finally, the identification becomes complete—the narrator quite literally becomes the "strange, provoking and formless sort of figure" of her hallucinations, creeping and skulking about the room. The successive stages of this process of identification, building toward the climactic scene in which John recoils and then faints at the sight, are clearly delineated and convincingly handled, and make for interesting and provocative class discussion.

SUSAN GLASPELL, "A Jury of Her Peers"

This story originally appeared in 1916 as a one-act play entitled *Trifles* and was reworked and published in its present form the following year. One can very easily imagine the action occurring on-stage, especially those scenes in which the men appear momentarily with their condescending but off-target comments, and then exit to allow the subversive drama of the three women, one of them only referentially present, to unfold. What the short story form contributes is the evocation of the bleak isolation of the farms in the vast emptiness of a Nebraska-Iowa kind of prairieland. Glaspell makes a special point of the particular loneliness in which the Wright farm is set, giving poignancy to Mrs. Hale's guilty lament that she seldom visited Minnie Wright because of the profound joylessness of the place.

We eventually come to understand that the source of much of that joylessness is Minnie's late husband. He is respected in the community because he is known as a hard worker, one who pays his bills and keeps his word. But as the story unfolds, we begin to see that there is very little correlation between what the male-dominated "public" culture understands as respectable and the intimate domestic world where the details of human relationships, especially qualities of human companionship, are worked out. Minnie Foster has been a gay, vivacious girl whose youth seems to have ended in cold, joyless, Siberia-like exile.

Being "married to the law" (as Mrs. Peters is said to be, since her husband is the sheriff), is an interesting concept. The "system" clearly belongs to the men, a fact of which their remarks keep us constantly aware. The women have a kind of "auxiliary" relationship to the men, who by tradition are more often seen in this frontier-like setting facing one another over the sights of Colt revolvers while their women anxiously keep the coffee hot. But in this situation, "the law" is seen pawing rudely, almost indecently through the private domain of Minnie Wright and comprehending none of it. One gets the feeling that if they do not hang her for the murder, they will hang her for her sticky cupboard and dirty roller-towel— her "failure" as a servant to one of the men who has been heroically wresting civilization from the bleak frontier.

The use of the word "jury" in the title raises another interesting issue: that of the interpretation of life and literature. In a trial, two (or more) versions of the same story are in contention with one another. The one that is most persuasive becomes, for all intents and purposes, "the truth." Here we can see a women's story and a men's story taking their separate shapes. The men show themselves incapable of interpreting the nuances of the feminine narrative, not because they are stupid, but because they act like any other occupation force in foreign territory. They cannot read the signs upon the landscape that are obvious to the "natives" of the place. Thus, the central action of the fiction has to do with the forging of a conspiracy between Mrs. Hale and Mrs. Peters. They keep to themselves a story that they are certain could or would not be adequately translated into the idiom of an alien male dialect.

GAIL GODWIN, "Dream Children"

This story operates upon the concealment of certain of its essential premises, first cultivating our sympathy for the central character, introducing us to the strangeness of her experience from her point of view. We are not suddenly confronted with the occult proposition that it is possible for two human souls or psyches or "dream selves" to meet and keep regular company together. In fact, readers need not consciously commit themselves to any such proposition. The story's *donne* is so beautifully introduced that such a possibility seems perfectly natural, regardless of one's convictions outside the boundaries of fiction.

Another essential piece of knowledge is concealed from us until we are thoroughly prepared to see things from this remarkable woman's point of view. She has lost both her child and at the same time her ability to have more children. The next morning, she is mistakenly given someone else's healthy baby to nurse, and for a few precious moments she is convinced that the horrors of the night before were merely a nightmare. The occurrence establishes within the story a pattern that makes the boundary between waking and dreaming less and less clear. Moreover, Mrs. McNair begins to speak of her "occult" experiences in terms of the profession she once followed and her husband still does: "He [the child] somehow found a will strong enough, or innocent enough, to project himself upon her still-floating consciousness, as clearly and believably as her own husband's image on the screen." In other words, the visions, the dreams, the hallucinations, the technology all combine, allowing the reader to feel quite comfortable with her view of the phenomenon. One can believe that the boy baby whom she was allowed to nurse that morning has somehow physically or spiritually bonded with her, so that in liminal moments he can launch himself toward the woman on the other coast. She, also in a state between waking and dreaming, is receptive to his "presence" because of her desperate need to love someone.

Mr. McNair has taken a mistress in the city, for which his wife seems to have given him permission. He is no longer a sexual partner, but a support and comforter who demands nothing. He is as much a "dream husband" as the boy is a "dream child." It is a marvelous suspension from life's usual responsibilities; she can ride recklessly over the pasture because she is not supporting anyone. She has no one to lose. This is both mad and sane, waking and dreaming, tragic and happy: "Was she a woman riding a horse and dreaming she was a mother who anxiously awaited her child's sleep; or was she a mother dreaming of herself as a free spirit who could ride her horse like the wind because she had nothing to fear?" Her answer is: "I am a woman, that's all I know. Who can explain such things?" The narrator comments as well that "she rode like the wind, a happy, happy woman."

And so, Mrs. McNair has found a way to survive with her unbearable pain. From this point of view, whether one calls her insane or deluded is beside the point. It is a solution, a place for her to put her love and yearning. Her husband fears a certain note in her laughter and the sudden bright flashes through her ordinary demeanor. And he is revolted by the kind of thinking expressed in the books she has been reading lately, looking for the support of other mature, intelligent adults who share her beliefs. But the bias of the narrative seems to come out squarely in favor of the escape from the tenets of realism. The form of this short story is doubling back toward the tale of the supernatural, now clothed in technological and psychological possibility. One does not quite know whether to applaud Mrs. McNair's madness or to hale her breakthrough in extrasensory communication. In this respect, the story has a good deal in common with Henry James's "The Turn of the Screw," which seems almost clinical or almost mystical, by turns.

NIKOLAI GOGOL, "The Overcoat"

Gogol's tale is a remarkably rich stew of social realism, fairy tale, moral fable, and political satire. While it may be said that "man is what he eats," in this tale it is more true that "clothes make the man." Akakii Akakiievitch's original character is as plain and threadbare as his old coat at the story's opening, but the thought of a new overcoat, despite the enormous sacrifices that it will require for him to buy it, begins to stimulate his imagination in mysterious ways. Nor is the tailor to whom he goes for the design of his coat a simple, straightforward cutter and sewer of fabric. Something about him makes us think of sorcerers and magicians. His descriptions of the glory of the garment transport Akakii into other worlds. He begins to dream of even *a finer* garment than the one the tailor is designing for him.

And the coat *does* seem almost magical. Those who ignored him before, or noticed him only to ridicule, suddenly take a new interest. He is no longer the simple fool he was at one time, who has a direct, honest competency at copying documents. For the first time, he commits an error in his work because his mind has become preoccupied with this new property. Also, because of his new appearance, he is suddenly visible as a social equal. He is even invited by one of his colleagues to a dinner party. But Akakii has also become vulnerable to the woes that beset people who own fine things. On the way home from the dinner party, thieves are attracted by the splendor of his coat, and rob him of it.

What *is* this coat, that works so many changes upon the life of this little scrivener? To be sure, it is like houses and automobiles and other material effects that clothe us bare-forked creatures. Besides keeping Akakii warm, it designates his status. It alters the way others perceive him and therefore the way he perceives himself. Being new, however, it constitutes a rather abrupt alternation of his identity, just as the title of the *certain important person* to whom he must apply to recover his stolen property is new. Both of them feel stiff and strange in their new garments. The General exaggerates his authoritarian gruffness, even though beneath that title he is actually quite merciful and tolerant. It is simply that he does not yet know how to wear his new identity with both dignity and charity. Therefore, when Akakii comes before him in his old, threadbare coat, there is such a vast gulf between them that they are incapable of recognizing one another's humanity. The General cannot see anything but Akakii's insignificance, and by the same token, Akakii cannot see anything of the General but his awesome power. As a result, the General's harsh manner literally frightens poor Akakii to death.

It is reported that Akakii's spirit continues to linger about the streets in the neighborhood where his coat was stolen, but be that as it may, the thief who stole Akakii's coat also steals the General's. This large-fisted, black-mustachioed man seems very mysterious. He, like the rain, falls upon the rich and poor alike. Naked we depart as naked we come into the world. At least the clerk and the General have that in common.

NADINE GORDIMER, "Home"

In the troubled world of South Africa in which most of Nadine Gordimer's fiction is set, Apartheid and its rigid racial laws touch virtually every aspect of national life. Attempts to insulate one's personal life from its social and political aspects are futile, and this is particularly true if one happens to belong to one of the racial groups whose activities and freedom the laws of Apartheid effectively circumscribe.

Teresa and Nils have attempted to make their peace with that world, even though the fact that Teresa's mixed black and Asian ancestry classifies her as Colored and therefore part of South Africa's disenfranchised majority. (In South Africa effective political and economic power resides in the hands of the white minority which comprises some 17% of the population; blacks comprise 71%, Coloreds 9%, and Asians 3%.) Though Teresa, with Nils's complicity, occasionally aids the activities of her activist brother Robert (Robbie), the life they have built for themselves is an insulated one defined by the daily routine of marriage and profession—routine which, we are told, serves to shield them from "what is really happening." (Their employment by the Institute places them within the apolitical "company of marine biologists who were content to believe all species are interesting and to inquire no further into questions of equality." The sudden arrest and detention of Robert and her mother and sister shatters the illusion of false security.

Gordimer's story is about what this event does to Teresa, to Nils, and to their relationship. Teresa's first discovery is that she loves the mother she thought she detested. Her discovery is not simply the discovery—the affirmation—of family obligation. In the context of racially divided South Africa her discovery also involves the recognition and affirmation of her place in the social order. These discoveries inevitably move Teresa to action. Her activities, just as inevitably, draw her away from Nils, from the white liberal community in which they live, and from the life and routine they have so carefully constructed. Teresa's attempts to aid her imprisoned family draws forth resources, energy, independence, determination, and courage that she has never before exhibited. Teresa is transformed by her experience, and transforms in Nils's eyes as well. All the comfortable assurances that he believes have characterized their life together are now seem thrown into doubt. As she moves further and further into the world of political activism and the state bureaucracy which deals with such matters, he is forced to recognize his own position as an outsider. In the face of Teresa's unexpected strength and determination, Nils is reduced to the role of uncomfortable spectator. His is a loneliness born out of what Gordimer elsewhere calls "the failure to connect." As a result, Nils misinterprets the reason for her absence. He becomes convinced that she has "found a lover, young like herself, brought up in comradely poverty, someone who had already been in prison, whose metier—outwitting those bastards of policeman, warders, government officials—was newly her own."

The ending of the story is at best ambiguous. To be sure, Nils achieves a measure of awareness and self-knowledge. He comes to understand that Teresa has not taken a lover, that she has rather, been acting "for them—for that house, the dark family of which he was not a member, her country, to which he did not belong." But what is also clear is that Teresa has affirmed the existence of realities which she can no longer ignore and that those realities exclude Nils. Their life together, if it continues, will be very different in its terms and conditions.

MARY GRIMM, "We"

This story, like the others in *Stealing Time* (1994), Mary Grimm's first published volume of short fiction, was first published in the *New Yorker*. "Perhaps the best of the lot," a writer for *Kirkus Reviews* noted in a pre-publication review,

> is the National Magazine Award-winning "We," a true knockout about three young Ohio women, their early marriages, their children, and their first decade as adults; their emotions settle like rust and their expectations lower with new sewing machines, Tupperware parties, recipe trading, book clubs, parties, illnesses, and aging husbands.

At first reading, "We" may remind us of one of the case studies out of Gail Sheehy's much-discussed 1976 best-seller *Passages*, a book named in a survey by the Library of Congress survey as one of the most influential books of our times. In that book, you will recall, Sheehy provided a roadmap for adult life, tracing the predictable changes we go through as we move through our 20s, 30s, 40s and into middle and old age.

In Grimm's story the narrator and her two friends, Suzanne and Virginia, negotiate their way through the years of their early marriage (when sex was everything) into the years of child-raising, which leaves them, by my count, something short of their mid 30s by the time the story reaches its conclusion. Much of class discussion, I expect, will focus on discovering through a careful examination of the narrator the values, attitudes, and beliefs that give shape and meaning to their suburban middle-class world. Some attention should also be given to the techniques that Grimm uses that makes that world a solid and realistic one. Other tantalizing questions will suggest themselves, such as those focussing on the whereabouts of the women's husbands, the one-time lovers who now seem to have all-too-willingly absented themselves.

Mary Grimm herself has offered an interesting way into the story through the comments about the story's origins which she provided the editor:

> The original title of "We" was "History of Feminism, Part IV," which is not a very good title. But it expresses some of my intention in the writing of the story, which I wanted to be about women who weren't the audience that people like Gloria Steinem were imagining: that is, women who had yearnings and regrets, but who perhaps hadn't put them into words, women who loved their children as much as the jobs they might have. And it was also about my own experience of being a mother—totally consuming, frightening even in the way that it took over what I thought of as my life. The story is also a tribute to a friendship: I had (and still have) a Suzanne in my life.

Certainly we can sympathize and empathize to a point with all three of these women. Their lives, though solid and respectable, have left them mildly discontented, though by no means desperate. What may end by disturbing us most, however, is not that the trio come to the kind of disillusionment and crisis that Sheehy had predicted would be their lot but rather that their response seems to be one of lowered expectations and a regret for the passing of "what we had together when there was no one else in the world but mothers and children."

Interestingly enough, the reviewer cited above criticizes Grimm's short stories for their "soft endings" and the fact that "one must strain to remember many of them even an hour after reading." Such comments are not without their justification, though one is moved to suggest that "soft endings" and the lack of memorability may indeed be an integral part of the lives of the generation of women—and men—that Mary Grimm has decided to write about.

THOMAS HARDY, "The Three Strangers"

This is another of those Hardy stories that takes as much of its point from the character of its setting as from the events that occur there. In this case, virtually the whole of the narrative action occurs within and about a small stone shepherd's cottage on the south downs of England. Neither the action nor the exposition of character is particularly breathtaking. The point of the story rests rather upon the number of ironies and coincidences that have their conjunction in this out-of-the-way place.

There is a considerable contrast between the outward appearance of this isolated and ancient cottage (especially in this weather) and the atmosphere inside, where a christening party is in progress with fiddle music, dancing, a bright, warm fire in the fireplace, and plenty of food and drink for the guests. The appearance of one stranger at the door asking for shelter from the rain, and then another shortly after, is alone rare enough in such a place, but when both settle themselves before the fire and enter into the spirit of the festivities, one singing the verses of a hanging song and the other joining in, the curiosity of the guests is mightily aroused. The fellow with the fine bass voice identifies himself as a wheelwright, the other reveals himself through riddles and verses to be a hangman on the way to Casterbridge to hang a sheep-stealer. Of course, the wheelwright is in fact the thief.

Unbelievably, a third stranger appears at the door of the cottage and looks in, only to bolt out guiltily. The assembled company is convinced that he must be the sheep-stealer (whom they now know to have escaped from prison in Casterbridge), and they form an impromptu posse to hunt him on the downs. One of the christening-party bears a remarkable likeness to Constable Elbow in *Measure for Measure*, and is the source of considerable humor, challenging the stranger when they finally come upon him, with "Your money or your life" rather than "You are under arrest," or some other appropriate phrase.

The sheep-thief never is apprehended; largely, it is suggested, because the country people shelter him from the law, feeling that the penalty is disproportionate to the crime and the circumstances under which it was committed. And as we reconsider the story, it is possible to begin to assess something of its local color. Hardy is interested in anything that suggests a persistence of ancient English attitudes, and he can still find something of that in county people like these. For example, it is not too surprising to find a Shakespearean Constable in this nineteenth-century setting, because in many respects nothing essential had changed between Elbow's days and this man's. The constable is concerned to have his official staff with the royal crest upon it, so that any blow he may let fall in the course of his duty will be an officially sanctioned one. His attitude may be "quaint" but it fairly resonates with centuries of hierarchical tradition. Further, the occasion of all these adventures is a chastening, one of those new beginnings that the country people felt were connected to the whole structure of fate. When it is learned that the stranger in gray is a hangman, the people draw back from him as if he were a visitor from the underworld. Hangmen are understandably not considered a sign of good fortune. But the residue of the whole scene is the eerie coincidence of the condemned man and his executioner coming to the same isolated cottage, and then sitting there singing together and toasting one another's health. In such places as this, things of this kind are wondered at and retold over and over again as a sign of the mysterious intelligence behind the appearance of things.

BRET HARTE, "Tennessee's Partner"

Modern critical attention to Bret Harte's classic story, which first appeared in the October 1869 issue of the *Overland Monthly*, began with a brief treatment by Brooks and Warren in their *Understanding Fiction* (1959). They concluded that "The difficulty with this story has to do with the credibility of the actions of Tennessee's partner....Bret Harte is so thoroughly obsessed with the pathos of the partner's loyalty that he has devoted no thought to the precise nature of the basis of that loyalty." Gray Scharnhorst (1992) believes that where Brooks and Warren, as well as other critics, go wrong is in their willingness to take the issue of friendship at its face value while ignoring the story's "subtle irony." "Harte has, in effect," Scharnhorst continues,

> set a trap for the unwary. "You could never be sure of Harte," as Howells recalled; he could only by chance be caught in earnest about anything and anybody." The narrator betrays as little expression in relating this story as the poker-faced Partner reveals in plotting revenge on the man who stole his wife....Harte deftly structures the story around the Partners elaborate scheme to avenge his loss of a wife, the act of victimization, which is central to western humor....Obviously, the miners in Sandy Bar expect the Partner to exact revenge....The Partner has already hatched his plot and he now bides his time. He exploits the opportunity to serve frontier justice when he appears in court at precisely the moment Tennessee's prosecution has become "irksomely thoughtful." The trial at this point becomes something of a poker game, with Tennessee folding his cards—"I don't take any hand in this yer game"—and the Partner in the role of the dealer.

The Partner summarizes the prosecution's case and then, shrewdly forestalls any possibility of the jury changing its mind by offering up a $1700 bribe. Tennessee, on his part, Scharnhorst contends, "understands the rules of the game played out in the courtroom. 'Euchred, old man!' he says to the Partner, then shakes his hand. The gesture is neither one of gratitude for the failed attempt to save his life nor one of friendly parting, but a way of congratulating the Partner for winning the pot." Such a reading certainly turns the concerns of Brooks and Warren upside down. It suggests that we need to read the story very much as we have come to read Mark Twain's "The Celebrated Jumping Frog of Calaveras County." "Far from simple, pathetic, and deeply loyal," William F. Conner observes (1980), "Tennessee's deadpan partner is complex, clever, and hard-boiled in his dogged individualism and firm sense of frontier justice."

Scharnhorst's interpretation still leaves the ending to be explained. Charles E. May (1977) argues that the Partner dies of guilt and remorse for having incited the men of Sandy Bar to lynch Tennessee. Scharnhorst, for his part, sees the Partner as being not unlike Hawthorne's Roger Chillingworth (*The Scarlet Letter*) who wastes away because he "has made revenge the *raison d'être* of his life."

Whatever problem the end causes, the thrust of the criticism on Bret Harte's story has moved in the direction suggested above. "It is not, in fact, the partner who is exploited and victimized by the events of the tale," Conner insists; "it is the popular-sentimental conceptions of friendship and matrimony complacently held by Harte's audience. Just as the partner successfully bamboozles the mining camp folk, so Harte tricks the readers all the while he seems to be trying to satisfy their pious presuppositions."

NATHANIEL HAWTHORNE, "My Kinsman, Major Molineux"

"We begin to live," wrote W. B. Yeats, "when we conceive of life as tragic." Many, especially perhaps young people and, it is said, Americans, find it hard to understand what he meant. But Hawthorne and his contemporary, Herman Melville, knew. They maintained their tragic view in the midst of nineteenth-century optimism. As America scrambled after its dream of industrial progress, Hawthorne looked insistently backward, to a darker era. He kept finding that darkness in the great expectations around him; therefore, many of his short stories and significant parts of his novels are built around some ironic joke. Reading "My Kinsman, Major Molineux," one feels uneasily that the joke is on oneself.

Hawthorne has constructed his story with two possible objects of sympathy, yet at the same time has opposed them to each other. It is difficult not to feel concerned about Robin, the young country visitor, "nearly eighteen years old." His mistreatment by the inhabitants of colonial Boston violates the rules of courtesy and hospitality. It is all too much like the treatment a stranger receives today—or at least fears he is likely to receive—in Boston, Los Angeles, Chicago, or whatever metropolis he must enter. It also resembles the indifference, even hostility, of city dwellers toward each other on freeways, for example. Robin is the outsider, and the local citizens represent the various powers that confuse him. The wayward young woman and the ingratiating innkeeper are well known to city visitors today. The "ill-favored fellow" with his face of black and red is the allegorized spirit of this morally as well as literally benighted place. Three appearances also give the old man's "hem hem" a nearly supernatural status; uncomprehending, self-absorbed, invariably condemning, he is the dominant human power. His house is the biggest and most beautiful; he walks at his own pace among the high and the low; heedless of all but his own anger and contempt, he is nevertheless wealthy and respectable, and so wields the authority these guarantee.

The elderly Major could scarcely contrast more with young Robin, whose very name brings to mind the harbinger of spring. The ironic joke is that these two are akin in their social predicament, as well as in their familial relationship. Both are outsiders to the urban mob. Old and young, often assumed to be natural opponents, are equally victims here. In the story's opening paragraphs, Hawthorne has told us that the Major represents the hated British crown. And yet, "his head grown gray in honor," he simultaneously represents order, civilized conduct, perhaps all that makes life tolerable. Nevertheless, his unsteady young kinsman is seduced by the mob. Robin mocks the old man, unaware that he, too, is an alien victim.

This was Hawthorne's message to the young American nation, new to the world, not yet a century old, portrayed here as the child of Rousseau and Voltaire. Where, then, are George Washington, Thomas Jefferson, and the other founding fathers? No graceful Mount Vernon or Monticello offers shelter here; gothic pillars refer us, instead, to the hag-ridden world of Cotton Mather, with adumbrations of Franz Kafka.

This tragic, or at least bitterly ironic, view also contrasts with "Rip Van Winkle," where civilization is rejuvenated and happily reentered. Yet, Washington Irving's hope for the New World was sketched in a pastoral setting, in the countryside, perhaps the very countryside that Robin has left behind. From Hawthorne's Boston to the "alabaster cities" of "America the Beautiful," time stretches out a long, long way.

The story opens for a discussion of all relationships with authority: those of students with teacher, citizens with government, and the utopian hopes that today remains attached to revolutionary movements. One could point out how Hawthorne's characterization of the Major as innocent, even honorable, supports a conservative opinion. In a more comprehensive work, King Lear for example, authority is portrayed as rigid, solipsistic, and irascible, although the king's tormentors are as bad or worse. The dreamlike setting of Hawthorne's tale also suggests fairy stories where, as in "Hansel and Gretel" or "Little Red Riding Hood," the elders are devouring. The darkness that softens the realistic elements of the scene also provides a transition into allegorical commentary, as does the "ill-favored fellow's" gradual change into a figure of fantasy. The latter's allegorical or fantastic role can suggest other Hawthorne "visions," that of young Goodman Brown, for instance, and many literary villains from ancient times to current science fiction.

NATHANIEL HAWTHORNE, "Young Goodman Brown"

The philosophical search that is the real action of this tale is allegorized as a journey into the darkness of a forest (cf. Conrad's "Heart of Darkness") where the hero, taking temporary leave of his Faith, has gone to confront the Prince of Darkness face to face. Once there,

Brown's steadfastness is first tested by the claim that both his father and grandfather were clients of Satan. Brown denies that any such thing is possible, but as the two walk deeper into the forest, he thinks that he glimpses Goody Cloyse, one of the town's most pious citizens, scurrying along a path toward the heart of the woods. Eventually, Brown finds himself on the edge of a clearing in which virtually every one of his neighbors can be seen, mixed with a sprinkling of heathen medicine men or "Pow Wows," standing before an altar dedicated to the Powers of Darkness. Just as Brown's own wife steps forward to be initiated into this company of the damned, Brown rushes out of his concealed place, and suddenly finds himself, as if waking from a dream, in another part of the forest. Soon afterward, though, he thinks he hears the sound of wind-borne voices passing overhead, and a pink ribbon just like those Faith wears in her cap comes fluttering down beside him.

Students nearly always want to make the crux of the matter the question of whether Brown "actually" witnessed the Black Mass or simply dreamed it. But that question is rather beside the point. Whether Brown slept or not, whether the journey into the forest is actual or a mere allegory of a journey into the depths of his own nature, he has experienced a *vision*, and in that vision is revealed to Brown the universal depravity of the human race. Of course, as people of experience know, the general culpability of humankind is easily documented. Even leaving aside the scriptural assertion that none of us is without sin, all one need do is pick up a newspaper for evidence of the "cussedness" of the race. What Brown sees in his vision is a revelation of the fallen nature of his fellow citizens—as if it had never before occurred to him.

Brown has lost his Faith; not his faith in God, but rather his faith in humanity. He is tempted by a vision of the weakness of the flesh (emblemized by his wife's pink ribbons), but he has such a sterile, self-centered conception of the sacred that he lacks all power of empathy or forgiveness. Like Gulliver, who is so revolted by the fundamental nature of his species as it is represented in the Yahoos that he cannot bear the company of his own wife and children, Brown is left bitter, suspicious, and isolated. But this is the natural result of having taken so shallow a view of the qualities of humanity in the first place, not realizing that there *must* be more to his fellow citizens than the pious exteriors they show to the public. When he does finally recognize their connections to the world and the flesh, he is convinced now that *this* is their sole reality. In refusing to extend any fellow feeling toward the race to which he too belongs, he is abandoning both hope and charity, without which his faith means little. The paradox is that he has wrestled temptation in the wilderness and *seems* to have won; but that infinitely resourceful Enemy has found a way to use the strength of Brown's conviction against him—by turning it into the sin of spiritual pride.

ERNEST HEMINGWAY, "Hills Like White Elephants"

Though the story is often discussed under the heading "point of view," it also provides an excellent example of how dialogue, held together with a minimum of description and narration, can be used to establish and reveal character. The dialogue, with its economy and its subtle undercurrent of powerful, yet largely controlled and understated emotions, bears close analysis and study. The words themselves, their ordering, and the nuances of tone that accompany them, are all crucially important here. Much of what is "said" between the two characters is said only by indirection or is left unsaid altogether—note the shifting use of pronouns whose antecedents often remain unclear. The distinctive qualities of Hemingway dialogue can be illustrated and clarified by reading selected passages aloud.

The sparse details of setting, with its symbolic juxtaposition of the hot, treeless, and barren foreground (where the action of the story takes place) over and against the hills, "fields of grain and trees" that lie across the river, also shed light upon the characters. Note that it is toward this further, fertile vista—toward the "hills [that look] like white elephants"—that Jig's attention is drawn. The fact that she responds to the sensual qualities of the setting in a way that the man does not—and presumably cannot—is crucial to our understanding of their separate temperaments and attitudes and the depth of their incompatibility and estrangement. The woman alone understands the final emotional, spiritual, and moral significance of the operation (the word "abortion" is never uttered). For him, the operation is a simple physical fact. Afterward, everything will be as before: "We can have everything." To which she replies with direct and devastating honesty, "No we can't. It isn't ours anymore…once they take it away, you never get it back."

Only once are we permitted to enter the mind of one of the characters. This occurs at the very end of the story where we are told that the other travelers "are waiting reasonably for the train." Students might be asked to consider the use of the word "reasonably" and what it contributes to the story. Consider also Jig's uses of the word "fine" which immediately follows: "I feel fine…There's nothing wrong with me. I feel fine."

ERNEST HEMINGWAY, "Indian Camp"

Like so many of Ernest Hemingway's Michigan stories, "Indian Camp" has strong autobiographical overtones. Hemingway's own father was, of course, a medical doctor, a general practitioner who had taken courses in obstetrics and on occasion delivered babies. He also took care of local Indian families in emergencies. The story's Uncle George, is Hemingway's own uncle, George Hemingway, who, we are told was not particularly happy to be included in one of his nephew's first short stories. Most of Hemingway's commentators also agree that Hemingway and his young protagonist, Nick Adams, are "intimately related." Finally, the story's setting, while not highly articulated, is deftly established by one who knew well the terrain in which it takes place.

"Indian Camp," is the first of some dozen stories that sequentially trace Nick Adams' initiation into the world of adult experience. Nick here is at his youngest. Hemingway's choice of name for his young protagonist is, of course, highly deliberate. Nick, at some level, is intended to be a "new Adam," a kind of everyman figure whose own rite of passage point the way to experiences that are universally shared. But his last name, suggests "Old Nick," Satan himself. As Joseph Defalco observes,

> Having thus named his character, Hemingway in one stroke characterizes the inherited tendencies of all men. The tension created by the implications of the association of these names is in itself archetypal in its suggestion of the eternal struggle between the forces of good and evil. But the hero in the Hemingway stories encounters evil in many guises, and it goes by many names, be it a wound— literal or psychological—terror in the night, or death, or anything else. Always, however, evil is inescapable and unpredictable. In many ways what the Hemingway hero must learn throughout the stories is the nature of evil, and the tension created by the struggle of opposing forces within himself provides the underlying dynamics of the learning process.

The "learning process" of which Defalco speaks begins with "Indian Camp." Areas and issues for fruitful classroom discussion include the following:

- First, of course, is the impact of the experience upon the protagonist: how the young Nick Adams responds, and what he learns. "Where are we going, Dad?" Nick wants to know, and in some sense the rest of the story is a working out of the answer to that question. The fact that he has embarked on a journey into new knowledge is made obvious in the story's opening scene as Nick sits in the rowboat, his father's protective arm around him. Nick's father has decided to take the boy with him in the apparent expectation that it will be a learning experience, a decision for which he will later express regret. (One can argue, of course, that he had no choice—that young Nick could not be left behind alone once Uncle George has decided to go.) Note that the father's answer to his son's question is similarly protective in its vague indirectness.

The journey motif is clear. "The classical parallel is too obvious to overlook," Joseph DeFalco remarks," for the two Indians function in a Charon-like fashion in transporting Nick, his father, and his uncle from their own sophisticated and civilized world of the white man into the dark and primitive world of the camp."

- The character of the father. What do we make of the fact that though he knows the reason for his visit, he fails to bring along the proper equipment, and must perform the Caesarean section with a jack-knife and fishing leader and without anesthetic? It is this omission that causes the woman to scream in pain and her already-wounded husband to commit suicide. How much blame are we to place upon the father? Is he, as some have claimed, insensitive, or is his failure to heed her screams a sign of the extraordinary single-minded focus and concentration he brings to the task of trying to save her life and the life of the baby? To have allowed her screams to have entered his consciousness, one can argue, is to risk botching the job. And, given the fact he is on vacation, roused from his tent by a request for help, and without the instruments he needs, shouldn't we rather praise him for doing the job with consummate skill under extraordinary circumstances?

One of the issues which the story explores (for some critics it is *the* issue) is the changing relationship between father and son. William Braasch Watson, for example, asserts that

> As the result of these experiences, the dynamic balance between the father and the son has gradually, almost imperceptibly, shifted by the end of the story. Although the doctor father is still answering young Nick's questions at the end as he had at the beginning, there are now more of them and their character has changed. So, also, has the quality of the father's answers. . . . By the end of the story . . . , Nick has learned the implications of his experience all too well. His questions go to the fundamental issues of life and death and to the differences between men and women, forcing the father on the defensive. It is he, now, who is being forced to play a role, forced to be a teacher even when there is little he can teach Nick, even if Nick does not understand all that has happened and does not wish to deal with it.

Subtle as it is, the dynamic between father and son is unalterable changed: "The story leaves the unmistakable impression that it is the son, despite his young age, who understands the world around him, a world in which violence and suffering exist, and that it is the father who cannot."

- The role and function of Uncle George. Consider the way in which by introducing another adult white male into the story Hemingway establishes a cypher or foil to the father-physician. For Joseph DeFalco, in his emotionality Uncle George is "a register against which the attitudes of Nick's father may be tested." Some critics have suggested that the cigar-giving Uncle George is in fact the father of the new-born Indian baby boy.
- The suicide of the husband, as he lies in the bunk with his wounded leg, merits consideration. At the very least one can say that his unnatural death by suicide contrasts with the unnatural birth taking place below, and that as a result young Nick Adams has been

136

almost simultaneously introduced this night to experiences which take place at farthest extremes of life itself.

- What of the story's title? What are the connotations and associations of the Indian camp? Words like "dark" and "primitive" surely come to mind. The story has many archetypal elements, and one of them surely resonates in the title which Hemingway chose to give his story.

- What are we to make of Nick's final comment? Are we, Earl Rovit suggests, to "smile bemusedly at Nick's naive confidence that he'll never die"? In the story Nick has come to know death and its reality for the first time. He has been in its presence. Does his comment undercut everything that has come before, as if to suggest that he has learned nothing from his experience? Or does it suggest that his education is as yet incomplete? That whatever he has learned and managed to internalize co-exists with the childish illusion of his own immortality, that he is only partly comprehending and still protected by innocence?

- There is also the descriptive passage in the story's second to last paragraph of the sun rising over the hills, the bass jumping, and the feel of the water ("warm in the sharp chill of the morning") as Nick trails his hand from the stern of the boat. This provides the context for Nick's final statement about death. Paul Smith, in his *Reader's Guide to the Short Stories of Ernest Hemingway*, makes the sensible suggestion that one needs to pay particular attention to the syntax of the sentence that follows:

It's four introductory phrases are more than adverbial. They serve as necessary conditions for the rest of the sentence: *only* in the early morning *and* on the lake *and* sitting in the stern of the boat *and* with his father rowing, could Nick 'feel *quite* sure that he would never die.' Which is not to say that elsewhere or at another time or alone he would be so certain—he was far from it when the Indian rowed and his father sat in the stern with his arm around him. So Nick's feeling is more reasonable and less illusory than it seems at first, and it returns our attention to the central issue of any male initiation story, the relationship between the father and son.

This early Hemingway story should make for excellent classroom discussion.

PAM HOUSTON, "How to Talk to a Hunter"

My assumption is that students will enjoy Pam Houston's story and that it will make for interesting classroom discussion. I also assume that much of the discussion will divide along gender lines, which is certainly the direction in which the story leads us. The female narrator and her relationship with her current male lover, "the hunter," is, of course, the story's subject. We learn a great deal about both of them, though we must keep in mind that everything we come to know about the hunter is filtered through either the prism of the narrative point of view or comes from the freely offered (though largely cliché-ridden) voices of the "best female friend" and the "best male friend."

The use of the future tense ("will") is interesting. It suggests that the narrator is telling the story for the sake of her female successor or successors—those who will replace her in the affections of the hunter. Does this mean that their relationship is, in fact, already at an end? Or, that she has convinced herself (in what may well be a self-fulfilling manner) that it soon will be? Or is she really attempting in self-defense to concoct (with the help of female and male friends) a scheme or stratagem for the present in an effort to hold together a relationship she finds continually at risk?

Other issues to be dealt with include the purpose and effect of those other "voices" as well

as the sardonic and detailed tone which the narrator adopts; the extent to which we can identify and describe the traditional elements of plot—beginning, middle, and end; the significance of the season of the year (Christmas) and the way it impacts the story; the image
of the narrator's dog, particularly as it dominates the story's final paragraph; and what the
narrator (and author) finally seems to be telling us about the relationship between men
and women (to what extent are we as readers being accused to generalize from the relationship reported here?). Also to be gauged through discussion is the student's final reaction
to the story. Do they like it? If so, why? If not, why not?

Students may find interesting, and provocative as well, the comments that Pam Houston offered on "How to Talk to a Hunter" upon the occasion of its inclusion in Richard
Ford's *The Best American Short Stories, 1990*:

> The first paragraph of "How to Talk to a Hunter" started out as a poem, which
> is one of the things that makes it different from all my other stories. I don't write
> poetry, so I was very surprised when it came out that way, and for half a second I
> thought maybe I could write poetry after all, but then I came to my senses and
> turned it into a story.
>
> Another thing that makes "Hunter" different from all my other stories is that it
> came to me all in a rush, ten straight hours at the computer, and after those first
> ten hours I never changed a word. I think that's mainly because it came out of my
> life's first moment of real desperation. I actually wrote the thing on Christmas
> Day. It is a story so frighteningly close to my own structures of fear and pain and
> need that I had to write it in the second person, even though (and also because)
> second person is the most transparent disguise.
>
> Now what I like about the story is the rhythm the second person created, the
> cadence, the sound. I consider "Hunter" to be my gift from the great writing gods,
> and I know the whole thing by heart. I probably shouldn't admit this but some-
> times when I'm driving up the canyon late at night I recite it to the empty car.[21]

ZORA NEALE HURSTON, "Spunk"

Hurston's fiction is characterized by its realistic rendering of rural southern black life
and by its artistic use of authentic black folklore (traditional legends, beliefs, legends, customs, and sayings) and black dialect. "Spunk," which depicts a world which Hurston herself knew at first hand, provides a particularly good example of the way in which such materials can be made to serve the purposes of literary art. Some notes and comments:

- Hurston's story is about adultery, jealousy, violence and murder, and revenge—forms of
  behavior that threaten and often destroy the fabric and continuity of family and community life. Yet in the world that Hurston writes about such behavior is absorbed into
  the routine of things and life, demonstrably, goes on. In large measure this has to do
  with the sense that the community has of itself and the abiding patterns, rituals, and
  beliefs which define its existence. This sense of community and its patterns are in evidence throughout the story, from the communal gathering at the village store which
  opens the story to the wake that marks its conclusion.
- Hurston's use of folklore is thus central to her story's success. As Robert Hemenway has
  observed in the introduction of his new edition of Hurston's *Mules and Men* (1978):
  "Black identity receives expression in Afro-American folklore because folklore permits

---

[21]Pam Houston, "Contributor's Notes," *The Best American Short Stories, 1990*, Richard Ford,
ed. (Boston: Houghton Mifflin Company, 1990), p. 349.

the presentation of emotions so deeply felt that they often cannot be openly articulated. Hurston Spunk Banks. How reliable a narrator is he? Elijah openly admires Spunk (the womanizer and adulterer) and attributes to him the quality of fearlessness. Elijah urges Joe to take on Spunk. He is also the source of what we know about the black bob-cat and about what happened at the sawmill. As the controlling prism on much of what happens in the story—and why—Elijah and his role are well worth close scrutiny.

JOHN IRVING, "Trying to Save Piggy Sneed"

Irving's story—or memoir—is clearly autobiographical. Irving's maternal grandmother, Helen Bates Winslow, died at Exeter, New Hampshire, a few days short of her 100th birthday, and not long after "Trying to Save Piggy Sneed" was first published in the *New York Times Book Review* on August 22, 1982. The places (and no doubt many of the people) that Irving writes about here have also been directly translated from the world of his youth. But having noted the obvious, it is probably important to point out to students (and perhaps to remind ourselves) that John Irving the narrator is not necessarily John Irving the author and that any narrator is finally as much of the author's creation as any fictional character and must be regarded as such.

As a memoir Irving's story has much to recommend it, particularly the author's ability to capture the details of place, time, and incident. No doubt all of us have, somewhere, a Piggy Sneed-like character to remind us not only of human misfortune but the insensitivity and downright cruelty of the young. In the face of the cruelty of the narrator and his peers stands the stately figure of the grandmother, a model of "good manners and kindness." Wellesley's oldest living English Major understands the "awful circumstances" that force Piggy "to live such a savage life." She treats him with decency and respect while making no concessions to his shortcomings and weaknesses. But having accepted life as it is, she has little patience for those who (like her grandson, the novelist) would suggest and explore its alternative possibilities.

Irving's story is, of course, ultimately about the imagination and the relationship of art (fiction) to life. Through the life and death of Piggy Sneed the narrator is introduced to "the possible power of my own imagination." By means of the stories he concocts for his fellow fire-fighters to "save" Piggy Sneed, the narrator comes, apparently for the first time, to understand "the writer's job." The grandmother is plainly wrong: being a writer is not "a lawless and destructive thing." Writing is a creative, life-affirming act precisely to the extent that it offers the reader glimpses of the various possibilities which life has to offer.

WASHINGTON IRVING, "The Legend of Sleepy Hollow"

At first glance, this tale is rather a strange one for a man of letters to have written, for it makes the bookish character an arrant fool and awards the laurels to a muscular boor. But taken with reference to Irving's typical stance regarding the making of a new mythology for the New World, one shouldn't be too surprised. Ichabod Crane is the stock comic butt, the Pedagogue from untold ages of past comedy, mainly dramatic, but in latter days equally well represented in the short story and the novel (one may think, for example, of Fielding's Mssrs. Square and Twackum). The reason that such characters make perfect thumping-blocks for physical comedy is that their attachment to learning has made them less "human" than the other characters. As a practical matter of comic response, highly stereotyped, mechanistic characters can absorb more abuse without stimulating the sympathy of the audience than can characters who have greater depth. They are "less human" because 1) they are traditionally enemies of the flesh (typically with the exception of their own); and 2) they are *superstitious*; that is, they have an almost barbaric regard for rote learning, for the letter of a thing at the expense of its spirit. In the seventeenth century, the Pedant was considered a "humours" character: one who has lost some portion of his divinely granted freedom of will to an overpowering obsession.

Ichabod Crane manages to contain a bit of nearly all these characteristics. He is all angles, his physique hanging together like an ill-strung puppet. But his chief characteristic is his profound superstition. He is only superficially educated, but what he has read, mainly Cotton Mather on witches and witchcraft, he believes without the slightest trace of critical intelligence. The "stitio" part of the word "superstition" is related etymologically to "stasis"—something that remains. "Superstition" is therefore something that remains, something "left over" from an earlier, more primitive form of belief. As a transmitter of culture, Ichabod is already something of a clog upon the spirit of the New World. Add to that his adherence to colonial legends of a headless Hessian soldier and the skinny, awkward teacher makes a perfect figure for comic explosion from the wedding rites of Brom Bones and Katrina Van Tassel.

WASHINGTON IRVING, "Rip Van Winkle"

Students seem to take Irving's tales very naturally, although they are likely to find the "framing" fiction of Knickerbocker somewhat off-putting. It may be argued, however, that Irving had more than quaintness in mind when he invented this gatherer of legend and folklore. Knickerbocker functions as a kind of mediating figure between the world of myth and legend and the world of historical fact. He pronounces the story of Rip Van Winkle as the kind of "legendary lore so invaluable to true history." One other framing device is interesting in this connection as well. At the head of the story, Irving-Knickerbocker cites a scrap of verse reminding us that we owe our name for Wednesday to Woden, "God of the Saxons."

What all this has to do with this light little tale about a man who falls asleep and does not awaken again for twenty years is hard to say. Certainly, the remark about the relevance of legend to "true history" is not calculated to make us believe the story in any literal sense, nor even to believe that someone once may have believed it. Still, Hendrick Hudson and his men making thunder in the Catskills with their game of bowls is part of a typology. They are like the company of gods around Woden, in some timeless, heroic Golden Age.

The village in which Rip and his wife live is like Sleepy Hollow—a sort of backwash or eddy in time where secular history is a relatively weak force and legends of the Old World hold the place in a kind of suspension. Still, it is a place of human dwelling, and about as near as it gets to the era of the meadhall brotherhood of warriors is in the group of old volunteers who gather at the inn to tell tall tales of their military exploits. Rip himself is descended from a family who were once warriors of a sort, but he is a sad case in the world of practical affairs. He is beloved by the whole village for his willingness to help the ladies and mind the children, but simply cannot keep his mind on his own business, and his wife has turned shrew from trying to get him to take some care of his own family.

However, Rip is not particularly of this world. His wife and the press of practical affairs are the effects of history, and the dreamer, Rip, is known in higher circles. The moment the strange-looking fellow in the old-fashioned Dutch breeches catches sight of him on the mountain, he calls him by name and takes him into the company of another timeless heroic brotherhood. Well, not *quite* timeless, for when Rip awakes, he and all his gear have aged. During his absence, history of the "linear" kind has visited his village. No longer does the cyclical mythology of the Old World hold the village in thrall. No more of "The king is dead, long live the king!" The New World view is of a history that for good or ill moves relentlessly forward. Rip has been caught between these opposing forces and has been outside of time but in it, too, has slept, but also has aged.

SHIRLEY JACKSON, "The Lottery"

This tale by Shirley Jackson has the distinction of being one of the very few pieces of literature ever to have been deemed unfit for reading by high-school students, for content unrelated to sexuality. What is so shocking about it is the suggestion that the moral leaders of an otherwise sane and respectable rural community (apparently American) could harbor such distorted values as to maintain the necessity for a regular seasonal sacrifice of their fellow beings. Here a ritualistic mechanism effectively causes ordinarily decent people so complete to withdraw their compassion that even the victim's children might contentedly participate in her death by stoning.

A distinct "anthropological" cast is given the story by Jackson's linking of this grim festival to an agricultural community's concern for the continuance of favorable growing conditions. What sacrifice has to do with insuring fertility has always been a controversial question amongst the experts. Some maintain that the offering is a simple *quid pro quo*: we mortals will surrender up something we value highly to show our devotion, and the deity will reward our sacrifice by bestowing the blessings of his or her plenty in return. The biblical story of Abraham and Isaac might be compared here. Certainly it is possible that what Jackson had in mind was simply the exploration of an alternative human history in which such rituals have persisted into the modern period, and there is nothing in the narrative incommensurate with such a reading.

On the other hand, one does not have to stretch very far to see that modern societies have and still do practice a kind of human sacrifice—perhaps not literally for "crops," but for their equivalent yield: for prosperity, for profits, either by shirking safety or environmental measures, or by the military defense of investments abroad. It is *possible* that Jackson is capable of this kind of political parable as well.

But it is not imperative that we interpret in such unsubtle ways as those suggested above. Jackson is as much exploring the social tendency toward sacrifice as she is exposing the consciousness of the profit motive. One might note, for example, that in the town where the ceremony takes place, the citizens have what most of us dream of in one phase of our utopian fantasies—real community, a closely knit, homogeneous society. What old man Warner is there to warn about is the failure of *mutual faith in an arbitrary horror*. Certainly reasonable people can agree about rational principles; but if they are indeed rational principles, they are always open to reasonable doubt, and there a multiplicity of opinion is the rule rather than the exception. But things like nationalism, warfare, capital punishment, racial and class hatred, are not rooted in reason; one is either with them or against them, for they have no rational variants. One should therefore not underestimate the fundamental seriousness of Pop Warner's point about community: as the Fascists learned, it is probably easier to hold the loyalty of a group around a piece of nonsense than around a reasoned principle.

Further, if there are few meaningful differences within a society by which to single out scapegoat figures—those upon whom all antisocial, centrifugal impulses might be vented for the reinforcement of the society's conformity and identity—then victims must be arbitrarily designated as "other." Those so identified are then expelled in the ritualistic "cleansing" of the body of the community, so that the community may become once again acceptable in the eyes of the deity. It should not be forgotten that Shirley Jackson wrote "The Lottery" in 1948, at the onset of the Cold War. After the comparative sense of camaraderie of World War II, there was a renewed distrust in this country for anything or anyone different, and McCarthyism was beginning to gather momentum.

At the same time, the full dimensions of the Nazi attempt to exterminate the European Jewish population were being revealed in newly captured film footage of those events. Jackson is unlikely to have been indifferent to the overwhelming question of why or how such things could have been perpetrated upon friends and neighbors and colleagues and schoolmates, social intimates in Germany perhaps more than anywhere else. But there is *no rationale* for the choice of victims in the story. It is not that Tessie Hutchinson is a "bad sport" about the outcome of the drawing; nor is she weak in character because she wishes her daughter and son-in-law to be included in the final draw to increase her own chances of escaping ostracism. (The very word, "ostracism," comes down to us from similar lotteries in which marked oyster shells were used as ballots). The point of the ritual, after all, is that Tessie may be declared "other" so that even her own family no longer recognizes their kinship with her. Their stones are cast at a stranger, if not at another entirely different species of being. Similarly, there is no *reason* for the Germans to have given the black dot to their Jewish fellow-citizens, suddenly declaring them "other"—no reason but to secure the solidarity of those *not* so designated. Here, to be one of the "chosen" has terrifying implications.

HENRY JAMES, "Four Meetings"

This story appeared in the first three editions of *Fiction 100*. It was then replaced by "Daisy Miller," a Jamesian classic with a similar theme. Reader surveys show that "Four Meetings" has been missed, undoubtedly because it teaches so well.

The brief review of some of the critical literature follows:

- For Krishna Vaid (1964), Caroline Spencer does come to understand by the time of the fourth meeting that she has been victimized. Up to that point, Vaid writes, "only the innocence of Caroline Spencer has been in evidence; now we see the dignity she has acquired through suffering." He continues,

   One of the best touches in the tale is the narrator's failure to provoke the heroine into voicing her regrets. She remains impenetrable to the end. The most he can bring her to express is contained in a look: "I took from her eyes, as she approached us, a brief but in tense appeal—the mute expression, as I felt, conveyed in the hardest little look she had yet addressed to me, of her longing to know what, as a man of the world in general and of the French world in particular, I thought of these allied forces now so encamped on the stricken field of her life."…It is not that the heroine does not realize what has happened, but that she realizes it only too well. Her resignation, however, remains equal to her bitterness.

- Leo Gurko (1970) focuses attention on the missing word in the story's opening paragraph: "I'm sorry to hear of her death, and yet when I think of it why *should* I be? The last time I saw her she was certainly not—!" "The reader's selection of the word represented by the dash," Gurko explains,

   will determine the meaning of the story, and incidentally, explain why the narrator decides not to feel regret. This being a story by James, several choices are possible. The ambiguity, however, is not pointlessly evasive. On the contrary, whatever the word chosen, the interpretation that follows is perfectly rational and clear.

Gurko then offers three "candidates": "happy," "uncompleted," and "alive."

"Happy" refers, of course to Caroline Spencer's state of mind, particularly during her third and fourth meeting with the narrator. She can hardly be happy over the way her life-long dream of Europe ends within thirteen hours in Harve (a "poor prosaic" city which, the narrator tells us, is "a place of convenience, nothing more; a place of transit, through which transit should be rapid"). "Uncompleted" refers to Caroline's experience, to the fact, as Gurko notes, that whatever her limitations, "she manages to live all the way up to that capacity." Moreover, there are signs that she has learned from her experience with the cousin and the "countess," that she is not taken in by the countess and her claims, even though she is unwilling or unable to rid herself of her house guest. "Why play host to a fraud?" Gurko asks. "Because fraudulent though she is, the countess is still a European—a low grade European to be sure, but better than none. Miss Spencer's dream has faded but it has not disappeared, and the countess is the agent that keeps the dream, at however low an ebb, alive." The third possibility, "alive," refers to the "psychic death" that comes with the slow, but final, destruction of her dream.

Gurko also discusses the role of the narrator, particularly in terms of James's revisions of the text which not only "magnify his role" but "make him a decidedly less pleasant person than in the earlier version." The issue that Gurko wishes to explore is the narrator's culpability and responsibility. Knowing the "truth" of things, why doesn't he intervene to "save" Caroline Spencer? What is the real nature of his interest in her? Is he, in the end, responsible for her death?

* Roger Seamon (1978), indicating that the story "has proved to be something of a puzzle to critics in recent years," begins by briefly tracing the criticism to date. The key to the story, he decides, is a "sympathetic understanding of character in a social context. We are not, in the final analysis, encouraged to judge the characters…, but to grasp the principle of their actions." Seamon then focuses on the narrator, who in each episode responds to Caroline Spencer's "need, but only part way, for after an initial movement toward her he pulls back." His attitude Seamon describes as an unconscious mixture of condescension, righteous indignation, and general irritation:

> The condescension means that he has judged her as unworthy and that he need not stoop. This protects him from his sense of failure in not responding generously to her. The righteous indignation is complex. It consists of anger at her passivity mingled, I think, with anger at himself. His emotional state, which is best, if inadequately, labelled as irritation, is the result of a compromise between his impulse to flee from her needs and his impulse to respond deeply to them. This is coupled with condescension, which is the tone of his telling and the way he tries to put aside an unresolved relationship. Here we have the basis of his character, the principle of his action, and this combines with Caroline's nature to form their mutual fate. She is in conflict, just like the narrator. She has strong needs, but she does not express them forcefully and openly, and this gives the narrator the chance to play out his conflict without ever having to acknowledge it. We have, then, a tale of suppressed feelings, and in each of their meetings a version of the same drama is enacted.

The remainder of Seamon's essay demonstrates this "drama" at work in each of the story's four meetings.
* W. R. Martin (1980) agrees with Seamon's analysis and extends it. "I believe the reader will understand the narrator's irritation more fully," Martin writes, "when he sees that the Countess's relation to Mr. Mixter in Section IV is not very unlike the narrator's to Caroline in Section I."
* Edward Wagenknecht (1984) has little sympathy for those who

lambast the narrator for his failure to save Miss Spencer as he ought to have done. Should he have taken an axe to the "Countess" and thrown Miss Spencer over his charger's neck so that he might ride off with her like young Lochinvar come out of the West? And, for that matter, what help can anybody, least of all a stranger quite without authority in the matter, give to an adult human being who is sufficiently the lamb to allow herself to be victimized and exploited by people who have no claim whatever upon her, as Miss Spencer does?

HENRY JAMES "The Real Thing"

The story (whose origins, as James explains in his *Notebooks*, is rooted in a real-life event) turns on the artist's "preference for the represented subject over the real one," the time-honored notion that art is not life but rather its distillation and translation. When models—such as the Monarchs—leave no room for the imagination, they cease to be useful to the artist. In this case "the real thing" (the Monarchs) are less useful to the cockney Miss Churm and the Italian Oronte (however otherwise implausible they may appear) because both are blessed with "a curious and inexplicable talent for imagination."

The story, which is often anthologized, belies its apparent simplicity. It is, as Earle Labor notes, a story that ultimately transcends platitudes and "esthetic cliché." Labor, in what is one of the best articles written to date, identifies "three major thematic levels in 'The Real Thing': (1) the social, (2) the esthetic, and (3) the moral." He then goes on to explain:

> James is quite explicit: socially speaking, Major and Mrs. Monarch have been and still are the real thing; they are, as the porter's wife immediately informs us, "a gentleman and a lady."…Unhappily, as the narrator complains, the real thing for society is "the wrong thing" for art. In the "deceptive atmosphere of art even the highest respectability may fail of being plastic." In other words, the real thing for the artist must be "the ideal thing."
>
> On a second and higher level of meaning…the real thing—esthetically—is the creative imagination of the artist himself. (1) cannot accommodate itself to (2), nor vice versa. It is from the conflict between these two levels of meaning that the tension within the story partially derives. The Monarchs prove to be utterly intractable for the artist's purposes. The painter's foolish attempt to amalgamate these incompatible elements almost ruins his project and, worse, perhaps irreparably mars his creative talent, if we are to accept the word of his esthetic conscience, Jack Hawley.…
>
> Notwithstanding his critical incisiveness, however, Jack Hawley is heartless. And this is the key to the third level of meaning in the story, a meaning that James skillfully withholds until his concluding sentence—a meaning so deftly manipulated that it has apparently been overlooked by most of James's critics.
>
> Following his friend's sound advice, the painter dismisses the pathetically inept Monarchs, who, according to Hawley, "did me a permanent harm, got me into false ways." Then he concludes with this enigmatic qualification: "If it be true I'm content to have paid the price—for the memory." An astounding concession for any artist to make! In essence, the narrator admits that he has been willing to sacrifice something of the artist's most precious gift, his creative talent, for something else termed vaguely as "the memory."…
>
> His attitude [towards the Monarchs] has changed radically from what it was at the beginning of the story. He is now involved with mankind. Though such involvement may have blurred his esthetic perspective, it has sharpened his moral insight; if he has lost something as an artist, he has gained infinitely more as a

man. From his painful experience with the Monarchs James's narrator emerges with a finer understanding of the human situation and with a new awareness of what constitutes "the real thing" in human relationships: compassion.

Labor's analysis provides a useful tool for getting at the story's complexity and allows us to deal with such key elements as plot, character, point of view, and, of course, theme.

SARAH ORNE JEWETT, "A White Heron"

"A White Heron" centers on Sylvia's climb up the pine tree. As she risks its dangers, she comes to resemble the endangered, tree-dwelling bird. Suspense builds in the hush of the early, faint light of dawn. We fear that this little girl will be mistaken for the bird, that a gun-shot will break the silence, and that she, not the bird, will fall to the ground.

Something—especially the young hunter—has seemed to menace Sylvia ever since his "aggressive" whistle startled her. But even before this meeting, Jewett builds the comparison that slowly emerges, like the forest in the dawn, between the heron and the girl. In that moment, when the two rest near each other in the same tree, we realize how steadily the parallel has developed. Afterward, the similarities seem to disappear. Rather than being identified with nature, Sylvia is permanently alienated from the articulate life around her, in which she has lived so intensely. And the cause of this radical separation is merely nature itself. Human companionship creates the gulf between her and her "woodland treasures." Her childhood ends not with a bang, but with a whisper of which even she is almost unaware. Just a slight change, almost unconscious and so gradual, that no one can say exactly when it occurs, makes all the difference.

In this story, the subtle changes involved in the very process of growing show how we are united with the rest of the natural world. Our involvement in life, and therefore necessarily in death, is our natural inheritance. But in this story, at least, something is added. To humans, and to them only, "natural" life brings both good and evil, joy and sorrow, and it often, or perhaps always, brings each of these contraries together.

The likeness between Sylvia and the white heron is prepared from the beginning. Her very name is Greek for woodland. Shy, "afraid of folks"; playing hide and seek not with other noisy children, but with the old cow Mistress Moolly; happy in the woods, Sylvy seems to be like the "elusive" bird. When the young man appears, she is "horror stricken." He is described then as "the enemy." Given these hints of violence, a reader might well think of rape. Instead, all proceeds gently. The young man, too, is a bit afraid. He feels his own "horrors," it turns out, regarding "primitive housekeeping." But Mrs. Tilley does well, and he in turn is kind to the little girl. Having been "vaguely thrilled by a dream of love," Sylvy even feels a pang when he leaves.

Through his visit, she has entered a new part of her life. While before she had been part of the woods, isolated from all except her grandmother—almost a wild creature—afterward she needs human, specifically male, companionship. Thus is she made ready for emotional and sexual fulfillment. In this way, too, nature has made sure that this instance of life will go on, that a new generation will follow Sylvia as they have her grandmother. This is the joy.

Yet, the story does not seem particularly joyful, but continues impartially, like a Greek tragedy. The pang that Sylvy feels as the young hunter leaves shows that a subtle violence has been done, not with his gun nor with the pen knife he has given her, but merely in the great natural course of things. Those stirrings of love have ended her woodland happiness, just as they have assured her growth into womanhood. Is her budding affection the cause of her growth, or its effect? As in life, no one can quite tell. Will love make Sylvia happy? Her grandmother, with her "hint of family sorrows," indicates the future.

Mrs. Tilley's life has been made happy through, or at least consoled by, her daughter's child. With similarly mixed results, the young man hunts and kills—and in a manner preserves—the things he loves. Reflecting on the story, one may recall that Cupid shoots his victims, too.

If the author had ended the story in the pine tree, if the nameless young man had shot Sylvy, we would have melodrama. If he had carried her off to live happily every after, we would have a fantasy or a romance. By rejecting both such pat endings, Jewett has included more significance than she could have achieved with either melodrama or romance. Realism is here the most effective artifice.

DOROTHY M. JOHNSON, "The Man Who Shot Liberty Valance"

As one would expect, the setting of this story is extremely important to its effect. The narrative takes place in a frontier town of the American West, and much of its atmosphere derives from the accretion of mythology concerning gunslingers and their pistol duels. The order of the narrative is fairly complex, starting with the funeral of Bert Barracune and the speculation as to why a certain senator and his wife should be attending the last rites of an obscure cowpoke. The bulk of the narrative is then presented in flashback, as an answer to the question raised in the opening scene.

The plot is fairly simple. Foster, a "greenhorn" from the east, has had his horse and equipment stolen, and has been beat up and set afoot on the prairie by the outlaw, Liberty Valance. A local cowboy, Bert Barracune, happens to run across the robbery victim and brings him to water, gives him food, and lends him his bedroll so that he might recover in solitude from his beating.

At this point, the story picks up on an ancient and honored variant of the "showdown," at least as old as Shakespeare's *Romeo and Juliet*. It is the variant in which the challenged man's response is retarded or delayed for some reason that he is unable or unwilling to explain to the waiting community. The typical situation in American western films is that an aging gunfighter has sickened of killing and renounces violence, refusing to pick up his guns despite the most outrageous provocations. The audience expectantly awaits the inevitable last straw when the gunman will finally give in to his indignation and kill someone. The code of righteous revenge is still very much alive in our literature, if not in our laws.

Ransome Foster virtually makes a study of craven manners, begging for food when he gets to town, accepting demeaning chores at the cafe (and getting handouts at the back door from Hallie). Later, he becomes a clerk and sweeper at the local store, teaches school, does everything, one might say, that "real men" in this mythic wild west wouldn't be caught dead doing. Of course, Foster is committing all these slanders against himself in order to "foster" his reputation as a pansy, knowing that the bully, Liberty Valance, will not be able to resist the temptation to make this gutless bookworm crawl before him in public. The point is summed up by Bert Barracune when he goes to fetch Foster from the remote spot where the latter has gone to practice his pistol-hand: "I come out to tell you that Liberty Valance is in town. He's interested in the dude that anybody can kick around—this here tenderfoot that boasts how he can read Greek." The hook has been skillfully baited; how could any self-respecting badman resist messing up such a Little Lord Fauntleroy?

So here at the center of the story is the time-honored facedown between two men in the middle of the deserted main street of a frontier town. Johnson has no desire to thwart our expectations. This is the equivalent of the stylized clashes between armored knights in Spenser's *The Faerie Queen*. Valance draws, Foster draws (too late); but the latter wakes up with a wound in his shoulder, believing he heard Valance fire twice. Of course it is Bert, unseen by anyone else, who has plugged the bully between the eyes. Foster's masculine honor has been retrieved, and he makes plans to return to his home in the East.

Hallie's affection for the dude is apparently kindled by those qualities in him that she does not find in the local males. Evidently, if Foster is not precisely a man's man, he can be a lady's man. Bert's part in making certain that Hallie gets her heart's desire is left deliberately vague, but what is hinted at is a kind of shotgun wedding in which Bert's quiet but armed insistence is enough to keep Ransome Foster a loyal and ambitious husband clear up to the Senate, providing Hallie with the kind of life Bert is certain she deserves.

JAMES JOYCE, "Araby"

Joyce's "Araby" provides a good example of the way in which lyrical and evocative imagery contributes to characterization and to the establishment of time. The story celebrates the rite of passage and the disenchantment and disillusionment which all too often is the fate of self-indulgent adolescent infatuation. The object of "confused adoration" is not Mangan's sister herself but rather the idealized image of the girl which the narrator has created out of his own romantic imagination. On the verge of adolescence (note how many of the images suggest an awakening, if still largely unconscious, sexuality), the boy becomes the victim not of some teenage enchantress but of his own extravagant romanticism. The quality and compelling nature of his vision is suggested not only by the blend of religious and romantic language in which it is described and celebrated, but by the unacknowledged daily ritual of courtly devotion that the boy performs on behalf of his beloved. As long as the object of affection can be viewed safely from a distance, the vision itself remains inviolable and intact. But in the aftermath of the boy's first actual encounter with Mangan's sister, in which he speaks to her of the "splendid bazaar" and promises to bring her "something," that vision becomes exposed to the realities and vicissitudes of a world he no longer can control. What begins as a chivalric quest to redeem a promise ends in a series of progressively disillusioning and deflating events. These final episodes are deftly handled: the anxiety caused by the uncle's late arrival home and the boy's delayed departure, the ride on the deserted train, the difficulty in gaining admission, and the silent, half-closed and rapidly darkening bazaar itself, whose commercial, artificial, and worldly aspects are all too visible in the weary-looking attendant, the men counting money on a salvar, and the banal dialogue carried on in English accents between the "two young gentlemen" with whom they are flirting, all combine to produce an epiphany of disenchantment, "anguish and anger." "I heard a voice call from one end of the gallery that the light was out."

Among the aspects of the story to be considered are the opening two paragraphs which describe North Richmond Street, the musty, uninhabited house of the dead priest, and the books and other artifacts which the priest has left behind. These details not only establish the locale of the story (and perhaps tell us something of Joyce's view of the dead-end and futile quality of Dublin life) but serve to introduce us to the sensibility and preferences of the narrator on the eve of his adventure. Notice particularly how the realistic detail of the first two paragraphs gives way to the lyricism of the third as we move more directly inside the narrator's recollected consciousness.

Point of view is obviously crucial to the story's success. "Araby" is told retrospectively by an older and wiser narrator who is still very much in touch with the sensations and emotions of the events themselves. Full maturity still eludes him; for in judging himself as "a creature driven and derided by vanity," it is clear that the narrator has yet to exorcise the emotions of pain, humiliation, and self-hatred which have attended his disillusionment. He has yet to attain the objectivity and detachment of the adult, able to look back and laugh at, even as he savors, what is after all a rather common, if bittersweet and confusing, experience in the process of coming of age.

JAMES JOYCE, "The Dead"

Gabriel Conroy is the character whose consciousness we are closest to in "The Dead," even though he is introduced into the action of the story after the scene of his aunts' party has already been set. His entrance draws considerable attention, because he is an important member of the festivities, the favorite nephew of the Misses Morkin. There is a great deal of excitement and bustle about the party's beginning, in contrast to the narrator's "cuts" to scenes of the snow falling softly and silently upon the monuments to dead heroes scattered throughout the city.

In the entrance hall, Gabriel makes a remark to Lily, the maid, who answers him in such a fashion as to reveal that she has in some way been bitterly disappointed in a relationship. Gabriel flinches at her remark, as if he is somehow personally touched by her reference to the emotional shallowness of men. Once upstairs, he finds himself dancing with Miss Ivors, who twits him about his publishing book reviews in a paper considered sympathetic to the established British authority. Mostly in play, she calls him a "West Briton." Again, Gabriel's reaction seems out of proportion to the provocation. In response to Miss Ivors' invitation to him to make a trip with several friends to the west of Ireland for the sake of rekindling their sense of Irish identity, Gabriel retorts that he is sick of his country and would gladly leave it if he could. It is some time before he is able to get himself back into the mood of the party.

The significance of Gabriel's exchange with Miss Ivors is not immediately clear. We know only that Gabriel's level of self-confidence fluctuates like that of most of us under similar circumstances, that he feels by turns superior and humiliated, affectionate and cold, generous and mean. At one point, he thinks of the grand impression his dinner speech is going to make and the next moment considers it a piece of inconsequential drivel. At one moment, he looks upon his aunts as ignorant old ladies, and the next he is fulsomely praising them as "the graces," at whose passing culture will be by so much impoverished.

At the dinner table, the conversation turns to the subject of singers, past and present, foreign and native. This discussion is preparatory to that moment when Gabriel will notice his wife Gretta poised upon the stairs, trying to catch the strains of an old Irish ballad being rendered above by the (slightly defective) tenor, Mr. D'Arcy. It is a moment that stirs Gabriel's affection and desire toward her, feelings heightened by the excitement of their staying in a rented room rather than returning immediately home. As he probes the reasons for Gretta's unusual pensiveness, she reveals that she has been reminded by the old song of someone else who used to sing it, a boy named Michael Furey, who died. How did he die? asks Gabriel. "I think he died for me," she replies. In that moment, he is overwhelmed by a vision of the pettiness of his life and the shallowness of his feelings in comparison with the profoundly poetic image of the young man standing in the rain, having left his sickbed to come one last time to bid his love farewell. How can the living compete—as orator, as singers, as lovers, as soldiers for the Grand Cause of Ireland? Only the past and its inhabitants, the dead, are real, and it is into this dreamland Golden Age that Gabriel begins to drift as he falls asleep. As for the rest, the waking and the living, it is all given over to the minute struggles, the moment-to-moment victories and defeats of the sort that he has experienced all evening at the party.

BEL KAUFMAN, "Sunday in the Park"

I like this story because of its simplicity—the way in which the author uses a brief encounter in the park to expose and explore human relationships. The setting and the occasion are deftly and concisely established in the very first paragraph, which begins in quietude and contentment and motionlessness and then, in the final two sentences, quickly erupts in a simple episode of violence between two young children, which generates the story.

The two fathers who confront one another over the sand-throwing incident are, of course, clearly different: the smaller man, the academic husband Morton, who wears glasses and reads the *Times* magazine section and who "was rarely angry" and "seldom lost his temper"; and his antagonist, the big man, who "seemed to be taking up the whole bench as he held the Sunday comics close to his face" and who spits "deftly." "As the story unfolds," writes Ronald J. Nelson ("The Battlefield in Kaufman's 'Sunday in the park,'" *English Language Notes*, XXX [September 19921, 61–68),

> it becomes clear that the ways in which the parents of both boys react to the situation typify opposing approaches to life. These conflicting perspectives broach one of the most difficult questions that people must somehow answer: "how to be" in any given situation, especially one that directly challenges a person's accustomed way of seeing things.

Between these two males suspended, if momentarily, is the wife who witnesses her husband's defeat and impotency. Though her first reaction is one of relief, she soon "senses" that implicit in the "unpleasant incident" is "a layer of something else," something "heavy and inescapable" that has something "acutely personal, familiar, and important" to do with her relationship with her husband. Beyond his reasonableness and a situation whose resolution she understands intellectually and knows she should dismiss as something "silly" and "not worth talking about," there is something deeper and more profound. This something is implicit in her final rebuke of her husband—a rebuke that is "cold and penetrating with contempt" and shocks even the speaker herself. What this means—or at least hints at—should make for interesting classroom discussion.

As Nelson notes in conclusion,

> How these two civilized people will cope with the dark forces that have lain dormant and that may surface at any time remains uncertain. What *is* certain, however, is that even the gentlest of people may be drawn into situations that test one's mettle, when deep-seated values are threatened. Perhaps the reader emerges from the story—as from Joseph Conrad's "Heart of Darkness" and Nathaniel Hawthorne's "Young Goodman Brown"—with an increased awareness that evil lurks within every human being and that it may raise its ugly head even in so unlikely a spot as a playground.

I found this story in an anthology entitled *Sudden Fictions: American Short-Short Stories*, edited by Robert Shapard and James Thomas (Salt Lake City: Gibbs M. Smith, Inc.— Peregrine Smith Books, 1986). The volume's thesis is that there is such a thing as a short-short story (from one to five pages in length) and that these stories are new, different ("unlike the modern notion of the story") and indeed even lack an agreed upon name. The assumption, according to editor Shapard, is that "something called the short-*short* story must be an even younger form than the short story. Short-*shorts* must be a sub-category. Or maybe a sub-sub category." The authors that Shapard and Thomas include in their collection (and some of the critics they cite) apparently agree. According to Stuart Dybek, one of the author-critics cited, "the short prose piece so frequently inhabits a No-Man's Land between prose and poetry, narrative and lyric, story and fable, joke and meditation, fragment and whole, that one of its identifying characteristics has been its protean shapes. Part of the fun of writing them is the sense of slipping between the scams." For Joyce Carol Oates, "Very short fictions are nearly always experimental, exquisitely calibrated, reminiscent of Frost's definition of a poem—a structure of words that consumes itself as it unfolds, like ice melting on a stove." Such comments suggest an interesting way to explore Kaufman's "Sunday in the Park" as well as other of the stories in this edition of *Fiction 100*.

GARRISON KEILLOR, "The Tip-Top Club"

Keillor's "The Tip-Top Club," which first appeared in a 1981 issue of the *Atlantic Monthly*, provides a perfect example of the kind of droll parody and satire that so entertained listeners to "A Prairie Home Companion." The audience of "The Tip-Top Club" is composed, in fact, of the kind of middle-class working folks ("older persons leading quiet lives and keeping busy with hobbies and children and grandchildren") who make up the Lake Wobegons of America. Yet, with the retirement of the self-effacing Bud Swenson we also learn that Lake Wobegons and its sister towns have a darker, less agreeable, and often unpleasant side to them. The audience which loves Bud Swenson is, after all, *the very same audience* that reviles his replacement Wayne Bargy. Middle America does not, it seems, take kindly to change or to those who call their attention to the depressing issues of the real world.

Some other notes and comments on the story:

- Keillor's story works, in large measure, because of the persona of its narrator and the serious, dead-pan, matter-of-fact manner of his delivery. He reports without, apparently, judging. Keillor's ability to reproduce the way in which people actually talk is one of the story's strengths. By accurately capturing speech patterns, Keillor is able to introduce with great economy a wide variety of familiar character types into his narrative. The story's narrator, of course, is not Garrison Keillor himself, and students need to be challenged to infer what the author's values and attitudes toward his subject may be and how they differ from those of the narrator. Keillor's humor almost always has its somber or serious side, and "The Tip-Top Club" is no exception.

- The Tip-Top Club gains and holds its audience precisely because of its pervasive and cheery optimism and its studied lack of controversy—a tone which is zealously protected by the show's unlisted telephone number and by the indefatigable Harlan and his tape loop machine. "No conversation about religion or politics was permitted, nor were callers allowed to be pessimistic or moody on the air." Topics of discussion are uniformly innocuous: "Vacations and pets were favorite Tip-Top topics, along with household hints, children, gardening, memories of long ago, favorite foods, great persons, good health and how to keep it, and of course the weather."

- Note the use of precise dates in recording important events in the history of the Club. Presumably, Club members remember such specifics, but their use is Keillor's way of reminding contemporary readers that the hey-day of the original Tip-Top Club hosted by Bud Swenson belonged to that tranquil period in American life that began with the close of World War II and ended with Vietnam. Bud, interestingly enough, retires on November 26, 1969. Two weeks earlier, about 300,000 persons had held an antiwar protest in Washington, D.C. The Tip-Top Club zealously excludes things foreign and unpleasant.

- The Tip-Toppers' response is one of ownership (they have, after all, been told that it is "*your* show"). The self-effacing Bud Swenson is "your recording secretary, chief cook and bottle washer" and they expect *him* to keep the faith. The response of listeners, on the other hand, is very much keyed to the personality, attitudes, and values of the announcer-host. Bud's voice, we are told, is "warm and reassuring." He has the capacity to edit reality on behalf of "the bright side." Bud quickly becomes the embodiment of his audience and loses his own identity in theirs. Once the tone and the "rules" have been established (the Club "hit full stride" in a matter of months), Bud Swenson becomes a listener, a neutral: "he seemed to lose whatever personality he had in the beginning." Put another way, Bud has *become* the collective personality of his devout listeners. Note that at age 65, he just fades away without mentioning his retirement on the air.

- What the Tip-Top Club listeners respond to is the *predictability* and the *changelessness* of the show, as reflected in its static format. Debates such as whether or not smoke-puffing discourages aphids "lasted for years." The format and its unvarying sameness obviously touches something deep in the psyche of the audience. (NBC's long-running "Tonight Show" under host Johnny Carson obviously has much the same appeal.)

- Ask students to consider how the values and attitudes of Roy Elmore, Jr., the pragmatic head of WLT, differ from those which he insists upon airing. Much the same thing can be said of the values and attitudes of Harlon and Alice. What does this suggest?
- Wayne Bargy, Bud Swenson's successor, has "little interest" in the old Tip-Top topics. "He was divorced and lived in an efficiency apartment (no lawns to keep up, no maintenance responsibilities) and had no pets or children." As opposed-to Bud Swenson's self-effacing neutrality, Wayne Bargy is egocentric (note his repeated use of the personal pronoun "I"). Wayne, the amateur psychologist, wants to probe within. He apologizes, expresses doubts, talks about his own life, and discusses depressing and unpleasant topics like divorce and "trying to understand people who may be different from ourselves." Whereas Bud had become indistinguishable from his listeners, Wayne feels alienated from them. Moreover, where Bud Swenson was a "listener" who merely reflected the concerns of his listeners, Wayne is a self-styled "communicator," who believes that "This show…[has] a tremendous opportunity to get people to open up their minds. He…[views] himself as an educator of sorts." What makes Wayne Bargy particularly threatening is that he is a man with a purpose and a message: "There's a lot of anger and violence out there—and I don't say people shouldn't feel that way, but I do feel people should be willing to change. Life is change. We all change." Bud Swenson and *his* audience explicitly denied that people should "feel that way."
- Wayne places his identity and uniqueness squarely before his readers and they don't like it. Club members remain united: not in support of the host of *their* show but against him. Again, this is the very *same* audience that unwaveringly supported Bud Swenson. Wayne Bargy may tap a different chord, but his audience is no less a responsive one.

GARRISON KEILLOR, "What Did We Do Wrong?"

Keillor's humorous story turns on a much-used, time-honored device. "What if?" the author asks. What would happen if the first woman to play major league baseball wouldn't play by the rules and openly defied the traditions of the game? How would such defiance impact he teammates, the opposition, the sports writing fraternity, and most importantly, the fans? What would happen, he wonders, if the first woman major leaguer, a woman with star-like capabilities, simply dared to be herself? For Annie Szemanski it is not even a case of being dared: she is what she is, thank you very much.

Baseball, of course, is not simply a game—it is *the* national pastime, with rules and traditions, some that are written down and codified, others that though unspoken are understood and adhered to (even worshipped) by everyone who plays or watches the game. Until now.

Baseball is clearly unprepared for the likes of Annie Szemanski. She is an absolute original, who defies categories and categorization. Though Keillor's story was first published in the *New Yorker* in 1985, it is set two years later, in 1987, perhaps as a way of indicating that his is a story for which the world was then not quite ready. The new century has now turned, some fifteen seasons have come and gone, and, as you will surely discover in you classroom, baseball is still not ready for this remarkable young woman.

When Annie Szemanski arrives in the big leagues, her difficulties begin. Her teammates on the Sparrows (quite a name for a major league team!) treat her "like dirt." The fact that she is a woman has everything to do with it. Manager Hemmie, the gnarled 61-year-old professional, on this point is direct and honest: "He disliked her purely because she was a woman—there was nothing personal about it. . . . Other than that, he thought she was a tremendous addition to the team."

The fans, on the other hand, are prepared to accept Annie, and to elevate her to a place in their pantheon of heroes. The Sparrows are, at best, a mediocre team, yet the fans turn out, 32,000 strong. They buy her souvenirs embossed with her name and applaud her with home-made banners made out of bedsheets. The fans are, in short, willingly signal her acceptance into "the game." Such accommodation extends even to hardened sportswriters like Arnie Brixius. When Annie is unable to chew tobacco in a "manly" sort of way, Arnie suggests banning the habit itself. "It's only this scribe's opinion," Arnie writes in his "Hot Box" column, "but isn't it about time baseball cleaned up its act and left the tobacco in the locker?"

Annie comes prepared to play. She plays a man's game with the physical gusto of men, taking out sliding runners with the best of them. She even instigates a brawl which empties the dugouts. She is then ejected from the game for swearing at the umpire, for "saying things to him . . . that he had never heard in his nineteen years of umpiring."

In the aftermath, women's groups—including the League of Women Voters—come to her rescue, declaring their "solidarity" with someone who is "a model for all women who are made to suffer guilt for their aggressiveness." Annie Szemanski, on her part, wants no part of being anyone's "role model," and she most certainly feels no "guilt" for her on-the-field "aggressiveness." As she later tells Gentleman Jim, the Sparrows "PR guy," "she wasn't there to be liked, she was there to play ball."

Despite her heroics in breaking new ground for women—the homerun in Fenway Park, for example—Annie remains adamant: she is not going to live up to anyone else's image of her. The fans simply cannot understand her behavior. They expect her to be like every other player with whom they have ever identified. "What Did We Do Wrong?" they ask in one banner hung from the upperdeck. They are so utterly convinced of the unspoken reciprocal relationship between player and fan, that they are willing to assume that they must somehow be to blame.

The fans back off, apologize, make excuses, even in the face of Annie's continuing unwillingness to understand, observe, and respect traditions and rules. She herself remains implacable, adding the sports writers to her list of those with whom she refuses to deal on any terms but her own. "It's who I am," Annie tells them as she parades naked to the showers.

What was first a local matter becomes a national one. A "high sign" delivered to a live camera television camera on NBC's "Game of the Week" sends the network into shock. Annie is fined $1,000 for "actions detrimental to the best interests of baseball." This too is part of the way that baseball does things and Gentleman Jim immediately is prepared to pay the fine without even asking either questions or permission. For Annie Szemanski, on the other hand, the "best interests of baseball" are largely irrelevant. The commissioner suggests an apology—again a time-honored ritual that immediately cures all ills and restores the offender to his (or now "her") rightful place in the order of things. The distraught fan, camping out at the entrance of Annie's apartment, summarizes it all well: "How can she do this to us? . . . Why can't she just play ball?" The answer, of course, is she can't and she won't.

There is much to discuss here. Students will, no doubt, react strongly, one way or another, to Annie's attitudes, values and behavior, and that is very much what Keillor intends. A good discussion can focus on how antithetical those attitudes, values, and behavior are to all the assumptions we so willingly, and unconsciously, make about our national sport. Also worthy of discussion is Keillor's masterful use of satire, much of which, as honest students will tell you, strikes pretty close to home.

STEPHEN KING, "The Man in the Black Suit"

Stephen King's considerable commercial success and popularity with general readers is well known. What is not nearly so well recognized is that King is also a writer of considerable literary ability, whose thematic treatment of evil firmly links him to the gothic tradition in American literature which includes such well known (and critically accepted) practitioners of the short story as Nathaniel Hawthorne, Edgar Allan Poe, Henry James, Flannery O'Connor, and Joyce Carol Oates.

King, who sets most of his novels and stories in New England, takes full advantage of its historical legends and traditions. He has in fact written with respect to "The Man in the Black Suit" that the story "comes from a long New England tradition of stories which deal with meeting the devil in the woods ('Young Goodman Brown' by Hawthorne, for instance)." The allusion to Hawthorne's story is a both cogent and suggestive. There is much about King's story that reminds us of Hawthorne's classic tale of the confrontation of good and evil, moral skepticism and faith, and the two stories make a most interesting pairing for the purposes of classroom discussion.

That discussion might well begin by quoting King's own statement about the story: "In 'The Man in the Black Suit,'" he has written, "I think I was writing about how the fear of evil is persistent, and how triumph over evil is, at best, temporary." King's comment seems very much on target, for the aged narrator makes it absolutely clear at the outset of the story that his entire life has been irremediably clouded by the event that took place on a Saturday afternoon some eighty years before. On that day for Gary, as for Hawthorne's Young Goodman Brown, evil in the shape of man clearly resembling the devil "comes out of the woods—the uncharted regions—to test the human soul." Though the motive that leads young Gary into the woods seems innocent enough (unlike the motive that compels Young Goodman Brown), the results of his journey are in fact much the same. In the depths of those woods—in Gary's case in a place where (significantly enough) the stream forks—both men encounter a figure dressed in black who they immediately recognize as the devil and subsequently undergo a rite of initiation.

In both stories the experience in the woods has all the trappings of a nightmarish dream, and can be so interpreted. The protagonists can, if they wish, come to see their experience as a transitory and hallucinatory one and, ultimately, dismiss it as such. (Gary, in fact, readily admits to his father and to himself that he had been asleep or drowsing in the moment before the appearance of the man in black. The possibility that his bizarre confrontation with the devil is, in fact, a dream is clearly suggested by Gary's easily understandable dreams of his dead brother, Dan, of the year before. The physical evidence of the devil's presence in the woods, as confirmed by Gary's father, on the other hand, points in the other direction.) But neither Goodman Brown nor Gary chooses to interpret his experience as a dream. Nor in the aftermath are they able to deal in a life affirming way with its implications.

Though Gary seeks "freedom" and "release" by writing down his experience of eighty years earlier in his journal, the clear implication of the story is that for him, as for Hawthorne's Puritan, there will be no relief. Like Brown, Gary has survived, but he has not managed to grow. Hawthorne ends his story with the following comment:

> And when he had lived long, and was borne to his grave, a hoary corpse, followed by Faith, an aged woman, and children and grand-children, a goodly procession, besides neighbors not a few, they carved no hopeful verse upon his tombstone; for his dying hour was gloom."

So too for Stephen King's Gary. In most of his fiction King presents children who are "better able to deal with fantasy and terror *on its own terms* than their elders are." But not so in "The Man in the Black Suit." Though Gary's experience in the woods with the man in the woods scarcely seems to be of his own making, it is, finally, his *inability* to come to grips with the experience that shapes and haunts his entire life and suggests the meaning and significance of King's story.

W. P. KINSELLA, "Shoeless Joe Jackson Comes to Iowa"

This is one story for which you will not have to ask, "Did you see the movie?" Everyone has seen Kevin Costner's performance in "Field of Dreams," released by Twentieth Century-Fox in 1989. The problem may well be not to let student opinion about the movie (for what story and film contain in terms of plot *are* different) unduly influence the way they approach Kinsella's original story." Your students can probably also tell you a good deal about the fallout of the movie. About the Shoeless Joe fan clubs inspired by the film, dedicated to restoring Jackson's name to a place of respect and a niche in Cooperstown, baseball's hallowed shrine. They can also tell you about the field in Iowa where the Costner movie was actually filmed, now a tourist attraction. Ah, Hollywood! It is the "kind of movie," *Chicago Sun-Times* critic Roger Ebert wrote, "[that] Frank Capra might have directed, and James Stewart might have starred in—a movie about dreams." Ebert, as usual, is right.

The story is about wish fulfillment and what might have been, about dreams, about the unfinished business between fathers and sons, and about the redemptive and affirmative power of love. Its center, I think, is the narrator's unfinished relationship with his dead father, a former minor league catcher, who returned from being gassed on a French battlefield during World War I, to live in a diminished world that came to be defined by Shoeless Joe Jackson and the Black Sox scandal. The scandal ended Jackson's baseball career and all that might yet have been his, just as the War ended the father's. From that point on both men had to settle for something far less. For the father (and later for the son) whatever might have been becomes symbolized by Shoeless Joe Jackson and his fall from grace.

The only place where such issues can now be resolved is in, and through, the imagination of the son. This is the meaning of the voice and its conditional statement, "If you build it, he will come." The voice is an open invitation to the narrator to construct a place in the imagination where the past and all its possibilities can again come alive and where old hurts can be healed. It is interesting that when "he comes," it is Annie who sees him first. Kinsella's story is not only about love in and for the past, it is about the shared love of the present, and the ways that love binds people together.

With Annie's understanding and support the narrator does "built it." He constructs a left field in a corner of his Iowa cornfield. By providing Jackson with the opportunity to play once again on a field where the bounce is "true," the narrator also, simultaneously, provides himself with the possibility of building a bridge by which he may yet achieve reconciliation with his father. Opening the way for Shoeless Joe opens the way for others.

"There are others," Jackson tells the narrator at the conclusion of the story. "If you were to finish the infield. . . ." To which the narrator responds, "Consider it done. . . . I know a catcher. . . . "He never made the majors, but in his prime he was good. Really good." The story ends here. In the movie, of course, redemption comes as Ray Kinsella comes face to face with his father as a young man, who has returned to play on the son's "field of dreams." In the story, however, such redemption, though prepared for, has not yet been achieved. A good way to approach the story, and to make all its details come together, is to use the prism of good old-fashioned Jungian psychology, where dreams have always had an acknowledged role.

Nevertheless, there is a great deal of the magical and mystical here, as well as the religious, all of it richly visual. The story speaks directly of "the magic growing closer" and of epiphanies. The thing to notice, of course, is just how Kinsella pulls it all off, without having the whole story simply topple into mawkishness and sentimentality. It is nice, I must admit, to find a contemporary story where the values are affirmative, where wives support their husband's fantasies, and where love is given and received unconditionally.

RUDYARD KIPLING, "They"

Kipling is so well known for his military and colonial tales that our most vivid picture of him (to Americanize the image) is of a kind of bluff and hardy Teddy Roosevelt type who writes avidly about the desirability of the "civilized" nations holding sway over the "uncivilized." However, in "They," one gets a chance to observe what a fine, sensitive stylist he can be. In this story, we see him exercising all the subtlety that we have come to expect of his contemporaries, Joseph Conrad and Henry James.

In fact this particular story has a great deal in common with one of James's most famous stories, "The Turn of the Screw," not simply because it involves children, and adult perceptions of them, but because both stories have as their setting a place where events are not easily explicable either as entirely psychological or as entirely supernatural. Of course, for both writers the opposition between these "realities" is not so much one of doctrine as of genre or style. Perhaps more than James, Kipling was sitting upon a wall between two literary modes. On the one hand, people at home wanted to hear what great adventures there were to be had "out there" on the colonial frontiers; on the other, he was as aware as any other first-hand observer how much waste, futility, and cruelty was to be reported against the system. Most times, he ends up trying to have it both ways, and it is this friction between the traditions of the romance and the program of literary realism that provides such interesting ambivalence in works like *The Man no Would Be King*.

Typically, then, at the opening of "They," the narrator is depicted as a thoroughly modern gentleman roaming freely about the countryside in his new automobile. But very soon, the reader gets to some familiar territory: an obscure track leads through a tangled wood, and the traveler suddenly finds himself arriving at a kind of Wonderland, in the back garden of a beautiful estate with fantastically shaped shrubbery, one of which (a knight on horseback with his lance aimed at the intruder's heart) seems to serve as a kind of guardian or gatekeeper to the enchanted realm. About these shrubs and fountains, and hanging out the upper-story windows, are a number of small children, charming to the stranger, yet unremarkable except for the extent of their shyness.

The great secret of the story is, of course, that these are not living children at all, but their shades—ghosts, who seem to inhabit a nearby wood, a kind of folkloric territory where the grief of bereft parents apparently keeps them on this side of the boundary of the perceivable for those who qualify, as obviously our narrator does. Evidently the blind mistress of the estate has special longings and sensitivities which allow her to be aware of the presence of these spirits, who come to romp through her house, though she cannot see them. At least that is what one is first led to assume through the comments of the narrator. However, the plot is so constructed as never to allow us to say with certainty whether the mistress of the estate actually perceives the presence of the children or is merely responding wistfully to what the "gifted" (which in this case means "bereft") say they see and hear. On his final visit to the estate, his hostess tells him that it is not for that the children come, but for the butler and his wife (who are of the right social class—i.e., not educated in skepticism to such phenomena—and have "borne and lost.") The tenant who comes to haggle with the mistress of the house is qualified in one way—he is obviously convinced that this is haunted territory—but because he lacks a generous heart, the spirits are merely terrifying him.

Of course, our narrator is another case altogether. Like Kipling, on the surface he is a modern, industrial-age realist, but in his heart he is still the old romancer who has come into this place through an enchanted wood, and who might otherwise have scoffed at the story and been deprived of his special privilege within it. Unaware, he sits patiently waiting for one of the tots to come and climb into his lap. But then with a shock, he recognizes by touch an old code, a game played with what must be (we now know) the spirit of a lost child of his own.

WILLIAM KITTREDGE, "We Are Not In This Together"

In an essay entitled "Grizzly" from his 1987 collection *Owning It All*, William Kittredge makes the following autobiographical statement which lies somewhere close to the origins of his story:

> A friend of mine, Mary Pat Mahoney, was killed by a grizzly in 1976, over in the Many Glaciers Campground of Glacier National Park, about a hundred and fifty yards from the Ranger Station. Contemplation of her death led me to a dream, a waking nightmare I learned to articulate at home in my bed the nights after she was dragged from her tent. It thinned any mountain man resolve I might ever have possessed to spend a pleasant campfire evening in the vicinity.

In a letter written to the current editor Kittredge goes still further:

> The story of her death was the strongest piece I ever read in *The Missoulian* (it was written by Diedre McNamer, who has done a number of "Talk of the Town" pieces for *The New Yorker*). I brooded about it for weeks, angered by the unfairness of things in irrational ways I didn't understand (and mostly still don't).
>
> They tell you to write from such emotions. So I did. "We Are Not In This Together" is a story about revenge, and for a long time it was a story as revenge. Which was stupid, as revenge always is. What you destroy is yourself (along with your ability to have a positive effect in the world). The story took a long time to write (three years) because it took me a long time to get that simple notion through my head. It's a story about learning, which is what stories are always about, coming to moments of insight, recognitions, or not.

Such comments are helpful. Halverson's nightmares, though triggered by an episode, are equally complex, bound up as they are with a primitive, unarticulated desire for revenge and with a desire for a past and a present that Halverson has clearly failed to come to grips with. The solution he chooses in this gripping story of man and nature is one of exorcism and spiritual renewal through confrontation.

For the following comments on Kittredge's rich and suggestive story, I am indebted to my colleague Terrill F. Dixon, who has allowed me to quote them in full. "Halverson," Dixon writes in his essay "Ways of Knowing Nature: Scientists, Poets, and Nature Writers View the Grizzly Bear," "clearly wants to avenge the girl's death, but other elements of the story tell us that his quest will be more complex than that. For one thing, park rangers in Glacier have already killed a bear with a belly full of human hair [though Halverson may not know this until Darby tells him at the end of the story], and the trip into Glacier will also take Halverson into territory which he used to travel with his father and which he has not entered since his father's death. He will also take this hunting trip and spiritual quest with Darby, the woman with whom he lives but with whom he cannot talk.

Once he is in the park's back-country, Halverson separates his bear hunt from what the rangers have already done; when the rangers fly over their campsite, he feels that 'we are not in this together.' His own deeper quest is not to be easily realized, however. Halverson kills one bear with his high-powered rifle only to find that death too distant for his purposes. He stalks the second bear with only a knife; he eats the purple-red berries that the bear feeds upon and he comes close enough to smell the bear's' odor of clean rot in the sunlight.' When Halverson starts to close with the bear, now standing on its hind-legs, Darby shoots it. Just as he and the bear are in it together, eating the same food, stalking each other, and confronting each other, so, finally, is Halverson in it with Darby. By letting her shoot the bear which would kill him, he tacitly acknowledges their partnership. The bear hunting in this complex story thus finally becomes more than revenge, it is also the means by which the half-person, Halverson, can move toward possible wholeness, can re-enter the worlds of the park, nature and family and the life of trust with Darby."

While Halverson is the story's focal character, Darby is an interesting character in her own right. She, too, is an inarticulate victim of nightmares, who has thus far been unwilling or unable to come to grips with her life. If Halverson's decision to hunt the bear is premeditated and ritualistic, hers is spontaneous. She too clearly senses the import of the journey. Note, if you will, that she attempts to reestablish communication through sex; note too that, though rebuffed, it is she who later wields the rifle (a clear symbol of masculine potency) that kills the bear, thereby saving Halverson's life. There is much to talk about here and students will doubtless be eager to discuss the story and its strange and powerful mixture of realism, symbolism, and myth.

RING LARDNER, "Haircut"

Lardner's story continues to wear well. Jonathan Yardley, a recent Lardner biographer, is certainly correct when he observes that "The story's enormous impact at the time of its publication and its subsequent appearance in countless anthologies are explained by its conciseness, its tone, and the skill with which it was constructed. Ring did not waste a word in telling it, and he told it exactly right: the barber's droning talk, his mindless laughter as he recalls Kendall's jokes, his unemotional reaction to a gruesome story—all create the mood of the tale at the same time delivering a terse, harsh, commentary on small-town more."

A survey of other critical comments suggest a number of potential approaches:

The practical joker, traditionally a beloved small-town figure, turns out to be miserable, brainless, and cruel; and the barber who admires him is just as bad. Ring was exposing the witlessness of a whole vein of the American comic tradition—the small-town wag who is generally accepted as a genuine humorist. Actually he is degraded and perverse; but there are still innumerable jackasses to laugh at him.

—Donald Elder

There is…another kind of deepening, not in content this time but in the way of presentation. Let us suppose that the narrator of the story had merely told us about people like the barber, people who had some tacit complicity in the card's jokes, and that he himself, the narrator, found such people reprehensible. Given this treatment, we would find ourselves in immediate agreement with his attitude. There would be no shock of the collision between the narrator's attitude and our own. But as things actually stand, there is a shock of collision between the narrator's attitude and our own, a growing need to reassess things and repudiate his attitude. In other words, Lardner has used an inverted and ironical method. The narrator does not represent the author's view, nor our own. The barber is there to belie, as it were, the meaning of the story, and by so doing to heighten our own feelings—even to irritate us to a fuller awareness of what is at stake in the story.

—Cleanth Brooks and Robert Penn Warren

Critical commentary on the story has praised Lardner's excellent use of the disingenuous narrator and his thorough condemnation of a small town that tolerates a Jim Kendall. The women characters should also be carefully considered for in their helplessness against sheer brutality, they confirm that society can tolerate astonishing behavior without serious protest.

—Elizabeth Evans

Whitey the barber is merely insensitive. Though not cruel himself, he provides an appreciative audience for the cruelties of others. It is not that he can't recognize cruelty when he sees it—he concedes that some of Jim's tricks were "a kind of a raw thing"—its just that he doesn't feel their cruelty....

Lardner's method is that of dramatic irony. He presents us with an imperceptive narrator who doesn't feel the horror of the narrative he tells us and who doesn't recognize its full implications. The chief effect of the story is the growing contrast between the admiration of the barber for Jim Kendall and the horror of the reader. The barber sets out to tell what a comical fellow Jim Kendall was, and succeeds in showing him as despicable.

—Laurence Perrine

The ending of the story is often cited as its major weakness. In the words of its critics, the ending is contrived, convenient, melodramatic (Yardley, calls it "a cliché"). But at least two scholars think differently. Charles May (1973) objects to the fact that such critics (and readers) have been all too willing to excuse Jim Kendall's death at the hands of a half-wit as accidental and thus guiltless. Rather, May suggests, "Lardner's satire is even more savage than we have heretofore thought. I suggest that his attack is not just on the practical joker and a small town's obtuse moral sense, but even more on the reader's willingness to approve of the extreme penalty for Jim as his just deserts for his practical jokes. The reader becomes as morally implicated in the death as the barber and the townspeople by accepting what was obviously their use of the idiot Paul to rid themselves of a troublemaker and prankster that they feared and fated." May cites as evidence the fact that Whitey the barber has been told by Doc Stair that Paul is getting better and "that they was times when he was as bright and sensible as anybody else." The same evidence can be cited both by critics who regard the ending not as an accident but as a deliberately contrived murder or by those who suggests that Kendall's death is actually the deliberately arranged suicide of a man whose life has disintegrated. Perhaps the most surprising suggestion comes from Hal Blythe and Charlie Sweet: not only does Whitey the barber understand what is going on and offers an apparent sanction of the killing, but he is, in fact, "the chief instigator of the town's deadly conspiracy."

D. H. LAWRENCE, "The Horse Dealer's Daughter"

This work treats one of Lawrence's favorite themes, the interconnectedness of love and death. As the story opens, the property of the once-prosperous horse farm is about to be sold, leaving the grown children of the horse dealer to find new means for themselves. There seems to be a barrier of some sort between the vital, "horsey" sons of the family and their only sister. She has become progressively more attached to the world of death where (in her mind) her late mother resides. The eldest brother, Joe, seems almost literally a horse, but he is giving up his freedom to "go into harness," marrying the daughter of the man he is going to work for, the steward of a neighboring estate. Following breakfast, Jack Fergusson, a close friend of the middle brother, Fred Henry, drops by to offer his condolences and farewells. Fergusson, a young, unmarried doctor, has depended a good deal upon his friendship with Fred Henry for the routine of his social life. Yet, Jack has hardly even spoken to his friend's sister, Mabel.

Of course, Mabel has had to hold herself aloof for a long time. In her youth, when the horse farm was a going concern, the kitchen was always filled with hired girls of "questionable reputation," and the men who came there were mainly coarse-talking horse dealers. Since the death of her mother and the decline of the farm under the inept management of her brothers, Mabel has dwindled into a mere housemaid, trying to sustain her dignity with the tradespeople of the town, while the family means grew steadily slimmer. All that is left seems to her to be connected with her dead mother, and when the farm is sold, we find that she fully intends to sacrifice her life to that last remaining dignity.

Jack Fergusson is intellectually isolated in the grimy coal mining and farming community and will be even more so when the residents of Oldmeadow have all gone. At the same time, though, the young doctor derives vitality from these people who either work the earth or work under it. And in the churchyard later that day, when Jack happens to catch Mabel's eye as she is tending the grave of her mother, he feels "a heavy power...which la[ys] hold of his whole being, as if he had drunk some powerful drug. He had been feeling weak and done before. Now life came back into him, he felt delivered of his own fretted, daily self." Mabel in that moment embodies the entire life cycle for him—erotic hypnosis, the vital force and its power of renewal, but also the death that awaits everything that is born. Jack's particular circumstances, his education, his work, even the round of social pleasures he enjoys with Fred Henry, are only "frettings" compared to this, Mabel is alluring, intoxicating, and brings out a kind of animal energy in him that makes him forget his fatigue and the sore throat that has been annoying him. At the same time, though, there are suggestions of a kind of bondage and loss of will that frightens him.

There is, in fact, an imaginistic linkage between the grave of Mabel's mother, the smell of the "rotting clay" at the bottom of the pond from which Jack pulls Mabel, and the clasp of the cold water about his knees (and terror of slipping beneath the surface). The same image appears in Mabel's embrace of his legs later, in the farmhouse, where he catches a glimpse of the "animal shoulder" that shows itself from beneath the blanket in which he has wrapped her naked body. At first, Mabel's naive assumption that this young doctor must love her because he has pulled her from the pond and removed her cold, wet clothing seems merely pathetic; but it is soon apparent that she has struck a chord very deep within him. Jack initially resists, thinking how his friends would laugh at him, a trained medical man, losing control of his feelings. But finally he surrenders, and his commitment is real and solid.

URSULA LE GUIN, "Horse Camp"

Ursula Le Guin's "Horse Camp," like so many other works of retrospective literature, recalls and celebrates (with the nostalgia that attaches itself to something forever lost) the exhilarating world of youth. Such works remind us of *what it is like to be young*, or, where we can particularly share the experience being celebrated, *what it was like to have once been young*. In this case it is the adolescent world of summer camp—not any summer camp, mind you, but "Horse Camp." Where adolescent girls are concerned, a world of meaning and significance lurks in the story's very title.

Norah, the younger of the two sisters, is the story's protagonist and focal character, and it is with her experience and growth that we are chiefly concerned. At the beginning of the story she stands apart with her older sister, Sal, in the paved parking lot waiting for the camp bus (a parking lot which is, interestingly enough, juxtaposed against "the far, insubstantial towers of downtown"). On the eve of her first camping experience, Norah is insecure and apprehensive, sheltered by her older sister, the mature ("light-foot and buxom") veteran camper—"quiet and serious," "cool, a tower of ivory."

The pastoral world of horse camp is clearly a world apart, and one of the strengths of the story, surely, is Le Guin's ability to capture and convey through the use of judicious detail the essential spirit of the place. At the center of this world are the horses and the legendary Meredy, the hero of a hundred adolescent stories: "Meredy said, Meredy did, Meredy knew...." Horses traditionally provide special objects of affection and emotional attachment for adolescent girls, as they clearly are for Norah and her sister. For Norah horses are connected with the ride itself ("once she had learned this by heart...[she] knew it forever, the purity, the pure joy") but with the kind of freedom that yields growth and a new and different sense of self. "I was afraid before I came here, thinks Norah, incredulous, remembering childhood." Given her new experiences, the lyrical ending of the story—the mad dash across the landscape ("cantering first and then running flat out, running wild, racing, heading for Horse Camp and the Long Pasture")—is a highly appropriate one, and serves as a final, highly appropriate, act of confirmation and celebration.

DORIS LESSING, "Wine"

The story is likely to prove difficult for students because so much that we would like to know is left unsaid. (In this respect, and others as well, "Wine" can be compared profitably with Hemingway's "Hills Like White Elephants.") For example, we can only speculate about the relationship, present and past, between the two nameless protagonists. Obviously, they know, and have known, each other well for some period of time, for both accept without comment each other's tired, languid state and the long moments of silence that punctuate their conversation. ("They accepted from each other," Lessing notes, "a sad irony; they could look at each other without illusion, steady-eyed.") Setting too—Paris in late winter—is important. Lessing spends a good deal of time, in so short a story, establishing its details. Note particularly how the present setting contrasts markedly with those of the two recollected episodes out of the past. The first of those two recollections (the woman's) is private—we alone have access to her mind; the second (the man's) is shared and becomes the point of contention between them. It is interesting that *she* deliberately draws the recollected incident from him by her questions and comments; and her reaction to it is both immediate and strong. The question on which the story finally turns is why? Is her response appropriate, and if so, in what way?

At some point, the title and its significance need to be considered. Initially the wine seems unimportant in the story; it is ordered and left standing untouched, like the coffee. But Lessing did entitle the story "Wine" and presumably we are meant to think about wine and its role in the story. The man orders the wine immediately after they have both begun to reminisce about other romances with other partners. Did he order it in an effort to restore a sense of romance with his current lover? Or did he simply order the wine because he was recalling a time when wine made him happy? ("It was a glorious night—gathering apples, the farmer shouting and swearing at us because we were making love more than working, and singing and drinking wine.") In the end, the wine seems both a symbol and a catalyst: a symbol of the romantic passion that is, at least temporarily, lacking between this man and woman; and a catalyst of their memories and ultimately of their conflict.

These are two satiated lovers in the winter of the year hearkening back to their youthful springtime. They are momentarily tired of one another in the cool, harsh morning light, and both of them long for some resurrection of youth, moonlight, and passion. The mere fact that the man is willing to describe his memory shows that he knows the woman very well, but it also shows that he is no longer concerned as he might be about hurting her. After all, he is daydreaming about another woman. As he tells his story, she enters it vicariously, merging it with a similar experience in her own past. She fails to see the selfless nobility of the young man's refusal to take advantage of a mere girl and empathizes entirely with the disappointed girl. By the end he seems to become for her a symbol of the thoughtless male who once shattered her own romantic dreams. Although they raise the wine and drink in the story's last line, it is possible to doubt that it will ever again produce for them the Bacchic delight of youth. As the woman puts it:

It's terrible. Terrible. Nothing could ever make up to her for that. Nothing, as long as she lived. Just when everything was most perfect, all her life, she'd suddenly remember that night, standing alone, not a soul anywhere, miles of damned empty moonlight....

The intrusion of the past upon the present leaves both the man and the woman troubled in this interval amid the cycles of their desire.

BERNARD MALAMUD, "The Magic Barrel"

"If you can love her," Salzman tells Leo about his wayward daughter, "then you can love anybody." This, of course, is precisely the point of Malamud's fable-like story of the young, cloistered, and unworldly rabbinical student who comes to confess to himself: "I am not...a talented religious person...I think...that I came to God not because I loved Him, but because I did not." Leo's realization is one of failure: "apart from his parents, he had never loved anyone"—"that he did not love God so well as he might, because he had not loved man." It is this realization that marks the crisis or turning point of the story and brings Leo to a new level of human awareness and commitment. No longer is his interest in wife and marriage a matter of practicality and convenience: "I want to be in love with the one I marry..."

Salzman, the matchmaker, is a comic figure out of Jewish folklore, a dealer in dreams who, Pan-like, partakes of both the supersalesman turned huckster *and* the supernatural—note his sudden, almost magical appearances and reappearances. Students will enjoy discussing and debating his role in the story. The ending, with its suggestive imagery, is deliberately ambiguous. Has Salzman deliberately maneuvered the rendezvous—cheap photograph and all? And what of his prayers for the dead? Are they prayers for Salzman himself and his own guilt—a confession that he has lured Leo to perdition? Or are they prayers of hope for resurrection and redemption through love and human suffering? Has Salzman finally failed as a matchmaker—or is this, in fact, his greatest triumph? What does Leo himself mean when he says to Salzman: "Put me in touch with her...Perhaps I can be of service"?

THOMAS MANN, "Death in Venice"

Mann's "Death in Venice"—whether one counts it as a short novella or long short story—is clearly one of the great works of Western literature. It tells the tragic story of the aging yet dedicated writer, Gustav Aschenbach, and his infatuation with the fourteen-year-old Polish boy, Tadzio, set against the background of a city often associated with death and decay (yet also with love and beauty). As Ignace Feuerlicht has noted 1968), "Aschenbach's encounter with Tadzio signifies the encounter of intellect with beauty, or spirit with life, an encounter which, according to Mann's views, is bound to be short, unsatisfactory, and fruitless." Most critics also agree with Feuerlicht's view that "Death in Venice" reflects Mann's belief that "fascination with death, destruction, and chaos, with the 'abyss,' is inherent in art." The philosophical and symbolic implications which underlie the story's narrative surface are, of course, clearly complex, and it will, no doubt, prove difficult and slow going for many students. It is for this reason that I have tried to provide a large number of "Questions for Study." Fortunately the plot itself is linear and fairly easy to follow. It breaks into five uneven sections or chapters (and includes two flashbacks) which suggests a good way to focus class discussion.

KATHERINE MANSFIELD, "Her First Ball"

The story, it is generally agreed, is firmly rooted in the author's own experience, a dance she attended in 1907 following her return to New Zealand from boarding school in England. "The description of every part of the dance hall is photographic, the stage with the chaperons and orchestra," recalled one of Katherine Mansfield's contemporaries, who was also present: "The decorations were the same. . . . The programmes with their pretty pencils, of which I still have some, the dressing room with its attendants, the benches, passages and double doors were all there." Mansfield even uses real names, perhaps as a way of recalling the immediacy of the original scene in a way that would help her to capture it in words.

The autobiographical element is important to the extent that it explains why Mansfield chose the first person point of view, and thus took on the difficulties imposed by having a narrator whose youth and limited social experience restricts her understanding. Mansfield meets the challenge and with brilliant economy, by using language rich with imagery to capture Leila's impressions and to convey both her excitement and emotion and the dizzying, enchanted world of the dance swirling around her. Note the images of light and dark and the way in which she uses words to suggest motion and music and to give her story its fairy-tale, dream-like quality. Despite Leila's shyness and inexperience, the world of her first ball is one in which the country-bred outsider quickly becomes caught up and spellbound.

The role of the balding fat man is, of course, a most ambiguous one. Who is he? What does he represent? Why has he kept attending such dances for 30 years? Having immediately understood Leila's innocence, what motivates him to dance with her and then to attempt to intrude his disturbing and disillusioning message? Despite her momentary awareness of the truth (or apparent truth) of what he says, Leila manages to capture the former magic of the evening and to save it. She returns to the dance floor and the magical illusion of timelessness returns. But what then, what next?

What of this ending? Are we to assume that Leila really has forgotten and dismissed the lesson about time, mortality and the illusions of life that the fat man has delivered? Or does she psychologically accept at some level the truth that "this first ball [was] only the beginning of her last ball after all"?

There are many questions to consider during class discussion, including the final one I pose in the text itself: "Do you finally consider the portrait of Leila a psychologically valid one?"

KATHERINE MANSFIELD, "Miss Brill"

Mansfield's late story "Miss Brill" has been praised as an impressive psychological portrait of a "marginal" woman—"a genteel . . . observer of life" who "sits on the sidelines and watches the game in all its striving, contending, cruelty, and passion" (Nathan, 1988). It has also been called Katherine Mansfield's "most famous sketch of a woman alone" (Fullbrook, 1986).

The outlines of the story are clear. Miss Brill receives life secondhand. During her Sunday trips to the park she vicariously lives through the lives and emotions of others, whose bits and pieces she witnesses as she sits on the park bench. Priding herself on her ability to interpret the behavior of those who enter her consciousness, Miss Brill fancies that she is the ever-receptive audience in a play. She also fancies that her presence is crucial to its very performance. It is this carefully constructed—and maintained—view of herself, and the meaning and purpose it gives to an otherwise drab and uneventful life, that is shattered by the cruel remarks of the young lovers. Ironically, she greets their arrival with pleasure. They are "hero and heroine" in yet another drama. Humiliated by their gratuitous remark, Miss

Brill returns to her psychologically safe and familiar room, but her happiness is gone—not just this Sunday, but, the ending suggests, for all the Sundays to follow. Miss Brill, who has made so many others the object of scrutiny, has now become scrutinized herself. With their cruel remarks, all the barriers she has so carefully erected against loneliness are swept away.

Kate Fullbrook in a single paragraph captures the woman Katherine Mansfield has created:

> Miss Brill lives alone in France, patching together an income from scraps of English teaching and from reading the newspaper to an invalid. She keeps herself going by reining her expectations in tightly with a chirpy, inconsequentiality of mind and with her conformity to a tattered notion of gentility. Her surroundings smack of the deprivation of a lone woman—a dark little room, her meagre treat of a honey-cake which she looks forward to each week as her only self-indulgence. She most significantly identifies herself with her furpiece, a decayed thing she keeps in a box under her bed, and which represents to her all the luxury and adventure in life that she convinces herself that she shares. She values, too, the sensuality and flirtatiousness of the fur, itself an emblem of the traditional man-fascinating ways out of poverty for a woman that she still obliquely believes apply to herself. But the fur, her only friend, is not what it used to be; even Miss Brill can see that.

Much of the artistry of the story lies in the use of point of view. By telling the story from Miss Brill's point of view, "in the vocabulary and cadences of her mind," "the author intensifies the emotional impact of events." The point of view also blunts the comic aspects of the story. These include Miss Brill's partial or inaccurate reading of situation and event (her "hierarchy of unrealities") as well as the sentimentality with which she invests them. From Miss Brill's perspective it is others who are odd: "Miss Brill had often noticed—there was something funny about nearly all of them. They were odd, silent, nearly all old, and from the way they stared they looked as though they'd just come from dark little rooms or even—cupboards!" Her own room, of course, is "like a cupboard."

As Sarah Sandley has observed (1994), by directing the narrative through the consciousness of a character "who is experienced at evading the present reality of a besetting situation" the narrative itself becomes "*about* the very process of creating narrative fiction." As Fullbrook observes, "The story portrays a consciousness distancing itself from its own suffering isolation with a tremendous degree of pain and yet with a dignity that is in itself a kind of virtue."

The tragedy of Miss Brill, Fullbrook continues, is that she is

> written off as a horror by a code that condemns her on grounds of sex, age, beauty, poverty, and singleness, the same code that Miss Brill herself uses to explain her disappointment with the old couple on the beach and which now comes full circle to indict her as less than human. This is a portrait of a woman caught by the contradictions of social preconceptions that she herself has internalised.

Though the episodes and encounters seem random, they do prepare us in various and subtle ways for the shock of recognition inflicted by the young lovers. Taken separately and together they also shed considerable light on the world in which Miss Brill lives and how she relates to that world. Note the many instances involving insensitive and discourteous behavior, which serves to expose the essential falseness of the sense of community that Miss Brill wants to believe exists among her cast of characters.

Miss Brill is identified throughout with her battered fur piece. As she prepares to venture on one of her Sunday forays into the park she carefully rubs "the life back into the dim little eyes." So complete is this identification that at the end Miss Brill mistakes her own tears of humiliation and defeat for those of the fox itself.

BOBBIE ANN MASON, "Shiloh"

The manifest content here is simple enough—almost insignificant. A young trucker has been injured and cannot drive any longer. His continuing presence at home very soon makes it apparent to his wife that the two of them have very little in common. She continues to grow and find new interests, while he seems to regress further into childishness, sensing that something is wrong between them but unable to grasp the complexities of the situation. Norma Jean's mother recommends a visit to the Shiloh battlefield in hopes that the experience will bring the couple together again, but what occurs there instead is that Norma Jean tells Leroy she is leaving him. The story ends amidst trivial, anticlimactic, muddled perceptions: Norma Jean has walked some distance away from Leroy to stand on the bluffs above the river. Is she going to throw herself off? No, but she seems to Leroy to be gesturing to him—or is she simply doing those exercises she does for her chest muscles? The sky is strangely pale, not "like a patient etherized upon a table," but rather "the color of the dust ruffle Mabel [has] made for their bed."

But for such a simple story about such insignificant people, this piece carries some mighty heavy-duty speculation about history, identity, and event. As Leroy sits by himself at the picnic table, he tries to envision the carnage of the battle of Shiloh, but he can think only of the pieces on the board game or of Virgil Mathis's drug raid on the local bowling alley, or how his mother-in-law reversed the fortunes of that battle, coming *from* Corinth—where she and her husband had spent their wedding night—*to* Shiloh, in bliss and triumph:

> ...and then Norma Jean was born, and then she married Leroy and they had a baby, which they lost, and now Leroy and Norma Jean are here at the same battleground.

And Shiloh becomes once again the scene of a defeat. But what is it that Mason is saying through these vastly unequal comparisons? Is it that the dissolution of this marriage is in any way commensurate with the horror and significance of the battle of Shiloh? The marriage may have lasted had not the couple lost their baby to SIDS, during the showing of *Dr. Strangelove* at a drive-in movie. That film ends with the nuclear destruction of the world. Isn't it a bit trite for one to say "the world ended" for Norma Jean and Leroy as well on that night?

To get some idea of the complexity of the "layering" of levels of significance in the story, one need merely look into the meaning of the characters' names. Mason opens up this question when she has Norma Jean announce to her husband one evening: "Your name means 'the king,'" followed by, "Norma comes from the Normans. They were invaders." Of course, "Norma Jean" was also Marilyn Monroe's real name, and Elvis Presley was called "The King." Leroy's injury reminds one of the crippled Fisher King of myth and "The Wasteland," and he certainly stands amidst the debris of the chivalric tradition, handed down from myth to medieval romance to the American cowboy to the trucker-knight of the road. His steed stands in the back yard rusting, while he does needlepoint design of a scene from the television romance, *Star Trek*.

But what are the modem terms of heroism and romance, anyway? What is the connection between love and war? What have Marilyn Monroe and the Norman conquest to do with any of this? Mabel sends the couple back to the Shiloh battleground because it was where she felt most real and whole and erotically fulfilled, where Norma Jean was conceived. But this ritualistic repetition does not heal her daughter's sterile marriage. In fact, the trip invokes the recollection of a very different kind of "courtship" when Norma Jean was eighteen and pregnant, faced with having to marry a boy she did not particularly love so that her mother would be spared embarrassment in the eyes of the community. Perhaps repetition and regression were once the "cure" for the terror of history, the men pretending generation after generation to be the heroic conquerors, home from the wars to be entertained by their Penelopes or Marilyns with old love songs, "Can't Take My Eyes Off of You" or "I'll Be Back."

But Norma Jean is quite at home with history. She may not be able to repeat the honeymoon dream of her mother, or to stand the idea of being closed up in Leroy's log house like the wife of Peter Pumpkin Eater; but she *can* keep in good physical condition and take composition courses at Paducah Community College. And if these things sound ridiculous, one must ask, "In comparison to what?" Of course, these are little people when compared with the idea of the Hero. But if men gain significance by repetition of the romantic archetype, so do they lose significance. Bobby Ann Mason presents the failure of the compulsion to repeat, and gives us a brave new woman instead. No, not Shakespeare's Miranda, and certainly not Marilyn Monroe, but fully herself, and fully historical.

GUY DE MAUPASSANT, "The Necklace"

Maupassant's classic tale illustrates how the accidental loss of a piece of borrowed jewelry and the genuine adversity that follows in its wake change the life and values of its middle-class heroine. Although "The Necklace" is sometimes criticized for its trick ending, and then dismissed on that basis (as if the ending is the only real point of interest), a careful reading of this apparently artless and simple story confirms that such a verdict is misplaced. The story, in fact, contains an inner consistency of character and motivation that makes the events themselves thoroughly plausible. The irony of the ending is thus anticlimactic and even in a sense unnecessary to the kind of story that Maupassant wishes to tell.

Despite the fact that Maupassant's tale is short, he devotes more than half of it establishing the character of Mme. Loisel and detailing events leading up to the ball and the loss of the necklace. The woman to whom we are introduced is hardly happy. "Feeling herself born for all the delicacies and all the luxuries" she does not have, Mme. Loisel wallows in a self-pity which leaves her "tortured" and "angry." Obsessed with material possessions and social status, she is motivated by a fierce pride that will not allow her to accept the drab realities of her middle-class life. It is her pride that initially leads her to reject "with disdain" the invitation which her husband has gone to "awful trouble" to obtain, and it is this same pride in the form of vanity ("there's nothing more humiliating than to look poor among other women who are rich") that motivates her to borrow the necklace from Mme. Forestier. That the jewels she borrows should be as false as the values that cause their borrowing is both ironic and symbolic.

Once the jewels are lost, and once the Loisels have bought time with a lie, the course of action which they adopt is completely in keeping with the middle-class values which they embody and represent. Rather than having to acknowledge the lie and accept the humiliation, they endure ten years of deprivation and near-poverty in order to make good on their obligation. Interestingly enough, still motivated by pride, Mathilde takes "her part...all of a sudden, with heroism." In the process, as the frequent use of the pronoun "they" suggests, their marriage becomes stronger even as adversity robs her of her beauty and leaves her looking old. "How life is strange and changeful!" Mme. Loisel muses. Mme. Loisel apparently has been "saved," for during these years she has purged herself of the misguided values that were the source of her original undoing.

Why then does she approach Mme. Forestier after ten years and tell the truth? Though many critics find this final scene implausible and contrived, Virgil Scott is substantially

correct when he writes that "this is not the same woman. It is not appearance that is important to her now, but the payment of an 'impossible' debt and pride in having accomplished
the difficult. Ten years before she wanted to be admired for her clothing, her jewels, her
youth. Now she wants to be respected for her character." And it is for this reason that she
smiles "with a joy which was proud and naive at once." Though there is, to be sure, irony
in the discovery that the original jewels were false, this fact in no way diminishes what
Mme. Loisel herself has accomplished and become.

GUY DE MAUPASSANT, "Rust"

In "Rust" Maupassant sensitively and humorously explores an important issue in sexuality about which convention, in his day as in ours, forbade open discussion. As a result, part
of Maupassant's goal in this story is to provide a roundabout definition of what he means by
the title "Rust." Note that in this "definition" we learn much about the causes, effects, and
potential cures for this form of "rust."

Students should like this story. They should be able to see how Maupassant establishes
the relationship between guns and male sexuality, much in the way Richard Wright does in
his story "The Man Who Was Almost a Man." The fiftyish M. Hector has transferred to hunting all of his sexual passion (as well as all his interest in life). Hunting has consumed his bach-
elorhood. In his fascination with guns and sport he has forsaken what might be considered
normal female companionship (and the normal sexuality that such companionship provides), and as a result another of his weapons is allowed to "rust" through disuse. Note that
Maupassant avoids crudity (a larger problem in his day, of course, than in our own) by
defining rust obliquely in roundabout terms that could not possibly corrupt the innocent but
that are completely unambiguous to experienced readers. M. Hector himself develops a
clearly Freudian pattern of symbolism when he explains to his friend. M. de Courville that
he went up to Paris because "Confound it; suppose I misfired!"

M. Hector decides on his own that the cure for his conditions is to be found among the
courtesans of Paris. He visits the best of them, "and they did everything they could. Yes...they
certainly did their best!" He tries a change in diet. He waits patiently. And yet he eventually
realizes that "the only thing I could do was...was...to withdraw, and I did so." In the end, of
course, Mme de Courville observes pragmatically that M. Hector has tried the wrong cure—
"he was frightened, that is all." She invites her friend Berthe to return confident that "When
a man loves his wife, you know...that sort of thing always comes right in the end." Maupassant
does not describe M. Hector's ailment or its potential cure with modern anatomical precision
because his readers would have found such writing tasteless and partly because the humor of the
story owes much to the hesitancy and obvious discomfort with which M. Hector attempts to
bring into service once more a weapon that he has kept locked up for too long.

There is, to be sure, considerable ambiguity in the story's closing sentence, but M. de
Courville's sudden embarrassment, coming after his earlier merriment at his friend's mishap,
seems to suggest that he too may have "misfired" on occasion—even though "When a man
loves his wife, you know [Could the emphasis be on *you*?]...that sort of thing always comes
right in the end."

HERMAN MELVILLE, "Bartleby the Scrivener"

In the opening of "Bartleby," one is struck by the narrators insistence upon how comfortably ensconced he is in the bosom of conventionality, "an eminently *safe* man" who
"do[es] a snug business among rich men's bonds and mortgages and title-deed." He stresses

his normality and reasonableness as a prelude to an experience he is about to relate concerning a singularly odd member of an already odd collection of individuals, the law-copyists or scriveners.

The device Melville uses as a way into the concerns he wishes to treat in his story is similar to that employed by Poe in his poem, "The Raven." That is, both writers create an enigmatic figure who keeps responding with the same word(s) over and over again to whatever question is posed. In their attempt to make sense of this "nonsense," both narrators are drawn into an exploration of their darkest, most thoroughly repressed preoccupations, and in both cases, those preoccupations concern the fear of death and (for want of a better term), "the void."

Makers of fictions are sometimes overly aware of the degree to which "real life" depends upon the majority's ongoing faith in some very shaky assumptions—such as the importance of their work to the world and the desirability of amassing goods far in excess of one's needs. Of course, none of us bears this burden of faith in absolute contentment, but the yoke rests most heavily upon the shoulders whose rewards are least. Turkey and Nippers, each of whom can "copy" (that is, faithfully reproduce what the cultural norms dictate) for half a day, between them are barely able to sustain what Conrad calls "the work of the world." It is no wonder that they are outraged by the refusal of their new colleague to help them maintain their flagging faith in the need to reproduce texts.

At first, the narrator himself shares his employees' outrage, but very soon it is sheer curiosity that draws him further and further under Bartleby's influence. There is awakened in the lawyer a certain speculative quality that the "safe" man of the opening self-description gives little hint of; Bartleby's presence provokes melancholy strains in the narrator's nature, stains of which he himself had been quite unaware, and the tone of the retelling reproduces the uncertainties of this man who ordinarily thinks of the values of his life as quite unproblematic. It seems for a time that the narrator will simply learn to live with this oddity in this life. In fact, he comes to the conclusion that divine Providence has installed the non-functional copyist in his office for some inscrutable reason known only to God. Bartleby is as calm and simple as death itself, and the direct opposite to the great parade of wealth and scramble for fortunes going on in that same quarter of the city, Wall Street.

The narrator's double perspective seems as if it might go unchallenged, but finally he can no longer bear his colleagues' concern over the odd situation their associate allows to persist in his office. It is like a sign of divided loyalties, as if the narrator were not entirely committed to the "real world" of bonds and mortgages and title-deeds. He is, in effect, given a choice between copying the manners and attitudes of his peers and the radical freedom that Bartleby represents which "sees through" life.

Bartleby refuses the meaningless reproduction of texts—and by extension, all social codes and artifacts—the original context of which we can never know. Certainly, the choice of the narrator is clear. He has followed Bartleby's vision as far as he dared and has at least understood what "I would prefer not to" means, and thus the anguished "All, Bartleby! All, humanity!" But the comfortable little man who takes such pleasure in the sheer pronunciation of the "rounded and orbicular"—sounding name of John Jacob Astor is the one who is delivering this tale—perhaps *must* deliver it—like some Wall Street version of Coleridge's Ancient Mariner.

HERMAN MELVILLE, "The Lightning-rod Man"

Much of Melville's fiction—and this certainly includes "Bartleby the Scrivener" and "The Lightning-rod Man"—set out to explore, in part at least, two opposing approaches to life: a positive optimism that is willing to accommodate itself to the world as it is, versus a negative pessimism that recoils before a universe that it either cannot or will not accept.

By the time Bartleby enters the law office of the narrator, it is clear he has weighed the world by his own standards, obscure as they are, and found it unacceptable. But, unlike the aggressive, openly defiant Captain Ahab of *Moby Dick*, Bartleby's resistance takes the form of an ever-increasing passivity and solitude, as symbolized by the loft brick wall and his own "dead wall reveries." His initial tractability and energy disappear, and instead he simply "prefers not to"—a courteous, dignified response which asserts the integrity of his own tragic vision of life.

The lawyer-narrator, on the other hand, is a man of accommodation, a prudential, "eminently sad" man who confesses his "profound conviction that the easiest way of life is the best." He has made his peace with the commercially-oriented world of Wall Street, and, in turn, has been rewarded with the "pleasantly remunerative" office of Mastery in Chancery. For all his expediency, however, the narrator is not a callous, indifferent human being; he is sympathetic to and deeply disturbed by the abject scrivener who steadfastly defies both "common usage" and "common sense." Bartleby makes him feel guilty and uneasy, though he attempts to mask that uneasiness by the slightly humorous, slightly cynical tone he adopts as he tells the story. But when, at length, he is confronted by the "inscrutable scrivener" huddled in death at the base of the prison wall, all he can utter is a plaintive "Ah, Bartleby! All, humanity," a confession that here is a universal mystery which his own widening understanding and genuine sympathy can neither penetrate nor remedy.

Though "The Lightning-rod Man," by contrast, is a humorous story (albeit one that has its center, unmistakably, a basic seriousness of purpose), its narrator's attitudes and values in many way's mirror those of the narrator of "Bartleby," and a comparison of the two story's should make for excellent classroom discussion. "The Lightning-rod Man" takes the form of an entertaining satire on professional doomsters and nay-sayers. Hershel Parker, in an important critical essay (1964), has demonstrated convincingly that it belongs to the genre of the humorous salesman or Yankee peddler story. Thanks to the spadework of Jay Leyda, we have also come to understand that "in the fall of 1853 [the story was first published in *Putnam's Monthly* Magazine in July of 1854] the Berkshires [where Melville was then living] was enduring an intense lightning-rod sales campaign, with advertisements and warnings and editorials on the subject in all the Berkshire papers" [Jay Leyda, *The Complete Short Stories of Herman Melville* (New York, 1949), p. xxvi], and that according to one family tradition Melville himself had an actual encounter with a lightning-rod salesman who chose to ply his trade in time of storm.

There are a number of profitable ways to approach the story as suggested by the growing body of critical attention that the story has received, particularly in recent years. Several of these approaches are suggested by the questions for study. An excellent source for the criticism and scholarship to 1986 is Lea Bertani Vozar Newman's *A Reader's Guide to the Short Stories of Herman Melville*.

SUSAN MINOT, "Lust"

Susan Minot has written to the editor as follows about the genesis and development of "Lust":

> I wrote the first versions of "Lust" while studying in the graduate writing program at Columbia. I remember being pleased at the liveliness of the discussion; the male students seemed particularly disturbed. The original version had many more names (of boys) in it, causing one classmate to ask, "Is she a slut?" Since I was not promoting that particular meaning I cut back many of the names to the masculine pronoun.

The story began as a light-hearted depicting of teenage sexual encounters and became darker as it went along. In this way, I suppose, it imitates life.

The response of Minot's classmates is both understanding and somewhat surprising, for as Christopher Lehmann-Haupt observes in reviewing *Lust and Other Stories* for the *New York Times*, there is "actually very little lust" involved in the story that the author wishes to tell. There are, to be sure, couplings and a kind of random casualness to the encounters that some readers may find disturbing, but the result, the aftermath, is one of sadness, regret, and emptiness. As the narrator notes in the story's final paragraph, "Their blank look tells you that the girl they were fucking is not there anymore. You seem to have disappeared."

What makes the story interesting, I think, is the successful way in which Susan Minot explores sex and sexuality and the nature of male-female relationships which, though focussed on teenagers and the inexperienced young, inevitably (and sadly) spreads across both generations and lifetimes.

The story's title is, of course, significant, for this is not a story about love, but about lust. Or, rather, it seems to be a story about how lust and sex manage to crowd out and negate the possibility of love and leaves the narrator "with an overwhelming sadness, an exclusive gaping worry" with "everything filling up finally and absolutely with death." It also leaves the narrator—having reported on her encounters with at least eighteen boys—with the final admission that "You haven't been able to—to what? To open your heart? You open your legs but can't, or don't dare, anymore, to open your heart." Lust and its culminating sex are easy; its love, finally, that is both difficult and elusive. In the truth of such an assertion lies maturity, adulthood, and the full and final affirmation of selfhood.

In addition to its obvious thematic concern, the story offers a good opportunity to discuss plot (or types of plot). Students, in fact, may have difficulty at first in recognizing this as a story at all. What they need to come to understand, of course, is that the plot of the story which is cumulative rather than linear—that the various encounters the female narrator (now older and wiser and looking backward in retrospect) reports on do logically and perhaps inevitably lead to the comments she delivers on her experiences with the boy-men who enter so briefly into her life.

Minot's story is filled with statements which not only expand our thematic understanding of the story, but which should make for provocative classroom discussion, For example,

> For a long time, I had Philip on the brain. The less they notice you, the more you got them on the brain.

> Teenage years. You know just what you're doing and don't see the things that start to get in their way.

> Sleeping with someone was perfectly normal once you had done it. You didn't really worry about it. But there were other problems. The problems had to do with something else entirely.

> The more girls a boy has, the better. He has a bright look, having reaped fruits blooming. He stalks around, sure-shouldered, and you have the feeling he's got more in him, a fatter heart, more stories to tell. For a girl, with each boy it's as though a petal gets plucked each time.

> After sex, you curl up like a shrimp, something deep inside you ruined, slammed in a place that sickens at slamming, and slowly you fill up with an overwhelming sadness, an exclusive gaping worry.

Without much encouragement, students should be willing to discuss the extent to which such observations about male-female relationships ring true to their own experience, and how. The challenge for the instructor will be to turn that discussion back upon the story itself and what Minot is finally trying to tell us.

ALICE MUNRO, "Meneseteung"

In choosing Alice Munro's "Meneseteung" for inclusion in *Best American Short Stories* for 1989, editor Margaret Atwood (herself, of course, an accomplished short story writer) made the following comment:

> "Meneseteung" is, for my money, one of Alice Munro's best and, in the manner of its telling, quirkiest stories yet. It purports to be about a minor sentimental 'poetess'...living in a small, raw, cowpat-strewn, treeless nineteenth-century town....Our sweet picture of bygone days is destroyed, and, in the process, our conceptions of how a story should proceed.

Atwood, of course, is correct. Moreover, it would seem to offer (as the Questions of Study suggest) a good place to begin classroom discussion of the story. "Meneseteung" most assuredly is an unconventional and aborted love story, whose plot and ending very much belie our expectations and our "poetic" sense of how things ought to be. It is not so much that small-town poetesses do not die as old-maid spinsters, but rather that when the potential for love comes—as it clearly does in the guise of the well-to-do widower Jarvis Poulter—we are led to expect a far different ending to the affair. Students should find this irony alone interesting.

Some additional comments and observations:

- The unnamed narrator (whose personality, values, attitudes, motives, and expectations we need to establish and explore in the course of discussion) goes to considerable length to reconstruct the life, appearance and personality of the long-dead poetess as well as the character and personality of the town in which she lived. The latter is, to be sure, as Atwood has reminded us, hardly the epitome of small town life as we often romanticize it. Meneseteung is by and large an unhappy place whose daily round of life is characterized by poverty, illness, insanity, and premature and accidental death. Interestingly enough, its residents seem to confirm and reinforce rather than mitigate or redeem their environment. They are unkind to their own (the town drunk Queen Aggie) and to strangers alike, who become the target for speculation and suspicion. Note that hometown eccentrics who cannot be cured by home-made remedies are sent off to the asylum as a matter of course.
- The town is not even redeemed by nature. Here the rural scenes are by no means pastoral—Meneseteung is a world of

> Manure piles...and boggy fields full of high, charred stumps, and great humps of brush waiting for a good day for burning. The meandering creeks have been straightened, turned into ditches with high, muddy banks. Some of the crop fields and pasture fields are fenced with big, clumsy uprooted stumps, others are held in a crude stitchery of rail fences. The trees have all second growth. No trees along the roads or lanes or around the farmhouses, except a few that are newly planted, young, and weedy looking.

- It is against such a background that we are introduced to the story of Almeda Roth and Jarvis Poulter. In so doing, Munro spends considerable time establishing the mores and sensibilities that govern the relationships of the town, particularly those that govern courtship and marriage. And it is precisely against such mores and sensibilities that Almeda and Jarvis Poulter grope toward one another and fail (grotesquely and tragically) to connect.

- Margaret Atwood concludes the introductory comments noted above with the observation by suggesting that the last seven lines of the story are "an epigraph for the act of writing itself." For Atwood the story is one that finally has something to say about literary art. I think that students will enjoy coming to grips with the implications of her statement, particularly in the context of their own discussion and understanding of the story.

ALICE MUNRO, "A Real Life"

Alice Munro contributed the following note about the source of her story to *Best American Short Stories 1992* in which it was republished:

> When I was finding out all sorts of things, a few years ago, about Albania in the early years of the twentieth century, I discovered the tradition of the Albanian Virgin. This was a woman who was allowed to own property, carry weapons, smoke and carouse with the men, and be waited on by women at table, all provided she gave up one thing—sex—forever and ever. It wasn't, then, inherent weakness of mind or body that made women unfit for lives of independence, unfit for companionship or conversation, it was sex pure and simple. I thought about how this had been true to some degree in my own society, which did contain the idea and the reality of the somewhat absurd, somewhat ridiculed, but often heroic and not unenvied, apparently not unhappy, sexless woman. So I made one of these the heroine of a romance. Then I had to have Millicent give her the final push, because Millicent believes that people should never be allowed to get out of happy endings.
>
> I got three stories out of that Albanian obsession and only one of them even mentions Albania.[22]

Munro's statement is both provocative and intriguing, and suggests an excellent entree into the story, though we must be careful to remember D. H. Lawrence's dictum to trust the tale and *not* its teller. Some other observations:

- Dorrie Beck is clearly the focal character of a story about three most interesting women. Dorrie is initially presented to us in precisely the kind of masculine terms that Munro uses above to describe the Albanian Virgin. Dorrie herself displays little interest in, or evidence of, the feminine. (In fact, we are later told that, until the day of her wedding she has never worn silk stockings or a brassiere.) She is "a big, firm woman with heavy legs," who has "remarkable strength for lugging furniture about, and could do a man's work." An expert hunter and trapper, her knowledge and skills rival or surpass the men of her Ontario community. She lives in a house whose furniture consists largely of her "traps and guns and the boards for stretching rabbit and muskrat skins." In such an environment housekeeping becomes irrelevant and largely nonexistent. Yet it is precisely these masculine attributes that attracts Wilkie Speirs, the rich Australian, to her.
- Their first meeting is hardly auspicious. Dorrie is late. She then arrives wearing a dress "suitable for a little girl or an old lady," "shoes that had been so recently and sloppily

---

[22]Alice Munro, "Contributors' Notes," *Best American Short Stories 1992* (Boston, 1993), p. 370.

cleaned that they left traces of whitener on the grass," and "wet hair...crimped...into place with bobby pins." She resembles, the narrator says, "a doll with a china head and limbs attached to a cloth body firmly stuffed with straw." Her opening conversation is about shooting the feral cat, and she even mistakes Mr. Speirs for the local minister (a man she might well be presumed to recognize). "Dorrie acknowledged the introduction and seemed unembarrassed by her mistake." Doubtless she was, for Dorrie Beck is clearly an original.

- Marriage (a marriage that without Millicent's push might well never have taken place) brings with it transformation. Removing her dead brother's coat (and symbolically leaving the world that he has largely defined and provided her), Dorrie emerges "gleaming, miraculous, like the pillar of salt in the Bible." The marriage that follows does precisely for Dorrie what the wise and caring Millicent (with her "absolute personal judgments") says it will: "Marriage takes you out of yourself and gives you a real life." I find particularly interesting the changes that Dorrie's marriage brings both before and after her husband's death.

- What of Muriel Snow, the piano teacher, with her penchant for flamboyant blue clothes, painted nails, crepe dresses, and Spanish perfume? Unlike Dorrie, Muriel openly courts masculine admiration and in fact gets herself in trouble in the community because of her "male friends." (Millicent calls her "bewitching.") Muriel freely jokes about getting married and challenges Porter to find her a husband. She too, we are told in the story's coda, undergoes transformation through marriage. But how different the apparent results. To what extent, we may well ask, does Muriel inherit "a real life"? And if, as Munro says, Dorrie Beck's story has "a happy ending," what can we say of the ending to Muriel's story?

- Millicent's relationship to both Dorrie and Muriel is also important. Muriel is not Millicent's first choice for best friend. Dorrie apparently is. Note that Millicent has married a man nineteen years her senior. Note too her attitude toward sex even within the context of marriage.

JOYCE CAROL OATES, "Four Summers"

The most powerful device in this story is repetition, which is finally revealed to be cyclicality as well. In the first section the girl, who will be the story's center of consciousness, is very young, probably about four, and still very attached to her mother. The mother is making a great fuss over "Sissy," whom she hugs in relief at finding safe. The end of the segment is marked by the little girl's first awareness of mortality: a bird has become caught in the water, and the boys are stoning it to death. She can remember saying to herself, "If the bird dies, then everything can die, I think."

In the second segment, set in the same locale, of course, only the father, the girl and one brother are in the scene. The mother is home with a new baby, and the girl has been displaced as the center of her mother's attention. The children's father is still torn between his own pleasure and his sense of duty to his family. Unlike the first vignette, however, this time he manages to break away from his friends to pay attention to the children. Silly, Jerry mutters, "All he does is drink....I hate him" and again, "I hate him, I wish he'd die." The narrator, perhaps eight or ten now, has a very keen eye for unpleasant detail: the trash strewn about, the mosquitoes, the flies clustering around spilled pop on the table, the bartenders dirty apron, and so forth. There is a suggestion that her longing for more idealized surroundings is related to the girl's awakening sexuality, for she also notices with approval the strength in her father's arms and the flatness of his stomach. The girl notices too, though, that her father is not only a heavy drinker, but does everything with a kind of unhealthy strenuousness. The three row to an island, where the children play for a while.

When they return to the boat, they find their father vomiting. The two are frightened by this, and the narrator fits the incident into the pattern of mortality with which she associates this place.

In the third segment, the girl is fourteen, and has been dragooned into coming along to the lake to help take care of her little sister. Typically for one of her age, she is bored with having to be out with the family and is rather ashamed of them. She thinks they are too loud: "I know everyone is staring at us." Her animosity toward her mother has really jelled by now. She is ashamed of the way her mother looks and can't believe she was ever the pretty young woman in the family photographs. Her attraction to the older man in the parking lot is clearly related to the feelings she has for her father; but when he begins kissing her she pulls away, frightened. The flirtation has gone beyond her understanding.

In the final section, the narrator is now a young woman, pregnant, and married to a man her own age. Her father is dead. They are visiting the same lakeside bar, and she sees a man there that she believes to be the one who had kissed her years before. She is attracted to him, but she wonders why he and his friends seem so worn out, so tired. Of course, it is simply age. As she looks at him, she begins to cry. She is crying for herself, for the other foreclosed possibilities of her life. She is young and pretty as her mother was when we first saw the family in this bar. She is once more made aware of the loss of her father, of the cycle of generations as it begins again, with her children, in this place. She tells herself that she loves her own life, the one she has chosen,

> I am terrified at being left with them. I watch the man at the door and think I could have loved him. I know it. I did nothing. I was afraid. Now he has left me here and what can I do?

The man is associated in her mind with the (necessarily) transcendent love she felt for her father, the kind of love that she now imagines might lift her out of the shadow of the mortality that she was deciphering the shape of, stage by stage, in her other visits to the lake. This is what lurks in the loss of her mother's first fixation upon her (associated with the dead bird), and in her realization of the limited nature of parental love (once thought boundless) as she hears her mother scream to her little sister that she was "an accident." The shadow has come still closer in the death of her father, and in her failure to take up the radical ecstasy offered by the stranger. And finally, her marriage and pregnancy have made her see (especially clearly in that place) that she is condemned to repeat the whole deadly pattern.

JOYCE CAROL OATES, "Where Are You Going, Where Have You Been?"

Like so many of the stories in Fiction 100, this is a story of initiation, the familiar rite of passage from childhood innocence to adult experience. But according to Joanne V. Creighton, "'Where Are You Going,' is more than a tale of the inevitable seduction of a young girl like Connie." In the process of recording the stages of Connie's sexual initiation, Oates also captures and exposes the false yet seductive values that define not only Connie herself but countless other members of her vain and spoiled middle-class generation: "the vacuousness, cheapness, and narcissism of...[those] who have nothing better to do than to stroll up and down a shopping center plaza looking for excitement. The implications of the title are that Connie has not been asked, 'Where are you going, where have you been?' with any rigor by her nagging mother and her indifferent father." Such an indictment, sadly, is as true today as it was at the time of the story's first publication in 1966. No doubt this explains, in part at least, why it "works" so well in the classroom.

Appropriately enough, as Marie Urbanski points out, the organizing metaphor of the story "the narrative's *zeitgeist* and *leitmotive*"—is popular music. "The recurring music… while ostensibly innocuous realistic detail, is in fact the vehicle of Connie's seduction and because of its intangibility, not immediately recognizable as such. Attesting to the significance of the *zeitgeist* in this narrative, 'Where Are You Going…'is dedicated to Bob Dylan, who contributed to making music almost religious in dimension among the youth. It is music—instead of an apple—which lures Connie, quickens her heartbeat; and popular lyrics which constitute Friend's conversation and cadence—his promises, threats, and the careless confidence with which he seduces her." This rather hostile view of popular music might well be contrasted with the more sympathetic treatment of music and musicians in "Sonny's Blues" by James Baldwin.

The dominating figure of the story is the sinister and thoroughly frightening Arnold Friend, and just what we are to make of him is, of course, central to our final understanding of Oates' tale. He is, to be sure, an elusive, enigmatic, and most suggestive figure. For Joyce W. Wegs, Friend combines the "grotesque portrait of a psychopathic killer masquerading as a teenager"; the demon lover of the traditional folk ballad "who carries away his helpless victim"; Satan, "the archdeceiver and source of grotesque horror…in disguise" whose entrance is explicitly prepared for in the portrayal of "popular music and its values as Connie's perverted version of religion"; and "the incarnation of Connie's unconsciously erotic desires and dreams but in uncontrollable nightmare form." Wegs' suggestions are supported by Joyce Carol Oates' own statement that "Arnold Friend is a fantastic figure: he is Death, he is the 'elf-knight' of the ballads, he is the Imagination, he is a Dream, he is a Lover, a Demon, and all that."

Oates' story is marvelously complex and more than repays careful analysis and discussion. One interesting line of inquiry, particularly relevant to users of *Fiction 100*, is set forth by Joan D. Winslow in her essay "The Stranger Within," which compares Oates' story with Nathaniel Hawthorne's "Young Goodman Brown." Both stories, Winslow believes, are concerned "with the human tendency to deny the evil inherent in human nature." And despite their obvious differences, Winslow also sees important similarities between Connie and Goodman Brown.

> The most significant similarity seems to be the connection with a sexual initiation. The [devil] figures [of Arnold Friend and Hawthorne's stranger in the forest] appear to the two protagonists at a time in their lives when both are entering into sexual experience. Brown is "three months married," and the marriage, we assume, has discovered in him a sexual passion he had been unaware of before and is having difficulty accepting.…Connie, if we are to take as true Arnold's statement, "You don't know what that is but you will," has not yet experienced sexual intercourse but she is moving toward it. She spends hours parked in dark alleys with the boys she meets. So far these tentative experiments with sex seem to her "sweet, gentle, the way it was in the movies and promised in songs." But she is conscious of another attitude about sex, which she rejects: "the way someone like June [her older sister] would suppose." These repressed negative feelings of revulsion, fear, and guilt appear to Connie in the projected figure of Arnold Friend. For Arnold proposes to become her lover and to initiate her fully into sensuality.… Her feelings cause her to associate Arnold with danger, nightmare, and death, just as Brown's guilt entangles sex with evil and loss of faith in virtuousness. Connie is moving tentatively toward an experience she—like Brown—will be unable to handle emotionally. Neither protagonist is able to accept the full reality of his/her sexual nature, but instead turns it into something evil and frightening and projects it in the form of a devil.

Winslow's article is well worth reading in its entirely in preparation for a class discussion exploring the many parallels between the two stories.

174

FLANNERY O'CONNOR, "A Good Man Is Hard to Find"

Flannery O'Connor's "A Good Man Is Hard to Find" is one of the author's most praised and most frequently anthologized and analyzed short stories. "One reason for its popularity," Fredrick Asals suggests, "may well be precisely that…[it] writes large the representative O'Connor themes and methods—comedy, violence, theological concern—and thus makes them quickly and unmistakably available. But another, surely, is the primordial appeal of the story, for 'A Good Man Is Hard to Find' captures a very old truth, that in the midst of life we are in death, in its most compelling modern form."

The story breaks itself into two separate halves. The first is given over to the family and their journey, and provides O'Connor with the opportunity to present her vision of the banality, superficiality, and absurdity of modern life. The dominant mode of presentation is comic. The author uses distortion, irony, and satire to particularize and expose her characters and the quality of the life they share with (or inflict upon) one another. The dominating figure is the grandmother and her self-righteous and sentimental piety, her condescending and xenophobic attitudes, and her pretension of Southern gentility ("anyone seeing her dead on the highway would know at once that she was a lady"). Note here and throughout how O'Connor utilizes imagery fusing the human and animal worlds as a technique for characterization.

The journey continues across Georgia toward the episode at The Tower with Red Sammy Butts. Butts views himself as a perpetual victim in a world in which "Everything is getting terrible." The grandmother's rejoinder that "People are certainly not nice like they used to be," and the example she cites to prove her argument further serve to reveal her character. She is, as Sister Kathleen Feeley notes, "A self-centered romantic…[who] arranges reality to suit herself when she can, and indulges in fantasy when she cannot." Their exchange also touches upon "goodness," a refrain that is to become central to the story.

It is, of course, the grandmother herself and her conscious or unconscious (but certainly selfish) forgetfulness which causes the accident and is responsible for the tragedy that follows. Now the pace of the story quickens. Comedy yields to crisis and crisis to tragedy. Though the ironic, detached narrative voice remains the same, the grandmother yields center stage to the Misfit, and the story itself, until this point apparently without direction, assumes a sharp and intense focus. The Misfit is one of O'Connor's most memorable grotesques. What we are to make of him, of the philosophy he utters, and of the precise meaning of the grandmother's attempt to embrace him as "one of my babies," constitutes the story's major interpretive problem.

Precise answers are elusive as the volume and diversity of the critical commentary suggests:

> The grandmother dominates the first half of the story; through its events one sees that her inability to grasp reality truly alienates her from its spiritual extensions. When the Misfit enters, he brings a different kind of alienation: he has an absolutely honest conviction of reality which embodies all reason and no faith. His agnosticism cuts him off from the supernatural world. The violent conflict of these two views marks the advent of grace.…Faith implies an acceptance of mystery, which, for the Misfit, is impossible, because he has to know "why." The story leaves open the possibility that the grandmother's mysterious action of love will open the Misfit's mind to the reality of mystery.
>
> —Sister Kathleen Feeley

"It's no real pleasure in life"—that is the existentialist's answer to the meaning of life and it is Flannery O'Connor's answer to that answer. Since the acceptance of Christ necessitates an act of faith, it is emotionally—not logically—convincing.

"If we could prove today that God did not exist," Voltaire said, "it would be necessary tomorrow to create him." "A Good Man Is Hard to Find" suggests the consequences if man refuses to perform that act; by rejecting the Christian view, the story suggests, man compounds original evil, he creates a world in which "there [is] not a cloud in the sky not any sun," in which "the line of woods [gapes] like a dark open mouth."

—Virgil Scott

The Misfit denies the resurrection in deed and thereby the possibility of ulti-mate meaning in life, yet seems in the end to imply a desire to accept it; he is at least painfully dissatisfied with the fruit of his choice. Although the grandmother seems initially to deny ultimate meaning in word, she plainly accepts it in both deed and word. The Misfit himself acknowledges how the extreme situation has revealed her essential goodness. "She would have been a good woman," he tells Bobby Lee, "if it had been somebody there to shoot her every minute of her life." Her appearance in death confirms the renewal implied in his words; her legs are crossed under her "like a child's" and "her face [is] smiling up at the cloudless sky."—Although it is the Misfit's word that illumines the grandmother's option and ours—the promise of renewal the belief in life offers—it is the grandmother's confession that reveals a sure basis of human goodness, the admission of our involvement in the sins of the world.

—John R. May

O'Connor's own remarks on this story…leave of course no doubt where she felt herself committed. Emphasizing the grandmother's recognition of The Misfit and calling it her "moment of grace," she insisted that the assumptions underlying her writing were those of "the central Christian mysteries"…And it would seem diffi-cult, watching the grandmother reach out to The Misfit as "one of (her) own babies" or responding to the overtones of her final posture…seriously to dispute this element in the story.

—Frederick Asals

As Asals suggests, Flannery O'Connor in her letters and other writings provides numer-ous hints and suggestions about the story and what it meant to her. But in the process, in a 1961 letter "To a Professor of English," she also delivered a timely warning about the interpretive process itself:

The meaning of a story should go on expanding for the reader the more he thinks about it, but the meaning cannot be captured in an interpretation. If teach-ers are in the habit of approaching a story as if it were a research problem for which any answer is believable so long as it is not obvious, then I think students will never learn to enjoy fiction. Too much interpretation is certainly worse than too little, and where feeling for a story is absent, theory will not supply it.

FRANK O'CONNOR, "Guests of the Nation"

Though first published more than fifty years ago, Frank O'Connor's "Guests of the Nation" continues to have a powerful and arresting effect upon the reader. William Tomory summarizes O'Connor's achievement well when he writes that

The story's starkness and lucidity beggar critical commentary; it is quite simply one of the most eloquent commentaries on the inhumanity of war. As in most great stories, the elements of character, plot, theme, and diction are deftly handled. In less than 5,200 words, O'Connor vividly individualizes six characters: the two Englishmen, the three Irish rebels, and the old woman whose cottage has been commandeered. The plot is fluid, inevitable in its relentless logicality once Donovan has punctured the halcyon serenity of the opening scene with his retaliatory notions. The theme receives no overt statement from character or narrator; the events and the characters' reactions to them speak plainly enough. The final line of the story approaches a thematic statement, but its colloquially rendered sentiment is natural enough given the traumatic event which occurred in the bog: "And anything that ever happened to me after I never felt the same about again."

O'Connor's story "works" extremely well in the classroom and offers any number of interesting and provocative topics for student writing.

The development of the story's plot, characterization, and conflict is perhaps best understood by directing students to a close study of each of the story's four sections. The atmosphere in section one is relaxed. The reality of civil war, though reported, is barely noticeable, and the emphasis is on the camaraderie which has developed between Bonaparte and Noble and their British prisoners. The four behave exactly as you would expect "chums" to: they joke and banter, engage in an ongoing, almost ritualistic, game of cards which the phlegmatic Belcher deliberately stops short of winning, and argue (at least Noble and Hawkins do) over politics and religion. The Britishers have made themselves at home—they are "guests" in a country not their own—and in their easy and amiable interactions with one another they underscore the possibility for human relationships that transcend, if temporarily, the differences of nationality, politics, and religion. The only disquieting notes—ones we are likely to overlook—are the waspish comments of the old woman. In the context of the atmosphere of the first section, her explanation of the origins of World War I have a comic ring about them. Her remarks, however, are prophetic: "nothing but sorrow and want can follow the people that disturb the hidden powers." "A queer old girl," Bonaparte calls her, but her words of warning resemble those of choral characters in Greek tragedy.

Section two introduces Jeremiah Donovan, and Bonaparte's observation that "it suddenly struck me that he had no great love for the two Englishmen," gives way to the more disturbing discovery that Belcher and Hawkins are hostages who may be shot in reprisal. It is important to understand how the impact of this discovery registers psychologically on both Bonaparte and Noble and how this impact, in turn, clarifies the story's conflict and intrudes a new tension.

Section three abruptly intensifies this tension with the news of the shootings in Cork. The suddenness with which the news is delivered serves to increase its emotional impact on both reader and character alike. The response of each of the characters is very much in keeping with what we have come to know about them. Donovan mumbles something about duty. Bonaparte feels sick and wishes the responsibility would pass from his hands. At the brink of crisis Bonaparte's empathy is underscored with the comment (concluding section three): "I had the feeling that it was worse on Noble than on me."

Section four carries the story's plot to what now is clearly an almost predetermined ending. The events of the section, and the way they are played off against setting and atmosphere, the conversation that ensures among the characters, and Bonaparte's own recollected observations upon those events, must be studied closely if one is to appreciate just how skillful O'Connor is in constructing the story's emotionally wrenching conclusion. Also to be considered are the final paragraphs when Bonaparte and Noble return to the old lady's House in the aftermath of the shootings. Here the silence, punctuated only by "the shrieking of the birds dying out over the bogs," sets a most appropriate stage for Bonaparte's quiet, earnest, and thoroughly convincing confession of initiation.

TILLIE OLSEN, "I Stand Here Ironing"

As William Van O'Connor once observed, Tillie Olsen "writes about anguish." The story, despite the difficulties imposed by the psychological order of events, is simple enough. A mother, who is in the middle of performing one of the household tasks that defines her maternity, meditates upon her nineteen-year-old daughter's past in an effort to explain her behavior to a psychologist or counselor (or, perhaps, given the statement "You must have seen it in her pantomimes," Emily's teacher). There is indeed anguish in responding to the request, "I stand here ironing," the story begins, "and what you asked me moves tormented back and forth with the iron." The mother's meditation moves backward in time, with occasional returns to the present as it intrudes back into her consciousness. She is trying to understand: "to render, to sift, to weigh, to estimate, to total" in order not to become "engulfed with all I did or did not do, with what should have been and what cannot be helped."

In the course of her meditative dialogue we learn a great deal about the mother and the details of her life. It has not been an easy one. Making certain that students understand the mother's difficulties (which may mean having to explain what it was like to have to struggle through the Depression of the 1930s and the years of World War II) and how they contribute to her development and the situation in which she now finds herself provides an interesting and helpful way of getting into the story and its larger dimensions. (Interestingly enough, there is certainly sufficient "modernity" about the mother's life for some students, regardless of age, to evoke empathy at once.) We also need to try to reconstruct Emily's lonely childhood and troubled adolescence and the way she came to see the world and respond to it.

Despite the fact that "I Stand Here Ironing" is often anthologized and now enjoys a reputation as something of "a classic," it has produced surprisingly little formal critical response. Perhaps the best to date is the article published by Joanne S. Frye in 1981 (see bibliographical section), who makes the following points:

- "In such statements as 'my wisdom came too late,' the story verges on becoming an analysis of parental guilt. But though the mother expresses frequent regret for her own past limitations and failings, she is not at all insisting on guilty self-laceration. Rather she is scorching for an honest assessment of the role of cultural necessity which nonetheless allows for individual responsibility....At the same time, she insists upon the power and significance of her own actions within those limiting circumstances: that, of course, is the premise for the whole narrative reconstruction of the past through the self-awareness founded in present knowledge."
- "Her actual absolution—to the extent that she is seeking absolution from parental guilt—does not come in the particular recognition of past success or failure. Rather it comes in the growing emphasis upon Emily's separateness and Emily's right to make her own imprint upon the world in which she lives."
- "The tension in Emily's personality—which has continually been defined as light and glimmering yet rigid and withheld—comes to a final focus in the self-mocking humor of her allusion to the most powerful cultural constraint on human behavior: nothing individual matters because 'in a couple of years we'll all be atom-dead....' Emily does not, in fact, succumb to that despairing view [and neither does her mother].... And when she (the mother) goes on from her despairing inability to 'total it all' to the story's conclusion, she recenters her thoughts on the tenuous balance between the powerful cultural constraints and the need to affirm the autonomy of the self in the face of those constraints: 'Let her be....There is still enough left to live by.'"
- "There cannot be—either for parent or for storytellers final coherence, a final access to defined personality, or a full sense of individual control. There is only the enriched understanding of the separateness of all people—even parents and children—and the necessity to perceive and foster the value of each person's autonomous selfhood."

- "The metaphor of the iron and the rhythm of the ironing establish a tightly coherent framework for the narrative probing of a mother-daughter relationship. But the fuller metaphorical structure of the story lies in the expansion of the metaphorical power of the relationship itself. Without ever relinquishing the immediate reality of motherhood and the probing of parental responsibility, Tillie Olsen has taken that reality and developed its peculiar complexity into a powerful and complex statement on the experience of responsible selfhood in the modern world."

Students may have a problem following the story's sequence of events or plot (covering nineteen years), which are ordered psychologically as they are recollected by the mother as she meditates on the past. While such a method places additional burdens on the reader (and forces us to read more carefully), it does add realism to the story by making it ring true to what we know of our own meditations and reveries. It also forces us to become participants in the reconstruction itself, and as such enlists our empathy on behalf of the mother and her situation.

Interesting as well is the question of who the students tend to sympathize with most—Emily or her mother—and how those sympathies may change in the course of class discussion. If the class is made up of traditional college-age students, it would be surprising if they did not, initially at least, take Emily's part. In the best of all situations, the class will contain some older students who can help the teacher provide the necessary balance and perspective.

DOROTHY PARKER, "Big Blonde"

> Popularity seemed to her to be worth all the work that had to be put into its achievement. Men liked you because you were fun, and when they liked you they took you out, and there you were. So, and successfully, she was fun. She was a good sport. Men liked a good sport.

This story might well be called "Requiem for a Party Girl." Hazel Morse is a party girl—not a prostitute, but a kind of American geisha, who has studied the art of entertaining men, has worked very hard at it, and up to a point has been fairly successful. Therefore, the course of her life is pretty much a steady slide into desperation. Having denied herself, feeling most comfortable with the kind of man who is affable and shallow, "lots of laughs," she makes the mistake of marrying one of the crowd she hangs around with in the bars. He is a hard drinker, but at the time Hazel does not have to drink much to be fun and lighthearted. She feels content being married because she does not have to perform all the time, entertaining her man when she is not in the mood for it. But in a short while, her husband finds married life too dull and drifts back to the loose, carefree, escapist society he and Hazel were part of before their marriage.

Eventually, Hazel is brought back to another version of her "good time girl" days by a neighbor who introduces her to a series of men, out-of-towners—salesmen, mostly—who have their serious attachments at home. And it is home, to a degree, that women like Hazel are to help them forget. They are never to insist upon their own needs, but always to be wholly selfless, available, and unserious. Any suggestion of pain or sadness must be strictly stifled, kept from spoiling the party. Hazel finds herself beginning to identify with the cab horses who are also responsible for giving the customers their joyrides, and then are beaten mercilessly when they finally collapse out of neglect. Hazel is not quite destitute; Parker does not have her character suffer particularly from material need. Rather, it is the deprivation of any significance or dignity to her life, any return for the affection or gaiety she is constantly required to furnish, pulling the load of other people's moods regardless of the state of her own emotions. Not that these people are asking any depth of attachment; that is the last thing they want. And so Hazel's life is slowly drained of any sense of worth or of being genuinely needed. More and more, liquor fills the space, keeps her anesthetized to the meaningless-ness around her, the nullification of her capacity for love. Finally, without passion, with a feeling of relief (almost of elation at her little joke about being "nearly dead"), Hazel attempts suicide. It is a very mixed blessing that she is discovered by her cleaning woman, who fetches a doctor to revive her. Now, the greatest thing she has to pray for is that "alco-hol will once again be her friend," deadening her senses enough so that she may pretend to be cheerful, for her manfriend, Art. Nettie urges her, "You cheer up now," because Nettie has her work. Something to do. She is necessary to the people who depend on her. Hazel replies, "Yeah," and "Sure." There is no escape, no rebirth, no renewal—just a reawakening to the same nightmare.

Hazel's story is extreme in some respects, certainly unrelievedly depressing, and gener-ically pathetic rather than tragic. But that's precisely the point, perhaps. Tragedy in the traditional sense takes place around the conflicting choices made by a towering ego, usually male. It is hard to say that Hazel Morse even chooses. She is placed upon a course in which the childhood value of being a "good girl" is purchased only at the price of her own selfhood. Dorothy Parker is not simply writing the story of a sadsack. The piece seethes with her own rage. She is far from being Hazel, perhaps, but to the degree that Hazel's fate is institutional rather than particular, Hazel is a kind of American Everywoman.

ROBERT PHILLIPS, "Surprise!"

At the request of the editor, author Robert Phillips addresses his story:

This story was written after a conversation I had with the wife of a friend. The friend was a noted American writer who was down on his luck. He'd lost his job as an editor in a New York publishing house; he'd accepted a contract for a new novel, yet hadn't written a word in seven years; and he was drinking heavily. Late every afternoon he began mixing vodka martinis. Late every evening he'd begin what his wife called "D & D"—Drinking and Dialing. He'd call up everyone he knew (and a few he didn't) and tell them his problems, or tell them off if he'd per-ceived some imagined slight. Once he called up a novelist who'd just won the Nobel Prize, to tell him what a lousy writer he was.

This of course is a terrible situation, but from it I concocted a comedy. At least when I read the story in public, the audience laughs.[23] The protagonist's inability to remember making dozens of phone calls results in a series of embarrassing intru-sions upon his household. And, embarrassing as it is, the protagonist obviously learns nothing from his ordeal, because at the story's end he discovers himself to be drinking and dialing once more.

The character, Elliott Fallick, appears in a number of interrelated stories I have been writing over a period of years. Some readers have objected to his surname, thinking it contrived or crude. Actually, I appropriated it from a Houston gossip columnist, even more improbably, French Fallick. With its echoes of "phallic," I thought the name ironic for my character, because in the stories he never seems able to bring anything to climax.

The story takes place somewhere north of New Jersey, north of New York City, north of White Plains, N.Y., as it is mentioned in the text. I had in mind a

---

[23]Perhaps I had in mind Ionesco's statement, "The comic alone is able to give us strength to bear the tragedy of existence."

wealthy Westchester County suburb, such as Chappaqua, Bedford, or Katonah, towns in which the very air smells of crisp bank notes. There is 6-acre zoning. Mercedes station wagons are parked at the train station, and every shopkeeper assumes your check is good. Setting is important to me in my fiction. As Henry James once said of Balzac, "The place in which an event occurred was in his view of equal moment with the event itself...it had a part to play; it needed to be made as definite as everything else." In my little story, social conventions of the upper middle class-bringing flowers and wine to the host; giving parties so large guests expect to have to park on the lawn—play a role in moving the comic situation forward. Guests keep dropping into Fallick's house like lovers dropping into a bed-room in a French farce.

"Surprise!" is set in the not-so-distant past, a time when the last generation of chain-smokers woke up coughing every morning, when guests drank martinis by the pitcherful. The evening trains from Grand Central and Penn Station to the suburbs all had bar cars, which were densely populated by people who claimed to be "unwinding" from the day.

The famous writer whose lifestyle triggered the idea for this story, incidentally, eventually joined Alcoholics Anonymous on his own volition. He spent the last decades of his life as a sober and productive human being. Eventually he pub-lished two more novels and another collection of short stories. He was well-reviewed in *The New York Times Book Review*. And his telephone bills were greatly reduced.

EDGAR ALLAN POE, "The Cask of Amontillado"

This is one of Poe's most concentrated stories, getting through its expository stages with incredible efficiency. The economy of the narrative is made possible mainly through the personal style of the first-person narrator. Much of what otherwise would have to come by way of description is available to the reader through direct inference. We are immediate intimates to his thought, if not co-conspirators in his chilling version of revenge.

We recognize the elements of the macabre of which Poe was such a master: the fas-cination with live entombment, the monomania of the narrator, the ancient aristocratic "house," which is both the building and the somewhat attenuated figure who is the fam-ily's last living representative. (Here we may say also that both house and master share ghastly secrets hidden within their darker recesses.) Most of these effects are the stock-in-trade of the gothic novel, originating in the eighteenth century out of the remnants of one of the most successful dramatic forms ever known, the revenge tragedy. Montresor may not look to us much like Hamlet, but he is certainly at least a cousin, and even much nearer kin to the sly malcontents who slink through the plays of Tourneur and Webster and Middleton.

In "The Cask of Amontillado," Fortunato is lured to his fate by his vanity over his sup-posed fine taste in wines. We are never informed by Montresor of the precise nature of the "thousand injuries" *supposedly* suffered by him at the hands of his intended victim, nor of the specific insult that has confirmed him in his resolve to take revenge; but in the exchanges between the two men, Fortunato appears to be much more obtuse than the slightly deferent Montresor. The conflict between them as it is actually presented in the story is one simply of temperament or personality. Fortunato's tendencies are to be bluff, loud, and self-assured. He is summed up by his name and costume as wealthy and showy, a "clown" who may be rather more boorish than comic. Montresor, on the other hand, is subtle and circumspect, as in his method for the disposition of his servants, and possesses a cunning and trenchant wit of the kind displayed when he answers his companion's question about whether he is a Mason by producing a trowel from beneath his cloak.

As for the method or his revenge, the well-spoken Montresor has invited his enemy into the bosom of his family. In fact, Fortunato is to be ensconced amid the very bones of Montresor's revered ancestors. The victim's consciousness of what is being done to him is as full and perfect as Montresor could wish. Fortunato is sobered from his intoxication almost immediately, and when he realizes his host is not engaging in some elaborate practical joke, screams in terror until the horror of his situation chokes off all sound. There have been no witnesses, and Montresor has cherished the secret of this perfect revenge for half a century. Finally, he simply *must* share the story that so neatly illustrates his cleverness, and so he reveals it to "you, who so well know the nature of my soul." Is this "you" a priest who is bound by an oath of confidentiality? Is it the reader? If so, why should we know his soul so well? Or is it a guard in a madhouse or prison, to one or another of whom Montresor has been relating his story for fifty years?

EDGAR ALLAN POE, "The Fall of the House of Usher"

As is generally known, Poe was an enthusiastic advocate of the idea that the short story ought to elicit a single concentrated mood or effect, with every detail of the work organically involved in the cultivation of that effect in the imagination of the reader. Certainly, *The Fall of the House of Usher* is an example of this practice, but it may be said in certain respects to be *about* it as well.

The organic interconnection of all the elements of the opening scene is obvious. Even the stories of the mansion itself are said to be arranged in such an order (like the words of a story) so as to reverberate to the psyches of those who dwell within. Even the lichen growing upon the walls is a part of the sentient fabric of the place. Of course, this is all standard gothic machinery of the sort one might find in such a novel as *The Castle of Otranto*. The sense of foreboding is stimulated by a mighty pile of adjectives with relatively little in the way of content to support them.

However, the story and the house are very much alike. We are invited into it by Poe, our host, who is, like the other host, Roderick Usher, a superior listener, sensitive enough to transmit to its the tiniest vibration from the dungeons below (which have already been identified, along with the rest of the house, as an extension of the host's psyche). What is it we are listening for? Certainly, there was plenty of Wordsworthian speculation, of which Poe was likely aware, about reawakening chords of our lost childhood through poetry; but we generally think of pleasant evocations in that connection. What does it mean to entomb a woman, thought dead, in the darkest and furthest reaches or the mansion (or mind) and then have her re-awakened by the guest's *reading?*—in the context of the narrative, the guest's reading aloud of the appropriate literary sound-effects. "Madman!" shouts Roderick Usher, as if to say, "Don't you know better than to be stirring up the dead past by creating sympathetic vibrations through your reading?"

It can be reasonably argued that Poe was intent upon exploring the dark side of the Wordsworthian aesthetic. The calling up of "nature" and of "natural feelings" can be problematic. The House of Usher stands so long as Roderick and his sister remain separated, but their embrace as she falls into his arms is like the combining of two mutually potentiating chemicals. All of the tensions and inhibitions are released at once and the formal structure collapses. Put in other terms, the qualities of dread and terror Poe is master of may well have their origin in oedipal guilt. To say so, however, is not much help, for the substance of his art is almost totally invested in the screens with which he disguises the springs of feeling.

EDGAR ALLAN POE, "The Purloined Letter"

There is no question that with the publication of Poe's "The Murders in the Rue Morgue" (1841), "The Mystery of Marie Roget" (1842–1843), and "The Purloined Letter" (1844) the detective story as we know it was born. Moreover, it arrived in full bloom. To be sure Poe seems to have borrowed the name of his French detective-hero C. Auguste Dupin from a character in some articles about the French Minister of Police, Francois Eugene Vidocq (1775–1857), which had appeared in *Burton's Gentleman's Magazine* in 1838, but in virtually every other respect Poe could claim to be the only American writer ever to invent a literary genre. Poe had a sense that these "tale of ratiocination," as he called them, were new and different. "These tales," he wrote to fellow writer Philip Pendleton Cooke in 1846,"…owe most of their popularity to being something in a new key. I do not mean to say that they are not ingenious—but people think them more ingenious than they are—on account of their method and *air* of method." As was often the case with Poe's critical pronouncements, he was largely correct.

"The Purloined Letter" contains every one of the three major elements of the classical detective story: a believable crime that is worth solving, an interesting, indeed unique, detective, and a method of detection. Note how many other elements that we more or less take for granted in the detective story are also there:

- The bumbling authorities, in this case "our old acquaintance, Monsieur G——, the Prefect of the Parisian Police," whose name Dupin kindly withholds. A master of method, but blind to much else, Monsieur G—— lacks the imagination necessary to solve any crime which is truly out of the ordinary.
- The detective, a man of leisure and intellect, who from the security of his armchair unflappably solves life's mysteries through his ability to know what to observe and then, aided by an intuition which helps to select which of the assembled clues are the correct ones, to follow those observations methodically through a process of association and analysis to their logical conclusion. Like so many of those who follow him, Dupin is reclusive, an outsider, a man of eccentricities, who prefers dark to daylight. He also smokes a meerschaum pipe! C. Auguste Dupin, in short, is the progenitor of virtually all those who have followed in his footsteps: Sherlock Holmes, Charlie Chan, Father Brown, Maigret, Miss Marple, Perry Mason, and Hercule Poirot.
- The detective's companion and confidante, a man of average intelligence who listens, observes, and reports the story to the reader. Who can doubt that the unnamed narrator of "The Purloined Letter" and Doyle's lovable Dr. Watson are not one and the same. It is to this confidante (and through this confidante to the reader) that the detective reports just how he has solved a crime which to others has seemed to have no solution. "You see," Holmes says to Watson, "but you do not observe," a remark which echoes a similar statement made by Dupin in "The Murders in the Rue Morgue" that "The necessary knowledge is of *what* to observe."
- An adversary or villain worthy of the detective's attention. The minister of "The Purloined Letter" matches this requirement perfectly for he is both a brilliant poet and mathematician, a combination which makes him a most worthy adversary because it is precisely these qualities which Dupin embodies as well.

What makes "The Purloined Letter" so interesting is the fact that the crime is known, the perpetrator is known, and the problem is not to solve "who done it," but to retrieve a letter that has already been stolen.

This story can, of course, be compared in interesting and productive ways with both Arthur Conan Doyle's "A Scandal in Bohemia" and "The Adventure of the Speckled Band." ("A Scandal in Bohemia," with its missing photograph which Irene Adler has cleverly hidden on the premises, has its antecedent in Poe's "The Purloined Letter," while "The

Adventure of the Speckled Band," an example of the locked-room mystery, was well-antic-ipated by Poe's "The Murders in the Rue Morgue.")

The debt which Doyle owes Edgar Allan Poe was, of course, enormous. Moreover, it was a debt that Doyle freely acknowledged. "You want strength, novelty, compactness, intensity, a single vivid impression upon the mind," Doyle wrote in his *Through the Magic Door* (1907), a statement that repeats almost verbatim the requirements that Poe had set forth in his seminal essay of 1846, "The Philosophy of Composition."

KATHERINE ANNE PORTER, "The Grave"

"The Grave" is the lyrical and subtle story of Miranda's initiation into knowledge of the mysterious and complex relationship between life and death. The plot is carefully con-structed; it consists or a brief prologue and an equally brief epilogue framing a central scene in which Miranda and her brother Paul discover "treasures" in the grave and then experi-ence the incident with the pregnant rabbit which Paul has killed. The relationship between life and death is introduced in the first paragraph, where we are told about the children's dead grandfather, the living grandmother who removed his bones "first to Louisiana and then to Texas" ("as if she had set out to find her own burial place"), and the final relocation of the family plot to "the big new public cemetery."

It is while innocently playing in the abandoned graves with their "pleasantly sweet, corrupt smell" that Miranda and Paul discover the silver dove and the gold ring which they promptly, and significantly, trade. The gold ring is the catalyst. Wearing it on her "rather grubby thumb," Miranda the nine-year-old feels the "vague stirrings" of femininity and sex-uality which give rise to thoughts of a cold bath, talcum powder, and the desire to replace her tomboyish clothes with "the most becoming dress she owned" and then sit demurely "in a wicker chair under the trees." Lagging behind with the "thought of just turning back and going home," Miranda joins Paul who is standing over the dead rabbit. As Sister M. Jose-lyn observes, it is in this brief incident, which climaxes with the discovery of the tiny still-born rabbits, that "all the symbols [of the story], the grave—death, burial, corruption, res-urrection, eternity; the dove—love, faithfulness, wisdom, the soul martyrdom; the ring—love, union, marriage, beauty, the cycle of existence, fidelity, permanency; the rabbits—life, death, birth, blood, prey, for a moment coalesce in a rich overflow of meaning." In wit-nessing the co-mingling of life and death, Miranda achieves a new, though indefinite, understanding which confirms "what she had always known": "She understood a little of the secret, formless intuitions in her own mind and body, which find been clearing up, taking form so gradually and so steadily she had not realized that she had learned what she had to know." The incident with all its ritualistic overtones is concluded with the promise of secrecy that Paul extracts from his sister.

The final scene of the story—some twenty years later—takes the form of a single con-cluding paragraph. It finds Miranda, now a woman, amid the indefiniteness of "a strange city of a strange country." Suddenly, without warning, the symbols of the earlier episode reappear, amidst the same kind of "mingled sweetness and corruption she had smelled that other day in the empty cemetery at home." The remembered moment does not last; the "dreadful vision faded," and the story closes upon the image of Paul, "whose childhood face she had forgotten, standing again in the blazing sunshine…a pleased sober smile in his eyes, turning the silver dove over and over in his hands." Though the reappearance of the ear-lier symbols is obvious, their meaning in the context of Miranda's final epiphany is not entirely clear. Dale Kramer, for example, interprets the episode in negative terms—that "the initiatory process—of learning the complexity of life-in-death and of sex—is ultimately thwarted by the self-protective devices of Miranda's personality." Sister M. Joselyn, on the other hand, finds in Miranda's vision "a final form of knowing." This view is supported by Daniel

Curley who sees the moment as a confirmation of the fact that life has order and meaning—"that what happens to us is not merely an event in the meaningless mass of experience."

MARY ROBISON, "Coach"

"Coach" is written as a series of scenes, or slices from a relatively short but crucial period in the life of a family in transition. The title character is perhaps on the brink of a relatively major career opportunity. He has been a teacher and coach in high schools up to this point and has been asked to coach freshmen at the university level. However, he has just learned through a rumor passed on to him by one of his players that he is (possibly) being considered for the varsity coaching position. At the same time, the life of his daughter, Daphne, is hovering on the brink of something new as well. She is of high-school age, and there seem to be several directions her life may take. We learn from a reminiscence of her father that as a little girl her life was happily centered upon his interests. She had "worn his colors," so to speak, but now there is some question about the direction her new maturity is going to take. There have been hints that Daphne was feeling somewhat less impressed by her father's position as high school coach; but now, his connections are beginning to open up her social life.

And it does seem that he is competing for her in some way. His two remarks to Bobby Stark seem closely related: first, that a coach's job depends upon kids, and secondly, that a coaching job is nothing without a man's family backing him, It is finally clear, whatever its terms, that the coach has won his struggle to hold his daughter. She enters the final scene wearing a pep-shirt, suggesting that her school spirit is a gauge of her rekindled enthusiasm for her father. The claustrophobic mood of the previous scene in which he suddenly appears in the doorway of the bedroom and momentarily blocks her exit is dissipated, or at least left suspended, as part of the ambiguous relationship between the two.

Over all this hangs another concern, that of the attempt by Sherry, Daphne's mother, to find a definition for herself outside her designation as "coach's wife." She has gone so far as to rent her own apartment where she may pursue her separate interests. The only one this seems to bother much is Daphne, who twice refers to her parents' "separation" and another time to their "leaving one another." Whatever the case, neither of the adults is willing to admit to anything so serious as that, in the last scene, Sherry comes into the kitchen, where the coach is drinking beer in celebration of the recent boost to his ego. He has asked Daphne to have a beer with him. Sherry must ask for a beer on her own. She wails that she cannot paint. "You *can* paint," the coach objects. To which she replies, "Let's face it,…." "An artist? The wife of a coach?" Of course, there is nothing in the natural course of things that prevents the wife of a coach from being an artist. But this seems to be her own judgment on her attempt to define herself apart from him. There is no question—he has an enormous ego, and it has just been given a tremendous lift. If Sherry has hoped to have some greater part in influencing her daughter's life, she has lost it. She cannot paint—not because she has not talent for it (though that may also be true), but because she has failed in her attempt to define a self out of which that activity might proceed. Implicitly, the coach has everything he has wanted—the job, and his family backing him. The story makes no explicit gesture toward the terms of his wife's and his daughter's surrender.

JO SAPP, "Nadine at 35: A Synopsis"

A synopsis, by definition, is a condensed statement or outline. The word serves as a more than adequate description of Jo Sapp's short story. Its protagonist, Nadine, is a cipher for many women, who at the age of 35 are confronted with an event beyond their control and forced to pick up and start life anew. Nadine's story is about aging, about changing, about moving into and through the various stages of one's life—stages which, however predictable, are nonetheless unsettling and more than a bit scary. As its ending suggests, it is also a story about the unpredictable (or is it the predictably unpredictable?). As such, the title, "Nadine at 35: A Synopsis," will do very nicely.

Jo Sapp has written me about the story and its genesis as follows:

> "Nadine" was . . . among my first published stories. I wrote it because David Ohle, a very talented writer who taught for a year at the University of Missouri, came into the classroom one Tuesday at the beginning of the semester, read three or four "minute" stories then said to the class something along the lines of "go forth and do similarly." Three to five pages, due Thursday. Some time Wednesday evening I sat at the typewriter and thumped at the keys fruitlessly for awhile, gave up in frustration, picked up a copy of *Woman's Day* and read a filler about the loss of brain cells. With no idea where I was going, I began there, and within an hour or less I had "Nadine."
>
> Of course there's more to it than that. Nadine, or someone very like her, had been lurking in the shadows for some time but whenever I tried to put anything down the effort seemed greater than the material warranted. This woman had something to say, but it wasn't precisely the thing that could be said in a traditional story without sounding like a made-for-TV movie. The short-short proved to be an ideal solution to the problem, allowing an ironic distance that brings another dimension to the piece.
>
> I hope and believe the story says something about fate and destiny and forbearance, but its ultimate lesson probably doesn't go much further than "shit happens."
>
> A final note: In the original "Nadine" [I] used a stronger word than "hell" and when I sent the story to NAR [*North American Review*] Robley Wilson returned it with a note suggesting that the word be softened. I agreed. Aside from that change and some slight polishing, the story stands pretty much as it was originally written that Wednesday night. The irony here is that I'm usually a very slow and methodical writer, taking weeks to accomplish what others do in days. There's a lesson here for budding perfectionists, I believe.

The slippage of brain cells which Sapp found in *Woman's Day* and which so worries Nadine is, I take it, a metaphor for the passage (or slippage) of time itself. At some point in our discussion we will need to consider the extent to which the metaphor really works and is effective. Some students may feel that it is contrived, forced, and unnecessary.

With or without the metaphor, Nadine is very aware that she is passing into early middle age (there is the ever-present reminder of the sagging "rump"). Whether this same awareness is what has sent her husband off on his "vacation from marriage" isn't entirely clear. Nadine apparently does not know, and the husband is obviously unwilling or unable to articulate the source or sources of his discontent. All she knows is that he has "earnestly" declared the need for "A year or two to find myself." The cliche is both obvious and infuriating.

In the wake of his departure, Nadine changes her appearance and her lifestyle. Left with three children, a dog, two cats and a goldfish, she simply does what she has to do to survive. Nadine too has an unfinished agenda and unfulfilled dreams. "She would like to return to school, to become a nuclear engineer, or perhaps a dietitian." But unlike her husband, who takes the money and disappears, Nadine does not have the luxury of such indulgences. Of necessity she finds a job and assumes a new independence. "That is the American way."

There is much to admire in Nadine. The voice that speaks to the reader is not Nadine's.

But the story is told from her point of view, almost if she herself were telling it. In fact, we are encouraged to identify the narrative voice—by turns, jaunty, comic, a bit irreverent, and thoroughly human—with Nadine's own. What is particularly remarkable, and likeable, about Nadine is that she is completely without self-pity. Nadine simply does what she has to do, and she does so with as much common sense, good humor, optimism, and lack of anger and hostility as anyone in her shoes is likely to be able to muster.

The synopsis that she provides of her own trials and triumphs is one that has been expanded to fill more than one full-length novel and screen play. Not only does she work hard, but "She finds, to her surprise, that she enjoys working, and is good at her job." She succeeds, is promoted, makes money, hires a housekeeper, and makes a new place for herself in the world. She even manages to attract the attention of the second vice president, who invites her to dinner and into an affair. Nadine has been looking for a lover, and in this case she apparently gets a promotion to boot. As the narrator says, with pointed reference to the departed husband, "She has found herself without really looking."

The end of her story comes quickly. For all her success, the mundane realities of everyday life nonetheless intrude. Nadine continues to be aware of the passage of time—the "twelve gray hairs at her left temple." The call from the outraged wife of the second vice president reminds Nadine, if she needs to be reminded, that everything comes with a price and has consequences.

The ending will surprise most students. I expect it will anger some of them. And it is on the ending that much of the discussion of the story can be expected to focus. Is Nadine's willingness to take her husband back into her life (with the same "What the hell" that she sent him forth) adequately prepared for by the narrative that proceeds it? Is her behavior consistent, justified, and otherwise explicable? Or does she give up too easily? Is she guilty of some sort of self-betrayal? What is there about Nadine and her story as we have come to understand it makes it plausible for her to come full circle, to move into the next stage of her life by resurrecting the comforts, securities, and problems of the old? Is this too "the American way"?

IRWIN SHAW, "The Girls in Their Summer Dresses"

Shaw's story has been much anthologized and, consequently, has drawn a great deal of critical commentary, not all of it in agreement. A sampling:

> This story is a very good example of the compact, well-made short story. The method is about as simple as possible, and a simple method is all that the material requires. Not much of the past needs to be told. We need only a minimum of individualization. The conflict between the two characters progresses in an obvious pattern of repetitions. The main movement is carried by dialogue, as though we were actually unseen eavesdroppers hearing the pair speak for themselves. The conclusion is quick and sharp. The point is clear and carries with its little ironic turn a serious idea—the failure of love through the failure to recognize the beloved as a person, as more than a convenience.
>
> —Cleanth Brooks and Robert Penn Warren (1959)

Shaw's third-person point of view is not restricted to either of his chief characters. He distances us from both and presents them from the outside, implying emotion and mood by action and speech. This "cool" presentation diminishes the overt emotionalism of the story; but emotion may be intensified by being hidden, and perhaps in the long run Shaw's objectivity and detachment sharpen our poignant awareness of what these young people have lost. Nor are the characters as flat as they may seem. Within the limits of a brief story Shaw suggests a great deal about the tensions and frustrations of monogamy....

In handling his theme Shaw avoids over-simplification. It would be easy to make Michael into a type of male chauvinist, the callous womanizing husband. Contrarily, it would be easy to turn Frances into the spoiled wife-child demanding what the world cannot give. But Frances and Michael do not fall easily into such types. They are bright, complex, sophisticated people. Nurtured on romantic illusions, they must face the hard truth that men and women do not easily escape their own egos. The truth is certainly not confined to them. The effort of our culture to harmonize romantic passion and monogamy has been heroic, but generally dissonance prevails. People cope as best they can: they divorce and try again, they pursue careers and wealth, most accept the humdrum of a shared existence by turns pleasant, frustrating, and boring. How Frances and Michael will cope we don't know. For the moment Frances calls the Stevensons, whose marriage, we may assume, is of this world—to which her own has now fallen.

—Thomas S. Kane and Leonard J. Peters (1976)

What is most impressive about the story is how much more the dialogue implies. What one senses most strongly about Michael and Frances's quarrel is that it is a ritual. Having no communication, they fall into the quarrel as a way of talk. This impression is conveyed through the fact that neither really listens to the other; it is almost as if they are speaking often-rehearsed lines in a play. In other stories, Shaw uses the device of the ritual quarrel to emphasize the emotional shallowness of a particular marriage.

James G. Giles (1983)

Michael will not accept his wife's description of his desire to look at women as a "kid's feeling." Indeed, she doesn't entirely believe that herself, because she thinks he probably has—or will—act on his fascination with women. Her "All right" in answer to Michael's assurances of fidelity points to the fact that everything is in fact all wrong. Their marriage is souring because she cannot believe in him and he cannot change (notice how at the crucial moment when Frances insists he is "going to make a move" Michael watches "the bartender slowly peel a lemon."). By the end of the story both of them have given up the idea of spending the day alone together, and their decision to call the Stevensons suggests how they will gradually drift apart in a bleak future.

Students will debate which character is more sympathetic. Some will find Michael's desire for and interest in women and life an appealing, natural quality, while others will find him something of a lecher and insensitive to his wife's feelings. Frances also evokes competing assessments: she wants a faithful husband but tries to draw promises from him that he cannot make. She expects him to renounce all desire except for her. Each wants more than either can have. Shaw seems to portray them as people who don't entirely understand themselves and will therefore never comprehend each other. He doesn't blame them so much as predict their mutual unhappiness for as long as they remain together. Shaw doesn't tell the story from either character's point of view because that would probably cause the reader to sympathize with one character more than the other. The story is, after all, about a *couple*.

—Michael Meyer, Ellen Darion, and Louise Kawada (1987)

The story does not say that love dies at such moments of candor as these young married people have come to. It does say that when we press, as Frances does, for certainty, the answer is very apt to be a distressing one. When Michael says, "I'll keep it to myself," he seems to be threatening as well as promising not to share with Frances some vital fraction of his life and spirit that he would have liked to open further if there were any way left to do so. Neither is at fault. Neither, in the nature of things, can be blamed for wasting the promise of the day.

To an extent this story echoes Hemingway's "Hills Like White Elephants" in manner as in theme.

—R. V. Cassill (1986)

[Michael and Frances] move from the spontaneous warmth of the opening to a guarded and self-conscious confrontation. Michael, certainly earnest enough to believe, explains that he enjoys watching attractive women. Frances, despite his reassurance, feels threatened, and she forces from him the confession that he would sometimes like to be free to sleep with other women. His answer wrings from her the offer of a divorce—so far has the emotional pendulum swung in a few moments. They move back from the edge of the abyss they have approached, and as Frances goes to call the Stevensons, that is, to surrender the day to the ordinary pursuits of an old married couple, he, not exactly ironically, displays the absolutely consistent and innocent nature of his affliction, as he watches his wife, "thinking what a pretty girl, what nice legs."

—Richard Abcarian and Marvin Klotz (1982)

LESLIE SILKO, "Yellow Woman"

Leslie Silko, one of the most gifted and exciting of our Native American writers, was born in Albuquerque, New Mexico, of mixed Pueblo, Anglo, and Mexican ancestry, but grew up some fifty miles to the west in Old Laguna, whose ancient Indian stories, customs, and traditions define, in her words, "everything I am as a writer and human being." The history of the Laguna Pueblo is an ancient one. It was populated as early as the beginning of the sixteenth century—well before the Spanish under Coronado first entered the region in 1540—by people who, according to tradition, had made their way south from the area of Mesa Verde a century before. It is the culture of the Laguna Pueblo, and the changes it has undergone in the gradual and often painful process of American acculturation, that provides the backdrop and themes for Leslie Silko's fiction.

Among these traditions are the Yellow Woman abduction stories which tell of Indian women being carried off forcibly by an evil spirit, not infrequently associated with the mountains. These traditions are discussed in A. LaVonne Ruoff's informative article "Ritual and Renewal: Keres Traditions in the Short Fiction of Leslie Silko." Like the unnamed woman protagonist of her story, Silko absorbed the Yellow Woman stories as part of the oral tradition of her cultural inheritance. "I used to wander around down there [along the banks of the river in Laguna]," she recalls, "and try to imagine walking around the bend and just happening to stumble upon some beautiful man. Later on I realized that these kinds of things that I was doing when I was fifteen are exactly the kinds of things out of which stories like the Yellow Woman story [came]. I finally put the two together: the adolescent longings and the stories around Laguna at the time about people who did, in fact just in recent times, use the river as a meeting place...."

"Yellow Woman" is a story of seduction and renewal, or, more precisely, a story of renewal *through* seduction. It begins, not with the initial afternoon encounter by the river, but the next morning, in the aftermath of lovemaking. We are not given details of how or why the narrator left the prosaic world of family and responsibility—a world of screen-doored houses, a baby playing on the floor with a husband named Al, and a mother and grandmother fixing Jell-O—though we can reconstruct motivation from the story that follows. Rather, at the moment the story beings, her physical separation from this other, more familiar world has been completed: "I tried to look beyond the pale red mesas to the pueblo. I knew it was there, even if I could not see it, on the sandrock hill above the river...."

Physical sensations dominate the opening paragraphs. Note the carefully constructed and perfectly fused images of a sight, sound, and touch. This is by no means accidental, for as Ruoff notes, "one of the themes of the story is the power which physical sensations and desire have to blot out thoughts of home, family, and responsibility." Having separated herself from the world of the pueblo, a world that no longer seems quite real to her, the narrator's "reality consists of immediate physical sensations combined with vague memory of the legends told by her grandfather which her own experience now parallels. The present begins when she touches her lover to tell him she is leaving—an unnecessary act if she really means to leave. The connection between legend and experience is made explicit when he calls her 'Yellow Woman,' although he stresses that it was she who suggested the parallel the night before."

Section two is set in Silva's mountain home. Isolated as she is, in a locale and situation which are unfamiliar, the narrator's mind ambivalently vacillates between the old life she has left and the new one upon which she has entered. Silko's use of first-person point of view makes convincing the narrator's genuine confusion about which life is "real" and commands authority. Nevertheless, her underlying psychological motives are complex. Her desire to identify herself with Yellow Woman, the victim of the legendary abduction tales, assuages her guilt and represents, at some level, a convenient form of self-deception which justifies her awakened sexual needs and the freedom to express them. It also helps her to understand and accept the powerful, fear-provoking influence which Silva exerts over her.

Silva himself is an intriguing character. A man of action—sensual, self-assured, independent—Silva lives a life apart in superior isolation. He makes no attempt to increase his dominance by assuming the mythical role she would have him play. Instead he tells her directly, "You will do what I want."

The encounter with the white rancher in section three marks the turning point of the story, and determines her "decision" to return home. Though the narrator senses during the incident "something ancient and dark" in Silva (which echoes, and perhaps reinforces, the fears she has felt earlier), there is no indication that her return is any more conscious or premeditated than the decisions that initially led her to accompany him into the mountains. Once again, she simply allows an unanticipated event to determine her action. But now the spell is broken. Ascending the ridge, "I looked down in the direction I had come from, but I couldn't see the place"—a statement that for her assumes the same kind of finality as her earlier observation by the river, quoted above. Without hesitation, though with a sadness relieved by a belief that "he will come back sometime and be waiting by the river," she follows on foot the path back to the village to resume a life that seems to have been scarcely interrupted by her absence.

The concluding section of the story, however brief, is rich with implications. To quote Ruoff once more,

> As she reaches her home, she is brought back to the realities of her own life by the smell of supper cooking and the sight of her mother instructing her grandmother in the Anglo art of making Jell-O.

This acculturation explains why the only member of her family for whom she feels an affectionate kinship is her dead grandfather, who loved the Yellow

Woman tales he passes on to his granddaughter. As her link to the mythological and historical past, he would understand that her disappearance was not a police matter because she had only been stolen by a kachina mountain spirit. For him, this would have been explanation enough; for her family, however, which no longer possesses this sense of unity with the past, she is forced to create the story of being kidnapped by a Navajo. Thus, the grandfather's belief in the tales in which the lives of the Pueblo people were inextricably intertwined with their goals has been transmitted to his granddaughter, who utilizes them as an explanation for her temporary escape from routine. Her conviction that her own experiences will serve the pueblo as a new topic for storytelling and that she herself will have to become a storyteller to explain away her absence indicates that the process will continue.

ISAAC BASHEVIS SINGER, "Gimpel the Fool"

"No doubt the entire world is imaginary," the narrator tells us (because, of course, he is a fool like Gimpel), "but it is only once removed from the true world." The "true world" is one in which everything that it is possible for humans to imagine is real. It is only the skepticism and cynicism prompted by the devil that keeps the rest of us from living as close to "reality" as fools like Gimpel (and implicitly Singer) do. The fallen world of appearances is uppermost in the minds of ordinary men and women because they are always letting their hope and innocence be drained away in contemplation of the limits of material probability. Gimpel is told stories of the wonderful and miraculous and always believes in the *possibility* of such things, even though experience tells him that those who fool him are probably lying. "Who knows, though," he reasons. Sometime they may be telling the truth, and he wouldn't want to miss such a miracle. The pleasure others get out of these jokes is simply a momentary sense of their superior skepticism, their greater acceptance of the limits of the fallen world. Gimpel believes when he is told that his new bride is chaste. He believes his wife when she tells him that the children are his. And he indeed has beautiful children whom he loves and who love him in return.

Eventually, however, Gimpel's wife Elka dies, and on her deathbed confesses to him that she has cuckolded him throughout their marriage, and that he is in fact the father of none of their children. For the first time, Gimpel sees the world as an absurd tissue of lies. "I imagined that, dead as she was, she was saying, 'I deceived Gimpel. That was the meaning of my brief life.'" It is following this revelation that the "Spirit of Evil" appears before Gimpel (looking, of course, the way he looks to the popular imagination, "with a goatish beard and horns, long-toothed, and with a tail"). He stirs Gimpel to his first vengeful, cynical act, a fundamentally symbolic act, the adulteration of "the staff of life." But very shortly, Gimpel expels the spite from his heart, buries the tainted bread, and leaves the town for good to wander the land as a beggar.

Gimpel is in search of no less than reality and finds it to be coextensive with the human imagination. He becomes a spinner of yarns, yarns about "improbable things that could never leave happened—about devils, magicians, windmills, and the like." When he dreams, he dreams about his wife looking just as she had when he first saw her in Frampole, and sometimes in the dream she weeps for him, strokes his face, and kisses him. Gimpel is thoroughly at peace and perfectly reconciled to his death: "When the time comes, I shall go joyfully," he says, "for whatever may be there, it will be real, without ridicule, without deception…there even Gimpel cannot be deceived."

"Gimpel the Fool" is a story about human dignity. In Singer's representation of Paradise, it is a place where the nagging philosophical problem of Reality and the human perception of it is simply erased. There will be no question of differences of perspective. Gimpel's dignity, which looks like foolishness to the ordinary mind, derives from his perception of the Universal even in this life. He has had to leave Frampole because his fellow citizens insisted upon their upside-down view of things. They thought that their dignity was enhanced by comparison with Gimpel's foolishness. But they are fallen beings, after all, and what it means to be fallen, to have lost one's innocence, is simply to have a depleted imagination.

JOHN STEINBECK, "The Chrysanthemums"

Two of the most telling sentences in this story by Steinbeck tell us: "Her face was eager and mature and handsome; even her work with the scissors was over-eager, over-powerful. The chrysanthemum stems seemed too small and too easy for her energy." Even the description of the woman's clothing has something to do with the equipment's overmatching the task. She is wearing heavy leather gloves, clodhopper shoes, a man's hat, and a huge corduroy apron with four gigantic pockets. But the flower garden that she is tending is fenced off from the "serious" part of the landscape, with its mountains and cattle and plowed and just-harvested fields. When her husband comes over to speak with her, he has just finished a weighty business deal, having sold the autumn crop of beef steers. He praises her gift for growing things, slightly undercutting the compliment with the qualifying phrase, "at least with flowers." He seems to have touched some hidden wound, for when he says smilingly that he wishes she could work such wonders in the apple orchard, she replies rather over-earnestly, "I could do it too." The whole scene is loaded with intimations of her untapped talents and energies. Are they childless? Is that what Steinbeck is hinting at, that the husband is unable to give her a child? Or does she feel her other gifts are placed in question by her inability to conceive? Or is it simply that her energies and talents are too great for the marginal role she is allowed in this huge, fertile landscape?

Her husband rides off to gather up the cattle he has sold and while he is away, an itinerant tinker drives into the yard with his ill-matched team of one horse and one donkey, suggesting again that the husband and wife, Elisa and Henry Allen, are another such sterilely matched couple. Elisa is immediately drawn to the tinker, because she feels that he, too, lives on the margins of the great world of "serious" business. As she talks to him about her chrysanthemums, she tries to convey to him a sense of the talent in her hands. What she says is something like the author himself might say about the art of writing—a feeling for which buds to cull and which to let grow, that goes like electricity from the hands through the arms to the body. She hopes so much for him to understand her talent, that she seems almost to grovel before him, in the kneeling posture she has assumed to select the plant-shoots she hopes he will take to give to another lonely woman somewhere. Of course, the tinker, the mender-of-holes and plugger-of-leaks, is a figure in numberless bawdy songs and jokes dating at least back to the middle ages. It is conceivable that Steinbeck may mean for us to understand Elisa Allen as unconsciously transmitting her sexual yearnings through the language of horticulture. On the other hand, when the tinker begins to insist upon the masculine dignity of his craft and his self-sufficiency, Elisa thinks to herself, "I could do that," meaning either, "I could go with you," or "I have the strength and cleverness to make a living for myself just as you do." In either case, the tinker claims that his kind of life would be impossible for a woman. When she later sees her cuttings dumped unceremoniously in the middle of the road, she realizes that the man took these carefully cultivated gifts of her magical hands as a way of flattering her into giving him the work that to *her* was unnecessary. She averts her eyes as she and her husband drive past. She cannot stand the thought of having her attempt to communicate her talent so nullified. In the car, she asks about prizefighters. Implicitly, she is asking whether it is true that men can use the talent in *their* hands to beat one another to a bloody pulp and be acclaimed for it? She is left without any confidence or importance or competence, and as they ride along, "she turn[s] up her collar so...[her husband] cannot see that she [is] crying weakly—like an old woman."

DANIEL STERN, "Brooksmith By Henry James"

In the following paragraphs, in a commentary especially written for *Fiction 100*, author Daniel Stern addresses his story:

The idea of putting a text by a previous writer at the heart of a piece of short fiction came to me one winter's day, while thinking about youth and its dreams. As I mulled over the elements of a story that was forming in my imagination, I suddenly realized that I could not only place a story by Henry James at the heart of my own story—but that my own story could actually be called by the same name.

It took a small leap of nerve, not to mention faith, but what got my pulse racing was this idea: that a text by a writer of the past whom I loved, could be basic to a fiction: as basic as a love affair, a trauma, a mother, a landscape, a lover, a job or a sexual passion.

Enter Brooksmith. As a young writer I had read Henry James' unforgettable story of a butler in a finely tuned English literary salon, a man so spoiled by the perfect literary and human exchanges he'd been part of for years, that when his master died, he could find no reason to go on living. This notion of someone with such limited prospects being spoiled for the life into which they'd been born and then imprisoned, lingered somewhere in my literary soul—as opposed to my regular soul—waiting for its moment.

That moment arrived when a friend of mine, a college teacher whose husband had died not long before, told me of a student she'd taught back in the sixties—a young black woman, trapped in a dead end life, faced with a destiny of being a prostitute and obsessed with finding a way out through education. To transform a British butler into a poor Brooklyn black woman. How could I resist?

Rarely have I drawn so directly from life in a piece of fiction. There was a "Celia," there was a "Zoe." And the central incident of the wrong story being assigned, actually happened. There, of course, the correspondence ended and imagination began. I had to create a narrator, one with problems of his own which would be affected by his discovery of Brooksmith. I had to create a background: the turbulent college years of the sixties. Most of all, I had to create a later fate for both the teacher and her cool, independent young black woman. Here, Zoe's passion to emancipate herself by becoming a nurse gave me the cue for Celia's illness. The rest wove itself naturally to a conclusion.

But it was while completing this transformation that I was the beneficiary of an unexpected stroke of good fortune. Leafing through Henry James' notebooks I came across the entry which tells us that Brooksmith had, himself, been based on someone in life: a ladies' maid with the evocative real life name of Past had given James the original idea. If I had ever doubted that there was a natural chain leading from life to literary characters and back again, I could now stop doubting. Brooksmith had been a woman—albeit a white, British woman—had become a man, a finely tuned butler at the perfect salon—and now was again to be a woman. The circle was complete.

There were apparently no boundaries separating life and literature. It was only a matter of finding and inventing the right connections.

I may mention, in passing, that Henry James got many of his best ideas by keeping his ears open at dinner tables. It is fitting that, at just such a dinner table, I first heard the name Brooksmith, and was launched on my adventure. I might suggest the same to any young person considering the strange destiny of becoming a writer of fiction.

ELIZABETH STROUT, "A Little Burst"

Students will, I think, rather enjoy this story of female revenge. Certainly they will understand, if not perhaps sympathize with, the reversal of roles on which the story turns. Usually the conflict among the recently-married is between the bride and her new mother-in-law. Here the situation is just the opposite. It is the mother-in-law, Olive Kitteridge, who is resentful. We leave her savoring the months of discomfort she intends to inflict on the unsuspecting (and apparently rather guiltless) "Dr. Sue."

What follows are the notes I found myself making as I prepared the story for *Fiction 100*. I include them in this form as a means of demonstrating (for anyone who might care) how I approach the task of bringing a new story to the text.

- It is important to note that Strout introduces the metaphor she will repeat as early as paragraph two. "All afternoon Olive has been fighting the sensation of moving under water, a panicky, dismal experience, since she has never managed to learn to swim." Later Olive will compare Suzanne, her daughter-in-law and rival, to an accomplished swimmer-diver: "It had been like watching some woman dive from a boat and swim easily to the dock. A reminder how some people could do things others could not."
- The story's conflict surely has to do with the fact that Suzanne has taken the place of Olive in the life of her only son, Christopher. Talk about the need to dominate and control! Not only has Olive seen to it that her podiatrist son remains a bachelor until he is well into his thirties but she has totally remained, until this very afternoon, in charge of his entire life. Even the house into which Christopher has brought Suzanne has been under her active supervision and management. "Now Suzanne (Dr. Sue is what Olive calls her in her head) will take over, and, coming from money, the way she does, she will probably hire a housekeeper, as well as a gardener." Olive herself has nicely managed these two roles until the arrival of Dr. Sue. "She [even] built the [Christopher's] house herself—well, almost."
- The bridegroom, Christopher Kitteridge, as we get to know him, is—a humorless, introverted, 38-year-old bachelor who combines the sensitivities of an artist with the skills of a podiatrist. He has few friends. The formidable and domineering Olive has had a clear hand in his making. What attracts Suzanne, a competent physician, to Christopher is left largely to our imagination. Theirs, we are told, has been a whirlwind courtship. Had it been longer, we suspect, Olive would have found a way to intervene.

Henry Kitteridge, Christopher's father and Olive's husband, appears to be rather ineffectual. He has little or no role in the story just as we suspect that he has had little or no role in his son's life.

- Note that Olive cannot conceive that Christopher's attraction for Suzanne may be anything more than sexual. Moreover, she points out that Suzanne is "small-breasted" and, later, that her bra is "small-cupped." This comes from someone whose only major source of satisfaction seems to be eating. Olive has allowed herself to become fat.
- This mother, who has done all she can to control the behavior of her son, has now, quite literally, camped out in his bridal bed.
- Olive's dress, which will later become the subject of ridicule, is indeed ridiculous: "gauzy green muslin with big reddish-pink geraniums printed all over it."
- We learn relatively little about Suzanne other than what Olive (or, rather, the narrator)

tells us. (It is important that we appreciate just how tightly Strout controls the story's angle of vision.) What we do "see" of Suzanne, however, is likely to increase our sympathy. Note, for example, when the small niece decides she doesn't want to sprinkle rose petals on the ground before the ceremony, Suzanne responds with gentle, good nature. Though Christopher is not smiling and is "stiff as driftwood" (as we suspect Olive is as well at this unexpected disruption), Suzanne calmly motions for the musician to proceed and for the ceremony to begin. There are no theatrics or emotional outbursts on her part—just the acceptance by a competent and sensitive adult of the behavior of a child. Later that same child will direct a series of innocent, yet telling, comments toward Mrs. Kitteridge, beginning with: "You look dead."

- Mrs. Kitteridge's behavior during the ceremony and throughout the day is very different. She is so nervous and anxious that she pictures herself having a heart attack on the lawn, and falling over dead just as her son says "I do." The symbolism of heart failure and its timing are obvious enough.
- As Olive lies in Christopher and Suzanne's bed, reviewing the events of the day as well as worrying over her son, present and past, she does seem to reach some positive appreciation of Suzanne and what marriage may do for her son:

> Still, Olive herself has worried about Christopher's being lonely. She was especially haunted this past winter by the thought of her son's becoming an old man, returning home from work in the darkness, after she and Henry were gone. So she is glad, really, about Suzanne. It was sudden, and will take getting used to, but, all things considered, Dr. Sue will do just fine. And the girl has been perfectly friendly to her.

Then she overhears Suzanne's comment about her green dress: "I couldn't believe it. I mean that she would really *wear* it." Olive, who "loves this dress," "is stunned in her underwater way." This snippet of conversation is followed by another telling remark: "He's had a hard time you know." Olive takes this comment personally as well.

Note how her attitude changes. She cannot bear the thought of having to return to the party to take her leave: "She is going to have to go back into the living room and kiss the cheek of that bride, who will be smiling and looking around, with her know-it-all-face." Olive is very much resentful of the competence that Suzanne seems to exude.

- At this point our knowledge of Olive and Christopher becomes a good deal greater. We learn that

  —Christopher has earlier talked of "just ending it all."
  —Olive's own father committed suicide 37 years before. His cries for help were dismissed by Olive because she was pregnant and had "disappointments of her own." Her willingness to dismiss her father's mood as the "blues" she now realizes was "The wrong response."
  —Christopher, who like her dead father "is not given to talk," was "scared of her" as a child.
  —Olive has her own "blackness": ". . . deep down there is a thing inside me, and sometimes it swells up like the head of a squid and shoots blackness through me."

- As the story ends, we find Olive succumbing to this "blackness." She wishes to "mark every item" that Suzanne has brought into Christopher's bedroom. As she surveys Suzanne's beige dress, now "pompously" hanging in her son's closet, it is the memory of the remark she has overheard about her own dress that clearly spurs her on: "For God's sake, what's wrong with a little *color*?" Olive shakes with anger.

- We leave Olive plotting about the future and the small, periodic anxieties and self-doubts she plans to introduce into the life of the otherwise calm and capable Dr. Sue. Note that Olive's hunger has now been sated. She will stop with Henry at Dunkin' Donuts on the way home, but *not* to eat. The surprises she has in mind are the "little bursts" of which she has earlier spoken—the little bursts on which "life depends." "Christopher doesn't need to be living with a woman who thinks she knows everything. Nobody knows everything, they shouldn't think they do."

The story, like the metaphor on which it turns, has great and hidden depths. There should be plenty of good discussion here.

ELIZABETH TALLENT, "No One's a Mystery"

The story's situation is commonplace enough: an older man cheats on his wife and engages in a two-year affair with a girl just now celebrating her eighteenth birthday. For that birthday he gives her a five-year diary whose prospective entries form the subject of conversation between them and whose differences generate the conflict and the story. The characterization of Jack, the married man, is interesting, particularly because he is seen exclusively through the eyes of the young protagonist-narrator. He exhibits, to be sure, sensuality (the reference to his crotch and the zipper of his Levis, for example), but much of the detail which help to establish his character seems rather unpleasant—from the dirty boots, the speed at which he drives, his cavalier attitude toward his wife, the way he makes the narrator ride on the dirty, pop-top strewn floor of his pickup. What this all suggests is a defining attitude of masculine carelessness, which, no doubt, students will be rather quick to pick up on.

Her view of life is a romantic one—or, one that seems to excuse the rather tawdry relationship of the present for the romantic possibilities of the future. It is this future, which she lays out for him as entries in her newly-acquired diary, which provides the central conflict and interest of the story.

His responses seem typical of the cynical and exploitative male who understands how their relationship will inevitably end and who seems willing through his comments to "let her down" gently to what lies ahead. Or is he? It is Jack who has made the present of the diary—who has deliberately given her a vehicle in which to record her present and provide an orderly record of her future. Is the nature of the gift really commensurate with the cynical attitudes he casually expresses? Or is he, in fact, trying to hold on to a romantic and meaningful present which he knows must inevitably slip away? There are good discussion possibilities for this story.

AMY TAN, "Young Girl's Wish"

Amy Tan's "Young Girl's Wish," a story of homecoming, discovery, and reconciliation, was published in the *New Yorker* on October 2, 1995. It also comprises Chapter XIII of *The Hundred Secret Senses*, Tan's collection of interrelated stories, published the same year.

American-born Olivia and her Chinese-born half-sister, Kwan, have come to China in the company of Olivia's husband, Simon (who she is the process of divorcing). The two women are very different, not only in terms of cultural background and upbringing but in temperament and personality as well. Their reasons for making the journey to China are also different. Olivia comes to China almost as a tourist to accompany her half-sister to the rural village of Changmian, Kwan's former home. Though China is the land of Olivia's ancestors, she has no understanding of its language and she feels little in the way of connectedness to its landscape, to the vibrant rhythms of its daily life, or to its legends and traditions. But Tan's story clearly implies that there are other, deeper psychological impulses at work in Olivia. There are things about China she has unconsciously learned from Kwan, and Olivia's discovery of what they are and what they mean constitutes a moment of epiphany and reintegration.

Olivia's discovery begins the moment that she, Kwan, and Simon enter Changmian, a place that "has avoided the detritus of modernization." "I feel," she says,

> as though we've stumbled on a fabled misty land, half memory, half illu-
> sion....Changmian looks like the carefully cropped photos found in travel
> brochures advertising "a charmed world of the distant past, where visitors can step
> back in time."

Her recognition quickly deepens beyond travel brochures: "'I feel like I've seen this place before,' I whispered to Simon." Then comes her epiphany:

> I gaze at the mountains and realize why Changmian seems so familiar. It's the
> setting for Kwan's stories, the ones that filter into my dreams. There they are: the
> archways, the cassia trees, the hills leading to Thistle Mountain. And being here, I
> feel as if the membrane separating the two halves of my life has finally been shed.

Olivia then looks up, and, as if on cue to celebrate the moment of her new wholeness, fifty tiny schoolchildren welcome her in English.

Kwan's own motive in returning to China and Changmian is far more clear. She is intent on wringing from her aunt, "Big Ma," the confession that she is sorry for having sent Kwan to the United States to live with Kwan's American family. Though as she enters her native village, Kwan momentarily fears that "I've become too American and now I see things with different eyes," she remains very much in touch with the traditions and culture of the China she learned about in childhood and then left behind. Sensing Big Ma's "yin" or spirit standing by the wall, Kwan intuitively knows that Big Ma is dead. From that experience she also intuits that the third of her wishes has in fact "already come true": Big Ma "was always sorry she sent me away. But she could never tell me this. Otherwise, I wouldn't have left her for a chance at a better life."

LEO TOLSTOY, "The Death of Ivan Ilyich"

Tolstoy, like many other serious modernists, was fascinated by the problem of how the ideas of human dignity, freedom, and authenticity were to be maintained in the face of a general collapse of faith in a loving God who, with his eye upon every sparrow that falls, once assured the special significance of each of our lives. As a kind of test case, the author chooses as the "hero" of his narrative a man whose success in life (translated into our own cultural terms) most of us might envy. True, he has his season of discontent, but through a combination of his efforts and a bit of good luck, he "lands on his feet," as we say, and continues his career in Petersburg under even better circumstances than before. Of course, we are purposely limited in our ability to empathize with Ivan because of the ironic tone of Tolstoy's narrative. His account of the hero's "failing in love" and marrying, for example, is absolutely flat and external, making the reader feel rather superior by comparison. But once again, as he keeps reminding us, the life of Ilyich is by no means the *least* of lives, but very much the norm for his class and period. The trick of the narrative is to keep us at a distance from the character of Ivan, so that when we are told he is quite the "usual" sort of person, we do not consider ourselves to belong to that category at all. We are always made to feel that our own lives are both more significant and more authentic than that of this little man who only does what is expected of a person of his place and time—just like the rest of us.

The fact that the narrative has as its beginning the end of Ivan's life is worth some attention. As Ivan's "remains" are being viewed, we see various of his friends and acquaintances in a typical funereal mood: thinking of the opportunities for advancement the position left vacant by Ilyich might open up, a bit elated that it is Ilyich and not themselves who is dead, and certain that when they must die, it will be a much more remarkable event. Out of this perceived indifference to Ilyich's death, the narrative of his life flows: this was an insignificant death; therefore, it must have been an insignificant life.

Of course, it is life that kills Ivan. He receives a bruise in the side while decorating the new home in Petersburg, and we assume this to be the "cause" of his fatal affliction. No one knows. The function of the doctors in this case is simply to make him believe that if he is a "good patient" he will recover. Their pretense is that there is something rational to be done about Ilyich's illness, but in fact they are totally ignorant of the real affliction and merely delay his confrontation to the fact that he is dying.

But in proportion to the narrative's indifference to Ivan's life, there is an increasingly more intimate account of the process of his death. We now begin to get particular details—particular evocations of the foul taste in his mouth, accounts of how he faces the pain through the long hours of the night, how his mood changes from hopeful to despairing, and back to hoping again. We begin to gain in sympathy with this dying man while the rest of the family, with the exception of the peasant servant, Gerasim, and possibly Ivan's young son, are made to seem shallow and indifferent. As the story progresses, it seems almost as if there were two separate races—the race of the living and the race of the dying. The living believe, despite the evidence before them, that they are immortal, and the dying are absolutely alone, unable to convey the least sense of their diverging experience. For a time, Ivan's wife chides him for not following the doctors' orders, so that he may be well again and so remove the inconvenience and embarrassment of his illness, but eventually it becomes clear that he will never join the living again, and his presence is rather like that of the giant cockroach in Kafka's "Metamorphosis."

As Ivan struggles more and more with the pain, comes more and more to admit to himself that he is dying, he begins to think of his illness as a special visitation upon himself, and he tries to find some reason, some fault that might explain his suffering, but there is none. He reviews his own life and finds it quite blameless, but at the same time it begins to reveal itself as quite meaningless as well. There was a time somewhere back in his childhood when he recalls having been vaguely happy, but since, his life has been a mere slide into nothingness. He can find no reason for his ever having existed. He has, as a servant of the state, judged others, has had the power and opportunity to make a difference in their lives, but he can think of no act of kindness or pity committed out of sympathy for the plight of his fellow humans.

The question that keeps recurring to him is, "Why *me?*" as if death were a peculiar insult to himself—as if it mattered whether his particular career had any meaning. But the moment he lets go of that persistent obsession with self, death comes easily, as a light opening out from the bottom of the "black sack" in which he had envisioned himself as struggling. In contrast with the peasant Gerasim's view of the common fate of the human race and the complete unity of life and death, Tolstoy places the illusion cultivated by the middle class to which Ilyich belongs that life is a kind of mad, individualist competition in which the competent "win" by surviving. The denial of death is so complete among the living that the dying seem as remote as if they were of another species. Tolstoy's narrative strategy has drawn us into a complete reversal of those attitudes, making even the relative success of Ivan's individual life seem petty in relation to the moment we must all confront. Childhood and death are to Tolstoy the moments of our greatest authenticity and unity as human beings. The rest is the mere imitation of manners.

JUDY TROY, "Ten Miles West of Venus"

Venus, we know from Judy Troy's other stories, is a small farming town located in Kansas. We have met this kind of place before. Venus is reminiscent, in fact, of Sherwood Anderson's Winesburg, Ohio. Both are small country villages populated by individuals who, to the community at large, seem for the most part to be leading ordinary and undistinguished lives in the American heartland. Beneath the surface of things, however, lurk darker realities. The stories of *Winesburg, Ohio*, strip aside appearances to reveal men and women whose lives are characterized by isolation, alienation, despair, frustration, and spiritual and emotional emptiness, much of it self-imposed and self-reinforcing. Winesburg is made of those whom Sherwood Anderson refers to as "grotesques," individuals whose thwarted dreams and desires result in lives lacking in fullness and completion.

While it is too much to say that Judy Troy is recasting Anderson's turn-of-the-century village in *fin de siecle terms*, the similarities are unmistakable. Her characters, like so many of Anderson's are aware of the inadequacies of their lives and to compensate make futile, in some cases self-destructive, efforts at revelation and communication. This is certainly true of all four of the characters to whom she introduces us here: the two on stage, the Reverend Franklin Sanders and Marvelle Lyle; and the two we simply hear about through Franklin Sanders' musings, Morgan Lyle and Gussie Dell.

The story's focal character is Franklin Sanders, a drab, cheerless 63-year-old Methodist minister. It is Sunday and Sanders is on his way to visit Marvelle Lyle, one of his parishioners, whose husband, Morgan Lyle, has recently committed suicide. The ostensible reason for his visit is to see if he can "coax" Marvelle into once again attending church. It is spring, a time of hope and promise. Yet as he makes the trip, Sanders is unaware of the world around him. He is preoccupied by what Gussie Dell, another of his parishioners, may or may not say during her weekly "Neighbor Talk" radio program. Gussie uses her radio show as a way of reaching out, though she does so in ways that the community apparently finds inappropriate and certainly does not understand. Her open discussion of taboo and unpleasant subjects is "embarrassing," and wins her few if any converts. Her freedom and spontaneity only unnerves people like Franklin Sanders.

The real reasons for Franklin's visit are psychologically complex. Though he ostensibly has come to console a widow and bring her back to the community of the Methodist church, his visit also has everything to do with an event that occurred 15 years before, on a day "like this day, a Sunday afternoon in spring." On that occasion, he and Marvelle had simultaneously entered the kitchen of the church, "walked toward each other and kissed passionately, as if they had planned it for months." Though Franklin has tried to push aside the memory of that event, a passion spontaneously expressed and mutually shared, he is unable to do so. "'You've always been an attractive woman,' he said quietly."

In response, Marvelle, who seems to be the more open and honest of the two, raises the issue of guilt. "The amazing thing," Marvelle tells Franklin, "is that it only happened once." To which Franklin responds: "No . . . it's that I allowed it to happen at all. . . . That was me not paying attention to God. . . ." That exchange and all that it implies is vital to our understanding of the story. Franklin's comment is particularly telling for it suggests how he has permitted his role as a minister to suppress even further a sexuality already thwarted by an unhappy marriage.

Several comments offer additional insight into the lives and psyches of these two characters. The first comes from Marvelle, who, like Franklin, gives signs of being emotionally wounded. That morning she has seen two deer in the woods below her house. "For a moment," she says, "I almost forgot about everything else." To which Franklin responds: "That's interesting . . . because that's what church services do to me." And then he adds: "I'd rather not be the one conducting them. I feel that more and more as I get older. I'd like to sit with the congregation and just partake." Their conversation is strained and elliptical, a

199

fact which underscores Franklin's inability and/or unwillingness to engage, understand, and articulate his true inner feelings.

Franklin Sanders, a man of God, is estranged and isolated from life and love. Just what Franklin would like to "partake" of is made clear by the story's conclusion. As he drives away from Marvelle's house, unable to concentrate on Billy Graham's sermon, his thoughts turn first to Gussie, who has questioned him about details of his newly-redecorated bedroom—details which, significantly, he cannot remember. His thoughts then turn to Marvelle, whose hair, dark eyes, and "every godless place" he remembers all too well. The final lines summarize the depth and extent of Franklin Sanders' self-imposed deprivation: love is something to which he has never considered himself entitled.

IVAN TURGENEV, "The Country Doctor"

Turgenev's doctor, as we are introduced to him in the framing episode, is not a particularly heroic or attractive figure. As Seymour Lainoff observes, the doctor is

a conventional practitioner, with a sharp eye for the dollar, deferring to his social superiors and snubbing his inferiors—a useful person, though hardly a noble one. He prescribes for his patient "the usual sudorific, ordered a mustard plaster to be put on, very deftly slid a five-rouble note up his sleeve, coughing dryly and looking away as he did so...."

His services rewarded, the doctor prepares to go, "but somehow fell into talk and remained."

Like Coleridge's Ancient Mariner, the doctor is a man compelled to tell a story, in this case the story of an imperfectly understood incident which has left him feeling vaguely troubled and guilty. (Note particularly how the doctor's nervousness and uncertainty are mirrored in his halting and broken speech.) The references to the game of Preference at the beginning and end of the story underscore the essentially complacent, routine, and prudential character of a life without risk in which the stakes are consistently "low." This complacency is temporarily broken one Lent "at the time of the thaw" (a period of the year symbolically suggesting both death *and* the possibility of the resurrection and renewal of life) when the doctor is suddenly summoned forth to the "little house with a thatched roof" where he encounters the beautiful dying girl. The "hellish" and chaotic conditions of his journey are important, for they not only underscore the power of nature but reinforce that fact that the doctor is now isolated and alone. Cut off from the comfortable and the familiar, his vulnerability as a human being is now very much exposed.

The details of what happens there—details which Turgenev handles with great economy and realism—constitute the vital center of the story. Love is kindled between doctor and patient in the face of a situation which the indecisive and vacillating doctor, for all his medical knowledge, cannot arrest. And in the process a rare moment of opportunity is offered and lost. To quote Lainoff once more:

the doctor could not rise to the great occasion of his life. If he had taken a courageous stand consistent with his love for Alexandra, he might have saved her life; or if that was impossible to accomplish, at least he would have risen to honesty in a testing situation. But he could not assert himself against the demands of convention: the impersonality expected of a doctor, the decorum customary in courtship and marriage, the dread of passionate expression. The doctor's nervousness, manifest throughout his narrative, indicates his awareness that in an essential way he has failed. The story incorporates a typical Turgenev theme, the inability of the socially comfortable to adopt the Heroic, a social course necessary for their salvation; it rises to universality in its suggestions of the conflict between body and spirit, inertia and initiative.

Just how much the doctor has lost is made clear by the reader's final glimpse of the man: having renounced "exalted sentiment," he is reduced once more to playing Preference for "low stakes," willing to settle for a life in which the winning of two and a half roubles leaves him "pleased with his victory" and in which he has married a "spiteful hag," "a merchant's daughter: seven thousand roubles dowry," who "luckily...sleeps all day."

JOHN UPDIKE, "A&P"

"A&P" wears extremely well. Even after thirty years, the story retains its vitality and humor, and students continue to love it, no doubt because they can immediately identify with Sammy's first-person rendition of his heroic, if reckless, gesture of independence and non-conformity. A good deal of the story's success can be traced directly to its language, to the authenticity of the narrative voice, whose vernacular manages to capture almost perfect the essential qualities of teenage humor: exaggeration, caricature, and brash judgments quickly, if at times a bit unfairly, rendered. Moreover, as Robert Detweiler notes, "the brash-ness and occasional mild vulgarity of the language balance nicely the inherent sentimen-tality of the action." For these reasons, "A&P" provides an excellent vehicle for discus-sions of the ways in which language and style are used in the creation of humor.

The central critical question concerns, of course, the motivation for Sammy's decision to quit. Sammy is no rebel; there is little in his narrative that would lead us to believe that he is going through some form of late adolescent rebellion or restlessness for which the episode in the A&P provides a convenient and necessary outlet. On the contrary, he responds to Lengel's comment that "Sammy you don't want to do this to your Mom and Dad" with an immediate "It's true. I don't." On one level, to be sure, his act of defiance is framed in the idealistic terms of the man of principle, for whom he is able to provide such appropriate rationalizations as "once you begin a gesture it's fatal not to go through with it." He also knows full well that such actions do have consequences ("I felt how hard the world was going to be to me hereafter").

Yet, it is also clear that Sammy's action in good measure surprises even Sammy himself and that his own explanations and comments only partially tell us what he is reacting to and why. A fuller, clear explanation is embedded within Sammy's monologue, in what he sees and describes *and* in the attitudes, values, and preferences he more or less unconsciously expresses. Here is a source for excellent class discussion. Queenie and her two friends attract Sammy because of the style and "class" they exude (Sammy has a well-developed eye for quality), because of their youth, beauty, and open sensuality, because of their reckless non-conformity, and because of the willingness, when pressed, to challenge authority. In every case these qualities stand in obvious marked contrast to the qualities and values mirrored in Sammy's own existence and in the everyday world of the A&P with its "sheep" and "hous-eslaves" and the staid and humorless Lengel. Seen in these terms, the underlying causes of Sammy's challenge to the establishment (A&P, Sunday school, "and the rest") become suf-ficiently clear and we can more fully appreciate the nature of Sammy's quixotic and courtly gesture—a gesture which goes unrequited, unacknowledged, and ironically, even unnoticed.

JOHN UPDIKE, "Here Come the Maples"

The upbeat-sounding title of the story is clearly ironic. It suggests the beginning of a marriage rather than the end. The separation, which was to only be a trial in the story

"Separating," which Updike had published the previous year (1975), has not worked. Richard and Joan Maple's 20-year marriage is over, and they are now going through the final stages of an uncontested "no-fault" divorce proceeding. This story can obviously be read and discussed with the earlier one. It is one of the 17 Maples stories, dealing with marriage, separation, and divorce, that comprise Updike's *Too Far to Go* (1979).

John Updike began writing about Richard and Joan in the mid-1960s, at a time, which as Alice and Kenneth Hamilton note, he was grappling with the issue of how to use the form of the short story to deal with the subject of marriage:

> As a "thing" to be reported, married love does not fit easily into short-story form. Each marriage, after all, is a developing experience in the context of a particular society caught up in the stream of history. In order to depict marriage and love as partners in a marriage know it, it is necessary for the writer to show something of the history of the individual marriage, and that means recording the passage of time and the accumulation of memories giving marriage its historical destiny, its unique and living character. Updike has attempted to provide historical perspective by making his married couples, in general, age along with their creator.

If many of the Maple stories succeed, it is because he managed to achieve precisely this effect. It allows Updike to trace the Maples' marriage as it evolves through its various stages. Those stages begin, as Robert Luscher has noted, "with early doubts, temptations, and overtures toward separation; next moving into increasing frustration, demystification, and adultery; then, bogging down in a series of arguments and stalemates; and finally culminating in a legal separation that renovates their vision of their marriage's enduring value." Next, as if inexorably, comes divorce.

As in "Separating," the "Here Come the Maples" story is told from Richard's point of view. There is much here that will be familiar to those who have read the earlier story: the same regret for the passing of life; the same sort of nostalgia for a time when love was new, when life and marriage seemed to hold out promise.

What is remarkable, given much of what we know has gone on before, is the lack of rancor. There is no assigned blame. This is a true "no-fault" divorce. It proceeds by careful juxtaposing scenes of beginning and end, while leaving out the long years of "middle" where the Maples' marriage has slowly atrophied and died. As he proceeds to Cambridge City Hall to obtain a copy of his marriage certificate, he thinks not of the divorce itself and the new life beyond, but conjures up memories of their wedding and honeymoon with its image of Hansel and Gretel, suggesting innocence.

These musings are interrupted by others occasioned by his reading of a "scholarly extract" on quantum physics which arrived in the same mail as the divorce affidavit. Richard cannot help but compare his marriage and its dissolution to the lesson it contains about the forces of nature which both bind couples together and draw them apart. "In life," Richard thinks, "there are four forces: love, habit, time, and boredom. Love and habit at short range are immensely powerful, but time, lacking a minus charge, accumulates inexorably, and with its brother boredom levels all." As Luscher suggests,

> Updike sets up an equation between the forces of nature and those that affect a relationship and leaves it purposely undeveloped: the correspondence set up (ranked in order of increasing strength) are gravity and love; the weak force and habit; electromagnetism and time; and the strong force and boredom.

There are none of the tears of the earlier story which Richard has used, Joan implies, as a crutch to make it seem as if it is Joan who has forced the issue. Rather the divorce proceeds with a kind of mechanical formality as scripted and without any embarrassing questions being asked. The marriage ends, as it had begun, with a formal ceremony. As in "Separating," "Here Comes the Maples" ends with a kiss, the kiss that Richard forgot to bestow on Joan to seal their wedding vows 20 years earlier. That he should do it now is clearly ironic, for the kiss, delivered without passion, signals the end of an important relationship rather than the beginning. There is so little emotion and pain. And perhaps that is precisely Updike's point.

As their marriage ends, Updike continues to use his equation from physics. As Luscher notes, "Even as they undo their marriage, the weaker forces of love and habit exert a pull; in the courtroom, Joan is 'the only animate object . . . that did not repel him.'"

And so the Maple stories find their conclusion. As Alice and Kenneth Hamilton have noted, in Updike's world "Marriage, in which two individuals must either share a common existence or destroy each others' happiness, becomes a test for the ability of contemporary man to understand his world—and, by natural consequence, himself."

JOHN UPDIKE, "Separating"

This story is vintage Updike, with its progressive revelation of layer after layer of social obligation, and detail after detail of married intimacy which, like the clay tennis court seem new and smooth and exciting, but has now suddenly become eroded and lumpy, the question left hanging is whether it will ever be repaired. In those days, the couple had the courage and energy to disturb things rather casually, like having a bulldozer come to scar and scrape and rearrange the landscape as if ". . .their marriage could rend the earth for fun." Both believed the new court would be a long-term investment in the improvement of their "game," but suddenly they have arrived at the moment he had dreaded: having to tell the children of the dissolution of the family they have known all their lives.

At this point, one can begin to see the difficulty of the artistic task Updike has set himself; the point of view the story takes—the consciousness it asks us to sympathize with—is that the character who is responsible for the destruction of the family over which he is grieving. Joan Maples is furious at her husband for weeping at dinner in front of the children and forcing to reveal the situation all at once. She had hoped to get him to face them one at a time, to have to tell each of them that he is deserting their mother for another woman. She reminds him she has spent the entire spring weeping; that is why she has no more tears left, and it is clear that Richard is just now beginning to realize the depth to which he is wounding others and maiming his own life. All summer, he has kept himself busy and oblivious fixing up the house, making it sound for his "ex-family" before leaving. Much of his guilt has been absorbed by this activity. But the dinner with the children suddenly forces him to face up to the dislocation, and he cannot control his tears. The climax of the story comes when Richard must face his eldest son alone and tell him what has happened. Instead of being funny or outraged as the other children have been, Richard, Jr., kisses his father and sobs, "Why?" totally unnerving Richard and causing the "pale face" of the other woman whose love awaits him on the far side of this ordeal to fade almost to nothing.

There is no simple resolution to the story. The conclusion is left hanging, as is the main character and probably the sympathy of the reader. It is easy to see that Richard is responsible for his own dilemma, and therefore "deserves" all the pain he gets in exchange for that which he is inflicting upon all those other people he loves. But if such a condemnation is merely a way out of the story, then the reader is missing the point. What Updike is attempting to capture is a fundamental rearrangement of the emotional landscape (as the bulldozers had rearranged the physical landscape) within the "world" of the story. All of these characters, including the shadowy other woman in her apartment across town, will emerge from these events with their lives drastically altered; there will be no putting things back the way they were. But to concentrate the effect, Updike makes the character most responsible for the changes also the one who is most defined by the terms of the past. Joan Maples has already changed, and of course that is another whole story. She seems already to have accepted her new circumstances: to her, Richard is already gone. But Updike centers the story upon the agent of change in the moment of his most intense realization of the irreversibility of those changes. The most conservative member of the family has disrupted it most radically and now looks bleakly upon what he has wrought. The effect may not be quite as thunderous as the moment of Oedipus' tragic realization, but Richard Maples is at least in the shadow of the same *anagnorisis*.

ALICE WALKER, "To Hell with Dying"

That this story occupies an important place in the Alice Walker canon seems clear enough from the decision by Harcourt Brace Jovanovich to republish it in illustrated book form for children. The decision, nevertheless, is a curious one. As Valerie Wilson Wesley points out in her *New York Times* book review, "the book's message about the healing power of love is far too subtle for most young readers to understand, and the first-person narrative, written from an adult's perspective, will puzzle them." "Most children," Wesley continues by way of illustration, "aren't worldly enough to understand such lines as 'Miss Mary loved her "baby," however, and worked hard to get him the "lil necessaries" of life, which turned out mostly to be women.'"

Wesley is correct. Though Alice Walker's story is *about* children, it is not a story *for* children. Nevertheless, her comments do take us to the critical center of the story: the author's extremely effective use of a first person point of view whose objectivity and gentle sense of irony blunts what in less skillful hands might well have become pure sentimentality. That the narrator is twenty-four years old and finishing her doctorate at a graduate school in Massachusetts far from home underscores the force of the story's theme and the meaning it holds for her.

The theme of Walker's story has to do with the redemptive, protective, life-affirming power of love, particularly as it finds expression within the family whose life it nourishes and sustains. The love that the narrator and her family have for the "melancholy and sad" Mr. Sweet is non-judgmental, freely and unconditionally given in spite of the "facts" of the old man's life. In the eyes of the conventional world, Mr. Sweet is a shiftless reprobate—"a diabetic and an alcoholic and a guitar player" who "lived down the road...on a neglected cotton farm." "Constantly on the verge of being blind and drunk" he is also periodically on the verge of death. Whether Mr. Sweet's death-bed performances are feigned for the sake of the attention that he knows will be forthcoming, or whether they are genuine—the product of declining health, the loneliness and depression of age, and congenital poverty—scarcely matters.

What does matter is the attitude of the narrator and her brothers and sisters who see Mr. Sweet through the tolerant and forgiving eyes of childhood. To them Mr. Sweet is "very kind," an "ideal playmate," and "not in the least a stingy sort of man." He is an adult who takes children and their games seriously and "had the grace to be shy with us, which is unusual in grown-ups." When Mr. Sweet is "feeling good" (and he has the "ability to be drunk and sober at the same time"), he wrestles and dances with the children, tells them stories about his life and early dreams, and plays "all sorts of sweet, sad, wonderful songs which he sometimes made up" on his old steel guitar, "in the old sad, sweet, down-home blues way." Without condescension he makes the narrator believe she is "his princess"—to "feel pretty at five and six, and simply outrageously devastating at the blazing age of eight and a half."

But if Mr. Sweet freely gives, he also freely receives. The children's gift is one of "revival" and "rehabilitation" through love. The effect of the "rite of Mr. Sweet's rehabilitation" upon the narrator and her attitudes about life and death, as she herself makes clear, has been profound. Her return home to witness Mr. Sweet's death—an episode now measured and understood in retrospect—has become an act of initiation and discovery. For once the "rite" of revival fails: "we had not learned that death was final when it did come. We thought nothing of triumphing over it so many times, and in fact became a trifle contemptuous of people who let themselves be carried away. It did not occur to us that if our father had been dying we could not have stopped it...." In Mr. Sweet's death she discovers her own vulnerability and mortality and the vulnerability and mortality that threatens her family. She registers "surprise" "to see that my father and mother looked old and frail." It is this lesson that she receives with Mr. Sweet's old steel guitar.

EUDORA WELTY, "Why I Live at the P.O."

In response to Katherine Anne Porter's suggestion that Sister suffers from schizophrenia, Eudora Welty told an interviewer in 1963 that

> It never occurred to me while I was writing the story (and it still doesn't) that I was writing about someone in serious mental trouble. I was trying to write about the way people who live away off from nowhere have to amuse themselves by dramatizing every situation that comes along by exaggerating it—"telling it." I used the exaggerations and the ways of talking I have heard all my life. It's just the way they keep life interesting—they make an experience out of the ordinary. I wasn't trying to do anything but show that. I thought it was cheerful, on the whole.

Welty's statement is helpful, for interpretations of the story vary widely. For one critic, "Why I Live at the P.O." is "a story about [Sister's] exasperation and frustration, loneliness and near-madness." Another critic characterizes Sister as "a solid and practical person struggling to keep her self-possession and balance in the midst of a childish, neurotic, and bizarre family." One thing is certain, however. Sister's long, humorous monologue—rooted very much in the oral tradition of Southern story-telling—is scarcely the narrative of an unbiased and objective observer. It is the degree and nature of this unreliability which makes Welty's story so interesting in the classroom.

The opening paragraph demands close attention. It establishes Sister's personality and narrative voice, the nature of her grievance, and the story's setting and characters; it also provides crucial information about past events and hints at the underlying motive which shapes Sister's attitude and actions—her jealousy of Stella-Rondo, exacerbated by the fact that her sister won the battle for the attentions of the absent Mr. Whitaker. (Sister's jealousy may, in fact, be well-founded. Note, for example, the implications of both halves of Stella-Rondo's name, while Sister is nameless. She is referred to only as "Sister" by the members of her family.) Sister masks this jealousy by a pronounced sense of self-righteous indignation and by rationalizing behavior that fails to see, much less to appreciate, any perspective or point of view other than her own.

The humor of the story flows from her language and tone, from her one-sided representations of the other characters, and from the unwavering logic of the method by which she pursues her revenge. No small part of the story's effect also depends, as Ruth Vande Kieft has pointed out, "on the implications of vulgarity which counter the comedy of the monologue in an ironic way. Marriage and family life are given their direction by the cheapest advertising, movies, and radio."

Welty's story is particularly useful in dealing with point of view and with the issue of the unreliable narrator. As Barbara McKenzie observes, "Although not all narrators are unreliable and not all unreliable narrators are as blatantly untrustworthy as Sister, 'Why I

Live at the P.O.' illustrates the importance of evaluating the position of *every* narrator in *every* story. This story also reaffirms the persistence of oral story-telling as a formalistic device within the genre of short fiction, and shows how an unreliable narrator can be used for comic effect."

W.D. WETHERELL, "Wherever That Great Heart May Be"

W.D. Wetherell's story is, to be sure, something of a tour de force. It introduces us to the late nineteenth-century New York of Herman Melville through a story that reaches down into the present. The story simultaneously operates, in fact, in three separate time frames: (1) the New York of the 1870s, when Donald Buskirk is fifteen and meets Herman Melville; (2) the world of 1946, when Donald Buskirk tells the story of his strange encounter with Captain Flanagan and the girl to Alan; and (3) the narrative present in which Alan, now in his full maturity, speaks to the reader and puzzles the meaning of his grandfather's tale. That tale, it is clear, has now become as much Alan's story as his grandfather's. He has absorbed that story and made it so much his own that he can narrate its facts and details to the reader with clarity and precision, though they belong to a world that he never knew— a world very different from his own.

Donald Buskirk is a man of many "elliptical" stories. Alan senses that his grandfather wants not only to talk about the past through his "autobiographic demonstrations" but to communicate it directly: "to communicate the past directly up my arm and not depend on sound waves or any intermediary that wasn't flesh." Though he is unable to frame and artic-ulate its precise significance, the incident on Sullivan Street, which Donald recounts to his grandson, has remained vivid in his memory for some seventy years. "I've never made much sense out of it," he tells Alan. "I go back often to try to puzzle things out." This is clearly an understatement. Not only has the incident remained a troubling one, but Alan surmises that it has had a permanent effect on his grandfather and his subsequent under-standing of the world. A "bad scare" is the way Alan puts it. Just what that lesson is, how-ever, Alan cannot decide. In fact, he cannot tell if it was meant to be a lesson at all. "I still can't decide," he notes, "whether it [the story] was meant as a lesson for my cocksure assumption or as another elliptical chapter in his autobiography."

The answer to this question takes us to the very heart of the story, and clearly has very much to do with the diametrically opposed views of the world expressed by the two princi-pals of the law firm of Wimpole and Bem. Wimpole and Bem (like the narrator and the abject scrivener in Melville's famous "Bartleby the Scrivener") are very different men. Alexan-der Wimpole is "fat, avuncular, and honest." His outlook on the world is positive and opti-mistic. Peregrine Bem, on the other hand, is described as "thin, avaricious, and cruel, and even then was showing signs of the mental instability that would lead to his breakdown and the dissolution of the firm." He looks at the world and humanity through glasses clouded by negativity and pessimism. Given their opposing attitudes it is hardly surprising that Wimpole and Bem should view Captain Flanagan and his situation so differently. And it is precisely between their two interpretations that Donald Buskirk uncomfortably finds himself sus-pended. Donald himself comes to sense this polarity during his second visit to the brownstone:

> Could both Wimpole *and* Bem be right? It was a new thought to him, and it
> was much too late, before he could put it into words, but this was the moment he
> first began to sense it—that opposite stories could be true, not in a literal way, but
> by the complicated, light-and-dark intertwining in which most truth resides.

This realization comes as close to a resolution of the "Puzzle" as the story provides. Yet, as Alan finally decides, for his grandfather "an answer didn't matter. For him the important thing was that he could continue to marvel at humanity after eighty long years; still find the world, for all his knowing, an enigma." An "enigma" it remains, for the story leaves plenty of questions unanswered: Who are Captain Flanagan and the girl, and what is the true nature of their relationship? What does Flanagan mean when he whispers to Donald "Not a word or we're lost!" and "Thank God you've come!" and then instructs him to "Go now and fetch help"? What are the girl's "devilish powers" that Flanagan alludes to? And, of course, what finally happens to them?

We never learn. But that doesn't matter. As Alan Buskirk suggests, his grandfather's story (and the lesson he has learned from it) is finally about the mystery, ambiguity, and enigma of life, as well as about its continuity as represented by the stories and the traditions that are handed down from one generation to another.

As suggested above, Wetherell's story can be delightfully (and instructively) paired with Melville's own famous story of New York, "Bartleby the Scrivener," which clearly served Wetherell as a source of inspiration. Wetherell knows Melville and the details of his life well, and has done a masterful job in recreating the New York world of Melville's custom house years.

LIZA WIELAND, "The Columbus School for Girls"

Wieland's Pushcart prize-winning story is, as its title suggests, a voyage or pilgrimage of discovery into what are, for the girls at Columbus, deep, uncharted, and clearly troubling waters. It begins, significantly enough, with the old anecdote about Columbus, Isabella, and the egg (on the eve of the discovery of America), suggesting perhaps that things are often not what they seem to be and that the obvious is not infrequently overlooked. Be that as it may, Wieland's story is clearly about adolescent initiation into a world of adult passion, ending in the narrator's admission that "We know what we need to know. This is the new world." For the word "new" in the final sentence we might well substitute the word "real."

The narrative point of view is carefully chosen. It is also clearly important to our understanding of the story. By restricting it to one of the Columbus girls, we come to understand incrementally as they do how very different the world of Emily and Bryan Jerman is from what it first seems to be. The girls—whose adolescent rebellions against the constraints of boarding school life do little to mask their innocence—have a crush on their English teacher, Bryan Jerman. (That crush prefigures, of course, the crush that Emily Jerman had years before on the school's gardener who died in a dormitory fire, presumably while having an affair with a Columbus student.) The girls not only romanticize their teacher, they also romanticize his thin, quiet and apparently bloodless wife, Emily, who holds herself for the most part remote and aloof from the daily life of the school. They identify with her through the figure of American poetess Emily Dickinson, the reclusive spinster of Amherst.

The trip to Amherst to visit the Dickinson Homestead and grave slowly strips away surfaces, veneers, and facades and gives these adolescent girls a brief, and frightening glimpse, into the passions and complexities of adult life. It also exposes the husband-wife relationship between the Jermans in ways that make the narrator and her friends plainly uncomfortable. For Emily Jerman the trip to Amherst is a trip into the past, not only the past of a dead poet but into her own. The fact that she would make the trip at all simply because a long-since dead gardener once gave her postcards speaks intimates a great deal about their relationship, though not necessarily, of course, that they were lovers. Be that as it may, the gardener clearly does represent Emily Jerman's own lost youth and girlhood years at Columbus (where, we discover, she was once as rebellious as her modern counterparts).

Emily Jerman drinks double vodkas, and under their influence she begins to reveal a side of her character and life that the girls have never seen. The next day, Emily "looks terrible" and the girls who so eagerly watch her every move are plainly disturbed:

We think something has happened to her during the night. At first we believe it has to do with love, but soon we see how wrong we are, how lost, and for a split second we wish we'd never left the Columbus School for Girls.

Her behavior intensifies and becomes more inexplicable when she arrives at the Dickinson Homestead in Amherst. First, Emily will not leave the van; then, when she does enter the house to join the tour, she is crying and walks "like she's walking in a trance." Whatever her actions mean (and we know that they are somehow connected both to the dead-gardener and her own past), Emily Jerman is in obviously great emotional pain. And, significantly, as the Columbus girls note, her husband cannot or will not reach out to help her and "we hate him for that." "We stare at the two of them," the narrator says,

> and all at once we know we will never remember anything Mr. Jerman has taught us, except this: that the world is a blind knot of electric and unspeakable desires.

Emily's emotional crisis only intensifies in the graveyard, where she verbally lashes out at her husband's attempt to correct an error in the Emily Dickinson poem she is reciting. (Significantly, she has substituted the word "lost" for the word "saved.") It is at the dinner after this event, when, again with the prompting of double vodkas, Emily Jerman tells her husband and the girls more about her secret life and the gardener, who is now explicitly linked with the Garden of Eden: "The gardener could do anything, bring anything back to life. He was a genius."

This scene and its revelations prefigures and prepares us for Emily's return to the Dickinson gravesite at the conclusion of the story. "You have to learn how to keep warm," she tells the girls while standing bathed in the van's headlights. "When I was your age, I learned how. When I was your age, I was on fire. On *fire*, do you understand." The girls understand, and what they understand is succinctly summarized by the narrator in the story's last sentences: "We know what we need to know. This is the new world."

Liza Wieland has written the editor about her story as follows:

> I came to the title for this story first, before any of it was written, while talking to a friend who said she'd heard a reading at the Columbus School for Girls (in Columbus, Ohio). It came into my head vividly as a place of strangeness, of both peculiar freedom and hard restriction, the kind of institution that would breed a curious, dangerous pack of narrators. The story itself comes from a trip I took with my own students to the Dickinson Homestead in Amherst, one of the most unusual and rewarding teaching experiences I have ever had. Brian Jerman was the name of a television sportscaster in Colorado Springs, where I was living when I wrote this story. One day, I heard him paged in the Denver airport, and all parts of the narrative fell together in that inexplicable, sidelong way stories sometimes come to us. Still, despite its being so much a gift, the story didn't write itself, not by a long shot. It grew by accretion, in layers, and I never, at any point in the writing, knew what was going to happen next.

JOY WILLIAMS, "Taking Care"

As the first sentence of this story announces, Jones, the central character, is a preacher, one who has "been in love all his life." We learn that his wife is in the hospital, dying of a pernicious blood disorder, and we are given a short, sharp description of the moment when she collapsed in her garden and told her husband for the first time that she was dying. The

Joneses have one daughter. She is said to have "fallen in with the stars"—whatever that means—has either become obsessed with astrology, or has picked up the "semi-official religion" of Hollywood, or both. In any case, she has left her husband, brought her dog and year-old daughter for her father to care for, and gone out into the mountains to meet the "nervous breakdown" she has foreseen in her astrological calculations. Her father seems as supportive of her as he can be under the circumstances, as he "slips a twenty dollar bill into...(her) suitcase and drives her to the airport." The letter that he receives from her sometime later mentions neither her child nor her dying mother, whose condition has further deteriorated.

One day, Jones is driving along with the smiling, gurgling baby when he sees a splendid snowshoe rabbit start up along the road, leaping splendidly, until it suddenly tumbles inertly in the snow—shot by a hunter, as it turns out. When he returns home, he plays some of his daughter's records and tries to think of her as the happy, playful child she was, but is only reminded of the frenetic nervous wreck she is, and of the many affairs she has had with men whom she has subsequently left. The recordings are Bruckner's *Te Deum* and Mahler's *Kindertotenlieder*. Jones's life, the omniscient narrator informs us, "has been devoted to apologetics. He is concerned with both justification and remorse. He has always acted rightly, but nothing has ever come of it."

If Jones is looking for a sign, his horizon remains terribly blank. His wife no longer recognizes him. He spends his days caring for the baby, listening to records, and letting the dog in and out. One Sunday, he baptizes the baby, saying, "*We are saved not because we are worthy. We are saved because we are loved.*" But he cannot swallow the communion bread he himself has cut. "Somewhere," says the narrator, "he has lost what he was looking for." And the days go on, with further scenes of Jones feeding the baby and taking care of the dog. We are given hints of a deep, silent change, like the brilliant images of food in the freezer, as if waiting to be brought out and made part of life again. But Jones can only think of his wife in the hospital, and everything he sees is distorted by his grief.

At Christmas, Mrs. Jones will be coming home for a few days. Jones finds himself feeling enraged at the passivity of the doctors. He wants to fight back, and that is a sign of renewed life in him. On the day he is to pick up his wife, he thinks of her as she was coming home from maternity care. He places their granddaughter in her arms as he meets her, and he feels now, "Isn't everything about to begin?" In Mexico, his daughter opens a silver egg, within which stand the miniature figures of a bride and groom. Jones has cleaned the house carefully for his wife's homecoming, and "Together they enter the shining rooms."

The story turns out to be a rather traditional one of near-despair and renewal, but its genius lies in the subtlety of the presentation. Williams herself knows how to "take care," that is, how simply to nurture the images until their delicate accretion leads naturally into the mood she wishes to achieve. Jones's "taking care" is an image of the day-to-day selflessness that leads him toward a regeneration he himself could not bring about, toward "grace" in the theological sense. But his patience is also a metaphor for the artistic achievement of the narrative in which he appears, which cannot, either, be brought about through the conscious willing of the artist—that is, "grace" in the aesthetic sense.

WILLIAM CARLOS WILLIAMS, "The Use of Force"

Williams' short story is, of course, directly related to his own career as a general practitioner of medicine, though, as usual, it is unwise to make too much of the story's autobiographical relevance. The story presents a familiar enough experience, one that students can no doubt easily relate to. The general outlines are also clear enough: a doctor, despite his patient's lack of cooperation and active resistance, probably saves her life through his "use of force." But to what extent have the ends justified the means? To the extent the girl's life is saved, they probably do. But note the very high price the doctor pays for the privilege. That "price" is what the story explores.

The major conflict of the story is between the doctor and his reluctant patient, and what their encounter finally reveals about the human capacity for physical violence when the will is checked and frustrated. But there are other conflicts in the story as well: the conflict within the doctor; the conflict within each parent; and the conflict within the girl; as well as the conflict between the two parents; the conflict between the parents and the doctor; and the conflict between the parents and their willful child. The conflict of the story is, in short, by no means a simple, one-dimensional one.

The doctor is not a cruel or brutal man. He is, in fact, a well-trained and competent physician, not only medically aware of what may be at stake if his diagnosis is diphtheria, but sensitive and observant as far as both Mathilda and her parents are concerned. He notices at once that the mother is "startled looking" (although the doctor's arrival has been expected) and that "I could see that they were all very nervous, eyeing me up and down distrustfully." He has been in such situations before: "As often in such cases, they weren't telling me more than they had to; it was up to me to tell them; that's why they were spending three dollars on me."

As the doctor's examination continues, he remains very much aware of the others in the room and their words and gestures. He is also clearly aware of his own limitations as a doctor. He proceeds using his "best professional manner." At least initially, he tells the story in a casual, matter-of-fact way, which suggests that he is what he appears to be—an experienced physician with a solid bed-side manner. As readers we are led to expect easily-obtained, informed, and successful diagnosis. Such expectations, ironically, turn out to be very much misplaced.

The response of the anxious parents is largely a stereotypical one. The parents are one-dimensional and representational. They are portrayed as being ineffectual and self-effacing. Even as the doctor tries to hide his loss of temper and control, they try to hide their own shame at their inability to control their own child, their fear over her condition, and their resentment of the doctor.

Mathilda does have something to hide. The child is single-minded, willful and perverse, tenaciously determined not to allow the doctor to know the truth of her condition. Her motive is, of course, an irrational one, based on a combination of fear and pain. But in the end her motive seems only slightly less irrational than that of the doctor who would pry her secret from her by brute force.

The plot moves through a very clear series of stages in which the doctor progressively sacrifices his cool detachment, self-control, and self-esteem in his contest with the child. Students should be encouraged to identify these successive stages as the doctor moves from simple to increased frustration and then into anger and overt brutality as he tries to force his diagnosis. In the end, the doctor, the very epitome of civilization, has thoroughly compromised himself in his contest with the irrationality of the "savage brat." The questions we are ultimately forced to ponder as readers are many, not the least of which is what has taken place in the doctor's understanding of himself.

Williams deliberately chooses to make the child a girl rather than a boy, and a photogenic girl at that. Students are not likely to overlook the fact that the increasing force with which the doctor forces himself upon the child has overtly sexual overtones. Both the language and the imagery, with its Freudian symbolism, certainly suggest violation. There is the matter of the girl's physical attractiveness which the doctor notes at the same time he notes her cold antagonism. As he tries to examine her, she becomes "flushed," her breathing greatly increases, their encounter becomes more and more physical. There is the wooden spatula that splinters as the doctor tries to probe her "mouth cavity," followed by the spoon which successfully forces entry. The girl begins to bleed. And finally there is the doctor's admission:

I could have torn the child apart in my own fury and enjoyed it. It was a pleasure to attack her. My face was burning with it.

In the end, Mathilda is "overpowered" by force—her secret membrane exposed. For discussion of the issue of rape as the story poses it, both pro and con, see the Diedrich (1967) and Wagner (1967) articles in the bibliography section of this manual.

Another line of inquiry that suggests itself involves a change in the story's point of view. What if the parents told the story? What if the mother or the father tried to narrate the events that unfold before them? And what of the child's point of view? How might the story be told through her eyes? What would disappear, of course, would be our understanding of the doctor's internal conflict as he is torn between reason and emotion? But might there be compensating gains? Or would other points of view so weaken or change the story that all its impact and force would be lost?

The story has become one of the favorites of the emerging fields of medical ethics and medical humanities. As Felice Aull observes,

> The story evokes with great immediacy a number of important issues about doctoring: the predicament of having quickly to assess a medical/social situation in an unfamiliar, even hostile, environment; the doctor's impressive powers of observation; his concern to do the right thing medically; the anxiety of the sick child's parents; the power which the doctor wields; the dark side of human nature which may allow such power to surface in unsavory ways and which the professional, like any rational person, has under most circumstances learned to control.

ELIZABETH WINTHROP, "The Golden Darters"

Elizabeth Winthrop tells us just about all we need to know to frame a good class discussion of her prize-winning story "The Golden Darters" in the "Contributors' Notes" which she wrote for *The Best American Short Stories, 1992*:

> One summer four years ago, I was between two projects and determined to take a rest from writing and from thinking about writing. So, for the first time in years, I did not bring my computer with me when I went up to spend August on a small island off the coast of Connecticut. But stories seem to happen to writers when we least expect them, even when we try to shut the door on them.
>
> I dropped by to have dinner with some old friends and after we ate, the husband gave me a tour of his fly-tying corner. Joe is my idea of a Renaissance man. He paints and takes martial arts, and Italian lessons and plays the piano. He is also a hunter and an avid fly fisherman. So on one hand it was not surprising that be had chosen fly-tying as a way of passing the hours of his convalescence from a disk operation. But tying flies seemed to be such a womanish business for a man as normally robust and active is Joe. I was impressed with his patience, his perseverance, and his small motor control. When he saw that my interest seemed to go beyond the usual polite responses of dinner guests, he invited me to sit down and tie a streamer with him.
>
> It was a grown woman who accepted the invitation but a twelve-year-old girl who lowered herself into that chair. A girl who used to hate to perform in front of any kind of audience, no matter how small or how encouraging, unless she was assured of success. A girl who forced herself to listen to a grown man's quietly delivered, yet imperative, instructions because she was so frightened of failing him and yet so angry at being put in that position. And at the end of the evening, it was a grown woman with an aching back and a story starting in her head who

211

stood up from the chair, whispered her good-byes, and with her golden darter tucked safely in a pocket, crawled home to bed.

In the days that followed, the story made its slow way on to paper. With no computer, I wrote it in longhand on a yellow legal pad. My friend Joe has seen it in its various drafts, and we have cheerfully argued back and forth about the direction it took. I think he wanted a story that dealt with trout season and hatching mayflies and a man's love of the river. But as I pointed out to him, I couldn't write that story because it was not mine. Mine was about a girl's coming of age and her rebellion against control. Perhaps for Joe, my story "hung upside down," but it was the only one I knew how to tell, a point which he finally and just as cheerfully conceded.

From Elizabeth Winthrop, "Contributors' Notes,"
The Best AmericanShort Stories, 1992, Robert Stone ed.
(Boston: Houghton Mifflin Company, 1993), pp. 377–378.

TOBIAS WOLFF, "Nightingale"

What is going on here? The human, psychological dimensions of Wolff's brief story seem clear enough. Dr. Booth, attempting to find a way to make his son Owen "grow up" by enrolling him in a military academy, ends up by having to confront the realities of his own conduct and a past which he has conveniently forgotten and certainly falsified. But what of the larger dimensions of the story? There is certainly something strange and otherworldly about Fort Steele Academy, its student body, and its all-too-absent commanding officer. Whatever is going on here is suggestive, and should make for interesting classroom discussion.

The Academy, a military school which promises to turn boys into men, is appropriately named Fort Steele. This is the kind of environment that Dr. Booth, a successful physician, wants, or at least thinks he wants, for his son, Owen. Nevertheless, as they drive toward Fort Steele, Dr. Booth is uneasy. Part of his unease has to do with the "lousy map," which makes the school hard to find. It also has to do with Dr. Booth's uncertainty about why he is there in the first place. Significantly, when he presses himself about why is is *really* sending Owen away from home, an environment in which Owen is comfortable, Dr. Booth has difficulty articulating a reason. In fact, as he pulls his car to a stop in front of the Academy, he deliberately shifts the burden of that question to his son: "Well? Owen? What do I want?"

Owen and his way of life bothers him. He is too "comfortable" in his adolescence:

> He was comfortable at home. He had his foolish dog, his lazy friends, the big house with all its sunny corners. When Dr. Booth went into the kitchen, there was Owen. In the living room, Owen again. The front yard, Owen; the back yard, the basement, the hammock—Owen!

Owen's comfort stands in sharp contrast to what Dr. Booth likes to remember about his own youth. That contrast makes Dr. Booth resentful and it is apparently this resentment that has caused him to conjure up for his own benefit—and for the benefit of his son and (presumably) for his wife—a falsified version of his own past.

The brochure announcing Fort Steele Academy just arrives in Dr. Booth's mailbox. It is not something he has sent for. The picture on the cover is not a terribly encouraging one. It shows two snow-covered cadets, in black uniforms standing ram-rod straight, guarding either side of the Academy's gate. Through that gate, as Commandant Colonel Karl's statement suggests, lies manhood. The message itself is delivered without warmth:

212

"It is no kindness to the young to pretend that life is not a struggle. The world belongs to men of will, and the sooner that lesson is learned, the better. We at Fort Steele are dedicated to teaching it by every means at our disposal."

Is Dr. Booth one of those "men of will"? Why should he want Owen to be one? From the moment the brochure arrives, Dr. Booth later admits, his course has been an almost predetermined one. "His wife had resisted at first, but in spite of his own doubts he bullied her along until she, like Owen, saw the futility of argument." Later Dr. Booth will come to judge his own rationale and actions as "baffling."

Dr. Booth does undergo a process of self-recognition, during which his veneer of smug self-assurance is put aside. That recognition begins as he watches his son being led away by Corporal Costello. He realizes then that Owen is simply Owen: "The distracted saunter he kept breaking into was not an accident of age, something to be outgrown or overcome: it was, in truth, nothing less than Owen himself." Increasingly unsure of himself, Dr. Booth seeks the assurance of others: "He wasn't going to leave his son here without some definite assurances." This is what sends him to see Colonel Karl, a man he knows only from the last page of the Academy brochure. Note the strange atmosphere that haunts the "windowless lounge" outside the Colonel's office with its grandfather clock, frozen in time. There Dr. Booth waits, until something leads him to the chapel (a building which on the aerial photograph of the Academy has been moved).

Dr. Booth's penultimate moment of self-revelation might well have come in the chapel, when he sits down in a chair which he instinctively knows is "a place of judgment . . . where you sat to have your faults revealed." That moment comes later, in the car, as Dr. Booth hurries back to the Academy to rescue his son. It is then that he is finally forced to confront fully what he has done, and why. Do students find his reasons valid and psychologically compelling, or is Dr. Booth engaging in yet another round of self-deceptions?

What of Fort Steele Academy itself? Its location on the map makes it difficult to find and, having found and left, equally difficult (and apparently impossible) to return to. Wolff's story suggests that the Academy belongs to another world, and another place and time. What of the apparently missing cadets and the absent commander, too busy this day to see the naturally-concerned, tuition-paying father of one of his school's newest recruits? What of the fact that the photograph of the Academy in the "windowless lounge" near Colonel Karl's office has been faked? And the fact that when the alarmed Dr. Booth rushes back to the Academy, "determined not to leave Owen in that place," all that he finds is an old military button? "Something must have happened here, long ago," he muses, "—that was why he'd been drawn to the place. A battle; boys became men, and were lost." Is it too late? Is Owen too now to be numbered among those who are "lost"? What, finally, of the story's title? To whom or what in the story does nightingale, a bird known for the sad quality of its song, refer?

TOBIAS WOLFF, "Say Yes"

Wolff's story, like so much modern and contemporary fiction, explores the meaning of a small, seemingly insignificant, event in the lives of two ordinary people. In this case it is a couple of indeterminate age who have been married long enough to know one another well. It is not that the rough edges have been worn away by familiarity, for they obviously have not been. Both Ann and her husband have personalities distinctively their own, and as a result are not immune to quarrels such as the one staged in that most domestic of all places, the kitchen.

On this occasion the question of interracial marriage, raised in the course of a casual evening's conversation, becomes the catalyst for a story which probes and defines the personalities of each of the characters and the nature of their relationship. The quarrel that ensures also comes close to ruining their evening.

In attempting to define the basic differences between Ann and her husband, students may well find themselves taking sides. That is all to the good, for the differences here are subtle and, just as in real life, there are no villains or ogres. And for whatever else it may signify, the story's culminating scene most certainly suggests that husband and wife are willing and able to reconcile their differences and relive once again the magic of surprise and new beginnings.

The unnamed husband is, of course, the story's protagonist. We come to see him as rather smug, self-satisfied, and sure of his views. He takes pleasure in being characterized by mutual friends as "such a considerate husband," an epithet which he has earned chiefly, it seems, through helping with the evening dishes. The story explores this "considerateness," with respect both to his wife's views and needs and to her integrity as a person.

When the subject of interracial marriage is raised, the husband states his views with the stubborn authority of one who seems to have a well-considered opinion. Ann clearly resents the tone of his presumed authority and, later, the way he attempts to destroy her argument and back her into a corner with simple answers to what she (and the reader) realizes is, after all, a complex issue. Her response (and we are led to believe that they have had "discussions" of this kind before) is to pinch her brows, bite her lower lip, and stare down at something. The husband senses this resistance. But in moments like this, rather than stop, back off and reconsider, his response is to bulldoze ahead. ("When he saw her like this he knew he should keep his mouth shut, but he never did. Actually it made him talk more.")

Despite appearances, he is far more sensitive and insecure than he appears. When his opinions meet resistance, he accuses Ann of implying that he is a "racist." Note carefully, if you will, Ann's argumentative strategy. Rather than challenge his dogmatism directly, her response is to draw him out by asking more questions. Ultimately, of course, the husband traps himself. Students may well come to feel that what we have here, essentially, is a "male" strategy opposing, and being opposed by, a "female" one.

The argument between them escalates, and one of the virtues of the story's brevity is that students can be asked to trace the debate, the strategies employed, and the emotions that become involved, on a line by line basis. Note that Ann betrays her emotional involvement by washing the dishes faster. Later, she "plunges" her hand in the water and cuts herself. Her wounded thumb serves as a convenient, if obvious, metaphor.

What is at stake here for the wounded Ann is her need to be recognized and loved for herself alone—for her individuality as a person. Love implies the willingness and the ability to transcend differences between people, be they differences of race, nationality, or circumstance.

When Ann retreats, obviously angry, her husband is hurt. And being hurt, "He had no choice but to demonstrate his indifference to her." To get even, he stubbornly cleans the kitchen to the point, significantly, that it "looked new, the way it looked when they were first shown the house, before they had ever lived here."

The husband's recovery begins in the peace of the garden and ends in the bedroom. There his better instincts assert themselves. "He felt ashamed that he had let his wife get him into a fight." Other sensations follow, culminating in a scene of reconciliation. The final victory—if victory it is—would nonetheless seem to belong to Ann. She has made her point, and the message seems to register as he waits in the darkness.

Wolff's story is characterized by its economy, by its dialogue, and by its comparative lack of descriptive detail. As such it provides a good example of the contemporary short story.

RICHARD WRIGHT, "The Man Who Was Almost a Man"

Dave's need for acceptance as a man and his identification of manhood with the gun he covets is established in the story's first paragraph: "One of these days he was going to get a gun and practice shooting, and they (the older fieldhands) couldn't talk to him as though he were a little boy." Almost seventeen, he feels acutely the inferiority of his status as he sees it reflected in the attitudes of those around him. On more than one occasion, they remind him, "You ain't nothing but a boy." Though the use of the limited omniscient point of view (we view the world from Dave's perspective) makes the reader generally sympathetic to his situation, it should not blind us to the shortcomings in Dave's character and to the fact that by the very standard of his own adolescent behavior, he is "nothing but a boy yit!"

Dave's efforts to get a gun are obviously devious ("He laid the catalogue down and slipped his arm around her waist, 'Aw, Mah, Ah done worked hard alla summer n ast yuh for nothings, is Ah, now?'"); and once he obtains her permission, he immediately breaks his promise to "bring it straight back to me." Inexperienced, he is exploited by Joe the shopkeeper, who overcharges him for an old gun which he then only has the slightest idea of how to use, and then stands "helpless," unable to aid the wounded Jenny. Later, when confronted by Hawkins, his father, and the crowd, his first reaction is to deny his own responsibility and lie. Still later, he lies again about what he has done with the gun. Physically, Dave is pictured as awkward (at home he "stumbled down the back steps," "groped back to the kitchen," "tumbled in a corner for the towel," and "bumped into a chair"); and his turbulent adolescent emotions are typified by his self-pitying complaints and his easily wounded pride.

In these and other ways, Wright makes it perfectly clear that Dave is unprepared physically, emotionally, and experientially to enter manhood, and that the major attraction of the gun is that it provides the "sense of power" and the ability to command "respect that he has not yet earned." The gun is, of course, a most appropriate symbol of masculinity, both within the context of the historical American experience and in the traditional lore of initiation ceremonies where the bestowal of a weapon is a crucial part of the rite of passage. At the end of the story, in the lingering aftermath of the derisive laughter that accompanies his disgrace, Dave fires the gun again. This time, he finally succeeds in firing the gun more or less correctly, and flush with pride and courage boards tile train rather than accept the humiliation of having to repay his debt to Hawkins. But even in rebellion, Dave's manhood continues to reside in the external object in his pocket, and only "somewhere" will he become a man.

It is also interesting to consider whether the accidental killing of Jenny may not be Dave's subconscious reaction to his own exploitation and subservience ("They treat me like a mule"), for he later *consciously* and deliberately expresses a desire to fire his gun at Jim Hawkins' house. The identification of Hawkins, the white man and boss, as an object of hatred and revenge is natural enough since the price exacted as payment for the mule is clearly excessive. Further, Hawkins has publicly humiliated not only Dave but Dave's father, who abjectly sides with Hawkins against his own son.

PATRICIA ZELVER, "Love Letter"

I like Zelver's "Love Letters" a great deal, and I think that students will respond well to the story. I like the story, I must confess, because as a parent who has had to contend with teenagers (and as someone who, as a teenager, once had to contend with parents), the story rings true for me. The situation and plot ring true, the characters ring true, and so does the dialogue.

"Love Letters" is a story about mothers and daughters, about parenting, about modern family life, about change and memory and the way in which we cope with the past as we get older and the kind of person we once were. Emily, the mother and the story's focal character, is the kind of person most of us would like to know—the kind of adult we would like to be. She understands and accepts the various members of her family (each of which is try-ingly outrageous in his or her own way) and she has long since come to terms with the inconsistencies and ironies of her daily existence (for example, her life in Vista Verde, the kind of upper-middle-class subdivision which her husband Richard, the social scientist, insists "no longer works"). In the face of the kind of provocations which in other fictions drive suburban housewives to alcohol, infidelity, or both—the fifteen-year-old Rebecca; her changeling sons, Adam and Andrew, in their cowboy outfits; Richard and his penchant for measuring life by statistics and norms—Emily wants only to maintain her own iden-tity. "I don't care about the Norm," she tells Richard. "I just care about me." Emily is the glue that holds the bunch together. Without her to take care of things "The house plants would wither; the dog, starve."

The central focus of story is on the relationship between Emily and Rebecca. Both char-acters ring absolutely true. If Rebecca is a caricature of the typical precocious fifteen-year-old woman-child, the portrait is close enough to the mark to make any father or mother wince. There is great candor in Emily's appraisal: "she isn't nice at all." Above all, the dia-logue between the two of them seems just right in word, phrase, and tone. Rebecca is the innocent but interested daughter, insistent on creating one stereotypical version of her mother or another. But Emily resists. "I refuse," she notes, "to provide her with a labeled and packaged Past...." Emily deals with Rebecca, and with the rest of her family, with a wry sense of humor and its unstated refrain that "this too will pass." As the story suggests, Emily is finally neither a wimp nor hero, but only someone who has put away the past in order to get on with the present. Like all the rest of us, she has confronted the realities, ambiguities, and ironies of life which all-too-often leave us feeling phantom-like and is simply intent, as the phrase goes, on keeping it all together.

V
Bibliography of Short Fiction Criticism

ALICE ADAMS, "His Women"

Chell, Clara. "Succeeding in Their Times: Alice Adams on Women and Work," *Soundings*, LXVIII (Spring 1985), 62–71. (G)[25]

Upton, Lee. "Changing the Past: Alice Adams' Revisionary Nostalgia," *Studies in Short Fiction*, XXVI (Winter 1989), 33–41. (G)

Waxman, Barbara Frey. *From the Hearth to the Open Road: A Feminist Study of Aging in Contemporary Literature* (New York, 1990), pp. 75–94. (G)

SHERWOOD ANDERSON, "I Want to Know Why"

Bishop, John Peale. *Collected Essays of John Peale Bishop*, (New York, 1975), pp. 146–165.

Brooks, Cleanth and Robert Penn Warren. *Understanding Fiction* (New York, 1959), pp. 324–330.

Brossard, Chandler. "Sherwood Anderson: A Sweet Singer, 'A Smooth Son of a Bitch,'" *American Mercury*, 72 (1951), 611–616.

Burhans, Clinton S., Jr. "The Complex Unity of *In Our Time*," Modern Fiction Studies," 14 (1968), 313–328.

Crawford, Nelson Antrim. "Sherwood Anderson, the Wistfully Faithful," *Critical Essays on Sherwood Anderson*," David D. Anderson, ed. (Boston, 1981), pp. 65–73.

Eckley, Grace. "I Want to Know Why," *Reference Guide to Short Fiction*, Noelle Watson, ed. (Detroit, 1994), pp. 748–749.

Ellis, James. "Sherwood Anderson's Fear of Sexuality: Horses, Men, and Homosexuality," *Studies in Short Fiction*, XXXX (Fall 1993), 595–601.

Fetterly, Judith. "Growing up Male in America: 'I Want to Know Why,'" *The Resisting Reader: A Feminist Approach to American Fiction*, Judith Fetterly, ed. (Bloomington, Ind., 1978), pp. 12–22.

Gado, Frank. "The Form of Things Concealed," Introduction to *Sherwood Anderson: The Teller's Tales* (Schenectady, N.Y., 1983), pp. 1–20.

Gross, Seymour. "Sherwood Anderson's Debt to *Huckleberry Finn*," *Mark Twain Journal*, XI (1960), 3–5, 24.

Howe, Irving. *Sherwood Anderson* (New York, 1951), pp. 154–157.

Lawry, Jon S. "The Artist in America: The Case of Sherwood Anderson," *Ball State University Forum*, 7 (1966), 15–26.

———. "Love and Betrayal in Sherwood Anderson's 'I Want to Know Why,'" *Shenandoah*, XIII (Spring 1962), 46–54.

Lesser, Simon O. "The Image of the Father: A Reading of 'My Kinsman, Major Molineux' and 'I Want to Know Why,'" *Partisan Review*, XXII (Summer 1955), 372–390.

---

[25](G) Denotes articles of general rather than specific interest. This list can be updated by referring to the annual bibliography of short fiction criticism published in *Studies in Short Fiction*.

Love, Glen A. "Horses and Men: Primitive and Pastoral Elements in Sherwood Anderson," *Sherwood Anderson: Centennial Studies*, Hilbert H. Campbell and Charles E. Modlin eds. (Troy, N.Y., 1976), pp. 253–258.

Marcus, Mordecai. "What is an Initiation Story?" *Journal of Aesthetics and Art Criticism*, XIX (1960–1961), 221–228.

Naugle, Helen H. "The Name 'Bildad,'" *Modern Fiction Studies*, XXII (1976–1977), 591–594.

Papinchak, Robert Allen. *Sherwood Anderson: A Study of the Short Fiction* (New York, 1992), pp. 32–34, 110–112, 122–128, 132–137.

Parish, John E. "The Silent Father in Anderson's 'I Want to Know Why,'" *Rice University Studies*, LI (Winter 1965), 49–57.

Raymund, Bernard. "The Grammar of Non-Reason: Sherwood Anderson," *Arizona Quarterly*, XII (1956), 48–60, 137–148.

Rideout, Walter B. "'I Want to Know Why' as Biography and Fiction," *Midwestern Miscellany*, XII (1984), 7–14.

Ringe, Donald A. "Point of View and Theme in 'I Want to Know Why'," *Critique*, III (Spring–Fall 1959), 24–39.

Sherbo, Arthur. "Sherwood Anderson's 'I Want to Know Why' and Messrs. Brooks and Warren," *College English*, XV (March 1954), 350–351.

Small, Judy J. *A Reader's Guide to the Short Stories of Sherwood Anderson* (New York, 1994), pp. 209–212.

Smith, Anneliese H. "Part of the Problem: Student Response to Sherwood Anderson's ' Want to Know Why?" *Negro American Forum*, VII (1973), 28–31.

West, Ray B. *The Short Story in America, 1900–1950* (Chicago, 1952), pp. 50–52.

JAMES BALDWIN, "Sonny's Blues"

Albert, Richard N. "The Jazz-Blues Motif in Baldwin's 'Sonny's Blues,'" *College Literature* XI (1984), 178–185.

Bieganowski, Ronald. "James Baldwin's Vision of Otherness: 'Sonny's Blues' and *Giovanni's Room*," *College Language Association Journal*, XXXII (1988), 69–90.

Bigsby, C. W. E. "The Divided Mind of James Baldwin," *The Second Black Renaissance: Essays in Black Literature* (Westport, Conn., 1980), pp. 105–138. (G)

Byerman, Keith E. "Words and Music: Narrative Ambiguity in 'Sonny's Blues,'" *Studies in Short Fiction*, XIX (Fall 1982), 367–372.

Cataliotti, Robert H. *The Music in African Fiction* (New York, 1995), pp. 148–156.

Clark, Michael. "James Baldwin's 'Sonny's Blues': Childhood, Light and Art," *College Language Association Journal*, XIX (December 1985), 197–205.

Cox, Clyde. "A Lasting Legacy: Brotherly Love and the Language of Jazz in 'Sonny's Blues'," *Mid-American Review*, X (1990), 127–135.

Duncan, Charles. "Learning to Listen in 'Sonny's blues,'" *Obsidian*, IX (Fall-Winter 1994), 1–10.

Featherstone, Joseph. "Blues for Mister Baldwin," *New Republic*, CLIII (November 27, 1965), 34–36.

Flibbert, Joseph. "Sonny's Blues," *Reference Guide to Short Fiction*, Noelle Watson, ed. (Detroit, 1994), p. 904.

Goldman, Suzy B. "James Baldwin's 'Sonny's Blues': A Message in Music," *Negro American Literature Forum*, VIII (Fall 197•), 231–233.

Gross, Theodore. "The World of James Baldwin," *Critique*, VII (Winter 1964–1965), 139–149.(G)

Harris, Trudier. *Black Women in the Fiction of James Baldwin* (Knoxville, 1985), pp. 78–82.

Hills, Penny C. and L. Rust. *How We Live* (New York, 1968), pp. 772–774.

Inge, Thomas M. "James Baldwin's Blues," *Notes on Contemporary Literature*, IV (September 1972), 8–11.

Jacoby, Jay Bruce. "The Music Is the Message: Teaching Baldwin's 'Sonny's Blues,'" *English Record*, iii, XIX (1978), 2–4.

Jones, Harry L. "Style, Form, and Content in the Short Fiction of James Baldwin," *James Baldwin: A Critical Evaluation*, Therman B. O'Daniel, ed. (Washington, 1977), pp. 143–145.

Lobb, Edward. "James Baldwin's Blues and the Function of Art," *International Fiction Review*, VI (Summer 1979), 143–148.

Macebuh, Stanley. *James Baldwin: A Critical Study* (New York, 1973), pp. 173–174.

Mosher, Marlene. "Baldwin's 'Sonny's Blues,'" *Explicator*, XL (Summer 1982), 59.

Murray, Donald C. "James Baldwin's 'Sonny's Blues': Complicated and Simple," *Studies in Short Fiction*, XIV (Fall 1977), 353–357.

Ognibene, Elaine R. "Black Literature Revisited: 'Sonny's Blues,'" *English Journal*, LX (January 1971), 36–37.

Ostendorf, Bernhard. James Baldwin, "Sonny's Blues," *Die Amerikanische Short Story der Gegenwart: Interpretationen*, Peter Freese, ed. (Berlin, 1976), pp. 194–204.

Pratt, Louis H. *James Baldwin* (Boston, 1978), pp. 32–34.

Reilly, John M. "'Sonny's Blues,': James Baldwin's Image of Black Community," *Negro American Literature Forum*, IV (July 1970), 56–60. Reprinted in *James Baldwin: A Critical Evaluation*, Therman B. O'Daniel, ed. (Washington, 1977), pp. 163–169.

Ro, Sigmund. "The Black Musician as Literary Hero: Baldwin's 'Sonny's Blues' and Kelley's 'Cry for Me,'" *American Studies in Scandinavia*, VII (1975), 17–48.

———. *Rage and Celebration: Essays on Contemporary Afro-American Writing* (Atlantic Heights, N.J., 1984), pp. 12–27.

Robertson, Patricia R. "Baldwin's 'Sonny's Blues': The Scapegoat Metaphor," *University of Mississippi Studies in English*, IX (1991), 189–198.

Savery, Pancho. "Baldwin, Bebop, and 'Sonny's Blues,'" *Understanding Others: Cultural and Cross-Cultural Studies and the Teaching of Literature*, Joseph Trimmer and Tilly Warnock, eds. (Urbana, Ill., 1992), pp. 166–168, 171–174.

Sylvander, Carolyn Wedin. *James Baldwin* (New York, 1980), pp. 116–117.

Tsomondo, Thorell. "No Other Tale to Tell: 'Sonny's Blues' and *Waiting for the Rain*," *Critique*, XXXVI (Spring 1995), 195–209.

Williams, Shirley Anne. "The Black Musician: The Black Hero as Light Bearer," *Give Birth to Brightness* (New York, 1973), pp. 145–166.

DONALD BARTHELME, "Cortés and Montezuma"

Bawer, Bruce. "Donald Barthelme," *New Criterion*, IX (January 1991), 22–30. (G)

Brans, Jo. "Embracing the World: An Interview with Donald Barthelme," *Southern Review*, LXVII (Spring 1982), 121–137. (G)

Brown, Rosellen. "Donald Barthelme: A Preliminary Account," *South Atlantic Quarterly*, XC (Summer 1991), 483–498 (G).

Courturie, Maurice and Regis Durand. *Donald Barthelme* (London, 1982). (G)

Cowley, Julian. "'weeping map intensive activity din': Reading Donald Barthelme," *University of Toronto Quarterly* LX (Winter 1990/1), 292–304. (G)

Dickstein, Morris. "Fiction at the Crossroads," *Gates of Eden* (New York, 1977), pp. 216–226. (G)

Ditsky, John. "'With Ingenuity and Hard Work, Distracted': The Narrative Style of Donald Barthelme," *Style*, IX (Summer 1975), 388–400. (G)

Domini, John. "Donald Barthelme: The Modernist Uprising," *Southwest Review*, LXXV (Winter 1990), 95–112. (G)

Fitzgerald, Sheila, ed. *Short Story Criticism: Excerpts from Criticism of the Works of Short Fiction Writers,* II (Detroit, 1989), pp. 24–58. (G)

Gass, William H. "The Leading Edge of the Trash Phenomenon," *Fiction and the Figures of Life* (New York, 1970), pp. 97–103. (G)

Gordon, Lois. *Donald Barthelme* (Boston, 1981). (G)

Guerard, Albert J. "Notes on the Rhetoric of Anti-Realism Fiction," *TriQuarterly,* XXX (Spring 1974), 3–50. (G)

Hiner, James. "I Will Tell the Meaning of Barthelme," *Denver Quarterly,* XIII (Winter 1979), 61–76.(G)

Johnson, R. E., Jr. "'Bees Barking in the Night': The End and Beginning of Donald Barthelme's Narrative," *Boundary 2,* V (1976), 71–92. (G)

Karl, Frederick R. *American Fictions: 1940–1980* (New York, 1983), pp. 384–396. (G)

Klinkowitz, Jerome. *Donald Barthelme: An Exhibition* (Durham, N. C., 1991). (G)

———. *Literary Disruptions: The Making of a Post–Contemporary American Fiction* (Urbana, Ill., 1975), pp. 62–81. (G)

Leitch, Thomas M. "Donald Barthelme and the End of the End." *Modern Fiction Studies,* XXVIII (Spring 1982),129–143. (G)

McCaffery, Larry. "Donald Barthelme: The Aesthetics of Trash," *The Metafictional Muse: The Works, of Robert Coover, Donald Barthelme, and William H. Gass* (Pittsburgh, 1982), pp. 99–150.(G)

———. "An Interview with Donald Barthelme," *Partisan Review,* XLIX, 2 (1982), 184–193. (G)

Molesworth, Charles. *Donald Barthelme's Fiction: The Ironist Saved From Drowning* (Columbia, Mo., 1982). (G)

O'Hara, J. D. "Donald Barthelme: The Art of Fiction LXVI," *Paris Review,* XXIII (Summer 1981), 180–210. (G)

Olsen, Lance. "Linguistic Pratfalls in Barthelme," *South Atlantic Review,* LI (November 1986), 69–77. (G)

———, ed. "Pre-texts to Barthelme," *Review of Contemporary Fiction,* XI (Summer 1991), 17–33. (G)

Owens, Clarke. "Donald Barthelme's Existential Acts of Art," *Since Flannery O'Connor: Essays on the Contemporary American Short Story,* Loren Logsdon and Charles W. Mayer, eds. (Macomb, Ill., 1987), pp. 72–82. (G)

Patteson, Richard F., ed. *Critical Essays on Donald Barthelme* (Boston, 1992).

Porush, David. "Fiction at the End of the Mechanical Age: Barthelme's Art 'which has not yet been invented,'" *Review Of Contemporary Fiction,* XI (Summer 1991), 83–93. (G)

Roe, Barbara L. *Donald Barthelme: A Study of the Short Fiction* (New York, 1992), pp. 62–63, 103–104.

Rother, James. "Parafiction: The Adjacent Universe of Barth, Barthelme, Punchon, and Nabokov," *Boundary 2,* V (Fall 1976), 21–44. (G)

Schmitz, Neil. "Donald Barthelme and the Emergence of Modern Satire," *Minnesota Review,* I (Fall 1971), 109–118. (G)

Stengel, Wayne B. *The Shape of Art in the Short Stories of Donald Barthelme* (Baton Rouge, 1985). (G)

Stott, William. "Donald Barthelme and the Death of Fiction," *Prospects: Annual of American Cultural Studies,* I (1975), 369–386. (G)

Trachtenberg, Stanley. *Understanding Donald Barthelme* (Columbia, S.C., 1990), pp. 214–220.

Warde, William B., Jr. "A Collage Approach: Donald Barthelme's Literary Fragments," *Journal of American Culture,* VIII (Spring 1985), 52–56. (G)

Wilde, Alan. *Middle Grounds: Studies in Contemporary American Fiction* (Philadelphia, 1987), pp.161–172. (G)

RICK BASS, "Antlers"

Lyons, Bonnie, and Bill Oliver. "Out of Boundaries: An Interview with Rick Bass," *Newl*, LIX, 3 (1993), 57–73. (G)

ANN BEATTIE, "Janus"

Beattie, Ann, and Neila C. Seshachari. "Picturing Ann Beattie: A Dialogue, Interview," *Weber Studies*, VII (Spring 1990), 12–36. (G)

Centola, Steven R. "Redefining the American Dream: Ann Beattie and the Pursuit of Happiness," *CLA Journal*, XXXIV (December 1990), 161–173.

Hornby, Nick. *Contemporary American Fiction* (London, 1992), pp. 7–29. (G)

Iyer, Pico. "The World According to Beattie," *Partisan Review*, L (1983), 548–553. (G)

McCaffery, Larry and Linda Gregory. "A Conversation with Ann Beattie," *Literary Review*, XXVII (Winter 1984), 165–177. (G)

McKinstry, Susan Jarey. "The Speaking Silence of Ann Beattie's Voices," *Studies in Short Fiction*, XXIV (Spring 1987), 111–117. (G)

Miller, Philip. "Beattie's 'Janus,'" *Explicator*, XLVI (Fall 1987), 48–49.

Montresor, Jaye Berman, ed. *The Critical Response to Ann Beattie* (Westport, Conn., 1993). (G)

Olster, Stacey. "Photographs and Fantasies in the Stories of Ann Beattie," *Since Flannery O'Connor: Essays on the Contemporary American Short Story*, Loren Logsdon and Charles W. Mayer, eds. (Macomb, Ill., 1987), pp.113–123. (G)

Segal, David, ed. *Short Story Criticism: Excerpts from Criticism of the Works of Short Fiction Writers*, XI (Detroit, 1992), pp. 1–35. (G)

Wilson, William S. "Ann Beattie's implications," *Mississippi Review*, XL–XLI (Winter 1985), 90–94, (G)

Wyatt, David. "Ann Beattie," *Southern Review*, XXVIII (January 1992), 145–159.

SAUL BELLOW, "Looking for Mr. Green"

Abbott, H. Porter. *Diary Fiction: Writing as Action* (Ithaca, N.Y., 1984), pp. 172–174.

Clayton, John Jacob. *Saul Bellow: In Defense of Man* (Bloomington, Ind., 1968), pp. 21–22.

Demarest, David P., Jr. "The Theme of Discontinuity in Saul Bellow's Fiction: 'Looking for Mr. Green' and 'A Father-to-Be,'" *Studies in Short Fiction*, VI (Winter 1969), 175–186.

Dowling, David. "Looking for Mr. Green," *Reference Guide to Short Fiction*, Noelle Watson, ed. (Detroit, 1994), pp. 780–782.

Friedrich, Marianne M. *Character and Narration in the Short Fiction of Saul Bellow* (New York, 1995), pp. 47–57.

Fuchs, Daniel. *Saul Bellow: Vision and Revision* (Durham, N.C., 1984), pp. 287–289.

Kiernan, Robert F. *Saul Bellow* (New York, 1989), pp. 121–124.

Kindiflen, Glenn A. "The Meaning of the Name 'Green' in Saul Bellow's 'Looking for Mr. Green,'" *Studies in Short Fiction*, XV (Winter 1978), pp. 104–107.

Nakajima, Kenji. "A Study of Saul Bellow's 'Looking for Mr. Green,'" *Kyushu American Literature*, XVIII (1977), 5–18.

Opdahl, Keith Michael. *The Novels of Saul Bellow: An Introduction* (University Park, Pa., 1967), pp.100–106.

Rodrigues, Eusebio L. "Koheleth in Chicago: The Quest for the Real in 'Looking for Mr. Green,'" *Studies in Short Fiction*, XI (Fall 1974), 387–393.

Shear, Walter. "Bellow's Fictional Rhetoric: The Voice of the Other," *Saul Bellow and the Struggle at the Center*, Eugene Hollahan, ed. (New York, 1996), pp. 189–202.

AMBROSE BIERCE, "An Occurrence at Owl Creek Bridge"

Ames, Clifford. "Do I Wake or Sleep? Technique as Content in Ambrose Bierce's Short Story, 'An Occurrence at Owl Creek Bridge,'" *American Literary Realism*, XIX (Spring 1987), 52–67.

Bahr, Howard W. "Ambrose Bierce and Realism," *Southern Quarterly*, I (July 1963), 309–331. (G)

Barrett, Gerald R. "From Fiction to Film," *From Fiction to Film: Ambrose Bierce's "An Occurrence at Owl Creek Bridge,"* Gerald R. Baffett and Thomas L. Erksine, eds. (Encino, Calif., 1973), pp. 2–37.

———. "Double Feature: Two Versions of a Hanging," *Ibid.*, pp. 189–211.

Bellone, Julius. "Outer Space and Inner Space: Robert Enrico's 'An Occurrence at Owl Creek Bridge,'" *Ibid.*, pp. 177–187.

Cheatham, George and Judy. "Bierce's 'An Occurrence at Owl Creek Bridge,'" *Explicator*, XLIII (Fall 1984), 46–47.

———. "Point of View in Bierce's 'Owl Creek Bridge,'" *American Literary Realism* (Spring and Autumn 1985), 219–225.

Comprone, Joseph J. "A Dual-Media Look at 'An Occurrence at Owl Creek Bridge,'" *Exercise Exchange*, XVII (Fall 1972), 14–17.

Conlogue, William. "Bierce's 'An Occurrence at Owl Creek Bridge,'" *Explicator*, XLVIII (Fall 1989), 37–38.

Crane, John Kenny. "Crossing the Bar Twice: Post-Mortem Consciousness in Bierce, Hemingway, and Golding," *Studies in Short Fiction*, VI (Summer 1969), 361–376.

Davidson, Cathy N. *The Experimental Fictions of Ambrose Bierce: Structuring the Ineffable* (Lincoln, Nebr., 1984), pp. 45–54, 125–130.

———. "Literary Semantics and the Fiction of Ambrose Bierce," *ETC: A Review of General Semantics* XXXI (September 1974), 263–271.

Erskine, Thomas L. "Language and Theme in 'An Occurrence at Owl Creek Bridge,'" *From Fiction to Film: Ambrose Bierce's "An Occurrence at Owl Creek Bridge,"* Gerald R. Barrett and Thomas L. Erskine, eds. (Encino, Calif., 1973), pp. 69–75.

Fabo, Kinga. "Ambrose Bierce: An Occurrence at Owl Creek Bridge," *Acta litteraria academie scientiarum Hungaricae*, XIV, 1–2 (1982), 225–232.

Fraser, Howard M. "Points South: Ambrose Bierce, Jorge Luis Borges, and the Fantastic," *Studies in Twentieth Century Literature*, I (1976), 173–181.

Fusco, Richard. *Maupassant and the American Short Story: The Influence of Form at the Turn of the Century* (University Park, Pa., 1994), pp. 112–115.

Geduld, Harry M. "Literature into Film: 'An Occurrence at Owl Creek Bridge,'" *Yearbook of Comparative Literature*, XXVII (1978),57–58.

Grenander, M. E. *Ambrose Bierce* (New York, 1971), pp. 93–96.

———. "Bierce's Turn of the Screw. Tales of Ironical Terror," *Western Humanities Review*, XI (Summer 1957), 257–264.

Hagopian, John V. and Martin Dolch, eds. *Insight: Analyses of American Literature* (Frankfurt, 1962), pp. 26–28.

Hartwell, Ronald. "What Hemingway Learned from Ambrose Bierce," *Research Studies*, XXXVIII (1970), 309–311.

Hayden, Brad. "Ambrose Bierce: The Esthetics of a Derelict Romance," *The Gypsy Scholar*, VII (Winter 1980), 11–13.

Joshi, S.T. *The Weird Tale* (Austin, Tex., 1990), pp. 163–164.

Linklin, Harriet Kramer. "Narrative Technique in 'An Occurrence at Owl Creek Bridge,'" *Journal of Narrative Technique*, XVIII (Spring 1988), 137–152.

Logan, F.J. "The Wry Seriousness of 'Owl Creek Bridge,'" *American Literary Review*, X (Spring 1977), 101–113.

May, Charles E. "The Occurence at Owl Creek Bridge," *Reference Guide to Short Fiction*, Noelle Watson, ed. (Detroit, 1994), p. 828.

Owens, David M. "Bierce and Biography: The Location of Owl Creek Bridge," *American Literary Realism*. XXVI (Spring 1994), 82–89.

Palmer, James W. "From Owl Creek Bridge to *La Rivière du Hibou*: The Film Adaptation of Bierce's 'An Occurrence at Owl Creek Bridge,'" *Southern Humanities Review*, XI (1977), 363–371.

Powers, James G. "Freud and Farquhar: An Occurrence at Owl Creek Bridge?" *Studies in Short Fiction*, XIX (Summer 1982), 278–281.

Shadoian, Jack. "So Who Is Peyton Farquhar?: The Question of Technique in "An Occurrence at Owl Creek Bridge,'" *From Fiction to Film: Ambrose Bierce's "An Occurrence at Owl Creek Bridge,"* Gerald R. Barrett and Thomas L. Erskine, eds. (Encino, Calif., 1973), p. 166–174.

Solomon, Eric. "The Bitterness of Battle: Ambrose Bierce's War Fiction," *Midwest Quarterly*, V (January 1964), 147–165.

Stoicheff, Peter. "'Something Uncanny': The Dream Structure in Ambrose Bierce's 'An Occurrence at Owl Creek Bridge,'" *Studies in Short Fiction*, XXX (Summer 1993), 349–357.

Welsh, James. "The First 'Occurrence' on Film: Charles Vidor and Ambrose Bierce," *From Fiction to Film: Ambrose Bierce's "An Occurrence at Owl Creek Bridge,"* Gerald R. Barrett and Thomas L. Erskine, eds. (Encino, Calif., 1973), pp. 160–165.

Wilson, Edmund. "Ambrose Bierce on The Owl Creek Bridge," *New Yorker*, XXVII (December 8, 1951), 159–170.

Wilt, Napier. "Ambrose Bierce and the Civil War," *American Literature*, I(1929), 260–285. (G)

Woodruff, Stuart C. *The Short Stories of Ambrose Bierce: A Study in Polarity* (Pittsburgh, 1964), pp. 153–163.

ELIZABETH BOWEN, "The Demon Lover"

Austin, Allan E. *Elizabeth Bowen* (Boston, 1989), pp. 73–75.

Bowen, Elizabeth. "The Demon Lover," *The Mulberry Tree: Writings of Elizabeth Bowen*, Hermione Lee, ed. (San Diego, 1987), pp. 94–99.

Calder, Robert L. "'A More Sinister Troth': Elizabeth Bowen's 'The Demon Lover' as Allegory," *Studies in Short Fiction*, XXXI (Winter 1994), 91–97.

Church, Margaret. "Social Consciousness in the Works of Elizabeth Bowen, Iris Murdoch, and Mary Lavin," *College Literature*, VII (Spring 1980), 158–163. (G)

Franstino, Daniel V, "Elizabeth Bowen's 'The Demon Lover': Psychosis or Seduction?" *Studies in Short Fiction*, XVII (Fall 1980), 483–487.

Glendinning, Victoria. *Elizabeth Bowen* (London, 1977). (G)

Greene, George. "Elizabeth Bowen: The Sleuth Who Bugged Tea Cups," *Virginia Quarterly Review*, LXVII (1991), 614–616.

Hardwick, Elizabeth. "Elizabeth Bowen's Fiction," *Partisan Review*, XVI November 1949), 1114–1121. (G)

Heath, William. *Elizabeth Bowen: An Introduction to Her Novels* (Madison, Wis., 196 1), pp. 106–108.

Hughes, Douglas A. "Cracks in the Psyche: Elizabeth Bowen's 'The Demon Lover,'" *Studies in Short Fiction*, X (Fall 1973), 411–413.

Jarrett, Mary. "Ambiguous Ghosts; The Short Stories of Elizabeth Bowen," *Journal of the Short Story in English*, VIII (Spring 1987), 71–79.

Kenney, Edwin, Jr. *Elizabeth Bowen* (London, 1981). (G)

Lassner, Phyllis. *Elizabeth Bowen* (Savage, Md., 1990). (G)

————. *Elizabeth Bowen: A Study of the Short Fiction* (New York, 1991), pp. 64–67.

Lee, Hermione. *Elizabeth Bowen: An Estimation* (London, 1981), pp. 160–161.

May, Charles E. "The Demon Lover," *Reference Guide to Short Fiction*, Noelle Watson, ed. (Detroit, 1994), pp. 688–689.

Mellors, John. "Dreams in War: Second Thoughts on Elizabeth Bowen," *London Magazine*, XIX (November 1979), 64–69. (G)

Mitchell, Edward. "Themes in Elizabeth Bowen's Short Stories," *Critique*, VIII (Spring-Summer 1966), 42–54. (G)

Saul, George Brandon. "The Short Stories of Elizabeth Bowen," *Arizona Quarterly*, XXI (Spring 1965), 53–59.

Snow, Lotus. "The Uncertain 'I': A Study of Elizabeth Bowen's Fiction," *Western Humanities Review*, IV (Autumn 1950), 299–310. (G)

KAY BOYLE, "Astronomer's Wife"

Bell, Elizabeth S. *Kay Boyle: A Study of the Short Fiction* (New York, 1992). (G)

Carpenter, Richard C. "Kay Boyle," *College English*. XV (November 1953), 81–87. (G)

Clark, Suzanne. "Revolution, the Women, and the Word," *Twentieth Century Literature*, XXXIV (Fall 1988). 322–333. (G)

Gronning, Robyn M. "Boyle's' Astronomer's Wife," *Explicator*, XLVI (Spring 1988), 51–53.

Slady, Paul. "Astronomer's Wife," *Reference Guide to Short Fiction*, Noelle Watson, ed. (Detroit, 1994), p. 626.

Spanier, Sandra Whipple. "Kay Boyle: In a Woman's Voice, " *Faith of a (Woman) Writer*, Alice Kessler-Harris and William McBrien, eds. (Westport, Conn., 1986), pp. 59–70. (G)

Votteler, Thomas, ed. *Short Story Criticism: Excerpts from the Criticism of the Works of Short Fiction Writers*, V (Detroit, 1990), pp. 51–77. (G)

RAY BRADBURY, "August 2002: Night Meeting"

Clareson, Thomas D. *Understanding Contemporary American Science Fiction: The Formative Period (1926–1970)* (Columbia, S.C., 1990), pp. 50–58. (G)

Forrester, Kent. "The Danger of Being Ernest: Ray Bradbury and *The Martian Chronicles*,"*Journal of General Education*, XXVIII (Spring 1976), 50–54. (G)

Gallagher, Edward J. "The Thematic Structure of *The Martian Chronicles*," Ray Bradbury, Martin Harry Greenberg and Joseph D. Olander, eds. (New York, 1980), pp. 55–82. (G)

Greenberg, Harry Martin, and Joseph D. Olander, eds. *Ray Bradbury* (New York, 1980). (G)

Grimsley, Juliet. *"The Martian Chronicles:* A Provocative Study," *English Journal*, LIX (December 1970),1239–1242. (G)

Johnson, Wayne L. "Mars, *The Martian Chronicles*, Other Mars Stories," *Ray Bradbury* (New York, 1990), pp. 106–119. (G)

McNelly, Willis E. "Ray Bradbury," *Science Fiction Writers: Critical Studies of the Major Authors from the Early Nineteenth Century to the Present Day*, E. F. Bleiler, ed. (New York, 1982), pp. 171–178. (G)

Mogen, David. *Ray Bradbury* (Boston, 1986), pp. 82–93. (G)

Moskowitz, Sam. *Seekers of Tomorrow: Masters of Modern Science Fiction* (New York, 1967). pp.351–370.(G)

Nolan, William F., ed. *The Ray Bradbury Companion* (Detroit, 1975). (G)

Platt, Charles. *Dream Makers: Science Fiction and Fantasy Writers at Work* (New York, 1987), pp.161–171.(G)

Rabkin, Eric S. "To Fairyland by Rocket: Bradbury Is *The Martian Chronicles*," *Ray Bradbury*, Martin Harry Greenberg and Joseph D. Olander, eds. (New York, 1980), pp. 110– 126. (G)

Reilly, Robert. "The Artistry of Ray Bradbury," *Extrapolation*, XIII (December 1971), 64–74. (G)

Slusser, George Edgar. *The Bradbury Chronicles* (San Bernadino, Ca., 1977). (G)

Sullivan, Anita T. "Ray Bradbury and Fantasy," *English Journal*, LXI (December 1972), 1309–1314. (G)

Touponce, William F. *Naming the Unnameable: Ray Bradbury and* (New York, 1996). (G)

———. *:Ray Bradbury* (New York, 1988)

———. *Ray Bradbury and the Poetics of Reverie: Fantasy, Science Fiction, and the Reader* (Ann Arbor, 1984). (G)

ALBERT CAMUS, "The Guest"

Artinian, Robert W. "The Bitter Sands: Camus; 'L'Hôte,'" *Notes on Contemporary Literature*, I (March 1971), 5–6.

Black, Moishe. "Camus's 'L'Hôte,' as a Ritual of Hospitality," *Nottingham French Studies* XXVIII (1989), 39–52.

Bovey, Shirley E. "Albert Camus' The Guest,'" *Notes on Contemporary Literature*, VII (March 1977), 9–10.

Braun, Lev. *Witness of Decline: Albert Camus, Moralist of the Absurd* (Rutherford, N.J., 1974), pp. 217–220.

Cervo, Nathan. "Camus' 'L'Hôte,'" *Explicator*, XLVIII (1990), 222–224.

Crant, Phillip. "Conflict and Confrontation: An Essay on Camus's 'L'hote,'" *University of South Florida Language Quarterly*, XII (Fall-Winter 1973), 43–46.

Ellison, David R. *Understanding Albert Camus* (Columbia, S.C., 1990), pp. 194–199.

Fitch, Brian T. *The Narcissistic Text: A Reading of Camus's Fiction* (Toronto, 1982).

Fortier, Paul A. "Le Decor Symbolique de 'L'Hôte' d'Albert Camus," *French Review*, LXVI (February 1973), 535–542.

Greenlee, James W. "Camus' 'Guest': The Inadmissible Complicity," *Studies in Twentieth Century Literature*, II (Spring 1978), 127–139.

Griem, Eberhard. "Albert Camus's 'The Guest': A New Look at the Prisoner," *Studies in Short Fiction*, XXX (Winter 1993), 95–98.

Grimaud, Michel. "Humanism and the "White Man's Burden': Camus, Daru, Meursault, and the Arabs," *Camus's "L'Etranger": Fifty Years On*, Adele King, ed. (New York, (1992), pp. 170–171, 175–180.

Grobe, E. P. "The Psychological Structure of Camus' 'L'Hôte,'" *French Review*, XLIII (1973), 357–376.

Gunter, G. O. "The Irony of Alienation in 'The Guest,'" *Notes on Contemporary Literature*, VIII (March 1978), 5–7.

Hurley, D.F. "Looking for the Arab: Reading the Readings of Camus's 'The Guest,'" *Studies in Short Fiction*, XXX (Winter 1993), 79–93.

Kroker, Arthur and David Cook. *The Postmodern Scene: Excremental Culture and Hyper-Aesthetics* (New York, 1986), pp. 206–208.

La Vallee-Williams, Martha. "Arabs in 'La femme adultere': from Faceless Other to Agent," *Revue Celfan/Celfan Review*, IV (May 1985), 6–10.

McDermott, John V. "Albert Camus' Flawed Guest," *Notes on Contemporary Literature*, XIV (May 1984), 5–7.

———. "Camus' Daru: Just How Humane?" *Notes on Contemporary Literature*, XV (May 1985), 11–12.

Minor, Anne. "The Short Stories of Albert Camus," *Yale French Studies*, XXV (Spring 1960), 75–80. (G)

O'Faolain, Sean. *Short Stories: A Study in Pleasure* (Boston, 1961), pp. 159–162.

Perrine, Laurence. "Camus' 'The Guest': A Reply," *Notes on Contemporary Literature*, VIII (September 1978), 4.

———. "Camus' 'The Guest': A Subtle and Difficult Story," *Studies in Short Fiction*, I (Fall 1963), 52–58.

———. "Daru: Camus' Humane Host," *Notes on Contemporary Literature*, XIV (November 1984), 11–12.

Rhein, Phillip H. *Albert Camus* (New York, 1969), pp. 125–126.

Rooke, Constance. "Camus' 'The Guest': The Message on the Blackboard," *Studies in Short Fiction*, XIV (Winter 1977), 78–81.

Showalter, Elaine. "Camus' Mysterious Guests: A Note on the Value of Ambiguity," *Studies in Short Fiction*, IV (Summer 1967), 348–350.

———. *Exiles and Strangers: A Reading of Camus' "Exile and the Kingdom"* (Columbus, Ohio, 1983), pp. 73–87.

Simon, John K. "Camus' Kingdom: The Native Host and the Unwanted Guest," *Studies in Short Fiction*, I (Summer 1964), 289–291.

Smith, Annette. "Algeria in the Work of Albert Camus," *Claremont Quarterly*, VII (July 1960), 5–13. (G)

Smith, Christopher. "The Guest," *Reference Guide to Short Fiction*, Noelle Watson, ed. (Detroit, 1994), pp. 726–727.

Sterling, Elwyn F. "A Story of Cain: Another Look at 'L'Hôte,'" *French Review*, LIV (1981), 524–529.

Stoltzfus, Ben. "Camus and the Meaning of Revolt," *Modern Fiction Studies*, X (Autumn 1964), 293–302. (G)

Storey, Michael. "The Guests of Frank O'Connor and Albert Camus," *Contemporary Literature Studies*, XXIII (1986), 250–262.

Tarrow, Susan. *Exile and Kingdom: A Political Reading of Albert Camus* (University, Ala., 1985), pp. 181–183.

Trilling, Lionel. *Prefaces to the Experience of Literature* (New York, 1979), pp. 166–169.

Womack, William R. and Francis S. Heck. "A Note on Camus' 'The Guest,'" *International Fiction and Review*, 11 (1975), 165.

RAYMOND CARVER, "Cathedral"

Alton, John. "What We Talk About When We Talk About Literature: An Interview with Raymond Carver," *Chicago Review*, XXXVI (Autumn 1988), 4–21. (G)

Bosha, Francis J. "Raymond Carver's 'Cathedral,'" *Thought Currents in English Literature*, LVII (1984), 149–151.

Boxer, David and Cassandra Phillips. "Will You Please Be Quiet, Please?: Voyeurism, Dissociation, and the Art of Raymond Carver," *Iowa Review*, X (Summer 1979), 75–90. (G)

Brown, Arthur A. "Raymond Carver and Postmodern Humanism," *Critique*, XXXI (Winter 1990), 125–136. (G)

Bugeja, Michael J. "Tarnish and Silver: An Analysis of Carver's 'Cathedral,'" *South Dakota Review*, XXIV, No. 3 (1986), 73–87.

Bullock, Chris J. "From Castle to Cathedral: The Architecture of Maculinity in Raymond Carver's 'Cathedral,'" *Journal of Men's Studies*, II, 4 (1994), 343–351.

Campbell, Ewing. *Raymond Carver: A Study of the Short Fiction* (New York, 1992), pp. 63–66, 135–139.

Carver, Maryann et. al. "Glimpses: Raymond Carver," *Paris Review*, 118 (Spring 1991), 260–303. (G)

Chenetier, Marc. "Living On/Off the 'Reserve': Performance, Interrogation, and Negativity in the Works of Raymond Carver," *Critical Angles: European Views of Contemporary American Culture*, Marc Chenetier, ed. (Carbondale, Ill., 1986), pp. 164–190. (G)

Clarke, Graham. "Investing the Glimpse: Raymond Carver and the Syntax of Silence," *The New American Writing: Essays on American Literature Since 1970*, Graham Clarke, ed. (New York 1990), pp. 165–190. (G)

Curnutt, Kirk. *Wise Economies: Brevity and Storytelling in American Short Stories* (Moscow, Ida., 1997), pp. 231–244. (G)

Cushman, Keith. "Blind, Intertextual Love: 'The Blind Man' and Raymond Carver's 'Cathedral.'" *Etudes Lawrenciennes* (May 1988), 125–128.

Engel, Monroe. "Knowing More Than One Imagines: Imagining More Than One Knows," *Agni*, XXXI-XXXII (1990), 167–169.

Facknitz, Mark A. R. "'The Calm,' 'A Small, Good Thing,' and 'Cathedral': Raymond Carver and the Rediscovery of Human Worth," *Studies in Short Fiction*, XXIII (Summer 1986), 287–296.

———. "Raymond Carver and the Menace of Minimalism," *CEA Critic*, LII (Fall 1989/Winter 1990), 62–73. (G)

Fontana, Ernest L. "Insomnia in Raymond Carver's Fiction," *Studies in Short Fiction*, XXVI (Fall 1989), 447–451. (G)

Gearhart, Michael William. "Breaking the Ties That Bind: In-articulation in the Fiction of Raymond Carver," *Studies in Short Fiction*, XXVI (Fall 1989), 439–446. (G)

Gentry, Marshall Bruce. "Woman's Voices in Stories by Raymond Carver," *CEA Critic*, LVI, i (1993), 86–95. (G)

———, and Wallace L. Stull, eds. *Conversations with Raymond Carver* (Jackson, Miss., 1990). (G)

Gilder, Joshua. "Less is Less," *New Criterion* (February 1983), 78–82. (G)

Grinnell, James W. "Raymond Carver: 'Cathedral'" *Studies in Short Fiction*, XXI (Winter 1984), 71–72.

Hathcock, Nathan. "'The Possibility of Resurrection': Revision in Carver's 'Feathers' and 'Cathedral,' *Studies in Short Fiction*, XXVIII (Winter 1991), 31–39.

Hornby, Nick. *Contemporary American Fiction* (London, 1992), pp. 30–52. (G)

Jansen, Reamy. "Being Lonely—Dimension of the Short Story," *Cross Currents*, XXXIX (1989–1990), 391–401, 419.

Lehmen, Daniel W. "Raymond Carver's Management of Symbol," *Journal of the Short Story in English*, XVII (1991), 43–58.

Lonnquist, Barbara C. "Narrative Displacement and Literary Faith: Raymond Carver's Inheritance from Flannery O'Connor," *Since Flannery O'Connor: Essays of the Contemporary American Short Story*, Loren Logsdon and Charles W. Mayer, eds. (Macomb, Ill., 1987), pp. 142–150. (G)

McCaffery, Larry and Linda Gregory. "An Interview with Raymond Carver," *Mississippi Review*, XL (Winter 1985), 62–82. (G)

Meyer, Adam. "Now You See Him, Now You Don't, Now You Do Again: The Evolution of Raymond Carver's Minimalism," *Critique*, XXX (Sumner 1989), 239–251.

———. *Raymond Carver* (New York, 1995), pp. 144–146.

Mullen, Bill. "A Subtle Spectacle: Television Culture in the Short Stories of Raymond Carver," *Critique*, 29 (Winter 1998), 99–114. (G)

Nesset, Kirk. "Insularity and Self-Enlargement in Raymond Carver's 'Cathedral,'" *Essays in Literature*, XXI, 1 (1994), 116–128.

———. *The Stories of Raymond Carver: A Critical Study* Athens, Ohio, 1995), pp. 66–70.

———. "'This Word Love': Sexual Politics and Silence in Early Raymond Carver," *American Literature* LXIII (June 1991), 292–313. (G)

O'Connell, Nicholas. *At the Field's End: Interviews with Twenty Pacific Northwest Writers* (Seattle, 1987), pp. 76–94. (G)

Powell, Jon. "The Stories of Raymond Carver: The Menace of Perpetual Uncertainty," *Studies in Short Fiction*, XXXI (Fall 1994), 647–656. (G)

Runyon, Randolph P. *Reading Raymond Carver* (Syracuse, 1992), pp. 181–185.

Saltzman, Arthur M. *Understanding Raymond Carver* (Columbia, S.C., 1988), pp. 151–154.

Shute, Kathleen. "Finding the Words: The Struggle for Salvation in the Fiction of Raymond Carver," *Hollins Critic*, XXIII (December 1987), 1–19.

Simpson Mona. "Raymond Carver," *Paris Review*, LXXXVIII (Summer 1983), 193–221. (G)

Stern, Carol Simpson. "Cathedral," *Reference Guide to Short Fiction*, Noelle Watson, ed. (Detroit, 1994), pp. 660–661.

Stull, William L. "Beyond Hopelessness: Another Side of Raymond Carver," *Philological Quarterly*, LXIV (Winter 1985), 1–15. (G)

Toolan, Michael. "Discourse Style Makes Viewpoint: The Example of Carver's Narrative in 'Cathedral,'" *Twentieth-Century Fiction From Text to Context*, Peter Verdonk and Jean Jacques Weber, eds. (London, 1995), pp. 126–137.

Votteler, Thomas, ed., *Short Story Criticism: Excerpts from the Criticism of the Works of Short Fiction Writers*, VIII (Detroit, 1991), pp. 1–62. (G)

VanderWeele, Michael. "Raymond Carver and the Language of Desire," *Denver Quarterly*, XXII (Summer 1987), 108–122.

Wolff, Tobias. "Raymond Carver Had His Cake and Ate it Too," *Esquire*, CXII, No.3 (1989), 240–242, 244, 247–258.

RAYMOND CARVER, "I Could See the Smallest Things"

Fontana, Ernest. "Insomnia in Raymond Carver's Fiction," *Studies in Short Fiction*, 26 (Fall 1989), 447–451.

Meyer, Adam. *Raymond Carver* (New York, 1995), pp. 95–96.

Trussler, Michael. "The Narrowed Voice: Minimalism and Raymond Carver," *Studies in Short Fiction*. 31 (Winter 1994), 23–37. (G)

RAYMOND CARVER, "What We Talk About When We Talk About Love"

Arias-Misson, Alain. "Absent Talkers," *Partisan Review*, XLIX, 4 (1982), 625–628.

Arons, Victoria. "Variance of Imagination," *Literary Review*, XXVII (Fall 1983), 147–152.

Atlas, James. "Less is Less," *Atlantic*, CCXLVII (June 6, 1981), 96–98.

Campbell, Ewing. *Raymond Carver: A Study of the Short Fiction* (New York, 1992), pp. 45–47.

Carlin, Warren. "Just Talking: Raymond Carver's Symposium," *Cross Currents*, XXVIII (Spring 1988), 87–92.

Cochrane, Hamilton E. "'Taking the Cure': Alcoholism and Recovery in the Fiction of Raymond Carver," *University of Dayton Review* XX (Summer 1989), 79–88.

Houston, Robert. "A Stunning Inarticulateness," *Nation*, CCXXXIII (July 4, 1981), 23–25.

Meyer, Adam. *Raymond Carver* (New York, 1995), pp. 108–111.

Runyon, Randolph P. *Reading Raymond Carver* (Syracuse, 1992), pp. 131–135.

Saltzman, Arthur M. *Understanding Raymond Carver* (Columbia, S.C., 1988), pp. 117–120.

Stonehill, Brian. "What We Talk About When We Talk About Love," *Reference Guide to Short Fiction*, Noelle Watson, ed. (Detroit, 1994), p. 967.

Stull, William L. "Beyond Hopelessville: Another Side of Raymond Carver," *Philological Quarterly*, LXIV (Winter 1985), 1–15.

JOHN CHEEVER, "The Country Husband"

Aldridge, John W. "John Cheever and the Soft Sell of Disaster, *The Devil in the Fire: Retrospective Essays on American Literature and Culture* (New York, 1972), pp. 235–240. (G)

Bracher, Frederick. "John Cheever and Comedy," *Critique*, VI (Spring 1963), 66–77. (G)

Brans, Jo. "Stories to Comprehend Life: An Interview with John Cheever," *Southwest Review*, LXV (Autumn 1980), 337–345. (G)

Chandler, Marilyn R. *Dwelling in the Text: Houses in American Literature* (Berkeley, 1991), pp.286–288.

Cheever, John. "Why I Write Short Stories," *Newsweek*, XCII (October 30, 1978), 24–25. (G)

Clesnick, Eugene. "The Domesticated Stroke of John Cheever," *New England Quarterly*, XLIV (December 1971), 531–552. (G)

Coale, Samuel. *John Cheever* (New York, 1977), pp. 28–33.

Collins, Robert C. "From Subject to Object and Back Again: Individual Identity in John Cheever's Fiction," *Twentieth Century Literature*, XXVIII (Spring 1982), 1–13. (G)

Crowley, John W. "John Cheever and the Ancient Light of New England," *New England Quarterly*, LVI (June 1983), 267–275. (G)

Dessner, Lawrence J. "Gender and Structure in John Cheever's 'The Country Husband,'" *Studies in Short Fiction*, XXXI (Winter 1994), 57–68.

Donaldson, Scott. *John Cheever: A Biography* (New York, 1988), pp. 141–143.

Flora, Joseph M. "The Country Husband," *Reference Guide to Short Fiction*, Noelle Watson, ed. (Detroit, 1994), pp. 674–675.

Hipkiss, Robert A. "'The Country Husband'—A Model of Cheever Achievement," *Studies in Short Fiction*, XXVII (Fall 1990), 577–585.

Hunt, George., S. J. *John Cheever: The Hobgoblin in Company of Love* (Grand Rapids, 1983), pp. 273–280.

Irving, John. "Facts of Living," *Saturday Review*, 5 (September 30, 1978), 44–46. (G)

Kazin, Alfred. "Our Middle-Class Storytellers," *Atlantic Monthly*, 222 (August 1968), 51–55. (G)

Kendle, Burton. "The Passion of Nostalgia in the Short Stories of John Cheever," *Critical Essays on John Cheever*, R. G. Collins, ed. (Boston, 1982), pp. 219–230.

Meanor, Patrick. *John Cheever Revisited* (New York, 1995), pp. 81–88.

Meisel, Robert. "The World of WASP," *Partisan Review*, XLVII (1980), 467–471. (G)

Meyer, Arlin G. "A Garden of Love After Eden," *The Cresset*, XLII (June 1979), 22–28. (G)

Moore, Stephen C. "The Hero on the 5:42: John Cheever's Short Fiction," *Western Humanities Review*, XXX (Spring 1976), 147–152. (G)

Morace, Robert A. "From Parallels to Paradise: The Lyrical Structure of Cheever's Fiction," *Twentieth Century Literature*, XXXV (Winter 1989), 502–528. (G)

Peden, William. *The American Short Story: Continuity and Change, 1940–1975* (Boston, 1975), pp.30–39.(G)

Rupp, Richard M. "Of That Time, of Those Places: The Short Stories of John Cheever," Critical Essays of John Cheever, R. G. Collins, ed. (Boston, 1982), pp. 231–251. (G)

Waldeland, Lynne. *John Cheever* (Boston, 1979), pp. 66–68, 74–75, 76–77.

———. "Isolation and Integration: John Cheever's 'The Country Husband,'" *Ball State University Forum*, XXVII (Winter 1986), 5–11.

ANTON CHEKHOV, "The Darling"

Bayuk, Milla. "The Submissive Wife Stereotype in Anton Chekhov's 'Darling,'" *College Language Association Journal*, XX (1977), 533–538.

Bitsilli, Peter M. *Chekhov's Art: A Stylistic Analysis* (Ann Arbor, 1983), pp. 93–96.

Durkin, Andrew R. "Chekhov's Narrative Technique," A *Chekhov Companion*, Toby W. Clyman, ed. (Westport, Conn., 1985), pp. 123–132. (G)

Evdokimova, Svetlana. "'The Darling': Femininity Scorned and Desired," *Reading Chekhov's Text*, Robert L. Jackson, ed. (Evanston, Ill., 1993), pp. 189–197.

Hahn, Beverly. *Chekhov: A Study of the Major Short Stories and Plays* (Cambridge, England, 1977), pp. 230–232.

Heidt, Barbara. "Chekhov (and Flaubert) on Female Devotion," *Ulbandus Review*, II, ii (1982), 166–174.

Kirk, Irina. *Anton Chekhov* (Boston, 1981), pp. 112–114.

Lainoff, Seymour. "Chekhov's 'The Darling,'" *Explicator*, XIII (February 1955), Item 24.

Lavrin, Janko. "Chekhov and Maupassant," *Slavonic Review*, V (June 1926), 1–24. (G)

Martin, David. "Chekhov and the Modern Short Story in English," *Neophilogus*, LXXI (January 1987), 129–143. (G)

May, Charles E. "Chekhov and the Modern Short Story," A *Chekhov Companion*, Toby W. Clyman, ed. (Westport, Conn., 1985), pp. 147–163. (G)

Peterson, Nadya. "The Languages of 'Darling,'" *Canadian-American Slavic Studies*, XXIV, ii (1990), 199–200, 203–215.

Poggioli, Renato. *The Phoenix and the Spider* (Cambridge, 1957), pp. 124–130.

Shaw, Valerie. *The Short Story: A Critical Introduction* (London, 1983), pp. 120–131. (G)

Sperber, Michael A. "The 'As If Personality and Chekhov's 'The Darling,'" *Psychoanalytic Review*, LVIII (1971),14–21.

Tolstoy, Leo. "The Darling," *The Works of Leo Tolstoy*, trans. by Aylmer Maude (London, 1929), XVIII, pp. 323–327.

Winner, Thomas. Chekhov and His Prose (New York, 1966), pp. 210–216.

ANTON CHEKHOV, "The Lady with the Dog"

Bayley, John. *The Short Story: Henry James to Elizabeth Bowen* (New York, 1988), pp. 185–186.

Callow, Philip. *Chekhov, The Hidden Ground: A Biography* (Chicago, 1998), pp. 313–316.

Gerlach, John. *Toward the End: Closure and Structure in the American Short Story* (University, Ala., 1985), pp. 131–132.

Hahn, Beverly. *Chekhov: A Study of the Major Short Stories and Plays* (Cambridge, Eng., 1977), pp. 252–263.

Lindheim, Ralph. "Chekhov' Major Themes," A *Chekhov Companion*, Toby W. Clyman, ed. (Westport, Conn., 1985), pp. 65–66.

Llewellyn Smith, Virginia. *Anton Chekhov and the Lady with the Dog* (Oxford, Eng., 1973), pp. 212–218.

Miller, Karl. *Doubles: Studies in Literary History* (New York, 1985), pp. 151–152.

Phelps, Gilbert. "'Indifference' in the Letters and Tales of Chekhov," *Cambridge Review*, 7 (1954), 211–213.

Rayfield, Donald. *Chekhov: The Evolution of His Art* (New York, 1975), pp. 197–200.

Stanion, Charles. "Oafish Behavior in 'The Lady with the Pet Dog," *Studies in Short Fiction*, 30 (Summer 1993), 402–403.

Van der Eng, Jan. "The Semantic Structure of 'Lady with Lapdog," *On the Theory of Descriptive Poetics: Anton P. Chekhov as Story-Teller and Playwright*, J. Van der Eng, J.M. Meijer, and H. Schmid, eds. (Lisse, The Netherlands, 1978), pp. 59–94.

Winner, Thomas. *Chekhov and His Prose* (New York, 1966), pp. 216–225.

KATE CHOPIN, "Athénaïse: A Story of a Temperament"

Bell, Pearl K. "Kate Chopin and Sarah Orne Jewett" *Partisan Review*, LV, ii (1988), 238–253. (G)

Bender, Bert. "Kate Chopin's Lyrical Short Stories," *Studies in Short Fiction*, XI (Summer 1974), 262–264.

Brown, Pearl L. "Awakened Men in Kate Chopin's Creole Stories," *ATQ*, 13 (March 1999), 69–82.

Cutter, Martha J. "Losing the Battle but Winning the War: Resistance to Patriarchal Discourse in Kate Chopin's Fiction," *Legacy*, XI, 1 (1994), 17–36.

Dyer, Joyce. "Gouvenail: Kate Chopin's Sensitive Bachelor," *Southern Literary Journal*, XIV (Fall 1981), 46–55.

———. "Night Images in the Work of Kate Chopin,", *American Literary Realism*, XIV (Autumn 1981), 223–224.

Ewell, Barbara C. Kate Chopin (New York, 1986), pp. 108–118.

Fletcher, Marie. "The Southern Woman in the Fiction of Kate Chopin," *Louisiana History*, VII (Spring 1966), 117–132. (G)

Jones, Anne Goodwyn. *Tomorrow Is Another Day: The Woman Writer in the South, 1859–1936* (Baton Rouge, 1981), pp. 135–182. (G)

Larson, Donald F. *Critical Survey of Short Fiction*, Frank Magill, ed. (Englewood Cliffs, N.J., 1981), III, pp. 1134–1135.

Lattin, Patricia Hopkins. "Kate Chopin's Repeating Characters," *Mississippi Quarterly*, XXXIII (Winter 1979–1980), 19–37. (G)

———. "The Search for Self in Kate Chopin's Fiction: Simple Versus Complex Vision," *Southern Studies*, XXI (Summer 1982), 225–235. (G)

Lohafer, Susan. *Coming to Terms with the Short Story* (Baton Rouge, 1983), pp. 115–132.

Newman, Judie. "Kate Chopin: Short Fiction and the Arts of Subversion," *The Nineteenth-Century American Short Story*, A. Robert Lee, ed. (Totowa, N.J., 1985), pp. 150–163. (G)

Rocks, James E. "Kate Chopin's Ironic vision," *Louisiana Review*, I (Winter 1972), 110–120. (G)

Rowe, Anne E. "Kate Chopin," *Fifty Southern Writers Before 1900*, Robert Bain and Joseph M. Flora, eds. (Westport, Conn., 1987), pp. 132–143. (G)

Schurbutt, Sylvia Bailey. "The Cane River Characters and Revisionist Mythmaking in the Works of Kate Chopin," *Southern Literary Journal*, XXV (Spring 1993), 24–23. (G)

Skeyersted, Per. *Kate Chopin: A Critical Biography* (Baton Rouge, 1969), pp. 112–115,130–132.

Skaggs, Peggy. *Kate Chopin* (New York, 1985), pp. 36–38.

Stein, Allen F. *After the Vows Were Spoken: Marriage in American Literary Realism* (Columbus, 1984), pp. 180–184.

Taylor, Helen. *Gender, Race, and Region in the Writings of Grace King, Ruth MeEnery Stuart, and Kate Chopin* (Baton Rouge, 1989), pp. 180–182.

Thomas, Heather K. "'The House of Style' in Kate Chopin's 'Athenaise,'" *Critical Essays on Kate Chopin*, Alice H. Petry, ed. (New York, 1996), pp. 207–217.

Toth, Emily. *Kate Chopin* (Austin, Tex., 1990), pp. 274–275, 298–301.

———. "Kate Chopin Thinks Back Through Her Mothers: Three Stories by Kate Chopin," *Kate Chopin Reconsidered: Beyond the Bayou*, Lynda S. Boren and Sara D. Davis, eds. (Baton Rouge, 1992), pp. 18–21, 24.

Ziff, Larzer. *The American 1890s: Life and Times of a Lost Generation* (New York, 1966), pp. 296–305. (G)

KATE CHOPIN, "The Storm"

Arner, Robert D. "Kate Chopin's Realism: 'At the 'Cadian Ball' and 'The Storm,'" *Markham Review*, 11, 2 (1970). 1–4.

Baker, Christopher. "Chopin's 'The Storm,'" *Explicator*, LII (Summer 1994), 225–226.

Bender, Bert. "Kate Chopin's Lyrical Short Stories," *Studies in Short Fiction*, XI (Summer 1974), 257–266.

Dyer, Joyce Coyne. "Epiphanies Through Nature in the Stories of Kate Chopin," *University of Dayton Review*, XVI (1983–1984), 75–81.

Elfenbein, Anna S. *Women on the Color Line: Evolving Stereotypes and the Writings of George Washington Cable, Grace King, and Kate Chopin* (Charlottesville, Va., 1989), pp. 139–142.

Ewell, Barbara C. *Kate Chopin* (New York, 1986), pp. 168–171.

Gaude, Pamela. "Kate Chopin's 'The Storm': A Study of Maupassant's Influence," *Kate Chopin Newsletter*, I (Fall 1975),1–6.

Girgus, Sam B. *Desire and the Political Unconscious in American Literature: Eros and Ideology* (New York, 1990), pp. 134–151. (G)

Seyersted, Per. *Kate Chopin: A Critical Study* (Baton Rouge, 1969), pp. 164–169.

Skaggs, Peggy. *Kate Chopin* (New York, 1985), pp. 61–62.

Toth, Emily. *Kate Chopin* (New York, 1990), pp, 318–322.

Wagner-Martin, Linda. "Recent Books on Kate Chopin," *Mississippi Quarterly*, XLII (Spring 1989),193–196. (G)

KATE CHOPIN, "The Story of an Hour"

Bender, Bert. "Kate Chopin's Lyrical Short Stories," *Studies in Short Fiction*, 11 (Summer 1974), 264–265.

Koloski, Bernard. *Kate Chopin: A Study of the Short Fiction* (New York, 1996), pp. 3–4, 132–134.

Miner, Madonne M. "Veiled Hints: An Affective Stylist's Reading of Kate Chopin's 'Story of an Hour,'" *Markham Review*, 11 (1982), 29–32.

Papke, Mary E. *Verging on the Abyss: The Social Fiction of Kate Chopin and Edith Wharton* (New York, 1990), pp. 62–64.

Seyersted, Per. *Kate Chopin: A Critical Biography* (Baton Rouge, 1969), pp. 57–59.

Skaggs, Peggy. *Kate Chopin,* (Boston, 1985), pp. 52–53.

———. "The Man-Instinct of Possession': A Persistent Theme in Kate Chopin's Stories," *Louisiana Studies*, 14 (1975), 177–185.

Toth, Emily. *Kate Chopin* (Austin, 1990), pp. 252–253, 284–285.

AGATHA CHRISTIE, "Witness for the Prosecution"

Bargainnier, Earl F. "Hercule Poirot," *The Gentle Art of Murder: The Detective Fiction of Agatha Christie* (Bowling Green, Ohio, 1980), pp. 44–66. (G)

Barnard, Robert. "Counsel for the Defense," *A Talent to Deceive: An Appreciation of Agatha Christie* (New York, 1980), pp. 107–126, (G)

Burgess, Granville. "'Witness for the Prosecution' (1948)," *The New Bedside, Bathtub & Armchair Companion to Agatha Christie*, Dick Riley and Pam McAllister, eds. (New York, 1986), pp. 175–176.

Cawelti, John G. *Adventure, Mystery, and Romance: Formula Stories in Art and Popular Culture* (Chicago, 1976), pp. 111–119. (G)

Crispin, Edmund. "The Mystery of Simplicity," *Agatha Christie: First Lady of Crime*, H. R. F. Keating, ed. (New York, 1977), pp. 39–48. (G)

Dueren, Fred. "Hercule Poirot: The Private Life of a Private Eye," *Armchair Detective*, VII (February 1974), 111–115. (G)

Gregg, Hubert. *Agatha Christie and All That Mousetrap* (London, 1980), pp. 109–111.

Grossvogel, David I. "Agatha Christie: Containment of the Unknown," *From Oedipus to Agatha Christie* (Baltimore, 1979), pp. 39–52. (G)

———. "Death Deferred: The Long Life, Splendid Afterlife and Mysterious Workings of Agatha Christie," *Art in Crime Writing: Essays on Detective Fiction*, Bernard Benstock, ed. (New York, 1983), pp. 1–17. (G)

Jenkinson, Philip. "The Agatha Christie Films," *Agatha Christie: First Lady of Crime*, H. R. F. Keating, ed. (New York, 1977), pp. 169–173.

Keating, H. R. F., ed. *Agatha Christie: First Lady of Crime* (New York, 1977). (G)

Knight, Stephen. *Form and Ideology in Crime Fiction* (Bloomington, Ind., 1981), pp. 107–134. (G)

Osborne, Charles. *The Life and Crime of Agatha Christie* (New York, 1982), pp. 14–18,27–29. (G)

Panek, LeRoy. *Watteau's Shepherds: The Detective Novel in Britain, 1914–1960* (Bowling Green, Ohio, 1979), pp. 38–63. (G)

Ramsey, G. C. "M. Hercule Poirot," *Agatha Christie: Mistress of Mystery* (New York, 1967), pp. 48–56. (G)

Robyns, Gwen. *The Mystery of Agatha Christie* (New York, 1978), pp. 150–159.

Routley, Erik. *The Puritan Pleasures of the Detective Story* (London, 1972), pp. 129–137. (G)

Symons, Julian. *Bloody Murder: From Detective Story to the Crime Novel, A History* (New York, 1985), pp. 118–119. (G)

Tennenbaum, Michael. "The Making of 'Witness for the Prosecution,'" *The New Bedside, Bathtub & Armchair Companion to Agatha Christie*, Dick Riley and Pam McAllister, eds. (New York, 1986), pp. 175–176.

Wagoner, Mary S. "Short Stories," *Agatha Christie* (Boston, 1986), pp. 15–32. (G)

SANDRA CISNEROS, "The House on Mango Street"

Cisneros, Sandra. "From a Writer's Notebook," *Americas Review*, XV, 1 (1987), 69–73.

Doyle, Jacqueline. "More Room of Her Own: Sandra Cisneros's *The House on Mango Street*," *Journal for the Society for the Study of the Multi-Ethnic Literature of the United States* (MELUS), 19 (Winter 1994), 5–35.

Gibson, Michelle. "The Unreliable Narrator in 'The House on Mango Street,'" *San Jose Studies*, XIX, 2 (1993), 4–44.

Guitierrez-Jones, Leslie S. "Different Voices: The Re-*Bildung* of the Barrio in Sandra Cisneros'

'The House on Mango Street,'" *Anxious Power: Reading, Writing, and Ambivalence in Narrative by Women*, Carol J. Singley and Susan E. Sweeney, eds. (Albany, 1993), pp. 295–314.

Kanoza, Theresa. "Esperanza's Mango Street: Home for Keeps in Sandra Cisneros' *The House on Mango Street*," *Notes on Contemporary Literature*, XXV (May 1995), 9.

Marek, Jayne E. "Difference, Identity, and Sandra Cisneros's *The House on Mango Street*," *Hungarian Journal of American Studies*, 1 (1996), 173–187.

Matchie, Thomas. "Literary Continuity in Cisneros' *The House on Mango Street*," *Midwest Quarterly*, XXXVII (Autumn 1995), 67–79.

McCracken, Ellen. "Sandra Cisneros' *The House on Mango Street: Community-Oriented Introspection and Demystification of Patriarchal Violence*," Ureaking Borders and Asuncion Horno-Delgado, eds. (Amherst, Mass., 1989), pp. 62–71.

Olivares, Julian. "Sandra Cisneros' *The House on Mango Street* and the Poetics of Space," *Chicana Creativity and Criticism: New Frontiers in American Literature*, Maria Herrera Subek and Maria Vira Montes, eds. (Albuquerque, 1996), 233–244.

Ricard, Serge. "La Desesperance d'Esperanza: Espace Reve, espace vecu dans 'The House on Mango Street,' de Cisneros," *L'Ice et láilleurs: Multilinguisme et multiculturalisme en Amerique du Nord: Espace seuils limites*, Jean Beringer, ed. (Bordeux, 1990), pp. 175–187.

Valdes, Maria Elenade. "The Critical Reception of Sandra Cisneros's *The House on Mango Street*," *Gender, Self, and Society*, Renate von Bardelben, ed. (Frankfurt, 1993), pp. 287–300.

———. "In Search of Identity in Cisneros' 'The House on Mango Street,'" *Canadian Review of American Studies*, XXIII, i (1992), 55–72.

SAMUEL L. CLEMENS, "The Celebrated Jumping Frog of Calaveras County"

Arnold, S. T., Jr. "Twain Bestiary: Mark Twain's Critters and the Tradition of Animal Portraiture in Humor of the Old Southwest," *Southern Folklore Review*, XLI (1977), 195–211.

Baender, Paul. "The 'Jumping Frog' as a Comedian's First Virtue," *Modern Philology*, LX (February 1963), 192–200.

Bellamy, Gladys. *Mark Twain as a Literary Artist* (Norman, Okla., 1950), pp. 146–149.

Branch, Edgar M. *The Literary Apprenticeship of Mark Twain* (Urbana, Ill., 1950), pp. 120–127.

———. "'My Voice Is Still for Setchell': A Background Study of Jim Smiley and His Jumping Frog,'" *PMLA*, LXXXII (December 1967), 591–601.

Brownell, George H. "Mark Twainiana," *American Book Collector*, V (April 1934), 124–126.

———. "The Mystery of 'Jim Greeley,'" *Twainian*. N.S. II (December 1942), 4–5.

Bryant, John. "Melville, Twain and Quixote: Variations on the Comic Debate," *Studies in American Humor*, NS, III, 1 (1994), 1–27.

Buckbee, Edna Bryan. "Mark Twain's Treasure Pile," *Pioneer Days of Angel's Camp* (Angel's Camp, Calif., 1932), pp. 21–35.

Clemens, Samuel L. "Private History of the 'Jumping Frog Story,'" *Literary Essays* (New York, 1897), pp. 100–110.

Cohen, Hennig. "Twain's Jumping Frog: Folktale to Life to Folktale," *Western Folklore*, XXII (January 1963), 17–18.

Coleman, Rufus A. "Mark Twain's Jumping Frog: Another Version of the Famed Story," *Montana Magazine of History*, III (Summer 1953), 29–30.

Covici, Pascal, Jr. *Mark Twain's Humor: The Image of a World* (Dallas, 1962), pp. 49–52.

Cox, James M. *Mark Twain: The Fate of Humor* (Princeton, 1966), pp. 24–32.

Cuff, Roger Penn. "Mark Twain's Use of California Folklore in His Jumping Frog Story," *Journal of American Folklore*, LXV (April-June 1952), 155–158.

Cunliffe, W. Gordon. "The Celebrated Jumping Frog of Calaveras County," *Insight I: Analyses of American Literature*, John V. Hagopian and Martin Dolch, eds. (Frankfurt, 1962), pp. 250–251.

DeVoto, Bernard. *Mark Twain's America* (Boston, 1932), pp. 174–178.

Eddings, Dennis W. "The Frog and the Rasm Redux: A Response to John Bryant," *Studies in American Humor*, BS, III, 2 (1995), 98–101.

Gibson, William. *The Art of Mark Twain* (New York, 1976), pp. 73–75.

Gillis, Steven E. "Jumping Frog Story: Gillis on Bret Harte: The Great Oak Plain," *Twainian*, XV (March–April 1956), 1–4.

Gerlach, John. *Toward the End: Closure and structure in the American Short Story* (University, Ala., 1985), pp. 60–65.

Lennon, Nigey. *Mark Twain in California: The Turbulent Years of Samuel Clemens* (San Francisco, 1982), pp. 83–85.

Lewis, Oscar. *The Origin of the Celebrated Jumping Frog of Calaveras County* (San Francisco, 1931).

Long, E. Hudson. *Mark Twain Handbook* (New York, 1957), pp. 134–136.

Lynn, Kenneth S. *Mark Twain and the Southwestern Humorists* (Boston, 1960), pp. 145–147.

Mellard, James M. *Four Modes: A Rhetoric of Fiction* (New York, 1973), pp. 22–25.

Michelson, Bruce. *Mark Twain on the Loose: A Comic Writer and the American Self* (Amherst, Mass., 1995), pp. 37–33.

Miller, Robert K. *Mark Twain* (New York, 1983), pp. 161–164.

Morrissey, Frank R. "The Ancestor of the 'Jumping Frog,'" *Bookman*, LIII (April 1921), 143–145.

Older, Fremont. "The Famous Jumping Frog Story...) the True Story," *Overland Monthly*, LXXXVII (April 1929), 101–102.

Paine, Albert Bigelow. *Mark Twain: A Biography* (New York, 1912), I, 270–273.

Rodgers, Paul C., Jr. "Artemus Ward and Mark Twain's 'Jumping Frog,'" *Nineteenth-Century Fiction*, XXVIII (December 1973), 273–286.

Rosenblum, Joseph. "The Notorious Jumping Frog," *Reference Guide to Short Fiction*, Noelle Watson, ed. (Detroit, 1994), pp. 825–826.

Rourke, Constance. *American Humor.– A Study of the National Character* (New York, 1931), pp. 204–221.

Schmidt, Paul. "The Deadpan on Simon Wheeler," *Southwest Review*, XLI (Summer 1956), 270–277.

Smith, Lawrence R. "Mark Twain's 'Jumping Frog': Toward an American Heroic Ideal," *Mark Twain Journal*, XX (Winter 1979–1980), 15–18.

Smith, Paul. "The Infernal Reminiscence: Mythic Patterns in Mark Twain's 'The Celebrated Jumping Frog of Calaveras County,'" *Satire Newsletter*, I (Spring 1964), 41–44.

Stone, Edward. "The Frog Jumper," *Mark Twain Journal*, XXI (Fall 1983), 47–50.

Taylor, J. Golden. "Introduction to 'The Celebrated Jumping Frog of Calaveras County" *American West*, 11 (Fall 1965), 73–76.

Wilson, James D. *A Reader's Guide to the Short Stories of Mark Twain* (Boston, 1987), pp. 163–176.

SAMUEL L. CLEMENS, "The Man That Corrupted Hadleyburg"

Allen, Charles A. "Mark Twain and Conscience," *Literature and Psychology*, VII (May 1957), 17–21.

Archer, William. "'The Man That Corrupted Hadleyburg'—A New Parable," *Critic*, XXXVII (November 1900), 413–415.

Bennet, Fordyce Richard. "The Moral Obliquity of 'The Man That Corrupted Hadley-burg,'" *Mark Twain Journal*, XXXI (Spring 1983), 10–11.

Bertolotti, David S. "Structural Unity in 'The Man That Corrupted Hadleyburg,'" *Mark Twain Journal*, XIV (Winter 1967–1968), 19–20.

Blues, Thomas. *Mark Twain and the Community* (Lexington, Ky., 1970), pp. 73–77.

Briden, Earl F. "Twainian Pedagogy and the No-Account Lessons of 'Hadleyburg,'" *Studies in Short Fiction*, XXVIII (Spring 1991), 125–134.

———, and Mary Prescott. "The Lie That I Am: Paradoxes of Identity in Mark Twain's 'Hadleyburg,'" *Studies in Short Fiction*, XXI (Fall 1984), 383–391.

Brodwin, Stanley. "Mark Twain's Mask of Satan: The Final Phase," *American Literature*, XLV (May 1973), 208–210.

Burhans, Clinton S., Jr. "The Sober Affirmation of Mark Twain's Hadleyburg," *American Literature*, XXXXIV (November 1962), 375–384.

Cardwell, Guy. "Mark Twain's Hadleyburg," *Ohio State Archives and Historical Quarterly*, LX (July 1951), 247–264.

Chard, Leslie F. "Mark Twain's 'Hadleyburg' and Fredonia, New York," *American Quarterly*, XVI (Winter 1964), 595–601.

Clark, George Pierce. "The Devil that Corrupted Hadleyburg," *Mark Twain Journal*, X (Winter 1956), 1–4.

Covici, Pascal. *Mark Twain's Humor: The Image of a World* (Dallas, 1962), pp. 189–205, 207–210.

Geismar, Maxwell. *Mark Twain: An American Prophet* (Boston, 1970), pp. 193–199.

Gibson, William M. *The Art of Mark Twain* (New York, 1976), pp. 89–95.

Gribben, Alan. "Those Other Thematic Patterns in Mark Twain's Writing," *Studies in American Fiction*, XIII (Autumn 1985), 185–200.

Harris, Susan K. "'Hadleyburg': Mark Twain's Dual Attack on Banal Theology and Banal Literature," *American Literary Realism*, XVI (Autumn 1983), 240–252.

Krause, Sidney J. "*The Pearl* and 'Hadleyburg': From Desire to Renunciation, *Steinbeck Quarterly*, VII (Winter 1974), 3–17.

Laing, Nita. "The Later Satire of Mark Twain," *Midwest Quarterly*, II (Autumn 1960), 35–48.

Lefcourt, Charles R. "Durrematt's 'Gullen' and Twain's 'Hadleyburg': The Corruption of Two Towns," *Revue des Langues Vivantes*, XXXIII (May–June 1967), 303–308.

Lorch, Fred. "Mark Twain's 'Morals' Lecture during the American Phase of His World Tour in 1895–1896," *American Literature*, XXVI (1954), 52–66.

McKeithan, Daniel M. "The Morgan Manuscript of 'The Man That Corrupted Hadley-burg,'" *Texas Studies in Literature and Language*, II (Winter 1961), 476–480.

McMahan, Elizabeth, ed. *Critical Approaches to Mark Twain's Short Stories* (Port Washington, N.Y., 1981) pp. 64–92.

MacNaughton, William R. *Mark Twain's Last Years as a Writer* (Columbia, Mo., 1979), pp. 100–103.

Male, Roy B. *Enter, Mysterious Stranger: American Cloistral Fiction* (Norman, Okla., 1979) pp. 22–24, 55–56.

Malin, Irving. "Mark Twain: The Boy as Artist," *Literature and Psychology*, VI (Summer 1961), 78–84.

Mandia, Patricia M. *Comic Pathos: Black Humor in Twain's Fiction* (Jefferson, N.C., 1991), pp. 68–82.

Marshall, W. Gerald. "Mark Twain's 'The Man That Corrupted Hadleyburg' and the Myth of Baucis and Philemon," *Mark Twain Journal*, II (Summer 1980), 4–7.

Michelson, Bruce. *Mark Twain on the Loose: A Comic Writer and the American Self* (Amherst, Mass., 1995), pp. 178–187.

Nebeker, Helen E. "The Great Corrupter or Satan Rehabilitated," *Studies in Short Fiction*, VIII (Fall 1971), 635–637.

Nye, Russel B. "Mark Twain in Oberlin," *The Ohio State Archaelogical and Historical Quarterly*, XLVII (1938), 69–73.

Park, Martha M. "Mark Twain's Hadleyburg: A House Built on Sand," *CLA Journal*, XVI (June 1973), 508–513.

Parsons, Coleman O. "The Devil and Samuel Clemens," *Virginia Quarterly Review*, XXIII (Autumn 1947), 595–600.

Rucker, Mary E. "Moralism and Determinism in 'The Man That Corrupted Hadleyburg,'" *Studies in Short Fiction*, XIV (Winter 1977), 49–54.

Rule, Henry B. "The Role of Satan in 'The Man That Corrupted Hadleyburg,'" *Studies in Short Fiction*, VI (Fall 1969), 619–629.

Scharnhorst, Gary. "Paradise Revisited: Twain's 'The Man That Corrupted Hadleyburg," *Studies in Short Fiction*, XVIII (Winter 1981), 59–64.

Scherting, Jack. "Poe's 'The Cask of Amontillado': A Source for Twain's 'The Man That Corrupted Hadleyburg,'" *Mark Twain Journal*, XVI (Summer 1972), 18–19.

Smith, Henry Nash. *Mark Twain: The Development of a Writer* (Cambridge, Mass., 1962), pp. 183–214.

Spangler, George M. "Locating Hadleyburg," *Mark Twain Journal*, XIV (Summer 1969), 20.

Summerfield, Carol. "The Man That Corrupted Hadleyburg," Reference Guide to Short Fiction, Noelle Watson ed. (Detroit 1994), pp. 790–791.

Varisco, Raymond. "A Militant Voice: Mark Twain's 'The Man That Corrupted Hadleyburg,'" *Revista/Review Inter-Americana*, VIII (Spring 1978), 129–137.

Werge, Thomas. "The Sin of Hypocrisy in 'The Man That Corrupted Hadleyburg' and *Inferno* XXIII," *Mark Twain Journal*, XVIII (Winter 1975–1976), 17–18.

Wilson, James D. *A Reader's Guide to the Short Stories of Mark Twain* (Boston, 1987), pp. 199–215.

JOSEPH CONRAD, "Heart of Darkness "

Achebe, Chinua. "An Image of Africa: Racism in Conrad's 'Heart of Darkness," *Joseph Conrad*, Andrew Michael Roberts, ed. (London, 1998), pp. 109–123.

Addison, Bill K. "Marlow, Aschenbach, and We," *Conradiana*, II (Winter 1970), 79–81.

Adelman, Gary. *Heart of Darkness: Search For the Unconscious* (Boston, 1997), pp. 61–88.

Alcorn, Marshall W. "Conrad and the Narcissistic Metaphysics of Morality," *Conradiana*, XIV (1984), 107–120.

Allen, Jerry. *The Thunder and The Sunshine* (New York, 1958), pp. 199–206.

Ambrosini, Richard. *Conrad's Fiction as Critical Discourse* (Cambridge, England, 1991), pp. 84–115.

Amur, G. S. "'Heart of Darkness' and 'The Fall of the House of Usher': The Tale of Discovery," *Criticism*, IX (Summer 1971), 59–70.

Anderson, Linda R. *Bennett, Wells and Conrad: Narrative in Transition* (New York, 1988), pp. 181–190.

Anderson, Walter E. "'Heart of Darkness': The Sublime," *University of Toronto Quarterly*, (Spring 1988), 404–421.

Andreach, Robert J. *The Slain and Resurrected God: Conrad, Ford and the Christian Myth* (New York, 1970), pp. 44–53.

Andreas, Osborn. *Joseph Conrad: A Study in Non-Conformity* (New York, 1959), pp. 46–54.

Anspaugh, Kelly. "Dante on His Head: 'Heart of Darkness,'" *Conradiana*, XXVIII (Summer 1995), 135–148.

Apter, T. E. *Fantasy Literature: An Approach to Reality* (Bloomington, Ind., 1982), pp. 13–19.

Arneson Richard J. "Marlow's Skepticism in 'Heart of Darkness,'" *Ethics* (April 1984), 420–440.

Arnold, J. A. "The Young Russian's Book in Conrad's 'Heart of Darkness,'" *Conradiana*, VIII (1976), 121–126.

Ashour, Radwa. "Significant Incongruities in Conrad's 'Heart of Darkness,'" *Neohelicon*, X (1983), 183–201.

Baines. Jocelyn. *Joseph Conrad: A Critical Biography* (New York, 1960), pp. 223–230.

Banjeree, A. "The Politicization of 'Heart of Darkness,'" *Literary Criterion*, XXVIII, 3 (1992), 14–22.

Baskett, Sam S. "Jack London's Heart of Darkness," *American Quarterly*, X (Spring 1958), 66–77.

Batchelor, John. *The Edwardian Novelists* (New York, 1992), pp. 36–45.

———. *The Life of Joseph Conrad* (Oxford, Eng., 1994), pp. 84–95.

Baum, Joan. "The 'Real' 'Heart of Darkness,'" *Conradiana*, VII (1975), 183–187.

Beebe, Maurice. "The Masks of Conrad," *Bucknell Review*, XI (December 1963), 42–47.

Bennett, Carl D. *Joseph Conrad* (New York,1991), pp. 75–83.

Benson, Donald R. "Ether, Atmosphere, and the Solidarity of Men and Nature in 'Heart of Darkness,'" *Beyond the Two Cultures: Essays on Science, Technology, and Literature*, Joseph W. Slade and Judith Y. Lee, eds. (Ames, Iowa, 1990), pp. 161–173.

———. "'Heart of Darkness': The Grounds of Civilization in an Alien Universe," *Texas Studies in Literature and Language*, VII (Winter 1966), 339–347.

Bergenholtz, Rita A. "Conrad's 'Heart of Darkness,'" *Explicator*, LIII (Winter 1995), 102–106.

Berger, Marjorie. "Telling Darkness," *English Literature in Transition*, XXV (1982), 199–210.

Bergstrom, Robert F. "Discovery of Meaning: Development of Formal Thought in the Teaching of Literature," *College English*, XLV (1983), 745–755.

Berman, Jeffrey. *Joseph Conrad: Writing as Rescue* (New York, 1977), pp. 53–67.

———. "Writing as Rescue: Conrad's Escape from the Heart of Darkness," *Literature and Psychology*, XXV (1975), 65–78.

Bernard, Kenneth. "Marlow's Lie," *English Record*, XII (April 1963), 47–48.

———. "The Significance of the Roman Parallel in Joseph Conrad's 'Heart of Darkness,'" *Ball State Teacher's College Forum*, V (Spring 1964), 29–31.

Berthoud, Jacques. *Joseph Conrad: The Major Phase* (Cambridge, England, 1978), pp. 41–63.

Billy, Ted. *A Wilderness of Words: Closure and Disclosure in Conrad's Short Fiction* (Lubbock, Tx., 1997), pp. 69–77.

Blake, Susan. "Racism and the Classics: Teaching 'Heart of Darkness,'" *CLA Journal*, XXV (June 1982), 396–404.

Bloom, Harold, ed. *Joseph Conrad's Heart of Darkness* (New York, 1987).

Bode, Rita. "'They...should be out of it': The Women in 'Heart of Darkness,'" *Conradiana*, XXVI (Spring 1994), 20–34.

Bongie, Chris. "Exotic Nostalgia: Conrad and the New Imperialism, " *Macropolitics of Nineteenth-Century Literature: Nationalism, Exoticism, Imperialism*, Jonathan Arac and Harriet Ritvo, eds. (Philadelphia, 1991), pp. 277–285.

Bouge, Ronald L. "The Heart of Darkness and Apocalypse Now," *Georgia Review*, XXXV (Fall 1981), 611–626.

Bouson, J. Brooks. *The Empathic Reader: A Study of the Narcissistic Character and the Drama of the Self* (Amherst, Mass., 1989), pp. 93–104.

Bowen, Robert O. "Loyalty and Tradition in Conrad," *Renascence*, X (Spring 1960), 125–131.

Boyle, Ted. "Marlow's Choice in 'Heart of Darkness,'" *The Modernists: Studies in a Literary Phenomenon: Essays in Honor of Harry T. Moore*, Lawrence B. Gamache and Ian S. Mac-Niven, eds. (Cranbury, N.J., 1987), pp. 92–102.

———. "Marlow's Lie in 'Heart of Darkness,'" *Studies in Short Fiction*, I (Winter 1964), 159–163.

————. *Symbol and Meaning in the Fiction of Joseph Conrad* (The Hague, 1965), pp. 85–115.

Bradbook, M. C. *Joseph Conrad: Poland's English Genius* (New York, 1965), pp. 27–31.

Bradshaw, Graham. "Mythos, Ethos, and the 'Heart of Darkness,'" *English Studies*, LXXII (April 1991), 160–172.

Brady, Marion B. "Conrad's Whited Sepulcher," *College English*, XXIV (October 1962), 24–29.

Brantlinger, Patrick. "'Heart of Darkness': Anti-Imperialism, Racism, or Imperialism?" *Criticism*, XXVII (Fall 1985), 363–385.

Brashers, H. C. "Conrad, Marlow, and Gautama Buddha: On Structure and Theme in 'Heart of Darkness,'" *Conradiana*, I (Summer 1969), 63–72.

Brink, Andre. "Woman and Language in Darkest Africa: The Quest for Articulation in Two Postcolonial Novels," *Liberator*, XIII, i (1992), 1–8.

Brooks, Peter. *Reading for the Plot* (New York, 1984), pp. 238–262.

Brooks, Randy M. "Blindfolded Women Carrying a Torch: The Nature of Conrad's Female Characters," *Ball State University Forum*, XVII (Autumn 1976), 28–32.

Bross, Addison C. "The Unextinguished Light of Belief: Conrad's Attitude Toward Women," *Conradiana*, II (Spring 1969–1970), 39–46.

Brown, Dennis. *The Modernist Self in Twentieth-Century Literature: A Study in Self-Fragmentation* (New York, 1989), pp. 22–28.

Brown, Douglas. "From 'Heart of Darkness' to *Nostromo*: An Approach to Conrad," *The Modern Age*, Boris Ford, ed. (Baltimore, 1961), 119–137.

Bruffee, Kenneth A. *Elegiac Romance, Cultural Change and the Loss of the Hero in Modern Fiction* (Ithaca, N.Y., 1983), pp. 96–132.

————. "The Lesser Nightmare: Marlow's Lie in 'Heart of Darkness,'" *Modern Language Quarterly*, XXV (September 1964), 322–329.

Bruss, Paul. *Conrad's Early Sea Fiction: The Novelist as Navigator* (Lewisburg, Pa., 1979), pp. 70–86.

Burgess, C. F. "Conrad's Pesky Russian," *Nineteenth-Century Fiction*, XXVIII (September 1963),189–193.

————. *The Fellowship of the Craft: Conrad on Ships and Seamen and the Sea* (Port Washington, N.Y., 1976), pp. 48–51, 70–72, 140–142.

Campbell, Ian. "Hogg's Confessions and 'The Heart of Darkness,'" *Studies in Scottish Literature*, XV (1980), 187–201.

Canario, John W. "The Harlequin," *Studies in Short Fiction*, IV (Spring 1967), 225–233.

Cheatham, George. "The Absence of God in 'Heart of Darkness,'" *Studies in the Novel*, XVIII (Fall 1986), 304–313.

Church, Andrea. "Conrad's 'Heart of Darkness,'" *Explicator*, XLV (Winter 1987), 35–36.

Clark, Michael. "'Heart of Darkness,'" *Explicator*, XXXIX (Spring 1981), 47.

Cleary, Thomas R. and Terry G. Sherwood. "Women in Conrad's Ironical Epic: Virgil, Dante and 'Heart of Darkness,'" *Conradiana*, XVI (1984), 183–194.

Clegg, Jerry S. "Conrad's Reply to Kierkegaard," *Philosophy and Literature*, XII, No. 2 (1988), 280–289.

Clews, Hetty. *The Only Teller: Readings in the Monologue Novel* (Victoria, B.C., 1985), pp. 132–141.

Clifford, James. "On Ethnographic Self-Fashioning: Conrad and Malinowski," *Reconstructing Individualism: Autonomy, Individuality, and the Self in Western Thought*, Thomas C. Heller et al. eds. (Stanford, 1986), pp. 140–161.

Coates, Paul. *The Double and the Other: Identity as Ideology in Post-Modern Fiction* (New York, 1988), pp. 72–77.

Cohen, Hubert. "The 'Heart of Darkness' in *Citizen Kane*," *Cinema Journal*, XII (Fall 1972), 11–25.

Cole, David W., and Kenneth B. Grant. "Conrad's 'Heart of Darkness,'" *Explicator*, 54 (Fall 1995) 24–26.

Collins, Harold R. "Kurtz, the Cannibals, and the Second-Rate Helmsman," *Western Humanities Review*, VII (Autumn 1954), 299–310.

Collins, Tracy J. R. "Eating, Food, and Starvation References in Conrad's 'Heart of Darkness,'" *Conradiana*, 30 (Summer 1998), 152–160.

Conrad, Joseph. *Congo Diary and Other Uncollected Pieces*, Zdzislaw Najder, ed. (Garden City, N.Y., 1978).

Cook, William J. "More Light on 'Heart of Darkness,'" *Conradiana*, III (September 1971), 4–14.

Cornwell, Gareth. "J. P. Fitzpatrick's 'The Outspan': A Textual Source for 'Heart of Darkness'?" *Conradiana*, 30 (Fall 1998), 203–212.

Coroneos, Con. "The Cult of 'Heart of Darkness,'" *Essays in Criticism*, XLV (January 1995), 1–23.

Cousineau, Thomas. "'Heart of Darkness': The Outsider Demystified," *Conradiana*, 30 (Summer 1998), 140–151.

Cox, C. B. *Conrad* (London, 1977), pp. 13–18.

———. *Joseph Conrad: The Modern Imagination* (London, 1974), I)p. 45–49.

Crews, Frederick. "The Power of Darkness," *Partisan Review*, XXXIV (Fall 1967), 507–525.

Curle, Richard, "Conrad's Diary," *Yale Review*, XV (January 1926), 254–266.

Cutler, F. W. "Why Marlow?" *Sewanee Review*, XXVI (January 1918), 28–38.

Cutler, Hugh Mercer. "Achebe on Conrad: Racism and Greatness in 'Heart of Darkness,'" *Conradiana*, 29, No 1 (1997), 30–40.

Dahl, James C. "Kurtz, Marlow, Conrad and the Human Heart of Darkness," *Studies in the Literary Imagination*, I (October 1968), 33–40.

Daitches, David. *The Novel in the Modern World* (Chicago, 1960), pp. 36–42.

Daleski, H. M. *Joseph Conrad: The Way of Dispossession* (New York, 1976), pp. 51–76.

Daniels, Patsy J. "Conrad's 'Heart of Darkness,'" *Explicator*, LIV (Spring 1996), 164–165.

Darras, Jacques. *Joseph Conrad and the West: Signs of Empire* (Totowa, N.J., 1982), pp. 37–96.

D'Avanzo, Mario. "Conrad's Motley as an Organizing Metaphor," *College Language Association Journal*, IX (March 1966), 289–291.

Dean, Leonard F., ed. *Joseph Conrad's "Heart of Darkness "* (Englewood Cliffs, N.J., 1960).

———. "Tragic Pattern in Conrad's 'Heart of Darkness,'" *College English*, VI (November 1944), 100–104.

De Koven, Marianne. *Rich and Strange: Gender, History, Modernism* (Princeton, 1991), pp. 89–100.

De Mille, Barbara. "*An Inquiry Into Some Points of Seamanship*: Narration as Preservation in 'Heart of Darkness,'" *Conradiana*, XVIII (1986), 94–104.

Dempsey, M. *"Apocalypse Now,"* *Sight and Sound*, XLIX (Winter 1980), 5–9.

Devers, James. "More on Symbols in Conrad's 'The Secret Sharer,'" *Conradiana*, XXVIII (Winter 1996), 66–76.

Devlin, Kimberly. "The Eye and the Gaze in 'Heart of Darkness': A Symptomological Reading, *Modern Fiction Studies*, XL (Winter 1994), 711–735.

Dhareshwar, Vivek. "The Song of the Sirens in 'The Heart of Darkness': The Enigma of Recit," *Boundary 2*, XV (Fall 1986/Winter 1987), 69–84.

Dilworth, T. "Listener and Lies in 'Heart of Darkness,'" *Review of English Studies*, XXXVIII (1987), 510–522.

Dobrinsky, Joseph. *The Artist in Conrad's Fiction: A Psychocritical Study* (Ann Arbor, 1989), pp. 1–25.

———. "From Whisper to Voice: Marlow's 'Accursed Inheritance' in 'Heart of Darkness,'" *Cahiers Victoriens and Edouardiens*, XVI (October 1982), 77–104.

Dowden, Wilfred S. *Joseph Conrad: The Imaged Style* (Nashville, 1970), pp. 71–85.

———. "The Light and the Dark: Imagery and Thematic Development in Conrad's 'Heart of Darkness,'" *Rice Institute Pamphlets*, LXIV (April 1957), 33–51.

Dudley, E. J. "Three Patterns of Imagery in Conrad's 'Heart of Darkness,'" *Revue des Langues Vivantes*, XXXI (1965), 568–578.

Edwards, Paul. "Clothes for the Pilgrimage: A Recurrent Image in 'Heart of Darkness,'" *Mosaic*, III (1971), 67–74.

Elbarbary, Samir. "'Heart of Darkness' and Late-Victorian Fascination with the Primitive and the Double," *Twentieth Century Literature*, XXXIX, i (1993), 113–118.

Elliot, Dorice W. "Hearing the Darkness: The Narrative Chain in Conrad's 'Heart of Darkness,'" *English Literature in Transition*, XXVIII (1985), 162–181.

Ellis, James. "Kurtz's Voice: The Intended as 'The Horror!" *English Literature in Transition*, XIX (1976), 105–110.

Emmett, V. J., Jr. "Carlyle, Conrad, and the Politics of Charisma: Another Perspective on 'Heart of Darkness,'" *Conradiana*, VII (1975), 145–153.

Engel, Wilson F. "Conrad, Marlow, and 'Falemian,'" *Conradiana*, IX (1977), 115–125.

Erdniast-Vulcan, Daphne. *Joseph Conrad and the Modern Temper* (Oxford, England, 1991), pp. 91–108.

Evans, Robert O. "Conrad's Underworld," *Modern Fiction Studies*, II (May 1956), 56–62.

———. "Further Comment on 'Heart of Darkness,'" *Modern Fiction Studies*, III (Winter 1957–1958), 358–360.

Farmer, Norman. "Conrad's 'Heart of Darkness,'" *Explicator*, XXII (March 1964), Item 51.

Faulkner, Peter. "Vision and Normality: Conrad's 'Heart of Darkness,'" *Ibadan Studies in English*, I (1969), 36–47.

Fayad, Mona. "The Problem of the Subject in Africanist Discourse: Conrad's 'Heart of Darkness' and Camus' 'The Renegade,'" *Comparative Literature Studies*, XXVII, No. 4 (1990), 298–312.

Feder, Lillian. "Marlow's Descent into Hell," *Nineteenth-Century Fiction*, IX (March 1955), 280–292.

Firmat, G. P. "*Don Quixote* in 'Heart of Darkness,'" *Comparative Literature Studies*, XII (December 1975), 374–383.

Fleishman, Avrom. *Conrad's Politics: Community and Anarchy in the Fiction of Joseph Conrad* (Baltimore, 1967), pp. 89–97.

Fleming, Bruce E. "Brothers Under the Skin: Achebe on 'Heart of Darkness,'" *College Literature* XIX–XX (October 1992–February 1993), 90–99.

Fogel, Aaron. *Coercion to Speak: Conrad's Poetics of Dialogue* (Cambridge, Mass., 1985), pp. 56–61.

———. "The Mood of Overhearing in Conrad's Fiction," *Conradiana*, XV (1983), 133–135.

Fowler, Doreen. "Marlow's Lie: A Terrible Truth," *CLA Journal*, XXII (March 1980), 287–295.

Fox, Claire. "Writing Africa with Another Alphabet: Conrad and Abish," *Conradiana*, XXII (1990), 111–125.

Fraser. Gail. *Interweaving Patterns in the Works of Joseph Conrad* (Ann Arbor, 1988), pp. 49–109.

———. "The Short Fiction," *The Cambridge Companion to Joseph Conrad*, J. H. Stape, ed. (Cambridge, Eng., 1996), pp. 25–44. (G)

Fraustino, Daniel V. "Self-Reliance in the '"Heart of Darkness,'" *Conradiana*, XXVII (Spring 1995), 74–80.

Friedman, Alan Warren. "Conrad's Picaresque Narrator: Marlow's Journey from *Youth* to *Chance*," *Multivalence: The Moral Quality of Form in the Modern Novel* (Baton Rouge, 1978), pp. 108–140.

Galef, David. "The Heart at the Edge of Darkness," *Journal of Modern Literature*, XVII (Summer 1990), 117–138.

———. "On the Margin: The Peripheral Characters in Conrad's 'Heart of Darkness,'" *Journal of Modern Literature*, XVII, i (1990), 117–138.

————. *The Supporting Cast: A Study of Flat and Minor Characters* (University Park, Pa., 1993), pp. 27–63.

Garrett, Peter K. *Scene and Symbol from George Eliot to James Joyce: Studies in Changing Fictional Mode* (New Haven, 1969), pp. 164–172.

Geary, Edward A. "An Ash Hollow: Woman as Symbol in 'Heart of Darkness,'" *Studies in Short Fiction*, XII (Fall 1976), 499–506.

Gekoski, R. A. *Conrad: The Moral World of the Novel* (London, 1978), pp. 72–90.

Gertzman, J. S. "Commitment and Sacrifice in 'Heart of Darkness': Marlow's Response to Kurtz.", *Studies in Short Fiction*. IX (Spring 1972), 187–196.

Gilbert, Sandra M. "Rider Haggard's Heart of Darkness," *Coordinates: Placing Science and Fantasy*, George E. Slusser, Eric Rabkin, and Robert Scholes, eds. (Carbondale Ill., 1983), pp. 136–138.

Gillespie, Gerald. "Savage Places Revisited: Conrad's 'Heart of Darkness' and Coppola's *Apocalypse Now*," *Comparatist*, IX (May 1985), 69–88.

Gilliam, Harriet. "Undeciphered Hieroglyphs: The Paleography of Conrad's Russian Characters," *Conradiana*, XII (1980), 37–50.

Gillon, Adam. *The Eternal Solitary: A Study of Joseph Conrad* (New York, 1960), pp. 104–108.

————. *Joseph Conrad* (Boston, 1982), pp. 68–81.

————. "Joseph Conrad and Shakespeare: Part Five *King Lear* and 'Heart of Darkness,'" *Polish Review*, XX, ii–iii (1975), 13–30.

Glassman, Peter J. *Language and Being: Joseph Conrad and the Literature of Personality* (New York, 1976), pp. 198–249.

Glenn, Ian. "Conrad's 'Heart of Darkness': A Sociological Reading," *Literature and History*, XIII (Autumn 1987), 238–256.

Godshalk, William Leigh. "Kurtz as Diabolical Christ," *Discourse*, XII (1969), 100–107.

Golanka, Mary. "Mr. Kurtz, I Presume? Livingstone and Stanley as Prototypes of Kurtz and Marlow," *Studies in the Novel*, XVII (Summer 1985), 194–202.

Golden, Kenneth L. "Joseph Conrad's Mr. Kurtz and Jungian *Enantiodromia*," *Interpretations*, XII (Fall 1981), 31–38.

Goldwyn, Merrill Harvey. "Nathaniel Hawthorne and Conrad's 'Heart of Darkness,'" *Conradiana*, XVI (1984), 73–78.

Goonetilleke, D. C. R. A. "Heart of Darkness," *Reference Guide to Short Fiction*, Noelle Watson, ed. (Detroit, 1994), p. 733.

————. "Ironies and Progress: Joseph Conrad and Imperialism in Africa," *Literature and Imperialism*. (Houndsmills, Eng., 1991), pp. 75–111.

Graham, Kenneth. *Indirections of the Novel: James, Conrad and Forster* (Cambridge, England, 1988), pp. 95–106.

Grant, Kenneth B. "Conrad's 'Heart of Darkness,'" *Explicator*, LIV (Fall 1995), 54–56.

Graver, Lawrence S. *Conrad's Shorter Fiction* (Berkeley, 1969), pp. 77–88.

Gray, Ethel M. "A Study of Conrad's 'Youth' and 'Heart of Darkness,'" *Revista de Literaturas Modernas*, VII (1968), 87–114.

Green, Jessie. "Diabolism, Pessimism, and Democracy: Notes on Melville and Conrad," *Modern Fiction Studies*, VIII (Autumn 1962), 287–305.

Gribble, Jennifer. "The Fogginess Of 'Heart of Darkness,'" *Sydney Studies in English*, XI (1985–1986), 83–94.

Griffith, John W. *Joseph Conrad and the Anthropological Dilemma* (Oxford, Eng., 1995), 46–55, ff.

Gross, Harvey. "Aschenbach and Kurtz: The Cost of Civilization," *Centennial Review*, VI (Spring 1962), 131–143.

Gross, Seymour. "Conrad and *All the King's Men*," *Twentieth-Century Literature*, III (April 1957), 27–32.

————. "A Further Note on the Function of the Frame in 'Heart of Darkness,'" *Modern Fiction Studies*, III (Summer 1957), 167–170.

Guerard, Albert J. *Conrad the Novelist* (Cambridge, Mass., 1958), pp. 34–48.

Guetti, James. "'Heart of Darkness' and the Failure of the Imagination," *Sewanee Review*, LXXIII (Summer 1965), 488–504.

———. *The Limits of Metaphor: A Study of Melville, Conrad, and Faulkner* (Ithaca, N.Y., 1967), pp. 46–68.

Guiterrez, Donald. "Uroboros, the Serpent and Conrad's 'Heart of Darkness,'" *Nantucket Review*, V (December 1973), 40–45.

Gurko, Leo. *Joseph Conrad: Giant in Exile* (New York, 1962), pp. 148–153.

Guth, Deborah. "Conrad's 'Heart of Darkness' as Creation Myth," *Journal of European Studies*, XVII (1987), 155–166.

Hagen, William M. "'Heart of Darkness' and the Process of *Apocalypse Now*," *Conradiana*, XIII (1981), 45–53.

Hampson, Robert. "Frazer, Conrad and the 'truth of primitive passion,'" *Sir James Frazer and the Literary Imagination: Essays in Affinity and Influence*, Robert Fraser, ed. (Houndsmills, Eng., 1990), pp. 172–191.

———. "'Heart of Darkness' and 'The Speech That Cannot Be Silenced,'" *English*, XXXIX (Spring 1990), 15–32.

———. *Joseph Conrad: Betrayal and Identity* (New York, 1992), pp. 106–116.

Hardy, Barbara. *Tellers and Listeners: The Narrative Imagination* (London, 1975), pp. 154–156.

Hardy, John Edward. "'Heart of Darkness': The Russian in Motley," *Man in the Modern Novel* (Seattle, 1964), pp. 17–33.

Harkness, Bruce, ed. *Conrad's "Heart of Darkness" and the Critics* (San Francisco, 1960).

Harper, George M. "Conrad's Knitters and Homer's Cave of the Nymphs," *English Language Notes*, I (September 1963), 53–57.

Haugh, Robert F. *Joseph Conrad: Discovery in Design* (Norman, Okla., 1957), pp. 35–55.

Hawkins, Hunt. "Conrad's Critique of Imperialism in 'Heart of Darkness,'" *Publications of the Modern Language Association*, XCIV (March 1979), 286–289.

———. "Conrad's 'Heart of Darkness': Politics and History," *Conradiana*, XXIV (1992), 207–217.

———. "Conrad and the Psychology of Colonialism," *Conrad Revisited: Essays for the Eighties*, Ross C. Martin, ed. (University, Ala., 1985), pp. 60–82.

———. "The Issue of Racism in 'Heart of Darkness,'" *Conradiana*, XIV (1982), 163–171.

———. "Joseph Conrad, Roger Casement and the Congo Reform Movement," *Journal of Modern Literature*, IX (1981/1982), 65–80.

Hawthorn, Jeremy. *Joseph Conrad: Language and Fictional Self-Consciousness* (Lincoln, Neb., 1979), pp. 7–36.

Hawthorn, Jeremy. *Joseph Conrad: Narrative Technique and Ideological Commitment* (London, 1990), pp. 171–202.

Hay, Eloise Knapp. "Cities Like White Sepulchres," *Conrad's Cities: Essays for Hans van Marle*, Gene M. Moore, ed. (Amsterdam, 1992), pp. 130–136.

———. *The Political Novels of Joseph Conrad* (Chicago, 1963), pp. 109–158.

———. "Rattling Talkers and Silent Soothsayers: 'Me Race for 'Heart of Darkness,'" *Conradiana*, XXIV (1992), 167–178.

Helder, Jack. "Fool Convention and Conrad's Hollow Harlequin," *Studies in Short Fiction*, XII (Fall 1975), 361–368.

Henricksen, Bruce. *Nomadic Voices: Conrad and the Subject of Narrative* (Urbana, Ill., 1992), pp. 47–80.

Hewitt, Douglas. *Conrad: A Reassessment* (Cambridge, England, 1952), pp. 16–30.

Hewitt, Douglas. *English Fiction of the Early Modern Period* (London, 1988), pp. 31–38.

———. "'Heart of Darkness' and Some 'Old and Unpleasant Reports,'" *Review of English Studies*, XXXVIII (1987), 374–376.

———. "Joseph Conrad's Hero: 'Fidelity' or 'The Choice of Nightmares,'" *Cambridge Journal*, II (August 1949), 658–687.

Heywood, Annemarie. "The Telling of the Tale: Conrad's 'Heart of Darkness,'" *Sheffield Papers on Literature and Society*, I (1976), 13–32.

Hoeppner, Edward H. "'Heart of Darkness': An Archeology of the Lie," *Conradiana*, XX, (1988), 137–146.

Hoffman, Stanton D. "The Hole in the Bottom of the Pail: Comedy and Theme in 'Heart of Darkness,'" *Studies in Short Fiction*, II (Winter 1965), 113–123.

Hollingsworth, Alan M. "Freud, Conrad, and the Future of an Illusion," *Literature and Psychology*, V (November 1955), 78–82.

Hooper, Myrtle J. "The Heart of Light: Silence in Conrad's 'Heart of Darkness,'" *Conradiana*, XXV (1993), 69–76.

Hopwood, Alison L. "Carlyle and Conrad: *Past and Present* and 'Heart of Darkness,'" *Review of English Studies*, XXIII (May 1972), 162–172.

Horner, Brother Patrick J. "'Heart of Darkness' and the Loss of the Golden Age," *Conradiana*, XI (1979), 190–192.

Hosilos, Lucila, "A Reliable Narrator: Conrad's Distance and Effects Through Marlow," *Diliman Review*, XVIII (April 1970), 154–172.

Houston, Gail. "Fictions to Live by: Honorable Intentions, Authorial Intentions and the Intended in 'Heart of Darkness,'" *Conradiana*, XXVIII (Winter 1996), 34–47.

Hubbard, Francis A. *Theories of Action in Conrad* (Ann Arbor, 1984), pp. 53–99.

Humphries, Reynold. "Language and 'Adjectival Insistence' in 'Heart of Darkness,'" *Conradiana* XXVI (Autumn 1994), 119–134.

———. "Restraint, Cannibalism and the 'Unspeakable Rites' in 'Heart of Darkness,'" *L'Epoque Conradienne*, (1990), 51–78.

———. "Taking the Figure Literally: Language and 'Heart of Darkness,'" *Etudes Anglaises*, XLVI, i (1993), 19–31.

Hunter, Allan. *Joseph Conrad and the Ethics of Darwinism* (London, 1983), pp. 15–78.

Hyland, Peter. "The Little Woman in 'Heart of Darkness,'" *Conradiana*, XX (1988), 3–11.

Inamdar, F. A. *Image and Symbol in Joseph Conrad's Novels* (Jaipur, India, 1979), pp. 43–70.

Jean-Aubrey, Georges. *Joseph Conrad in the Congo* (Boston, 1926).

Jean-Aubrey, Gérard. *The Sea Dreamer: A Definitive Biography of Joseph Conrad* (New York, 1957), pp. 163–171.

Jenkins, Ruth Y. "A Note on Conrad's Sources: Ernest Dowson's 'The Statute of Limitations' as Source for 'Heart of Darkness,'" *English Language Notes*, XXIV (March 1987), 39–42.

Johnson, Bruce. *Conrad's Models of Mind* (Minneapolis, 1971), pp. 70–88.

———. "'Heart of Darkness' and the Problem of Emptiness." *Studies in Short Fiction*, IX (Fall 1972), 387–400.

———. "Names, Naming, and the 'Inscrutable' in Conrad's 'Heart of Darkness,'" *Texas Studies in Literature and Language* (1971), 675–688.

Johnson, A. James M. "Victorian Anthropology, Racism, and 'Heart of Darkness,'" *Ariel*, 28 (October 1997), 111–131.

Jones, Michael. *Conrad's Heroism: A Paradise Lost* (Ann Arbor, 1985), pp. 66–80.

Kam, Rose Sallberg. "Silverberg and Conrad, Explorers of Inner Darkness," *Extrapolation*, XVII (December 1975), 18–27.

Kaplan, Harold. *The Passive Voice: An Approach to Modern Fiction* (Athens, Ohio, 1966), pp. 131–138.

Karl, Frederick R. "Introduction to the Danse Macabre: Conrad's 'Heart of Darkness,'" *Modern Fiction Studies*, XIV (Summer 1968), 143–156.

———. *Joseph Conrad, The Three Lives: A Biography* (New York, 1979), pp. 289–292, 457–460.

———. *A Reader's Guide to Joseph Conrad* (New York, 1960), pp. 133–140.

Kauvar, Gerald B. "Marlow as Liar," *Studies in Short Fiction*, V (Spring 1968), 290–292.

Kawin, Bruce F. *The Mind of the Novel: Reflexive Fiction and the Ineffable* (Princeton, 1982), pp. 52–66.

Kelleher, Victor. "Conrad and Barth: Nihilism Revisited," *Unisa English Studies*, XXI (1983), 19–22.

Kerf, René. "Symbol Hunting in Conradian Land," *Revue des Langues Vivantes*, XXXII (1966), 266–277.

Ketterer, David. "'Beyond the Threshold' in Conrad's 'Heart of Darkness,'" *Texas Studies in Literature and Language*, XI (Summer 1969), 1013–1022.

Kettle, Arnold. "The Greatness of Joseph Conrad," *Modern Quarterly*, III (Summer 1948), 64–70.

Kharbutli, Mahmoud K. "The Treatment of Women in 'Heart of Darkness,'" *Dutch Quarterly Review of Anglo-American Letters*, XVII (1987), 237–248.

Kimbrough, Robert H., ed. Joseph Conrad "Heart of Darkness" An *Authoritative Text, Background and Sources, Criticism* (New York, 1971).

Kinkead-Weekes, Mark. "'Heart of Darkness' and the Third-World Writer," *Sewanee Review*, XCVIII (January–March 1990), 31–49.

Kirby, David. *The Sun Rises in the Evening: Monism and Quietism in Western Culture* (Metuchen, N.J. 1982), pp. 110–117.

Kirschner, Paul. *Conrad: The Psychologist as Artist* (Edinburgh, 1968), pp. 42–48.

Kishler, Thomas C. "Reality in 'Heart of Darkness,'" *College English*, XXIV (1963), 561–562.

Kisner, Sister Mary R. "The Lure of the Abyss for the Hollow Man: Conrad's Notion of Evil," *Conradiana*, II (Spring 1969–1970), 85–99.

Kitonga, Ellen Mae. "Conrad's Image of African and Coloniser in 'Heart of Darkness,'" *Busara*, III (1970), 33–35.

Klein, Herbert G. "Charting the Unknown: Conrad, Marlow, and the World of Women," *Conradiana*, XX, (1988), 147–157.

Knapp, Bettina A. *Exile and the Writer: Exoteric and Esoteric Experience—A Jungian View* (State College, Pa., 1991), pp. 49–74.

Knight, Diana. "Structuralism I: Narratology: Joseph Conrad, 'Heart of Darkness,'" *Literary Theory and Work: Three Texts*, Douglas Tallack, ed. (Totowa, N.J., 1987), pp. 9–28.

Knox-Shaw, Peter. *The Explorer in English Fiction* (New York, 1986), pp. 136–163.

Krasner, James. *The Entangled Eye: Visual Perception and the Representation of Nature in Post-Darwinian Narrative* (New York, 1992), pp. 122–138.

Krieger, Murray. "Joseph Conrad: Action, Inaction, and Extremity: 'Heart of Darkness,'" *The Tragic Victim* (New York, 1960), pp. 154–165.

Krupat, Arnold. "Antonymy, Language and Value in Conrad's 'Heart of Darkness,'" *Missouri Review*, III, i (1979), 63–85.

Kurman, George and Roger W. Rouland. "Conrad's 'Heart of Darkness' as Pretext for Barth's 'Night-Sea Journey': The Colonist's Passage Upstream," *International Fiction Review*, XX, 1 (1993), 3–13.

La Bossiere, Camille R. *Joseph Conrad and the Science of Unknowing* (Frederickton, Canada, 1979), pp. 71–74.

Land, Stephen K. *Paradox and Polarity in the Fiction of Joseph Conrad* (New York, 1984), pp. 67–78.

Laskowski, Henry J. "'Heart of Darkness' A Primer for the Holocaust," *Virginia Quarterly Review*, LVIII (Winter 1982), 93–110.

Leavis, F. R. "Joseph Conrad," *Scrutiny*, X (June 1941), 23–32.

Lee, Robert F. *Conrad's Colonialism* (The Hague, 1969), pp. 40–49.

Lemon, Lee T. *Approaches to Literature* (New York, 1969), pp. 213–219.

Leondopoulos, Jordan. *Still the Moving World: Intolerance, Modernism and "Heart of Darkness"* (New York, 1991), pp. 21–35.

Lessenich, Rolf P. "Joseph Conrad: The Pilgrim's Progress and the Pilgrim's Regress," *Conradiana*, XIV (1982), 205–216.

Lester, John. "Captain Rom: Another Source for Kurtz?" *Conradiana*, XIV (1982), 112.

———. *Conrad and Religion* (New York, 1988), pp. 61–63, 94–97, 117–119, 146–148.

Levenson, Michael. "On the Edge of the 'Heart of Darkness," *Studies in Short Fiction*, XXIII (Spring 1986), 153–157.

———. Modernism and the Fate of Individuality: Character and Novelistic Form from Conrad to Woolf (New York, 1991), pp. 1–77.

———. "The Value of Facts in 'Heart of Darkness,'" *Nineteenth-Century Fiction*, XL (December 1985), 261–280.

Levin, Gerald. "The Skepticism of Marlow," *Twentieth-Century Fiction*, III (January 1958), 177–184.

———. "Victorian Kurtz," *Journal of Modern Literature*, VII (September 1979),433–440.

Levine, Paul. "Joseph Conrad's Blackness," *South Atlantic Quarterly*, LXIII (Spring 1964), 198–206.

Lincoln, Kenneth H. "Comic Light in 'Heart of Darkness,'" *Modern Fiction Studies*, XVIII (Summer 1972), 183–197.

Lindenbaum, Peter. "Hulks with One and Two Anchors: The Frame, Geographical Detail, and Ritual Process in 'Heart of Darkness,'" *Modern Fiction Studies*, XXX (Winter 1984), 703–710.

Loe, Thomas. "'Heart of Darkness' and the Short Novel," *Conradiana*, XX (1988), 33–44.

London, Betty. "Reading Race and Gender in Conrad's Dark Continent" *Criticism*, XXX (Summer 1989), 235–252.

Lord, George deF. *Trials of the Self: Heroic Ordeals in the Epic Tradition* (Hamden, Conn., 1983), pp. 192–216.

Lorsch, Susan E. *Where Nature Ends: Literary Response to the Designification of Landscape* (Rutherford, N.J., 1983), pp. 109–114.

Lothe, Jakob. *Conrad's Narrative Method* (Oxford, England. 1989), pp. 21–44.

———. "From Conrad to Coppola to Steiner," *Conradiana*, VI, 1 (1975), 10–13.

Low, Anthony. "Drake and Franklin in 'Heart of Darkness,'" *Conradiana*, II (Spring 1969–1970), 128–131.

———. "'Heart of Darkness': The Search for an Occupation," *English Literature in Transition*, XII, i (1969), 1–9.

Lucas, Michael A. "Conrad's Adjectival Eccentricity," *Style*, XXV (Spring 1991), 123–150. (G)

Lynn, David H. *The Hero's Tale: Narrators in the Early Modern Novel* (New York, 1989), pp. 12–27.

McCall, Dan. "The Meaning in Darkness: A Response to a Psychological Study of Conrad," *College English*, XXIX (May 1968), 620–627.

McCarthy, Patrick A. "'Heart of Darkness' and the Early Novels of H. G. Wells: Evolution, Anarchy, Entropy," *Journal of Modern Literature*, XIII (March 1986), 37–60.

McClure, John H. *Kipling and Conrad: The Colonial Fiction* (Cambridge, Mass., 198 1), pp. 131–154.

———. "Problematic Presence: The Colonial Other in Kipling and Conrad," *The Black Presence in English Literature*, David Dabydeen ed. (Manchester, England, 1985), pp. 159–162.

———. "The Rhetoric of Restraint in 'Heart of Darkness,'" *Nineteenth-Century Fiction*, XXXII (December 1977), 310–326.

McConnell, Daniel J. "'The Heart of Darkness' in T. S. Eliot's 'The Hollow Men,'" *Texas Studies in Literature and Language*, IV (Summer 1962), 141–153.

McIntyre, Allan J. "Psychology and Symbolism: Correspondence Between 'Heart of Darkness' and 'Death in Venice,'" *Hartford Studies in Literature*, VII (1975), 216–232.

McLaughlan, Juliet. "Conrad's 'Three Ages of Man': The 'Youth' Volume," *Polish Review*, XX, ii–iii (1975), 189–202.

———. "The 'Something Human' in 'Heart of Darkness,'" *Conradiana*, IX (1977), 115–125.

———. "The 'Value' and 'Significance' of 'Heart of Darkness,'" *Conradiana*, XV (1983), 3–21.

Madden, David. "Romanticism and the Hero-Witness Relationship in Four Conrad Stories," *Ohio University Review*, X (1968), 5–22.

Madden, Fred. "Marlow and the Double Horror of 'Heart of Darkness,'" *Midwest Quarterly*, XXVII (Summer 1986), 504–517.

Mahood, N. M. *The Colonial Encounter: A Reading of Six Novels* (Totowa, N.J., 1977), pp. 4–36.

Mandel, Miriam B. "Significant Patterns of Color and Animal Imagery in Conrad's 'Heart of Darkness,'" *Neophilologus*, LXXIII (January 1989), 305–319.

Mansell, Darrel. "Trying to Bring Literature Back Alive: The Ivory in Joseph Conrad's 'Heart of Darkness,'" *Criticism*, XXXIII (1991), 205–215.

Martin, David M. "The Diabolic Kurtz: The Dual Nature of His Satanism in 'Heart of Darkness,'" *Conradiana*, VII (1975), 175–177.

———. "The Function of the Intended in Conrad's 'Heart of Darkness,'" *Studies in Short Fiction*, XI (Winter 1974), 27–33.

Maud, Ralph. "The Plain Tale of 'Heart of Darkness,'" *Humanities Association Bulletin*, XVII (Autumn 1966), pp. 13–17.

Maxwell, J. C. "Mr. Stephens on 'Heart of Darkness,'" *Essays in Criticism*, XX (January 1970), 118–119.

Meckier, Jerome. "The Truth About Marlow," *Studies in Short Fiction*, XIX (Fall 1982), 373–379.

Mellard, James. "Myth and Archetype in 'Heart of Darkness,'" *Tennessee Studies in Literature*, XIII (1968), 1–15.

Melnick, Daniel. "The Morality of Conrad's Imagination: 'Heart of Darkness' and *Nostromo*," *Missouri Review*, V (1982), 139–156.

Meyer, Bernard C. *Joseph Conrad: A Psychoanalytic Biography* (Princeton, 1967), pp. 154–159.

Meyers, Jeffrey. *Fiction and the Colonial Experience* (Ipswich, Mass., 1973), pp. 58–67.

———. "Savagery and Civilization in *The Tempest, Robinson Crusoe*, and 'Heart of Darkness,'" *Conradiana*, II (Spring 1969–1970), 171–179.

Milbauer, Asher Z. *Transcending Exile: Conrad, Nabokov, I. B. Singer* (Miami, 1985), pp. 17–21.

Miller, Christopher L. *Black Darkness: Africanist Discourse in French* (Chicago, 1985), pp. 169–183.

Miller, J. Hillis. "'Heart of Darkness' Revisited," *Conrad Revisited: Essays for the Eighties*, Ross C. Martin, ed. (University, Ala., 1985), pp. 31–50.

Miller, Karl. *Doubles: Studies in Literary History* (New York, 1985), pp. 260–265.

Milne, Fred L. "Marlowe's Lie and the Intended: Civilization as the Lie in 'Heart of Darkness,'" *Arizona Quarterly*, XLIV (Spring 1988), 106–112.

Montag, George E. "Marlow Tells the Truth: The Nature of Evil in 'Heart of Darkness,'" *Conradiana*, III (May 1971), 93–97.

Morf, Gustav. *The Polish Shades and Ghosts of Joseph Conrad* (New York, 1976), pp. 200–205.

Morrissey, L. J. "The Tellers in 'Heart of Darkness': Conrad's Chinese Boxes," *Conradiana*, XIII (1981), 141–148.

Moseley, Edwin M. *Pseudonyms of Christ in the Modern Novel: Motifs and Methods* (Pittsburgh, 1962), pp. 16–21.

Moser, Thomas. *Joseph Conrad: Achievement and Decline* (Cambridge, Mass., 1957), pp. 78–81.

Moynihan, William T. "Conrad's 'The End of the Tether': A New Reading," *Modern Fiction Studies*, IV (Summer 1958), 173–177.

Mudrick, Marvin. *Conrad* (Englewood Cliffs, N.J., 1966), pp. 38–42, 45–54.

———. "The Originality of Conrad," *Hudson Review*, XI (Winter 1958–1959), 545–553.

Murfin, Ross, ed. *Heart of Darkness: A Case Study of Contemporary Criticism* (Boston, 1989).

Murray, David. "Dialogics: Joseph Conrad 'Heart of Darkness,'" *Literary Theory at Work*, Douglas Tallack, ed. (Totowa, N.J., 1987), pp. 5–134.

247

Na, Yong-Gyun. "The Original Sin Motif in 'Heart of Darkness,'" *Studies in English Literature* (1972), 97–107.

Nalbantian, Suzanne. *Seeds of Decadence in the Late Nineteenth-Century Novel: A Crisis in Values* (New York. 1983), pp. 104–112.

Narvette, Susan J. "The Anatomy of Failyre in Joseph Conrad's 'Heart of Darkness,'" *Texas Studies in Literature and Language*, XXXV, iii (1993), 279–315.

Nazareth, Peter. "Out of Darkness: Conrad and Other Third World Writers," *Conradiana*, XIV (1982), 173–187.

Neilson, Renn G. "Conrad's 'Heart of Darkness,'" *Explicator*, XLV (Spring 1987), 41–42.

Nettles, Elsa. "'Heart of Darkness' and the Creative Process," *Conradiana*, V (1973), 66–73.

Ober, Warren. "'Heart of Darkness': 'The Ancient Mariner' a Hundred Years Later," *Dalhousie Review*, XLV (Autumn 1965), 333–337.

O'Hanlon, Redmond. *Joseph Conrad and Charles Darwin: The Influence of Scientific Thought on Conrad's Fiction* (Atlantic Heights, N.J., 1984), pp. 99–101.

Ong, Walter J. "Truth in Conrad's Darkness," *Mosaic*, XI (Fall 1977), 151–163.

Owens, Guy, Jr. "A Note on 'Heart of Darkness,'" *Nineteenth-Century Fiction*, XII (September 1957), 168–169.

Owens, Robert F. "Kurtz's Fetish," *Conradiana*, X (1978), 155–159.

Padmini, Mongia. "Empire, Narrative and the Feminine in *Lord Jim* and 'Heart of Darkness,'" *Contexts for Conrad*, Own Knowles and Wieslaw Krajke, eds. (Boulder, Co., 1993), pp. 135–150.

Page, Norman. *A Conrad Companion* (New York, 1986), pp. 141–144.

Palmer, John A. *Joseph Conrad's Fiction: A Study in Literary Growth* (Ithaca, N.Y., 1968), pp. 1–45. (G)

Parr, Susan R. *The Moral of the Story: Literature, Values, and American Education* (New York, 1982), pp. 79–87.

Parrinder, Patrick. "'Heart of Darkness': Geography as Apocalypse," *Fin de Siecle, Fin du Globe: Fears and Fantasies of the Late Nineteenth Century*, John Stokes, ed. (New York, 1992), pp. 85–101.

Parry, Benita. *Conrad and Imperialism: Ideological Boundaries and Visionary Frontiers* (London, 1983), pp. 20–39.

Pecora, Vincent. "'Heart of Darkness' and the Phenomenology of Narrative Voice," *English Literary History*, LII (Winter 1985), 993–1015.

———. "Metropolitan Ironies: Conrad's 'Heart of Darkness,'" *Conradiana*, XXIV (1992), 179–189.

———. *Self and Form in Modern Narrative* (Baltimore, 1989), pp. 149–175.

Pérez Firmat, Gustavo. "*Don Quixote* in 'Heart of Darkness': Two Notes," *Comparative Literature*, XII (December 1975), 374–383.

Perlis, Alan D. "Coleridge and Conrad: Spectral Illuminations, Widening Frames," *Journal of Narrative Technique*, XII (Fall 1982), 167–176.

Perry, John Oliver. "Action, Vision, or Voice: The Moral Dilemmas in Conrad's Tale-Telling," *Modern Fiction Studies*, X (Spring 1964), 3–14.

Peters, Bradley T. "The Significance of Dream Consciousness in 'Heart of Darkness' and *Palace of the Peacock*," *Conradiana*, XXII (1990), 127–141.

Phillips, Gene D. *Conrad and Cinema: The Art of Adaptation* (New York, 1995) pp. 125–143.

———. "Nightmares at Noon: Nicholas Roeg's Television Version of Conrad's 'Heart of Darkness,'" *Conradiana*, 29 (Summer 1997), 150–155.

Pierce, William P. "An Artistic Flaw in 'Heart of Darkness,'" *Conradiana*, I (Summer 1969), 72–80.

Pinsker, Sanford. "Conrad's Curious 'Natives': Fatalistic Machiavellians/Cannibals with Restraint," *Conradiana*, XIV (1982), 199–204.

———. *The Languages of Joseph Conrad* (Amsterdam, 1978), pp. 43–49.

Pitt, Rosemary. "The Exploration of Self in 'Heart of Darkness' and Woolf's *The Voyage Out, Conradiana*, X (1978),141–154.

Pittock, Murray. "Rider Haggard and 'Heart of Darkness,'" *Conradiana*, XIX (1987), 206–208.

Purdy, Dwight H. *Joseph Conrad's Bible* (Norman, Okla., 1984), pp. 65–70.

Pym, J. "*Apocalypse Now*: An Errand Boy's Journey," *Sight and Sound*, XLIX (Winter 1980), 9–10.

Rael, Elsa. "Joseph Conrad: Master Absurdist," *Conradiana*, II (Spring 1969–1970), 163–170

Raskin, Jonah. "'Heart of Darkness': The Manuscript Revisions," *Review of English Studies*, XVIII (February 1967), 30–39.

Raval, Suresh. *The Art of Failure: Conrad's Fiction* (Boston, 1986), pp. 19–44.

Rawson, C. J. "Conrad's 'Heart of Darkness,'" *Notes and Queries*, VI (March 1959), 110–111.

Reeves, Charles Eric. "A Voice of Unrest: Conrad's Rhetoric of the Unspeakable," *Texas Studies in Literature and Language*, XXVII (Fall 1985), 284–310.

Reid, Stephen A. "The 'Unspeakable Rites' in 'Heart of Darkness,'" *Modern Fiction Studies*, IX (Winter 1963), 347–356.

Reilly, Joseph J. "The Shorter Stories of Joseph Conrad," *Of Books and Men* (New York, 1942), pp. 79–92.

Reilly, Patrick. *The Literature of Guilt: From Gulliver to Golding* (Iowa City, 1988), pp. 46–68.

Renner, Stanley. "The Garden of Civilization: Conrad, Huxley, and the Ethics of Evolution," *Conradiana*, VII (1975), 115–116.

———. "Kurtz, Christ and the 'Heart of Darkness,'" *Renascence*, XXVIII (Winter 1976), 95–104.

Ressler, Steve. *Joseph Conrad: Consciousness and Integrity* (New York, 1988), pp. 7–23.

Richardson, J. A. "James S. Jameson and 'Heart of Darkness,'" *Notes and Queries*, XL, i (1993), 64–66.

Ridd, Carl. "Saving the Appearances in Conrad's 'Heart of Darkness,'" *Studies in Religion, A Canadian Journal*, II (1972), 93–113.

Riddley, Florence. "The Ultimate Meaning of 'Heart of Darkness,'" *Nineteenth-Century Fiction*, XVIII (June 1963), 43–53.

Rising, Catherine. *Darkness at Heart: Fathers and Sons in Conrad* (Westport, Conn., 1990), pp. 40–50.

Rogers, William N. "The Game of Dominoes in 'Heart of Darkness,'" *English Language Notes*, XIII (Summer 1975), 42–45.

Roussel, Royal. *The Metaphysics of Darkness: A Study in the Unity of Conrad's Fiction* (Baltimore, 1971), pp. 72–79.

Roy, V. K. *The Romance of Illusions: A Study of Joseph Conrad* (Delhi, India, 1971), pp. 193–215.

Ruthven, K. K. "The Savage God: Conrad and Lawrence," *Critical Quarterly*, X (Spring-Summer 1968), 41–46.

Ruppel, Richard. "'Heart of Darkness' and the Popular Exotic Stories of the 1890s," *Conradiana*, XXI (1989), 3–14.

Ryf, Robert S. *Joseph Conrad* (New York, 1970), pp. 16–21.

Saalmann, Dieter. "Christa Wolf's *Storfall* and Joseph Conrad's 'Heart of Darkness,' The Curse of the 'Blind Spot,'" *Neophilologus*, LXXVI, i (1992), 19–28.

Saha, P. K. "Conrad's 'Heart of Darkness,'" *Explicator*, XLV (Winter 1987), 34–35.

———. "'Heart of Darkness,'" *Explicator*, XLVI (Winter 1988), 21.

Sanders, Charles. "Conrad's 'Heart of Darkness,'" *Explicator*, XXIV (September 1965), Item 2.

Sarvan, Charles Ponnuthurai, and Paul Balles. "Buddhism, Hinduism, and the Conradian Darkness," *Conradiana*, XXVI (Spring 1994), 70–75.

Sarvan, C. P. "Racism and 'Heart of Darkness,'" *International Fiction Review*, VII (Winter 1980), 6–10.

Saveson, John E. "Conrad's View of Primitive Peoples in *Lord Jim* and 'Heart of Darkness,'" *Modern Fiction Studies*, XVI (Summer 1970), 163–183.

Scheick, William J. *Fictional Structure and Ethics: The Turn-of-the-Century English Novel* (Athens, Ga., 1990), pp. 114–128.

Schleifer, Ronald. *Rhetoric and Death: The Language of Modernism and Postmodern Discourse Theory* (Urbana, Ill., 1990), pp. 192–197.

Schug, Charles. *The Romantic Genesis of the Modern Novel* (Pittsburgh, 1979), pp. 133–188.

Schwartz, Daniel R. *Conrad: Almayer's Folly to Under Western Eyes* (Ithaca, N.Y., 1980), pp. 63–75.

———. "Teaching 'Heart of Darkness': Towards a Pluralistic Perspective, *Conradiana*, XXIV (1992), 190–206.

Schwartz, Nina. "The Ideologies of Romanticism in 'Heart of Darkness,'" *New Orleans Review*, XIII (1986), 84–95.

Seidel, Michael. *Exile and the Narrative Imagination* (New Haven, 1986), pp. 44–70.

———. "Isolation and Narrative Power: A Meditation on Conrad by the Boundaries," *Criticism*, XXVII (Winter 1985), 73–95.

Seltzer, Leon. *The Vision of Melville and Conrad* (Athens, Ohio, 1970), pp. 1–7.

Sexton, Mark S. "Kurtz's Sketch in Oils: Its Significance to 'Heart of Darkness.'" *Studies in Short Fiction*. XXIV (Fall 1987) 387–392.

Shaffer, Brian W. *The Blinding Torch: Modern British Fiction and the Discourse of Civilization* (Amherst, Mass., 1993), pp. 47–57.

———. "'Civilization' Under Western Eyes: Lowry's *Under the Volcano* as a Reading of Conrad's 'Heart of Darkness,'" *Conradiana*, XXII (1990), 143–156.

———. ", Progress and Civilization and all the Virtues': Teaching 'Heart of Darkness' via 'An Outpost of Progress,'" *Conradiana*, XXIV (1992). 219–231.

———. "'Rebarbarizing Civilization': Conrad's African Fiction and Spencerian Sociology," *PMLA*, CVIII, i (1993), 45–58.

———. "Teach the Conflicts: 'Heart of Darkness' in the Classroom," *Conradiana*, XXIV (1992), 163–166.

Shaffett, C. "Operation and Mind Control: Apocalypse Now and the Search for Clarity," *Journal of Popular Films and Television*, VIII (Spring 1980), 34–43.

Sherry, Norman. *Conrad's Western World* (Cambridge, England, 1971), pp. 339–350.

Shetty, Sandya. "'Heart of Darkness': Out of Africa Some New Thing Never Comes," *Journal of Modern Literature*, XV, iv (1989), 461–474.

Shukla, Narain Prasad. "The Flame Image in 'Heart of Darkness,'" *Literary Criterion*, XIV, ii (1979), 38–45.

Simpson, David. *Fetishism and Imagination: Dickens, Melville, Conrad* (Baltimore, 1982), pp. 97–99.

Singh, Frances B. "The Colonialistic Bias of 'Heart of Darkness,'" *Conradiana*, X (1978), 41–54.

Skinner, John. "The Oral and the Written: Kurtz and Gatsby Revisited," *Journal of Narrative Technique*, XVII (Winter 1987), 131–140.

Smith, Steve. "Marxism and Ideology: Joseph Conrad, 'Heart of Darkness,'" *Literary Theory at Work*, Douglas Tallack, ed. (Totowa, N.J., 1987), pp. 181–200.

Spinner, Kaspar. "Embracing the Universe: Some Annotations to Joseph Conrad's 'Heart of Darkness,'" *English Studies*, XLIII (October 1962), 420–423.

Stallman, Robert W. "Conrad and The Great Gatsby," *Twentieth-Century Literature*, I (April 1955), 5–12.

Stampfl, Barry. "Conrad's 'Heart of Darkness,'" *Explicator*, XLIX (Spring 1991), 162–165.

——— . "Marlow's Rhetoric of (Self–) Deception in 'Heart of Darkness,'" *Modern Fiction Studies*, XXXVII (Summer 1991), 183–196.

Stark, Bruce K. "Kurtz's Intended: The Heart of 'Heart of Darkness,'" *Texas Studies in Literature and Language*, XVI (Fall 1974), 535–555.

Staten, Henry. "Conrad's Mortal Word," *Critical Inquiry*, XII (1986), 720–740.

Stein, William Bysshe. "Buddhism and the 'Heart of Darkness,'" *Western Humanities Review*, XI (Summer 1957), 281–285.

———. "Conrad's East: Time, History, Action, and 'Maya,'" *Texas Studies in Literature and Language*, VII (Autumn 1965), 265–283.

———. "The 'Heart of Darkness': Budhisattva Scenaria," *Orient/West*, IX (September–October 1964), 37–46.

———. "The Lotus Posture and the 'Heart of Darkness,'" *Modern Fiction Studies*, II (Winter 1956–1957), 235–237.

Steiner, Joan E. "Modem Pharisees and False Apostles: Ironic New Testament Parallels in Conrad's 'Heart of Darkness,'" *Nineteenth-Century Literature*, XXXVII (June 1982), 75–96.

Stephane, Nelly. "La Morale au coeur de Tenebres," *Europe*, LXX (June–July 1992), 64–68.

Stephens, R.C. "'Heart of Darkness': Marlow's 'Spectral Moonshine,'" *Essays in Criticism*, XIX (July (1969), 273–284.

Stewart, David H. "Kipling, Conrad and the Dark Heart," *Kipling Journal*, LXVII, 265 (1993), 22–32.

Stewart, Garret. *Death Sentences: Styles of Dying in British Fiction* (Cambridge, Mass., 1984), pp.146–152.

———. "Lying as Dying in 'Heart of Darkness,'" *PMLA*, XCV (May 1980), 319–331.

Stewart, J. I. M. *Joseph Conrad* (New York, 1968), pp. 77–85.

Stone, Carol, and Fawzia Afzal-Khan. "Gender, Race and Narrative in Joseph Conrad's 'Heart of Darkness,'" *Conradiana*, 29 (Autumn 1997), 221–234.

Straus, Nina Pelikan. "The Exclusion of the Intended From Secret Sharing in Conrad's 'The Heart of Darkness,'" *Joseph Conrad*, Andrew Michael Roberts, ed. (London, 1998), pp. 171–188.

Sugg, Richard P. "The Triadic Structure of 'Heart of Darkness,'" *Conradiana*, VII (1975), 179–182.

Sullivan, Zoreh T. "Civilization and Its Darkness: Conrad's 'Heart of Darkness' and Ford's *The Good Soldier*," *Conradiana*, VIII (1976), 110–120.

———. "Enclosure, Darkness, and the Body: Conrad's Landscape," *Centennial Review*, XXV (Winter 1981), 59–79.

Tanner, Tony. "'Gnawed Bones' and 'Artless Tales'—Eating and Narration in Conrad," *Partisan Review*, XLV (1982), 94–97.

Tennant, Roger. *Joseph Conrad* (New York, 1981), pp. 57–63.

Tessitore, John. "Freud, Conrad, and 'Heart of Darkness,'" *College Literature*, VII (Winter 1980), 30–40.

Thale, Jerome. "Marlow's Quest," *University of Toronto Quarterly*, XXIV (July 1955), 351–358.

———. "The Narrator as Hero," *Twentieth-Century Literature*, III (July 1957), 69–73.

Thorburn, David. *Conrad's Romanticism* (New Haven, 1974), pp. 135–146.

Thornton, L. "Conrad, Flaubert, and Marlow: Possession and Exorcism," *Comparative Literature*, XXXIV (Spring 1982), 146–156.

Thumboo, Edwin. "Some Plain Reading: Marlow's Lie in 'Heart of Darkness,'" *Literary Criterion*, XVI, iii (1981), 12–22.

Tick, Stanley. "Conrad's 'Heart of Darkness,'" *Explicator*, XXI (April 1963), Item 68.

Tindall, William York. "Apology for Marlow," *From Jane Austen to Joseph Conrad*, Robert C. Rathburn and Martin Steinmann, Jr., eds. (Minneapolis, 1958), pp. 274–285.

———. *The Literary Symbol* (Bloomington, Ind., 1955), pp. 86–91.

Todorov, Tzvetan. "Knowledge in the Void: 'Heart of Darkness,'" *Conradiana*, XXI (1989), 161–172.

Tretheway, Eric. "Language, Experience, and Selfhood in Conrad's 'Heart of Darkness,'" *Southern Humanities Review*, XXII (Spring 1988), 101–111.

Unger, Leonard. *The Man in the Name* (Minneapolis, 1956), pp. 195–200, 207–211.

Verleun, Jan. "Conrad's 'Heart of Darkness' and the Intended," Neophilologus, LXVII (October 1983), 623–629.

———. "Marlow and the Harlequin," Conradiana, XIII (1981), 195–220.

Vidan, Ivo. "'Heart of Darkness' in French Literature," Studies in Joseph Conrad, Claude Thomas, ed. (Montpellier, 1975), pp. 167–204.

Visiak, E. H. The Mirror of Conrad (New York, 1956), pp. 224–231.

Vitoux, Pierre. "Marlow: The Changing Narrator of Conrad's Fiction," Studies in Joseph Conrad, Claude Thomas, ed. (Montpellier, 1975), pp. 87–90.

Votteler, Thomas, ed. Short Story Criticism: Excerpts from Criticism of the Works of Short Fiction Writers, IX (Detroit, 1992), pp. 139–208. (G)

de Vries, Jetty. Conrad Criticism 1965–1985: "Heart of Darkness" (Groningen, Netherlands, 1988).

Walcutt, Charles C. Man's Changing Masks: Modes and Methods of Characterization in Fiction (Minneapolis, 1966), pp. 93–102.

Wallenstein, Jimmy. "'Heart of Darkness': The Smoke-and-Mirrors Defense," Conradiana, 29 (Autumn 1997), 205–220.

Warner, Oliver. Joseph Conrad (London, 1951), pp. 138–142.

Watson, Wallace. "'The Shade of Old Flaubert' and Maupassant's 'Art Impeccable (Presque)': French Influence on the Development of Conrad's Marlow," Journal of Narrative Technique, VII (Winter 1977), 37–56.

Watt, Ian. Conrad in the Nineteenth Century (Berkeley, 1979), pp. 126–253.

———. "Impressionism and Symbolism in 'Heart of Darkness,'" Southern Review, XIII (Winter 1977), 96–113.

———. "Marlow, Henry James, and 'Heart of Darkness,'" Ninteenth-Century Fiction, XXXIII (1978), 159–174.

Watts, C. T. "'Heart of Darkness': The Covert Murder-Plot and the Darwinian Theme," Conradiana, VII (1975), 137–145.

———. "Nardeau and Kurtz: A Footnote to 'Heart of Darkness,'" Notes and Queries, XXI (June 1974), 226–227.

Watts, Cedric. "Conrad and the Myth of the Monstrous Town," Conrad's Cities: Essays for Hans von Marle, Gene M. Moore, ed. (Amsterdam, 1992), pp. 22–23, 24.

———. The Deceptive Test: An Introduction to Covert Plots (Totowa, N.J., 1984), pp. 21–24, 74–84.

———. "Heart of Darkness," The Cambridge Companion to Joseph Conrad, J. H. Stape, ed. (Cambridge, Eng., 1996), pp. 45–62.

West, Roger. "Conrad's 'Heart of Darkness,'" Explicator, L (Summer 1992), 222–223.

White, Allan. "Joseph Conrad and the Rhetoric of Enigma," Joseph Conrad, Andrew Michael Roberts, ed. (London, 1998), pp. 235–246.

White, Allon. The Uses of Obscurity: The Fiction of Early Modernism (London, 1981), pp. 108–122.

White, Andrea. Joseph Conrad and the Adventure Tradition: Constructing and Deconstructing the Imperial Subject (Cambridge, Eng., 1993), pp. 167–192.

Whitehead, Lee M. "The Active Voice and the Passive Eye: 'Heart of Darkness' and Nietzsche's The Birth of Tragedy," Conradiana, VII (1975), 121–135.

Wilcox, Stewart C. "Conrad's 'Complicated Presentations' of Symbolic Imagery in 'Heart of Darkness,'" Philological Quarterly, XXXIX (January 1960), 1–17.

Wiley, Paul. Conrad's Measure of Man (New York, 1970), pp. 61–64.

———. "Conrad's Skein of Ironies," 'Heart of Darkness,' An Annotated Text, Backgrounds and Sources, Criticism, Robert Kimbrough, ed. (New York, 1971), pp. 200–205.

Williams, George Walton. "The Turn of the Tide in 'Heart of Darkness,'" Modern Fiction IX (Summer 1963), 171–173.

Willy, Todd G. "Measures of the Heart and of the Darkness: Conrad and the Suicides of 'New Imperialism,'" Conradiana, XIV (1982), 189–198.

———. "The 'Shamefully Abandoned' Kurtz: A Rhetorical Context for 'Heart of Darkness'", *Conradiana*, X (1978), 99–112.

Wilson, Reuel K. "Ivan Turgenev's *Rudin* and Joseph Conrad's 'Heart of Darkness': A Parallel Interpretation," *Comparative Literature Studies*, XXXII, 1 (1995), 26–41.

Wilson, Robert. *Conrad's Mythology* (Troy, N.Y., 1987), pp. 44–48.

Winnington, Peter. "Conrad and Cutcliffe Hyne: A New Source for 'Heart of Darkness,'" *Conradiana*, XVI (1984), 163–182.

Wirth-Nesher, Hana. "The Strange Case of 'The Turn of the Screw' and 'Heart of Darkness,'" *Studies in Short Fiction*, XVI (Fall 1979), 317–325.

Wollaeger, Mark A. Joseph Conrad and the Fictions of Skepticism (Stanford, Calif, 1990), pp. 57–77.

Woodring, Carl. *Nature into Art: Cultural Transformations in Nineteenth-Century Britain* (Cambridge, Mass., 1989), pp. 209–212.

Wright, Walter F. *Romance and Tragedy in Joseph Conrad* (New York, 1966), pp. 143–160.

Yarrison, Betsy C. "The Symbolism of Literary Allusion in 'Heart of Darkness,'" *Conradiana*, VII (1975), 155–164.

Yoder, Albert C. "Oral Artistry in Conrad's 'Heart of Darkness': A Study in Oral Aggression," *Conradiana*, II (Winter 1969–1970) 65–78.

Young, Gloria L. "Quest and Discovery: Joseph Conrad's and Carl Jung's African Journeys," *Modern Fiction Studies*, XXVIII (Winter 1982–1983), 583–589.

Yurick, S. "*Apocalypse Now:* Capital Flow," *Cineaste*, IX (Winter 1980), 21, 23.

Zabus, Chantel. "Answering Allegations Against 'Alligator' Writing in '"Heart of Darkness,' and 'Mister Johnson,'" *Shades of Empire in Colonial and Post Colonial Literature*, C. C. Barfoot and Theo D'Haen, eds. (Atlanta, 1993), pp. 117–138.

Zak, William F. "Conrad, F. R. Leavis, Whitehead: 'Heart of Darkness' and Organic Holism," *Conradiana*, IV (January 1972), 5–24.

Zhang, Weiwen. "A Tentative Comment on Conrad's 'Heart of Darkness,'" *Foreign Literature Studies*, XXXVII, i (1985), 39–45.

JOSEPH CONRAD, "The Secret Sharer"

Abdou, Sherlyn. "Ego Formation and the Land/Sea Metaphor in Conrad's 'Secret Sharer'" *Poetics of the Elements in the Human Condition: The Sea*, Anna-Teresa Tymienieck, ed. (Dordrecht, 1985), pp. 67–76.

Adelman, Gary. *Heart of Darkness: Search for the Unconscious* (Boston, 1987), pp. 50–53.

Andreach, Robert J. *The Slain and Resurrected God: Conrad, Ford and the Christian Myth* (New York, 1970), pp. 39–44.

Andreas, Osborn. *Joseph Conrad: A Study in Non-Conformity* (New York, 1959), pp. 135–138.

Baines, Jocelyn. *Joseph Conrad: A Critical Biography* (New York, 1960), pp. 355–359.

Barnett, Louise K. '*The Whole Circle of the Horizon*': The Circumscribed Universe of '*The Secret Sharer*,'" *Studies in the Humanities*, VIII (March 1981), 5–9.

Batchelor, John. *The Life of Joseph Conrad* (Oxford, Eng., 1994), pp. 187–189.

Bennett, Carl D. *Joseph Conrad* (New York, 1991), pp. 113–115.

Benson, Carl. "Conrad's Two Stories of Initiation," *Publications of the Modern Language Association*, LXIX (March 1954), 46–56.

Bidwell, Paul. "Leggatt and the Promised Land: A New Reading of 'The Secret Sharer,'" *Conradiana*, III, No. 2 (1971–1972), 26–34.

Billy, Ted. *A Wilderness of Words: Closure and Disclosure in Conrad's Short Fiction* (Lubbock, Tx., 1997), pp. 20–27.

Bouson, J. Brooks. *The Empathic Reader: A Study of the Narcissistic Character and the Drama of the Self* (Amherst, Mass., 1989), pp. 92–92.

Boyle, Ted E. *Symbol and Meaning in the Fiction of Joseph Conrad* (The Hague, 1965), pp. 133–142.

Brown, P. L. "The Secret Sharer and the Existential Hero," *Conradiana*, III (1971–1972), 22–30.

Burjorjee, Dinshaw M. "Comic Elements in Conrad's 'The Secret Sharer,'" *Conradiana* VIII, i (1975), 51–61.

Carabine, Keith. "The Secret Sharer: A Note on the Dates of Its Composition," *Conradiana*, XIX (1987), 209–213.

Carson, Herbert L. "The Second Self in 'The Secret Sharer,'" *Cresset*, XXXIV (#1 1970), 11–13.

Coates, Paul. *The Double and the Other: Identity as Ideology in Post-Modern Fiction* (New York, 1988), pp. 56–58.

Cohen, Michael. "Sailing Through 'The Secret Sharer': The End of Conrad's Story," *Massachusetts Studies in English*, X (Fall 1985), 102–109.

Cox, C. B. *Joseph Conrad: The Modern Imagination* (Totowa, N.J., 1974), pp. 138–150.

Curley, Daniel. "Legate of the Ideal," *Conrad's Secret Sharer and the Critics*, Bruce Harkness, ed. (Belmont, Calif., 1962), pp. 75–82.

———. "The Writer and His Use of Material: The Case of 'The Secret Sharer,'" *Modern Fiction Studies*, XIII (Summer 1967), 179–194.

Daleski, H. M. *Joseph Conrad: The Way of Dispossession* (New York, 1977), pp. 171–183.

———. "'The Secret Sharer': Questions of Command," *Critical Quarterly*, XVII (Autumn 1975), 268–279.

Davis, W. Eugene. "The Structure of Justice in 'The Secret Sharer,'" *Conradianal* XXVII (Spring 1995), 64–73.

Dawson, Anthony B. "In the Pink: Self and Empire in 'The Secret Sharer,'" *Conradiana*, XXII, No. 3 (1990), 185–196.

Day, Robert A. "The Rebirth of Leggatt," *Literature and Psychology*, XIII (Summer 1963), 74–81.

Dazey, Mary Ann. "Shared Secret or Secret Sharing in Conrad's 'The Secret Sharer,'" *Conradiana*, XVIII (1986), 201–203.

Devers, James. "More on Symbols in Conrad's 'The Secret Sharer,'" *Conradiana*, 28, No. 1 (1996), 66–76.

Dilworth, Thomas R. "Conrad's Secret Sharer at the Gate of Hell," *Conradiana*, IX (1977), 203–218.

Dobrinsky, Joseph. *The Artist in Conrad's Fiction: A Psychocritical Study* (Ann Arbor, 1989), pp. 63–76.

———. "The Two Lives of Conrad in 'The Secret Sharer,'" *Cahiers Victoriens et Edouardiens*, XXI (April 1985), 33–49.

Dowden, Wilfred S. *Joseph Conrad: The Imaged Style* (Nashville, 1970), pp. 141–145.

Durin, Jean. "Brinksmanship in 'Heart of Darkness' and 'The Secret Sharer,'" *L'Epoque Conradienne* (1987), 97–104.

Dussinger, Gloria R. "'The Secret Sharer': Conrad's Psychological Study," *Texas Studies in Literature and Language*, X (Winter 1969), 599–608.

Eggenschwiler, David. "Narcissus in 'The Secret Sharer': A Secondary Point of View," *Conradiana*, XI (1979), 23–40.

Evans, Frank B. "The Nautical Metaphor in 'The Secret Sharer,'" *Conradiana*, VII (1975), 3–16.

Evans, Robert O. "Conrad: A Nautical Image," *Modern Language Notes*, LXXII (February 1957), 98–99.

Faatz, Anita J. "An Illustration of the Experience of Change in Conrad's 'The Secret Sharer,'" *Journal of the Otto Rank Association*, V (June 1970), 31–37.

Facknwitz, Mark A. R. "Cryptic Allusions and the Moral of the Story: The Case of Joseph Conrad's 'The Secret Sharer,'" *Journal of Narrative Technique*, XVII (Winter 1987), 115–130.

Folsom, James K. "The Legacy of 'The Secret Sharer,'" *Bulletin of the Rocky Mountain Modern Language Association*, XXV (March 1971), 16–21.

Foye, Paul F., Bruce Harkness, and Nathan L. Marvin. "The Sailing Maneuver in 'The Secret Sharer,'" *Journal of Modern Literature*, II (September 1971), 119–123.

Fraser, Gail. *Interweaving Patterns in the Works of Joseph Conrad* (Ann Arbor, 1988), pp. 111–133.

Gilley, Leonard. "Conrad's 'The Secret Sharer,'" *Midwest Quarterly*, VIII (July 1967), 319–330.

Gillon, Adam. *Joseph Conrad* (Boston, 1982), pp. 153–156.

Graver, Lawrence. *Conrad's Short Fiction* (Berkeley, 1969), pp. 149–158.

Guerard, Albert. *Conrad the Novelist* (Cambridge, 1958), pp. 21–29.

Hamilton, S. C. "'A Cast-Anchor Devils' and Conrad: A Study of Persona and Point of View in 'The Secret Sharer,'" *Conradiana*, II (Spring 1960–1970), 111–121.

Hampson, Robert. *Joseph Conrad: Betrayal and Identity* (New York, 1992), pp. 191–195.

Harkness, Bruce. "The Secret of 'The Secret Sharer' Bared," *College English* XXVII (October 1965), 55–61.

Haugh, Robert F. *Joseph Conrad: Discovery in Design* (Norman, Okla., 1957), pp. 78–82.

Hawthorn, Jeremy. *Multiple Personality and the Disintegration of Literary Character: From Oliver Goldsmith to Sylvia Plath* (New York, 1983), pp. 84–90.

Hewitt, Douglas. *Joseph Conrad: A Reassessment* (Chester Springs, Pa., 1969), pp. 70–79

Hoffman, Charles G. "Point of View in 'The Secret Sharer,'" *College English*, XXIII (May 1962), 651–654.

Johnson, Barbara and Marjorie Garber. "Secret Sharing: Reading Conrad Psychoanalytically," *College English*, XLIX (1987), 629–640.

Johnson, Bruce. *Conrad's Models of Mind* (Minneapolis, 1971), pp. 126–129.

Jones, Michael. *Conrad's Heroism: A Paradise Lost* (Ann Arbor, 1985), pp. 101–112.

Kane, Thomas S. "The Dark Ideal: A Note on 'The Secret Sharer,'" *CEA Critic*, XXXVI (November 1973), 28–30.

Karl, Frederick R. *A Reader's Guide to Joseph Conrad* (New York, 1960), pp. 230–236.

Karl, Frederick R. and Marvin Magalaner. *A Reader's Guide to Great Twentieth-Century English Novels* (New York, 1959), pp. 83–86.

Keppler, C. F. *The Literature of the Second Self* (Tucson, 1972), pp. 112–115.

Kirschner, Paul. *Conrad: The Psychologist as Artist* (Edinburgh, 1968), pp. 118–127.

Land, Stephen K. *Paradox and Polarity in the Fiction of Joseph Conrad* (New York, 1984), pp. 167–173.

Leiter, Louis. "Echo Structures: Conrad's 'The Secret Sharer,'" *Twentieth-Century Literature*, V (January 1960) 159–175.

Loe, Thomas. "The Secret Sharer," *Reference Guide to Short Fiction*, Noelle Watson, ed. (Detroit, 1994), 890–891.

Lothe, Jakob. *Conrad's Narrative Method* (Oxford, Eng., 1989), pp. 57–71.

Madden, David. "Romanticism and the Hero-Witness Relationship in Four Conrad Stories," *Ohio University Review*, X (1968), 10–12.

Madison, R. D. "The Secret Maneuver in 'The Secret Sharer,'" *Conradiana*, XIV (1982), 233–236.

Marsh, D. R. C. "Moral Judgment in 'The Secret Sharer,'" *English Studies in America*, III (March 1960), 57–70.

Martin, Jacky. "A Topological Re-reading of 'The Secret Sharer,'" *Recherches Anglaises et Americaines*, XV (1982), 51–66.

Meisel, Perry. *The Myth of the Moderns: A Study in British Literature and Criticism After 1850* (New Haven, 1987), 232–236.

Miller, Karl. *Doubles: Studies in Literary History* (New York, 1985), pp. 255–257.

Miller, Norma. "All is Vanity Under the Sun: Conrad's Floppy Hat as Biblical Allusion," *Conradiana*, 30 (Spring 1998), 64–67.

Milne, Fred L. "Conrad's 'The Secret Sharer,'" *Explicator*, XLIV (Spring 1986), 38–39.

Moore, Aluyat. "Conrad's Technique of 'The Secret Sharer,'" *L'Epoque Conradienne*, II (1976), 35–53.

Moser, Thomas. *Joseph Conrad: Achievement and Decline* (Cambridge, Mass., 1957), pp. 138–141.

Mudrick, Marvin. *Conrad* (Englewood Cliffs, N.J., 1966), pp. 75–82.

———. "Conrad and the Terms of Modern Criticism," *Hudson Review*, VII (Autumn 1954), 424–426.

Murphy, Michael. "'The Secret Sharer': Conrad's Turn of the Winch," *Conradiana*, XVIII (1986), 193–200.

O'Brien, Juston. "Camus and Conrad: An Hypothesis," *Romanic Review*, LVIII (October 1967), 196–199.

O'Hara, J. D. "Unlearned Lessons in 'The Secret Sharer,'" *College English*, XXVI (March 1965), 444–450.

Orel, Harold. *The Victorian Short Story: Development and Triumph of a Literary Genre* (Cambridge, England, 1986), pp. 168–172.

Otten, Terry. *After Innocence: Vision of the Fall in Modern Literature* (Pittsburgh, 1982), pp. 42–51.

———. "The Fall and After in 'The Secret Sharer,'" *Southern Humanities Review*, XII (Summer 1978), 221–230.

Paccaud, Josiane. "The Alienating Imaginary and the Symbolic Law in Conrad's 'The Secret Sharer,'" *L'Epoque Conradienne* (1987), 89–96.

———. "Under the Other's Eyes: Conrad's 'The Secret Sharer,'" *The Conradian*, XII (1987), 59–73.

Page, Norman. *A Conrad Companion* (New York, 1986), pp. 156–159.

Palmer, John A. *Joseph Conrad's Fiction: A Study of Literary Growth* (Ithaca, N.Y., 1968), pp. 221–230.

Powell, Marian C. "An Approach to Teaching 'The Secret Sharer,'" *English Journal*, LVI (January 1967), 49–53, 96.

Phillips, Gene D. *Conrad and Cinema: The Art of Adaptation* (New York, 1995), pp. 85–89.

Quinones, Ricardo J. *The Changes of Cain: Violence and the Lost Brother in Cain and Abel Literature* (Princeton, 1991), pp. 109–121.

Rahv, Philip. "Fiction and the Criticism of Fiction," *Kenyon Review*, XVIII (Spring 1956), 276–299.

Rashkin, Esther. *Family Secrets and the Psychoanalysis of Narrative* (Princeton, N.J., 1992), pp. 49–63.

Reilly, Joseph J. "The Shorter Stories of Joseph Conrad," *Of Books and Men* (New York, 1942), pp. 79–92.

Ressler, Steve. "Conrad's 'The Secret Sharer': Affirmation of Action," *Conradiana*, XVI (1984), 195–214.

———. *Joseph Conrad: Consciousness and Integrity* (New York, 1988), pp. 80–97.

Roberts, Edgar V. "The Setting of Conrad's Story 'The Secret Sharer,'" *Writing Themes About Literature* (Englewood Cliffs, N.J., 1969), pp. 48–51.

Robinson, E. Arthur. "Conrad's 'The Secret Sharer,'" *Explicator*, XVIII (February 1960), Item 28.

Rogers, Robert. *A Psychological Study of the Double in Literature* (Detroit, 1970), pp. 42–46.

Rosen, John B. "The L Shaped Room in 'The Secret Sharer,'" *Claflin College Review*, I, i (1976), 4–8.

Ryan, Alvan S. "The Secret Sharer," *Insight II: Analyses of British Literature*, John V. Hagopian and Martin Doich, eds. (Frankfurt, 1964), pp. 70–76.

Said, Edward W. *Joseph Conrad and the Fiction of Autobiography* (Cambridge, 1966), pp. 125–132.

St. Aubyn, F. C. "The Secret Sharers: Conrad and Schehadé," *Revu de Littérature Comparée*, XLVII (July–September 1973), 456–464.

Schenck, Mary-Lou. "Seamanship in Conrad's 'The Secret Sharer,'" *Criticism*, XV (Winter 1973), 1–15.

Schwartz, Daniel R. *Conrad: The Later Fiction* (London, 1982), pp. 1–10.

Sherry, Norman. *Conrad's Eastern World* (Cambridge, England, 1966), pp. 253–269.

———. "*Lord Jim* and 'The Secret Sharer,'" *Review of English Studies*, XVI (November 1965), 378–392.

Simmons, J. L. "The Dual Morality in Conrad's 'The Secret Sharer,'" *Studies in Short Fiction*, II (Spring 1965), 209–220.

Simons, Kenneth. *The Ludic Imagination: A Reading of Joseph Conrad* (Ann Arbor, 1985), pp. 95–104.

Stallman, R. W. "Conrad and 'The Secret Sharer,'" *Accent*, IX (Spring 1949), 131–143.

Stein, Allen F. "Conrad's Debt to Cooper: *The Sea Lion* and 'The Secret Sharer,'" *Conradiana*, VIII (1976), 247–252.

Steiner, Joan E. "Conrad's 'The Secret Sharer: Complexities of the Doubling Relationship," *Conradiana*, XII (I 980), 173–186.

Stewart, J. I. M. *Joseph Conrad* (New York, 1968), pp. 232–240.

Tennant, Roger. *Joseph Conrad* (New York, 1981), pp. 57–63.

Thomas, Mark Ellis. "Doubling and Difference in Conrad: Secret Sharer,' *Lord Jim*, and *The Shadow Line*," *Conradiana*, XXVIII (Autumn 1995), 222–234.

Thorburn, David. *Conrad's Romanticism* (New Haven, 1974), pp. 140–146.

Trilling, Lionel. *Prefaces to Experience of Literature* (New York, 1979), pp. 107–111.

Troy, Mark. "'…Of No Particular Significance Except to Myself': Narrative Posture in Conrad's 'The Secret Sharer,'" *Studia Neophilologica*, XLVI, 1 (1984), 35–50.

Walcutt, Charles C. "Interpreting the Symbol," *College English*, XIV (May 1953), 452–454.

Watts, Cedric. *The Deceptive Text: An Introduction to Covert Plots* (Totowa, N.J., 1984), pp. 84–90.

———. "The Mirror-Tate: An Ethico-Structural Analysis of Conrad's 'The Secret Sharer,'" *Critical Quarterly*, XIX (Autumn 1977), 25–37.

West, Ray B., Jr. and Robert Wooster Staliman. *The Art of Fiction* (New York, 1960), pp. 490–498.

Westbrook, Wayne W. "Dickens's Secret Sharer, Conrad's Mutual Friend," *Studies in Fiction*, XXIX (Spring 1992), 205–214.

White, James F. "The Third Theme in 'The Secret Sharer,'" *Conradiana*, XXI (1989), 37–46.

Wiley, Paul. *Conrad's Measure of Man* (Madison, 1954), pp. 94–97.

Williams, Porter. "'The Brand of Cain in 'The Secret Sharer,'" *Modern Fiction Studies*, X (Spring 1964), 27–30.

JOSEPH CONRAD, "Youth"

Andreas, Osborne. *Joseph Conrad: A Study in Non-Conformity* (New York, 1959), pp. 43–45.

Baines, Jocelyn. *Joseph Conrad: A Critical Biography* (London, 1960), pp. 210–212.

Billy, Ted. *A Wilderness of Words: Closure and Disclosure in Conrad's Short Fiction* (Lubbock, Tx., pp. 54–63.

Bonney, William W. *Thorns and Arabesques: Contexts of Conrad's Fictions* (Baltimore, 1980), pp. 24–26.

Boyle, Ted E. *Symbol and Meaning in the Fiction of Joseph Conrad* (The Hague, 1965), pp. 116–124.

Bruss, Paul. *Conrad's Early Sea Fiction* (Lewisburg, PA, 1979), pp. 58–69, 160–163.

Burgess, C. F. *The Fellowship of the Craft: Conrad on Ships and Seamen and the Sea* (Port Washington, NY, 1976), pp. 62–64.

Conrad, Joseph. "Author's Notes," *Youth and Two Other Stories* (New York, 1925), pp. ix–xii.

Crawford, John. "Another Look at 'Youth,'" *Research Studies*, XXXVII (1969), 154–156.

Emmett, V. J., Jr. "'Youth': Its Place in Conrad's *Oeuvre*," *Connecticut Review*, IV (1970), 49–58.

Gillon, Adam. *Joseph Conrad* (Boston, 1982), pp. 63–68.

Gonzalez, N. V. M. "Time as Sovereign: A Reading of Conrad's 'Youth,'" *Literary Apprentice* (University of the Philippines, 1954), 106–122.

Gordan, John D. *Joseph Conrad: The Making of a Novelist* (Cambridge, MA, 1940), pp. 264–266.

Graver, Lawrence. *Conrad's Shorter Fiction* (Berkeley, 1969), pp. 70–77.

Gray, Ethel M. "A Study of Conrad's 'Youth' and 'Heart of Darkness,'" *Revista de Literaturas Modernas*, VII (1968), 87–114.

Gurko, Leo. *Joseph Conrad: Giant in Exile* (New York, 1962), pp. 79–82.

Haugh, Robert. *Joseph Conrad: Discovery in Design* (Norman, OK, 1957), pp. 20–24.

Jean-Aubry, Gérard. *The Sea Dreamer: A Definitive Biography of Joseph Conrad* (New York, 1957), pp. 93–99.

Karl, Frederick R. *A Reader's Guide to Joseph Conrad*, Revised Edition (New York, 1969), pp. 133–134.

Krieger, Murray. "Conrad's 'Youth': A Naive Opening to Art and Life," *College English*, XX (March 1959), 275–280.

Land, Stephen K. *Paradox and Polarity in the Fiction of Joseph Conrad* (New York, 1984), pp. 66–67.

Levin, Gerald H. "The Skepticism of Marlow," *Twentieth-Century Literature*, III (January 1958), 177–184.

McLaughlan, Juliet. "Conrad's 'Three Ages of Man': The 'Youth' Volume," *Polish Review*, XX (1975) 189–202.

Madden, David. "Romanticism and the Hero-Witness Relationship in Four Conrad Stories," *Ohio University Review*, X (1968), 8–10.

Mathews, James W. "Ironic Symbolism in Conrad's 'Youth,'" *Studies in Short Fiction*, XI (Spring 1974), 117–123.

Moser, Thomas. *Joseph Conrad: Achievement and Decline* (Cambridge, MA, 1957), pp. 43–49.

Newhouse, Neville H. *Joseph Conrad* (New York, 1969), pp. 77–78.

Owen, Guy. "Crane's 'The Open Boat' and Conrad's 'Youth,'" *Modern Language Notes*, LXXII (February 1958), 100–102.

Page, Norman. *A Conrad Companion* (New York, 1986), pp. 139–141.

Pinsker, Sanford. *The Languages of Joseph Conrad* (Amsterdam, 1978).

Schwarz, Daniel R. *Conrad: The Later Fiction* (London, 1982), pp. 1–10.

Smith, J. Oates. "The Existential Comedy of Conrad's 'Youth,'" *Renascence*, XVI (Fall 1963), 22–28.

Sullivan, Ernest W. "The Genesis and Evolution of Joseph Conrad's 'Youth': A Revised and Copy-edited Typescript Page," *Review of English Studies*, XXXVI (November 1985), 522–534.

Tennant, Roger. *Joseph Conrad* (New York, 1981), pp. 34–37.

Thomas, Lloyd S. "Conrad's 'Jury Rig' Use of the Bible in 'Youth,'" *Studies in Short Fiction*, XVII (Winter 1980), 79–82.

Tindall, William Y. "Apology for Marlow," *From Jane Austen to Joseph Conrad: Essays in Memory of James T. Hillhouse*, Robert C. Rathburn and Martin Steinmann, eds. (Minneapolis, 1958), pp. 278–282.

Unger, Leonard. *The Man in the Name* (Minneapolis, 1956), pp. 240–242.

Vitoux, Pierre. "Marlow: The Changing Narrator of Conrad's Fiction," *Studies in Conrad*, Claude Thomas, ed. (Montpellier, France, 1975), pp. 84–87.

Watson, Wallace. "'The Shade of Old Flaubert' and Maupassant's 'Art Impeccable (Presque)': French Influence on the Development of Conrad's Marlow," *Journal of Narrative Technique*, VII (Winter 1977), 37–56.

Weston, John Howard. "'Youth': Conrad's Irony and Time's Darkness," *Studies in Short Fiction*, XI (Fall 1974), 399–407.

Wills, J. H. "A Neglected Masterpiece: Conrad's 'Youth,'" *Texas Studies in Language and Literature*, IV (Spring 1963), 591–601.

Willy, Todd G. "The Call to Imperialism in Conrad's 'Youth': An Historical Reconstruction," *Journal of Modern Literature*, VIII (1980), 39–50.

Wright, Walter F. *Romance and Tragedy in Joseph Conrad* (Lincoln, NB, 1949), pp. 9–12.

STEPHEN CRANE, "The Blue Hotel"

Beaver, Harold. "Stephen Crane: Interpreting the Interpreter," *The Nineteenth-Century American Short Story*, A. Robert Lee, ed. (Totowa, N.J., 1985), pp. 120–133.

Bergon, Frank. *Stephen Crane's Artistry* (New York, 1975), pp. 124–131.

Berryman, John. *Stephen Crane* (New York, 1950), pp. 208–214.

Cady, Edward. *Stephen Crane* (New York, 1962), pp. 155–157.

Cate, Hollis. "Seeing and Not Seeing in 'The Blue Hotel,'" *College Literature*, IX (1982), 150–152.

Church, Joseph. "The Determined Stranger in Stephen Crane's 'Blue Hotel,'" *Studies in the Humanities*, XVI (December 1989), 99–110.

Collins, Michael J. "Realism and Romance in the Western Stories of Stephen Crane," *Under the Sun: Myth and Realism in Western American Literature*, Barbara H. Meldrum, ed. (Troy, N.Y., 1985), pp. 144–146.

Cox, James T. "Stephen Crane as Symbolic Naturalist: An Analysis of 'The Blue Hotel,'" *Modern Fiction Studies*, III (Summer 1957), 147–158.

Davison, Richard Allan. "Crane's 'Blue Hotel' Revisited: The Illusion of Fate," *Modern Fiction Studies*, XV (Winter 1969–1970), 537–540.

Deamer, Robert Glen. "Remarks on the Western Stance of Stephen Crane," *Western American Literature*, XV (Summer 1980), 123–141.

———. "Stephen Crane and the Western Myth," *Western American Literature*, VII (Summer 1972), 111–123.

Dean, James L. "The Wests of Howells and Crane," *American Literary Realism, 1870–1910*, X (Summer 1977), 254–266.

Dillingham, William B. "'The Blue Hotel' and the Gentle Reader," *Studies in Short Fiction*, I (Spring 1964), 224–226.

Dooley, Patrick K. *The Pluralistic Philosophy of Stephen Crane* (Urbana, Ill., 1993), pp. 90–92.

Ellis, James. "The Game of High-Five in 'The Blue Hotel,'" *American Literature*, XLIX (November 1977), 440–442.

Feaster, John. "Violence and the Ideology of Capitalism: A Reconsideration of Crane's 'The Blue Hotel,'" *American Literary Realism*, XXV, No. I (1992), 80–94.

Gibson, Donald B. "'The Blue Hotel' and the Idea of Human Courage," *Texas Studies in Literature and Language*, VI (Autumn 1964), 388–397.

———. *The Fiction of Stephen Crane* (Carbondale, Ill., 1968), pp. 106–118.

Gleckner, Robert F. "Stephen Crane and the Wonder of Man's Conceit," *Modern Fiction Studies*, V (Autumn 1959), 271–281.

Greenfield, Stanley B. "The Unmistakable Stephen Crane," *Publications of the Modern Language Association*, LXXIII (December 1958), 565–568.

Grenberg, Bruce L. "Metaphysic of Despair: Stephen Crane's 'The Blue Hotel,'" *Modern Fiction Studies*, XIV (Summer 1968), 203–213.

Gross, David S. "The Western Stories of Stephen Crane," *Journal of American Culture*, XI (Winter 1988), 15–21.

Gullason, Thomas A. "An Early Draft of 'The Blue Hotel,'" *Stephen Crane Newsletter*, III (1968), 1–2.

Halliburton, David. *The Color of the Sky: A Study of Stephen Crane* (New York, 1989), pp. 206–226.

Holton, Milne. *Cylinder of Fiction: The Fiction and Journalistic Writings of Stephen Crane* (Baton Rouge, 1972), pp. 233–241.

Johnson, George W. "Stephen Crane's Metaphor of Decorum," *Publications of the Modern Language Association*, LXXVIII (June 1963), 254–255.

Juan-Navarro, Santiago. "Reading Reality: The Tortuous Path to Perception in Stephen Crane's 'The Open Boat' and 'The Blue Hotel,'" *Revista Canaria de Estudios Ingleses*, (November 1989), 43–48.

Katz, Joseph. "An Early Draft of 'The Blue Hotel,'" *Stephen Crane Newsletter*, III (Fall 1968) 1–3.

———. *Stephen Crane: The Blue Hotel*, Merrill Literary Casebook Series (Columbus, Ohio, 1970).

Keenan, Richard C. "The Sense of an Ending: Jan Kadar's Distortion of Stephen Crane's 'The Blue Hotel,'" *Literature/Film Quarterly*, XVI (1988), 265–268.

Kent, Thomas. *Interpretation and Genre: The Role of Generic Perception in the Study of Narrative Texts* (Lewisburg, Pa., 1986), pp. 124–127, 137–143.

———. "The Problem of Knowledge in 'The Open Boat' and 'The Blue Hotel,'" *American Literary Realism*, XIV (Autumn 1981), 262–268.

Kimball, Sue L. "Circles and Squares: The Designs of Stephen Crane's 'The Blue Hotel,'" *Studies in Short Fiction*, XVII (Fall 1980), 425–430.

Kinnamon, Jon M. "Henry James, The Bartender in Stephen Crane's 'The Blue Hotel,'" *Arizona Quarterly*, XXX (Summer 1974), 160–163.

Klotz, Marvin. "Stephen Crane: Tragedian or Comedian, 'The Blue Hotel,'" *University Kansas City Review*, XXVII (Spring 1961), 170–174.

Knapp, Bettina. *Stephen Crane* (New York, 1987), pp. 158–161.

Knapp, Daniel. "Son of Thunder: Stephen Crane and the Fourth Evangelist" *Nineteenth-Century Fiction*, XXIV (December 1969), 253–291.

Kowalewski, Michael. *Deadly Musings: Violence and Verbal Form in American Fiction* (Princeton, 1993), pp. 123–129.

LaFrance, Marston. *A Reading of Stephen Crane* (London, 1971), pp. 221–232.

Levenson, J. C. "Introduction," *Stephen Crane: Tales of Adventure*, Fredson Bowers (Charlottesville, Va., 1970), pp. xv-cxxxi.

Lewis, Anthony. "Teaching the Western Stories of Stephen Crane," *American Renaissance and American West: Proceedings of the Second University of Wyoming American Studies Conference*, Christopher S. Durer, Herbert R. Dieterich, Henry J. Laskowsky, and James W. Welke, eds. (Laramie, Wyo., 1992), pp. 97–103. (G)

McFarland, Ronald E. "The Hospitality Code and Crane's 'The Blue Hotel,'" *Studies in Short Fiction*, XVIII (Fall 1991), 447–451.

Maclean, Hugh N. "The Two Worlds of 'The Blue Hotel,'" *Modern Fiction Studies*, V (Autumn 1959), 260–270.

Monteiro, George, "Crane's Coxcomb," *Modern Fiction Studies*, XXXI (1985), 295–305.

Murphy, Brenda. "'The Blue Hotel': A Source in *Roughing It*," *Studies in Short Fiction*, XX (Winter 1983), 39–44.

Narveson, Robert. "Conceit in 'The Blue Hotel,'" *Prairie Schooner*, XLIII (Summer 1969), 187–191.

———. "Notes on 'The Blue Hotel,'" *Prairie Schooner*, XLIII (Summer 1969), 193–199.

Oriard, Michael. *Sporting with the Gods: The Rhetoric of Play in American Culture* (Cambridge, England, 1991), pp. 246–248.

Osborn, Neal J. "Crane's 'The Monster' and 'The Blue Hotel,'" *Explicator*, XXIII (October 1964), Item 10.

Pierce, J. F. "Stephen Crane's Use of Figurative Language in 'The Blue Hotel,'" *Studies by Members of the South Central Modern Language Association*, XXXIV (Winter 1974), 160–164.

Pilgrim, Tim A. "Repetition as a Nihilistic Device in Stephen Crane's 'The Blue Hotel,'" *Studies in Short Fiction* XI (Spring 1974), 125–129.

Proudfit, Charles L. "Parataxic Distortion and Process in Stephen Crane's 'The Blue Hotel,'" *Hartford Studies in Literature* XV (1984), 47–53.

Quinn, Brian T. "A Contrastive Look at Stephen Crane's Naturalism as Depicted in 'The Open Boat' and 'The Blue Hotel,'" *Studies in English Language and Literature*, XLII (1992), 55–61.

Robertson, Jamie. "Stephen Crane, Eastern Outsider in the West and Mexico," *Western American Literature*, XIII (Fall 1978), 255–257.

Satterwhite, Joseph M. "Stephen Crane's 'The Blue Hotel': The Failure of Understanding," *Modern Fiction Studies*, II (Winter 1956–1957), 238–241.

Schroeder, John W. "Stephen Crane Embattled," *University of Kansas City Review*, XVII (Winter 1950), 119–129.

Stallman, Robert Wooster. "Stephen Crane: A Revaluation," *Critiques and Essays on Modern Fiction, 1920–1951: Representing the Achievement of Modern American and British Critics*, John W. Aldridge, ed. (New York, 1952), pp. 244–269. (G)

Starr, Alvin. "The Concept of Fear in the Works of Stephen Crane and Richard Wright," *Studies in Black Literature*, VI (Summer 1975), 6–10.

Stone, Edward. *A Certain Morbidness: A View of American Literature* (Carbondale, Ill., 1969), pp. 53–69.

Sutton, Walter. "Pity and Fear in 'The Blue Hotel,'" *American Quarterly*, IV (Spring 1952), 73–76.

Van Der Beets, Richard. "Character as Structure: Ironic Parallel and Transformation in 'The Blue Hotel,'" *Studies in Short Fiction*, V (Spring 1968), 294–295.

Vanouse, Donald. "Popular Culture in the Writings of Stephen Crane," *Journal of Popular Culture*, X (Fall 1976), 424–430. (G)

Voss, Arthur. *The American Short Story* (Norman, Okla., 1973), pp. 162–164.

Ward, J. A. "'The Blue Hotel' and 'The Killers,'" *CEA Critic*, XXI (September 1959), 7–8.

Weinig, Sister Mary Anthony. "Heroic Convention in 'The Blue Hotel,'" *The Stephen Crane Newsletter*, II (Spring 1968), 6–7.

Weiss, Daniel. "'The Blue Hotel': A Psychoanalytic Study," in *Stephen Crane, A Collection of Critical Essays*, Maurice Bassan, ed. (Englewood Cliffs, N.J., 1967), pp. 154–164.

———. *The Critical Agonistes: Psychology, Myth and the Art of Fiction* (Seattle, 1985), pp. 100–107.

West, Ray B. "Stephen Crane: Author in Transition, *American Literature*, XXXIV (May 1962), 215–228.

Westbrook, Max. "Stephen Crane's Social Ethic," *American Quarterly*, XIV (Winter 1962), 593–595.

Wolford, Chester L. *The Anger of Stephen Crane: Fiction and the Epic Tradition* (London, 1983), pp. 101–114.

———. "The Eagle and the Crow: High Tragedy and Epic in 'The Blue Hotel,'" *Prairie Schooner*, LI (Fall 1977), 260–274.

———. *Stephen Crane: A Study of the Short Fiction* (Boston, 1989), pp. 30–34, 115–117.

Wolter, Jurgen. "Drinking, Gambling, Fighting, Paying: Structure and Determinism in 'The Blue Hotel,'" *American Literary Realism*, XII (Autumn 1979), 295–298.

Wycherly, H. Alan. "Crane's 'The Blue Hotel': How Many Collaborators?" *American Notes & Queries*, IV (February 1966), 88.

STEPHEN CRANE, "The Bride Comes to Yellow Sky"

Agee, James. *Agee on Film: Five Film Scripts* (Boston, 1964), pp. 355–390.

Barnes, Robert. "Crane's 'The Bride Comes to Yellow Sky,'" *Explicator*, XVI (April 1958), Item 39.

Bassan, Maurice. "The 'True West' of Sam Shepard and Stephen Crane," *American Literary Realism*, XXVIII (Winter 1996), 11–17.

Bellman, Samuel I. "The Bride Comes to Yellow Sky," *Reference Guide to Short Fiction*, Noelle Watson, ed. (Detroit, 1994), pp. 655–656.

Bergnon, Frank. *Stephen Crane's Artistry* (New York, 1975), pp. 94–95, 123–124.

Bernard, Kenneth. "'The Bride Comes to Yellow Sky': History as Elegy," *English Record*, XVII (April 1967), 17–20.

Bloom, Edward A. *The Order of Fiction* (New York, 1964), pp. 100–104.

Burns, Shannon and James Levernier. "Crane's 'The Bride Comes to Yellow Sky,'" *Explicator*, XXXVII (Fall 1978), 36–37.

Cook, Robert G. Stephen Crane's 'The Bride Comes to Yellow Sky,'" *Studies in Short Fiction*, II (Summer 1965), 368–369.

Ferguson, S. C. "Crane's 'The Bride Comes to Yellow Sky,'" *Explicator*, XXI (March 1963), Item 59.

Folsom, James K. *The American Western Novel* (New Haven, 1966), pp. 91–94.

Gerlach, John. *Toward the End: Closure and Structure in the American Short Story* (University, Ala., 1985), pp. 70–73.

Gross, David S. "The Western Stories of Stephen Crane," *Journal of American Culture*, XI (Winter 1988), 15–21.

Halliburton, David. *The Color of the Sky: A Study of Stephen Crane* (New York, 1989), pp. 227–235.

Holton, Milne. *Cylinder of Vision: The Fiction and Journalistic Writing of Stephen Crane* (Baton Rouge, 1972), pp. 226–233.

Knapp, Bettina L. *Stephen Crane* (New York, 1987), pp. 155–156.

LaFrance, Marston. *A Reading of Stephen Crane* (Oxford, England, 1971), pp. 210–214.

Levenson, J. C. *Stephen Crane: Tales of Adventure* (Charlottesville, Va., 1970), pp. lxxiii–lxxvi.

Marovitz, Sanford E. "Scratchy the Demon in 'The Bride Comes to Yellow Sky,'" *Tennessee Studies in Literature*, XVI (1971), 137–140.

Monteiro, George. "Stephen Crane's 'The Bride Comes to Yellow Sky,'" *Approaches to the Short Story*, Neil D. Isaacs and Louis H. Leiter, eds. (San Francisco, 1963), pp. 221–238.

Overton, James P. "'The Game' in 'The Bride Comes to Yellow Sky,'" *Xavier University Studies*, IV (March 1965), 3–11.

Petry, Alice H. "Crane's 'The Bride Comes To Yellow Sky,'" *Explicator*, XLII (1983), 45–47.

Robertson, Jamie. "Stephen Crane, Eastern Outsider in the West and Mexico," *Western American Literature*, XIII (1978), 251–252.

Roth, Russell. "A Tree in Winter: The Short Fiction of Stephen Crane," *New Mexico Quarterly*, XXIII (Summer 1953), 191–193.

Solomon, Eric. *Stephen Crane: From Parody to Realism* (Cambridge, Mass., 1967), pp. 252–257.

Stein, William Bysshe. "Stephen Crane's Homo Absurdus," *Bucknell Review*, VIII (May 1959), 184–186.

Teague, David W. *American Literature and Art: The Rise of a Desert Aesthetic* (Tucson, 1997), pp. 80–88.

Tibbetts, A. M. "Stephen Crane's 'The Bride Comes to Yellow Sky,'" *English Journal*, LIV (April 1965), 314–316.

Vorpahl, Ben Merchant. "Murder by the Minute: Old and New in 'The Bride Comes to Yellow Sky,'" *Nineteenth-Century Fiction*, XXVI (September 1971), 196–218.

West, Ray B. *The Art of Writing Fiction* (New York, 1968), pp. 134–140.

———. "The Use of Action in 'The Bride Comes to Yellow Sky,'" *Reading the Short Story* (New York, 1968), pp. 17–23.

Wolford, Chester L. *The Anger of Stephen Crane* (Lincoln, Neb., 1983).

———. "Classical Myth Versus Realism in Crane's 'The Bride Comes to Yellow Sky,'" *Under the Sun: Myth and Realism in Western American Literature*, Barbara Howard Meldrum, ed. (Troy, N.Y., 1985), pp. 129–136.

———. *Stephen Crane: A Study of the Short Fiction* (Boston, 1989), pp. 26–30.

Zanger, Jules. "Stephen Crane's 'Bride' as Countermyth of the West," *Great Plains Quarterly*, XI, ii (1991), 157–165.

Zinck, Catherine. "Literature and Life: The Moment the Bride Comes to Yellow Sky," *Arizona English Bulletin*, XXXI (Fall 1988), 18–20.

ARTHUR CONAN DOYLE, "A Scandal in Bohemia"

Atkinson, Michael. *The Secret Marriage of Sherlock Holmes and Other Eccentric Readings* (Ann Arbor, 1996), pp. 41–63.

Barolsky, Paul. "The Case of the Domesticated Aesthete," *Virginia Quarterly Review*, XL (1984), 438–452. (G)

Cawelti, John G. *Adventure, Mystery, and Romance: Formula Stories in Art and Popular Culture* (Chicago, 1976), pp. 80–96. (G)

Clausen, Christopher. "Sherlock Holmes, Order, and the Late-Victorian Mind," *Georgia Review*, XXXVIII (Spring 1984), 104–123. (G)

Conroy, Peter. "The Importance of Being Watson," *Texas Quarterly*, XXI (Spring 1978), 84–103. (G)

Cox, Allison and J. Randolf. "'A Scandal in Bohemia': Bohemian Scandals of 1891," *The Baker Street Dozen*, P. J. Doyle and E. W. McDiarmid, eds. (New York, 1987), pp. 120–125.

Cox, Don Richard. *Arthur Conan Doyle* (New York, 1985), pp. 49–50.

Dakin, D. Martin. *A Sherlock Holmes Commentary* (Newton Abbot, England, 1972), pp. 38–48.

Eames, Hugh. "Sherlock Holmes-Arthur Conan Doyle," *Sleuths, Inc.: Studies in Problem Solvers* (Philadelphia, 1978), pp. 9–47. (G)

Hare, Cyril. "The Classic Form," *Crime in Good Company: Essays on Criminals and Crimewriting*, Michael Gilbert, ed. (London, 1959), pp. 55–84. (G)

Harrison, Michael. "Sherlock Holmes and the King of Bohemia: The Solution of a Royal Mystery," *Beyond Baker Street: A Sherlockian Anthology*, Michael Harrison, ed. (Indianapolis, 1976), pp. 137–172.

Jaffe, Jacqueline A. *Arthur Conan Doyle* (Boston. 1987), pp. 31–49. (G)

Kestner, Joseph A. *Sherlock's Men: Masculinity, Conan Doyle, and Cultural History* (Aldershot, Eng., 1997). (D)

Knight, Stephen. *Form and Ideology in Crime Fiction* (Bloomington, Ind., 1981), pp. 67–106. (G)

Kramm, Pascale. "'A Scandal in Bohemia' and Sherlock Holmes's Ultimate Mystery Solved," *English Literature in Transition*, 39, No. 2 (1996), 193–203.

Krasner, James. "Watson Falls Asleep: Narrative Frustration and Sherlock Holmes," *English Literature in Transition*, 40, No. 4 (1997), 424–436. (G)

Lambert, Gavin. "The Final Problem: Sir Arthur Conan Doyle," *The Dangerous Edge*, Gavin Lambert, ed. (New York, 1976), pp. 31–63. (G)

La Vallo, Frank. "The Case of the Deathless Detective," *Texas Quarterly*, XI (Summer 1968), 180–199. (G)

Moorman, Charles. "The Appeal of Sherlock Holmes," *Southern Quarterly*, XIV (January 1976), 71–92. (G)

Murch, A. M. *The Development of the Detective Novel* (New York, 1958), pp. 167–191. (G)

Ousby, Ian. *Bloodhounds from Heaven: The Detective in English Fiction from Godwin to Doyle* (Cambridge, 1976), pp. 140–175. (G)

Peterson, Audrey. "Arthur Conan Doyle and the Great Detective," *Victorian Masters of Mystery: From Wilkie Collins to Conan Doyle* (New York, 1984), p. 197–217. (G)

Poston, Lawrence. "City versus Country: A Holmesian Variation on an Old Theme," *Etudes Anglaises*, XXXIII (April–June 1980), 156–170. (G)

Priestman, Martin. *Detective Fiction and Literature: The Figure On the Carpet* (New York, 1991), pp. 81–83.

Otis, Laura. "The Empire Bites Back: Sherlock Holmes as an Imperial Immune System," *Studies in Twentieth Century Literature*, 22 (Winter 1998), 31–60. (G)

Putney, Charles R., Joseph A. Cutshall King, and Sally Sugarman. *Sherlock Holmes: Victorian Sleuth to Modern Hero* (Lanham, Md., 1996). (G)

Redmond, Donald A. *Sherlock Holmes: A Study in Sources* (Kingston, Canada, 1982), p. 35–39.

Routley, Frank. *The Puritan Pleasures of Detective Fiction* (London, 1971), pp. 17–59. (G)

Segal, David, ed. *Short Story Criticism: Excerpts from Criticism of the Works of Short Fiction Writers*, XII (Detroit, 1993), 47–76. (G)

Stowe, William W. "From Semiotics to Hermeneutics: Modes of Detection in Doyle and Changler," *The Poetics of Murder: Detective Fiction and Literary Theory*, Glenn W. Most and William W. Stowe, eds. (New York, 1983), pp. 366–383. (G)

Strong, L. A. G. "The Crime Story: An English View," *Crime in Good Company: Essays on Criminals and Crime-writing*, Michael Gilbert, ed. (London, 1959), pp. 149–162. (G)

Symons, Julian. *Bloody Murder. From the Detective Story to the Crime Novel: A History* (New York, 1985), pp. 64–73. (G)

Truzzi, Marcello. "Sherlock Holmes: Applied to Social Psychology," *The Sign of the Three: Dupin, Holmes, and Pierce*, Umberto Eco and Thomas A. Sebeck, eds. (Bloomington, Ind., 1983), pp. 55–80. (G)

Van Dover, J. K. *You Know My Method: The Science of the Detective* (Bowling Green, Ohio, 1994), pp. 71–78. (G)

Wilson, Daniel. "Sherlock Holmes and the Social History of the Victorian Age," *North Dakota Quarterly*, XLIV (Spring 1976), 51–72. (G)

RALPH ELLISON, "King of the Bingo Game"

Deutsch, Leonard J. "Ellison's Early Fiction," *Negro American Literature Forum*, VII (Summer 1973), 57–58.

Guereschi, Edward. "Anticipations of *Invisible Man*: Ralph Ellison's 'King of the Bingo Game,'" *Negro American Literature Forum*, VI (Winter 1972), 122–124.

Herman, David J. "Ellison's' King of the Bingo Game:' Finding Naturalism's Trapdoor," *English Language Notes*, XXIX (September 1991), 71–74.

Hoeveler, Diane L. "Game Theory and Ellison's 'King of the Bingo Game,'" *Journal of American Culture*, XV, No. 2 (1992), 39–42.

O'Meally, Robert G. *The Craft of Ralph Ellison* (Cambridge, Mass., 1980), pp. 74–76.

Real, Willi. "Ralph Ellison, 'King of the Bingo Game,'" *The Black American Short Story in the 20th Century: A Collection of Critical Essays*, Peter Bruck, ed. (Amsterdam, 1977), pp. 111–127.

Saunders, Pearl I. "Symbolism in Ralph Ellison's 'King of the Bingo Game,'" *CLA Journal*, XX (September 1976), 35–39.

Schor, Edith. *Visible Ellison: A Study of Ralph Ellison's Fiction* (Westport, Conn., 1993), pp. 48–51.

Snyder, Phillip A. "King of the Bingo Game," *Reference Guide to Short Fiction*, Noelle Watson, ed. (Detroit, 1994), pp. 766–767.

LOUISE ERDRICH, "Mauser"

Blak, Hans. "Toward a Native American 'Realism': The Amphibious Fiction of Louise Erdrich," *Neo-Realism in Contemporary American Fiction*, Kristiann Versluys, ed. (Amsterdam, 1992), pp. 145–170. (G)

Bonetti, Kay. "An Interview with Louise Erdrich and Michael Dorris,"" *Missouri Review*, XI (1988), 79–99. (G)

Erdrich, Louise. "Whatever is Really Yours: An Interview with Louise Erdrich," interview with Joseph Bruchac, *This Way: Interviews with American Indian Poets*, Joseph Bruchac, ed. (Tucson, 1987), pp. 73–86. (G)

Ferguson, Suzanne. "The Short Stories of Louise Erdrich's Novels," *Studies in Short Fiction*, 33 (Fall 1996), 541–559. (G)

Jaskoski, Helen. "From Time Immemorial: Native American Traditions in Contemporary Short Fiction," *Since Flannery O'Connor: Essays on the Contemporary American Short Story*, Loren Logsdon and Charles W. Mayer, eds. (Macomb, Ill., 1987), pp. 54–71. (G)

Magalaner, Marvin. "Louise Erdrich: Of Cars, Time, and the River," *American Women Writing Fiction: Memory, Identity, Family, Space*, Mickey Pearlmen, ed. (Lexington, Ky., 1989), pp. 95–108. (G)

Rainwater, Catherine. "Reading between Worlds: Narrativity in the Fiction of Louise Erdrich," *American Literature*, LXII (September 1990), 405–422. (G)

White, Sharon and Glenda Burnside. "On Native Ground: An Interview with Louise Erdrich and Michael Dorris," *Bloomsbury Review*, VIII (July/August 1988), 16–22. (G)

WILLIAM FAULKNER, "Barn Burning"

Billingslea, Oliver. "Fathers and Sons: The Spiritual Quest in Faulkner's 'Barn Burning,'" *Mississippi Quarterly*, XLIV (1991), 287–308.

Bowen, James K. and James A. Hamby. "Colonel Sartoris Snopes and Gabriel Marcel: Allegiance and Commitment," *Notes on Mississippi Writers*, III (Winter 1971), 101–107.

Bradford, M. E. "Family and Community in Faulkner's 'Barn Burning,'" *Southern Review*, XVII (April 1981), 332–339.

Broer, Lawrence R. "William Faulkner: 'Barn Burning,'" *Instructor's Manual for the Art of Fiction*, Third Edition, R. F. Dietrich and Roger H. Sundell, eds. (New York, 1978), pp. 55–64.

Brooks, Cleanth. *William Faulkner: First Encounters* (New Haven, 1983), pp. 16–19.

Brown, Suzanne Hunter. "Appendix A: Reframing Stories," *Short Story Theory at a Crossroads*, Susan Lohafer and Jo Ellyn Carey, eds. (Baton Rouge, 1989), pp. 311–327.

Cackett, Kathy. "'Barn Burning': Debating the American Adam," *Notes on Mississippi Writers*, 21 (1989), 1–17.

Carothers, James B. "Faulkner's Short Stories: 'And Now What's to Do,'" *New Directions in Faulkner Studies*, Doreen Fowler and Ann J. Abadie, eds. (Jackson, Miss., 1984), pp. 202–227. (G)

———. *William Faulkner's Short Stories* (Ann Arbor, 1985), pp. 60–64.

———. "The Road to *The Reivers*," *"A Cosmos of My Own": Faulkner and Yoknapatawpha 1980*, Doreen Fowler and Ann J. Abadie, eds. (Jackson, Miss., 1981), pp. 95–124.

Comprone, Joseph J. "Literature and the Writing Process: A Pedagogical Reading of William Faulkner's 'Barn Burning,'" *College Literature*, IX (1982), 1–21.

Cox, James M. "On William Faulkner and 'Barn Burning,'" *The American Short Story*, II, Calvin Skaggs, ed. (New York, 1980), pp. 403–406.

Cox, Leland H. *William Faulkner: Biographical Reference Guide* (Detroit, 1982), pp. 279–281.

Crackett, Kathy. "'Barn Burning': Debating the American Adam," *Notes on Mississippi Writers*, XXI, i (1989), 1–17.

Crocker, Michael W. and Robert C. Evans. "Faulkner's 'Barn Burning' and O'Connor's 'Everything That Rises Must Converge," *College Language Association Journal*, XXXVI (June 1993), 371–383.

Dowling, David. *William Faulkner* (New York, 1989), 144–156. (G)

Edwards, C. H. "A Conjecture on the Name Snopes," *Notes on Contemporary Literature*, VIII (November 1978), 9–10.

Eldred, Janet Carey. "Narratives of Socialization: Literacy in the Short Story," *College English*, LIII (October 1991), 686–700.

Fisher, Marvin. "The World of Faulkner's Children," *University of Kansas City Review*, XXVII (October 1960), 13–18.

Flora, Joseph M. "Barn Burning," *Reference Guide to Short Fiction*, Noelle Watson, ed. (Detroit 1994), pp. 637–638.

Fowler, Virginia C. "Faulkner's 'Barn Burning': Sarty's Conflict Reconsidered," *College Language Association Journal*, XXIV (June 1981), 513–521.

Franklin, Phyllis. "Sarty Snopes and 'Barn Burning,'" *Mississippi Quarterly*, XXVI (Summer 1968), 189–193.

Gadden, Richard. *Fictions of Labor: William Faulkner and the South's Long Revolution* (Cambridge, Eng., 1997), pp. 123–129.

Hadley, Charles. "Seeing and Telling: Narrational Functions in the Short Story, " *Discourse and Style*, II, J. P. Petit, ed. (Lyon, France, 1980), pp. 63–68.

Hall, Joan Wylie. "Faulkner's Barn Burners: Abe Snopes and the Duke of Marlborough," *Notes on Mississippi Writers*, XXI, ii (1989), 65–68.

Hiles, Jane. "Kinship and Heredity in Faulkner's 'Barn Burning,'" *Mississippi Quarterly*, XXXVIII (Summer 1985), 329–337.

Hogan, Michael. "Grammatical Tenuity in Fiction," *Language and Style*, XIV (Winter 1981), 13–19.

Holmes, Edward. *Faulkner's Twice Told Tales: His Re-Use of His Materials* (The Hague, 1966), pp. 31-34.

Howell, Elmo. "Colonel Sartoris Snopes and Faulkner's Aristocrats," *Carolina Quarterly*, XI (Summer 1959), 13–19.

Johnston, Kenneth G. "Time of Decline: Pickett's Charge and the Broken Clock in Faulkner's 'Barn Burning,'" *Studies in Short Fiction*, XI (Fall 1974), 434–436.

Jones, Diane Brown. *A Reader's Guide to the Short Stories of William Faulkner* (New York, 1994), pp. 3–32.

Loges, Max L. "Faulkner's 'Barn Burning,'" *Explicator*, 57 (Fall 1998), 43–45.

Matthews, John T. "Faulkner and Proletarian Literature," *Faulkner in Cultural Context*, Donald M. Kartiganer and Ann J. Abadie, eds. (Jackson, Miss., 1997), pp. 28–29, 172–174.

Mitchell, Charles. "The Wounded Will of Faulkner's 'Barn Burning,'" *Modern Fiction Studies*, XI (Summer 1965), 185–189.

Moreland, Richard C. "Compulsive and Revisionary Repetition: Faulkner's 'Barn Burning' and the Craft of Writing Difference," *Faulkner and the Craft of Fiction: Faulkner and Yoknapatawpha, 1987*, Doreen Fowler and Ann J. Abadie, eds. (Jackson, Miss., 1989), pp. 59–67.

———. *Faulkner and Modernism: Rereading and Rewriting* (Madison, 1990), pp. 3–22, 130–139.

Nicolet, William P. "Faulkner's 'Barn Burning,'" *Explicator*, XXXIV (November 1975), 25.

Parr, Susan R. *The Moral of the Story: Literature, Values, and American Education* (New York, 1982), pp. 131–136.

Phillips, Gene D. *Fiction, Film, and Faulkner: The Art of Adaptation* (Knoxville, 1988), pp. 174–179.

Pierce, Constance. "William Faulkner," *Critical Survey of Short Fiction*, Frank N. Magill, ed. (Englewood Cliffs, N.J., 1981), IV, 1365–1366.

Polk, Noel. *Children of the Dark House: Text and Context in Faulkner* (Jackson, Miss., 1996), pp. 26–29.

Reed, Joseph P. *Faulkner's Narrative* (New Haven, 1973), pp. 43–47.

Ross, Stephen M. *Fiction's Inexhaustible Voice: Speech and Writing in Faulkner* (Athens, Ga., 1989), pp. 13–15.

Sartoris, Brenda Eve. "Cornbote: A Feudal Custom and Faulkner's 'Barn Burning,'" *Studies in American Fiction* XI (Spring 1983), 91–94.

Skaggs, Merrill M. "Story and Film of 'Barn Burning': The Difference a Camera Makes," *Southern Quarterly*, XXI (Winter 1983), 5–15.

Stein, William Bysshe. "Faulkner's Devil," *Modern Language Notes*, LXXVI (December 1961), 731–732.

Trilling, Lionel. *The Experiences of Literature* (New York: 1967), pp. 745–748.

Volpe, Edmond L. "'Barn Burning': A Definition of Evil," *Faulkner: The Inappeased Imagination. A Collection of Essays*, Glen O. Carey, ed. (Troy, N.Y., 1980), pp. 75–82.

Watson, James G. "The American Short Story: 1930–1945," *The American Short Story, 1900–1945: A Critical History*, Philip Stevick, ed. (Boston, 1984), pp. 126–138. (G)

Wilson, Gayle Edward. "'Being Pulled Two Ways': The Nature of Sarty's Choice in 'Barn Burning,'" *Mississippi Quarterly*, XXIV (Summer 1971), 279–288.

Zender, Karl F. "Character and Symbol in 'Barn Burning,'" *College Literature*, XVI (1989), 48–49.

WILLIAM FAULKNER, "Dry September"

Bache, William B. "Moral Awareness in 'Dry September,'" *Faulkner Studies*, III (Winter 1954), 53–57.

Bassett, John E. "Gradual Progress and *Intruder in the Dust*," *Vision and Revisions: Essays on Faulkner*, John E. Bassett, ed. (Locust Hill, Conn., 1986), pp. 167–179.

Blotner, Joseph. "Continuity and Change in Faulkner's Life and Art," *Faulkner and Idealism: Perspectives from Paris*, Michael Gresser and Patrick Samway, S. J., eds. (Jackson, Miss., 1983), pp. 15–26.

Carey, Glenn O. "Social Criticism in Faulkner's 'Dry September,'" *English Record*, XV (December 1964), 27–30.

Carothers, James B. "The Myriad Heart: The Evolution of the Faulkner Hero," *"In a Cosmos of My Own": Faulkner and Yoknapatawhpa*, Doreen Fowler and Ann J. Abadie, eds. (Jackson, Miss., 1981), pp. 252–283.

Crane, John K. "But the Days Grow Short: A Reinterpretation of Faulkner's 'Dry September,'" *Twentieth-Century Literature*, XXXI (Winter 1985), 410–420.

Douglas, Ellen. "Faulkner's Women," *"In a Cosmos of My Own": Faulkner and Yoknapatawhpa*, Doreen Fowler and Ann J. Abadie, eds. (Jackson, Miss., 1981) pp. 149–167.

Dressner, L. J. "'Dry September': Decadence Domesticated," *College Literature*, XI (1984), 151–162.

Faulkner, Howard. "The Stricken World of 'Dry September,'" *Studies in Short Fiction*, X (Winter 1973), 47–50.

Ford, Arthur L. "Dust and Dreams: A Study of Faulkner's 'Dry September,'" *College English*, XXIV (December 1962), 219–220.

Griffin, William J. "How to Read Faulkner: A Powerful Plea for Ignorance," *Tennessee Studies in Literature*, I (1956), 27–34.

Johnson, Ira. "Faulkner's 'Dry September' and Caldwell's 'Saturday Afternoon': An Exercise in Practical Criticism," *Tradition et innovation, litterature et paralitterature: Actes du Congres de Nancy* (Paris, n.d.), pp. 269–278.

Jones, Diane Brown. *A Reader's Guide to the Short Stories of William Faulkner* (New York, 1994), pp. 169–203.

Kerr, Elizabeth M. "William Faulkner and the Southern Concept of Woman," *Mississippi Quarterly*, 15 (1961–1962), 1–16.

McDermott, John V. "Faulkner's Cry for a Healing Measure: 'Dry September,'" *Arizona Quarterly*, XXXII (Spring 1976), 31–34.

Moore, Janice Townley. "Faulkner's 'Dry September,'" *Explicator*, XLI (Spring 1982), 47–48.

Mortimer, Gail L. *Faulkner's Rhetoric of Loss: A Study in Perception and Meaning* (Austin, TX, 1983), pp. 55–57.

Page, Sally R. *Faulkner's Women: Characterization and Meaning* (DeLand, FL, 1972), pp. 99–103.

Parr, Susan R. *The Moral of the Story: Literature, Values, and American Education* (New York, 1982), pp. 79–87.

Pryse, Marjorie. *The Mask and the Knowledge: Social Stigma in Classic American Fiction* (Columbus, OH, 1979), pp. 92–98.

Putzel, Max. *Genius of Place: William Faulkner's Triumphant Beginnings* (Baton Rouge, 1985), pp. 223–228.

Reed, Joseph W. *Faulkner's Narrative* (New Haven, 1973), pp. 50–55.

Rogalus, Paul. "Faulkner's 'Dry September,'" *Explicator*, 48 (1990), 211–212.

Skei, Hans H. *William Faulkner: The Short Story Career* (Oslo, 1981), pp. 59–60.

Steward, J. F. "The Infernal Climate of Faulkner's 'Dry September,'" *Research Studies* (Washington State University), XLVII (December 1979), 238–243.

Szeky, Annamaria R. "The Lynching Story," *Studies in English and American*, IV (1978), 181–199.

Vickery, John B. "Ritual and Theme in Faulkner's 'Dry September,'" *Arizona Quarterly*, XVIII (Spring 1962), 5–14.

Volpe, Edmond L. "'Dry September': Metaphor for Despair," *College Literature*, 16 (1989), 60–65.

Waggoner, Hyatt H. *William Faulkner: From Jefferson to the World* (Lexington, Ky., 1959), pp. 196–199.

Weiss, Daniel. "William Faulkner and the Runaway Slave," *Northwest Review*, VI (Summer 1963), 71–79.

Winslow, Joan D. "Language and Destruction in Faulkner's 'Dry September,'" *College Language Association Journal*, XX (March 1977), 380–386.

Wolfe, Ralph H. and Edgar F. Daniels. "Beneath the Dust of 'Dry September,'" *Studies in Short Fiction*, I (Winter 1964), 158–159.

WILLIAM FAULKNER, "A Rose for Emily"

Allen, Charles A. "William Faulkner: Comedy and the Purpose of Humor," *Arizona Quarterly*, XVI (Spring 1960), 59–60.

Allen, Dennis W. "Horror And Perverse Delight: Faulkner's 'A Rose for Emily,'" *Modern Fiction Studies*, XXX (Winter 1984), 685–695.

Arensberg, Mary and Sara E. Schyfter. "Hairolglyphics in Faulkner's 'A Rose for Emily': Reading the Primal Trace," *Boundary 2*, XV (Fall 1986 [Winter 1987], 123–134.

Armour, Richard. "William Faulkner," *A Rose for Emily*, Thomas M. Inge (Columbia, Oh., 1970), pp. 73–75.

Barber, Marion. "The Two Emilys: A Ransom Suggestion to Faulkner?" *Notes on Mississippi Writers*, V (Winter 1973), 103–105.

Barnes, Daniel R. "Faulkner's Miss Emily and Hawthorne's Old Maid," *Studies in Short Fiction*, IX (Fall 1972), 373–377.

Barth, J. Robert. "Faulkner and the Calvinist Tradition," *Thought*, XXXIX (March 1964), 100–120.

Birk, John F. "Tryst Beyond Time: Faulkner's 'Emily' and Keats," *Studies in Short Fiction*, XXVIII (Spring 1991), 203–213.

Blythe, Hal. "Faulkner's 'A Rose for Emily,'" *Explicator*, XLVII (Winter 1989), 49–50.

Bride, Sister Mary, O.P. "Faulkner's 'A Rose for Emily,'" *Explicator*, XX (May 1962), Item 78.

Brooks, Cleanth. "A Note on Faulkner's Early Attempts at the Short Story," *Studies in Short Fiction*, 10 (1973), 381–388.

———. *William Faulkner: Toward Yoknapatawpha and Beyond* (New Haven, 1978), pp. 382–388.

Brooks, Cleanth and Robert Penn Warren. *Understanding Fiction* (New York, 1959), pp. 350–354.

Brown, Suzanne Hunter. "Reframing Stories," *Short Story Theory at a Crossroads*, Susan Lohafer and Jo Ellvn Clarev. eds. (Baton Rouge, 1989), pp. 317–327.

Burduck, Michael L. "Another View of Faulkner's Narrator in 'A Rose for Emily,'" *University of Mississippi Studies in English*, 8 (1990), 209–211.

Burns, Maggie. "A Good Rose Is Hard to Find: Southern Gothic as Signs of Social Dislocation in Faulkner and O'Connor," *Image and Ideology in Modern Postmodern Discourse*, David B. Downing and Susan Bazargan, eds. (Albany, 1991), pp. 108–113, 117–121.

Campbell, Harry Modean and Ruel E. Foster. *William Faulkner: A Critical Appraisal* (Norman, Okla., 1951), pp. 90–100.

Clements, Arthur L. "Faulkner's 'A Rose for Emily,'" *Explicator*, XX (May 1962), Item 78.

Crossman, Robert. "How Readers Make Meaning," *College Literature*, IX (1982), 207–215.

Daremo, John. "Insight into Horror: The Narrator in Faulkner's 'A Rose for Emily,'" *A Short Guide to Writing About Literature*, Sylvan Bamett, ed. (Boston, 1975), pp. 108–111.

Davis, William V. "Another Flower for Faulkner's Bouquet: Theme and Structure in 'A Rose for Emily,'" *Notes on Mississippi Writers*, VII (Fall 1974), 34–38.

Dillon, George L. "Styles of Reading," *Poetics Today*, III, ii (1982), 77–88.

Doyle, Charles C. "Mute Witnesses: Faulkner's Use of a Popular Riddle," *Mississippi Folklore Register*, XXIV (1990), 53–55.

Duvall, John N. *Faulkner's Marginal Couple: Invisible, Outlaw, and Unspeakable Communities* (Austin, Tex.), pp. 127–128.

Edwards, C. Hines, Jr. "Three Literary Parallels to Faulkner's 'A Rose for Emily,'" *Notes on Mississippi Writers*, 7 (1974), 21–25.

Ferguson, James. *Faulkner's Short Fiction* (Knoxville, 1991), pp. 129–130.

Fetterley, Judith. *The Resisting Reader: A Feminist Approach to American Fiction* (Bloomington, Ind., 1978), pp. 12–22.

Garrison, Joseph M., Jr. "'Bought Flowers' in 'A Rose for Emily,'" *Studies in Short Fiction*, XVI (Fall 1979), 341–344.

Going, William T. "Chronology in Teaching 'A Rose for Emily,'" *Exercise Exchange*, V (February 1958), 8–11.

———. "Faulkner's 'A Rose for Emily,'" *Explicator*, XVI (February 1958), Item 27.

Gold, Joseph. "Dickens and Faulkner: The Uses of Influence," *Dalhousie Review*, XLIX (Spring 1969), 69–79.

Hagopian, John V. and Martin Dolch. "Faulkner's 'A Rose for Emily'" *Explicator*, XXIT (April 1964), Item 68.

———. *Insight I, Analyses of American Literature* (Frankfurt, 1962), pp. 42–50.

Hall, Alice Petry. "Faulkner's 'A Rose for Emily,'" *Explicator*, XLIV (Spring 1986), 52–54.

Hall, Donald. *To Read Literature: Fiction, Poetry, Drama* (New York, 1981), pp. 10–16.

Happel, Nikolaus. "William Faulkner's 'A Rose for Emily,'" *Die Neuren Sprachen*, XII (1962), 396–404.

Hays, Peter L. "Who Is Faulkner's Emily?" *Studies in American Fiction*, XVI (Spring 1988), 105–110.

Heller, Terry. "The Telltale Hair: A Critical Study of William Faulkner's 'A Rose for Emily,'" *Arizona Quarterly*, XXVIII (Winter 1972), 301–318.

Hendricks, William O. "'A Rose for Emily': A Syntagmatic Analysis," *PTL: A Journal for Descriptive Poetics and Theory of Literature*, II (April 1977).

Hines, Edward C., Jr. "Three Literary Parallels to Faulkner's 'A Rose for Emily,'" *Notes on Mississippi Writers*, VII (Spring 1974), 21–25.

Hinkle, James. "Some Yoknapatawpha Names," *New Directions in Faulkner Studies*, Doreen Fowler and Ann J. Abadie, eds. (Jackson, Miss., 1984), pp. 191–194.

Hochman, Baruch. *Character in Literature* (Ithaca, N.Y., 1985), pp. 149–152.

Holland, Norman N. "Fantasy and Defense in Faulkner's 'A Rose for Emily,'" *Hartford Studies in Literature*, IV (1972), 1–25.

Howell, Elmo. "Faulkner's 'A Rose for Emily,'" *Explicator*, XIX (January 1961), Item 26.

———. "A Note on Faulkner's Emily as a Tragic Heroine," *Serif*, III (September 1966), 13–15.

Hunter, William B., Jr. "A Chronology for Emily," *Notes on Modern American Literature*, IV (Summer 1980), 18.

Inge, M. Thomas. *William Faulkner: A Rose for Emily* (Columbus, Ohio, 1970).

Jacobs, John T. "Ironic Allusion in 'A Rose for Emily,'" *Notes on Mississippi Writers*, XIV (1982), 77–79.

Jay, Gregory S. *America the Scrivener: Deconstruction and the Subject of Literary History* (Ithaca, N.Y., 1990), pp. 331–334.

Johnson, C. W. M. "Faulkner's 'A Rose for Emily,'" *Explicator*, VI (May 1948), Item 45.

Jones, Diane Brown. *A Reader's Guide to the Short Stories of William Faulkner* (New York, 1994), pp. 87–141.

Kempton, Kenneth. *The Short Story* (Cambridge, Mass., 1947), pp. 104–106.

Kerr, Elizabeth M. "William Faulkner and the Southern Concept of Woman," *Mississippi Quarterly*, 15 (1961–1962), 1–16.

Kobler, J. F. "Faulkner's 'A Rose for Emily,'" *Explicator*, XXXII (April 1974), Item 65.

Kurtz, Elizabeth Carney. "Faulkner's 'A Rose for Emily,'" *Explicator* XLIV (Winter 1986), 40.

Landeira, Ricardo Lopez. "'Aura,' 'The Aspern Papers,' 'A Rose for Emily': A Literary Relationship," *Journal of Spanish Studies: Twentieth Century*, 3 (1975), 125–143.

Levitt, Paul. "An Analogue for Faulkner's 'A Rose for Emily,'" *Papers on Language Literature*, IX (1973), 91–94.

Lind, Ilse Dusoir. "Faulkner's Women," *The Maker and the Myth: Faulkner and Yoknapatawhpa*, Evans Harrington and Ann J. Abadie, eds. (Jackson, Miss., 1978), pp. 89–104.

Littler, Frank A. "The Tangled Thread of Time: Faulkner's 'A Rose for Emily,'" *Notes on Mississippi Writers*, XIV (1982), 80–85.

Long, Elizabeth. *The American Dream and the Popular Novel* (Boston, 1985), pp. 55–57.

Lopez Landeira, Ricardo. "'Aura,' 'The Aspern Papers,' 'A Rose for Emily': A Literary Relationship," *Journal of Spanish Studies: Twentieth Century*, III (Fall 1975), 125–143.

Lupack, Barbara Tepa. "The Two Tableaux in Faulkner's 'A Rose for Emily,'" *Notes Contemporary Literature*, XI (May 1981), 6–7.

McGlynn, Paul D. "The Chronology of 'A Rose for Emily,'" *Studies in Short Fiction*, (Summer 1969), 461–462.

McLendon, Carmen Chaves. "A Rose for Rosalina: From Yoknapatawpha to Opera Dos Mortos," *Comparative Literature Studies*, XIX (Winter 1992), 450–458.

Mellard, James M. "Faulkner's Miss Emily and Blake's 'Sick Rose': Invisible Worm, *Nachtraglichkeit*, and Retrospective Gothic," *Faulkner Journal*, II (Fall 1986), 37–45.

Montenyohl, Eric L. "Folklore and Faulkner: Toward an Expansion of the Relations of Folklore and Literature," *Motif*, VII (February 1989), 1, 4, 6.

Moore, Gene M. "Of Time and Its Mathematical Progression: Problems of Chronology Faulkner's 'A Rose for Emily,'" *Studies in Short Fiction*, XXIX (Spring 1992), 195-204.

Muller, Gilbert H. "Faulkner's 'A Rose for Emily,'" *Explicator*, XXXIII (May 1975), 79.

Nebecker, Helen E. "Chronology Revised," *Studies in Short Fiction*, VIII (Summer 1971), 471–473.

———. "Emily's Rose of Love: A Postscript," *Bulletin of the Rocky Mountain Modern Language Association*, XXIV (1970), 190–191.

———. "Emily's Rose of Love: Thematic Implications of Point of View in Faulkner's 'A Rose for Emily,'" *Bulletin of the Rocky Mountain Modern Language Association*, XXIV (March 1970), 3–13.

Page, Sally R. *Faulkner's Women: Characterization and Meaning* (Deland, Fla., 1972), pp. 99–103.

Perry, Menakhem. "Literary Dynamics: How the Order of a Text Creates Its Meanings," "Poet Today, I (Autumn 1979), 35–64, 311–361.

Petry, Alice Hall. " Faulkner's 'A Rose for Emily,'" *Explicator*, XLIV (Spring 1986), 52–54.

Pierce, Constance. "William Faulkner," *Critical Survey of Short Fiction*, Frank N. Magill, (Englewood Cliffs, N.J., 1981), IV, 1360–1363.

Putzel Max. *Genius of Place: William Faulkner's Triumphant Beginnings* (Baton Rouge, 1985), pp. 220–223.

Reed, Jose W. *Faulkner's Narrative* (New Haven, 1973), pp. 12–21, 87–89.

Rodman, Isaac. "Irony and Isolation: Narrative Distance i Faulkner's A Rose for Emily,'" *Faulkner Journal*, VIII (Spring 1993) 3–12.

Scherting, Jack. "Emily Grierson's Oedipus Complex: Motif, Motive, and Meaning in Faulkner's 'A Rose for Emily,'" *Studies in Short Fiction*, XVII (Fall 1980), 397–405.

Schwab, Milinda. "A Watch for Emily," *Studies in Short Fiction*, XXVIII (Spring 1991), 215–217.

Shiroma, Mikio. "A Rose for Tobe: A New View of Faulkner's First Short Story," *Kyushu American Literature*, 27 (1986), 21–27.

Skei, Hans. *William Faulkner: The Novelist as Short Story Writer* (Oslo, 1985), pp. 108–113.

Skinner, John L. "'A Rose for Emily': Against Interpretation," *Journal of Narrative Technique*, XV (Winter 1985), 42–57.

Snell, George. "The Fury of William Faulkner," *Western Review*, XI (Autumn 1946), 35–37.

Stafford, T. J. "Tobe's Significance in 'A Rose for Emily,'" *Modern Fiction Studies*, XIV (Winter 1968–1969), 451–453.

Stevens, Aretta. "Faulkner and 'Helen,'" *Poe Newsletter*, I (October 1968), 31.

Stewart, James T. "Miss Havisham and Miss Grierson," *Furman Studies*, IV (Fall 1958), 21–23.

Stone, Edward. *A Certain Morbidity: A View of American Literature* (Carbondale, Ill., 1969), pp. 85–100.

———. "Usher, Poquelin, and Miss Emily: The Progress of Southern Gothicism," *Georgia Review*, XIV (Winter 1960), 433–443.

Strandberg, Victor, "A Rose for Emily," *Reference Guide to Short Fiction*, Noelle Watson, ed. (Detroit 1994), p. 877.

Stronks, James. "A Poe Source for Faulkner? 'To Helen' and 'A Rose for Emily,'" *Poe Newsletter*, I (April 1968), 11.

Sullivan, Ruth. "The Narrator in 'A Rose for Emily,'" *Journal of Narrative Technique*. I (September 1971), 159–178.

Tefs, Wayne A. "Norman N. Holland and 'A Rose for Emily': Some Questions Concerning Psychoanalytic Criticism," *The Sphinx*, I (Summer 1974), 50–57.

Wallace, James M. "Faulkner's 'A Rose for Emily,'" *Explicator*, L (Winter 1992), 105–107.

Watkins, Floyd C. "The Structure of 'A Rose for Emily,'" *Modern Language Notes*, LXIX (November 1954),508–510.

Weaks, Mary Louise. "The Meaning of Miss Emily's Rose," *Notes on Contemporary Literature*, XI (November 1981), 11–12.

West, Ray B., Jr. "Atmosphere and Theme in Faulkner's 'A Rose for Emily,'" *Perspective*, 11 (Summer 1949), 239–245.

————. "Faulkner's 'A Rose for Emily,'" *Explicator*, VII (October 1948), Item 8.

————. *Reading the Short Story* (New York, 1968), pp. 79–85.

Winchell, Mark Royden. "For All the Heart's Endeavor: Romantic Pathology in Browning and Faulkner," *Notes on Mississippi Writers*, 15, No. 2 (1983), 57–63.

Wilson, G. R., Jr. "The Chronology of Faulkner's 'A Rose for Emily' Again," *Notes on Mississippi Writers*, V (Fall 1972), 56–62.

Woodward, Robert H. "The Chronology of 'A Rose for Emily,'" *Exercise Exchange*, XIII (March 1966), 17–19.

F. SCOTT FITZGERALD, "Winter Dreams"

Boggan, J. R. "A Note on 'Winter Dreams,'" *Fitzgerald Newsletter*, No. 13 (Spring 1961), 1–2.

Burhans, Clinton S. "'Magnificently Attuned to Life': The Value of 'Winter Dreams,'" *Studies in Short Fiction*, VI (Summer 1969), 401–412.

Cowley, Malcolm. "F. Scott Fitzgerald: The Romance of Money," *Western Review*, XVII (Summer 1953), 245–255.

Daniels, Thomas E. "The Text of 'Winter Dreams,'" *Fitzgerald/Hemingway Annual 1977*, Margaret M. Duggan and Richard Laymen, eds. (Detroit, 1977), pp. 77–100.

Fahey,William A. *F. Scott Fitzgerald and the American Dream* (New York, 1973), pp. 145–149.

Flibbert, Joseph. "Winter Dreams," *Reference Guide to Short Fiction*, Noelle Watson, ed. (Detroit, 1994), pp. 975–976.

Gallo, Rose. *F. Scott Fitzgerald*, (New York, 1978), pp. 90–92.

Gross, Barry. "Fitzgerald's Midwest: 'Something Gorgeous Somewhere'—Somewhere Else," *Midamerica*, VI (1979), 111–126.

Harding, Brian. "'Made for—or against—the Trade': The Radicalism of Fitzgerald's Saturday Evening Post Stories," *Scott Fitzgerald: The Promises of Life*, A. Robert Lee, ed. (London, 1989), pp. 113–130.

Isaacs, Neil D. "'Winter Dreams' And Summer Sports," *The Short Stories of F. Scott Fitzgerald*, Jackson R. Bryer, ed. (Madison, 1982), pp. 199–207.

Ishikawa, Akiko. "From 'Winter Dreams' to The Great Gatsby," *Persica (Journal of the English Society of Okayama)*, No. 5 (January 1978), 79–92.

Kane, Patricia. "F. Scott Fitzgerald's St. Paul: A Writer's Use of Material," *Minnesota History*, XLV (Winter 1976), 141–148.

Kuehl, John. *F. Scott Fitzgerald: A Study of the Short Fiction* (Boston, 1991), pp. 64–68.

Lehan, Richard D. *F. Scott Fitzgerald and the Craft of Fiction* (Carbondale and Edwardsville, Ill., 1966), pp. 94–95.

Long, Robert Emmet. *The Achieving of The Great Gatsby: F. Scott Fitzgerald, 1920–1925* (Lewisburg, Pa., 1979), pp. 67–70.

Mangum, Bryant. "F. Scott Fitzgerald," *Critical Survey of Short Fiction*, Frank N. Magill, ed. (Englewood Cliffs, N.J.. 1981). IV, pp. 1371–1372.

————. *A Fortune Yet: Money in the Art of F. Scott Fitzgerald's Short Stories* (New York, 1991), pp. 53–55.

Miller, James E., Jr. *The Fictional Technique of F. Scott Fitzgerald* (The Hague, 1957), pp. 83–87.

Petry, Alice Hall. *Fitzgerald's Craft of Short Fiction: The Collected Stories, 1920–1935* (Ann Arbor, 1989), pp. 123–124, 136–137.

Pike, Gerald. "Four Voices in 'Winter Dreams,'" *Studies in Short Fiction*, XXIII (Summer 1986), 315–320.

Roulston, Robert, and Helen H. Roulston. *The Winding Road to West Egg: The Artistic Development of F. Scott Fitzgerald* (Lewisburg, Pa., 1995), pp. 115–122.

RICHARD FORD, "Rock Springs"

Crowe, David. "Resisting Reduction: Closure in Richard Ford's *Rock Springs* and Alice Munro's *Friend of My Youth*," *Canadian Literature*, 146 (Autumn 1995), 51–64. (G)

Lee, Don. "About Richard Ford," *Ploughshares*, 22 (Fall 1996), 226–235. (G)

MARY WILKINS FREEMAN, "A New England Nun"

Bader, Julia. "The Dissolving Vision: Realism in Jewett, Freeman, and Gilman," *American Realism: New Essays* Eric J. Sunquist, ed. (Baltimore, 1982), pp. 176–198. (G)

Barnstone, Aliki. "Houses Within Houses: Emily Dickinson and Mary Wilkins Freeman's 'A New England Nun,'" *Centennial Review*, XXVIII, No. 2 (1984), 129–145.

Brand, Alice Garden. "Mary Wilkins Freeman: Misanthropy as Propaganda," *New England Quarterly*, L. (March 1977), 83–100.

Brown, Lynda. "Anderson's Wing Biddlebaum and Freeman's Louisa Ellis," *Studies in Short Fiction*, XXVII (Summer 1990), 413–414.

Buell, Lawrence. *New England Literary Culture: From Revolution Through Renaissance* (Cambridge, England, 1986), pp. 345–347.

Csicsila, Joseph. "Louisa Ellis and the Unpardonable Sin: Alienation from the Community of Human Experience as Theme in Mary Wilkins Freeman's 'A New England Nun,'" *American Literary Realism*, 30 (Spring 1998), 1–13.

Daniel, Janice. "Redefining Place: *Femes Covert* in the Stories of Mary Wilkins Freeman," *Studies in Short Fiction*, 33 (Winter 1996), 69–76.

Donovan, Josephine. *New England Local Color Literature: A Woman's Tradition* (New York, 1983).

Foster, Edward. *Mary E. Wilkins Freeman* (New York, 1959), pp. 105–109.

Gardner, Kate. "The Subversion of Genre in the Short Stories of Mary Wilkins Freeman," *New England Quarterly*, LXV (1992), 461–463.

Hirsch, David H. "Subdued Meaning In 'A New England Nun,'" *Studies in Short Fiction*, II (Spring 1965), 124–136.

Levy, Babette May. "Mutations in New England Local Color," *New England Quarterly*, XIX (Summer 1946), 338–358.

Pennell, Melissa McFarland. "The Liberating Will: Freedom of Choice in the Fiction of Mary Wilkins Freeman," *Critical Essays on Mary Wilkins Freeman*, Shirley Marchalonis, ed. (Boston, 199 1), pp. 207–221.

Petry, Alice Hall. "Freeman's New England Elegy," *Studies in Short Fiction* XXI (Winter 1984), 68–70.

Pyrse, Marjorie. "'Distilling Essences': Regionalism and 'Women's Culture,'", *American Literary Realism*, XXV, No. 2 (1993), 3–6.

————. "An Uncloistered 'New England Nun,'" *Studies in Short Fiction*, XX (Fall 1983), 289–295.

Quina, James H. "Character Types in the Fiction of Mary Wilkins Freeman," *Colby Library Quarterly*, IX (December 1971), 432–439. (G)

Reichardt, Mary R. *A Web of Relationships: Women in the Short Stories of Mary Wilkins Freeman* (Jackson, Miss., 1992), pp. 91–93.

Romines, Ann. *The Home Plot: Women, Writing and Domestic Ritual* (Amherst, 1992), pp. 102–106.

Westbrook, Perry D. *Mary Wilkins Freeman* (Boston, 1988), pp. 38–41.

————. "A New England Nun," *Reference Guide to Short Fiction*, Noelle Watson, ed. (Detroit, 1994), pp. 819–820.

Ziff, Larzer. *American 1890s: Life and Times of a Lost Generation* (New York, 1966), 275–305. (G)

CARLOS FUENTES, "Aura"

Alazraki, Jaime. "Theme and System in Carlos Fuentes' Aura," *A Critical View: Carlos Fuentes*, Robert Brody and Charles Rossman, eds. (Austin, Tex., 1982), pp. 95–105.

Beaudin, Emilio Bejel y Elizabethann. "'Aura' de Fuentes: La liberación de los espacios simultaneos," *Hispanic Review*, XLVI (Autumn 1978), 465–473.

Dauster, Frank. "The Wounded Vision: *Aura, Zona sagrada*, and *Cumpleaños*," *A Critical View: Carlos Fuentes*, Robert Brody and Charles Rossman, eds. (Austin, Tex., 1982), pp. 106–120.

DeGuzman, Daniel. *Carlos Fuentes* (New York, 1972), pp. 84–85, 118–125.

Faris, Wendy B. *Carlos Fuentes* (New York, 1983), pp. 69–78.

————. "'Without Sin, and with Pleasure': The Erotic Dimensions of Fuentes' Fiction," *Novel*, XX (Fall 1996), 62–77.

Garcia Nunez, Fernando. "La poetics narrative de Carlos Fuentes." *Bulletin Hispanique*, XCIV, i (1992), 264–272.

Landeira, Ricardo Lopez. "'Aura,'" 'The Aspern Papers,'" 'A Rose for Emily': A Literary Relationship," *Journal of Spanish Studies: Twentieth Century*, 3 (1975), 125–143.

Leavitt, Morton P. "Joyce and Fuentes: Not Influence but Aura," *Comparative Literature Studies*, XIX (Summer 1982), 254–271.

López Landeira, Ricardo. "'Aura,' 'The Aspern Papers,' 'A Rose for Emily': A Literary Relationship," *Journal of Spanish Studies: Twentieth Century*, III (Fall 1975), 125–143.

de Oliveira, Celso. "Carlos Fuentes and Henry James: The Sense of the Past," *Arizona Quarterly*, XXXVII (Autumn 1981), 237–244.

Olsen, Lance. *Ellipse of Uncertainty: An Introduction to Post–Modern Fantasy* (Westport, Conn., 1987), pp. 51–68.

Perez, Janet. "Aspects of the Triple Lunar Goddess in Fuentes' Short Fiction," *Studies in Short Fiction*, XXIV (Spring 1987), 131–138.

————. "Aura," *Reference Guide to Short Fiction*, Noelle Watson, ed. (Detroit, 1994), pp. 628–629.

Reeve, Richard M. "Carlos Fuentes and the New Short Story in Mexico," *Studies in Short Fiction*, VIII (Winter 1971), 169–179. (G)

Sommers, Joseph. *After the Storm: Landmarks of the Modern Mexican Novel* (Albuquerque, 1968), pp. 178–181.

Titiev, Janice G. "Witchcraft in Carlos Fuentes' 'Aura,'" *Revista de Estudios Hispanicos*, XV (1981), 396–405.

Weiss, Jason. "An Interview with Carlos Fuentes," *Kenyon Review* NS, V (Fall 1983), 105–118. (G)

GABRIEL GARCÍA MÁRQUEZ, "A Very Old Man with Enormous Wings"

Bell-Villada, Gene]. *García Márquez: The Man and His Work* (Chapel Hill, N.C., 1990) 136–137.

Byk, John. "From Fact to Fiction: Gabriel García Márquez and the Short Story," *Mid-American Review*, VI, 2 (1986), 111–116. (G)

Dauster, Frank. "The Short Stories of García Márquez," *Books Abroad*, XLVII (Summer 1973), 466–470. (G)

Dreifus, Claudia. "Playboy Interview: Gabriel García Márquez," *Playboy*, XXX (February 1983), 65–77, 172–178. (G)

Epstein, Joseph. "How Good Is Gabriel García Márquez?" *Plausible Prejudices: Essays on American Writing* (New York, 1985), pp. 171–187. (G)

Foster, David William. *Studies in the Contemporary Spanish-American Short Story* (Columbia, Mo., 1979), pp. 39–50, 51–62. (G)

Friedman, Mary L. "The Paradigm of the Outsider in the Work of GabrielGarcía Márquez," *Justina: Momenaje a Justina Ruiz de Conde en Su ochenta cumpleanos*, Elena Gascon-Vera and Joy Renjilian, eds. (Erie, Pa., 1992), pp. 142–143.

Gerlach, John. "The Logic of Wings: García Márquez, Todorov, and the Endless Resources Fantasy," *Bridges to Fantasy*, George E. Slusser, Eric S. Rabkin and Robert Scholes, ed (Carbondale, Ill., 1982).

Janes, Regina. *Gabriel García Márquez: Revolution in Wonderland* (Columbia, Mo. 1981), pp. 75–76.

———. "A Very Old Man with Enormous Wings," *Reference Guide to Short Fiction*, Noelle Watson, ed. (Detroit, 1994), p. 958–959.

Kutzinski, Vera M. "The Logic of Wings: Gabriel García Márquez and Afro-American Literature," Harold Bloom, ed. *Gabriel García Márquez: Modern Critical Views* (New York, 1989), pp. 176–182.

McFarland, Ronald E. "Community and Interpretive Commmunities in Stories by Hawthorne, Kafka, and García Márquez," *Studies in Short Fiction*, XXIX (Fall 1992), 551–559.

McGuirk, Bernard and Richard Cardwell. *Gabriel García Márquez: New Readings* (Cambridge, England, 1987). (G)

McMurray, George R. *Gabriel García Márquez* (New York, 1977), pp. 116–119.

McNerney, Kathleen. *Understanding García Márquez* (Columbia, S.C., 1989). (G)

Malm, Ulf. "Reading Gabriel García Márquez: Hyperbole and Intertext in Four Stories," *Studia Neophilologica*, LXI, 1 (1989), 77–88.

Morello Frosch, Marta. "The Common Wonders of García Márquez's Recent Fiction," *Books Abroad*, XLVII (Summer 1973), 496–501. (G)

Oberhelman, Harley D. *Gabriel García Márquez: A Study of the Short Fiction* (Boston, 1991), pp. 37–39.

Olsen, Lance. "Misfires in Eden: García Márquez and Narrative Frustration," *Ellipse of Uncertainty: An Introduction to Postmodern Fantasy* (Westport, Conn., 1987), pp. 85–100. (G)

Peel, Roger M. "The Short Stories of Gabriel García Márquez," *Studies in Short Fiction*, VIII (Winter 1971), 159–168. (G)

Simon, John. *The Sheep from the Goats: Selected Literary Essays of John Simon* (New York, 1989), pp. 375–381. (G)

Updike, John. "Living Death," *The New Yorker*, LXI (May 20, 1985), 118, 121–125. (G)
Williams, Raymond L. Gabriel García Márquez (Boston, 1984), pp. 93–97.

CHARLOTTE PERKINS GILMAN, "If I Were a Man"

Fishkin, Shelley Fisher. "'Making a Change': Strategies of Subversion in Gilman's Journalism and Short Fiction," *Critical Essays on Charlotte Perkins Gilman*, Joanne B. Karpinski, ed. (New York, 1992), pp. 240–241.

CHARLOTTE PERKINS GILMAN, "The Yellow Wall-Paper"

Allen, Polly Wynn. *Building Domestic Liberty: Charlotte Perkins Gilman's Architectural Feminism* (Amherst, Mass., 1988).

Ammons, Elizabeth. *Conflicting Stories: American Women Writers at the Turn into the Twentieth Century* (New York, 1990), pp. 34–43.

Bader, Julia. "The Dissolving Vision: Realism in Jewett, Freeman, and Gilman," *American Realism: New Essays*, Eric J. Sunquist, ed. (Baltimore, 1982), pp. 192–196.

Bak, John S. "Escaping the Jaundiced Eye: Foucauldian Panopticism in Charlotte Perkins Gilman's 'The Yellow Wallpaper," *Studies in Short Fiction*, XXXI (Winter 1994), 39–46.

Berman, Jeffrey. *The Talking Cure: Literary Representations of Psychoanalysis* (New York, 1985). pp. 51–59.

Biamonte, Gloria A. "'...There Is a Story, If We Could Only Find It': Charlotte Perkins Gilman's 'The Giant Wisteria,'" *Legacy*, V (Fall 1988), 33–38.

Chandler, Marilyn R. *Dwelling in the Text: Houses in American Literature* (Berkeley, 1991), pp.139–147.

Curnutt, Kirk. *Wise Economies: Brevity and Storytelling in American Short Stories* (Moscow, Ida., 1997), pp. 117–131.

De Koven, Marianne. "Gendered Doubleness and the Origins of the Modernist Form," *Tulsa Studies in Woman's Literature*, VIII (Spring 1989), 38–35.

———. *Rich and Strange: Gender, History, Modernism* (Princeton, 1991), pp. 39–47.

DeLamotte, Eugenia C. "Male and Female Mysteries in 'The Yellow Wallpaper,'" *Legacy*, V, (Spring 1988), 3–14.

Dimock, Wai-Chee. "Feminism, New Historicism, and the Reader," *American Literature*, LXIII (December 1991), 601–622.

Dock, Julia Bates, Daphne Ryan Allen, Jennifer Palais, and Kristen Tracy, "'But One Expects That': Charlotte Perkins Gilman's 'The Yellow Wallpaper' and the Shifting Light of Scholarship," *PMLA*, CXI (January 1996), 52–65.

DuPlessis, Rachel B. *Writing Beyond the Ending: Narrator Strategies of Twentieth-Century Women Writers* (Bloomington, Ind., 1985), pp. 91–93.

Erskine, Thomas, and Connie L. Richards. *Charlotte Perkins Gilman, "The Yellow Wallpaper* (New Brunswick, N.J., 1993).

Feldstein, Richard. "Reader, Text, and Ambiguous Referentiality in 'The Yellow Wall-Paper, *Feminism and Psychoanalysis*, Richard Feldstein and Judith Roof, eds. (Ithaca, N.Y., 1989), pp. 269–279.

Fetterley, Judith. "Reading About Reading: 'A Jury of Her Peers,' 'The Murders in the Rue Morgue,' 'The Yellow Wallpaper,'" *Gender and Reading*, Elizabeth A. Flynn and Patrocino P. Schweikart, eds. (Baltimore, 1986), pp. 159–164.

Fleenor, Juliann Evans. "The Gothic Prism: Charlotte Perkins Gilman's Gothic Stories and her Autobiography," *Charlotte Perkins Gilman: The Woman and Her Work*, Sheryl L. Meyering, ed. (Ann Arbor, 1989), pp. II 7–131.

Gilbert, Sandra M. and Susan Gubar. *The Madwoman in the Attic: the woman Writer and the Nineteenth-Century Literary Imagination* (New Haven, 1979), pp. 89–92.

Gilman, Charlotte Perkins. "Why I Wrote 'The Yellow Wallpaper," *The Captive Imagination: A Casebook on "The Yellow Wallpaper,"* Catherine Golden, ed. (New York, 1992), pp. 51–53.

Girgus, Sam B. *Desire and Political Unconscious in American Literature: Eros and Ideology* (New York, 1990), pp. 133–134.

Golden, Catherine, ed. *The Captive Imagination: A Casebook on "The Yellow Wallpaper"* (New York, 1992).

———. "'Overwriting' the Rest Cure: Charlotte Perkins Gilman's Literary Escape from S. Weir Mitchell's Fictionalization of Women, *Critical Essays on Charlotte Perkins Gilman*, Joanne B. Karpinski, ed. (New York, 1992), pp. 144–158.

———. "The Writing of 'The Yellow Wallpaper': A Double Palimpsest," *Studies in American Fiction*, XVII (Autumn 1989), 193–201.

Hanley-Peritz, J. "Monumental Feminism and Literature's Ancestral House: Another Look at 'The Yellow Wallpaper,'" *Women's Studies*, XII (1986), 113–128.

Hedges, Elaine. "Afterword," in Charlotte Perkins Gilman, *The Yellow Wall-Paper*, Elaine Hedges, ed. (Old Westbury, N.Y., 1973), pp. 37–63.

———. "'Out at Last'? 'The Yellow Wallpaper' after Two Decades of Feminist Criticism," *Critical Essays on Charlotte Perkins Gilman*, Joanne B. Karpinski, ed. (New York, 1992), pp. 222–233; *The Captive Imagination: A Casebook on "The Yellow Wallpaper,"* Catherine Golden, ed. (New York, 1992), pp. 319–333.

Herndl, Diane P. *Invalid Women: Figuring Feminine Illness in American Fiction and Culture, 1840–1940* (Chapel Hill, 1993), pp. 112–113, 129–133, 141–149.

Hill, Mary A. "Charlotte Perkins Gilman: Feminist's Struggle with Womanhood," *Massachusetts Review*, XXI (Fall 1980), 503–526. (G)

———. *Charlotte Perkins Gilman: The Making of a Radical Feminist* (Philadelphia, 1980), pp. 150–152, 185–186.

Hume, Beverly A. "Gilman's 'interminable grotesque': The Narrator of 'The Yellow Wallpaper,'" *Studies in Short Fiction*, XXVIII (Fall 1991), 477–484.

Jacobus, Mary. "An Unnecessary Maze of Sign-Reading," *Reading Women: Essays in Feminist Criticism* (New York, 1986), pp. 229–248; *The Captive Imagination: A Casebook on "The Yellow Wallpaper,"* Catherine Golden, ed. (New York, 1992), pp. 277–295.

Johnson, Greg. "Gilman's Gothic Allegory: Rage and Redemption in 'The Yellow Wallpaper,'" *Studies in Short Fiction*, XXVI (Fall 1989), 521–530.

Johnston, Georgia. "Exploring Lack and Absence in the Body/Text: Charlotte Perkins Gilman Prewriting Irigay," *Women's Studies*, XI, i (1992), 75–86.

Kasmer, Lisa. "Charlotte Perkins Gilman's 'The Yellow Wallpaper': A Symptomatic Reading," *Literature and Psychology*, XXXVI (1990), 1–15.

Kennard, Jean E. "Convention Coverage or How to Read Your Own Life," *Charlotte Perkins Gilman: The Woman and Her Work*, Sheryl L. Meyering, ed. (Ann Arbor, 1989), pp. 75–94.

———. "Convention Coverage or How to Read Your Own Life," *New Literary History*, XIII (Autumn 1981), 69–88.

King, Jeannette and Pam Morris. "On Not Reading Between the Lines: Models of Reading in 'The Yellow Wallpaper,'" *Studies in Short Fiction*, XXVI (Winter 1989), 23–32.

Kolodny, Annette. "A Map for Rereading: Or, Gender and the Interpretation of Literary Texts," *New Literary History*, XI (Spring 1980), 453–467.

Lane, Ann J. "The Fictional World of Charlotte Perkins Gilman," *The Charlotte Perkins Gilman Reader*, Ann J. Lane, ed. (New York, 1980), pp. ix–xiii. (G)

————. *To Herland and Beyond: The Life and Work of Charlotte Perkins Gilman* (New York, 1990), pp. 124–132.

Lanser, Susan S. "Feminist Criticism, 'The Yellow Wallpaper,' and the Politics of Color in America," *Feminist Studies*, XV (Fall 1989), 415–441.

Long, Charles. "Gilman's 'The Yellow Wallpaper,'" *Explicator*, L (Fall 1991), 32–33.

MacPike, Loralee. "Environment as Psychopathological Symbolism in 'The Yellow Wall Paper,'" *American Literary Realism*, VIII (Summer 1975), 286–288.

Marston, Peter J., and Bambi Rockwell. "Charlotte Perkins Gilman's 'The Yellow Wallpaper': Rhetorical Subversion in Feminist Literature'" *Women's Studies in Communication*, XI (Fall 1991), 58–72.

Masse, Michelle. *In the Name of Love: Women, Masochism, and the Gothic* (Ithaca, N.Y., 1992), pp. 29–39.

Michaels, Walter B. *The Gold Standard and the Logic of Naturalism: American Literature at the Turn of the Century* (Berkeley, 1987), pp. 9–13.

Owens, E. Suzanne. "The Ghostly Double Behind the Wallpaper in Charlotte Perkins Gilman's 'The Yellow Wallpaper,'" *Haunting the House of Fiction: Feminine Perspectives on Ghost Stories by American Women*, Lynette Carpenter and Wendy K. Kolmar, eds. (Knoxville, 1991), pp. 64–79.

Parr, Susan R. *The Moral of the Story: Literature, Values, and American Education* (New York, 1982), pp. 79–87.

Pearce, Lynne, and Sara Mills. "Marxist-Feminism," *Feminist Readings/Feminists Reading*, Sara Mills, et al., eds. (Charlottesville, Va., 1989), pp. 208–219.

Pringle, Mary Beth. "'La Poetique de L'Espace' in Charlotte Perkins Gilman's 'The Yellow Wallpaper,'" *French-American Review*, III (1978/1979), 15–22.

Robinson, Fred M. *Comic Moments* (Athens, Ga., 1992), pp. 93–97.

Schnöee-Schilling, Beate. "'The Yellow Wallpaper': A Rediscovered 'Realistic' Story," *American Literary Realism*, VIII (Summer 1975), 284–286.

Schweninger, Lee. "Reading the Garden in Gilman's 'The Yellow Wallpaper," Isle, II (Winter 1996), 25–44.

Segal, David, ed. *Short Story Criticism: Excerpts from Criticism of the Works of Short Fiction Writers*, XIII (Detroit, 1993), pp. 119–125, 128–141, 145–175.

Shumaker, Conrad. "Realism, Reform, and the Audience: Charlotte Perkins Gilman's Unreadable Wallpaper," *Arizona Quarterly*, XLVII (Spring 1991), 81–93.

————. "Too Terribly Good to Be Printed': Charlotte Gilman's 'The Yellow Wallpaper,'" Aı *an Literature*, LVII (December 1985), 588–599.

Smith, Marsha A. "The Disoriented Male Narrator and Societal Conversion: Charlotte Perkins Gilman's Utopian Vision," *ATQ*, III (March 1989), 123–133.

Spaull, Sue, and Elaine Millard. "The Anxiety of Authorship," *Feminist Readings/Feminists Reading*, Sara Mills, et al., eds. (Charlottesville, Va., 1989), pp. 131–133.

Tallack, Douglas. *The Nineteenth-Century American Short Story: Language, Form and Ideology* (London, 1993), pp. 218–241.

Treichler, Paula A. "Escaping the Sentence: Diagnosis and Discourse in 'The Yellow Wallpaper,'" *Feminist Issues in Literary Scholarship*, Shari Benstock, ed. (Bloomington, Ind., 1987), pp. 62–78.

Veeder, William. "Who is Jane? The Intricate Feminism of Charlotte Perkins Gilman," *Arizona Quarterly*, XLIV (Autumn 1988), 40–79.

Wagner-Martin, Linda. "Gilman's 'The Yellow Wallpaper': A Centenary," *Charlotte Perkins Gilman: The Woman and Her Work*, Sheryl L. Meyering, ed. (Ann Arbor, 1989), pp. 51–64.

————. "The Yellow Wall Paper." *Reference Guide to Short Fiction*, Noelle Watson, ed. (Detroit, 1994), pp. 981–982.

Wiesenthal, C. S. "'Unheard-of-Contradictions': The Language of Madness in C. P. Gilman's 'The Yellow Wallpaper,'" *Wascana*

Will, Barbara. "The Nervous Origins of the American Western," *American Literature*, 70 (June 1998), 293–316.

SUSAN GLASPELL, "A Jury of Her Peers"

Aarons, Victoria. "A Community of Women: Surviving Marriage in the Wilderness," *Portraits of Marriage in Literature*, Anne C. Hargrove and Maurine Magliocco, eds. (Macomb, Ill., 1984), pp. 145–148.

Alkalay-Gut, Karen. "Jury of Her Peers: The Importance of Trifles," *Studies in Short Fiction*, XXI (Winter 1984), 1–9.

Fetterley, Judith. "Reading About Reading: 'A Jury of Her Peers,' 'The Murders in the Rue Morgue,' and 'The Yellow Wallpaper,'" *Gender and Reading*, Elizabeth A. Flynn and Patrocino P. Schweikart, eds. (Baltimore, 1986), pp. 159–164.

Hedges, Elaine. "Small Things Reconsidered: Susan Glaspell's 'A Jury of Her Peers,'" *Women's Studies*, XII, (1986), 89–110.

Kolodny, Annette. "A Map for Rereading: Or, Gender and the Interpretation of Literary Texts," *New Literary History*, XI (1980), 451–467.

Madden-Simpson, Janet, ed. *Trifles and A Jury of Her Peers* (New York, 1991).

Makowsky, Veronica. *Susan Glaspell's Century of American Women* (New York, 1993), pp. 61–64.

Mustazza, Leonard. "Generic Translation and Thematic Shift in Susan Glaspell's *Trifles* and 'A Jury of Her Peers,'" *Studies in Short Fiction*, XXVI (Fall 1989), 489–496.

Quinn, Laura. "Trifles as Treason: Coming to Consciousness as a Gendered Reader," *Reader Response in the Classroom: Evoking and Interpreting Meaning in Literature*, Nicholas Karolides, ed. (New York, 1992), pp. 187–197.

Stein, Karen. "The Women's World of Glaspell's Trifles," *Women in American Theatre* (New York, 1981), pp. 2351–2354.

Sterne, Richard Clark. *Dark Mirror: The Sense of Injustice in Modern European and American Literature* (New York, 1994), pp. 245–246.

Waterman, Arthur E. *Susan Glaspell* (New York, 1966), pp. 28–30.

GAIL GODWIN, "Dream Children"

Allen, John Alexander. "Researching Her Salvation: The Fiction of Gail Godwin," *Hollins Critic*, XXV (April 1988), 1–9. (G)

Cargill, Mary Terrell. "O'Connor, Godwin, and a Memphis Murder," *Publications of the Mississippi Philological Society* (1993), 1–6.

Cheney, Anne. "Gail Godwin and Her Novels," *Southern Women Writers: The New Generation* Tonette Bond, ed. (Tuscaloosa, Ala., 1990), 204–235.

Hill, Jane. *Gail Godwin* (New York, 1992). (G)

Mickelson, Anne Z. *Reaching Out: Sensitivity and Order in Recent American Fiction by Women* (Metuchen, N.J., 1979), pp. 68–86. (G)

Rhodes, Carolyn. "Gail Godwin and the Ideal of Southern Womanhood," *Southern Quarterly*, XXI (Summer 1983), 54–66. (G)

Wimsatt, Mary Ann. "Gail Godwin's Evolving Heroine: The Search for Self," *Mississippi Quarterly*, XLII (Winter 1988–1989), 27–46. (G)

NIKOLAI GOGOL, "The Overcoat"

Bailey, James. "Some Remarks about the Stricture of Gogol's 'Overcoat,'" *Mnemozina: Studia Litteraria Russica in Honorem Vsevolod Setchkarev*, Joachim Baer and Norman W. Ingham, eds. (Munich, 1974), pp. 13–22.

Baumgarten, Murray. "Gogol's 'The Overcoat' As a Picaresque Epic," *Dalhousie Review*, LXVI (Summer 1966), 186–199.

Bernheimer, Charles C. "Cloaking the Self: The Literary Space of Gogol's 'Overcoat,'" *Publications of the Modern Language Association*, XV (January 1975), 53–61.

Brombert, Victor. "Meanings and Indeterminacy in Gogol's 'The Overcoat,'" *Literary Generations: A Festschrift in Honor of Edward D. Sullivan*, Alain Toumayan, ed. (Lexington, Ky., 1992), pp. 48–54.

Bryner, Cyril. "Gogol's 'The Overcoat,' in World Literature," *Slavonic and East European Review*, XXXII (1954), 499–509.

Chizhevsky, Dmitri. "On Gogol's 'The Overcoat,'" *Dostoevsky and Gogol: Texts and Criticism*, Priscilla Meyer and Stephen Rudy, eds. (Ann Arbor, 1979), pp. 137–160.

Clyman, Toby. "The Hidden Demons in Gogol's 'Overcoat,'" *Russian Literature*, VII (1979), 601–610.

De Jong, A. "Gogol," *Nineteenth-Century Russian Literature: Studies of Ten Russian Writers*, John Fennell, ed. (London, 1973), pp. 100–106.

Driessen, F. C. *Gogol as a Short-Story Writer: A Study of His Technique of Composition*, Ian F. Finlay, trans. (The Hague, 1965), pp. 182–214.

Eichenbaum, Boris. "The Structure of Gogol's 'The Overcoat,'" *Russian Review*, XXII (October 1963), 377–399.

Erlich, Victor. *Gogol* (New Haven, 1969), pp. 143–157.

Fanger, Donald. *The Creation of Nikolai Gogol* (Cambridge, Mass., 1979), pp. 153–163.

Hippisley, Anthony. "Gogol's 'The Overcoat': A Further Interpretation," *Slavic and East European Review*, XX (1976), 121–129.

Holquist, James M. "The Devil in Mufti: The Märchenwelt in Gogol's Short Stories," *Publications of the Modern Language Association*, LXXXII (October 1967), 360–362.

Hyde, G. M. "Melville's 'Bartleby' and Gogol's 'The Overcoat,'" *Essays in Poetics: Journal of the Neo-Formalist Circle*, I (1976), 32–48.

Jackson, Robert L. *Dialogues with Dostoevsky: The Overwhelming Questions* (Stanford, 1993), pp. 200–203.

Karlinsky, Simon. *The Sexual Labyrinth of Nikolai Gogol* (Cambridge, 1976), pp. 135–144.

Konick, Willis. "The Theme of Brotherhood in Gogol's 'The Overcoat,'" *Proceedings: Pacific Northwest Conference on Foreign Languages*, Walter Kraft, ed., XXIV (1973), 253–258.

Landry, Hilton. "Gogol's 'The Overcoat,'" *Explicator*, XIX (May 1961), Item 54.

Larvin, Janko. *Gogol* (London, 1926), pp. 117–127.

Lindstrom, Thais. *Nikolai Gogol* (New York, 1974), pp. 88–96.

McFarlin, Harold A. "'The Overcoat' as a Civil Service Episode," *Canadian-American Slavic Studies*, XIII (1979), 235–253.

Marder, Herbert. "The Overcoat," *Reference Guide to Short Fiction*, Noelle Watson, ed. (Detroit, 1994), pp. 839–840.

Martin, Mildred A. "The Last Shall Be First: A Study of Three Russian Short Stories," *Bucknell Review*, VI (March 1956), 12–23.

Mersereau, John. *Russian Romantic Fiction* (Ann Arbor, 1983), pp. 301–306.

Meyer, Priscilla. "False Pretenders and the Spectral City: 'A May Night' and 'The Overcoat,'" *Essays on Gogol: and the Russian Word*, Susanne Fusso and Prscilla Meyers, eds. (Evanston, Ill., 1992), pp. 65–72.

Mills, Judith Oloskey. "Gogol's 'Overcoat': The Pathetic Passages Reconsidered," *Publications of the Modern Language Association*, LXXXIX (October 1974), 1106–1111.

Nabokov, Vladimir. *Nikolai Gogol* (Norfolk, Conn., 1944), pp. 140–149.

Nilsson, Nils Ake. "On the Origins of Gogol's 'The Overcoat,'" Edward V. Lawler and Eliza W. Trahan, trans., *Gogol's "Overcoat": An Anthology of Critical Essays*, Elizabeth Traban, ed. (Ann Arbor, 1982), pp. 61–72.

O'Faolain, Sean. *Short Stories: A Study in Pleasure* (Boston, 1961), pp. 493–495.

Oinas, Felix J. "Akakij Akakievic's Ghost and the Hero Orestes," *Slavic and East European Journal*, XX (1976), 27–33.

O'Toole, L. Michael. *Structure, Style and Interpretation in the Russian Short Story* (New Haven, 1982), pp, 20–36.

Peace, R. A. "Gogol: 'The Greatcoat,'" *The Voice of a Giant: Essays on Seven Russian Classics*, Roger Cockrell and David Richards, eds. (Exeter, England, 1985), pp. 27–40.

Peppard, Victor. "Who Stole Whose Overcoat and Whose Text Is It?" *South Atlantic Review*, LV, I (1990), 63–80.

Profitt, Edward. "Gogol's 'Perfectly True' Tale: 'The Overcoat' And Its Mode of Closure," *Studies in Short Fiction*, XIV (Winter 1977), 35–40.

Rancour-Laferriere, Daniel. *Out From Under Gogol's Overcoat: A Psychoanalytic Study* (Ann Arbor, 1982).

Rohrberger, Mary. "Nickolai Vasilyevich Gogol," *Critical Survey of Short Fiction*, Frank N. Magill, ed. (Englewood Cliffs, N.J., 1981), IV, pp. 1499–1550.

Rowe, William Woodin. *Through Gogol's Looking Glass* (New York, 1976), pp. 113–118.

Schillinger, John. "Gogol's 'The Overcoat' as a Travesty of Hagiography," *Slavic and European Journal*, XVI (Spring 1972), 36–41.

Seemann, K. D. "Eine Heiligentegende als Vorbild von Gogols 'Mantel,'" *Zeitschrift für Slavische Philologie*, XXXOOO (1967), 7–21.

Setchkarev, Vsevolod. *Gogol: His Life and Works* (New York, 1965), pp. 216–226.

Shephard, Elizabeth C. "Pavlov's 'Demon' and Gogol's 'Overcoat,'" *Slavic Review*, XXXIII (1974), 288–301.

Sherry, Charles, "The Fit of Gogol's 'Overcoat': An Ontological View of Narrative Form," *Genre*, VII (March 1974), 1–29.

Simmons, Ernest J. *Introduction to Russian Realism* (Bloomington, Ind., 1965), pp. 59–61.

Slonimsky, Alexander. "The Technique of the Comic in Gogol," *Gogol from the Twentieth Century: Eleven Essays*, Robert A MaGuire, ed. (Princeton, 1974), pp. 332–335.

Stilman, Leon, "Gogol's 'Overcoat'—Thematic Pattern and Origins," *American Slavic and East European Review*, XI (April 1952), 138–148.

Trahan, Elizabeth W., ed. *Gogol's "Overcoat": An Anthology of Critical Essays* (Ann Arbor, 1982).

Troyat, Henri. *Divided Soul: The Life of Gogol* (New York, 1973), pp. 305–308.

Tschizewskij, Dmitrij. "The Composition of Gogol's 'Overcoat,'" E. V. Lawler and Elizabeth W. Trahan, trans., *Russian Literature TriQuarterly*, XIV (Winter 1976), 378–401.

van der Eng, Jan. "Bashmachkin's Character: A Combination of Comic, Grotesque, Tragicomical and Tragic Elements," *Gogol's Overcoat: An Anthology of Critical Essays*, Elizabeth Trahan, ed. (Ann Arbor, 1982), pp. 73–85.

Waszink, Paul M. "Mythical Traits in 'The Overcoat,'" *Slavic and East European Journal*, XXII (1978), 287–300.

Wissemann, Heinz. "The Ideational Content of Gogol's 'Overcoat,'" *Gogol's Overcoat: An Anthology of Critical Essays*, Elizabeth Trahan, ed. (Ann Arbor, 1982), pp. 86–105.

Woodward, James B. "The Threadbare Fabric of Gogol's 'Overcoat,'" *Canadian-Slavic Studies*, I (Spring 1967), 95–104.

Zeldin, Jesse. *Nikolai Gogol's Quest for Beauty: An Exploration into His Works* (Lawrence, Kans., 1978), pp. 53–59, 155–162.

NADINE GORDIMER, "Home"

Bazin, Nancy Topping. "An Interview with Nadine Gordimer," *Contemporary Literature*, XXXVI (Winter 1995), 571–587. (G)

Colleran, Jeanne. "Archive of Apartheid: Nadine Gordimer's Short Fiction at the End of the Interregnum," *The Later Fiction of Nadine Gordimer*, Bruce King, ed. (New York, 1993), pp. 237–245.

Githii, Ethel W. "Nadine Gordimer's Selected Stories," *Critique*, XXII, No. 3 (1981), 45–54. (G)

Ettin, Andrew V. *Betrayals of the Body Politic: The Literary Commitments of Nadine Gordimer* (Charlottesville, Va., 1993), pp. 109–111.

Head, Dominic. *Nadine Gordimer* (New York, 1995). (G)

Ingersoll, Earl and Stan S. Rubin. "A Voice from a Troubled Land: A Conversation with Nadine Gordimer," *Ontario Review*, XXVI (Spring–Summer 1987), 5–14. (G)

Margarey, Kevin. "'Cutting the Jewel: Facets of Art in Nadine Gordimer's Short Stories," *Southern Review* (Adelaide), VII (February 1974), 3–28. (G)

Smyer, Richard I. "Africa in the Fiction of Nadine Gordimer," *Ariel*, XVI (April 1985), 15–29. (G)

Trump, Martin. "The Short Fiction of Nadine Gordimer," *Research in African Literatures*, XVII (1986), 341–369. (G)

Wade, Michael. "Nadine Gordimer," *Essays on Contemporary Postcolonial Fiction*, Hedwig Bock and Albert Wertheim, eds. (Munich, 1986), pp. 115–148. (G)

THOMAS HARDY, "The Three Strangers"

Alexander, Anne. *Thomas Hardy: The "Dream Country" of His Fiction* (London, 1987), pp. 156–180. (G)

Brady, Kristin. *The Short Stories of Thomas Hardy* (New York, 1982), pp. 6–12.

Cassis, A. F. "A Note on the Structure of Hardy's Stories," *Colby Library Quarterly*, Series X (March 1974), 297–296. (G)

Fischler, Alexander. "Theatrical Techniques in Thomas Hardy's Short Stories," *Studies in Short Fiction*, III (Summer 1966), 435–445. (G)

Guerard, Albert J. *Thomas Hardy: The Novels and Stories* (London, 1949). (G)

Hagopian, John V. and Martin Dolch, eds. *Insight II, Analyses of Modern British Literature* (Frankfurt, 1965), pp. 171–175.

Hornback, Bert G. *The Metaphor of Chance: Vision and Technique in the Works of Thomas Hardy* (Athens, Ohio, 1971), pp. 11–14.

Howe, Irving. "A Note on Hardy's Stories," *Hudson Review*, XIX (Summer 1966–1967), 259–266. (G)

Marroni, Francesco. "'The Three Strangers' and the Verbal Representation of Wessex," *Thomas Hardy Journal*, VIII, 2 (1992), 26–39.

O'Connor, William Van. "Cosmic Irony in Hardy's 'The Three Strangers,'" *English Journal* XLVII (May 1958), 248–254, 262.

Page, Norman. "Hardy's Short Stories: A Reconsideration," *Studies in Short Fiction*, XI (Winter 1974), 75–84. (G)

Quinn, Marie A. "Thomas Hardy and the Short Story," *Budmouth Essays on Thomas Hardy*, F. B. Pinion, ed. (London, 1976), pp. 74–85. (G)

Ray, Martin. *Thomas Hardy: A Textual Study of the Short Stories* (Aldershot, Eng., 1997), pp. 8–13.

Roberts, Edgar V. "An Analysis of the Structure of the 'Three Strangers' by Thomas Hardy," *Writing Themes about Literature* (Englewood Cliffs, N.J., 1969), pp. 88–90.

Roberts, James L. "Legend and Symbol in Hardy's 'The Three Strangers,'" *Nineteenth-Century Fiction*, XVII (September 1962), 191–194.

Smith, J. B. "Dialect in Hardy's Short Stories," *Thomas Hardy Annual*, III (1985), 79–92. (G)

Wilson, Keith. "Hardy and the Hangman: The Dramatic Appeal of 'The Three Strangers,'" *English Literature in Transition*, XXIV (1981), 155–160.

BRET HARTE, "Tennessee's Partner"

Brooks, Cleanth and Robert Penn Warren. *Understanding Fiction* (New York, 1959), pp. 181–184.

Burton, Linda. "For Better or Worse/Tennessee and His Partner: A New Approach to Bret Harte," *Arizona Quarterly*, XXXVI (Autumn 1980), 211–216.

Canby, Henry Seidel. *The Short Story in English* (New York, 1909), pp. 280–298. (G)

Conner, William F. "The Euchring of Tennessee: A Reexamination of Bret Harte's 'Tennessee's Partner,'" *Studies in Short Fiction*, XVII (Spring 1980), 113–120.

Hill, Archibald. "Principles Governing Semantic Parallels," *Texas Studies in Literature and Language*, I (Autumn 1959), 363–365.

Hutchinson, E. R. "Harte's 'Tennessee's Partner,'" *Explicator*, XXII (October 1963), Item 10.

Loomis, C. Grant. "Bret Harte's Folklore," *Western Folklore* XV (January 1956), 19–22. (G)

May, Charles E. "Bret Harte's 'Tennessee's Partner': The Reader Euchred," *South Dakota Review*, XV (Spring 1977), 109–117,

Morrow, Patrick D. "Bret Harte, Popular Fiction, and the Local Color Movement," *Western American Literature*, VIII (Fall 1973), 123–132. (G)

———. "The Predicament of Bret Harte," *American Literary Realism*, V (Summer 1972), 181–188. (G)

Pattee, Fred Lewis. *A History of American Literature Since 1900* (New York, 1968), pp. 63–82. (G)

Scharnhorst, Gary. *Bret Harte* (New York, 1992), pp. 29–31.

Shaw, Valerie. *The Short Story: A Critical Introduction* (London, 1983), pp. 90–91.

Stevens, J. David. "'She war a woman': Family Roles, Gender, and Sexuality in Bret Harte's Western Fiction," *American Literature*, 69 (September 1997), 571–593.

White, James G. "The Death of Tennessee's Partner," *Quarterly of the Tuolumne County Historical Society*," IV (January–March 1965), 122–124.

NATHANIEL HAWTHORNE, "My Kinsman, Major Molineux"

Abenethy, P. L. "The Identity of Hawthorne's Major Molineux," *American Transcendental Quarterly*, XXXT (Summer 1976), 5–8.

Abrams, Robert E. "The Psychology of Cognition in 'My Kinsman, Major Molineux,'" *Philological Quarterly*, LVIII (Summer 1979), 336–347.

Adams, Joseph D. "The Societal Initiation and Hawthorne's 'My Kinsman, Major Molineux': The Night Journey Motif," *English Studies Colloquium* (East Meadow, N.Y.), I (1976), 1–19.

Adams, Richard P. "Hawthorne's Provincial Tales," *New England Quarterly*, XXX (March 1957), 39–57.

Allen, Mary. "Smiles and Laughter in Hawthorne," *Philological Quarterly*, LTI (January 1973), 119–128.

Allen, Walter. *The Short Story in English* (New York, 1980), pp. 30–33.

Allison, Alexander W. "The Literary Contexts of 'My Kinsman, Major Molineux,'" *Nineteenth-Century Fiction*, XXIII (December 1968), 304–311.

Autrey, Max L. ""My Kinsman, Major Molineux': Hawthorne's Allegory of the Urban Movement," *College Literature*, XII (1985), 211–221.

Baker, S. "Hawthorne's Evidence," *Philological Quarterly*, LXI (Fall 1982), 479–483.

Becker, Jolin E. *Hawthorne's Historical Allegory* (Port Washington, N.Y., 1971), pp. 7–13.

Benoit, Raymond. "Hawthorne's Ape Man: 'My Kinsman, Major Molineux,'" *American Transcendental Quarterly*, XIV (1972), 8–9.

Bier, Jesse. "Hawthorne's 'My Kinsman, Major Molineux,'" *Explicator*, XXXVIII (Summer 1980), 40–41.

Bremer, Sidney H. "Exploding the Myth of Rural America and Urban Europe: 'My Kinsman, Major Molineux' and 'The Paradise of Bachelors and the Tartarus of Maids,'" *Studies in Short Fiction*, XVIII (Winter 1981), 49–57.

Broes, Arthur T. "Journey into Moral Darkness: 'My Kinsman, Major Molineux' as Allegory," *Nineteenth-Century Fiction*, XIX (September 1964), 171–184.

Brown, Dennis. "Literature and Existential Psychoanalysis: 'My Kinsman, Major Molineux' and 'Young Goodman Brown,'" *Canadian Review of American Studies*, IV (Spring 1973), 65–73.

Budick, Emily Miller. *Fiction and Historical Consciousness: The American Romance Tradition* (New Haven, 1989), pp. 113–118.

Cameron, Sharon. *The Corporeal Self: Allegories of the Body in Melville and Hawthorne* (Baltimore, 1981), pp. 144–155.

Carlson, Patricia Ann. *Hawthorne's Functional Settings: A Study of Artistic Method* (Amsterdam, 1977), pp. 131–137.

Carpenter, Richard C. "Hawthorne's Polar Explorations: 'Young Goodman Brown' and 'My Kinsman, Major Molineux,'" *Nineteenth-Century Fiction*, XXIV (June 1969), 45–56.

Cervo, Nathan A. "The Gargouille Anti-Hero: Victim of Christian Satire," *Renascence*, XXII (Winter 1970), 69–77.

Cohen, Hazel. "The Rupture of Relations: Revolution and Romance in Hawthorne's 'My Kinsman, Major Molineux,'" *English Studies in America*, XXIX (1986), 19–30.

Colacurcio, Michael J. *The Province of Piety: Moral History in Hawthorne's Early Tales* (Cambridge, 1984), pp. 130–153.

Collins, Michael J. "Hawthorne's Use of Clothing in 'My Kinsman, Major Molineux,'" *Nathaniel Hawthorne Journal*, VIII (1978), 171–172.

Connors, Thomas E. "'My Kinsman, Major Molineux': A Reading," *Modern Language Notes*, LXXIV (April 1959), 299–302.

Crews, Frederick C. *The Sins of the Fathers: Hawthorne's Psychological Themes* (New York, 1966), pp. 72–79.

D'Alanzo, Mario L. "The Literary Sources of 'My Kinsman, Major Molineux': Shakespeare, Coleridge, and Milton," *Studies in Short Fiction*, X (Spring 1973), 121–136.

Dauber, Kenneth. "Hawthorne and the Authority of Intimacy," *Thoreau Quarterly*, XVI (Winter/Spring 1984), 59–61.

Davison, Richard Allan. "Redburn, Pierre, and Robin: Melville's Debt to Hawthorne?" *Emerson Society Quarterly*, XLVII (Second Quarter 1967), 32–34.

Deamer, Robert Glen. "Hawthorne's Parricidal Vision of the American Revolution: 'My Kinsman, Major Molineux,'" *The Importance of Place in the American Literature of Hawthorne, Thoreau, Crane, Adams, and Faulkner: American Writers, American Culture, and the American Dream* (Lewiston, N.Y., 1990), pp. 55–62.

Dennis, Carl. "How to Live in Hell: The Bleak Vision of Hawthorne's 'My Kinsman, Major Molineux,'" *University Review*, XXXVII (Summer 1971), 250–258.

Dolan, Paul J. *Of War and War's Alarms: Fiction and Politics in the Modern World* (New York, 1976), pp. 16–35.

Donohue, Agnes McNeill. *Hawthorne: Calvin's Ironic Stepchild* (Kent, Ohio, 1985), pp. 195–199, 201–210.

Doubleday, Neal Frank. *Hawthorne's Early Tales: A Critical Study* (Durham, N.C., 1972), pp. 227–238.

Duban, James. "Robins and Robinarchs in 'My Kinsman, Major Molineux,'" *Nineteenth-Century Fiction*, XXXVIII (December 1983), 271–288.

Dunne, Michael. *Hawthorne's Narrative Strategies* (Jackson, Miss., 1995), pp. 162–164.

Dusenberg, Robert. "Hawthorne's Merry Company: The Anatomy of Laughter in the Tales and Short Stories," *Publications of the Modern Language Association*, LXXXII (May 1967), 285–288.

Eldred, Janet Carey. "Narratives of Socialization: Literacy in the Short Story," *College English*, LIII (October 1991), 686–700.

England, A. B. "Robin Molineux and the Young Ben Franklin: A Reconsideration," *Journal of American Studies*, VI (August 1972), 181–188.

England, Eugene. "Hawthorne and the Virtue of Sin," *Literature & Belief*, III (1983), 109–120.

Fass, Barbara. "Rejection of Paternalism: Hawthorne's 'My Kinsman, Major Molineux' and Ellison's Invisible Man," *CLA Journal*, XIV (March 1971), 317–323.

Fogle, Richard Harter. *Hawthorne's Fiction: The Light and the Dark* (Norman, Okla., 1964), pp.104–116.

Fossum Robert H. *Hawthorne's Inviolable Circle: The Problem of Time* (Deland, Fla., 1972), pp. 26–31.

———. "The Shadow of the Past: Hawthorne's Historical Tales," *Claremont Quarterly*, XI (1963), 45–56.

Franzosa, John. "Locke's Kinsman, William Molyneux: The Philosophical Context of Hawthorne's Early Tales," *ESQ, A Journal of the American Renaissance*, XXIX (1983), 1–15.

Freese, Paul. "'Rising in the World' and 'Wanting to Know Why': The Socialization Process as Theme of the American Short Story," *Archiv für das Studium der Neuren Sprachen und Literaturen*, CCXVIII (1981), 290–294.

Freese, Peter. "Robin und seine vielen Verwandten: zur Rezeptionsgeschichte von Nathaniel Hawthorne," *Die englische und americanische Kurzqeschichte*, Klaus Lubbers, ed. (Darmstadt, Germany, 1990), pp. 12–27.

Girgus, Sam B. *Desire and the Political Unconscious in American Literature: Eros and Ideology* (New York, 1990), pp. 56–59.

Gollin, Rita. *Nathaniel Hawthorne and the Truth of Dreams* (Baton Rouge, 1979), pp. 115–123.

Grayson, Robert C. "The New England Sources of 'My Kinsman, Major Molineux,'" *American Literature*, LIV (December 1982), 545–559.

Gross, Seymour. "Hawthorne's 'My Kinsman, Major Molineux': History as Moral Adventure," *Nineteenth-Century Fiction*, XII (September 1957), 97–109.

———. "Hawthorne Versus Melville," *Bucknell Review*, XIV (December 1957), 89–109.

Hagopian, John V. and Martin Dolch, eds. *Insight I: Analyses of American Literature* (Frankfurt, 1962), pp. 67–73.

Henderson, Harry B., III. *Versions of the Past: The Historical Imagination in American Fiction* (New York, 1974), pp. 109–114.

Herbert, T. Walter, Jr. "Doing Cultural Work: 'My Kinsman, Major Molineux' and the Construction of the Self-Made Man," *Studies in the Novel*, XXIII (Spring 1991), 20–27.

Herndon, Jerry A. "Hawthorne's Dream Imagery," *American Literature*, XLVI (January 1975), 538–545.

Hoffman, Daniel F. *Form and Fable in American Literature* (New York, 1964), pp. 113–125.

Houston, Neal B. and Fred A. Rodewald. "'My Kinsman, Major Molineux': A Re-Evaluation," *Proceedings Conference College Teachers of English* (Texas), XXXIV (1969), 18–22.

Johnson, Claudia D. *The Productive Tension of Hawthorne's Art* (University, Ala., 1981), pp. 27–29.

Jones, Bartlett C. "The Ambiguity of Shrewdness in 'My Kinsman, Major Molineux,'" *Mid-Continent American Studies Journal*, III (Fall 1962), 42–47.

Kay, Donald. "Hawthorne's Use of Laughter in Selected Short Stories," *Xavier University Studies*, X (Fall 1971), 27–32.

Kimmey, John L. "Pierre and Robin: Melville's Debt to Hawthorne," *Emerson Society Quarterly*, XXXVIII (First Quarter 1965), 90–92.

Kozcikowski, Stanley J. "'My Kinsman, Major Molineux' as Mock-Heroic," *American Transcendental Quarterly*, XXXI (Summer 1976), 20–21.

Leavis, Q. D. "Hawthorne as Poet," *Sewanee Review*, LIX (Spring 1951), 198–205.

Lesser, Simon O. "The Image of the Father," *Partisan Review*, XXII (Summer 1955), 372–390.

Leverenz, David. "Historicizing Hell in Hawthorne's Tales," *New Essays on Hawthorne's Major Tales*, Millicent Bell, ed. (New York, 1993), pp. 101–132.

———. *Manhood and the American Renaissance* (Ithaca, N.Y., 1989), pp. 231–239.

Liebman, Sheldon W. "Robin's Conversion: The Design of 'My Kinsman, Major Molineux,'" *Studies in Short Fiction*, VIII (Summer 1971), 443–457.

Machor, James L. *Pastoral Cities: Urban Ideals and the Symbolic Landscape of America* (Madison, 1987), pp. 193–198.

———. "Pastoralism and the American Urban Ideal: Hawthorne, Whitman, and the Literary Pattern," *American Literature*, LIV (October 1982), 329–353.

McNamara, Leo. "Irish and American Politics in the 18th Century and Nathaniel Hawthorne's 'My Kinsman, Major Molineux,'" *Eire-Ireland*, XXIV (Fall 1988), 20–32.

McWilliams, John P., Jr. *Hawthorne, Melville, and the American Character: A Looking-glass Business* (Cambridge, England, 1984), pp. 85–88.

———. "Thorough-Going Democrat and 'Modern Tory': Hawthorne and the Puritan Revolution of 1776," *Studies in Romanticism*, XV (Fall 1976), 567–571.

Male, Roy B. *Hawthorne's Tragic Vision* (Austin, Tex., 1957), pp. 48–53.

Martin, Terence. *Nathaniel Hawthorne* (Boston, 1983), pp. 98–104.

Marzec, Marcia S. "'My Kinsman, Major Molineux' as Theo-Political Allegory," *American Transcendental Quarterly*, I (December 1987), 273–289.

Mellard, James M. *Four Modes: A Rhetoric of Modern Fiction* (New York, 1973), pp. 136–138.

Mellow, James R. *Nathaniel Hawthorne in His Times* (Boston, 1980), pp. 61–64.

Miller, John N. "The Pageantry of Revolt in 'My Kinsman, Major Molineux,'" *Studies in American Fiction*, XVII (Spring 1989), 51–64.

Millington, Richard H. *Practicing Romance: Narrative Form and Cultural Engagement in Hawthorne's Fiction* (Princeton, 1992), pp. 40–41.

Murphy, Denis M. "Poor Robin and Shrewd Ben: Hawthorne's Kinsman," *Studies in Short Fiction*, XV (Spring 1978), 185–190.

Newberry, Frank. *Hawthorne's Divided Loyalties: England and America in His Works* (Cranbury, N.J., 1987), pp. 62–65.

Newman, Franklin B. "'My Kinsman, Major Molineux': An Interpretation," *University of Kansas City Review*, XXI (March 1955), 203–212.

Newman, Lea Bertani Vozar. *A Reader's Guide to the Short Stories of Nathaniel Hawthorne* (Boston, 1979), pp. 217–230.

Nilson, Helge N. "Hawthorne's 'My Kinsman, Major Molineux,'" *American-Norvegica*, Vol. 4 (Oslo, 1973), pp. 123–136.

Nitzche, J. C. "House Symbolism in Hawthorne's 'My Kinsman, Major Molineux,'" *American Transcendental Quarterly*, XXXVIII (Spring 1978), 167–175.

Paul, Louis. "A Psychoanalytic Reading of Hawthorne's 'Major Molineux': The Father Manqué and the Protégé Manqué," *American Imago*, XVIII (Fall 1961), 279–288.

Pearce, Roy Harvey. "Hawthorne and the Sense of the Past, or the Immortality of Major Molineux," *English Literary History*, XXI (December 1954), 327–349.

———. "Robin Molineux on the Analyst's Couch: A Note on the Limits of Psychoanalytic Criticism," *Criticism*, I (1959), 83–90.

Pinsker, Sanford. "Hawthorne's 'Double-Faced Fellow'—A Note on 'My Kinsman, Major Molineux,'" *Nathaniel Hawthorne Journal 1972* (Washington, 1973), pp. 255–256.

Reed, Michael D. "Robin and His Kinsman: A Psychoanalytic Re-Examination of 'My Kinsman, Major Molineux,'" *Journal of Evolutionary Psychology*, XL (April 1982), 94–103.

Ringe, Donald A. "Hawthorne's Night Journey," *American Transcendental Quarterly*, X (Spring 1971), 27–32.

Rohrberger, Mary. *Hawthorne and the Modern Short Story* (The Hague, 1966), pp. 31–39.

Rohrberger, Mary and Samuel H. Woods, Jr. *Reading and Writing About Literature* (New York, 1971), pp. 77–84.

Rose, Marilyn G. "Theseus Motif in 'My Kinsman, Major Molineux,'" *Emerson Society Quarterly*, XLVII (Second Quarter 1967), 21–23.

Rowe, Joyce. *Equivocal Endings in Classic American Novels* (New York, 1988), pp. 14–28.

Russell, John. "Allegory and 'My Kinsman, Major Molineux,'" *New England Quarterly*, XL (September 1967), 432–440.

Scott, Jon C. "Hawthorne's 'My Kinsman, Major Molineux' and the American Ideal," *Michigan Academician*, IV (Fall 1971), 197–203.

Sharma, T. R. S. "Diabolic World and Naive Hero in 'My Kinsman, Major Molineux,'" *Indian Journal of American Studies*, I (1971), 35–43.

Shaw, Peter. "Fathers, Sons and the Ambiguities of Revolution in 'My Kinsman, Major Molineux,'" *New England Quarterly*, XLIX (December 1976), 559–576.

———. "Their Kinsman, Thomas Hutchinson: The Boston Patriots and His Majesty's Royal Governor," *Early American Literature*, XI (Fall 1976), 183–190.

Shulman, Robert. *Social Criticism and Nineteenth-Century American Fictions* (Columbia, Mo., 1987), pp, 114–124.

Simpson, Lewis P. "John Adams and Hawthorne: The Fiction of the Real American Revolution," *Studies in the Literary Imagination*, IX (Fall 1976), 1–17.

Smith, Julian. "Coming of Age in America: Young Ben Franklin and Robin Molineux,' *American Quarterly*, XVII (Fall 1965), 550–558.

———. "Historical Ambiguity in 'My Kinsman, Major Molineux,'" *English Language Notes*, VIII (December 1970), 115–120.

Stein, William Bysshe. "Teaching Hawthorne's 'My Kinsman, Major Molineux'" *College English*, XX (November 1958), 83–86.

Stout, Janis P. *Sodoms in Eden: The City in American Fiction Before 1860* (Westport, Conn., 1976), pp. 94–96.

Stephenson, Will, and Mimosa. "Molineux in the Underworld: Virgil, Yes; Homer, No," *Nathaniel Hawthorne Review*, XVIII, 2 (1992), 19–20.

Stubbs, John Caldwell. *The Pursuit of Form: A Study of Hawthorne and the Romance* (Urbana, 1970), pp. 67–71.

Thompson, G. R. *The Art of Authorial Presence: Hawthorne's Provincial Tales* (Durham, N. C., 1993), pp. 120–158.

Thorpe, Dwayne. "'My Kinsman, Major Molineux': The Identity of the Kinsman," *Topic: 18*, IX (Fall 1969), 53–63.

Trilling, Lionel. *Prefaces to the Experience of Literature* (New York, 1979), pp. 69–73.

Van Der Beets, Richard and Paul Witherington. "My Kinsman, Brockden Brown: Robin Molineux and Arthur Mervyn," *American Transcendental Quarterly*, I (1969), 13–15.

Wagenknecht, Edward. *Nathaniel Hawthorne: The Man, His Tales and Romances* (New York 1989), pp. 66–72.

Waggoner, Hyatt, *Hawthorne: A Critical Study* (Cambridge, 1955), pp. 46–53.

———. *The Presence of Hawthorne* (Baton Rouge, 1979), pp. 27–30, 157–159.

Wallins, Roger P. "Robin and the Narrator in 'My Kinsman, Major Molineux,'" *Studies in Fiction*, XII (Spring 1975), 173–179.

Warren, Robert Penn. "Hawthorne Revisited: Some Remarks on Hellfiredness," *Sewanee Review*, LXXXI (January–March 1973), 85–93.

Wyatt–Brown, Bertram. *Southern Honor: Ethics and Behavior in the Old South* (Oxford, England, 1983), pp. 4–14.

Zajkowski, Robert. "Renaissance Psychology and Hawthorne's 'My Kinsman, Major Molineux,'" *Nathaniel Hawthorne Journal*, VIII (1978), 159–168.

NATHANIEL HAWTHORNE, "Young Goodman Brown"

Abcarian, Richard. "The Ending of 'Young Goodman Brown,'" *Studies in Short Fiction* (Spring 1966), 343–345.

Abel, Darrel. "Black Glove and Pink Ribbon: Hawthorne's Metonymic Symbols," *New Quarterly*, XLII (June 1969), 163–180.

———. *The Moral Picturesque: Studies in Hawthorne's Fiction* (West Lafayefte, Ind., 1988), pp.130–141.

Adams, Richard P. "Hawthorne's Provincial Tales," *New England Quarterly*, XXX (March 1957), 39–57.

Allen, Walter. *The Short Story in English* (New York, 1980), pp. 33–38.

Alkana, Joseph. "Hawthorne's Drama of the Imagination and the Family," *Philological Quarterly* LXIX (Spring 1990), 217–231.

Apseloff, Sanford and Marilyn. "'Young Goodman Brown': The Goodman," American & Queries, XX (1982), 103.

Baker, S. "Hawthorne's Evidence," *Philological Quarterly*, LXI (Fall 1982), 479–483.

Becker, Isadore H. *The Ironic Dimension in Hawthorne's Short Fiction* (New York, 1971) 68–72.

Becker, John E. *Hawthorne's Historical Allegory* (Port Washington, N.Y., 1971), pp. 13–21.

Bell, Michael Davitt. *Hawthorne and the Historical Romance of New England* (Princeton, 1971), pp. 76–81.

Benoit, Raymond. "'Young Goodman Brown': The Second Time Around," *Nathaniel Hawthorne Review*, XIX (Spring 1993), 18–21.

Boudreau, Gordon V."The Summons of Young Goodman Brown," *Greyfriar* XII (1972), 15–24.

Brown, Dennis. "Literature and Existential Psychoanalysis: 'My Kinsman, Major Molineux' and 'Young Goodman Brown,'" *Canadian Review of American Studies*, IX (Spring 1973), 65–73.

Budick, Emily Miller. *Fiction and Historical Consciousness: The American Romance Tradition* (New Haven, 1989), pp. 79–97.

———. "The World as Specter: Hawthorne's Historical Art," *PMLA*, CI (1986), 218–225.

Buell, Lawrence. *New England Literary Culture: From Revolution Through Renaissance* (New York, 1986), pp. 73–77.

Campbell, Harry M. "Freudianism, American Romanticism, and 'Young Goodman Brown,'" *CEA Critic*, XXXIII (March 1971), 3–6.

Capps, Jack L. "The Arc of Rebirth in 'Young Goodman Brown,'" *Explicator*, XL (Spring 1982), 25.

Cargas, Harry J. "The Arc of Rebirth in 'Young Goodman Brown,'" *New Laurel Review*, IV (1975), 5–7.

Carlson, Patricia Ann. *Hawthorne's Functional Settings: A Study of Artistic Method* (Amsterdam, 1977), pp. 128–131.

Carpenter, Richard C. "Hawthorne's Polar Explorations: 'Young Goodman Brown' and 'My Kinsman, Major Molineux,'" *Nineteenth-Century Fiction*, XXIV (June 1969), 45–56.

Cherry, Fannye N. "The Sources of Hawthorne's 'Young Goodman Brown,'" *American Literature*, V (January 1934), 342–348.

Christophersen, Bill. "'Young Goodman Brown' As Historical Allegory; A Lexical Link," *Studies in Short Fiction*, XXIII (Spring 1986), 202–204.

Cifelli, Edward M. "Typology: A New Ambiguity in 'Young Goodman Brown,'" *CEA Critic*, XLI (March 1979), 16–17.

Clark, James W., Jr. "Hawthorne's Use of Evidence in 'Young Goodman Brown,'" *Essex Institute Historical Collections*, CXI (January 1975), 12–34.

Cohen, B. Bernard. "Deodat Lawson's *Christ's Fidelity* and Hawthorne's 'Young Goodman Brown,'" *Essex Institute Historical Collections*, CVI (October 1968), 348–370.

———. *Guide to Nathaniel Hawthorne* (Columbus, Ohio, 1970), pp. 25–28.

———. "*Paradise Lost* and 'Young Goodman Brown,'" *Essex Institute Historical Collections*, XCIV (July 1958), 282–296.

Cohran, Robert W. "Hawthorne's Choice: The Veil or the Jaundiced Eye," *College English*, XXIII (February 1962), 342–346.

Colacurcio, Michael J. "'Certain Circumstances': Hawthorne and the Interest of History," *New Essays on Hawthorne's Major Tales*, Millicent Bell, ed. (New York, 1993), pp. 37–66.

———. *The Province of Piety: Moral History in Hawthorne's Early Tales* (Cambridge, Mass., 1984), pp. 283–313.

———. "Visible Sanctity and Spector Evidence: The Moral World of Hawthorne's 'Young Goodman Brown,'" *Essex Institute Historical Collections*, CX (October 1974), 259–299.

Coldiron, A. E. B. "Laughter as Thematic Marker in 'Young Goodman Brown,'" *Nathaniel Hawthorne Review*, XVII (Spring 1991), 19.

Connolly, Thomas E. "Hawthorne's 'Young Goodman Brown': An Attack on Puritanic Calvinism," *American Literature*, XXVIII (January 1957), 370–375.

Cook, Reginald. "The Forest of Goodman Brown's Night: A Reading of Hawthorne's 'Young Goodman Brown,'" *New England Quarterly*, XLIII (September 1970), 473–481.

Crews, Frederick C. *The Sins of the Fathers: Hawthorne's Psychological Themes* (New York, 1966), pp. 98–106.

Dameron, J. Lasley. "Faust, the Wandering Jew, and the Swellowed Serpent: Hawthorne's Familiar Literary Analogues," *Nathaniel Hawthorne Review*, XX (Spring 1994), 10–15.

Davidson, Frank. "'Young Goodman Brown'—Hawthorne's Intent," *Emerson Society Quarterly*, XXXI (Second Quarter 1963), 68–71.

Davis, William V. "Hawthorne's 'Young Goodman Brown,'" *Nathaniel Hawthorne Journal 1973* (Englewood, Colo., 1973), pp. 198–199.

Dessner, Lawrence Jay. "Malamud's Echoes of Hawthorne's 'Young Goodman Brown,'" *Notes on Contemporary Literature*, 29 (March 1999), 6–8.

Dickson, Wayne. "Hawthorne's 'Young Goodman Brown,'" *Explicator*, XXIX (January 1971), Item 44.

Doubleday, Neal Frank. *Hawthorne's Early Tales: A Critical Study* (Durham, N.C., 1972), pp. 202–212.

Easterly, Joan E. "Lachrymal Imagery in Hawthorne's 'Young Goodman Brown,'" *Studies in Short Fiction* XXIX (Summer 1991), 339–343.

Eberwein, Jane D. "'My Faith Is Gone!': 'Young Goodman Brown' and Puritan Conversion," *Christianity & Literature*, XXXII (1982), 23–32.

Ensor, Allison. "'Whispers of a Bad Angel': A *Scarlet Letter* Passage as Commentary on Hawthorne's 'Young Goodman Brown,'" *Studies in Short Fiction*, VII (Summer 1970), 467–469.

Erisman, Fred. "'Young Goodman Brown': Warning to Idealists," *American Transcendental Quarterly*, XIV (1972), 156–158.

Ferguson, J. M., Jr. "Hawthorne's 'Young Goodman Brown,'" *Explicator*, XXVIII (December 1969), Item 32.

Fogle, Richard H. "Ambiguity and Clarity in Hawthorne's 'Young Goodman Brown,'" *New England Quarterly*, XVIII (December 1945), 448–465.

———. *Hawthorne's Fiction: The Light and The Dark* (Norman, Okla., 1952), pp. 15–32.

———. "Weird Mockery: An Element of Hawthorne's Style," Style, II (Fall 1968), 191–202.

Fossum, Robert H. Hawthorne's Inviolable Circle: The Problem of Time (Deland, Fla., 1972), pp. 52–56.

Gallagher, Edward J. "The Concluding Paragraph of 'Young Goodman Brown,'" Studies in Short Fiction, XII (Winter 1975), 29–30.

Gaston, Warren. "'Young Goodman Brown': A Criticism," Littérature, VI (Spring 1965), 26–30.

Girgus, Sam B. Desire and the Political Unconscious in American Literature: Eros and Ideology (New York, 1990), pp. 59–66.

Gollin, Rita. Nathaniel Hawthorne and the Truth of Dreams (Baton Rouge, 1979), pp. 123–128.

Gordon, Caroline and Allen Tate. The House of Fiction (New York, 1950), pp. 36–39.

Grayson, Robert C. "Curdled Milk for Babes: The Role of the Catechism in 'Young Goodman Brown,'" Nathaniel Hawthorne Review, XVI (Spring 1990), 1, 3–6.

Gross, Seymour L. "Hawthorne's Moral Realism," Emerson Society Quarterly, XXV (Fourth Quarter 1961), 11–13.

———. "Hawthorne Versus Melville," Bucknell Review, XIV (December 1966), 89–109.

Grunes, Dennis. "Allegory Versus Allegory in Hawthorne," American Transcendental Quarterly, XXXII (Fall 1976), 14–19.

Guerin, Wilfred L., Earle G. Labor, Lee Morgan, and John R. Willingham. A Handbook of Critical Approaches to Literature (New York, 1966), pp. 35–44, 57–65, 100–104, 139–141, 163–172.

Hagopian, John V. and Martin Dolch, eds. Insight I, Analyses of American Literature (Frankfurt, 1962), pp. 73–78.

Harmsel, Henrietta Ten. "'Young Goodman Brown' and 'The Enormous Radio,'" Studies in Short Fiction, IX (Fall 1972), 407–408,

Hale, John K. "The Serpentine Staff in 'Young Goodman Brown,'" Nathaniel Hawthorne Review, XIX (Spring 1993), 17–18.

Harris, Kenneth Marc. Hypocrisy and Self Deception in Hawthorne's Fiction (Charlottesville, Va., 1988), pp. 42–45.

Hoffman, Daniel G. Form and Fable in American Fiction (New York, 1965), pp. 149–168.

Hollinger, Karen. "'Young Goodman Brown': Hawthorne's 'Devil in Manuscript': A Rebuttal," Studies in Short Fiction, XIX (Fall 1982), 381–384.

Hostetler, Norman H. "Narrative Structure and Theme in 'Young Goodman Brown,'" Journal of Narrative Technique, XII (Fall 1982), 221–228.

Humma, John B. "'Young Goodman Brown' and the Failure of Hawthorne's Ambiguity," Colby Library Quarterly, Series IX (December 1971), 425–431.

Hurley, Paul J. "'Young Goodman Brown's 'Heart of Darkness,'" American Literature, XXXVII (January 1966), 410–419.

Irwin, John T. American Hieroglyphics (Baltimore, 1980), pp. 254–255.

Jayne, Edward. "Pray Tarry With Me Young Goodman Brown," Literature and Psychology XXIX, 3 (1979), 110–113.

Johnson, Claudia D. The Productive Tension of Hawthorne's Art (University, Ala., 1981), pp. 30–35.

———. "'Young Goodman Brown' and Puritan Justification," Studies in Short Fiction, XI (Spring 1974), 200–203.

Jones, Madison. "Variations on a Hawthorne Theme," Studies in Short Fiction, XV (Summer 1978), 278–280.

Keil, James C. "Hawthorne's 'Young Goodman Brown': Early Nineteenth-Century and Puritan Construction of Gender, New England Quarterly, LXIX (March 1996), 33–55.

Kennelly, Laura B. "Hawthorne and Goldsmith? British History in 'Young Goodman Brown' and Biographical Stories," Journal of American Studies, XXIII (August 1989), 295–297.

Kesterson, David B. "Nature and Theme in 'Young Goodman Brown,'" Dickinson Review, II (1968), 42–46.

Kim, Chong–Un. "Hawthorne's 'Young Goodman Brown,'" *English Language and Literature*, IX (1960), pp. 140–155.

Klammer, Enno. "The Fatal Flaw in 'Young Goodman Brown,'" *Cresset*, XXVIII (February 1965), 8–10.

Krumpelmann, John T. "Hawthorne's 'Young Goodman Brown' and Goethe's *Faust*," *Die Neueren Sprachen*, V (1956), 516–521.

Lang, H. J. "How Ambiguous Is Hawthorne?" *Hawthorne: Twentieth-Century Views*, A. N. Kaul, ed. (Englewood Cliffs, N.J., 1966), pp. 86–98.

Leibowitz, Herbert A. "Hawthorne and Spenser: Two Sources," *American Literature*, XXX (January 1959), 459–464

Levin, David. *In Defense of Historical Literature* (New York, 1967). pp. 77–87.

———. "Shadows of Doubt: Specter Evidence in Hawthorne's 'Young Goodman Brown,'" *American Literature*, XXXIV (November 1962), 344–352.

Levine, Robert. *Conspiracy and Romance: Studies in Brockden Brown, Cooper, Hawthorne, and Melville* (Cambridge, England, 1989), pp. 127–129.

Levy, Leo B. "The Problem of Faith in 'Young Goodman Brown,'" *Journal of English and Germanic Philology*, LXXIV (July 1975), 375–387.

Liebman, Sheldon W. "The Reader in 'Young Goodman Brown,'" *Nathaniel Hawthorne Journal 1975* (Englewood, Colo., 1975), pp. 156–169.

Loving, Jerome. "Pretty in Pink: 'Young Goodman Brown' and New World Drama," *Critical Essays on Hawthorne's Short Stories*, Albert J. von Frank, ed. (Boston, 1991), pp. 219–231.

Lynch, James J. "The Devil in the Writings of Irving, Hawthorne, and Poe," *New York Folklore Quarterly VII* (Summer 1952), 111–131.

McCullen, Joseph T. "Young Goodman Brown: Presumption and Despair," *Discourse*, II (July 1959), 145–157.

McKeithan, D. M. "Hawthorne's 'Young Goodman Brown,'" *Modern Language Notes*, LXVI (February 1952), 93–96.

Male, Roy B. *Hawthorne's Tragic Vision* (Austin, Tex., 1957), pp. 76–80.

Manheim, L. F. "Outside Looking In: Evidence of Primal-Scene Fantasy in Hawthorne's Fiction," *Literature and Psychology*, XXXI (1981), 4–15.

Martin. Terence. *Nathaniel Hawthorne* (Boston, 1983), pp. 81–87.

Matheson, Terence J. "'Young Goodman Brown': Hawthorne's Condemnation of Conformity," *Nathaniel Hawthorne Journal*, VIII (1978), 137–145.

Matthews, James W. "Antinomianism in 'Young Goodman Brown,'" *Studies in Short Fiction*, III (Fall 1965), 73–75.

Matthiessen, F. O. *The American Renaissance* (New York, 1941), pp. 282–284.

May, Charles E. "Young Goodman Brown," *Reference Guide to Short Fiction*, Noelle Watson, ed. (Detroit, 1994), p. 982.

Miller, Edwin Haviland. *Salem Is My Dwelling Place: A Life of Nathaniel Hawthorne* (Iowa City, Ia., 1991), pp. 111–112.

Miller, Paul W. "Hawthorne's 'Young Goodman Brown': Cynicism or Meliorism?" *Nineteenth-Century Fiction*, XIV (December 1959), 255–264.

Mills, Barriss. "Hawthorne and Puritanism," *New England Quarterly*, XXI (March 1948), 78–102. (G)

Minock, Daniel W. "Hawthorne and the Rumor About the Governor's Lady," *American Notes & Queries*, XIII (1975), 87–88.

Morsberger, Robert E. "The Woe That Is Madness: Goodman Brown and the Face of Fire," *Nathaniel Hawthorne Journal 1973* (Englewood, Colo., 1973), pp. 177–182.

Mosher, Harold F. "The Source of Ambiguity in Hawthorne's 'Young Goodman Brown': A Structuralist Approach," *Emerson Society Quarterly*, XXVI (1980), 16–25.

Newman, Lea Bertani Vozer. *A Reader's Guide to the Short Stories of Nathaniel Hawthorne* (Boston, 1979), pp. 333–348.

Norris, Christopher D. "Deconstructing 'Young Goodman Brown,'" *American Transcendental Quarterly*, II (March 1988), 23–33.

Park, Yangkeun. "Application of Discourse Analysis to Literature: Reinterpretation of Hawthorne's 'Young Goodman Brown,'" *Journal of English Language and Literature*, XXXVII (1991), 901–919.

Paulits, Walter J. "Ambivalence in 'Young Goodman Brown,'" *American Literature*, XLI (January 1970), 577–584.

Ponder, Melinda M. *Hawthorne's Early Narrative Art* (Lewiston, N.Y., 1990), pp. 52–62.

Reynolds, Larry J. "Melville's Use of 'Young Goodman Brown,'" *American Transcendental Quarterly*, XXXI (Summer 1976), 12–14.

Ringe, Donald A. "Hawthorne's Night Journeys," *American Transcendental Quarterly*, X (Spring 1971), 27–32.

Robinson, E. Arthur. "The Vision of Goodman Brown: A Source and Interpretation," *American Literature*, XXXV (May 1963), 218–225.

Rohrberger, Mary. *Hawthorne and the Modern Short Story* (The Hague, 1966), pp. 39–47.

St. Armand, Barton Levi. "'Young Goodman Brown' as Historical Allegory," *Nathaniel Hawthorne Journal 1973* (Englewood, Colo., 1973), pp. 183–197.

Scoville, Samuel. "To Conceive of the Devil," *English Journal*, LVIII (May 1969), 673–675.

Shaw, Patrick W. "Checking Out Faith and Lust: Hawthorne's 'Young Goodman Brown' and Updike's 'A&P,'" *Studies in Short Fiction*, XXIII (Summer 1986), 321–323.

Shear, Walter. "Cultural Fate and Social Freedom in Three American Short Stories," *Studies in Short Fiction*, XXIX (Fall 1992), 543–549.

Shriver, Margaret M. "'Young Goodman Brown,'" *Études Anglaises*, XXX (October–December 1977), 407–419.

Sisk, John P. "The Devil and American Epic," *Hudson Review*, XL (Spring 1987), 31–47.

Smoot, Jeanne J. "'Young Goodman Brown'—Puritan Don Juan: Faith in Tirso and Hawthorne," *Post Script*, I (1983), 42–48.

Stephenson, Will, and Mimosa. "An Additional Source for the Serpentine Staff in 'Young Goodman Brown,'" *Nathaniel Hawthorne Review*, XX (Fall 1994), 31–32.

Stoehr, Taylor. "'Young Goodman Brown' and Hawthorne's Theory of Mimesis," *Nineteenth-Century Fiction*, XXIII (March 1969), 393–412.

Swenson, William G. *Great Themes in Short Fiction* (New York, 1975), pp. 69–72.

Tharpe, Jac. *Nathaniel Hawthorne: Identity and Knowledge* (Carbondale, Ill., 1967), pp. 74–77.

Tritt, Michael. "'Young Goodman Brown' and the Psychology of Projection," *Studies in Short Fiction*, XXIII (Winter 1986), 113–117.

Wagenknecht, Edward. *Nathaniel Hawthorne: The Man, His Tales and Romances* (New York, 1989), pp. 57–66.

Walcutt, Charles C. *Man's Changing Masks: Modes and Methods of Characterization in Fiction* (Minneapolis, 1966), pp. 124–130.

Walsh, Thomas F. "The Bedeviling of Young Goodman Brown," *Modern Language Quarterly*, XIX (December 1958), 331–336.

Whelan, Robert E. "Hawthorne Interprets 'Young Goodman Brown,'" *Emerson Society Quarterly*, LXII (Winter 1971), 3–6.

Williamson, James L. "'Young Goodman Brown': Hawthorne's Devil in Manuscript," *Studies in Short Fiction*, XVIII (Spring 1991), 155–162.

Winkelman, Donald A. "Goodman Brown, Tom Sawyer, and Oral Tradition," *Keystone Folklore Quarterly*, X (Spring 1965), 43–48.

Wolf, Bryan Jay. *Romantic Re-Vision: Culture and Consciousness in Nineteenth-Century American Painting and Literature* (Chicago, 1982), pp. 141–144.

Zanger, Jules. "'Young Goodman Brown' and 'A White Heron': Correspondences and Illuminations," *Papers on Language and Literature*, XXVI (Summer 1990), 346–357.

ERNEST HEMINGWAY, "Hills Like White Elephants"

Abdoo, Sherlyn. "Hemingway's 'Hills Like White Elephants,'" *Explicator*, XLIX (Summer 1991), 238–240.

Barbour, James. "Fugue State as a Literary Device in 'Cats in the Rain' and 'Hills Like White Elephants,'" *Arizona Quarterly*, XLIV (Summer 1988), 98–106.

Brown, Nancy Hemond. "Aspects of the Short Story: A Comparison of Jean Rhys's 'The Sound of the River' with Ernest Hemingway's "Hills Like White Elephants,'" *Jean Rhys Review*, I, i (1986), 2–13.

Chatman, Seymour. "Towards a Theory of Narrative," *New Literary Theory*, VI (1975), 295–318.

Consigny, Scott. "Hemingway's 'Hills Like White Elephants,'" *Explicator*, XLVIII (Fall 1989), 54–55.

Curnutt, Kirk. *Wise Economies: Brevity and Storytelling in American Short Stories* (Moscow, Ida., 1997), pp. 159–172.

DeFalco, Joseph. *The Hero in Hemingway's Short Stories* (Pittsburgh, 1963), pp. 168–172.

Elliott, Gary D. "Hemingway's 'Hills Like White Elephants,'" *Explicator*, XXXV (Summer 1977), 22–23.

Fleming, Robert E. "An Early Manuscript of Hemingway's 'Hills Like White Elephants,'" *Notes on Modern American Literature*, VII (Spring-Summer 1983), Item 3.

Fletcher, Mary Dell. "Hemingway's 'Hills Like White Elephants,'" *Explicator*, XXXVIII (Summer 1980), 16–18.

Flora, Joseph M. *Ernest Hemingway: A Study of the Short Fiction* (Boston, 1989), pp. 33–35, 38–39.

Gerlach, John C. *Toward the End: Closure and Structure in the American Short Story* (University, Ala., 1985), pp. 112–115.

Giger, Romeo. *The Creative Void: Hemingway's Iceberg Theory* (Bern, 1977), pp. 37–50.

Gilligan, Thomas Maher. "Topography in Hemingway's 'Hills Like White Elephants,'" *Notes on Modern American Literature*, VIII (Spring–Summer 1984).

Gilmour, David R. "Hemingway's 'Hills Like White Elephants,'" *Explicator*, XLI (Summer 1983), 47–49.

Grebstein, Sheldon. *Hemingway's Craft* (Carbondale, Ill, 1973), pp. 110–113.

Grimes, Larry E. *The Religious Design of Hemingway's Early Fiction* (Ann Arbor, 1985), pp. 71–73.

Gullason, Thomas A. "The 'Lesser' Renaissance: The American Short Story in the 1920s," The American Short Story, 1900–1945: A Critical History, Philip Stevick, ed. (Boston, 1984), pp. 85–92. (G)

Gurko, Leo. *Ernest Hemingway and the Pursuit of Heroism* (New York, 1968), pp. 191–193.

Hannum, Howard L. "'Jig Jig to dirty ears': White Elephants to Let," *Hemingway Review*, XI (Fall 1991), 46–54.

Hardy, Donald E. "Presupposition and the Coconspirator," *Style*, XXVI (1992), 6–8.

Hays, Peter L. *Ernest Hemingway* (New York, 1990), pp. 56–58.

Hildy, Coleman. "'Cat' and 'Hills': Two Hemingway Fairy Tales," *Hemingway Review*, XII (Fall 1992), 67–72.

Hollander, John. "Hemingway's Extraordinary Reality," Ernest Hemingway, Harold Bloom, ed. (New York, 1985), pp. 211–216.

Hughes, Kenneth J. *Signs of Literature: Language, Ideology and Literary Text*, (Vancouver, 1986), pp. 157–166.

Jain, S. P. *Hemingway: A Study of His Short Stories* (New Delhi, 1985), pp. 77–80.

———. "'Hills Like White Elephants': A Study," *Indian Journal of American Studies*, I (1970), 33–38.

Johnston, Kenneth G. "'Hills Like White Elephants': Lean, Vintage Hemingway," *Studies in American Fiction*, X (1982), 233–238.

———. *The Tip of the Iceberg: Hemingway and the Short Story* (Greenwood, Fla., 1987), pp. 125–134.

Kelly, Lionel. "Hemingway and Fitzgerald: Two Short Stories," *Re-reading the Short Story*, Clare Hanson, ed. (New York, 1989), 98–104.

Kobler, J. F. "Hemingway's 'Hills Like White Elephants,'" *Explicator*, XXXVIII (Summer 1980), 6–7.

Kozikowski, Stanley. "Hemingway's 'Hills Like White Elephants,'" *Explicator*, LII (Winter 1994), 107–109.

Kraus, W. Keith. "Ernest Hemingway's 'Hills Like White Elephants': A Note on a 'Reasonable' Source," *English Record*, XXI (December 1970), 23–27.

Lamb, Robert Paul. "Hemingway and the Creation of Twentieth-Century Dialogue," *Twentieth-Century Literature*, 42 (Winter 1996), 453–480. (G)

Lanier, Doris. "The Bittersweet Taste of Absinthe in Hemingway's 'Hills Like White Elephants,'" *Studies in Short Fiction*, XXVI (Summer 1989), 279–288.

Lansky, Ellen. "Two Unfinished Beers: A Note on Drinking in Hemingway's 'Hills Like White Elephants,'" *Dionysus: The Literature of Addiction Triquarterly*, V, 2 (1993), 28–30.

Lid, Richard. "Hemingway and the Need for Speech," *Modern Fiction Studies*, VIII (Winter 1962–1963), 403–407.

Maynard, Reid. "Leitmotif and Irony in Hemingway's 'Hills Like White Elephants,'" *University Review*, XXXVII (Summer 1971), 273–275.

Messent, Peter. *Ernest Hemingway*, pp. 89–92.

Nagel, James. "Hills Like White Elephants," *Reference Guide to Short Fiction*, Noelle Watson, ed. (Detroit, 1994), pp. 735–736.

O'Brien, Timothy D. "Allusion, Word-Play, and the Central Conflict in Hemingway's 'Hills Like White Elephants,'" *Hemingway Review*, XII (Fall 1992), 19–25.

Organ, Dennis. "Hemingway's 'Hills Like White Elephants,'" *Explicator*, XXXVII (Summer 1979), 11.

Passey, Laurie. "Hemingway's 'Hills Like White Elephants,'" *Explicator*, XLVI (Summer 1988), 32–33.

Rao, P. G. Rama. *Ernest Hemingway: A Study in Narrative Technique* (New Delhi, 1980), pp. 102–104.

Renner, Stanley. "Moving to the Girl's Side of 'Hills Like White Elephants,'" *Hemingway Review*, XV (Fall 1995), 27–41.

Rodriques, Eusebio L. "'Hills Like White Elephants': An Analysis," *Literary Criterion*, V (1962), 105–109.

Sipiora, Philip. "Hemingway's 'Hills Like White Elephants,'" *Explicator*, XLII (Spring 1984), 50.

Smiley, Pamela. "Gender-Linked Miscommunication in 'Hills Like White Elephants,'" *Hemingway Review*, VIII (Fall 1988), 2–12.

Smith, Paul. "Hemingway's Luck," *Hemingway Review*, VII (Fall 1987), 38–42.

———. *A Reader's Guide to the Short Stories of Ernest Hemingway* (Boston, 1989), pp. 204–212.

Stampfl, Barry. "Similes as Thematic Clues in Three Hemingway Stories," *Hemingway Review*. X (Spring 1991), 30–38.

Trilling, Lionel. *Prefaces to the Experience of Literature* (New York, 1979), pp. 145–149.

Urgo, Joseph. "Hemingway's 'Hills Like White Elephants,'" *Explicator*, XLVI (Spring 1988), 35–37.

Weeks, Lewis E., Jr. "Hemingway's Hills: Symbolism in 'Hills Like White Elephants,'" *Studies in Short Fiction*, XVII (Winter 1980), 75–77.

Whitlow, Roger. *Cassandra's Daughters: The Women in Hemingway* (Westport, Conn., 1984), pp. 93–96.

Wright, Austin McGiffert. *The American Short Story in the Twenties* (Chicago, 1961), pp. 370–373.

ERNEST HEMINGWAY, "Indian Camp"

Adair, William. "A Source for Hemingway's 'Indian Camp,'" *Studies in Short Fiction*, 28 (Winter 1991), 93–95.

Benson, Jackson J. "Ernest Hemingway as Short Story Writer," *The Short Stories of Ernest Hemingway: Critical Essays*, Jackson J. Benson, ed. (Durham, N.C., 1975), pp. 272–310. (G)

Bayley, John. *The Short Story: Henry James to Elizabeth Bowen* (New York, 1988), pp. 78–80.

Bernard, Kenneth. "Hemingway's 'Indian Camp,'" *Studies in Short Fiction*, 2 (Spring 1965), 291.

Burhans, Clinton S. "The Complex Unity of *In Our Time*," *Modern Fiction Studies*, 14 (1968), 313–328.

DeFalco, Joseph. *The Hero in Heminway's Short Stories* (Pittsburgh, 1963), pp. 27–33.

Flora, Joseph M. "A Closer Look at the Young Nick Adams and His Father," *Studies in Short Fiction*, 14 (1977), 75–78.

———. *Hemingway's Nick Adams* (Baton Rouge, 1982), pp. 22–35.

Grimes, Larry. "Night, Terror and Morning Calm: A Reding of Hemingway's 'Indian Camp' as a Sequel to 'Three Shots,'" *Studies in Short Fiction*, 12 (1976), 413–415.

———. *The Religious Design of Hemingway's Early Fiction* (Ann Arbor, 1985), pp. 55–58.

Hannum, Howard L. "The Case of Dr. Henry Adams," *Arizona Quarterly*, 44, No. 2 (1988), 40–43.

Johnston, Kenneth G. "In the Beginning: Hemingway's 'Indian Camp,'" *Studies in Short Fiction*, 15 (1978), 102–104.

Joost, Nicholas. *Ernest Hemingway and the Little Magazines: The Paris Years* (Barre, Mass., 1968), pp. 84–86.

Lynn, Kenneth. *Hemingway* (New York, 1987), pp. 227–229.

Meyers, Jeffrey. "Hemingway's Primitivism and 'Indian Camp,'" *Twentieth-Century Literature*, 34 (Summer 1988), 117–120.

Monteiro, Geoge. "The Limits of Professionalism: A Sociological Approach to Faulkner, Fitzgerald and Hemingway," *Criticism*, 15 (Spring 1973), 145–155.

Montgomery, Constance. *Hemingway in Michigan* (New York, 1966, 1977), pp. 56–64.

Nashal, Chaman. *The Narrative Pattern in Ernest Hemingway's Fiction* (Rutherford, N.J., 1971), pp. 87–91.

Nichols, Olivia Murray. "An Example of Folklore in Hemingway's 'Indian Camp,'" *Kentucky Folklore Record*, 27 (1981), 33–35.

Oldsey, Bernard. "Hemingway's Beginnings and Endings," *College Literature*, 7 (Fall 1980), 213–238.

Penner, Dick. "The First Nick Adams Story," *Fitzgerald/Hemingway Annual* (1975), 195–202.

Rovit, Earl and Garry Brenner. *Ernest Hemingway* (Boston, 1986), pp. 160, 161.

Shaw, Samuel. *Ernest Hemingway*, (New York, 1973), pp. 29–31.

Slatoff, Walter. *The Look of Distance: Reflections on Suffering & Sympathy in Modern Literature—Audubon to Agee, Whitman to Woolf* (Columbus, Ohio, 1985), pp. 21–24.

Smith, Paul. "Hemingway's Early Manuscripts: The Theory and Practice of Omission," *Journal of Modern Literature*, 10 (July 1983), 268–288.

———. *A Reader's Guide to the Short Stories of Ernest Hemingway* (Boston, 1989), pp. 34–42.

———. "The Tenth Indian and the Thing Left Out," *Ernest Hemingway: The Writer in Context*, James Nagel, ed. (Madison, Wisc., 1984), pp. 53–74.

Strong, Amy Lovell. "Screaming Through Silence: The Violence of Race in 'The Doctor and the Doctor's Wife' and 'Indian Camp,'" *Hemingway Review*, 16 (Fall 1996), 18–32.

Strong, Paul. "The First Nick Adam Stories," *Studies in Short Fiction*, 28 (Winter 1991), 83–91.

Tanselle, G. Thomas. "Hemingway's 'Indian Camp,'" *Explicator* 20 (February 1962), Item, 53.

Wainwright, J. Andrew. "The Far Shore: Gender Complexities in Hemingway's 'Indian Camp,'" *Dalhousie Review*, 66 (1986), 181–187.

Waldhorn, Arthur. *A Reader's Guide to Ernest Hemingway* (New York, 172), pp. 54–55.
Watson, William Braasch. "The Doctor and the Doctor's Son: Immortalities in 'Indian Camp.'" *Hemingway: Up in Michigan Perspectives*, Frederic J. Svoboda and Joseph J. Waldmeir, eds. (East Lansing, Michigan, 1995), pp. 37–45.
Wolter, Jurgen C. "Caesareans in an Indian Camp," *Hemingway Review*, 13, No. 1 (1993), 92–94.
Workman, Brooke. *In Search of Ernest Hemingway: A Model for Teaching a Literature Seminar* (Urbana, Ill., 1979), pp. 11–18.
Young, Philip. "'Big World Out There': The Nick Adams Stories," *The Short Stories of Ernest Hemingway: Critical Essays*, Jackson J. Benson, ed. (Durham, N.C., 1975), pp. 29–45.
———. "Letter to the Editor," *Studies in Short Fiction*, 3 (Fall 1965), ii–iii.

ZORA NEALE HURSTON, "Spunk"

Bone, Robert. *Down Home: A History of Afro-American Short Fiction From Its Beginnings to the End of the Harlem Renaissance* (New York, 1975), pp. 122–123, 141–150.
Cobb-Moore, Geneva. "Zora Neale Hurston as Local Colorist," *Southern Literary Journal*, XXVI (Spring 1994), 25–34.
Hale, Dale G. "Hurston's 'Spunk' and Hamlet," *Studies in Short Fiction*, XXX (Summer 1993), 397–398.
Hemenway, Robert E. *Zora Neale Hurston: A Literary Biography* (Urbana, Ill., 1977). (G)
Howard, Lillie P. *Zora Neale Hurston* (New York, 1980). (G)
Perry, Margaret. *Silence to the Drums: A Survey of the Literature of the Harlem Renaissance* (Westport, Conn., 1976), pp. 121–124.

JOHN IRVING, "Trying to Save Piggy Sneed"

Budd, John. "The Inadequacy of Brevity: John Irving's Short Fiction, XXVI (Spring 1985), 4–6. (G)
Campbell, Josie P. *John Irving: A Critical Companion* (Westport, Conn., 1998), pp. 7–8.
McCaffrey, Larry. "An Interview with John Irving," *Contemporary Literature*, XXIII (Winter 1982), 1–18. (G)
Miller, Gabriel. *John Irving* (New York, 1982). (G)
Priestly, Michael. "An Interview with John Irving," *New England Review* (Summer 1979), 489–504. (G)
Reilly, Edward C. "Life Into Art: Some Notes on Irving's Fiction," *Notes on Contemporary Literature*, XIII (September 1983), 8–9. (G)
———. *Understanding John Irving* (Columbia, S.C., 1991). (G)
Shostak, Debra. "Plot as Repetition: John Irving's Narrative Experiments," *Critique*, XXXVII (Fall 1995), 51–70. (G)

WASHINGTON IRVING, "The Legend of Sleepy Hollow"

Achilles, Jochen. "Washington Irving: 'The Legend of Sleepy Hollow'—ein prekarer amerikanischer Traum vom guten Leben," *Die englische und amerikanische Kurzgeschichte*, Klaus Lubbers, ed. (Darmstadt, Germany, 1990), pp. 1–11.
Bedell, Rebecca. "John Quidor and the Demonic Imagination: 'Ichabod Crane Flying from the Headless Horseman (c. 1828)," *Yale Journal of Criticism*, 11 (Spring 1998), 111–118.

Bone, Robert A. "Irving's Headless Hessian: Prosperity and the Inner Life," *American Quarterly*, XV (Summer 1963), 167–175.

Bowden, Mary W. *Washington Irving* (Boston, 1981), pp. 72–74.

Brooks, E. L. "A Note on Irving's Sources," *American Literature*, XXV (May 1953), 229–230.

Bruner, Marjorie. "'The Legend of Sleepy Hollow': A Mythological Parody," *College English*, XXV (January 1964), 274, 279–283

Clark, James W., Jr. "Washington Irving and New England Witchlore," *New York Folklore Quarterly*, XXIX (December 1973), 304–311.

Clendenning, John. "Irving and the Gothic Tradition," *Bucknell Review*, XII (May 1964), 90–98.

Coad, Oral Sumner. "The Gothic Element in American Literature before 1835," *Journal of English and German Philology*, XXIV (January 1925), 72–93.

Conley, Patrick T. "The Real Ichabod Crane," American Literature, XL (March 1968), 70–71.

Curnutt, Kirk. *Wise Economies: Brevity and Storytelling in American Short Stories* (Moscow, Ida., 1997), pp. 27–41.

Current-Garcia, Eugene. "Irving Sets the Pattern: Notes on Professionalism and the Art of the Short Story," *Studies in Short Fiction*, X (Fall 1973), 327–341. (G) See, also, Eugene Current-Garcia, *The American Short Story Before 1850: A Critical History* (Boston, 1985), pp. 25–41.

Daigrepont, Lloyd M. "Ichabod Crane: Inglorious Man of Letters," *Early American Literature*, XIX (1984), 68–81.

Daniels, Howell. "Washington Irving and the Land of Was," *The Nineteenth-Century American Short Story*, A. Robert Lee, ed. (Totowa, N.J., 1985), pp. 40–56. (G)

Eby, Cecil D., Jr. "Ichabod Crane in Yoknapatawpha," *Georgia Review*, XVI (Winter 1962), 465–469.

Eckley, Wilton, "The Legend of Sleepy Hollow," *Reference Guide to Short Fiction*, Noelle Watson, ed. (Detroit 1994), pp. 771–772.

Guttmann, Allen. "Washington Irving and the Conservative Imagination,", *American Literature*, XXXVI (May 1964), 165–173.

Hedges, William L. *Washington Irving: An American Study, 1802–1832* (Baltimore, 1965), pp. 141–143.

Hoffman, Daniel G. "Irving's Use of American Folklore in 'The Legend of Sleepy Hollow,'" *PMLA*, LXVII (June 1953), 425–435.

———. "Prefigurations: 'The Legend of Sleepy Hollow,'" *Form and Fable in American Fiction* (New York, 1961), pp. 83–96.

Kempton, Kenneth. *The Short Story* (Cambridge, Mass., 1947), pp. 79–81.

Leary, Lewis. "The Two Voices of Washington Irving," *From Irving to Steinbeck: Studies in American Literature in Honor of Harry R. Warfel*, Motley Deakin and Peter Lisca, ed (Gainesville, Fla., 1972), pp. 13–26.

McClary, Ben H. "Ichabod Crane's Scottish Origin," *Notes & Queries*, XV (January 1968), 29.

Malin, Irving. "Secret Oppositions," *Approaches to the Short Story*, Neil D. Isaacs and Lou H. Leiter, eds. (San Francisco, 1963), pp. 56–63.

Martin, Terence. "Rip, Ichabod, and the American Imagination," *American Literature*, XX (May 1959), 137–149.

Mellard, James M. *Four Modes: A Rhetoric of Modern Fiction* (New York, 1973), pp. 119–122.

Mengeling, Marvin. "Irving's Knickerbocker Folktales," *American Transcendental Quarterly*, XL (1978), 355–364. (G)

Messenger, Christian K. *Sport and the Spirit of Play in American Fiction: Hawthorne Faulkner* (New York, 1981), pp. 41–44.

Pajak, E. "Washington Irving's Ichabod Crane: American Narcissus," *American Imago*, XXXVIII (1981), 127–135.

Piacentino, Ed. "'Sleepy Hollow' Comes South: Washington Irving's Influence on Old Southern Humor," *Southern Literary Journal*, 30 (Fall 1997), 27–42.

Plummer, Laura, and Michael Nelson. "'Girls can take care of themselves': Gender and Storytelling in Washington Irving's 'The Legend of Sleepy Hollow,'" *Studies in Short Fiction*, XXX (Spring 1993), 175–185.

Pochmann, Henry A. "Irving's German Sources in *The Sketch Book*," *Studies in Philology*, XXVII (July 1930), 477–507.

Reed, Herbert. "Ichabod Crane and Washington Irving," *Staten Island Historian*, XXIV (April–June 1963), 9–11.

Reed, Kenneth T. "On These Women! These Women!: Irving's Shrews and Coquettes," *American Notes and Queries*, VIII (June 1970), 147–150.

Reichart, Walter A. *Washington Irving and Germany* (Ann Arbor, 1957), pp. 30–32.

———. "Washington Irving's Interest in German Folklore," *New York Folklore Quarterly*, XI (Autumn 1957), 181–192,

Ringe, Donald A. *American Gothic: Imagination and Realism in Nineteenth-Century Fiction* (Lexington, Ky., 1982), pp. 92–94.

———. "Irving's Use of the Gothic Mode," *Studies in Literary Imagination*, VIII (Spring 1974 51–65. (G)

———. "New York and New England: Irving's Criticism of American Society," *American Literature*, XXXVIII (January 1967), 455–467.

———. *The Pictorial Mode: Space and Time in the Art of Bryant, Irving, and Cooper* (Lexington, Ky., 1971), pp. 188–190.

Rodes, Sara P. "Washington Irving's Use of Traditional Folklore," *Southern Folklore Quarterly*, XX (September 1956), 143–153.

Roth, Martin. *Comedy and America: The Lost World of Washington Irving* (Port Washington, N.Y., 1976), pp. 161–168.

———. "The Final Chapter of Knickerbocker's New York," *Modern Philology*, LXVI (February 1969), 248–255.

Rubin-Dorsky, Jeffrey. *Adrift in the Old World: The Psychological Pilgrimage of Washington Irving* (Chicago, 1988), pp. 104–111, 115–120.

———. "Washington Irving and the Genesis of the Fictional Sketch," *Early American Literature*, XXI (Winter 1986/1987), 226–247. (G)

———. "Washington Irving as an American Romantic," *The Old and the New World Romanticism of Washington Irving*, Stanley Brodwin, ed. (Westport, Conn., 1986), pp. 35–48.

———. "The Value of Storytelling: 'Rip Van Winkle' & 'The Legend of Sleepy Hollow' in the Context of *The Sketch Book*," *Modern Philology*, LXXXII (May 1985), 393–406.

Seed, David. "The Art of Literary Tourism: An Approach to Washington Irving's *Sketch Book*," *Ariel*, XIV (April 1983), 68–82.

Seelye, John. "Root and Branch: Washington Irving and American Humor," *Nineteenth-Century Fiction*, XXXVIII (March 1984), 415–425.

Shaw, Valerie. *The Short Story: A Critical Introduction* (London, 1983), pp. 159–165. (G)

Shear, Walter. "Time in 'Rip Van Winkle' and 'The Legend of Sleepy Hollow,'" *Midwest Quarterly*, XVII (January 1876), 158–172.

Smith, Herbert F. "The Spell of Nature in Irving's Famous Stories," *Washington Reconsidered: A Symposium*, Ralph M. Aderman, ed. (Hartford, Conn., 1969), pp. 18–21. See, also, *American Transcendental Quarterly*, V (First Quarter 1970), 14–18.

Springer, Haskell S., "Creative Contradictions in Irving," *Washington Irving Reconsidered: A Symposium*, Ralph M. Aderman, ed. (Hartford, Conn., 1969), pp. 14–18.

———. "Introduction," *Rip Van Winkle and the Legend of Sleepy Hollow* (Tarrytown, 1974), pp. 7–15.

Strobridge, Truman S. and Edwin Tumbladh. "Lieutenant Ichabod Crane, United States Marine Corps," *Proceedings of the New Jersey Historical Society*, LXXXIV (July 1966), 170–173.

von Frank, Albert J. " The Man That Corrupted Sleepy Hollow," *Studies in American Fiction*, XV (Autumn 1987), 129–143.

WASHINGTON IRVING, "Rip Van Winkle"

Barbarese, J. T. "Landscape of the American Psyche," *Sewanee Review*, C (1992), 599–603.

Beebe, Richard T. "Hunter's Syndrome: Gargoyles—Washington Irving—'Rip Van Winkle,'" *Bulletin of the History of Medicine*, XLIV (1970), 582–585.

Beranger, Jean. "Analyses structurales de 'Rip Van Winkle,'" *Revuew Française de-Études Américaines*, V (April 1978), 33–45.

Bowden, Mary Weatherspoon. *Washington Irving* (Boston, 1981), pp. 59, 61–63.

Brooke, Rose Christine. *A Rhetoric of the Unreal* (Cambridge, England, 1981), pp. 106–112.

Brooks, Elmer L. "A Note on the Source of 'Rip Van Winkle,'" *American Literature*, XXV (January 1954), 495–496.

Cameron, Kenneth W. "The Long-Sleep-and-Changed-World Motif in 'Rip Van Winkle,'" *Emerson Society Quarterly*, XIX (Second Quarter 1960), 35–36.

Clendenning, John. "Irving and the Gothic Tradition," *Bucknell Review*, XII (May 1964), 90–98.

Curnutt, Kirk. *Wise Economies: Brevity and Storytelling in American Short Stories* (Moscow, Ida., 1997), pp. 27–33.

Current-Garcia, E. "Irving Sets the Pattern: Notes on Professionalism and the Art of the Short Story," *Studies in Short Fiction*, X (Fall 1973), 327–341. (G)

Dawson, William P. "'Rip Van Winkle' as Bawdy Satire: The Rascal and the Revolution," *ESQ: A Journal of the American Renaissance*, XXVII (1981), 198–206.

Daigrepont, Lloyd M. "'Rip Van Winkle' and the Gnostic Vision of History," *Clio*, XV (Fall 1985), 47–59.

Fetterley, Judith. *The Resisting Reader: A Feminist Approach to American Fiction* (Bloomington, Ind., 1978), pp. 1–11.

Fiedler, Leslie A. *Love and Death in the American Novel* (Cleveland, 1962), pp. 332–336.

Gerlach, John C. *Toward the End: Closure and Structure in the American Short Story* (University, Ala., 1985), pp. 41–47.

Haberly, David T. "Form and Fiction in the New World Legend," *Do Americans Have a Common Literature?*, Gustavo Perez Firmat, ed. (Durham, 1990), pp. 47–53.

Hagopian, John V. and Martin Dolch, eds. *Insight I. Analyses of American Literature* (Frankfurt, 1962), pp. 123–128.

Hedges, William L. *Washington Irving: An American Study, 1802–1832* (Baltimore, 1965), pp. 137–141.

Heiman, Marcel. "'Rip Van Winkle': A Psychoanalytic Note on the Story and Its Author," *American Imago*, XVI (Spring 1959), 3–47.

Kann, David. "'Rip Van Winkle': Wheels within Wheels," *American Imago*, XXXVI (Summer 1979), 178–196.

Karcher, Carolyn. "Patriarchal Society, Matriarchal Family in Irving's 'Rip Van Winkle' and Child's 'Hilda Silfvering,'" *Legacy*, II (Fall 1985), 31–53.

Krumpelmann, John T. "Revealing the Source of Irving's 'Rip Van Winkle,'" *Monatshefte*, XLVII (November 1955), 361–362.

Larson, Charles R. "Dame Van Winkle's Burden," *Colorado Quarterly*, XVII (Spring 1969), 407–410.

Lee, Helen. "Clue Patterns in 'Rip Van Winkle,'" *English Journal*, LX (February 1966), 192–194, 200.

LeFevre, Louis. "Paul Bunyan and Rip Van Winkle," *Yale Review*, XXXVI (Autumn 1946), 66–76.

Lloyd, Francis W. "Irving's 'Rip Van Winkle,'" *Explicator*, IV (February 1946), Item 26.

Loving, Jerome. *Lost in the Customhouse: Authorship in the American Renaissance* (Iowa City, Ia., 1993), pp. 10–13.

Lynen, John F. *The Design of the Present: Essays on Time and Form in American Literature* (New Haven, 1969), pp. 153–166.

Martin, Terence. "Rip, Ichabod, and the American Imagination," *American Literature*, XXXI (May 1959), 137–149.

Mengeling, Marvin E. "Characterization in 'Rip Van Winkle,'" *English Journal*, LIII (December 1964), 643–646.

———. "Structure and Tone in 'Rip Van Winkle': The Irony of Silence," *Discourse*, IX (Autumn 1966), 457–463.

Pearce, Colin D. "Changing Regimes: The Case of Rip Van Winkle," *Clio*, XXII (Winter 1993), 115–128.

Pease, Donald E. *Visionary Compacts: American Renaissance Writings in Cultural Contexts* (Madison, 1987), pp. 12–17.

Plung, Daniel L. "'Rip Van Winkle': Metempsychosis and the Quest for Self-Reliance," *Rocky Mountain Review*, XXXI (1977), 65–80.

Pochmann, Henry A. "Irving's German Sources in *The Sketch Book.*" *Studies in Philology*, XXVII (July 1930), 477–507.

Reed, Kenneth R. "Oh, These Women! These Women!: Irving's Shrews and Coquettes," *American Notes and Queries*, VIII (June 1970), 147–150.

Reichart, Walter. "Concerning the Source of Irving's 'Rip Van Winkle,'" *Monatshefte*, XLVIII (February 1956), 94–95.

Ringe, Donald A. "New York and New England: Irving's Criticism of American Society," *American Literature*, XXXVIII (January 1967), 455–467.

Rodes, Sara P. "Washington Irving's Use of Traditional Folklore," *Southern Folklore Quarterly*, XX (September 1956), 143–153.

Roth, Martin. *Comedy in America: The Lost World of Washington Irving* (Port Washington, N.Y., 1976), pp. 151–161.

———. "The Final Chapter of Knickerbocker's *New York*," *Modern Philology*, LXVI (February 1969), 248–255.

Rubin-Dorsky, Jeffrey. *Adrift in the Old World: The Psychological Pilgrimage of Washington Irving* (Chicago, 1988), pp. 73–76, 100–104, 110–115.

Schik, Berthold. "Washington Irving: 'Rip Van Winkle,'" *Interpretationen zu Irving, Melville und Poe*, Hans Finger, ed. (Frankfurt, 1971) pp. 7–21.

Seed, David. "The Art of Literary Tourism: An Approach to Washington Irving's 'Sketch Book,'" *Ariel*, XIV (April 1983), 67–82.

Shear, Walter. "Cultural Fate and Social Freedom in Three American Short Stories," *Studies in Short Fiction*, XXIX (Fall 1992), 543–549.

———. "Time in 'Rip Van Winkle' and 'The Legend of Sleepy Hollow,'" *Midwest Quarterly*, XVII (January 1976), 158–172.

Smith, Herbert F. "The Spell of Nature in Irving's Famous Stories," *American Transcendental Quarterly*, V (First Quarter 1970), 18–21.

Springer, Haskell S. "Creative Contradictions in Irving," *American Transcendental Quarterly*, V (First Quarter 1970), 14–18.

Thompson, John B. "The Genesis of the Rip Van Winkle Legend," *Harper's Monthly Magazine*, LXVII (September 1983), 617–622.

Vance, W. Silas. "Mrs. Rip Van Winkle," *American Mercury*, LXXXVI (April 1958), 118–121.

Waldhorn, Arthur and Hilda. *The Rite of Becoming* (New York, 1966), pp. 273–274, 286–292.

Wells, Robert V. "While Rip Napped: Social Change in Late Eighteenth-Century New York," *New York History*, LXXI (January 1990), 5–23.

Wetzel, George. "Irving's 'Rip Van Winkle,'" *Explicator*, X (June 1952), Item 54.

Williams, Stanley T. *The Life of Washington Irving* (New York, 1935), I, pp. 183–187.

Wilson, Christopher Kent. "John Quidor's 'The Return of Rip Van Winkle' at the National Gallery of Art: The Interpretation of American Myth," *American Art Journal*, 19 (Spring 1985), 73–88.

Wolf, Bryan Jay. *Romantic Re-Vision: Culture and Consciousness in Nineteenth-Century American Painting and Literature* (Chicago, 1982), pp. 153–167.

Woodward, Robert H. "Dating the Action of 'Rip Van Winkle,'" *New York Folklore Quarterly*, XV (Spring 1959), 70.

Young, Philip. "Fallen From Time: The Mythic Rip Van Winkle," *Kenyon Review*, XXII (Autumn 1960), 547–573.

Yongue, Patricia Lee. "*The Professor's House* and 'Rip Van Winkle,'" *Western American Literature*, XVIII (Winter 1984), 281–297.

Zlogar, Richard J. "'Accessories That Covertly Explain': Irving's Use of Dutch Genre Painting in 'Rip Van Winkle,'" *American Literature*, LIV (March 1982), 44–62.

SHIRLEY JACKSON, "The Lottery"

Allen, Barbara. "A Folkloristic Look at Shirley Jackson's 'The Lottery,'" *Tennessee Folklore Society Bulletin*, XLVI (December 1980), 119–124.

Bagchee, Shyamal. "Design of Goodness in Shirley Jackson's 'The Lottery,'" *Notes on Contemporary Literature* IX (September 1979), 8–9.

Bobbitt, Randy. "The Spiral of Silence: A Sociological Interpretation of Shirley Jackson's 'The Lottery,'" *Notes on Contemporary Literature*, XXIV (January 1994), 8–9.

Brinkman, Horst. "Shirley Jackson's 'The Lottery,'" *In Die amerikanische Short Story der Gegenwart*, Peter Freese, ed. Berlin 1976), pp. 101–109.

Brooks, Cleanth and Robert Penn Warren. *Understanding Fiction* (New York, 1959), pp. 72–76.

Cervo, Nathan. "Jackson's 'The Lottery,'" *Explicator*, L (Spring 1992), 183–185.

Chaves, Ruthanne. "Student-Teacher Dramatization in 'The Lottery,'" *Exercise Exchange*, XV (Fall 1972), 6.

Church, Joseph. "Getting Taken in 'The Lottery,'" *Notes on Contemporary Literature*, XVI (September 1988), 10–11.

Coulthard, A. R. "Jackson's 'The Lottery,'" *Explicator*, XLVIII (1990), 226–228.

Egan, James. "Sanctuary: Shirley Jackson's Domestic and Fantastic Parables." *Studies in Weird Fiction*, VI (1989), 15–24.

Friedman, Lenemaja. *Shirley Jackson* (Boston, 1975), pp. 63–67.

Gibson, James M. "An Old Testament Analogue for 'The Lottery,'" *Journal of Modern Literature*, XI (March 1984), 193–195.

Gordon, Caroline and Allen Tate. *The House of Fiction* (New York, 1960), pp. 72–76.

Hagopian, John V, and Martin Dolch, eds. *Insight I, Analyses of American Literature* (Frankfurt, 1962), pp. 129–132.

Hall, Joan Wylie. *Shirley Jackson: A Study of the Short Fiction* (New York, 1993), pp. 48–53, 124–128, 171–174, 179–183.

Heller, Terry. "Shirley Jackson," *Critical Survey of Short Fiction*, Frank N. Magill, ed. (Englewood Cliffs, N.J., 1981), V, pp. 1672–1673.

Herrick, Casey. "Shirley Jackson's 'The Lottery,'" *Bulletin of Bibliography* XVVI (June 1989), 120–121.

Hilton, James. "The Focus of a Dream," *New York Herald Tribune Book Review* (May 1, 1949), 4.

Jackson, Shirley. "Biography of a Story," *Come Along with Me*, Stanley Edgar Hyman, ed. (New York, 1968), pp. 211–224.

Kittredge, Mary. "The Other Side of Magic: A Few Remarks about Shirley Jackson" *Discovering Modern Horror Fiction*, Darrell Schweitzer, ed. (Mercer Island, Wash.)

Kosenko, Peter. "A Marxist/Feminist Reading of Shirley Jackson's 'The Lottery,'" *New Orleans Review*, XII (Spring 1985), 27–32.

Lainoff, Seymour, "Jackson's 'The Lottery,'" *Explicator*, XII (March 1954), Item 34.

Nebeker, Helen E. "'The Lottery': Symbolic Tour de Force," *American Literature*, XLVI (March 1974), 100–107.

Oehlschlaeger, Fritz. "The Stoning of Mistress Flutchinson: Meaning and Context in 'The Lottery,'" *Essays in Literature*, XV (Fall 1988), 259–265.

Oppenheimer, Judy. *Private Demons: The Life of Shirley Jackson* (New York, 1988), pp. 127–133.

Robert, Edgar W. "Shirley Jackson's Dramatic Point of View in 'The Lottery,'" *Writing Themes About Literature* (Englewood Cliffs, N.J., 1973), pp. 61–64.

Schaub, Danielle. "Shirley Jackson's Use of Symbols in 'The Lottery,'" *Journal of the Short Story in English*, XIV (Spring 1990), 79—86.

Swenson, William G. *Great Themes in Short Fiction* (New York, 1975), pp. 43–46.

Wagner-Martin, Linda. "The Lottery," *Reference Guide to Short Fiction*, Noelle Watson, ed. (Detroit, 1994), 783–784.

Whittier, Gayle. "'The Lottery' as Misogynist Parable," *Women's Studies*, XVIII, 4 (1991), 353–356.

Williams, Richard H. " A Critique of the Sampling Plan Used in Shirley Jackson's 'The Lottery,'" *Journal of Modern Literature* VII (September 1979), 543–544.

Yarmove, Jay A. "Jackson's 'The Lottery,'" *Explicator*, LII (Summer 1994), 242–244.

HENRY JAMES, "Four Meetings"

Albers, Christina E. *A Reader's Guide to the Short Stories of Henry James* (New York, 1997), pp. 263–278.

Aziz, Magbool. "'Four Meetings': A Caveat for James Critics," *Essays in Criticism*, XVIII (July 1968), 258–274.

Bosanquet, Theodora. "The Revised Version," *Little Review*, V (August 1918), 56–62.

Buitenhuis, Peter. *The Grasping Imagination: The American Writings of Henry James* (Toronto, 1970), pp. 173–176.

Clair, John. *The Ironic Dimension in the Fiction of Henry James* (Pittsburgh, 1965), pp. 1–16.

Gargano, James W. "The 'Look' as a Major Event in James's Short Fiction," *Arizona Quarterly*, 35 (Winter 1979), 308–320.

Griffin, Robert J. "Notes Toward an Exegesis: 'Four Meetings,'" *University of Kansas City Review*, XXIX (October 1962), 45–49.

Gurko, Leo. "The Missing Word in Henry James 'Four Meetings,'" *Studies in Short Fiction*, VII (Spring 1970), 298–307.

Iwase, Shitsuyu. "Henry James: 'Four Meetings' Revised," *Queries*, III (June 1962), 9–22.

Jones, Leonidas M. "James's 'Four Meetings,'" *Explicator*, XX (March 1962), Item 55.

Kelley, Cornelia P. *The Early Development of Henry James* (Urbana, Ill., 1930), pp. 259–261.

Kraft, James. *The Early Tales of Henry James* (Carbondale and Edwardsville, Ill., 1969), pp. 99–102.

Martin, W. R. "The Narrator's 'Retreat in James's 'Four Meetings,'" *Studies in Short Fiction*, XVII (Fall 1980), 497–499.

Morgan, Alice. "Henry James: Money and Morality," *Texas Studies in Language and Literature*, 12 (1970), 75–92.

Seamon, Roger. "Henry James's 'Four Meetings': A Study of Irritability and Condescension," *Studies in Short Fiction*, XV (Spring 1978), 155–163.

Stowe, William W. *European Travel in Nineteenth-Century American Culture* (Princeton, N.J., 1994), pp. 180–182, 183–184.

Tartella, Vincent. "James's 'Four Meetings': Two Texts Compared," *Nineteenth-Century Fiction*, XV (June 1960), 17–28.

Vaid, Krishna Baldev. *Technique in the Tales of Henry James* (Cambridge, 1964), pp. 36–41.

Vanderbilt, Kermit. "Notes Largely Musical on Henry James's 'Four Meetings,'" *Sewanee Review*, LXXXI (October–December 1973), 739–752.

Wagenknecht, Edward. *The Tales of Henry James* (New York, 1984), pp. 9–12, 216.

HENRY JAMES, "The Real Thing"

Albers, Christina E. *A Reader's Guide to the Short Stories of Henry James* (New York, 1997), pp. 767–799.

Anderson, Quentin. *The American Henry James* (New Brunswick, N. J., 1957), pp. 142–146.

Auchard, John. *Silence in Henry James: The Heritage of Symbolism and Decadence* (University Park, Pa., 1986), pp. 37–39.

Banta, Martha. "Artists, Models, Real Things, and Recognizable Types," *Studies in the Literary Imagination*, XVI (Fall 1983), 7–34.

Baxter, Annette K. "Independence vs Isolation: Hawthorne and James on the Problem of the Artist," *Nineteenth-Century Fiction*, 10 (1955), 225–231.

Beaver, Harold. "'The Real Thing' and Unreal Things: Conflict of Art and Society in Henry James," *Fabula*, I (March 1983), 53–69.

Berkelman, Robert. "Henry James and 'The Real Thing,'" *University of Kansas City Review*, XXVI (Winter 1959), 93–95.

Bernard, Kenneth. "The Real Thing in James's 'The Real Thing,'" *Brigham Young University Studies*, V (Autumn 1962), 31–32.

Briden, E. F. "James's Miss Churm: Another of Eliza's Prototypes?," *Shaw Review*, XIX (January 1976), 17–21.

Fadiman, Clifton. "A Note on 'The Real Thing,'" *The Short Stories of Henry James* (New York, 1945), pp. 216–217.

Farnsworth, Robert. "The Real and the Exquisite in James's 'The Real Thing,'" *Literary Criterion*, 7, No. 4 (1967), 29–31.

Foff, Arthur and Daniel Knapp. "Analysis of 'The Real Thing,'" *Story: An Introduction to Prose Fiction* (Belmont, Cal., 1964), pp. 366–368.

Fusco, Richard. *Maupassant and the American Short Story: The Influence of Form at the Turn of the Century* (University Park, Pa., 1994), pp. 187–193.

Gale, Robert L. "H. J's J. H. in 'The Real Thing,'" *Studies in Short Fiction*, XIV (Fall 1977), 396–398).

———. "A Note on Henry James's 'The Real Thing,'" *Studies in Short Fiction*, I (Fall 1963), 65–66.

Gargano, James W. "The 'Look' as a Major Event in James's Short Fiction,," *Arizona Quarterly*, XXXV (Winter 1979), 303–320.

Henricksen, Bruce. "'The Real Thing': Criticism and the Ethical Turn," *Papers on Language and Literature*, XXVII (Fall 1991), 473–495.

Higgins, Charles. "Photographic Aperture: Coburn's Frontispiece to James's New York Edition," *American Literature*, 53 (1981), (661–675).

Horne, Helen. "Henry James: 'The Real Thing,' (1890): An Attempt at Interpretation," *Die Neuren Sprachen*, II (May 1959), 214–219.

Kehler, Harold. "James's 'The Real Thing,'" *Explicator*, XXV (May 1967), Item 79.

Labor, Earle. "James's 'The Real Thing': Three Levels of Meaning," *College English*, XXXIII (February 1962), 376–378.

Lackey, Kris. "Art and Class in 'The Real Thing," *Studies in Short Fiction*, 26 (Spring 1989), 190–192.

Lainoff, Seymour. "A Note on Henry James's 'The Real Thing,'" *Modern Language Notes*, LXXI (March 1956), 192–193.

Leavis, Q. D. "Henry James: The Stories," *Scrutiny*, 14 (Spring 1947), 223–229.

Lee, Woo-Kun. "The Real Approach to James's 'The Real Thing,'" *Journal of English Language and Literature*, II (1983), 21–31.

Lester, Pauline. "James's Use of Comedy in 'The Real Thing,'" *Studies in Short Fiction*, XV (Winter 1978), 33–38.

Lycette, Ronald L. "Perceptual Touchstones for the Jamesian Artist-Hero," *Studies in Short Fiction*, XIV (Winter 1977), 55–62.

McMurray, Andrew. "'In Their Own Language': Sarah Orne Jewett and the Question of Non-human Speaking Subjects," *Isle: Interdisciplinary Studies in Literature and the Environment*, 61 (Winter 1999), 51–63.

Marquardt, William F. "A Practical Approach to 'The Real Thing,'" *English "A" Analyst* (Northwestern University, 1949), 1–8.

Mellard, James M. *Four Modes: A Rhetoric of Modern Fiction* (New York, 1973), pp. 157–161.

Mueller, Lavonne. "Henry James: The Phenomenal Self in 'The Real Thing,'" *Forum*, VI (Spring 1968), 46–50.

Munson, Gorham, "'The Real Thing': A Parable for Writers of Fiction," *University of Kansas City Review*, XVI (Summer 1950), 261–264.

Nordloh, David. "First Appearance of Henry James's 'The Real Thing': The McClure Papers as Bibliographical Resources," *Papers of the Bibliographical Society of America*, LXXVIII, I (1984), 69–71.

Pendleton, James D. "The James Brothers and 'The Real Thing,'" *South Atlantic Bulletin*, XXXVIII, 4 (1973), 3–10.

Powers. Lyall H. "Henry James and the Ethics of the Artist: 'The Real Thing' and 'The Liar,'" *Texas Studies in Literature and Language*, III (Autumn 1961), 360–368.

Raeth, Claire. "The Real Approach to 'The Real Thing,'" *English "A" Analyst* (Northwestern University, 1949), 1–5.

Ron, Moshe. "A Reading of 'The Real Thing,'" *Yale French Studies*, LVIII (1979), 190–212.

Sanders, Thomas. *The Discovery of Fiction*, (Glenview, Ill., 1967), pp. 289–303, 331–333.

Shaw, Valerie. *The Short Story: A Critical Introduction* (London, 1983), pp. 69–75.

Smith, Virginia Llewellyn. *Henry James and the Real Thing*, A Modern Reader's Guide (New York, 1994), pp. 1–5.

Stone, Edward, ed. *Henry James: Seven Stories and Studies* (New York, 1961).

Telotte, J. P. "The Right Way with Reality: James's 'The Real Thing,'" *Henry James Review*, VI (Fall 1984), 8–14.

Thorberg, Raymond. "Henry James and 'The Real Thing': 'The Beldonald Holbein,'" *Southern Humanities Review*, III (1968), 78–85.

Toor, David. "Narrative Irony in Henry James' 'The Real Thing,'" *University Review*, XXXIV (Winter 1967), 95–99.

Uroff, "Perception in James's 'The Real Thing,'" *Studies in Short Fiction*, IX (Winter 1972), 41–46.

Vielledent, Catherine. "Representation and Reproduction: A Reading of Henry James's 'The Real Thing,'" *Interface: Essays on History, Myth, and Art in American Literature*, Daniel Royat, ed. (Montepelier, France, 1985), pp. 31–49.

Wagenknecht, Edward. *The Tales of Henry James* (New York, 1984), pp. 68–70.

Walcutt, Charles Child. "The Illusion of Action in Henry James," *Man's Changing Mask: Modes and Methods of Characterization in Fiction* (Minneapolis, 1966), pp. 175–211.

Whitsitt, Sam. "A Lesson in Reading: Henry James's 'The Real Thing,'" *Henry James Review*, XVI (Fall 1995), 304–314.

Wright, Walter. "'The Real Thing,'" *Research Studies of the State College of Washington*, XXV (March 1957), 85–90.

SARAH ORNE JEWETT, "A White Heron"

Ammons, Elizabeth. "The Shape of Violence in Jewett's 'A White Heron,'" *Colby Library Quarterly*, XXII (March 1986), 6–16.

Atkinson, Michael. "The Necessary Extravagance of Sarah Orne Jewett: Voices of Authority in 'A White Heron,'" *Studies in Short Fiction*, XIX (Winter 1982), 71–74.

Bader, Julia. "The Dissolving Vision: Realism in Jewett, Freeman, and Gilman," *American Realism: New Essays* Eric J. Sunquist, ed. (Baltimore, 1982), pp. 176–198. (G)

Bell, Pearl K. "Kate Chopin and Sarah Orne Jewett," *Partisan Review*, LV (1989), 238–253.

Bell, Michael Davitt, *The Problem of American Realism: Studies in the Cultural History of a Literary Idea* (Chicago, 1993), pp. 188–192.

Brenzo, Richard. "Free Heron or Dead Sparrow: Sylvia's Choice in Sarah Orne Jewett's 'A White Heron,'" *Colby Library Quarterly*, XIV (1978), 36–41.

Cary, Richard. *Sara Orne Jewett* (New York, 1962), pp. 101–105.

Curnutt, Kirk. *Wise Economies: Brevity and Storytelling in American Short Stories* (Moscow, Ida., 1997), pp. 101–115.

Donovan, Josephine. *New England Local Color Literature., A Women's Tradition* (New York, 1983), pp. 107–109.

———. *Sarah Orne Jewett* (New York, 1980), pp. 69–72.

———. "Silence or Capitulation: Prepatriarachal 'Mothers' Gardens' in Jewett and Freeman," *Studies in Short Fiction*, XXIII (Winter 1996), 43–48.

———. "A Woman's Vision of Transcendence: A New Interpretation of the Works of Sarah Orne Jewett," *Massachusetts Review*, XXI (Summer 1980), 365–380. (G)

Eakin, Paul John. "Sarah Orne Jewett and the Meaning of Country Life," *American Literature* XXXVI (January 1967), 508–531. (G)

Ellis, James. "The World of Dreams: Sexual Symbolism in 'A White Heron,'" *Nassau Review*, III, iii (1977), 3–9.

Gerlach, John C. *Toward the End., Closure and Structure in the American Short Story* (University, Ala., 1985), pp. 66–69.

Griffith, Kelly, Jr. "Sylvia as Hero in Sarah Orne Jewett's 'A White Heron,'" *Colby Library Quarterly*, XXI (March 1985), 22–27.

Held, George. "Heart to Heart with Nature: Ways of Looking at 'A White Heron,'" *Colby Library Quarterly*, XVIII (1982),55–65.

Heller, Terry. "The Rhetoric of Communion in Jewett's 'A White Heron,'" *Colby Quarterly* XXVI (September 1990), 182–194.

Heller, Terry. "Sarah Orne Jewett," *Critical Survey of Short Fiction*, Frank N. Magill, (Englewood Cliffs, N.J., 1981), V, 1697–1698.

Hovet, Theodore R. "American's 'Lonely Country Child': The Theme of Separation in Sarah Orne Jewett's 'A White Heron,'" *Colby Library Quarterly*, XIV (September 1978), 166–171.

———. "Once Upon a Time: Sarah Orne Jewett's 'A White Heron' as a Fairy Tale," *Studies in Short Fiction*, XV (Winter 1978), 63–68.

Jobes, Katherine T. "From Stowe's Eagle Island to Jewett's 'A White Heron,'" *Colby Library Quarterly*, X (December 1974), 515–521.

Johns, Barbara A. "'Mateless and Appealing': Growing into Spinsterhood in Sarah Orne Jewett," *Critical Essays on Sarah Orne Jewett*, Gwen L. Nagel, ed. (Boston, 1984), pp. 153–157.

Joseph, Sheri. "Sarah Orne Jewett's White Heron: An Imported Metaphor," *American Literary Realism*, XXVII (Spring 1995), 81–84.

Kelchner, Heidi. "Unstable Narrative Voice in Sarah Orne Jewett's 'A White Heron,'" *Colby Library Quarterly*. XXVIII (1992), 85–92.

Levy, Babette May. "Mutations in New England Color," *New England Quarterly*, XIX (September 1946), 338–358. (G)

Lutwack, Leonard. *Birds in Literature* (Gainesville, 1994), pp. 205–207.

Martin, Jay. *Harvests of Change: American Literature, 1865–1914* (Englewood Cliffs, N.J., 1967), pp. 142–148. (G)

Mobley, Marilyn S. *Folk Roots and Mythic Wings in Sarah Orne Jewett and Toni Morrison* (Baton Rouge, 1991), pp. 49–58.

Moreno, Karen K. "'A White Heron': Sylvia's Lonely Journey,'" *Connecticut Review*, XIII, i (191), 81–85.

Nagel, Gwen L. "A White Heron," *Reference Guide to Short Fiction*, Noelle Watson, ed. (Detroit, 1994), pp. 969–970.

Orr, Elaine. "Reading Negotiation and Negotiated Reading: A Practice with/in 'A White Heron' and 'The Revolt of "Mother,"'" *CEA Critic*, LIII (Spring/Summer 1991), 49–65.

Pool, Eugene Hillhouse. "The Child Is Sarah Orne Jewett," *Appreciation of Sarah Orne Jewett: 29 Interpretive Essays*, Richard Carey, ed. (Waterville, Me., 1973), pp. 223–228.

Renza, Louis M. *"A White Heron" and the Question of Minor Literature* (Madison, 1984).

Roman, Margaret. *Sarah Orne Jewett: Reconstructing Gender* (Tuscaloosa, Ala., 1992), pp. 190–192.

Rosenblum, Joseph. "A New England Heron on the Natchez Trace: Sarah Orne Jewett's 'A White Heron' As Possible Source for Eudora Welty's 'A Still Moment,'" *Notes on Mississippi Writers* XII, No. 2 (1990), 69–74.

Shaw, Valerie. *The Short Story: A Critical Introduction* (London, 1983), pp. 172–174.

Sherman, Sarah Way. *Sarah Orne Jewett: An American Persephone* (Hanover, N.H., 1989), pp. 154–169.

Singley, Carol J. "Reaching Lonely Heights: Sarah Orne Jewett, Emily Dickinson, and Female Initiation," *Colby Library Quarterly*, XXII (1986), 76–80.

Smith, Gayle L. "The Language of Transcendence in Sarah Orne Jewett's 'A White Heron,'" *Colby Library Quarterly*, XIX (March 1983), 37–44.

Stevenson, Catherine Bames. "The Double Consciousness of the Narrator in Sarah Orne Jewett's Fiction," *Colby Library Quarterly*, XI (March 1975), 1–12.

Votteler, Thomas, ed. *Short Story Criticism: Excerpts from Criticism of the Works of Short Fiction Writers*, VI (Detroit, 1990), pp. 148–183. (G)

Zanger, Jules. "'Young Goodman Brown' and 'A White Heron,': Correspondences and Illuminations," *Papers on Language and Literature*, YXVI (Summer 1990), 346–357.

DOROTHY M. JOHNSON, "The Man Who Shot Liberty Valance"

Alter, Judy. *Dorothy Johnson* (Boise, Id. 1980). (G)

———. "Dorothy M. Johnson," *Fifty Western Writers: A Bio-Bibliographical Sourcebook*, Fred Erisman and Richard W. Etulain, eds. (Westport, Conn., 1982), pp. 228–236. (G)

Bredahl, A. Carl, Jr. *New Ground: Western American Narrative and the Literary Canon* (Chapel Hill, 1989), pp. 153–155. (Film Version)

Hitt, Jim. *The American West from Fiction (1823–1976) into Film (1909–1986)* (Jefferson, N.C., 1990), pp. 262–264.

Mathews, Sue and James W. Healey. "The Winning of the Western Fiction Market: An Interview with Dorothy M. Johnson," *Prairie Schooner*, LII (Summer 1978), 158–167. (G)

Meldrum, Barbara H. "Dorothy Johnson's Short Fiction: the Pastoral and the Uses of History," *Western American Literature*, XVII (November 1982), 213–226.

Simon, William. "Liberty Valance Lives: Movies, Myths & Men," *Southwest Media Review*, III (Spring 1985), 64–69.

JAMES JOYCE, "Araby"

Atherton, J. S. "'Araby,'" *James Joyce's Dubliners: Critical Essays*, Clive Hart, ed. (London, 1969), pp. 39–47.

Barney, Rick, *et al.* "The MURGE Project: 'Araby' as Story and Discourse," *James Joyce Quarterly*, XVIII (Spring 1981), 237–254.

Baechler, Lea. "Voices of Unexpected Lyricism in Two Dubliners Stories," *James Joyce Quarterly* XXVIII (Winter 1991), 361–376.

Barisonzi, Judith. "Who Eats Pigs' Cheeks? Food and Class in 'Araby,'" *James Joyce Quarterly*, XXVIII (Winter 1991), 518–519.

Beck, Warren. *Joyce's Dubliner's: Substance, Vision, and Art* (Durham, N.C., 1969), pp. 96–109.

Beja, Morris. *James Joyce: A Literary Life* (London, 1992), pp. 31–39. (G)

Benstock, Bernard. "Arabesques: Third Position of Concord," *James Joyce Quarterly*, V (Fall 1967), 30–39.

———. "The Road to *Dubliners*," *James Joyce* (New York, 1985), pp. 23–47. (G)

Bidwell, Bruce and Linda Heffer. *The Joycean Way: A Topographic Guide to Dubliners & A Portrait of the Artist as a Young Man* (Baltimore, 1982), pp. 70–74.

Blythe, Hal, and Charlie Sweet. "Diptych in 'Araby': The Key to Understanding the Boy's 'Anguish and Anger,'" *Notes on Modern Irish Literature*, VI (1994), 16–18.

Bowen, Zak. *Musical Allusions in the Works of James Joyce* (Albany, 1974), pp. 13–14.

Brandabur, Edward. *A Scrupulous Meanness: A Study of Joyce's Early Work* (Urbana, Ill., 1971), pp. 49–56.

Brooks, Cleanth and Robert Penn Warren. *Understanding Fiction* (New York, 1959), pp. 189–192.

Brown, Terence. "The Dublin of *Dubliners*," *James Joyce: An International Perspective*, Suheil Badi Busbrui and Bernard Benstock, eds. (Totowa, N.J., 1982), pp. 11–18. (G)

Brugaletta, John J. and Mary H. Hayden. "The Motivation for Anguish in Joyce's 'Araby,'" *Studies in Short Fiction*, XV (Winter 1978), 11–17.

Burto, William. "Joyce's 'Araby,'" *Explicator*, XXV (April 1967), Item 67.

Carens, James F. "In Quest of a New Impulse: George Moore's *The Untilled Field* and James Joyce's *Dubliners*," *The Irish Short Story: A Critical History*, James F. Kilroy, ed. (Boston, 1984), pp. 75–77.

Collins, Ben L. "Joyce's 'Araby' And the Extended Simile," *James Joyce Quarterly*, IV (Winter 1967), 84–90.

Coulthard, A. R. "Joyce's 'Araby,'" *Explicator*, LII (Winter 1994), 97–99.

Cronin, Edward J. "James Joyce's Trilogy and Epilogue: 'The Sisters,' 'An Encounter,' 'Araby,' and 'The Dead,'" *Renascence*, XLI (Summer 1979), 229–248.

Dadufalza, Concepción D. "The Quest of the Chalice-Bearer in James Joyce's 'Araby,'" *Diliman Review*, VII (July 1959), 317–325.

———. "Aspects of Milton's Paradise Lost in James Joyce's 'Araby,'" *James Joyce Quarterly*, XXXIII (Fall 1969), 113–115.

Doloff, Steven. "On the Road with Loyola: St. Ignatius' Pilgrimage as Model for James Joyce's 'Araby,'" *James Joyce Quarterly*, XXVIIII (Winter 1991), 555–517.

Egan, Joseph J. "Romantic Ireland, Dead and Gone; Joyce's 'Araby' As National Myth," *Colby Library Quarterly*, XV (September 1979), 188–193.

Elbarbary, Samir. "The Theme of Idealised Love in 'Araby,'" *Journal of English*, XV (September 1987), 58–67.

Flynn, Elizabeth A. "Gender and Reading," *Gender and Reading: Essays on Readers, Texts, and Contexts*, Elizabeth A. Flynn and Patrocinio P. Schwiekart, eds. (Baltimore, 1986), pp. 367–388.

Freimarck, John. "'Araby': A Quest for Meaning," *James Joyce Quarterly*, VII (Summer 1970), 366–368.

French, Marilyn. "Missing Pieces in Joyce's *Dubliners*," *Twentieth-Century Literature*, XXIV (Winter 1978), 450–452.

Friedman, Stanley. "Joyce's 'Araby,'" *Explicator*, XXIV (January 1966), Item 43.

Fuller, James A. "A Note on Joyce's 'Araby,'" *CEA Critic*, XX (February 1958), 8.

Garrison, Joseph M. "The Adult Consciousness of the Narrator in Joyce's 'Araby,'" *Studies in Short Fiction*, X (Fall 1973), 416–419.

Gifford, Don. *Notes for Joyce* (New York, 1967), pp. 37–41.

Going, William T. "Joyce's 'Araby,'" *Explicator*, XXVI (January 1968), Item 39.

Hahn, H. George. "Tarsicius: A Hagiographical Allusion in Joyce's 'Araby,'" *Papers on Language and Literature*, XXVII (Summer 1991), 381–385.

Hamilton, Alice. "Between Innocence and Experience: From Joyce to Updike," *Dalhousie Review*, XLIX (Spring 1969), 102–104.

Hanson, Claire. *Short Stories and Short Fictions, 1880–1980* (New York, 1985), pp. 56–63. (G)

Head, Dominic. *The Modernist Short Story: A Study of Theory and Practice* (Cambridge, Eng., 1992), pp. 50–53.

Henke, Suzette A. *James Joyce and the Politics of Desire* (New York, 1990), pp. 19–21.

Herring, Phillip F. *Joyce's Uncertainty Principle* (Princeton, 1987), pp. 26–34.

Hirsch, David H. "Linguistic Structure and Literary Meaning," *Journal of Literary Semantics*, 1 (1972), 80–88.

Ingersoll, Earl G. *Engendered Trope in Joyce's Dubliners* (Carbondale, Ill., 1996), pp. 44–54.

Johnson, James D. "Joyce's 'Araby' And Romans VII and VlII," *American Notes and Queries*, XIII (November 1974), 38–40.

Kershner, R. B. *Joyce, Bakhtin, and Popular Literature: Chronicles of Disorder* (Chapel 1989), pp, 46–60.

LaHood, Marvin J. "A Note on the Priest in Joyce's 'Araby,'" *Revue des Langues Viva* XXXIV, No. I (1968), 24–25.

Lang, Frederick K. "Rite East of Joyce's 'Araby,'" *Journal of Ritual Studies*, I (Summer 1987) 111–120.

Leonard, Garry M. "The Question and the Quest: The Story of Mangan's Sister," *Modern Fiction Studies*, XXXV (Autumn 1989), 459–477.

———. *Reading Dubliners Again: A Lacanian Perspective* (Syracuse, 1993), pp. 73–94.

Litz, A. Walton, *James Joyce* (New York, 1966), pp. 51–53.

Lyons, John O. "James Joyce and Chaucer's Prioress," *English Language Notes*, II (December 1964), 127–132.

Magalaner, Marvin and Richard M. Kain. *Joyce: The Man, The Work, The Reputation* (New York, 1956), pp. 77–79.

Mandel, Jerome. "The Structure of 'Araby,'" *Modern Language Studies*, III (Spring 1973), 48.

Mellard, James M. *Four Modes: A Rhetoric of Modern Fiction* (New York, 1973), pp. 335–337.

Morrissey, L. J. "Joyce's Narrative Strategies in 'Araby,'" *Modern Fiction Studies*, XXVIII (Spring 1982), 45–52.

Morse, Donald E. "'Sing Three Songs of Araby': Theme and Structure in Joyce's 'Araby,'" *College Literature*, V (Spring 1978), 125–132.

Norris, Margot. "Blind Streets and Seeing Houses: Araby's Dim Glass Revisted," *Studies in Short Fiction*, 32 (Summer 1995), 309–318.

Peake, C. H. *James Joyce: The Citizen and the Artist* (Stanford, Calif., 1977), pp. 19–21.

Peters, Margot. "The Phonological Structure of James Joyce's 'Araby,'" *Language and Style*, VI (Spring 1973), 135–144.

Peterson, Richard F. *James Joyce Revisited* (New York, 1992), pp. 28–29.

Riquelme, John Paul. *Teller and Tale in Joyce's Fiction: Oscillating Perspectives* (Baltimore, 1983), pp. 106–108.

Robbins, Susan. "Anguish and Anger," *Virginia English Bulletin*, XXXVI (Winter 1986), 59–61.

Roberts, Robert P. "'Araby' and the Palimpsest of Criticism: Or *Through a Glass Eye Darkly*," *Antioch Review*, XXVI (Winter 1966–1967), 469–489.

Robinson, David W. "The Narration of Reading in Joyce's 'The Sisters,' 'An Encounter', and 'Araby,'" *Texas Studies in Literature and Language*, XXIX (1987), 387–392.

Rosowski, Susan L. "Joyce's 'Araby' and Imaginative Freedom," *Research Studies*, XLIV (September 1976), 183–188.

Russell, John. "From Style to Meaning in 'Araby,'" *College English*, XXVIII (November 1966), 170–171.

———. *Style in Modern British Fiction: Studies in Joyce, Lawrence, Forster, Lewis and Green* (Baltimore, 1978), pp. 27–31.

Ryf, Robert S. *A New Approach to Joyce* (Berkeley, 1962), pp. 63–65.

San Juan, Epifanio. *James Joyce and the Craft of Fiction: An Interpretation of Dubliners* (Rutherford, N.J., 1972), pp. 54–67.

Skau, Michael and Donald L. Cassidy. "Joyce's 'Araby,'" *Explicator*, XXXV (Winter 1976), Item 5.

Somerville, Jane. "Money in *Dubliners*," *Studies in Short Fiction*, XII (Spring 1975), 115–116.

Sosnoski, James J. "*Story and Discourse* and the Practice of Literary Criticism: 'Araby,' A Test Case," *James Joyce Quarterly*, XVIII (Spring 1981), 255–265.

Stein, William Bysshe. "Joyce's 'Araby': Paradise Lost," *Perspective*, XII (Spring 1962), 215–222.

Stone, Harry. 'Araby' and the Writings of James Joyce," *Antioch Review*, XXV (Fall 1965), 375–410.

Thorn, Eric. "James Joyce: Early Imitations of Structural Unity," *Costerus*, IX (1973), 232–234.

Tindall, William York. *A Reader's Guide to James Joyce* (New York, 1959), pp. 19–21.

Torchiana, Donald B. *Backgrounds for Joyce's Dubliners* (Boston, 1986), pp. 52–67.

Turaj, Frank. "'Araby' and *Portrait*: Stages of Pagan Conversion," *English Language Notes*, VII (March 1970), 209–213.

Walzl, Florence L, "The Liturgy of the Epiphany Seasons and the Epiphanies of Joyce," *PMLA* (September 1965), 436–450.

———. "Pig's Cheeks in 'Araby,'" *Cahiers Victoriens & Edouardiens*, XVI (October 1982), 175–176.

Wachtel, Albert. *The Cracked Looking-glass: James Joyce and the Nightmare of History* (Cranbury, N.J., 1992), pp. 32–37.

Waxman, Robert E. "Invitations to Dread: John Updike's Metaphysical Quest," *Renascence*, XXIX (Summer 1977), 201–210.

Wells, Walter. "John Updike's 'A&P', A Return to Araby," *Studies in Short Fiction*, XXX (Spring 1993), 127–133.

Werner, Craig Hansen. *Dubliners: A Pluralistic World* (Boston, 1988), pp. 37–41, 53–54, 75–77.

West, Ray B. *The Art of Writing Fiction* (New York, 1968), pp. 241–246.

JAMES JOYCE, "The Dead"

Ames, Christopher. *The Life of the Party: Festive Vision in Modern Fiction* (Athens, Ga., 1991), pp. 45–57.

Anspaugh, Kelly. "'Three Mortal Hour(i]s': Female Gothic in Joyce's 'The Dead,'" *Studies in Short Fiction*, XXXI (Winter 1994), 1–12.

Averill, Deborah M. *The Irish Short Story from George Moore to Frank O'Connor* (Lanham, Md., 1982), pp. 59–65.

Avery, Bruce. "Distant Music: Sound and the Dialogics of Satire in 'The Dead,'" *James Joyce Quarterly* XXVIII (Winter 1991), 473–497.

Baker, Christopher. "The Dead Art of 'The Dead,'" *English Studies*, LXIII (December 1982), 531–534.

Bayley, John. *The Short Story: Henry James to Elizabeth Bowen* (New York, 1988), pp. 150–168.

Barolsky, Paul. "Gretta's Name," *James Joyce Quarterly*, XXVIII (Winter 1991), 519–520.

———. "Joyce's Distant Music," *Virginia Quarterly Review*, LXV (Winter 1989), 111–118.

Beck, Warren. *Joyce's Dubliners: Substance, Vision, and Art* (Durham, N.C., 1969), pp. 303–360.

Begnal, Michael H. "The Dead," *Reference Guide to Short Fiction*, Noelle Watson, ed. (Detroit, 1994), p. 683.

Beja, Morris. "One Good Look at Themselves: Epiphanies in Dubliners," *Joyce Centenary Essays*, Richard E. Peterson, Alan M. Cohn, and Edmund L. Epstein, eds. (Carbondale, Ill., 1983), pp. 3–14. (G)

Benstock, Bernard. "'The Dead,'" *James Joyce's Dubliners: Critical Essays*, Clive Hard, ed. (London, 1969), pp. 153–169.

———. "Joyce's Rheumatics: The Holy Ghost in *Dubliners*," *Southern Review*, XIV (January 1978), 1–15. (G)

Bidwell, Bruce and Linda Heffer. *The Joycean Way: A Topographic Guide to Dubliners & A Portrait of the Artist as a Young Man* (Baltimore, 1982), pp. 106–111.

Bierman, Robert. "Structural Elements in 'The Dead,'" *James Joyce Quarterly*, IV (Fall 1966), 42–45.

Billigheimer, Rachel V. "The Living in Joyce's 'The Dead,'" *CLA Journal*, XXXI (June 1988), 472–483.

Blum, Morgan. "The Shifting Point of View: Joyce's 'The Dead' and Gordon's 'Old Red,'" *Critique*, I (Winter 1956), 45–66.

Bogorad, Samuel N. "Gabriel Conroy as 'Whited Sepulchre': Prefiguring Imagery in 'The Dead,'" *Ball State University Forum*, XIV (Winter 1973), 52–58.

Bowen, Zack and James F. Carens, eds. *A Companion to Joyce Studies* (Westport, Conn., 1984), pp. 209–216.

Bowen, Zack. "Joyce's Prophylactic Paralysis: Exposure in *Dubliners*," *James Joyce Quarterly*, XIX (1982), 269–273.

———. *Musical Allusions in the Works of James Joyce* (Albany, 1974), pp. 18–23.

Boyd, John D. "Gabriel Conroy's Secret Sharer," *Studies in Short Fiction*, XVII (Fall 1980), 499–501.

Boyd, John D. and Ruth A. "The Love Triangle in Joyce's 'The Dead,'" *University of Toronto Quarterly*, XLII (Spring 1973), 202–217.

Boyle, Robert. "Ellmann's Revised Conroy," *James Joyce Quarterly*, XXI (1984), 257–264.

Boyle, Robert S. J. and Thomas F. Staley. "The He and the She of it: The Furnace Image in 'The Dead,'" *James Joyce Quarterly*, XVI (Spring 1979), 361–364.

Brandabur, Edward. "Arrayed for the Bridal: The Embodied Vision of 'The Dead,'" *Joyce's The Dead*, William T. Moynihan, ed. (Boston, 1965), pp. 108–119.

———. *A Scrupulous Meanness: A Study of Joyce's Early Work* (Urbana, Ill., 1971), pp. 115–126.

Brivic, Sheldon R. *Joyce Between Freud and Jung* (Port Washington, N.Y., 1980), pp. 87–93.

Brown, Homer Obed. *James Joyce's Early Fiction: The Biography of a Form* (Cleveland, 1973), pp. 89–103.

Brown, Richard. *James Joyce* (New York, 1992). pp. 17–27.

Brunsdale, Mitzi M. *James Joyce: A Study of the Short Fiction* (New York, 1993) pp. 36–47.

Burke, Daniel. *Beyond Interpretation: Studies in the Modern Short Story* (Troy, N.Y., 1991), pp, 27–47.

Burke, Kenneth. "'Stages' in 'The Dead,'" *Dubliners: Text, Criticism, and Notes*, Robert Scholes and A. Walton Litz, eds, (New York, 1969), pp. 410–416.

Carens, James F. "In Quest of a New Impulse: George Moore's *The Untitled Field* and James

Joyce's *Dubliners*," *The Irish Short Story: A Critical History*, James F. Kilroy, ed. (Boston, 1984), pp. 88–92.

Carpenter, William. *Death and Marriage: Structural Metaphors for the Work of Art in Joyce and Mallarme* (New York, 1988), pp. 56–60.

Carson, John F. "John Huston's 'The Dead': An Irish Encomium," *Proteus*, VII, No. 2(1991), 26–28.

Chambers, Ross. "Gabriel Conroy Sings for His Support, or Love Refused ('The Dead')," *Story and Situation: Narrative Seduction and the Power of Fiction* (Minneapolis, 1984), pp. 181–204.

Conboy, Sheila C. "Exhibition and Inhibition: The Body Scene in *Dubliners*," *Twentieth-Century Literature*, XXXVII (1991), 407–408, 412–415.

Corcoran, Marlena G. "Language, Character, and Gender in the Direct Discourse in *Dubliners*," *Style*, XXV (1991), 446–449.

Cosgrove, Brian. "Male Sexuality and Female Rejection: Persistent Irony in Joyce's 'The Dead,'" *Irish University Review*, 26 (Spring/Summer 1996), 37–47.

Cox, Roger L. "Johnny the Horse in Joyce's 'The Dead,'" *James Joyce Quarterly*, IV (Fall 1966), 36–42.

Cronin, Edward J. "James Joyce's Trilogy and Epilogue: 'The Sisters,' 'An Encounter,' 'Araby,' and 'The Dead,'" *Renascence*, XLI (Summer 1979), 229–248.

Daiches, David. *The Novel and the Modern World* (Chicago, 1960), pp. 73–82.

Damon, Philip. "A Symphasis of Antipathies in 'The Dead,'" *Modern Language Notes*, LXXIV (February 1959), 111–114.

Deane, Paul. "Motion Picture Techniques in James Joyce's 'The Dead,'" *James Joyce Quarterly*, VI (Spring 1969), 231–236.

Delaney, Paul. "Joyce's Political Development and the Aesthetics of *Dubliners*," *College English*, XXXIV (November 1972),256–266.

DiBattista, Maria. *First Love: The Affections of Modern Fiction* (Chicago, 1991), pp. 29–31.

Dilworth, Thomas. "Sex and Politics in 'The Dead,'" *James Joyce Quarterly*, XXIII (Winter 1986), 157–171.

Doherty, Gerald. "Shades of Difference: Tropic Transformations In James Joyce's 'The Dead,'" *Style*, XXIII (Summer 1989), 225–237.

———. "Undercover Stories: Hypodiegetic Narration in Joyce's 'The Dead,'" *Journal Of Narrative Technique*, XXII (Winter 1992), 35–47.

Doloff, Steven. "Ibsen's A Doll's House and 'The Dead,'" *James Joyce Quarterly*, XXI (Winter 1994), 111–114.

Dunleavy, Gareth W. "Hyde's Crusade for the Language and the Case of the Embarrassing Packets," *Studies*, XXI (1984), 307–319.

Dunleavy, Janet Egleson. "The Ectoplasmic Truth-Tellers of 'The Dead,'" *James Joyce Quarterly*, XXI (Summer 1984), 307–319.

Eggers, Tillie. "What is a woman…a Symbol of?" *James Joyce Quarterly*, XVIII (1981), 379–395.

Ellmann, Richard. "The Backgrounds of 'The Dead,'" *Kenyon Review*, XX (Autumn 1958), 507–528.

———. *James Joyce* (New York, 1959), pp. 252–263.

Erzgraber, Willi. "Der Korrespondenzprinzip in James Joyce's 'The Dead,'" *Germanisch-Romanische Monatsschrift*, XXXIII (1983), 146–166.

Fairhall, James. *James Joyce and the Question of History* (Cambridge, England, 1993), pp. 84–86.

Feeley, John. "James Clarence Mangan in Joyce's 'The Dead,'" *English Language Votes*, XX (March–June 1983), 27–30.

———. "Joyce's 'The Dead' and the Browning Quotation," *James Joyce Quarterly*, XX (Fall 1982), 87–96.

Finney, Michael. "Why Greta Falls Asleep: A Postmodern Sugarplum," *Studies in Short Fiction*, 32 (Summer 1995), 475–481.

Foster, John W. "Passage Through 'The Dead,'" *Criticism*, XV (Spring 1973), 91–108.

Fransson, R. "A Little Too Familiar: A Brownie Among 'The Dead,'" *James Joyce Quarterly*, XXV (Winter 1988), 262–264.

French, Marilyn. "Missing Pieces in Joyce's Dubliners," *Twentieth-Century Literature*, XXIV (Winter 1978), 46–71.

Friedrich, Gerhard. "Bret Harte as a Source for James Joyce's 'The Dead,'" *Philological Quarterly*, XXXIII (October 1954), 442–444.

———. "The Perspective of Joyce's Dubliners," *College English*, XXVI (March 1965), 421–426.

Frizler, Paul. "John Huston's Film of James Joyce's 'The Dead,'" *Proteus*, VII, No. 2 (1991), 22–25.

Gandolfo, Anita. "A Portrait of the Artist as Critic: Joyce, Moore and the Background of 'The Dead,'" *English Literature in Transition*, XXII (1979), 239–250.

Garrett, Roland. "Six Theories in the Bedroom of 'The Dead,'" *Philosophy and Literature*, XVI (1992), 115–127.

Ghiselin, Brewster. "The Unity of Joyce's *Dubliners*," *Accent*, XVI (Summer 1956), 207–212.

Gifford, Don. *Notes for Joyce* (New York, 1967), pp. 74–84.

Going, William T. "Joyce's Gabriel Conroy and Robert Browning: The Cult of 'Broadcloth,'" *Papers on Language and Literature*, XIII (Spring 1977), 202–207.

Gordon, Caroline and Allen Tate. *The House of Fiction* (New York, 1960), pp. 279–282.

Gottfried, Roy. "'Scrupulous meanness' reconsidered: *Dubliners* as Stylistic Parody," Joyce in Context, Vincent J. Cheng and Timothy Martin, eds. (Cambridge, Eng., 1993), pp. 167–168.

Haas, Robert. "Music in *Dubliners*," *Colby Quarterly*, XXVIII (March 1992), 19–33.

Halper, Nathan. *The Early James Joyce* (New York, 1973), pp, 28–33.

———. *Studies in Joyce* (Ann Arbor, 1983), pp. 151–155.

Handy, William J. "Joyce's 'The Dead,'" *Modern Fiction: A Formalist Approach* (Carbondale, Ill., 1971), pp. 29–61.

Hardy, Barbara. *Tellers and Listeners: The Narrative Imagination* (London, 1975), pp. 223–226.

Harty, John. "'The Dead,'" *Explicator*, XLVI (Winter 1988), 23–24.

Heller, Vivian. *Joyce, Decadence, and Emancipation* (Urbana, Ill., 1995), pp. 33–41.

Henke, Suzette A. *James Joyce and the Politics of Desire* (New York, 1990), pp. 49–49.

———. "Through a Cracked Looking-glass: Sex Role Stereotypes in *Dubliners*," *International Perspectives on James Joyce*, Gottlieb Gaiser, ed. (Troy, N.Y., 1986), pp. 2–31. (G)

Herring, Phillip F. *Joyce's Uncertainty Principle* (Princeton, 1997), pp. 71–75.

Higgins, Joanna. "A Reading of the Last Sentence of 'The Dead,'" *English Language Notes*, XVII (March 1990), 203–207.

Hodgart, Matthew. *James Joyce: A Student's Guide* (London, 1978), pp. 52–56.

Hogan, Patrick Colm. *Joyce, Milton, and the Theory of Influence* (Gainesville, 1995), pp. 93–97.

Humma, John B. "Gabriel and the Bedsheets: Still Another Reading of the Ending of 'The Dead,'" *Studies in Short Fiction*, X (Spring 1973), 207–209.

Hunter, Robert. "Joyce's 'The Dead,'" *James Joyce Quarterly*, VII (Summer 1970), 365.

Hutton, Virgil. "James Joyce's 'The Dead.'" *East-West Review*, II (Winter 1965–1966), 124–139.

Ingersoll, Earl G. *Engendered Trope in Joyce's Dubliners* (Carbondale, Ill., 1996), pp. 145–162.

———. "The Gender of Travel in 'The Dead,'" *James Joyce Quarterly*, XXX (1993), 41–50.

Johnsen, William A. "Joyce's 'Dubliners' and the Futility of Modernism," *James Joyce and Modern Literature*, W. J, McCormarck and Alistair Stead, eds. (London, 1982), pp. 17–20.

Kaye, Julian B. "The Wings of Daedalus: Two Stories in *Dubliners: Modern Fiction Studies*, IV (Spring 1958), 31–41.

Keen, William P. "The Rhetoric of Spacial Focus in Joyce's *Dubliners*," *Studies in Short Fiction*, XVI (Summer 1979), 201–203.

Kelleher, John V. "Irish History and Mythology in James Joyce's 'The Dead,'" *Review of Politics*, XVII (July 1965), 424–433.

Kelly, John S. "Afterword," James Joyce's *Dubliners*, Hans W. Gabler and Walter Hettche, eds. (New York, 1993), pp. 269–275.

Kelly, Joseph. *Our Joyce: From Outcast to Icon* (Austin, Tx., 1998), pp. 168–172.

Kennelly, Brendan. "the Irishness of 'The Dead' by James Joyce," *Moderna Sprak*, LVI (1967), 239–242.

Kenner, Hugh. *Dublin's Joyce* (Bloomington, Ind., 1956), pp. 62–68.

Kershner, R. B. *Joyce, Bakhtin, and Popular Literature: Chronicles of Disorder* (Chapel Hill, 1989), pp. 138–150.

Kim, Hwan Hee. "Plot and Epiphany in the Short Story," *Journal of English Language and Literature*, 41 (Winter 1995), 1043–1060.

Knox, George. "Michael Furey: Symbol Name in Joyce's 'The Dead,'" *Western Humanities Review*, XIII (Spring 1959), 221–222.

Kopper, Edward A., Jr. "Joyce's 'The Dead,'" *Explicator*, XXVI (February 1968), Item 46.

Kupers, Herbert. "The Dead," *Analyses of Twentieth-Century British and American Fiction*, V, Hermann J. Weiand, ed. (Frankfurt, 1981), pp. 135–143.

Ledden, Patrick J. "Letter: Some Comments on Vincent Cheng's 'Empire and Patriarchy in 'The Dead'" *Joyce Studies Annual 5* (1994), 202–207.

Leonard, Garry. *Advertising and Commodity Culture in Joyce* (Gainesville, Fla., 1998), pp. 72–97.

———. "Joyce and Lacan: 'The Woman' as a Symptom of 'Masculinity' in'The Dead,'" *James Joyce Quarterly*, XXVIII (Winter 1991), 451–472.

———. *Reading Dubliners Again: A Lancanian Perspective* (Syracuse, 1993), pp. 1–26.

Levenson, Michael. "Living History in 'The Dead,'" *The Dead: Complete Authoritative Text with Biographical and Historical Contexts, Critical History, and Essays from Five Contemporary Critical Perspectives*, Daniel R. Schwartz, ed. (New York, 1994), pp. 163–177.

Levin, Richard and Charles Shattuck. "First Flight to Ithaca: A New Reading of Joyce's *Dubliners*," *Accent*, IV (Winter 1944), 96–99.

Linguanti, Elsa. "Joyce's 'The Dead, and the Epiphany of the Reader," *Strumenti Critici*, VIII (January 1993), 113–130.

Litz, A. Walton. *James Joyce* (New York, 1966), pp. 55–59.

Loc, Thomas. "'The Dead' as Novella," *James Joyce Quarterly*, XXVIII (Winter 1991), 485–497.

Logan, Dorothy. "Joyce's 'The Dead,'" *Explicator*, XXXII (October 1973), Item 16.

Loomis, C. C. "Structure and Sympathy in Joyce's 'The Dead,'" *Publications of the Modern Language Association*, LXXV (March 1960), 149–151.

Lucente, Gregory L. "Encounters and Subtexts in 'The Dead': A Note on Joyce's Narrative Technique," *Studies in Short Fiction*, XX (Fall 1983), 281–287.

Ludwig, Jack Barry. "The Snow," *James Joyce's Dubliners: A Critical Handbook*, James R. Baker and Thomas F. Staley, eds. (Belmont, Calif, 1969), pp. 159–162.

Lytle, Andrew. "A Reading of Joyce's 'The Dead,'" *Sewanee Review*, LXXVII (Spring 1969), 193–216.

McDermott, Hubert. "Conroy and Coffin in Joyce's 'The Dead,'" *Notes & Queries*, N.S. 27 (December 1980), 533.

McFate, Patricia Ann. "Gabriel Conroy and Ned Carmady: A Tale of Two Irish Geese," *College Literature*, V (Spring 1978), 125–132.

McIntire, Janice E. "Gretta's 'Angels': The Significance of Naming in 'The Dead,'" *Notes on Modern Irish Literature*, 9 (1997), 55–59.

McKenna, John P. "An Ill-Stared Magus," *James Joyce Quarterly*, IX (Fall 1971), 126–128.

———. "Joyce's 'The Dead,'" *Explicator*, XXX (September 1971), Item 1.

MacDonagh, Donagh, "Joyce and 'The Lass of Aughrim," *Hibernia*, XXXI (June 1967), 21.

————. "The Lass of Aughrim or the Betrayal of James Joyce," *Hibernia*, XXXIII (June 1969), 6–26.

MacNicholas, John. "Comic Design in Joyce's 'The Dead,'" *Modern British Literature*, I (Fall 1976), 56–65.

Maddox, Lucy B. "Gabriel and Otello: Opera in 'The Dead,'" *Studies in Short Fiction*, XXIV (Summer 1987), 271–277.

Magalaner, Marvin and Richard M. Kain. *Joyce: The Man, The Work, The Reputation* (New York, 1956), pp. 92–98.

Mansell, Darrel, "William Holman Hunt's *The Awakening Conscience* and James Joyce's 'The Dead,'" *James Joyce Quarterly*, XXIII (Summer 1986), 487–491.

Menghan, Rod. "Military Occupation in 'The Dead,'" *Re: Joyce: Text, Culture, Politics*, John Brannigan, Geoff Ward, and Julian Wolfreys, eds. (London, 1998), pp. 77–86.

Miller, Milton. "Definition by Comparison: Chaucer, Lawrence and Joyce," *Essays in Criticism*, III (October 1953), 369–381.

Morrissey, L. J. "Inner and Outer Perception in Joyce's 'The Dead,'" *Studies in Short Fiction*. XXV (Winter 1988), 21–29.

Moseley, Virginia. *Joyce and the Bible* (DeKalb, Ill., 1967), pp. 19–31.

————. "'Two Sights for Ever in a Picture' in Joyce's 'The Dead,'" *College English*, XXVI (March 1965), 426–433.

Mosher, Harold F. "The Narrated and Its Negatives: The Nonnarrated and the Disnarrated in Joyce's *Dubliners*," *Style*, XXVII (1993), 421–424.

Moynihan, William T., ed. *Joyce's The Dead* (Boston, 1965).

Munich, Adrienne A. "Form and Subtext in Joyce's 'The Dead,'" *Modern Philology*, LXX (November 1984), 173–184.

Murphy, Mary C. "Petronius in Dublin: The Influence of Petronius' 'Dinner at Trimalchio's' on James Joyce's 'The Dead,'" *Essays in Literature*, II (March 1974), 1–10.

Murphy, Sean P. "Passing Boldly into the Other World of (W)Holes: Narrativity and Subjectivity in James Joyce's 'The Dead,'" *Studies in Short Fiction*, 32 (Summer 1995), 463–474.

Nilsen, Kenneth. "Down Among the Dead: Elements of Irish Language and Mythology in James Joyce's 'The Dead,'" *Canadian Journal of Irish Studies*, XII (June 1986), 23–34.

Norris, Margot. *Joyce's Web: The Social Unraveling of Modernism* (Austin, Tx., 1992), pp. 97–118.

————. "Not the Girl She Was at All: Women in 'The Dead,'" *The Dead: Complete Authoritative Text with Biographical and Historical Contexts, Critical History, and Essays from Five Contemporary Critical Perspectives*, Daniel R. Schwartz, ed. (New York, 1994), pp. 190–205.

————. "Stifled Back Answers: The Gender Politics of Art in Joyce's 'The Dead,'" *Modern Fiction Studies*, XXXV (Autumn 1989), 479–503.

O'Brien, Darcy. *The Conscience of James Joyce* (Princeton, 1968), pp. 16–21.

O'Connor, Frank. *The Lonely Voice: A Study of the Short Story* (Cleveland, 1963), pp. 123–126.

O'Hehir, Brendan P. "Structural Symbol in Joyce's 'The Dead,'" *Twentieth-Century Literature*, III (April 1957), 3–13.

O'Leary, Joseph S. "The Musical Structure of 'The Dead,'" *The Harp: ISAIL-Japan Bulletin*, 11 (1996), 29–40.

Osteen, Mark. "Gabriel's Sarcasm: A Lost Line in 'The Dead,' *James Joyce Quarterly*, XXV (Winter 1988), 259–262.

Owens, Collin. "The Mystique of the West in Joyce's 'The Dead,'" *Irish University Review*, XXII (Spring 1992), 80–91.

Parrinder, Patrick. *James Joyce* (Cambridge, England, 1984), pp. 66–70.

Peake, C. H. *James Joyce: the Citizen and the Artist* (Stanford, Calif, 1977), pp. 45–55.

Pearce, Sandra Manoogian. "Edna O'Brien's 'Lantern Slides' and Joyce's 'The Dead': Shadows of a Bygone Era," *Studies in Short Fiction*, 32 (Summer 1995), 437–446.

Pecora, Vincent P. "'The Dead' and the Generality of the Word," *PMLA*, CI (1986), 233–234.

———. *Self and Form in Modern Narrative* (Baltimore, 1989), pp. 227–238.

Pederson, Ann. "Uncovering 'The Dead': A Study in Adaptation," *Literature/Film Quarterly*, XXI, i (1993), 69–70.

Peterson, Richard F. *James Joyce Revisited* (New York, 1992), pp. 30–31.

Pillipp, Frank. "Narrative Devices and Aesthetic Perception in Joyce's and Houston's 'The Dead,'" *Literature Film Quarterly*, xxi, i (1993), 61–68.

Rabate, Jean-Michael. *James Joyce, Authorized Reader* (Baltimore, 1991), pp. 41–46.

———. "Silence in Dubliners," *James Joyce: New Perspectives*, Colin MacCabe, ed. (Bloomington, Ind., 1982), pp. 64–68.

Reilly, Seamus. "Rehearing 'Distant Music' in 'The Dead,'" *James Joyce Quarterly*, 35 (Fall 1997), 149–151.

Rice, Thomas J. "Dante...Browning. Gabriel...Joyce: Allusion and Structure in 'The Dead,'" *James Joyce Quarterly*, XXX (1992), 29–40.

———. "The Geometry of Meaning in *Dubliners*: A Euclidean Approach," *Style*, XXV (1991), 399–440.

Riikonen, H. K., ed. *Joyce by Lamplight: Finnish Readings of "The Dead"* (Turku, Finland, 1989).

Riquelme, John Paul. "For Whom the Snow Taps: Style and Repetition in 'The Dead,'" *The Dead: Complete Authoritative Text with Biographical and Historical Contexts, Critical History, and Essays from Five Contemporary Critical Perspectives*, Daniel R. Schwartz, ed. (New York, 1994), pp. 219–233.

———. "Joyce's 'The Dead': The Dissolution of the Self and the Police," *Style*, XXV (1991), 488–505.

———. *Teller and Tale in Joyce's Fiction: Oscillating Perspectives* (Baltimore, 1983), pp. 121–130.

Rix, Walter T. "James Joyce's 'The Dead': The Symbolist Inspiration and Its Narrative Reflection," *Critical Approaches to Anglo-Irish Literature*, Michael Allen and Angela Wilcox, eds. (Totowa, N.J., 1989), pp. 145–165.

Robinowitz, Peter, "'A Symbol of Something': Interpretive Vision in 'The Dead,'" *The Dead: Complete Authoritative Text with Biographical and Historical Contexts, Critical History, and Essays from Five Contemporary Critical Perspectives*, Daniel R. Schwartz, ed. (New York, 1994), pp. 137–149.

Robinson, Eleanor, "Gabriel Conroy's Cooked Goose," *Ball State University Forum*, XI (Spring 1970), 25.

Ryf, Robert S. *A New Approach to Joyce* (Berkeley, 1962), pp. 72–76.

San Juan, Epifanio. *James Joyce and the Craft of Fiction: An Interpretation of Dubliners* (Rutherford, N.J., 1972), pp. 209–233.

Scarry, John. "Dating Parkinson's 'Prime' in Joyce's 'The Dead,'" *Notes and Queries*, XXIII (January 1976), 21–22.

———. "The 'Negro Chieftain' and Disharmony in Joyce's 'The Dead,'" *Revue des Langues Vivantes*, XXXIX, No. 2 (1973), 182–183.

———. "'Poor Georgina Burns' in Joyce's 'The Dead,'" *English Language Notes*, X (December 1972), 123–126.

———. "William Parkinson in Joyce's 'The Dead,'" *Journal of Modern Literature*, III February 1973), 105–107.

Scheuerle, William H. "'Gabriel Hounds' and Joyce's 'The Dead,'" *Studies in Short Fiction*, II (Summer 1965), 369–371.

Schmidt, Hugo. "Hauptmann's Michael Kramer and Joyce's 'The Dead,'" *PMLA*, LXXX (March 1965), 141–142.

Scholes, Robert E. "Some Observations on the Text of *Dubliners*: 'The Dead,'" *Studies in Bibliography*, XV (1962), 191–205.

Scott, Bonnie K. "James Joyce: A Subversive Geography of Gender," *Irish Writing: Exile and Subversion*, Paul Hyland and Neil Sammells, eds. (New York, 1991), pp. 161–164.

Senn, Fritz. "Not Too Scrupulous Always," *James Joyce Quarterly*, IV (Spring 1967), 244.

———. "Reverberations," *James Joyce Quarterly*, III (Spring 1966), 222.

Sherry, Vincent B. "Joyce's Monologues in 'The Dead' and Browning's Thought-Tormented Music," *College Literature*, XI (1984), 134–140.

Shields, David. "A Note on the Conclusion of Joyce's 'The Dead,'" *James Joyce Quarterly*, XXII (Summer 1985), 427–428.

Scholes, Robert. *In Search of Joyce* (Urban, Ill., 1992), pp. 17–34.

Shout, John D. "Joyce at Twenty-Five, Huston at Eighty-One: 'The Dead', *Literature/Film Quarterly*, XVII, No. 2 (1989), 91–94.

Shurgot, Michael W. "Windows of Escape and the Death Wish of Man: Joyce's 'The Dead," *Eire-Ireland*, XVII, iv (1982), 58–71.

Schwartz, Daniel R. "A Critical History of 'The Dead," *The Dead: Complete Authoritative Text with Biographical and Historical Contexts, Critical History, and Essays from Five Contemporary Critical Perspectives*, Daniel R. Schwartz, ed. (New York, 1994), pp. 63–84.

———, ed. *The Dead: Complete Authoritative Text with Biographical and Historical Contexts, Critical History and Essays from Five Contemporary Critical Perspectives* (New York, 1994).

Sisson, Annette. "Constructing the Human Conscience in Joyce's *Dubliners*," *Midwest Quarterly*, XXX (1989), 496–502.

Smith, Thomas F. "Color and Light in 'The Dead,'" *James Joyce Quarterly*, II (Summer 1965), 304–309.

Sperber, Michael. "Shame and James Joyce's 'The Dead,'" *Literature and Psychology*, XXXVII, Nos. 1 & 2 (1991), 62–71.

Spoo, Robert. "Uncanny Returns in 'The Dead': Ibsenian Intertexts and the Estranged Infant," *Joyce: The Return of the Repressed*, Susan F. Friedman, ed. (Ithaca, N.Y., 1993), pp. 89–113.

Stanzel, Franz K. "Consonant and Dissonant Closure in 'Death in Venice' and 'The Dead,'" *Neverending Stories: Toward a Critical Narratology*, Fehn, Ingeborg Hoestery, and Maria Tatar, eds. (Princeton, 1992), pp. 114–123.

Stone, William B. "Teaching 'The Dead': Literature in the Composition Class," *Conference on Composition and Communication*, XIX (October 1968), 229–231.

Tate, Allen. "'The Dead,'" *Dubliners: Text, Criticism, and Notes*, Robert Scholes and A. Walton Litz, eds. (New York, 1969), pp. 404–410.

Taylor, Gordon O. "Joyce 'After Joyce: Oates's 'The Dead,'" *Southern Review*, XIX (July 1983), 596–605.

Theoharis, Theoharis C. "Hedda Gabler and 'The Dead,'" *English Literary History*, L (Winter 1983), 791–809.

Tindall, William York. *A Reader's Guide to James Joyce* (New York, 1959), pp. 42–49.

Torchiana, Donald T. *Backgrounds for Joyce's Dubliners* (Boston, 1986), pp. 223–257.

———. "The Ending of 'The Dead': I Follow Saint Patrick," *James Joyce Quarterly*, XVIII (Winter 1981), 123–132.

———. "James Joyce's Method in *Dubliners*," *The Irish Short Story*, Patrick Rafroidi and Terence Brown, eds. (Atlantic Highlands, N.J., 1979), pp. 134–140.

Trilling, Lionel. *Prefaces to the Experience of Literature* (New York, 1979), pp. 112–117.

Wagner, C. Roland. "A Birth Announcement in 'The Dead,'" *Studies in Short Fiction*, 32 (Summer 1995), 447–462.

Wales, Katie. *The Language of James Joyce* (New York, 1992), 47–55.

Walzl, Florence L. "Ambiguity in the Structural Symbols of Gabriel's Vision in Joyce's 'The Dead,'" *Wisconsin Studies in Literature*, II (1965), pp. 60–69.

———. "Dubliners," *A Companion to Joyce Studies*, Zack Bowen and James F. Carens, eds. (Westport, Conn., 1984), pp. 209–216.

———. "Gabriel and Michael: The Conclusion of 'Me Dead,'" *James Joyce Quarterly*, IV (Fall 1966), 17–31.

Ware, Thomas C. "A Miltonic Allusion in Joyce's 'The Dead,'" *James Joyce Quarterly*, VI (Spring 1969), 273–274.

Weir, David. *James Joyce and the Art of Mediation* (Ann Arbor, 1996), pp. 78–85.

———. "Gnomon is an Island: Euclid and Bruno in Joyce's Narrative Practice," *James Joyce Quarterly* XXVIII (Winter 1991 343–360.

Werner, Craig Hansen. *Dubliners: A Pluralistic World* (Boston, 1988), pp. 39–41, 56–72.

———. *James Joyce and the Art of Mediation* (Ann Arbor, 1996), pp. 78–85.

Wheatley-Lovoy, Cynthia D. "The Rebirth of Tragedy: Nietzsche and Narcissus in 'A Painful Case' and 'The Dead,'" *James Joyce Quarterly*, XXXIII (Winter 1996), 177–194.

Williams, Trevor. *Reading Joyce Politically* (Gainesville, Fla., 1997), pp. 91–96.

———. "Resistance to Paralysis in *Dubliners*," *Modern Fiction Studies*, XXX (Autumn 1989), 437–457.

Wright, David G. *Characters of Joyce* (Totowa, N.J., 1983), pp. 26–29.

———. "Interactive Stories in *Dubliners*," *Studies in Short Fiction*, 32 (Summer 1995), 285–293.

Yee, Cordell D. K. *The Word According to James Joyce: Reconstructing Representation* (Lewisburg, Pa., 1997), pp. 25–26; 95–98.

Yin, Xiaoling. "The Paralyzed and the Dead: A Comparative Reading of 'The Dead' and 'In a Tavern,'" *Comparative Literature Studies*, XXIX (192), 276–278, 281–288, 292, 294.

Zasadimsky, Eugene. "Joyce's 'The Dead,'" *Explicator*, XL (Winter 1982), 3–4.

BEL KAUFMAN, "Sunday in the Park"

Nelson, Robert J. "The Battlefield in Bel Kaufman's 'Sunday in the Park,'" *English Language Notes*, XXX, No. 1 (1992), 61–68.

GARRISON KEILLOR, "The Tip–Top Club"

Fedo, Michael. *The Man from Lake Wobegon: An Unauthorized Biography of Garrison Keillor* (New York, 1987). (G)

Greasley, Philip. "Garrison Keillor's Lake Wobegon: The Contemporary Oral Tale," *Mid-America Review*, XIV (1987), 126–136. (G)

La Roche, Jacques, and Calude J. Fouillade. "A Socio-Cultural Reading of *Lake Wobegon Days* or Can You Go Home Again to Mid-America?" *Revue Francaise, D'etudes Americaines*, XLII (1989), 427–438. (G)

Lee, Judith Yaross. *Garrison Keillor: A Voice of America* (Jackson, Miss., 1991), pp. 130–131.

Scholl, Peter A. "Garrison Keillor and the News from Lake Wobegon," *Studies in American Humor*, IV (Winter 1985–1986), 217–228. (G)

Traub, James. "The Short and Tall Tales of Garrison Keillor," *Esquire*, XCVII (May 1982), 108–117.(G)

Wilbers, Stephen. "Lake Wobegon: Mythian Place and the American Imagination," *American Studies*, XXX (Spring 1989), 5–20. (G)

STEPHEN KING, "The Man in the Black Suit"

Beahm, George, ed. *The Stephen King Companion* (Kansas City, Mo., 1989). (G)

Collings, Michael R. *The Annotated Guide to Stephen King* (Mercer Island, Wash., 1986). (G)

———. *The Many Facets of Stephen King* (Mercer Island, Wash., 1985). (G)

————. *Scaring Us to Death: The Impact of Stephen King on Popular Culture* (San Bernadino, Ca., 1997). (G)

————. *The Stephen King Phenomenon* (San Bernadino, Ca., 1987). (G)

————, and Boden Clarke, eds. *The Work of Stephen King: An Annotated Bibliography and Guide* (San Bernadino, Ca., 1996) (G)

————, and David Engebretson. *The Shorter Works of Stephen King* (Mercer Island, Wash., 1985). (G)

Davis, Jonathan P. *Stephen King's America* (Bowling Green, Ohio, 1994) (G)

Hansen, Clare. "Stephen King: Powers of Horror," *American Horror Fiction: From Brockden Brown to Stephen King*, Brian Docherty, ed. (London, 1990), pp. 135–154. (G)

Heppenstand, Gary, and Ray B. Browne, eds. *The Gothic World of Stephen King: Landscapes of Nightmare* (Bowling Green, 1987). (G)

Lant, Kathleen Margaret and Theresa Thompson, eds. *Imagining the Worst; Stephen King and the Representation of Women* (Westport, Conn., 1998). (G)

Magistrale, Tony, ed. *The Dark Descent: Essays Defining Stephen King's Horrorscope* (Westport, Conn., 1992). (G)

————. *Landscape of Fear: Stephen King's American Gothic* (Bowling Green, Ohio, 1988). (G)

————. *The Moral Voyages of Stephen King* (Mercer Island, Wash., 1990). (G)

————. *Stephen King, The Second Decade: Dance Macabre to the Dark Half* (New York, 1992) (G)

Reino, Joseph. *Stephen King: The First Decade, Carrie to Pet Sematary* (Boston, 1988) (G)

Winter, Douglas E. *Stephen King: The Art of Darkness* (New York, 1984). (G)

KINSELLA, W. P., "Shoeless Joe Jackson Comes to Iowa"

Westbrook, Deanne. *Ground Rules: Baseball and Myth* (Urbana, Ill., 1996), pp. 125–167. (G)

RUDYARD KIPLING, "They"

Birkenhead, Lord (Frederick W. F. Smith). *Rudyard Kipling* (New York, 1978), pp. 314–316.

Bodelsen, C. A. *Aspects of Kipling's Art* (New York, 1964), pp. 97–98.

Dobré, Bonamy. *Rudyard Kipling, Realist and Fabulist* (London, 1967), pp. 101–102, 158–159.

Eckley, Wilton. "Rudyard Kipling," *Critical Survey of Short Fiction*, Frank N. Magill, ed. (Englewood Cliffs, N.J., 1981), V, 1751–1753.

Hanson, Clare. "Limits and Renewals: The Meaning of Form in the Stories of Rudyard Kipling," *Kipling Considered*, Phillip Mallett, ed. (New York, 1989), pp. 85–97. (G)

————. *Short Stories and Short Fictions, 1880–1980* (New York, 1985), pp. 39–44. (G)

Harbord, R. E. *Readers Guide to Rudyard Kipling's Work* (Kent, England, 1965–1966), IV, 1922–1932.

Harrison, James. *Rudyard Kipling* (Boston, 1982), pp. 96–98.

Hart, Walter Morris. *Kipling: The Story Writer* (Berkeley, 1918), pp. 194–202.

Hopkins, R. Thursdon. *Rudyard Kipling: A Literary Appreciation* (London, 1915), pp. 67–71.

Kemp, Sandra. *Kipling's Hidden Narrative* (Oxford, England, 1988), pp. 44–49.

Laski, Marghanita. *From Palm to Pine: Rudyard Kipling Abroad and at Home* (New York, 1987), pp. 128–129.

Lyon, John. "Half-Written Tales: Kipling and Conrad," *Kipling Considered*, Phillip Mallett, ed. (New York, 1989), pp. 115–134.(G)

Mallett, Phillip. "They," *Reference Guide to Short Fiction*, Noelle Watson, ed. (Detroit 1994), pp. 926–927.

Mason, Philip. *Kipling: The Glass, the Shadow and the Fire* (New York, 1975), pp. 204–208.

Page, Norman. *A Kipling Companion* (New York, 1984), pp. 127–128.

Peck, Harry Thurston. "Mr. Kipling's *Traffics and Discoveries*" *Bookman*, XX (October 1904), 155–157.

Penzoldt, Peter. *The Supernatural in Fiction* (London, 1952), pp, 134–142.

Pritchett, V. S. "Kipling's Short Stories," *The Living Novel and Later Appreciations* (New York, 1964), pp. 175–182. (G)

Robson, W. W. "Kipling's Later Stories," *Kipling's Mind and Art: Selected Critical Essays.* Andrew Rutherford, ed. (Stanford, 1964), pp. 265–268.

Schwarz, John H. "Hardy and Kipling's 'They,'" *English Literature in Translation*, XXXIV, No. 1 (1990), 7–16.

Scott-Giles, C. W. and Mrs. Scott-Giles. "Note on 'They,'" *Kipling Journal*, XXXV (September 1968), 18–20.

Shanks, Edward. *Rudyard Kipling: A Study in Literature and Political Ideas* (London, 1940), pp.252–256.

Shaw, Valerie. *The Short Story: A Critical Introduction* (London, 1983), pp. 95–107. (G)

Stewart, J. I. M. "Kipling," *Eight Modern Readers* (Oxford, Eng., 1963), pp. 223–293. (G)

———. *Rudyard Kipling* (New York, 1966), pp. 131–134.

Tompkins, J. M. S. *The Art of Rudyard Kipling* (London, 1959), pp. 203–204.

Wilson, Angus. *The Strange Ride of Rudyard Kipling: His Life and Works* (New York, 1977), pp. 264–266.

WILLIAM KITTREDGE, "We Are Not in This Together"

Carver, Raymond. "Foreword," *William Kittredge, We Are Not in This Together* (Townsend, Wash., 1984), pp. vii–x.

Gonzalez, Ray and Ida Steven. "The Myth of Ownership: An Interview with William Kittredredge," *Bloomsbury Review*, VII (July/August 1988), 4–15. (G)

RING LARDNER, "Haircut"

Anderson, Sherwood. "Four American Impressions," *New Republic*, XXXII (October 11, 1922), 171–173. (G)

Berryman, John. "The Case of Ring Lardner," *Commentary*, xxii (November 1956) 416–423. (G)

Blythe, Hal. "Lardner's 'Haircut,'" *Explicator*, XLIV (Spring 1986), 48–49.

Blythe, Hal and Charlie Sweet. "The Barber of Civility: The Chief Conspirator of 'Haircut'" *Studies in Short Fiction*, XXIII (Fall 1986), 450–453.

———. "Why Whitey Tells His Tale: The Penitent Narrator of Lardner's 'Haircut,'" *Notes on Contemporary Literature*, 29 (January 1999), 2–4.

Bordewyck, Gordon. "Comic Alienation: Ring Lardner's Style," *Markham Review* XI (Spring 1982), 51–57. (G)

Brooks, Cleanth and Robert Penn Warren. *Understanding Fiction* (New York, 1959), p 145–150.

Cervo, Nathan. "Lardner's 'Haircut,'" *Explicator*, XLVII (Winter 1989), 47–48.

Core, George. "Haircut," *Reference Guide to Short Fiction*, Noelle Watson, ed. (Detroit, 1994), p. 730.

Cowlishaw, Brian T. "The Reader's Role in Ring Lardner's Rhetoric," *Studies in Short Fiction*, XXXI (Spring 1994) 207–216.

Elder, Donald. *Ring Lardner: A Biography* (Garden City, N.Y., 1956), p. 238.

Evans, Elizabeth. *Ring Lardner* (New York, 1979), pp. 61–63.

Geismar, Maxwell. "Introduction," *The Ring Lardner Reader* (New York, 1963), pp. xv–xxxiv. (G)

Gilead, Sarah. "Lardner's Discourses of Power," *Studies in Short Fiction*, XXII (Summer 1985), 332–333.

Goldstein, Melvin. "A Note on a Perfect Crime," *Literature and Psychology*, XI (1961), 65–67.

Hagopian, John V. *Insight I: Analyses of American Literature* (Frankfurt, 1962), pp. 140–144.

Hasley, Louis. "Ring Lardner: Ashes of Idealism," *Arizona Quarterly*, XXVI (1970), 219–232. (G)

Moseley, Merritt. "Ring Lardner and the American Humor Tradition," *South Atlantic Review*, XLVI (January 1981), 42–60. (G)

Kasten, M. C. "The Satire of Ring Lardner," *English Journal*, XXXVI (April 1947), 192–195. (G)

May, Charles E. "Lardner's 'Haircut,'" *Explicator*, XXXI (May 1973), Item 69.

Patrick, Walton R. *Ring Lardner* (New York, 1963), pp. II 4–117.

Pellow, C. Kenneth. "Ring Lardner: Absurdist Ahead of His Time," *Aethlon*, VI, 2 (1989), 111–117. (G)

Robinson, Douglas. "Ring Lardner's Dual Audience and the Capitalist Double Bind," *American Literary History*, IV (1992), 266–268.

———. *Ring Larder and the Other* (New York, 1992), 175–180, 181–191.

Webb, Howard W., Jr. "The Development of a Style: The Lardner Idiom," *American Quarterly*, XII (I 960), 482–492.

———. "Mark Twain and Ring Lardner," *Mark Twain Journal*, XI, 2 (1960), 13–15. (G)

———. "The Meaning of Ring Lardner's Fiction: A Re-Evaluation," *American Literature*, XXXI (January 1960), 434–445. (G)

———. "Ring Lardner's Idle Common Man," *Bulletin of the Central Mississippi Valley American Studies Association*, I (Spring 1958), 6–13. (G)

Yardley, Jonathan. *Ring: A Biography Of Ring Lardner* (New York, 1977), pp. 287–289.

D. H. LAWRENCE, "The Horse Dealer's Daughter"

Becker, George J. "Short Stories and Novellas," *D. H. Lawrence* (New York, 1980), 113–130. (G)

Betsky-Zweig, S. "Floughtingly in the Fine Black Mud': D. H. Lawrence's 'The Horse Dealer's Daughter,'" *Dutch Quarterly Review*, III (I 973), 159–164.

Brooks, Cleanth, John T. Purser, and Robert Penn Warren. *An Approach to Literature* (New York, 1952), pp. 186–188.

Cox, James. "Pollyanalytics and Pedagogy: Teaching Lawrence's Short Stories," *D. H. Lawrence Review*, VIII (1976), 74–77. (G)

Ford, George H. *Double Measure: A Study of the Novels and Stories of D. H. Lawrence* (New York, 1965) pp. 91–96.

Gremelova, Anna. "Thematic and Structural Diversification D. H. Lawrence's Short Story in the Wake of World War I," *Litteraria Praaensia*, II, iv (1992), 62–64.

Gullason, Thomas A. "Revelation and Evolution: A Neglected Dimension of the Short Story," *Studies in Short Fiction*, X (Fall 1973), 347–352.

Harris, Janice Hubbard. *The Short Fiction of D. H. Lawrence* (New Brunswick, N.J., 1984), 125–129.

Herbert, Michael. "The Horse Dealer's Daughter," *Reference Guide to Short Fiction*, Noelle Watson, ed. (Detroit, 1994), 739.

Higashida, Chiaki. "On the Prose Style of D. H. Lawrence," *Studies in English Literature* (Tokyo University), XIX (1939), 545–566. (G)

Junkins, Donald. "D. H. Lawrence's 'The Horse-Dealer's Daughter,'" *Studies in Short Fiction*, VI (Winter 1969), 210–212.

Krishnamurthi, M. G. *D. H. Lawrence: Tale as Medium* (Mysore, India, 1970), pp. 83–89.

Leavis, F. R. *D. H. Lawrence: Novelist* (New York, 1956), pp. 311–315.

McCabe, Thomas H. "Rhythm as Form in Lawrence: 'The Horse-Dealer's Daughter," *Publications of the Modern Language Association*, LXXXVII (January 1972), 64–68.

Meyers, Jeffrey. "D. H. Lawrence and Tradition: 'The Horse Dealer's Daughter,'" *Studies in Short Fiction*, XXVI (Summer 1989), 346–351.

O'Faolain, Sean. *Short Stories: A Study in Pleasure* (Boston, 1961), pp. 461–464.

Padhi, Bibhti. *D. H. Lawrence: Modes of Fictional Style* (Troy, N.Y., 1989), pp. 85–88.

Philips, Steven R. "The Double Pattern of D. H. Lawrence's 'The Horse Dealer's Daughter,'" *Studies in Short Fiction*, X (Winter 1973), 94–97.

Pinion, F. B. "Shorter Stories," *A D. H. Lawrence Companion: Life, Thought, and Works* (London, 1978), pp. 218–248. (G)

Rehder, Jessie. *The Story at Work* (New York, 1963), pp. 240–241.

Roberts, Edgar V. "The Idea in D. H. Lawrence's 'The Horse Dealer's Daughter' that Man's Destiny Is to Love," *Writing Themes About Literature* (Englewood Cliffs, N.J., 1969), pp. 59–61.

Ryals, Clyde de L. "D. H. Lawrence's 'The Horse-Dealer's Daughter,'" *Literature and Psychology*, XII (Spring 1962), 39–43.

Schneider, Raymond. "The Visible Metaphor," *Communication Education*, XXV (March 1976), 121–126,

Schorer, Mark. *The Story* (New York, 1950), pp. 326–329.

Stewart, Jack F. "Eros and Thanatos in Lawrence's 'The Horse-Dealer's Daughter,'" *Studies in the Humanities*, XII (June 1985), 11–21.

DORIS LESSING "Wine"

Atack, Margaret. "Towards a Narrative Analysis of 'A Man and Two Women," *Notebooks/ Memoirs/ Archives: Reading and Rereading Doris Lessing*, Jenny Taylor, ed. (London, 1982), pp. 135–163. (G)

Brewster, Dorothy. *Doris Lessing* (New York, 1965). (G)

Burkom, Selma R, "'Only Connect': Form and Content in Works of Doris Lessing," *Critique* XI (1968), 51–68. (G)

Butcher, Margaret K. "'Two Forks of a Road': Divergence and Convergence in the Short Stories of Doris Lessing," *Modern Fiction Studies*, XXVI (Spring 1980), 55–61. (G)

Gardiner, Judith Kegan. "Gendered Choices: History and Empathy in the Short Fiction of Doris Lessing," *Rhys, Stead, Lessing and the Politics of Empathy* (Bloomington, Ind., 1989), pp. 83–120. (G)

Hanson, Clare. "Free Stories: The Shorter Fiction of Doris Lessing," *Doris Lessing Newsletter*, IX (Spring 1985), 7–8, 14. (G)

Knapp, Mona. *Doris Lessing* (New York, 1984), pp. 75–85. (G)

McDowell, Frederick P. W. "The Fiction of Doris Lessing: An Interim View," *Arizona Quarterly*, XXI (Winter 1965), 315–345. (G)

Stitzel, Judith. "Reading Doris Lessing," *College English*, XL (January 1979), 498–504. (G)

Sukenick, Lynn, "Feeling and Reason in Doris Lessing's Fiction," *Contemporary Literature*, XIV (Autumn 1973), 515–535. (G)

Thorpe, Michael. *Doris Lessing* (Essex, England, 1973). (G)

Votteler, Thomas, ed. *Short Story Criticism: Excerpts from Criticism of the Works of Short Fiction Writers*, VI (Detroit, 1990), pp. 184–221.

BERNARD MALAMUD, "The Magic Barrel"

Aarons, Victoria. "Compassion and Redemption in Malamud's Short Fiction." *Studies in American Fiction*, XX (Spring 1992), 57–73. (G)

Abramson, Edward A. *Bernard Malamud Revisted* (New York, 1993). (G)

Adler, Brian. "Akedah and Community in 'The Magic Barrel,'" *Studies in American Jewish Literature*, X (Fall 1991), 188–196.

Bluefarb, Sam. "Bernard Malamud: The Scope of Caricature," *English Journal*, LIII (May 1964), 319–326, 335.

Dessner, Lawrence Jay. "Malamud's Echoes of Hawthorne's 'Young Goodman Brown,'" *Notes on Contemporary Literature*, 29 (March 1999), 6–8.

———. "Malamud's Revisions to The Magic Barrel," *Critique*, XXX (Summer 1989), 252–260.

———. "The Playfulness of Bernard Malamud's 'The Magic Barrel,'" *Essays in Literature*, XV (Spring 1988), 87–101.

Foff, Arthur. "Strangers Amid Ruins," *Northwest Review*, II (Fall–Winter 1958), 68–77. (G)

Gealy, Marcia B. "Malamud's Short Stories: A Reshaping of Hasidic Tradition," *Judaism*, XXVIII (Winter 1979), 51–61. (G)

Gerlach, John C. *Toward the End: Closure and Structure in American Short Story* (University, Ala., 1985), pp. 128–130.

Gittleman, Sol. *From Shtetl to Suburbia: The Family in Jewish Literary Imagination* (Boston, 1978), pp. 161–164.

Goldman, Mark. "Bernard Malamud's Comic Vision and the Theme of Identity," *Critique*, VII (Winter 1964–1965), 92–109. (G)

Gunn, Giles B. "Bernard Malamud and the High Cost of Living," *Adversity and Grace*, Nathan A. Scott, ed. (Chicago, 1968), pp. 59–85. (G)

Hershinow, Sheldon J. *Bernard Malamud* (New York, 1980), pp. 128–131.

Hoffer, Bates. "The Magic in Malamud's Barrel," *Linguistics in Literature*, II (Fall 1977), 1–26.

Karl, Frederick R. *American Fictions: 1940–1980* (New York, 1983), pp. 243—244.

Kemer, David. "A Note on the Source of 'The Magic Barrel,'" *Studies in American Jewish Literature*, IV (Spring 1978), 32–35.

Klein, Marcus. *After Alienation: American Novelists in Mid-Century* (Cleveland, 1964), pp. 277–280.

Kumar, Shiv P. "Marionettes in Taleysim: Yiddish Folkfigures in Two Malamud Stories," *Indian Journal of American Studies*, VIII (July 1977), 18–24.

Marcus, Steven. "The Novel Again," *Partisan Review*, XXIX (Spring 1962), 171–195.

May, Charles E. "Something Fishy in 'The Magic Barrel,'" *Studies in American Fiction*, XIV (Spring 1986), 93–98.

Miller, Theodore C. "The Minister and the Whore: An Examination of Bernard Malamud's 'The Magic Barrel,'" *Studies in the Humanities*, III (October 1972), 43–44.

Peden, William. *The American Short Story: Continuity and Change, 1940–1975* (Boston, 1975), pp.116–121.(G)

Pinsker, Sanford. "The Magic Barrel," *Reference Guide to Short Fiction*, Noelle Watson, ed. (Detroit, 1994), pp. 788–789.

———. *The Schlemiel as Metaphor: Studies in the Yiddish and American Jewish Novel* (Carbondale, Ill., 1971), pp. 88–93.

Raban, Jonathan. *The Technique of Modern Fiction* (South Bend, Ind., 1969), pp. 129–132.

Ray, Laura Krugman. "Dickens and 'The Magic Barrel,'" *Studies in American Jewish Literature*, IV (Spring 1978), 35–40.

Reynolds, Richard. "'The Magic Barrel': Pinye Salzman's Kadish," *Studies in Short Fiction*, X (Winter 1973), 100–102.

Richman, Sidney. *Bernard Malamud* (New York, 1966), pp. 118–123.

Rovit, Earl H. "Bernard Malamud and the Jewish Literary Tradition," *Critique*, III (Winter-Spring 1960), 3–10.

Sloan, Gary. "Malamud's Unmagic Barrel," *Studies in Short Fiction*, XXXII (Winter 1995), 11–19, 39–57.

Solotaroff, Robert. *Bernard Malamud: A Study of the Short Fiction* (Boston 1989), pp. 35–37.

Stegel, Ben. "Through a Glass Darkly: Bernard Malamud's Painful View of the Self," *The Fiction of Bernard Malamud*, Richard Astro and Jackson J. Benson, eds. (Corvallis, Ore., 1977), pp. 117–147. (G)

———. "Victims in Motion: Bernard Malamud's Sad and Bitter Clowns," *Northwest Review*, V (Spring 1962), 69–80.

Storey, Michael L. "Pinye Salzman, Pan, and 'The Magic Barrel,'" *Studies in Short Fiction*, XVIII (Spring 1981), 180–183.

Trilling, Lionel. *Prefaces to the Experience of Literature* (New York, 1979), pp. 170–174.

Walden, Daniel. "Bernard Malamud, An American Jewish Writer and His Universal Heroes," *Studies in American Jewish Literature*, VII (Fall 1988), 153–161. (G)

THOMAS MANN, "Death in Venice"

Albright, Daniel. *Personality and Impersonality: Lawrence, Woolf and Mann* (Chicago, 1978), pp. 226–235.

Alexander, Doris. *Creating Literature Out of Life* (University Park, Pa., 1996), pp. 7–21.

Amory, Frederic. "The Classical Style of 'Der Tod in Venedig,'" *Modern Language Review*, LIX (July 1964), 399–409.

Apter, T. E. *Thomas Mann: The Devil's Advocate* (New York, 1978), pp. 50–57.

Baron, Frank. "Sensuality and Morality in Thomas Mann's 'Tod in Venedig,'" *Germanic Review*, XLV (March 1970), 115–125.

Bergenholtz, Rita A. "Mann's 'Death in Venice,'" *Explicator*, 55 (Spring 1997), 145–147.

Bovey, John. "'Death in Venice': Structure and Image," *Twice a Year*, No. 5 and No. 6 (1940), 238–246.

Braverman, Albert, and Larry David Nachman. "The Dialectic of Decadence: An Analysis of Thomas Mann's 'Death in Venice,'" *Germanic Review*, XLV (November 1970), 289–298.

Bryson, Cynthia B. "The Imperative Daily Nap; or, Aschenbach's Dream in 'Death in Venice," *Studies in Short Fiction*, XXIX (Spring 1992), 181–194.

Church, Margaret. "'Death in Venice': A Study of Creativity," *College English*, XXIII (1962), 648–651.

Cohn, Dorrit. "The Second Author of 'Der Tod in Venedig,'" *Critical Essays on Thomas Mann* Inta N. Ezergailis, ed. (Boston, 1988), pp. 124–133.

Cosigny, Scott. "Aschenbach's 'Page and a Half of Choicest Prose': Mann's Rhetoric of Irony," *Studies in Short Fiction*, XIV (1977), 359–367.

Del Caro, Adrian. "Philosophizing and Poetic License in Mann's Early Fiction," *Approaches to Teaching Thomas Mann's "Death in Venice" and Short Other Fiction*, Jeffrey B. Berlin, ed. (New York, 1992), 46–48.

Dyson, A. E. "The Stranger God: 'Death in Venice,'" *Critical Quarterly*, XIII (Spring 1971), 5–20.

Engelberg, Edward. *Elegiac Fictions: The Motif of the Unlived Life* (University Park, Pa., 1989), pp. 96–103.

Feuerlicht, Ignace. *Thomas Mann* (New York, 1968), pp. 117–126.

Frank, Bernhard. "Mann's 'Death in Venice,'" *Explicator*, XLV, i (1986), 31–32.

Frey, John R. "'Die Stumme Begegnung,' Beobachtungen zur Funktion des Blicks im 'Tod in Venedig,'" *German Quarterly* XLI (1968), 177–195.

Furst, Lilian R. "Reading 'Nasty' Great Books," *The Hospitable Canon: Essays on Literary Play, Scholarly Choice, and Popular Pressures*, Virgil Nemoianu and Robert Royals, eds. (Philadelphia, 1991), pp. 40–50.

———. *Through the Lens of the Reader: Exploration of European Narrative* (Albany, 1992), pp. 54–66.

Gillespie, Gerald. "Man and the Modernist Tradition," *Approaches to Teaching Thomas Mann's "Death in Venice" and Other Short Fiction*, Jeffrey B. Berlin, ed. (New York, 1992), 98–104.

Good, Graham. "The Death of Language in 'Death in Venice,'" *Mosaic*, V (Spring 1972), 43–52.

Gray, Ronald. *The German Tradition in Literature, 1871–1945* (London, 1965), pp. 145–156.

Gronicka, Andre von. Myth Plus Psychology: A Style Analysis of 'Death in Venice,'" *Germanic Review*, XXXI (October 1956), 191–205.

Gross, Harvey. "Aschenbach and Kurtz: The Cost of Civilization," *Centennial Review*, VI (Spring 1962), 131–143.

Gustafson, Lorraine. "Xenophon and 'Der Tod in Venedig,'" *German Review*, XXI (October 1946), 209–214.

Hafele, Josef, and Hans Stammel. *Thomas Mann: Der Tod in Venedig* (Frankfurt, 1992).

Heilbut, Anthony. *Thomas Mann: Eros and Literature* (New York, 1996), pp. 42–44, 246–268, 402–404.

Heller, Erich. *The Ironic German: A Study of Thomas Mann* (Boston, 1958), pp. 98–115.

Hofmiller, Josef "Thomas Mann 'Tod in Venedig,'" *Merkur* IX (June 1955), 305–520.

Jonas, Isadore B. *Thomas Mann and Italy*, Betty Crouse, trans. (University, Ala., 1969), pp. 34–41.

Kirchberger, Lida. "'Death in Venice' and the Eighteenth Century," *Monatshefte*, LVIII (Winter 1966), 321–334.

Kohut, Heinz. "'Death in Venice' by Thomas Mann: A Story About Disintegration of Artistic Sublimation," *Psychoananalytic Quarterly*, XXVI (1957), 206–228.

Krotkoff, Herta. "Zur Symbolik in Thomas Mann's 'Tod in Venedig,'" *Modern Language Notes*, I, XXXII (1967), 445–453,

Lehnert, Herbert. "Thomas Mann's Early Interest in Myth and Erwin Rohde's *Psyche*," *PMLA*, LXXIX (June 1964), 297–304.

Leppmann, Wolfgang. "Time and Place in 'Death in Venice'," *German Quarterly*, XLVIII (1975), 66–75.

Leser, Esther H. *Thomas Mann's Short Fiction: An Intellectual Biography*, Mitzi Brunsdale, ed. (Rutherford, N.J., 1989), pp. 161 –180.

Luft, Hermann. *Der Konflikt zwischen Geist und Sinnlichkeit in Thomas Manns Tod in Venedig* (Frankfurt, 1976).

McNamara, Eugene. "'Death in Venice': The Disguised Self," *College English*, XXIV (December 1962), 233–234.

McWilliams, James R. *Brother Artist: A Psychological Study of Thomas Mann's Fiction* (Lanham, Md., 1983), pp. 147–158.

———. "The Failure of a Repression: Thomas Mann's 'Tod in Venedig,'" *German Life and Letters*, XX (1967), 233–241.

Marson, E. L. *The Ascetic Artist: Prefiguration in Thomas Mann's Der Tod in Venedig* (Frankfurt, 1979).

Martin, Robert K. "Gender,, Sexuality, and Identity in Mann's Short Fiction," *Approaches* to Teaching Thomas Mann's "Death in Venice" and Short Other Fiction, Jeffrey B. Berlin, ed. (New York, 1992), 63–66.

Mautner, Franz H. "Die Griechischen Anklange in Thomas Mann's 'Tod in Venedig,'" Monatshefte, XLIV (I 962), 20–26.

Michael, Wolfgang. "Stoff und Idee im 'Tod in Venedig,'" Deutsche Vierteljahrsschrift fur Literaturwissenschaft und Geistegeschichte, XXXIII (1959), 13–19.

Mileck, Joseph. "A Comparative Study of 'Die Betrogene' and 'Der Tod in Venedig,'" Modern Language Forum, XLII (December 1957), 124–129.

Nicholls, R. A. Nietzsche in the Early Works of Thomas Mann (Berkeley, 1955), pp. 77–91.

Reed, T. J. Thomas Mann: The Uses of Tradition (London, 1974), pp. 144–178.

Reilly, Patrick. The Literature of Guilt: From "Gulliver" to Golding (Iowa City, 1988), pp. 69–91.

Rey, W. H. "Tragic Aspects of the Artist in Thomas Mann's Works," Modern Language Quarterly, XIX (1958), 197–203.

Rockwood, Heidi M. "Mann's 'Death in Venice,'" Explicator, XXXIX, iv (I 981), 34.

Rosenthal, M. L. "The Corruption of Aschenbach," University of Kansas City Review, XIV (1947), 49–56.

Rotkin, Charlotte. "Form and Function: The Art and Architecture of 'Death in Venice,' Midwest Quarterly (1988), 497–505.

Schuster, George N. "Art at War with the Good," Great Moral Dilemmas in Literature, Past and Present, R. M. MacIver, ed. (New York, 1956), pp. 25–36.

Seyppel, Joachim H. "Two Variations on a Theme: Dying in Venice (Thomas Mann and Ernest Hemingway)," Literature and Psychology, VII (1957), 8–12.

Slochower, Harry. "Thomas Mann's 'Death in Venice,'" American Imago, XXVI (Summer 1969), 123–144.

Smith, Christopher. "Death in Venice," Reference Guide to Short Fiction, Noelle Watson, ed. (Detroit, 1994), pp. 685–686.

Smith, Herbert 0. "Prologue to the Great War: Encounters with Appolo and Dionysus in 'Death in Venice,'" Focus on Robert Graves, I (Winter 1992), 36–42.

Stanzel, Franz K. "Consonant and Dissonant Closure in 'Death in Venice' and 'The Dead,'" Neverending Stories: Toward a Critical Narratology, Ann Fehn, Ingeborg Hoesterey, and Maria Tatar, eds. (Princeton, N.J., 1992), pp. 114–123.

Stewart, Walter K. "'Der Tod in Venedig': The Path to Insight," German Review, LIII (1978), 50–55.

Stock, Irvin. Ironic Out of Love: The Novels of Thomas Mann (Jefferson, N. C., 1994), 32–35.

Strue, Troman S., and E. L. Marson. "The Ascetic Artist: Prefigurations in Thomas Mann's 'Tod in Venedig,'" Seminar: A Journal of Germanic Studies, XVI, No. 2 (1980), 120–122.

Tarbox, Raymond. "'Death in Venice': The Aesthetic Object as Dream Guide," American Imago, XXVI (Summer 1969), 123–144.

Thomas, R. Hinton. Thomas Mann: The Mediation of Art (Oxford, England, 1956), pp. 59–84.

Timms, Edward. "'Death in Venice' as Psychohistory," Approaches to Teaching Thomas Mann's "Death in Venice" and Short Other Fiction, Jeffrey B. Berlin, ed. (New York, 1992), 63–66.

Traschen, Isadore. "The Uses of Myth in 'Death in Venice,'" Modern Fiction Studies, XI (Summer 1965), 165–179.

Travers, Martin. Thomas Mann (New York, 1992), pp. 48–59.

Urdang, Constance. "Faust in Venice: The Artist and the Legend in 'Death in Venice,'" Accent, XVIII (1958), 253–267.

Venable, Vernon. "Poetic Reason in Thomas Mann," Virginia Quarterly Review, XIV (1938), 61–76.

Watt, Cedric. The Deceptive Text: An Introduction to Covert Plots (Totowa, N.J., 1984), pp. 167–175.

Wiegmann, Hermann. Die Erzahlungen Thomas Mann: Interpretationen und Realien (Bielefeld, Germany, 1992), pp. 186–201.

Wiese, Benno von. *Die deutsche Novelle von Goethe bis Kafka* (Dusseldorf, 1956), pp. 304–324.

Winkler, Michael. "Tadzio-Anastasios: A note on 'Der Tod in Venedig,'" *Modern Language Notes*, XCI I (1977), 607–609.

Woodward, Anthony. "The Figure of the Artist in Thomas Mann's *Kroger* and 'Death in Venice,'" *English Studies in Africa*, IX (September 1966), 158–167.

Wright, Cuthbert. "Eros," *Dial*, LXXVIII (1925), 420–425.

KATHERINE MANSFIELD, "Her First Ball"

Franklin, Carol. "Mansfield and Richardson: A Short Story Dialectic," *Australian Literary Studies*, 11 (1983), 224–233.

Hankin, C. A. *Katherine Mansfield and Her Confessional Stories* (New York, 1983), pp. 216–218.

Klein, Don W. "An Eden for Insiders: Katherine Mansfield's New Zealand," *College English*, 27 (1965), 207–209.

Nathan, Rhoda B. *Katherine Mansfield* (New York, 1988), pp. 46–50.

KATHERINE MANSFIELD, "Miss Brill"

Berkman, Sylvia. *Katherine Mansfield: A Critical Study* (New Haven, 1951), pp. 162–163.

Daly, Saralyn. *Katherine Mansfield* (New York, 1994), pp. 82–83.

Fullbrook, Kate. *Katherine Mansfield* (Bloomington, Ind., 1986), pp. 103–106.

Gargano, James W. "Mansfield's 'Miss Brill,'" *Explicator*, 19 (November 1960), Item 10.

Hull, Robert L. "Alientation in 'Miss Brill,'" *Studies in Short Fiction*, 5 (Fall 1967), 74–75.

Madden, David. "Katherine Mansfield's 'Miss Brill,'" *University Review*, 31 (December 1964), 89–92.

Nathan, Rhoda B. *Katherine Mansfield* (New York, 1988), pp. 91–92.

Orvis, Mary. *The Art of Writing Fiction* (New York, 1948), pp. 14–15.

Sanders, Thomas E. *The Discovery of Fiction* (Chicago, 1967), pp. 138–145.

BOBBIE ANN MASON, "Shiloh"

Barnes, Linda Adams. "The Freak Endures: The Southern Grotesque from Flannery O'Connor to Bobbie Ann Mason," *Since Flannery O'Connor: Essays on the Contemporary American Short Story*, Loren Logsdon and Charles W. Mayer, eds. (Macomb, Ill., 1987), pp. 133–141. (G)

Blythe, Hal, and Charlie Sweet. "The Ambiguous Grail Quest in 'Shiloh,'" *Studies in Short Fiction*, XXXII (Spring 1995), 223–226.

———. "Bird Imagery in Mason's 'Shiloh'" *Notes on Contemporary Literature*, XXV (November 1995), 2–3.

———. "Goodbye, Norma Jean: The Transformation Motif in 'Shiloh,'" *Notes on Contemporary Literature*, 29 (March 1999), 5–6.

———. "Mason's 'Shiloh': Another Civil War," *Notes on Contemporary Literature*, XXV (September 1995), 5–6.

Brinkmeyer, Robert H., Jr. "Finding One's History: Bobbie Ann Mason and Contemporary Southern Literature," *Southern Literary Journal*, XIX (Spring 1987), 20–33.

Bucher, Tina. "Changing Roles and Finding Stability: Women in Bobbie Ann Mason's *Shiloh and Other Stories*," *Border States*, 8 (1991), 54.

Cooke, Stewart J. "Mason's 'Shiloh'" *Explicator*, LI (Spring 1993), 196–199.

Curnutt, Kirk. *Wise Economies: Brevity and Storytelling in American Short Stories* (Moscow, Ida., 1997), pp. 217–229.

Giannone, Richard. "Bobbie Ann Mason and the Recovery of Mystery," *Studies in Short Fiction* XXVII (Fall 1990), 553–566.

Henring, Barbara. "Minimalism and the American Dream: 'Shiloh' by Bobbie Ann Mason and 'Preservation' by Raymond Carver," *Modern Fiction Studies* XXXV (Winter 1989), 689–698.

Hornby, Nick. *Contemporary American Fiction* (London, 1992), pp. 77–80.

Levy, Andrew. *The Culture and Commerce of the American Short Story* (New York, 1993), pp. 108–125.

Lohafer, Susan. "Stops on the Way to 'Shiloh': A Special Case for Literary Empiricism," *Style*, XXVII (1993) 395–406.

Lyons, Bonnie and Bill Oliver. "An Interview with Bobbie Ann Mason," *Contemporary Literature*, XXXII (Winter 1991), 449–470. (G)

Morphew, G. O. "Downhome Feminists in *Shiloh and Other Stories*, *Southern Literary Journal*, XXII (Spring 1989), 41–49.

Pollack, Harriet. "From *Shiloh* to *In Country* to *Feather Crown*: Bobbie Ann Mason, Women's History, and Southern Fiction," *Southern Literary Journal*, XXVIII (Spring 1996), 95–116.

Ryan, Maureen. "Stopping Places: Bobbie Ann Mason's Short Stories," *Women Writers of the Contemporary South*, Peggy Whitman Prenshaw, ed. (Jackson, Miss., 1984), pp. 283–294. (G)

Smith, Michael. "Bobbie Ann Mason, Artist and Rebel: An Interview," *Kentucky Review*. VIII (Autumn 1988), 56–63. (G)

Thompson, Terry. "Mason's 'Shiloh'" *Explicator*, LIV (Fall 1995), 54–58.

White, Leslie. "The Function of Popular Culture in Bobbie Ann Mason's *Shiloh and Other Stories* and *In Country*," *Southern Quarterly*, XXVI (Summer 1988), 69–79. (G)

Wilhelm, Albert E. "An Interview With Bobbie Ann Mason," *Southern Quarterly*, XXVI (Winter 1988), No. 2.

———. "Making Over or Making Off: The Problem of Identity in Bobbie Ann Mason's Short Fiction," *Southern Literary Journal*, XVIII (Spring 1986), 76–82. (G)

———. "Private Rituals: Coping with Change in the Fiction of Bobbie Ann Mason," *Southern Literary Journal*, XXVIII (Winter 1987), 271–282.

GUY DE MAUPASSANT, "The Necklace"

Bement, Douglas. *Weaving the Short Story* (New York, 1931), pp. 72–74.

Brooks, Cleanth and Robert Penn Warren. *Understanding Fiction* (New York, 1959), pp. 112–115.

Donaldson-Evans, Mary. "The Last Laugh: Maupassant's 'Les Bijoux' and 'La Purure,'" *French Forum*, LIV, 1 (1980), 163–174.

Lavrin, Janko. "Chekhov and Maupassant," *Slavonic Review*, (June 1926), 1–24. (G)

Matthews, J. H. "Theme and Structure in Maupassant's Short Stories," *Modern Languages*, XLII (December 1962), 136–144. (G)

O'Faolain, Sean. *The Short-Story* (New York, 1951), pp. 176–179.

Saint-Armand, Pierre. "Tales of Adornment: Fictions of the Feminine," *Literature and Psychology*, XXXVIII, iii (1992), 6–14.

Shaw, Valerie. *The Short Story: A Critical Introduction* (London, 1983), pp. 56–57.

Smith, Christopher. "The Necklace," *Reference Guide to Short Fiction*, Noelle Watson, ed. (Detroit, 1994), p. 818.

Steegmuller, Francis. *Maupassant: A Lion in the Path* (New York, 1949), pp. 203–210.
Sullivan, Edward D. *Maupassant: The Short Stories* (Great Neck, N.Y., 1962), pp. 19–20.

HERMAN MELVILLE, "Bartleby the Scrivener"

Abearian, Richard, "The World of Love and the Spheres of Fright: Melville's 'Bartleby the Scrivener,'" *Studies in Short Fiction*, I (Spring 1964), 207–215.

Abrams, Fred. "*Don Quixote* and Melville's 'Bartleby the Scrivener,'" *Studies in Short Fiction*, XVIII (Summer 1981), 323–324.

Abrams, Robert E. "'Bartleby' and the Fragile Pageantry of the Ego," *Journal of English Literary History*, XLV (Fall 1978), 488–500.

Anderson, Walter E. "Form and Meaning in 'Bartleby the Scrivener,'" *Studies in Short Fiction*, XVIII (Fall 1981), 383–393;

Ayo, Nicholas. "Bartleby's Lawyer on Trial," *Arizona Quarterly*, XXVIII (Spring 1972), 27–38.

Bach, Bert C. "Melville's Theatrical Mask: The Role of Narrative Perspective in His Short Fiction," *Studies in the Literary Imagination*, II (April 1969), 43–55.

Barbara, Patricia. "What If Bartleby Were a Woman?" *The Authority of Experience*, Arlyn Diamond and Lee R. Edwards, eds. (Amherst, Mass., 1977), pp. 212–223.

Barnett, Louise K. "Bartleby as Alienated Worker," *Studies in Short Fiction*, XI (Fall 1974), 379–385.

———. *Authority and Speech: Language, Society and Self in the American Novel* (Athens, Ga., 1993), pp. 77–87.

Barry, Elaine. "Herman Melville: The Changing Face of Comedy," *American Studies International*, XVI (1978), 19–33.

Beja, Morris. "Bartleby and Schizophrenia," *Massachusetts Review*, XIX (1978), 555–568.

Bender, Bert. "Melville's Shock of Genius and His Three Tales of the Shock Unrecognized," *Forum*, XIII (Winter 1976), 24–30.

Benoit, Raymond. "*Bleak House* and 'Bartleby the Scrivener,'" *Studies in Short Fiction*, XXI (Summer 1984), 272–273.

Bergmann, Hans. "'Turkey on His Back': 'Bartleby' and New York Words," *Melville Society Extracts*, XL (September 1992), 16–19.

Bergmann, Johannes Dietrich. "'Bartleby' and *The Lawyer's Story*," *American Literature*, XLVII (November 1975), 432–436.

———. "Melville's Tales," *A Companion to Melville Studies*, John Bryant, ed. (Westport, Conn., 1986), pp. 253–256.

Bernstein, John. *Pacificism and Rebellion in the Writings of Herman Melville* (The Hague, 1964), pp. 166–171.

Berthold, Michael C. "The Prison World of Melville's *Pierre* and 'Bartleby,'" *ESQ XXXIII* (4th Quarter 1987), 237–252.

Bickley, R. Bruce, Jr. *The Method of Melville's Short Fiction* (Durham, N.C., 1975), pp. 26–44.

Bigelow, Gordon E. "The Problem of Symbolist Form in Melville's 'Bartleby the Scrivener,'" *Modern Language Quarterly*, XXI (September 1970), 345–358.

Billy, Ted. "Eros and Thanatos in 'Bartleby,'" *Arizona Quarterly*, XXXI (Spring 1975), 21–32.

Bluestone, George. "'Bartleby': The Tale, the Film,' *The Melville Annual 1965, A Symposium: Bartleby the Scrivener*, Howard P. Vincent, ed. (Kent, Ohio, 1966), pp. 45–54.

Bollas, Christopher. "Melville's Lost Self: 'Bartleby,'" *American Imago*, XXXI (Winter 1974), 401–411.

Bowen, James K. "Alienation and Withdrawal are Not the Absurd: Renunciation and Preference in 'Bartleby the Scrivener,'" *Studies in Short Fiction*, VIII (Fall 1971), 633–635.

Brennan, Matthew C. "Melville's Bartleby as an Archetypal Shadow," *Journal of Evolutionary Psychology*, XIII, iii–v (1992), 318–331.

Brodwin, Stanley. "To the Frontiers of Eternity: Melville's Crossing in 'Bartleby the Scrivener,'" *Bartleby the Inscrutable: A Collection of Commentary on Herman Melville's Tale "Bartleby the Scrivener,"* Thomas M. Inge, ed. (Hamden, Conn., 1979), pp. 174–196.

Browne, Ray B. "The Affirmation of 'Bartleby,'" *Folklore International Essays in Traditional Literature, Belief, and Custom in Honor of Wayland Debs Hand*, D.K. Wilgus, ed. (Hatboro, Pa., 1967), pp. 11–21.

———. *Melville's Drive to Humanism* (Lafayette, Ind., 1971), pp. 152–168.

Bulger, Thomas. "'Bartleby,'Burton and the Artistic Temperament," *Melville Society Extracts*, CI (June 1995), 14–17.

Burling, William J. "Commentary on 'Bartlebty': 1968–1979," *Arizona Quarterly*, XXXVII (Winter 1981), 347–354.

Busch, Frederick. "Thoreau and Melville as Cellmates," *Modern Fiction Studies*, XXIII (Summer 1977), 239–242.

Cervo, Nathan A. "Melville's 'Bartleby'—*Imago Dei*," *American Transcendental Quarterly*, XIV (Spring 1972), 152–156.

———. "A Note on Melville's "Bartleby the Scrivener,'" *Journal of the Pre-Raphaelite Studies*, VI (November 1985), 96.

Chase, Richard. *Herman Melville: A Critical Study* (New York, 1949), pp. 143–149.

Clark, Michael. "Witches and Wall Street: Possession Is Nine-Tenths of the Law," *Texas Studies in Language and Literature*, XXV (Spring 1983), 55–76.

Cohen, Hennig. "Bartleby's Dead Letter Office," *Melville Society Extracts*, X (1972), 5–6.

Colwell, James L. and Gary Spitzer. "'Bartleby' and 'The Raven': Parallels of the Irrational," *Georgia Review*, XXIII (Spring 1969), 37–43.

Conarroe, Joel L. "Melville's Bartleby and Charles Lamb," *Studies in Short Fiction*, V (Winter 1968), 113–118.

Conkling, Chris, "Misery of Christian Joy: Conscience and Freedom in 'Bartleby the Scrivener,'" *Literature and Belief*, I (1981), 79–89.

Cornwell, Ethel F. "Bartleby the Absurd," *International Fiction Review*, IX, ii (1982), 93–99.

Craver, Donald H. and Patricia R. Plante. "Bartleby or, The Ambiguities," *Studies in Short Fiction*, XX (Spring–Summer 1983), 132–136.

Curnutt, Kirk. *Wise Economies: Brevity and Storytelling in American Short Stories* (Moscow, Ida., 1997), pp. 57–70.

D'Avanzo, Mario L. "Melville's 'Bartleby' and Carlyle," *The Melville Annual 1965, A Symposium: Bartleby the Scrivener*, Howard P. Vincent, ed. (Kent, Ohio, 1966), pp. 113–139.

———. "Melville's 'Bartleby' and John Jacob Astor," *New England Quarterly*, XLI (June 1968), 259–264.

Davidson, Cathy R. "Courting God and Mammon: The Biographer's Impasse in Melville's 'Bartleby the Scrivener,'" *Delta*, VI (April 1978), 47–60.

Davidson, Frank. "'Bartleby': A Few Observations," *Emerson Society Quarterly*, XXVII (Second Quarter 1962), 25–32.

Demure, Catherine. "La Vibration du monde," *Europe*, LXIX (1991), 100–108.

Dew, Marjorie. "The Attorney and the Scrivener: Quoth the Raven, 'Nevermore,'" *The Melville Annual 1965, A Symposium: Bartleby the Scrivener*, Howard P. Vincent, ed. (Kent, Ohio, 1966), pp. 94–103.

Dillingham, William B. *Melville's Short Fiction, 1853–1856* (Athens, Ga., 1977), pp. 18–55.

Ditsky, John. "Melville's Bartleby: A Shakespearean Source?" *New Laurel Review*, IX (Spring–Fall 1979), 43–45.

Douglas, Ann. *The Feminization of American Culture* (New York, 1977), pp. 315–317.

Duban, James. "Chipping with a Chisel: The Ideology of Melville's Narrators," *Texas Studies in Literature and Language*, XXXI (Fall 1989), 341–385. (G)

Eitner, Walter H. "The Lawyer's Rockaway Trips in 'Bartleby, the Scrivener,'" *Melville Society Extracts*, LXXVIII (September 1989), 14–16.

Eliot, Alexander. "Melville and Bartleby," *Furioso*, III (Fall 1947), 11–21.

Emery, Allan Moore. "The Alternatives of Melville's 'Bartleby,'" *Nineteenth-Century Fiction*, XXXI (September 1976), 170–187.

Evans, Walter. "Hawthorne and 'Bartleby the Scrivener,'" *American Transcendental Quarterly*, LVII (July 1985), 45–58.

Felheim, Marvin. "Meaning and Structure in 'Bartleby,'" *College English*, XXIII (February 1962), 369–376.

Fiene, Donald M. "Bartleby the Christ," *American Transcendental Quarterly*, VII (Summer 1970), 18–23.

Firchow, Peter E. "Bartleby: Man and Metaphor," *Studies in Short Fiction*, V (Summer 1968), 342–348.

Fisher, Marvin. "'Bartleby,' Melville's Circumscribed Scrivener," *Southern Review*, X (Winter 1974), 59–79.

———:. *Going Under: Melville's Short Fiction and the American 1850s* (Baton Rouge, 1977), pp.179–199.

Fogle, Richard H. "Melville's 'Bartleby': Absolutism, Predestination, and Free Will," *Tulane Studies in English*, IV (1954), 125–135.

———. *Melville's Shorter Tales* (Norman, Okla., 1960), pp. 14–27.

Foley, Brian. "Dickens Revised: 'Bartleby' and *Bleak House*," *Essays in Literature*, XII (Fall 1985), 241–250.

Franklin, H. Bruce. *The Victim as Criminal and Artist: Literature from the American Prison* (New York, 1978), pp. 56–60.

———. *The Wake of the Gods: Melville's Mythology* (Stanford, 1963), pp. 126–136.

Friederich, Reinhard H. "Asleep with Kings and Counselors: A Source Note on Bartleby in the Tombs," *Melville Society Extracts*, LVIII (May 1984), 13–15.

Friedman, Maurice. "Bartleby and the Modern Exile," *The Melville Annual 1965, A Symposium: Bartleby the Scrivener*, Howard P. Vincent, ed. (Kent, Ohio, 1966), pp. 64–81.

———. *Problematic Rebel: Melville, Dostoevsky, Kafka, Camus* (Chicago, 1970), pp. 82–92.

Friedman, Michael II. "*Pickwick Papers* as a Source for the Epilogue to Melville's 'Bartleby the Scrivener,'" *Studies in Short Fiction*, XXXI (Spring 1984), 147–151.

Frost, Graham Nicol, "Up Wall Street Towards Broadway: The Narrator's Pilgrimage in Melville's 'Bartleby the Scrivener,'" *Studies in Short Fiction*, XXIV (Summer 1987), 263–270.

Gale, Robert L. "'Bartleby'—Melville's Father-in-Law," *Annali Instituto Universitario Orientale, Napoli, Sezione Germanica*, V (1962), 57–72.

Gardner, John. "'Bartleby': Act and Social Commitment," *Philological Quarterly*, XLIII (January 1964), 87–98.

Gibson, William M. "Herman Melville's 'Bartleby the Scrivener' and 'Benito Cereno,'" *The American Renaissance, The History of an Era: Essays and Interpretations*, George Hendrick, ed, (Frankfurt, 1961), 107–116.

Giddings, T. H. "Melville, the Colt-Adams Murder, and 'Bartleby,'" *Studies in American Fiction*. II (Autumn 1974), 123–132.

Gilmore, Michael T. "'Bartleby the Scrivener' and the Transformation of the Economy," *American Romanticism and the Marketplace* (Chicago, 1985), pp. 132–145.

Goldleaf, Steven. "Bartleby the Scrivener," *Reference Guide to Short Fiction*, Noelle Watson, ed. (Detroit, 1994), P. 639.

Gordon, Andrew. "Dead Letter Offices: Joseph Heller's *Something Happened* and Herman Melville's 'Bartleby the Scrivener,'" *Notes on Contemporary Literature*, XII (November 1982), 2–4.

Green, John M. "Bartleby the Perfect Pupil," *ATQ*, VII (March 1993), 65–75.

Grenberg, Bruce L. *Some Other World to Find. Quest and Negation in the Works of Herman Melville* (Urbana, Ill., 1989), pp. 165–176.

Guido, Auguste. "Considcrazioni su Bartleby," *Studi Americani*, III (1957), 99–108.

Gupta, R. K, "'Bartleby': Melville's Critique of Reason," *Indian Journal of American Studies*, IV (June–December 1974), 66–71.

Hagopian, John V. "Bartleby the Scrivener," *Insight I: Analyses of American Literature*, John V. Hagopian and Martin Dolch, eds. (Frankfurt, 1962), pp. 145–149.

Hale, John K. "Bartleby's Stilted Speech," *Melville Society Extracts*, XCVI (March 1994), 12–13.

Hamilton, William. "Bartleby and He: The Strange Hermeneutic of Herman Melville," *Melville Society Extracts*, LXXVIII (September 1989), 12–14.

Hardwick, Elizabeth. "Bartleby in Manhattan," *Bartleby in Manhattan and Other Essays* (New York, 1983), pp. 217–231.

Harmon, Maryhelen C. "Melville's 'Borrowed Personage': Bartleby and Thomas Chatterton," *ESQ*, XXXIII (1st Quarter 1987), 35–44.

Hattenhauer, Darryl. "Bartleby as Horological Chronometer: Yet another View of Bartleby the Doubloon," *American Transcendental Quarterly*, II (March 1989), 35–40.

Hays, James S. "Emptiness and Plentitude in 'Bartleby the Scrivener' and *The Crying of Lot 49*," *Essays in Literature*, XXIII (Fall 1995), 285–299.

Hildebrand, William K. "'Bartleby' and the Black Conceit," *Studies in Romanticism*, XXVII (Summer 1999), 289–313.

Hoag, Ronald Wesley, "The Corpse in the Office: Mortality, Mutability and Salvation in 'Bartleby, the Scrivener,'" *ESQ*, XXXVIII (2nd Quarter 1992), 119–142.

———. "The Last Paragraph of 'Bartleby,'" *Reconciliations: Studies in Honor of Richard Harter Fogle*, Mary L. Johnson and Seraphic D. Leyda, eds. (Salzburg, 1983), pp. 153–160.

Hoffman, Charles G. "The Shorter Fiction of Herman Melville," *South Atlantic Quarterly*, LII (July 1953), 418–421.

Howard, Francis K. "The Catalyst of Language: Melville's Symbol," *English Journal*, LVII (September 1968), 925–831.

Hyde, G. M. "Melville's 'Bartleby' and Gogol's 'The Overcoat,'" *Essays in Poetics: Journal of the Neo-Formalist Circle*, I (1976), 32–48.

Inge, Thomas M., ed. *Bartleby the Inscrutable: A Collection of Commentary on Herman Melville's "Bartleby the Scrivener "* (Hamden, Conn., 1979).

Jay, Gregory S. *America the Scrivener: Deconstruction and the Subject of Literary History* (Ithaca, 1990), pp. 19–27.

Jennings, Margaret. "Bartleby the Existentialist," *Melville Society Extracts*, XXII (Fall 1974), 8–10.

Joswick, Thomas P. "The 'Incurable Disorder' in 'Bartleby,'" *Delta*, VI (April 1978), 79–93.

Kelley, Wyn. *Melville's City: Literary and Urban Form in Nineteenth-Century New York* (New York, 1996), pp. 201–207.

Keppler. C. F. *The Literature of the Second Self* (Tucson, Ariz,, 1972), pp. 115–120.

Kirby, David. *Herman Melville* (New York, 1993), pp. 136–143.

———. *The Sun Rises in the Evening: Monism and Quietism in Western Culture* (Metuchen, N.J., 1982), pp. 57–64.

Kissane, Leedice. "Dangling Constructions in Melville's 'Bartleby,'" *American Speech*, XXXVI (October 1961), 192–200.

Knight, Karl F. "Melville's Variations of the Theme of Failure: 'Bartleby' and *Billy Budd*," *Arlington Quarterly*, II (Autumn 1969), 44–58.

Kopley, Richard. "The Circle and Its Center in 'Bartleby the Scrivener,'" *American Transcendental Quarterly*, II (September 1988), 191–206.

Kornfeld, Milton. "'Bartleby' and the Presentation of Self in Everyday Life," *Arizona Quarterly*, XXXI (Spring 1975), 51–56.

Kuebrich, David. "Melville's Doctrine of Assumptions: The Hidden Ideology of Capitalist Protection in 'Bartleby,'" *New England Quarterly*, LXIX (September 1996), 381–405.

Leary, Lewis. "B is for Bartleby," *Bartleby the Inscrutable: A Collection of Commentary on Herman Melville's Tale "Bartleby the Scrivener,"* Thomas M. Inge, ed. (Hamden, Conn., 1979), pp. 13–27.

Lee, A. Robert. "Voices Off and On: Melville's Piazza and Other Stories," *The Nineteenth-Century American Short Story*, A. Robert Lee, ed. (Totowa, N.J., 1985), pp. 76–102. (G)

Levy, Leo B. "Hawthorne and the Idea of 'Bartleby,'" *Emerson Society Quarterly*, XLVII (Second Quarter 1967), 66–69.

Lindon, Mathieu. "Description d'un combat," *Delta*, VI (April 1978), 5–27.

McCall, Dan. *The Silence of Bartleby* (Ithaca, N.Y., 1989).

McCarthy, Paul. *"The Twisted Mind": Madness in Herman Melville's Fiction* (Iowa City, 1990), 100–104.

MacLaine, Allan H. "Melville's 'Sequel' to 'Bartleby the Scrivener' and Dickens' 'Story of the Bagman's Uncle' in *Pickwick Papers*: An Unnoticed Link," *American Transcendental Quarterly*, LX (June 1986), 37–39.

McWilliams, John P., Jr. *Hawthorne, Melville, and the American Character: A Looking-Glass Business* (Cambridge, England, 1984), pp. 179–181.

Mathews, James M. "'Bartleby': Melville's Tragedy of Humors," *Interpretations*, X (1978), 41–48.

Marcus, Mordecai. "Melville's Bartleby as a Psychological Double," *College English*, XXIII (February 1962), 365—368.

Marter, Robert F. "'Bartleby the Scrivener' and the American Short Story," *Genre*, VI (December 1973), 428–447.

Marx, Leo. "Melville's Parable of the Walls," *Sewanee Review*, LXI (Autumn 1953), 602–627.

McNamara, Leo F. "Subject, Style, and Narrative Technique in 'Bartleby' and 'Wakefield,'" *Michigan Academician*, III (Spring 1971), 41–46.

Mendez, Charlotte Walker. "Scriveners Forlorn: Dickens's Nemo and Melville's Bartleby," *Dickens Studies Newsletter*.

Meyer, Janice Jones. "'Bartleby the Scrivener': Performing the Narrator's Inner Conflict in Chamber Theatre," *Communication Education*, XXVI (November 1977), 348–351.

Meyer, William E., Jr. "'Bartleby,' An American Story," *Forum*, XXIV (Summer 1983), 75–81.

Middleton, F. "Source for 'Bartleby,'" *Extracts*, XV (1973), 9.

Miller, Edwin Haviland. *Melville* (New York, 1975), pp. 262–264.

Miller, J. Hillis. *Versions of Pygmalion* (Cambridge, Mass., 1990), pp. 147–178.

Miller, Lewis H., Jr. "'Bartleby' and the Dead Letter," *Studies in American Fiction*, VIII (Spring 1980), 1–12.

Mills, Nicolaus C. "Prison and Society in 19th Century American Fiction," *Western Humanities Review*, XXIV (Autumn 1970), 325–331.

Mitchell, Charles. "Melville and the Spurious Truths of Legalism," *Centennial Review*, XII (Winter 1968), 110–126.

Mitchell, Thomas R. "Dead Letters and Dead Men: Narrative Purpose in 'Bartleby, the Scrivener,'" *Studies in Short Fiction*, XXVII (Summer 1990), 329–338.

Moldenhauer, Joseph. "'Bartleby' and 'The Custom-House,'" *Delta English Studies*, VII (1978), 21–62.

Mollinger, Robert N. *Psychoanalysis and Literature: An Introduction* (Chicago, 1981), pp. 85–96.

Monteiro, George. "'Bartleby the Scrivener' and Melville's Contemporary Reputation," *Studies in Bibliography*, XXIV (1971), 195–196.

———. "Melville's 'Timothy Quicksand' and the Dead-Letter Office," *Studies in Short Fiction*, IX (Spring 1972), 198–201.

Moore, Jack B. "Ahab and Bartleby: Energy and Indolence," *Studies in Short Fiction*, I (Summer 1964), 291–294.

Morris, Wright. "The Lunatic, the Lover, and the Poet," *Kenyon Review*, XXVII (Autumn 1965), 727–737.

Morsberger, Robert E. "'I Prefer Not To': Melville and the Theme of Withdrawal," *University College Quarterly*, X (November 1964), 24–29.

Morse, David. *American Romanticism*, Vol. II (Totowa, N.J., 1987), pp. 73–77.

Mottram, Eric. "Orpheus and Measured Forms: Law, Madness and Reticence in Melville," *New Perspectives on Melville*, Faith Pullin, ed. (Kent, Ohio, 1978), pp. 232–236.

Murphy, Michael. "'Bartleby the Scrivener': A Simple Reading," *Arizona Quarterly*, XLI (Summer 1985), 143–151.

Mushabac, Jane. *Melville's Humor: A Critical Study* (Hamden, Conn., 1981), pp. 110–120.

Newman, Lea Bertani Vozar. *A Reader's Guide to the Short Stories of Herman Melville* (Boston, 1986), pp. 19–78.

Norman, Liane. "Bartleby and the Reader," *New England Quarterly*, XLIV (March 1971), 22–39.

Oakland, John. "Romanticism in Melville's 'Bartleby' and *Pierre*," *Modern Spräk*, LXX (1976), 209–219.

Oliver, Egbert S. "'Cock-A-Doodle-Do!' and Transcendental Hocus-pocus," *New England Quarterly*, XXI (June 1948), 202–216.

———. "A Second Look at 'Bartleby,'" *College English*, VI (May 1945), 431–439.

Parker, Hershel. "Dead Letters and Melville's 'Bartleby,'" *Resources for American Literary Studies*, IV (Spring 1977), 209–212.

———. "Melville's Satire of Emerson and Thoreau: An Evaluation of the Evidence," *American Transcendental Quarterly*, No. 7 (Summer 1970), 61–67.

———. "The 'Sequel' in 'Bartleby,'" *Bartleby the Inscrutable: A Collection of Commentary on Herman Melville's Tale "Bartleby the Scrivener,"* Thomas M. Inge, ed. (Hamden, Conn., 1979), pp. 159–165.

Patrick, Walton R. "Melville's 'Bartleby' and the Doctrine of Necessity," *American Literature*, XLI (March 1969), 39–54.

Perry, Dennis R. "'Ah, Humanity': Compulsion Neuroses in Melville's 'Bartleby,'", *Studies in Short Fiction*, XXIV (Fall 1987), 407–415.

Pinsker, Sanford. "'Bartleby the Scrivener': Language as Wall," *College Literature*, II (Winter 1975), 17–27.

Plumstead, A. W. "'Bartleby': Melville's Venture into a New Genre," *The Melville Annual 1965, A Symposium: Bartleby the Scrivener*, Howard P. Vincent, ed. (Kent, Ohio, 1966), pp. 82–93.

Pops, Martin Leonard. *The Melville Archetype* (Kent, Ohio, 1970), pp. 121–132.

Post-Lauria, Sheila. "Canonical Texts and Context: The Example of Herman Melville's 'Bartleby, the Scrivener: A Story of Wall Street,'" *College Literature*, XX, 2 (1993), 196–205.

Pribek, Thomas. "An Assumption of Naivete: The Tone of Melville's Lawyer," *Arizona Quarterly*, XLI (Summer 1985), 131–142.

———. "Melville's Copyists: The 'Bartenders' of Wall Street," *Papers on Language and Literature*, XXII (Spring 1986), 176–186.

———. "The 'Safe' Man of Wall Street: Characterizing Melville's Lawyer," *Studies in Short Fiction*, XXIII (Spring 1986), 191–195.

Randall, David S. "Neutered Narration and the Scriptive Fate of the Spirit of Resentment: 'Bartleby the Scrivener' and Herman Melville," *Boundary 2*, XV (Fall 1986/Winter 1987), 85–106–

Randall, John H., III. "Bartleby vs. Wall Street: New York in the 1850's," *Bulletin of the New York Public Library*, LXXVIII (Winter 1975), 138–144.

Reynolds, David S. *Beneath the American Renaissance: The Subversive Imagination in the Age of Emerson and Melville* (New York, 1988), pp. 295–296.

Riddle, Mary-Madeleine G. *Herman Melville's Piazza Tales* (Gothenburg, 1985), pp. 58–74.

Robbillard, Douglas. "The Dead Letter Office," *Melville Society Extracts*, XCVI (March 1994), 8–9.

———. "Monroe Edwards and Melville's Bartleby," *English Language Notes*, XV (1978), 291–294.

Rogers, Robert. *A Psychoanalytic Study of the Double in Literature* (Detroit, 1970), pp. 67–70.

Rogin, Michael Paul. *Subversive Genealogy: The Politics and Art of Herman Melville* (New York, 1983), pp. 192–201.

Ross, Robert. "'Bartleby the Scrivener': An American Cousin," *Post Script*, I (1983), 27–33.

Roudant, Jean. "A propos de 'Bartleby': Compilation," *Delta*, VI (April 1978), 37–42.

Roundy, Nancy. "'That Is All I Know of Him': Epistemology and Art in Melville's 'Bartleby,'" *Essays in Arts and Sciences*, IX (1980), 33–43.

Rovit, Earl. "Purloined, Scarlet, and Dead Letters in *Classic American Literature*," XCVI (1998), 426–430.

Rowe, John C. *Through the Custom-House: Nineteenth-Century American Fiction and Modern Theory* (Baltimore, 1982), pp. 118–124.

Rozenberg, Helene. "Huis-clos dans 'Bartleby,'" *Delta*, VI (April 1978), 29–35.

Ryan, Steven T. "The Gothic Formula of 'Bartleby.'" *Arizona Quarterly*, XXXIV (Winter 1978), 311–316.

St. Armand, Barton Levi. "Curtis's 'Bartleby': An Unrecorded Melville Reference," *Papers of the Bibliographical Society of America*, LXXI (1977), 219–220.

Sanderlin, Reed. "A Re-examination of the Role of the Lawyer-Narrator in Melville's 'Bartleby,'" *Interpretations*, X (1978), 49–55.

Schaffer, Carol. "Unadmitted Impediments, Unmarriageable Minds: Melville's 'Bartleby' and 'I and My Chimney,'" *Studies in Short Fiction*, XXIV (Spring 1987), 93–101.

Schatt, Stanley. *"Bartleby the Scrivener": A Casebook for Research* (Dubuque, Iowa, 1972).

Schechter, Harold. "Bartleby the Chronometer," *Studies in Short Fiction*, XIX (Fall 1982), 359–366.

Schehr, Lawrence R. "Dead Letters: Theories of Writing in 'Bartleby the Scrivener,'" *Enclitic*, VII, i (1983), 96–103.

Sealts, Merton M., Jr., "The Reception of Melville's Short Fiction," *ESQ: A Journal of the American Renaissance*, XXV (1st Quarter 1979), 43–57. (G)

Seelye, John. "The Contemporary 'Bartleby,'" *American Transcendental Quarterly*, VII (Summer 1970), 12–18.

———. *Melville: The Ironic Diagram* (Evanston, Ill., 1970), pp. 96–99.

Senn, Wemer. "Reading Melville's Mazes: An Aspect of the Short Stories," *English Studies*, LXV (February 1984), 27–35. (G)

Shulman, Robert. *Social Criticism and Nineteenth-Century American Fictions* (Columbia, Mo., 1987), pp. 6027.

Shustertnan, David. "The 'Reader Fallacy' and 'Bartleby the Scrivener,'" *New England Quarterly*, XLV (March 1972), 118–124.

Silver, A. "The Lawyer and the Scrivener," *Partisan Review*, XLVIII (1981), 409–424.

Singleton, Marvin. "Melville's 'Bartleby': Over the Republic, a Ciceronian Shadow," *Canadian Review of American Studies*, VI (1975), 165–173.

Short, Byron C. *Cast By Means of Figures: Herman Melville's Rhetorical Development* (Amherst, Mass., 1992), pp. 127–130.

Smith, Herbert F. "Melville's Master in Chancery and His Recalcitrant Clerk,'" *American Quarterly*, XVII (Winter 1965), 734–741.

Smith, Peter A. "Entropy in Melville's 'Bartleby the Scrivener,'" *Centennial Review*, XXXII (Spring 1988), 155–162.

Soloman, Pearl Chesler. *Dickens and Melville in Their Time* (New York, 1975), pp. 34–36, 78–84.

Solomon, Susan and Ritchie Darling. *Bartleby: An Essay* (Amherst, Mass., 1969).

Spector, Robert D. "Melville's 'Bartleby' and the Absurd," *Nineteenth-Century Fiction*, XVI (September 1961), 175–177.

Springer, Norman. "Bartleby and the Terror of Limitations," *Publication of the Modern Language Association*, LXXX (September 1965), 410–418.

Stark, John. "Melville, Lemuel Shaw, and 'Bartleby,'" *Bartleby the Inscrutable: A Collection of Commentary on Herman Melville's Tale "Bartleby the Scrivener,"* Thomas M. Inge, ed. (Hamden, Conn. 1979), pp. 166–173.

Stein, Allen F. "The Motif of Voracity in 'Bartleby,'" *Emerson Society Quarterly,* XXI (First Quarter 1975), 29–34.

Stein, William Bysshe. "Bartleby: The Christian Conscience," *The Melville Annual 1965, A Symposium: Bartleby the Scrivener,* Howard P. Vincent ed. (Kent, Ohio, 1966), pp. 104–112.

Stempel, Daniel and Bruce M. Stillians. "'Bartleby the Scrivener': A Parable of Pessimism," *Nineteenth-Century Fiction,* XXVII (December 1972), 268–282.

Sten, Christopher. "Bartleby the Transcendentalist: Melville's Dead Letter to Emerson," *Modern Language Quarterly,* XXV (March 1974), 30–44.

Stern, Milton R. "Towards 'Bartleby the Scrivener,'" *The Stoic Strain in American Literature: Essays in Honour of Marston LaFrance,* Duane J. MacMillan, ed. (Toronto, 1979), pp. 19–41.

Stone, Edward. *A Certain Morbidness: A View of American Literature* (Carbondale, Ill., 1969), pp. 32–42.

———. "Bartleby and Miss Norman," *Studies in Short Fiction,* IX (Summer 1972), 271–274.

Stout, Janis P. "The Encroaching Sodom: Melville's Urban Fiction," *Texas Studies in Literature and Language,* XVII (Spring 1975), 170–173.

———. *Sodoms in Eden: The City in American Fiction Before 1860* (Westport, Conn., 1976), pp.136–138.

Sullivan, William P. "Bartleby and Infantile Autism: A Naturalistic Explanation," *Bulletin of the Virginia Association of College English Teachers,* III (Fall 1976), 43–60.

Swann, Charles. "Dating the Action of 'Bartleby,'" *Notes and Queries,* XXXII (1985), 357–358.

Tallack, Douglas. *The Nineteenth-Century American Short Story: Language, Form and Ideology* (London, 1993), pp. 2148–180.

Thomas, Brook. "The Legal Fictions of Herman Melville and Lemuel Shaw," *Critical Inquiry,* XI (1984), 24–51.

Trilling, Lionel. *Prefaces to the Experience of Literature* (New York, 1979), pp. 74–78.

Tuerck, Richard. "Melville's 'Bartleby' and Isaac D'Israeli's *Curiosities of Literature,* Second Series," *Studies in Short Fiction,* VII (Fall 1970), 647–649.

Vann, J. Don. "Pickwick and 'Bartleby,'" *Studies in American Fiction,* VI (Autumn 1978), 235–237.

Vogel, Dan. "Bartleby/Job/America," *Midwest Quarterly,* XXXV (1994), 151–161.

Voss, Arthur. *The American Short Story: A Critical Survey* (Norman. Okla., 1973), pp. 39–41.

Walton, Patrick R. "Melville's 'Bartleby' and the Doctrine of Necessity," *American Literature,* XLI (March 1969), 39–54.

Warwick, Wadlington. *The Confidence Game in American Literature* (Princeton, 1975), pp. 113–123.

Wasserstrom, William. "Melville the Mannerist: Form in the Short Fiction," *Herman Melville: Reassessments* (Totowa, N.J., 1984), pp. 135–156. (G)

Weiner, Susan. *Law in Art: Melville's Major Fiction and Nineteenth Century American Law* (New York, 1992), pp. 91–111.

Weinstein, Arnold. *Nobody's Home: Speech, Self, and Place in American Fiction from Hawthorne to DeLillo* (New York, 1993), pp. 25–43.

Weinstein, Cindy. "Melville, Labor, and the Discourse of Reception," *The Cambridge Companion to Herman Melville,* Robert S. Levine, ed. (Cambridge, Eng., 1998), pp. 214–216.

Weisbuch, Robert. "Melville's 'Bartleby' and the Dead Letter of Charles Dickens," *Atlantic Double-Cross: American Literature and British Influence in the Age of Emerson* (Chicago, 1986), pp. 36–54.

Wells, Daniel A. "'Bartleby the Scrivener,' Poe, and the Duyckinck Circle," *Emerson Society Quarterly* XXI (First Quarter 1975), 35–39.

Widmer, Kingsley. "Bartleby," *The Literary Rebel* (Carbondale and Edwardsville, Ill., 1965), pp. 48–59.

———. "Melville's Radical Resistance: The Method and Meaning of 'Bartleby,'" *Studies in the Novel*, I (Winter 1969), 444–458.

———. "The Negative Affirmation: Melville's 'Bartleby,'" *Modern Fiction Studies*, VIII (Autumn 1962), 276–286.

———. *The Ways of Nihilism: A Study of Herman Melville's Short Novels* (Los Angeles, 1970), pp. 91–125.

Wilson, James C. "'Bartleby': The Walls of Wall Street," *Arizona Quarterly*, XXXVII (Winter 1981), 335–346.

———. "The Significance of Petra in 'Bartleby,'" *Melville Society Extracts*, LVII (February 1984), 10–12.

Wright, Nathalia. "Melville and 'Old Burton,' with 'Bartleby' as an Anatomy of Melancholy," *Tennessee Studies in Literature*, XV (1970), 1–13.

Zeinick, Stephen. "Melville's 'Bartleby': History, Ideology, and Literature," *Marxist Perspective*, II (Winter 1979–1980), 74–92.

Zink, David D. "Bartleby and the Contemporary Search for Meaning," *Forum*, VIII (Summer 1970), 46–50.

Zlogar, Richard J. "Body Politic in 'Bartleby': Leprosy, Healing, and Christ-ness in Melville's 'Story of Wall-Street,'" *Nineteenth-Century Literature*, 53 (March 1999), 505–529.

Zuppinger, Renaud. "'Bartleby': Prometheus Revisited. Pour une problématique que de la confiance, ou, la sortie du soutcrain," *Delta* VI (April 1978), 61–77.

HERMAN MELVILLE, "The Lightning-Rod Man"

Bickley, R. Bruce, Jr. *The Method of Melville's Short Fiction* (Durham, 1975), pp. 67–71.

Brack, Vida K. and O. M. Brack. "Weathering Cape Horn: Survivors in Melville's Minor Short Fiction," *Arizona Quarterly*, XXVIII (1972), 61–73.

Campbell, Marie A. "A Quiet Crusade: Melville's Tales of the Fifties," *American Transcendental Quarterly*, VII (1970), 8–12.

Dillingham, William. *Melville's Short Fiction, 1853–1856* (Athens, Ga., 1977), pp. 172–178.

Emery, Allan Moore. "Melville on Science: 'The Lightning-Rod Man,'" *New England Quarterly*, LVI (1983), 555–568.

Fisher, Marvin. *Going Under: Melville's Short Fiction and the American 1850s* (Baton Rouge, 1977), pp. 118–124.

Fogle, Richard Harter. *Melville's Shorter Tales* (Norman, Okla., 1960), pp. 55–58.

Hoffman, Charles G. "The Shorter Fiction of Herman Melville," *South Atlantic Quarterly*, LII (1953), 414–430.

Kimpel, Sgt. Ben Drew. "'The Lightning-Rod Man,'" *American Literature*, XVI (1944), 30–32.

Mastriano, Mary. "Melville's 'The Lightning-Rod Man,'" *Studies in Short Fiction*, XIV (1977), 29–33.

Newman, Lea Bertani Vozar. *A Reader's Guide to the Short Stories of Herman Melville* (Boston, Mass., 1986), pp. 269–282.

Oliver, Egbert Samuel. "Herman Melville's 'The Lightning-Rod Man,'" *Philadelphia Forum* XXXV (1956), 4–5, 17.

Parker, Hershel. "Melville's Salesman Story," *Studies in Short Fiction*, 1 (1964), 154–158.

Shusterman, Alan. "Melville's 'The Lightning-Rod Man': A Reading," *Studies in Short Fiction*, IX (1972), 165–174.

Stater, Judith. "The Domestic Adventurer in Melville's Tales," *American Literature*, XXXVII (1965), 267–279.

Stockton, Eric W. "A Commentary on Melville's 'The Lightning-Rod Man,'" *Papers of the Michigan Academy of Science, Arts, and Letters*, XL (1955), 321–328.

Verdier, Douglas L. "Who Is the Lightning-Rod Man?" *Studies in Short Fiction*, XVIII (1981), 273–279.

Werge, Thomas A. "Melville's Satanic Salesman: Scientism and Puritanism in 'The Lightning-Rod Man,'" *Newsletter of the Conference of Christianity and Literature*, XXT (1972), 6–12.

Young, Philip. *The Private Melville* (University Park, Pa., 1993), pp. 75–85.

ALICE MUNRO, "Meneseteung"

Blodgett, E. D. *Alice Munro* (Boston, 1988). (G)

Canitz, A. E. Christa, and Roger Seamon. "The Rhetoric of Fictional Realism in the Stories of Alice Munro," *Canadian Literature*, 150 (Autumn 1996), 67–80. (G)

Carscallen, James. *The Other Country: Patterns in the Writing of Alice Munro* (Toronto, 1993). (G).

———. "Three Jokers: The Shape of Alice Munro's Stories," *Centre and Labyrinth: Essays in Honour of Northrop Frye*, Eleanor Cook, Chaviva Hosek, Jay Macpherson, Patricia Parker, and Julian Patrick, eds. (Toronto, 1983), pp. 128–146. (G)

Dahlie, Hallvard. "Alice Munro," *Canadian Writers and Their Works*, Fiction Series, Robert Lecker, Jack David, and Ellen Quigley, eds. (Toronto, 1985), pp. 215–256. (G)

———. "The Fiction of Alice Munro," *Ploughshares*, IV (Summer 1978), 56–71. (G)

———. "Unconsummated Relationships: Isolation and Rejection in Alice Munro's Stories," *World Literature Written in English*, XII (April 1972), 42–48. (G)

Ditsky, John. "The Figure in the Linoleum: The Fictions of Alice Munro," *Hollins Critic*, XXII (June 1985), 1–10. (G)

Dombrowski, Eileen. "'Down to Death': Alice Munro and Transcience." *The University of Windsor Review*, XIV (Fall-Winter 1978), 21–29. (G)

Fitzpatrick, Mary Anne. "'Projection' in Alice Munro's *Something I've Been Meaning to Tell You*," *The Art of Alice Munro: Saying the Unsayable* (Waterloo, Canada, 1984), pp. 15–20. (G)

Fitzgerald, Sheila. *Short Story Criticism: Excerpts from Criticism of the Works of Short Fiction Writers*, III (Detroit, 1989), pp. 319–350. (G)

Forceville, Charles. "Language, Time and Reality: The Stories of Alice Munro," *External and Detached: Dutch Essays on Contemporary Canadian Literature*, Charles Forceville, August J. Fry, and Peter J. de Voogd, eds. (Amsterdam, 1988), pp. 37–44. (G)

Fowler, Rowena. "The Art of Alice Munro: *The Beggar Maid* and *Lives of Girls and Women*," *Critique*, XXV (Summer 1984), pp. 189–198. (G)

Hancock, Geoff. "An Interview with Alice Munro," *Canadian Fiction Magazine*, XLIII (1982), 75–114. (G)

Hiscock, Andrew. "'Longing for a Human Climate': Alice Munro's *Friend of My Youth* and the Culture of Loss," *Journal of Commonwealth Literature*, 32, No. 2 (1997), 36–37.

Hoy, Helen. "'Dull, Simple, Amazing and Unfathomable': Paradox and Double Vision in Alice Munro's Fiction," *Studies in Canadian Literature*, V (Spring 1980), 100–115. (G)

Houston, Pam. "A Hopeful Sign: The Making of Metonymic Meaning in Munro's 'Meneseteung,'" *Kenyon Review*, XIV, No. I (1992), 85–91.

Irvine, Loma. "Questioning Authority: Alice Munro's Fiction," *CEA Critic*, L (Fall 1987), 57–66. (G)

Keith, W. J. *A Sense of Style: Studies in the Art of Fiction in English-Speaking Canada* (Toronto, 1989), 155–174, (G)

Macdonald, Rae McCarthy. "A Madman Loose in the World: The Vision of Alice Munro." *Modern Fiction Studies*, XXII (Autumn 1976), 365–374. (G)

Martin, W. R. "Alice Munro and James Joyce," *Journal of Canadian Fiction*, XXIV (1979), 120–126. (G)

Mayberry, Katherine J. "'Every Last Thing...Everlasting': Alice Munro and the Limits of Narrative," *Studies in Short Fiction*, XXIX (Fall 1992), 531–541. (G)

Murphy, Georgeann. "The Art of Alice Munro: Memory, Identity, and the Aesthetics of Conviction," *Canadian Women Writing Fiction*, Mickey Pearlman ed. (Jackson, Miss., 1993), pp. 12–27. (G)

New, W. H. "Pronouns and Propositions: Alice Munro's Short Stories," *Open Letter*, V (Summer 1976), 40–49. (G)

Noonan, Gerald. "The Structure and Style in Alice Munro's Fiction," *Probably Fictions: Alice Munro's Narrative Acts*, Louis K. MacKendrick, ed. (Downsview, Canada, 1983), pp. 163–180. (G)

Orange, John. "Alice Munro and a Maze of Time," *Probable Fictions: Alice Munro's Narrative Acts*, Louise K. MacKendrick, ed. (Downsview, Canada, 1983), pp. 83–98. (G)

Osachoff, Margaret Gail. "'Treacheries of the Heart': Memoir, Confession, and Meditation in the Stories of Alice Munro," *Probable Fictions: Alice Munro's Narrative Acts*, Louis K. MacKendrick, ed. (Downsview, Canada, 1983), pp. 61–82. (G)

Redekop, Magdalene. *Mothers and Other Clowns: The Stories of Alice Munro* (London, 1992), pp. 216–228.

Ross, Catherine Sheldrick. "'At Least Part Legend': The Fiction of Alice Munro," *Probably Fictions: Alice Munro's Narrative Acts*, Louis K. MacKendrick, ed. (Downsview, Canada, 1983), pp. 112–126. (G)

Strouck, David. "Alice Munro," *Major Canadian Authors: A Critical Introduction* (Lincoln, 1984), pp. 257–272. (G)

————. *Modern Canadian Authors: A Critical Introduction to Canadian Literature in English* (Lincoln, 1988), pp. 257–272. (G)

Struthers, J. R. "Reality and Ordering: The Growth of a Young Artist in Lives of Girls and Women," *Modern Canadian Fiction*, Carole Gerson, ed. (Richmond, Canada, 1980), 164–174. (G)

Stubbs, Andrew. "Fictional Landscape: Mythology and Dialectic in the Fiction of Alice Munro," *World Literature Written in English*, XXIII (1984), 53–62. (G)

Thacker, Robert. "Connection: Alice Munro and Ontario," *American Review of American Studies*, XIV (Summer 1984), pp. 213–226. (G)

Thomas, Sue. "Reading Female Sexual Desire in Alice Munro's *Lives of Girls and Women*,", *Critique*, XXXVI (Winter 1995), 107–120. (G)

Wall, Kathleen. "Representing the Other Body: Frame Narrative in Margaret Atwood's 'Giving Birth' and Alice Munro's 'Meneseteung,'" *Canadian Literature*, 154 (Autumn 1997), 74–90.

Woodcock, George. "The Plots of Life: The Realism of Alice Munro," *Queen's Quarterly*, XCIII (Summer 1986), 235–250. (G)

JOYCE CAROL OATES, "Four Summers"

Barza, Steven. "Joyce Carol Oates: Naturalism and the Aberrant Response," *Studies in American Fiction*, VII (1979) 141–153. (G)

Bender, Eileen T. "Between the Categories: Recent Short Fiction by Joyce Carol Oates," *Studies in Short Fiction*, XVII (Fall 1980).

Cushman, Keith. "A Reading of Joyce Carol Oates's 'Four Summers,'" *Studies in Short Fiction*, XVIII (Spring 1981), 137–146.

Johnson, Greg. *Joyce Carol Oates: A Study of the Short Fiction* (New York, 1994), pp. 54–55.

Norman, Torborg. *Isolation and Contact: A Study of Character Relationships in Joyce Carol Oates's Short Stories, 1963–1980* (Goteborg, Sweden, 1984), pp. 169–170.

Pickering, Samuel F., Jr. "The Short Stories of Joyce Carol Oates," *Georgia Review*, XXVIII (Summer 1974), 218–226. (G)

Votteler, Thomas, ed. *Short Story Criticism: Excerpts from Criticism of the Works of Short Fiction Writers*, VI (Detroit, 1990), pp. 222–256. (G)

JOYCE CAROL OATES, "Where Are You Going, Where Have You Been?"

Allen, Mary. *The Necessary Blankness: Women in Major American Fiction of the Sixties* (Urbana, Ill., 1976), pp. 141–143.

Coulthard, A. R. "Joyce Carol Oates's 'Where Are You Going, Where Have You Been?' as Pure Realism," *Studies in Short Fiction*, XXVI (Fall 1989), 505–510.

Creighton, Joanne V. *Joyce Carol Oates* (Boston, 1979), pp. 117–120.

———. "Joyce Carol Oates' Craftsmanship in *The Wheel of Love*," *Studies in Short Fiction*, XV (Fall 1978), 380–383.

Daly, Brenda. "An Unfilmable Conclusion: Joyce Carol Oates at the Movies," *Journal of Popular Culture*, XXIII (Winter 1989), 101–114.

Dessommes, Nancy Bishop. "O'Connor's Mrs. May and Oates's Connie: An Unlikely Pair of Religious Initiates," *Studies in Short Fiction*, XXXI (Summer 1994), 433–450.

Easterly, Joan. "The Shadow of a Satyr in Oates's 'Where Are You Going, Where Have You Been?' *Studies in Short Fiction*, XXVII (Fall 1990), 537–543.

Friedman, Ellen G. *Joyce Carol Oates* (New York, 1980), pp. 10–13.

Fulkerson, Tahita. "Not-so-strange bedfellows: A Pedagogical Pairing of Henry James's 'Four Meetings' and Joyce Carol Oates' 'Four Summers,'" *Teaching English in the Two-Year College*, XII (February 1985), 39–42.

Gentry, Marshall Bruce. "O'Connor's Legacy in Stories by Joyce Carol Oates and Paula Sharp," *Flannery O'Connor Bulletin*, XXIII (1994–1995), 44–60.

Gerlach, John C. *Toward the End: Closure and Structure in the American Short Story* (University, Ala., 1985), pp. 120–122.

Gillis, Christina Marsden. "'Where Are You Going, Where Have You Been?': Seduction, Space, and a Fictional Mode," *Studies in Short Fiction*, XVIII (Winter 1981), 65–70.

Gratz, David K. "Oates's 'Where Are You Going, Where Have You Been'?'" *Explicator*, XLV (Spring 1987), 55–56.

Harty, Kevin J. "Archetype and Popular Lyric in Joyce Carol Oates's 'Where Are You Going, Where Have You Been?'" *Pennsylvania English*, VII (1980–1981), 26–28.

Healey, James. "Pop Music and Joyce Carol Oates' 'Where Are You Going, Where Have You Been?'" *Notes on Modern American Literature*, VII (Spring-Summer 1983), Item 5.

Hurley, D. F. "Impure Realism: Joyce Carol Oates's 'Where Are You Going, Where Have You Been?'" *Studies in Short Fiction*, XXVIII (Summer 1991), 371–375.

Hurley, C. Harold. "Cracking the Secret Code in Oates' 'Where Are You Going, Where Have You Been?'" *Studies in Short Fiction*, XXIV (Winter 1987), 62–66.

Jeanotte, M. Sharon. "The Horror Within: The Short Stories of Joyce Carol Oates," *Sphinx: A Magazine of Literature and Society*, II, No. 4 (1977), 25–36.

Johnson, Greg. *Joyce Carol Oates: A Study of the Short Fiction* (New York, 1994), pp. 148–151.

———. *Understanding Joyce Carol Oates* (Columbia, S.C., 1987), pp. 98–103.

Kowalewski, Michael. *Deadly Musing: Violence and Verbal Form in American Fiction* (Princeton, 1993), pp. 27–29.

Moser, Don. "The Pied Piper of Tucson: He Cruised in a Golden Car, Looking for Action," *Life* (March 4, 1966), 19–24, 80–90.

Oates, Joyce Carol. "'Where Are You Going, Where Have You Been?' and 'Smooth Talk': Short Story into Film, *(Woman) Writer: Occasions and Opportunities* (New York, 1988), pp. 316–321.

Norman, Torborg. *Isolation and Contact: A Study of Character Relationships in Joyce Carol Oates's Short Stories, 1963–1980* (Goteborg, Sweden, 1984), pp. 168–169.

Petry, Alice Hill. "Who Is Ellie? Oates' 'Where Are You Going, Where Have You Been?'" *Studies in Short Fiction*, XXV (Spring 1988), 155–157.

Piwinski, David J. "Oates's 'Where Are You Going, Where Have You Been?'" *Explicator*, XLIX (Spring 1991), 195–196.

Quirk, Tom. "A Source for 'Where Are You Going, Where Have You Been?'" *Studies in Short Fiction*, XVIII (Fall 1981), 413–419.

Robson, Mark B. "Joyce Carol Oates's 'Where Are You Going, Where Have You Been?' Arnold Friend as Devil, Dylan, and Levite," *Publications of the Mississippi Philological Association* (1985), 98–105.

———. "Oates's 'Where Are You Going, Where Have You Been,'" *Explicator*, XL (Summer 1982), 59–60.

Rubin, Larry. "Oates's 'Where Are You Going, Where Have You Been?'" *Explicator*, XLII (Summer 1984), 57–60.

Schulz, Gretchen and J. R. Rockwood. "In Fairyland, Without a Map: Connie's Exploration Inward in Joyce Carol Oates' 'Where Are Are You Going, Where Have You Been?'" *Literature and Psychology*, XXX (1980), 155–167.

Showalter, Elaine, ed. *Where Are You Going, Where Have You Been?* (New Brunswick, N.J., 1994).

Sullivan, Walter. "Where Have All the Flowers Gone?: The Short Story in Search of Itself," *Sewanee Review*, LXXVIII (Summer 1970), 535–537.

Tierce, Mike and John Michael Craflon. "Connie's Tambourine Man: A New Reading of Arnold Friend," *Studies in Short Fiction*, XXII (Spring 1985), 219–224.

Urbanski, Marie. "Existential Allegory: Joyce Carol Oates's 'Where Are You Going, Where Have You Been?' *Studies in Short Fiction*, XV (Spring 1978), 200–203.

Wagner-Martin, Linda. "Where Are You Going, Where Have You Been?" *Reference Guide to Short Fiction*, Noelle Watson, ed. (Detroit, 1994), p. 968.

Wegs, Joyce W. "'Don't You Know Who I Am?': The Grotesque in Oates's 'Where Are You Going, Where Have You Been?'" *Journal of Narrative Technique*, V (January 1975), 66–72.

Weinberger, G. J. "Who Is Arnold Friend?: The Other Self in Joyce Carol Oates's 'Where Are You Going, Where Have You Been?'", *American Imago*, XLV (Summer 1988), 205–215.

Winslow, Joan D. "The Stranger Within: Two Stories by Oates and Hawthorne," *Studies in Short Fiction*, XVII (Summer 1980), 263–268.

FLANNERY O'CONNOR, "A Good Man Is Hard to Find"

Anastaplo, George. "Can Beauty 'Hallow Even the Bloodiest Tomahawk'?" *Critic*, XLVIII, 2 (1993), 2–18.

Asals, Frederick, ed. *Flannery O'Connor, "A Good Man Is Hard to Find"* (New Brunswick, N.J., 1983).

———. *Flannery O'Connor: The Imagination Of Extremity* (Athens, Ga., 1982), pp. 142–154.

Bandy, Stephen C. "'One of my Babies': The Misfit and the Grandmother," *Studies in Short Fiction*, 33 (Winter 1996), 107–117.

Bartlett, Beverly. "Flannery O'Connor's 'A Good Man Is Hard to Find,'" *Linguistics in Literature*, VI (1981), 49–58.

Bellamy, Michael O. "Everything off Balance: Protestant Election in Flannery O'Connor's

'A Good Man Is Hard to Find,'" *Flannery O'Connor Bulletin*, VIII (Autumn 1979), 116–124.

Blythe, Hal and Charlie Sweet, "The Misfit: O'Connor's 'Family,' Man as Serial Killer," *Notes on Contemporary Literature*, XXV (January 1995), 3–5.

———. "O'Connor's 'A Good Man Is Hard to Find,'" *Explicator*, L, (Spring 1992), 185–187.

———. "O'Connor's 'A Good Man Is Hard to Find,'" *Explicator*, 55, (Fall 1996), 49–51.

Bonney, William. "The Moral Structure of 'A Good Man Is Hard to Find,'" *Studies in Short Fiction* XXVII (Summer 1990), 347–356.

Brinkmeyer, Robert H., Jr. *The Art and Vision of Flannery O'Connor* (Baton Rouge, 1989), pp. 160–162, 185–188.

Brittain, Joan Tucker. "O'Connor's 'A Good Man is Hard to Find,'" *Explicator*, XXVI (September 1967), Item 1.

Brown, Ashley. "Grotesque Occasions," *The Spectator*, CCXXI (September 6,1968), 330–332.

Browning, Preston M., Jr. *Flannery O'Connor* (Carbondale and Edwardsville, Ill., 1974), pp. 54–59.

———. "Flannery O'Connor and the Grotesque Recovery of the Holy," *Adversity and Grace: Studies in Recent American Literature*, Nathan A. Scott, ed. (Chicago, 1968), pp. 143–147.

Bryant, Hallman B. "Reading the Map in 'A Good Man Is Hard to Find,'" *Studies in Short Fiction*, XVIII (Summer 1981), 301–307.

Burns, Maggie. "A Good Rose Is Hard to Find: Southern Gothic as Signs of Social Dislocation in Faulkner and O'Connor," *Image and Ideology in Modern Postmodern Discourse*, David B. Downing and Susan Bazargan, eds. (Albany, 1991), pp. 108–113, 117–121.

Carlson, Thomas M. "Flannery O'Connor: The Manichaean Dilemma," *Sewanee Review*, LXXVII (Spring 1969), 254–276.

Church, Joseph. "An Abuse of the Imagination in Flannery O'Connor's 'A Good Man Is Hard to Find,'" *Notes on Contemporary Literature*, XX (May 1990), 8–10.

Clark, Michael. "Flannery O'Connor's 'A Good Man Is Hard to Find': The Moment of Grace," *English Language Notes*, XXIX (December 1991), 66–69.

Coulthard, A. R. "Flannery O'Connor's Deadly Conversions," *Flannery O'Connor Bulletin*, XIII (Autumn 1984), 87–98.

Currie, Sheldon. "A Good Grandmother Is Hard to Find: Story as Exemplum," *Antigonish Review*, No. 81–82 (1990), 147–156.

Di Renzo, Anthony. *American Gargoyles: Flannery O'Connor and the Medieval Grotesque* (Carbondale, Ill., 1993), pp. 134–149, 153–160.

Donahoo, Ronald. "O'Connor's Ancient Comedy: Form in 'A Good Man Is Hard to Find,'" *Journal of the Short Story in English*, XVI (Spring 1991), 29–39.

Dowell, Bob. "The Moment of Grace in the Fiction of Flannery O'Connor," *College English*, XXVII (December 1965), 235–239.

Doxey, William S. "A Dissenting Opinion of Flannery O'Connor's 'A Good Man Is Hard to Find,'" *Studies in Short Fiction*, X (Spring 1973), 199–204.

Drake, Robert. "'The Bleeding Stinking Mad Shadow of Jesus' in the Fiction of Flannery O'Connor," *Comparative Literature Studies*, III (1966), 183–196. (G)

Driskell, Leon V. and Joan T. Brittain. *The Eternal Crossroads: The Art of Flannery O'Connor* (Lexington, Ky., 1971), pp. 67–72.

Eggenschwiler, David. *The Christian Humanism of Flannery O'Connor* (Detroit, 1972), pp. 46–52, 91–92.

Ellis, James. "Watermelons and Coca-Cola in 'A Good Man Is Hard to Find': Holy Communion in the South," *Notes on Contemporary Literature*, VIII (May 1978), 7–8.

Evans, Elizabeth. "Three Notes on Flannery O'Connor," *Notes on Contemporary Literature*, III (May 1973), 11–15.

Evans, Robert C. "Poe, O'Connor, and the Mystery of The Misfit," *Flannery O'Connor Bulletin*, 25 (1996–1997), 1–12.

Feeley, Sister Kathleen. *Flannery O'Connor: Voice of the Peacock* (New Brunswick, N.J., 1972), pp. 69–76.

Gentry, Marshall Bruce. *Flannery O'Connor's Religion of the Grotesque* (Jackson, Miss., 1986), pp. 31–39, 108–112.

Giannone, Richard. *Flannery O'Connor and the Mystery of Love* (Urbana, Ill., 1989), pp. 46–53.

Gordon, Caroline and Allen Tate. *The House of Fiction* (New York, 1960), pp. 384–386.

Gossett, Thomas F. "Flannery O'Connor on Her Fiction," *Southwest Review*, LIX (Winter 1974), 34–42.

Hamblen, Abigail Ann. "Flannery O'Connor's Study of Innocence and Evil," *University Review*, XXIV (Summer 1968), 295–297.

Hawkins, Peter S. *The Language of Grace: Flannery O'Connor, Walker Percy, and Iris Murdoch* (Cambridge, Mass., 1983), pp. 40–50.

Hendin, Josephine. *The World of Flannery O'Connor* (Bloomington, Ind., 1970), pp. 148–151.

Hurd, Myles R. "The Misfit as Parracide in Flannery O'Connor's 'A Good Man Is Hard to Find," *Notes on Contemporary Literature*, XXII, iv (1992), 5–7.

Ireland, Patrick J. "The Place of Flannery O'Connor in Our Two Literatures: The Southern and National Literary Traditions," *Flannery O'Connor Bulletin*, VII (Autumn 1978), 55–58.

Jones, Madison. "A Good Man's Predicament," *Southern Review*, XX (1984), 836–841.

Kessler, Edward. *Flannery O'Connor and the Language of Apocalypse* (Princeton, 1986), pp. 60–63.

Kinney, Arthur F. "Flannery O'Connor and the Fiction of Grace," *Massachusetts Review*, XVII (Spring 1986), 71–96.

———. "A Good Man Is Hard to Find," *Reference Guide to Short Fiction*, Noelle Watson, ed. (Detroit, 1994), pp. 721–722.

Kitagaki, Muncharu. "The Valley of the Shadow of Death: An interpretation of Flannery O'Connor's 'A Good Man Is Hard to Find,'" *Studies in Humanities*, LXXXV (February 1966), 51–66.

Kropf, C. R. "Theme and Setting in 'A Good Man Is Hard to Find,'" *Renascence*, XXIV (Summer 1972), 177–180, 206.

Lasseter, Victor. "The Children's Names in Flannery O'Connor's 'A Good Man Is Hard to Find,'" *Notes on Modern American Literature*, VI, i (1982), Item 6.

———. "The Genesis of Flannery O'Connor's 'A Good Man Is Hard to Find,'" *Studies in American Fiction*, XX (Autumn 1982), 227–232.

Leonard, Douglas Novich. "'A Good Man Is Hard to Find,'" *Interpretations*, XIV (Spring 1983), 48–54.

Loomis, Jeffrey B. "Miltonic Patterns in Flannery O'Connor's 'A Good Man Is Hard to Find,'" *Cithara* XXIV (November 1984), 41–58.

Lorentzen, Melvin E. "A Good Writer Is Hard to Find," *Imagination and the Spirit: Essays in Literature and the Christian Faith Presented to Clyde S. Kilby*, Charles A. Huttar, ed. (Grand Rapids, 1971), pp. 417–435.

McBride, Mary. "Paradise Not Regained: Flannery O'Connor's Unredeemed Pilgrims in the Garden of Evil," *South Central Bulletin*, XL (Winter 1980), 154–155.

McFarland, Dorothy Tuck. *Flannery O'Connor* (New York, 1976), pp. 17–22.

McMullen, Joanne Halleran. *Writing Against God: Language as Message in the Literature of O'Connor* (Macon, Ga., 1996), pp. 34–36, 62–64, 70–76, 117–119.

Marks, W. S. "Advertisements for Grace: Flannery O'Connor's 'A Good Man is Hard to Find,'" *Studies in Short Fiction*, IV (Fall 1966), 19–27.

Martin, Carter W. *The True Country: Themes in the Fiction of Flannery O'Connor* (Nashville, 1969), pp. 163–167.

Martin, Sister M., O.P. "O'Connor's 'A Good Man Is Hard to Find,'" *Explicator*, XXIV (October 1965), Item 19.

May, John R. *The Pruning Word: The Parables of Flannery O'Connor* (Notre Dame, Ind., 1976), pp. 60–64.

Mellard, James M. *Four Modes: A Rhetoric of Modern Fiction* (New York, 1973), pp. 39–42.

Merton, Thomas. "The Other Side of Despair: Notes on Christian Existentialism," *Critic*, XXIV (October–November 1965), 12–23.

Mills, Jerry Leath, "Samburan Outside of Toombsboro: Conrad's Influence on 'A Good Man Is Hard to Find,'" *South Atlantic Quarterly*, LXXXIV (Spring 1995),186–196.

Montgomery, Marion. "Grace: A Tricky Fictional Agent," *Flannery O'Connor Bulletin*, IX (Autumn 1980), 19–29.

———. "Miss Flannery's 'Good Man,'" *Denver Quarterly*, III (Autumn 1968), 1–19.

Napier, James. "Tragic and Comic Interplay in O'Connor's 'A Good Man Is Hard to Find,'" *CEA Forum*, XII (December 1981), 3–6.

Nisly, Paul W. "The Mystery of Evil: Flannery O'Connor's Gothic Power," *Flannery O'Connor Bulletin*, XI (Autumn 1982), 25–35.

Ochshorn, Kathleen G. "A Cloak of Grace: Contradiction in 'A Good Man Is Hard to Find,'" *Studies in American Fiction*, XVIII (Spring 1990), 113–117.

O'Connnor, Flannery. *The Habit of Being*, Sally Fitzgerald, ed. (New York, 1979), P. 437.

Orvell, Miles. *Flannery O'Connor: An Introduction* (Jackson, Miss., 1991), pp. 130–136.

———. *Invisible Parade: The Fiction of Flannery O'Connor* (Philadelphia, 1972), pp. 130–136.

Owens, Mitchell. "The Function of Signature in 'A Good Man Is Hard to Find,'" *Studies in Short Fiction*, 28 (Winter 1996), 101–106.

Paulson, Suzanne Morrow. *Flannery O'Connor: A Study of the Short Fiction* (Boston, 1988), pp. 85–91.

Pearce, Richard. *Stages of the Clown: Perspectives on Modern Fiction from Dostoyevsky to Beckett* (Carbondale, Ill., 1970), pp. 69–71.

Portch, Stephen R. "O'Connor's 'A Good Man Is Hard to Find,'" *Explicator*, XXXVII (Fall 1978), 19–20.

Quinn, John S., S.J. "A Reading of Flannery O'Connor," *Thought*, XLVIII (1973), 520–531.

Reesman, Jeanne Campbell. "Women, Language, and the Grotesque in Flannery O'Connor and Eudora Welty," *Flannery O'Connor: New Perspectives*, Sura P. Rath and Mary Neff, eds. (Athens, Ga., 1996), pp. 38–56. (G)

Renner, Stanley. "Secular Meaning in 'A Good Man is Hard to Find,'" *College Literature*, IX (1982), 123–132.

Richard, Claude. "Desire and Destiny in 'A Good Man Is Hard to Find,'" *Delta*, II (1976), 61–74.

Rubin, Louis D., Jr. "The Ladies of the South," *Sewanee Review*, LXIII (1955), 671–681.

Scheick, William J. "Flannery O'Connor's 'A Good Man Is Hard to Find' and G. K. Chesterton's *Manalive*," *Studies in American Fiction*, XI (Autumn 1983), 241–245.

Shinn, Thelma J. "Flannery O'Connor and the Violence of Grace," *Contemporary Literature*, IX (1968), 58–73.

Sloan, Gary. "O'Connor's 'A Good Man Is Hard to Find,'" *Explicator*, 57 (Fall 1998), 118–120.

Spivey, Ted. R. *Flannery O'Connor: The Woman, the Thinker, the Visionary* (Macon, Ga., 1995), pp. 122–125.

Stephens, Martha. *The Question of Flannery O'Connor* (Baton Rouge, 1973), pp. 17–36.

Sullivan, Walter. "Southerners in the City: O'Connor and Percy," *The Comic Imagination in American Literature*, Louis D. Rubin, ed. (New Brunswick, N.J., 1973), pp. 324–344.

Sweet-Hurd, Evelyn. "Finding O'Connor's Good Man," *Notes on Contemporary Literature*, XIV (May 1994), 9–10.

Tate, J. O. "A Good Source Is Not So Hard to Find," *Flannery O'Connor Bulletin*, IX (Autumn 1980), 98–103.

Thompson, Terry. "The Killers in O'Connor's 'A Good Man Is Hard to Find,'" *Notes on Contemporary Literature*, XVI (September 1986), 4.

Walls, Doyle W. "O'Connor's 'A Good Man Is Hard to Find,'" *Explicator*, XLVI (Winter 1988), 43–47.

Walters Dorothy. *Flannery O'Connor* (New York, 1973), pp. 70–73.

White, Terry. "Allegorical Evil, Existential Choice in O'Connor, Oates, and Styron, *Midwest Quarterly*, XXXIV (1993), 383, 386–388.

Whitt, Margaret Earley. *Understanding Flannery O'Connor* (Columbia S.C., 1995), 43–48.

Weinstein, Arnold. *Nobody's Home: Speech, Self, and Place in American Fiction from Hawthorne to DeLillo* (New York, 1993), pp. 115–119.

Woodward, Robert H. "A Good Route Is Hard to Find: Place Names and Setting in O'Connor's 'A Good Man Is Hard to Find,'" *Notes on Contemporary Literature*, III (November 1973), 2–5.

Wynne, Judith F. "The Sacramental Irony of Flannery O'Connor," *Southern Literary Journal*, VII (Spring 1976), 33–49.

FRANK O'CONNOR, "Guests of the Nation"

Averill, Deborah. *The Irish Short Story from George Moore to Frank O'Connor* (Lanham, Md., 1982). pp. 249–251.

Brenner, Gerry. "Frank O'Connor's Imprudent Hero," *Texas Studies in Literature and Language*, X (Fall 1968), 457–469. (G)

Bordwyk, Gordon. "Quest for Meaning: The Stories of Frank O'Connor," *Illinois Quarterly*, XLI (Winter 1978), 37–47. (G)

Briden, E. F. "'Guests of the Nation,' A Final Irony," *Studies in Short Fiction*, XIII (Winter 1976) 79–81

Chatalic, Roger. "Frank O'Connor and the Desolation of Reality," *The Irish Short Story*, Patrick Rafroidi and Terence Brown, eds. (Atlantic Highlands, N.J., 1979), pp. 189–201. (G)

Crider, J.R. "Jupiter Pluvius in 'Guests of the Nation,'" *Studies in Short Fiction*, XXIII (Fall 1986), 407–411.

Gordon, Caroline and Allen Tate. *The House of Fiction* (New York, 1960), pp, 441–444.

Hanson, Clare. *Short Stories and Short Fictions, 1880–1980* (New York, 1985), pp. 88–96. (G)

Hildebidle, John. *Five Irish Writers: The Errand of Keeping Alive* (Cambridge, Mass., 1989), pp. 179–181.

Kilroy, James F. "Setting the Standards: Writers of the 1920s and 1930s," *The Irish Short Story: A Critical History*, James F. Kilroy, ed. (Boston, 1984), pp), 106–107.

Kavanagh, Patrick. "Coloured Balloons: A Study of Frank O'Connor," *Journal of Irish Literature*, VI (January 1977), 40–49.

Liberman, Michael. "Unforeseen Duty in Frank O'Connor's 'Guests of the Nation,'" *Studies in Short Fiction*, XXIV (Fall 1987), 438–441.

Matthews, James H. "'Magical Improvisation': Frank O'Connor's Revolution," *Eire-Ireland*, X (Winter 1975), 3–13. (G)

———. "Women, War, and Words: Frank O'Connor's First Confessions," *Irish Renaissance Annual I*, I (1980), 73–112. (G)

Murphy, Kate. "Grappling with the World," *Twentieth-Century Literature*, XXXVI (Fall 1990), 310–343. (G)

O'Malley, Jerome F. "The Broken Pattern of Ritual in the Stories of Frank O'Connor," *Eire-Ireland*, XXIII (Spring 1988), 45–59. (G)

Owes, Cóilín. *Critical Survey of Short Fiction*, Frank Magill, ed. (Englewood Cliffs, N.J., 1981), V, pp. 1989–1991.

Peterson, Richard F. "Frank O'Connor and the Modern Irish Short Story," *Modern Fiction Studies*, XXVIII (Spring 1982), 53–67.

———. "Guests of the Nation," *Reference Guide to Short Fiction*, Noelle Watson, ed. (Detroit 1994), pp. 727–728.

Prosky, Murray. "The Pattern of Diminishing Certitude in the Stories of Frank O'Connor," *Colby Library Quarterly*, Series IX (June 1971), 311–321.

Robinson, Patricia. "O'Connor's 'Guests of the Nation,'" *Explicator*, XLV (Fall 1986), 58.

Renner, Stanley. "The Theme of Hidden Powers: Fate vs. Human Responsibility in 'Guests of the Nation,'" *Studies in Short Fiction*, XXVII (Summer 1990), 371–377.

Saul, George Brandon. "A Consideration of Frank O'Connor's Short Stories," *Colby Library Quarterly*, Series VI (December 1963), 329–342. (G)

Stokey, Michael L. "The Guests of Frank O'Connor and Albert Camus," *Comparative Literature Studies*, XXIII (1986), 250–262.

Thompson, Richard. *Everlasting Voices: Aspects of the Modern Irish Short Story* (Troy, N.Y., 1989), pp. 19–22.

———. "A Kingdom of Commoners: The Moral Art of Frank O'Connor," *Eire-Ireland*, XIII (Winter 1978), 65–80. (G)

Tomory, William N. *Frank O'Connor* (Boston, 1980), pp. 29–31, 80–81.

Warner, Alice, *A Guide to Anglo-Irish Literature* (New York, 1981), pp. 79–88. (G)

TILLIE OLSEN, "I Stand Here Ironing"

Bauer, Helen Pike. "'A Child of Anxious, Not Proud, Love': Mother and Daughter in Tillie Olsen's 'I Stand Here Ironing,'" *Mother Puzzles: Daughters and Mothers in Contemporary American Literature*, Mickey Pearlman, ed. (New York, 1989), pp. 35–39.

Boucher, Sandy. "Tillie Olsen: The Weight of Things Unsaid," *Ms*, (September 1974), 26–30. (G)

Burkom, Selman, and Margaret Williams. "De-Riddling Tillie Olsen's Writings," *San Jose Studies*, II, 1 (1976), 65–83.

Cainer, Constance. "'No One's Private Ground': A Bakhtinian Reading of Tillie Olsen's *Tell Me a Riddle*," *Feminist Studies*, XVIII (1992), 260–264.

Culver, Sara. "Extending the Boundaries of the Ego: Eva in 'Tell Me a Riddle,'" *Midwestern Miscellany*, X (1982), 38–48.

Cunneen, Sally. "Tillie Olsen: Storyteller of Working America," *The Christian Century*, XCVII (May 21, 1980), 570–574.

Dawahare, Anthony. "'That Joyous Certainty,'" History and Utopia in Tillie Olsen's Depression-Era Literature," *Twentieth-Century Literature*, 44 (Fall 1998), 261–275. (G)

Ellman, Richard. "The Many Forms Which Loss Can Take," *Commonweal*, LXXV (October 8, 1961), 295–296.

Faulkner, Mara. *Protest and Possibility in the Writing of Tillie Olsen* (Charlottesville, Va., 1993), pp. 117–120.

Fry, Joanne S. "'I Stand Here Ironing': Motherhood as Experience and Metaphor," *Studies in Short Fiction*, XVIII (Summer 1981), 287–292.

Jacobs, Naomi. "Earth, Air, Fire and Water in 'Tell Me a Riddle,'" *Studies in Short Fiction*, XXIII (October 1986), 401–406.

Kamel, Rose. "Literary Foremothers and Writers, Silences: Tillie Olsen's Autobiographical Fiction, *MELUS*, XII, 2 (1985), 55–72.

Lidoff, Joan. "Fluid Boundaries: The Mother-Daughter Story," *Texas Studies in Literature and Language*, XXXV (1993), 410–411.

Niehus, Edward L., and Teresa Jackson. "Polar Stars, Pyramids, and 'Tell Me a Riddle,'" *American Notes and Queries*, XXIV, 5–6 (1986), 77–83.

Martin, Abigail. *Tillie Olsen* (Boise, Idaho, 1984). (G)

McElhiny, Annette Bennington. "Alternative Responses to Life in Tillie Olsen's Work," *Frontiers*, II, 1 (1977), 76–91.

O'Connor, William Van. "The Short Stories of Tillie Olsen," *Studies in Short Fiction*, I (Fall 1963), 21–25. (G)

Peterman, Michael A. "'All That Happens, One Must Try to Understand': The Kindredness of Tillie Olsen's 'Tell Me a Riddle' and Margaret Laurence's *The Stone Angel*," *Margaret Laurence: An Appreciation*, Christl Verduyn, ed. (Peterborough, N.H., 1988), pp. 70–88.

Roberts, Nora Ruth. *Three Radical Women Writers: Class and Gender in Meridel Le Sueur, Tillie Olsen, and Josephine Herbst* (New York, 1996), pp. 100–105,

Rosenfelt, Deborah. "From the Thirties: Tillie Olsen and the Radical Tradition," *Feminist Studies*, VII, 3 (1981), 70–81.

Segal, David, ed. *Short Story Criticism: Excerpts from Criticism of the Works of Short Fiction Writers*, XI (Detroit, 1992), pp. 162–200. (G)

Van O'Connor, William. "The Short Stories of Tillie Olsen," *Studies in Short Fiction*, I (Fall 1963), 21–25. (G)

Yalom, Marilyn. "Tillie Olsen," *Women Writers of the West Coast: Speaking of Their Lives and Careers*, Marilyn Yalom, ed. (Santa Barbara, Ca., 1983), pp. 57–66. (G)

DOROTHY PARKER, "Big Blonde"

Keats, John. *You Might as Well Live: The Life and Times of Dorothy Parker* (New York, 1970), pp, 143–147.

Kinney, Arthur F. "Big Blonde," *Reference Guide to Short Fiction*, Noelle Watson, ed. (Detroit 1994), pp. 645–646.

———. *Dorothy Parker* (Boston, 1978), pp. 136–137.

Labrie, Ross. "Dorothy Parker Revisited," *Canadian Review of American Studies*, VII (Spring 1976), 48–56. (G)

Lansky, Ellen. "Female Trouble: Dorothy Parker, Katherine Anne Porter and Alcoholism," *Literature and Medicine*, 17 (Fall 1998), 212–230.

Orvis, Mary. *The Art of Writing Fiction* (New York, 1948), pp. 161–164,

EDGAR ALLAN POE, "The Cask of Amontillado"

Adler, Jacob H. "Are There Flaws in 'The Cask of Amontillado'? *Notes & Queries*, CXCIX (January 1954), 32–34.

Bales, Kent. "Poetic Justice in 'The Cask of Amontillado,'" *Poe Studies*, V (June 1972), 51.

Benton, Richard P. "The Cask of Amontillado," *Reference Guide to Short Fiction*, Noelle Watson, ed. (Detroit, 1994), pp. 658–659.

———. "Poe's 'The Cask' and the 'White Webwork Which Gleams,'" *Studies in Short Fiction*, XXVIII (Spring 1991), 183–194.

Bonaparte, Marie. *The Life and Works of Edgar Allan Poe: A Psycho-Analytic Interpretation* (London, 1949), pp. 505–510.

Burduck, Michael L. *Grim Phantasms: Fear in Poe's Short Fiction* (New York, 1992), pp. 78–83.

Carolan, Katherine. "'The Cask of Amontillado': Some Further Ironies," *Studies in Short Fiction*, XI (1974), 195–199.

Cecil, L. Moffitt. "Poe's Wine List," *Poe Studies*, V (June 1972), 41–42.

Clendenning, John. "Anything Goes: Comic Aspects of 'The Cask of Amontillado,'" *American Humor. Essays Presented to John C Gerber*, O. M. Brack, ed. (Scottsdale, Ariz., 1977), pp. 13–25.

Cooney, James F. "'The Cask of Amontillado': Some Further Ironies," *Studies in Short Fiction*, XI (Spring 1974), 195–196.

Cruz, I. R. "Literary Theory in Mathematical Language," *CEA Forum*, VI (December 1975), 15, 17.

Cunliffe, W. Gordon and John V. Hagopian. "The Cask of Amontillado," *Insight I: Analyses of American Literature*, John V. Hagopian and Martin Dolch, eds. (Frankfurt, 1962), pp. 203–207.

Current-Garcia, Eugene. "Poe's Short Fiction," *The American Short Story Before 1850: A Critical History* (Boston, 1985), pp. 59–83. (G)

Dameron, J. Lasley. "The Poe Theme in Junior High Literature," *Interpretations*. II (1969), 11–18.

Davidson, Edward H. *Poe: A Critical Study* (Cambridge, 1964), pp. 201–203.

Dedmond, Francis B. "An Additional Source of Poe's 'The Cask of Amontillado,'" *Notes & Queries*, CXCVII (May 1952), 212–214.

———. "'The Cask of Amontillado' and the 'War of the Literati,'" *Modern Language Quarterly*, XV (June 1954), 13 7–146.

Doxey, William S. "Concerning Fortunato's 'Courtesy,'" *Studies in Short Fiction*, IV (Spring 1967), 266.

Dwight, Eleanor. "Edith Wharton and 'The Cask of Amontillado,'" *Poe and Our Times: Influences and Affinities*, Benjamin Franklin Fisher, ed. (Baltimore, 1986), pp. 49–57.

Engel, Leonard W. "Victim and Victimizer: Poe's 'The Cask of Amontillado,'" *Interpretations*, XV (Fall 1983), 26–30.

Felheim, Marvin, Sam Moon, and Donald Pearce. "The Cask of Amontillado,'" *Notes & Queries*, N.S. I (October 1954), 447–449.

Foote, Dorothy Norris. "Poe's 'The Cask of Amontillado,'" *Explicator*, XX (November 1961), Item 27.

Fossum, Richard H. "Poe's 'The Cask of Amontillado,'" *Explicator*, XVII (November 1958), Item 16.

Freehafer, John. "Poe's 'Cask of Amontillado': A Tale of Effect," *Jahrbuch für Amerikastudien*, XIII (1968), 134–142.

Frieden, Ken. *Genius and Monologue* (Ithaca, N.Y., 1985), pp. 166–168.

Garber, Frederick. *The Autonomy of the Self from Richardson to Huysmans* (Princeton, 1982), pp.237–241.

Gargano, James W. "'The Cask of Amontillado': A Masquerade of Motive and Identity," *Studies in Short Fiction*, IV (Winter 1967), 119–126.

———. *The Masquerade Vision in Poe's Short Stories* (Baltimore, 1977), pp. 9–11.

Harkey, J. H. "A Note on Fortunato's Coughing," *Poe Newsletter*, III (June 1970), 22.

Harris, Kathryn Montgomery. "Ironic Revenge in Poe's 'The Cask of Amontillado,'" *Studies in Short Fiction*, VI (Spring 1969), 333–335.

Henniger, F. J. "The Bouquet of Poe's Amontillado," *South Atlantic Bulletin*, XXXV (March 1970), 35–40.

Hoffman, Daniel. *Poe Poe Poe Poe Poe Poe Poe* (Garden City, N.Y., 1973), pp. 218–221.

Jacoby, Jay. "Fortunato's Premature Demise in 'The Cask of Amontillado,'" *Poe Studies*, XII (1979), 30–31.

Jacobs, Edward Craney. "A Possible Debt to Cooper," *Poe Studies*, IX (June 1976), 23.

Kempton, Kenneth P. *The Short Story* (Cambridge, Mass., 1954), pp. 86–91.

Kennedy, J. Gerald. *Poe, Death, and the Life of Writing* (New Haven, 1987), pp. 138–143.

Ketterer, Richard. *The Rationale of Deception in Poe* (Baton Rouge, 1979), pp. 110–112.

Kirkham, E. Bruce. "Poe's Amontillado, One More Time," *American Notes & Queries*, XXIV (May–June 1986), 144–145.

Kishel, Joseph F. "Poe's 'The Cask of Amontillado,'" *Explicator*, XLI (Fall 1982), 30.

Knapp, Bettina L. *Edgar Allan Poe* (New York, 1984), pp. 178–180.

Knox, Helene. "Poe's 'The Cask of Amontillado,'" *Explicator*, XLI (Fall 1982), 30–31.

Kozikowski, Stanley J. "A Reconsideration of Poe's 'The Cask of Amontillado,'" *American Transcendental Quarterly*, XXIX (1978), 269–280.

Levine, Stuart. *Edgar Poe: Seer and Craftsman* (Deland, Fla., 1972), pp. 80–92.

———. "Masonry, Impunity, and Revolution," *Poe Studies*, XVII (June 1984), 22–23.

Mabbott, Thomas O. "Poe's 'Cask of Amontillado,'" *Explicator*, XXV (November 1966), Item 30.

May, Charles E. *Edgar Allan Poe: A Study of the Short Stories* (New York, 1991), pp. 79–81.

Moon, Sam. "'The Cask of Amontillado,'" *Notes & Queries*, CXCIX (October 1954), 448.

Nevi, Charles N. "Irony and 'The Cask of Amontillado,'" *English Journal*, LVI (March 1967), 461–463.

Otten, Charlotte. "Poe, the Puritans, and the Hate Ethic," *Cresset*, XXXII (March 1969), 16–17.

Pearce, Donald. "'The Cask of Amontillado,'" *Notes and Queries*, CXCIX (October 1954), 448–449.

Pittman, Philip. "Method and Motive in 'The Cask of Amontillado,'" *Malahat Review*, XXXIV (1975), 87–100.

Pollin, Burton R. *Discoveries in Poe* (Notre Dame, Ind., 1970), pp. 29–37.

———. "Notre-Dame de Paris in Two of Poe's Tales," *Revue des Longues Vivantes*, XXXIV (August 1968), 354–365.

Punter, David. *The Literature of Terror: A History of Gothic Fictions From 1765 to the Present Day* (London, 1980), pp. 207–210.

Randall, John H. "Poe's 'The Cask of Amontillado' and the Code of the Duello," *Studia Germanica Gandensia*, V (1963), 175–184.

Rasor, C. L. "Possible Sources of 'The Cask of Amontillado,'" *Furman Studies*, XXXI (1949), 46–50.

Rea, Joy. "Poe's 'The Cask of Amontillado,'" *Studies in Short Fiction*, IV (Fall 1966), 57–69.

———. "In Defense of Fortunato's Courtesy," *Studies in Short Fiction*, IV (Spring 1967), 261–269.

Reynolds, David S. "Poe's Art of Transformation: 'The Cask of Amontillado,'" *New Essays on Poe's Major Tales*, Kenneth Silverman, ed. (Cambridge, England, 1993), pp. 93–112.

Robertson, Patricia. "Poe's 'The Cask of Amontillado'—Again," *Publications of the Arkansas Philological Association*, XIV (Spring 1988), 39–46.

Rocks, James E. "Conflict and Motive in 'The Cask of Amontillado,'" *Poe Studies*, V (June 1972), 50–51.

Scherting, Jack. "Poe's 'The Cask of Amontillado': A Source for Twain's 'The Man That Corrupted Hadleyburg," *Mark Twain Journal*, XVI (Summer 1972), 18–19.

Schick, Joseph S. "The Origin of 'The Cask of Amontillado,'" *American Literature*, VI (March 1934), 18–21.

Shurr, William H. "Montressor's Audience in 'The Cask of Amontillado,'" *Poe Studies*, X (June 1977), 28–29.

Silverman, Kenneth. *Edgar A. Poe: Mournful and Never-Ending Remembrance* (New York, 1991), 316–317.

Snow, Edward R. "The Roving Skeleton of Boston Bay," *Yankee*, XXV (April 1961), 52–55, 109–110.

Sorenson, Peter J. "William Morgan, Freemasonry, and 'The Cask of Amontillado,'" *Poe Studies*, XXII (December 1989), 45–47.

Spisak, James W. "Narration as Seduction, Seduction as Narration," *CEA Critic*, XVI (January 1979), 26–29.

Steele, Charles W. "Poe's 'The Cask of Amontillado,'" *Explicator*, XVIII (April 1960), Item 43.

Stepp, Walter. "The Ironic Double in Poe's 'The Cask of Amontillado,'" *Studies in Short Fiction*, XIII (Fall 1976), 447–453.

Stewart, Kate. "The Supreme Madness: Revenge and the Bells in 'The Cask of Amontillado'" *University of Mississippi Studies in English* V (1987), 51–57.

White, Patrick. "'The Cask of Amontillado': A Case for the Defense," *Studies in Short Fiction*, XXVI (Fall 1989), 550–555.

EDGAR ALLAN POE, "The Fall of the House of Usher"

Abel, Darrel. "A Key to the House of Usher," *University of Toronto Quarterly*, XVIII (January 1949), 176–185.

Allison, John. "Coleridgean Self-Development: Entrapment and Incest in 'The Fall of the House of Usher,'" *South Central Review*, V (1988), 40–47.

Amur, G. S. "'Heart of Darkness' and 'The Fall of the House of Usher,'" *Literary Criticism*, IX (Summer 1971), 59–70.

Auerbach, Jonathan. *The Romance of Failure: First-Person Fictions of Poe, Hawthorne, and James* (New York, 1989), pp. 47–51.

Bachinger, Katrina. *The Multi-Man Genre and Poe's Byrons*, Salzburg Studies in English Literature, James Hogg, ed. (Salzburg, 1987), pp. 1083.

———. "The Poetic Distance of 'House of Usher,'" Romantic Assessment, James Hogg, ed., *Studies in Nineteenth-Century Literature*, Salzburg Studies in English Literature, No. 87 (Salzburg, 1979), pp. 61–74.

Bailey, J. 0. "What Happens in 'The Fall of the House of Usher'?" *American Literature*, XXXV (January 1964), 445–466.

Barberese, J. T. "Landscapes of the American Psyche," *Sewanee Review*, C (1992), 603–609.

Beebe, Maurice. "The Fall of the House of Pyncheon," *Nineteenth-Century Fiction*, XI (June 1956), 4–8.

———. "The Universe of Roderick Usher," *The Personalist*, XXXVII (Spring 1956), 147–160.

Bell, Michael Davitt. *The Development of American Romance* (Chicago, 1980), pp. 108–112.

Biegailowski, Ronald. "The Self-Consuming Narrator in Poe's 'Ligeia' and 'Usher,'" *American Literature*, LX (March 1988), 175–187.

Bonaparte, Marie. *The Life and Works of Edgar Allan Poe: A Psycho-Analytic Interpretation* (London, 1949), pp. 237–250.

Bradfield Scott. *Dreaming Revolution: Transgression in the Development of American Romance* (Iowa City, 1993), pp. 86–92.

Brennan, Matthew C. "Tumerian Topography: The Paintings of Roderick Usher," *Studies in Short Fiction*, XXVII (Fall 1990), 605–608.

Brooks, Cleanth and Robert Penn Warren. *Understanding Fiction* (New York, 1943), pp. 202–205.

Budick, E. Miller. "'The Fall of the House of Usher': A Reappraisal of Poe's Attitudes Toward Life and Death," *Southern Literary Journal*, IX (Spring 1977), 30–50.

Buranelli, Vincent. *Edgar Allan Poe* (New Haven, 1961), pp. 77–78.

Burduck, Michael L. *Grim Phantasms: Fear in Poe's Short Fiction* (New York, 1992), pp. 70–75.

Butler, David W. "Usher's Hypochondriasis: Mental Alienation and Romantic Idealism in Poe's Gothic Tales," *American Literature*, XLVIII (March 1976), 1–12.

Cameron, Kenneth W. "Three Notes on Poe," *American Literature*, IV (January 1933), 385–386.

Carlson, Eric W., ed. *Edgar Allan Poe: The Fall of the House of Usher* (Columbus, Ohio, 1971).

Carton, Evan. *The Rhetoric of American Romance: Dialect and Identity in Emerson, Dickinson, Poe, and Hawthorne* (Baltimore, 1985), pp. 72–76.

Caws, Mary Ann. *Reading Frames in Modern Fiction* (Princeton, 1985), pp. 109–118.

Chandler, Marilyn R. *Dwelling in the Text: Houses in American Literature* (Berkeley, 1991), pp. 47–62.

Clifton, Michael. "Down Hecate's Chain: Infernal Inspiration in Three of Poe's Tales, " *Nineteenth-Century Fiction*, XLI (September 1986), 217–227.

Cohen, Hennig. "Roderick Usher's Tragic Struggle," *Nineteenth-Century Fiction*, XIV (December 1959), 270–272.

Cronin, James. "Poe's Vaults," *Notes and Queries*, CXCVIII (September 1953), 395–396.

Crossley, Robert. "Poe's Closet Monologues," *Genre*, X (Summer 1977), 226–230.

Dameron, J. Lashley. "Arthur Symons on Poe's 'The Fall of the House of Usher,'" *Poe Studies*, IX (1976), 46–49.

Davidson, Edward H. *Poe: A Critical Study* (Cambridge, Mass., 1957), pp. 196–198.

Davis, Jeff. "The Lady Madeline as a Symbol," *Annotator*, 11 (April 1954), 8–11.

Davis, Richard Beale. "Haunted Palace and Haunted Place," *Notes and Queries*, CCIV (September 1959), 336–337.

Elbert, Monika M. "'The Man of the Crowd' and The Man Outside the Crowd: Poe's Narrator and the Democratic Reader,'" *Modern Language Studies*,", XXI, iv (1991), 19–20, 21–24, 25.

Engel, Leonard W. "The Journey from Reason to Madness: Edgar Allan Poe's 'The Fall of the House of Usher,'" *Essays in Arts and Sciences*, XIV (May 1985), 23–31.

Evans, Walter. "'The Fall of the House of Usher' and Poe's Theory of the Tale," *Studies in Short Fiction*, XIV (Spring 1977), 137–144.

Fagin, N. Bryllion. *The Histrionic Mr. Poe* (Baltimore, 1949), pp. 200–203.

Falk, Doris V. "Poe and the Powers of Animal Magnetism," *Publications of the Modern Language Association*, LXXXIV (March 1969), 536–546.

Feidelson, Charles, Jr. *Symbolism in American Literature* (Chicago, 1953), pp. 39–42.

Fisher, Benjamin F. "Playful 'Germanism' in 'The Fall of the House of Usher': The Storyteller's Art," *Ruined Eden of the Present: Hawthorne, Melville, and Poe*, G. R. Thompson and Virgil L. Lockke, eds. (West Lafayette, Ind., 1981), pp. 355–374.

———. "Poe's 'Usher' Tarred and Feathered," *Poe Studies*, VI (December 1973), 49.

Flory, Wendy Stallard. "Usher's Fear and the Flaw in Poe's Theories of the Metamorphosis of the Senses," *Poe Studies*, VII (June 1974), 17–19.

Frank, Frederick S. "Poe's House of the Seven Gothics: The Fall of the Narrator in 'The Fall of the House of Usher,'" *Orbis Litterarum*, XXXIV (1979), 331–351.

Gargano, James W. "'The Fall of the House of Usher': An Apocalyptic Vision," *University of Mississippi Studies in English*, III (1982), 53–63.

———. *The Masquerade Vision in Poe's Short Stories* (Baltimore, 1977), pp. 12–14.

Garmon, Gerald. "Roderick Usher: Portrait of the Madman as Artist," *Poe Studies*, V (June 1972), 11–14.

Garrison, Joseph M., Jr. "The Function of Terror in the Work of Edgar Allan Poe," *American Quarterly*, XVIII (Summer 1966), 136–150.

Gerlach, John S. *Toward the End: Closure and Structure in the American Short Story* (University, Ala., 1985), pp. 30–35.

Girgus, Sam B. "Poe and R. D. Laing: The Transcendental Self," *Studies in Short Fiction*, XIII (Summer 1976), 299–309.

Gold, Joseph, "Reconstructing the 'House of Usher,'" *Emerson Society Quarterly*, XXXVII (Fourth Quarter 1964), 74–76.

Goodwin, K. L. "Roderick Usher's Overrated Knowledge," *Nineteenth-Century Fiction*, XVI (September 1961), 173–175.

Gordon, Caroline and Allen Tate. *The House of Fiction* (New York, 1960), pp. 114–117.

Gray, Richard. "Edgar Allen Poe and the Problem Of Regionalism," *The United States South: Regionalism and Identity*, Valeria G. Lerda and Tjebbe Westendorp, eds. (Rome, 1991), pp. 84–90.

Griffith, Clark. "Poe and the Gothic," *Papers on Poe: Essays in Honor of John Ward Ostrom*, Richard P. Veler, ed. (Springfield, Ohio, 1972), pp. 21–27.

Grillou, Jean-Louis. "'The Fall of the House of Usher': Un cryptogramme alchimique?" *Du fantasque en litterature*, Max Duperray, ed. (Aix-en-Provence, France, 1990), pp. 111–126.

Guilds, John C., Jr. "Poe's Vaults Again," *Notes and Queries*, CCII (May 1957), 220–221.

Hafley, James. "A Tour of the House of Usher," *Emerson Society Quarterly*, XXXI (Second Quarter 1963), 18–20.

Halliburton, David. *Edgar Allan Poe: A Phenomenological View* (Princeton, 1973), pp. 278–299.

Hammond, J. R. *An Edgar Allan Poe Companion* (Totowa, N.J., 198 1), pp. 69–73.

Hansen, Thomas S. "Poe's 'German' Source for 'The Fall of the House of Usher': The Arno Schmidt Connection," *Southern Humanities Review*, XXVII (Spring 1992), 101–112.

————, and Burton R. Pollin. *The German Face of Edgar Allan Poe: A Study of Literary References in His* Works (Columbia, S.C., 1995), 60–66.

Harding, Brian. *American Literature in Context, II: 1830–1865* (London, 1982), pp. 48–55, 66–67.

Hartley, Lodwick. "From Crazy Castle to the House of Usher: A Note Toward a Source," *Studies in Short Fiction*, II (Spring 1965), 256–261.

Heller, Terry. *The Delights of Terror: An Aesthetics of the Tales of Terror* (Urbana, Ill., 1987), pp.127–146.

Hill, Archibald A. "Principles Governing Semantic Parallels," *Texas Studies in Literature and Language*, I (Autumn 1959), 356–365.

Hill, John. "Poe's 'The Fall of the House of Usher' and Frank Norris' Early Short Stories," *Huntington Library Quarterly*, XXVI (1962), 111–112.

Hill, John S. "The Dual Hallucination in 'The Fall of the House of Usher,'" *Southern Review*, XLVIII (Autumn 1963), 396–402.

Hoeveler, Diane L. "The Hidden God and the Abjected Woman in 'The Fall of the House of Usher,'" *Studies in Short Fiction*, XXIX (Summer 1992), 385–394.

Hoffman, Daniel. *Poe Poe Poe Poe Poe Poe Poe* (Garden City, N.Y., 1973), pp. 295–316.

Hoffman, Gerhard. "Space and Symbol in the Tales of Edgar Allan Poe," *Poe Studies*, (1979), 3–8.

Hoffman, Michael J. "The Discovery of the Void: The House of Usher and Negative Romanticism," *The Subversive Vision: American Romanticism in Literature* (Port Washington, N.Y., 1972), pp. 19–29.

Howes, Craig. "Burke, Poe and 'Usher': The Sublime and Rising Woman," *Emerson Society Quarterly*, XXXI (1985), 173–189.

————. "'The Fall of the House of Usher' and Elgiac Romance," *Southern Literary Journal*, XIX (Fall 1986), 68–78.

Hungerford, Edward. "Poe and Phrenology," *American Literature*, II (November 1930), 225–227.

Jay, Gregory S. *America the Scrivener: Deconstruction and the Subject of Literary History* (Ithaca, 1990), 177–183.

Johansen, Ib, "The Madness of the Text: Deconstruction of Narrative Logic in 'Usher,' 'Berenice,' and 'Doctor Tarr and Professor Fether,'" *Poe Studies*, XXII (June 1989), 1–9.

Jordan, Cynthia S. "Poe's Re-Vision: The Recovery of the Second Story," *American Literature*, LIX (March 1987), 1–19.

————. *Second Stories: The Politics of Language Form and Gender in Early American Fiction* (Chapel Hill, 1989), pp. 140–145, 149–153.

Kaplan, Louise J. "The Perverse Strategy in 'The Fall of the House of Usher,'" *New Essays on Poe's Major Tales*, Kenneth Silverman, ed. (Cambridge, England, 1993), pp. 46–64.

Kendall, Lyle H., Jr. "The Vampire Motif in 'The Fall of the House of Usher,'" *College English*, XXIV (March 1963), 450–453.

Kennedy, J. Gerald. *Poe, Death, and the Life of Writing* (New Haven, 1987), pp. 86–88.

Ketterer, Richard. *The Rationale of Deception in Poe* (Baton Rouge, 1979), p. 192–198.

Kim, Hwan Hee. "Plot and Epiphany in the Short Story," *Journal of English Language and Literature*, 41 (Winter 1995), 1043–1060.

Kinkead-Weekes, Mark. "Reflections On, and In, 'The Fall of the House of Usher,'" *Edgar Allan Poe: The Design of Order*, A. Robert Lee, ed. (Totowa, N.J., 1987), pp. 17–34.

Knapp, Bettina L. *Edgar Allan Poe* (New York, 1984), pp. 134–139.

La Cassagnere, Christian. "Desastre obscur: angoisse et ecriture dans 'The Fall of the House of Usher'" d'Edgar Allan Poe, *Visages de l'angoisse*, Christian La Cassagnere, ed. (Clermont-Ferrand, France, 1989), pp. 303–324.

Lawrence, David Herbert. *Studies in Classic American Literature* (New York, 1923), pp. 110–116.

Levin, Harry. *The Power of Blackness* (New York, 1958), pp. 159–161.

Levin, Stuart. *Edgar Poe: Seer and Craftsman* (Deland, Fla., 1972), pp. 38–41.

Levy, Maurice. "Poe and the Gothic Tradition," *Emerson Society Quarterly*, XVIII (1972), 19–28.

Lippe, George B. von der. "Beyond the House of Usher: The Figure of E. T. A. Hoffman in the Works of Poe," *Modern Language Studies*, IX (Winter 1978–1979), 33–41.

Ljungquist, Kent. *The Grand and the Fair: Poe's Landscape Aesthetics and Pictorial Techniques* (Potomac, Md., 1984), pp. 100–106.

———. "Howitt's 'Byronian Rambles' and the Picturesque Setting of 'The Fall of the House of Usher,'" *ESQ*, XXXIII (4th Quarter 1987), 224–236.

Lynen, John F. *The Design of the Present: Essays on Time and Form in American Literature* (New Haven, 1969), pp. 229–238.

Mabbott, Thomas Olive. "The Books in the House of Usher," *Books at Iowa*, XIX (November 1973).

———. "Poe's 'The Fall of the House of Usher,'" *Explicator*, XV (November 1956), Item 7.

———. "Poe's Vaults," *Notes and Queries*, CXCVIII (December 1953), 542–543.

MacAndrew, Elizabeth. *The Gothic Tradition in Fiction* (New York, 1979), pp. 195–199.

Marks, Alfred H. "Two Rodericks and Two Worms: 'Egotism, Or, The Bosom Serpent,'" *Publications of the Modern Language Association*, LXXIV (December 1959), 607–612.

Marrs, Robert L. "'The Fall of the House of Usher': A Checklist of Criticism Since 1960," *Poe Studies*, V, No. I (1972), 23–24.

Marsh, John L. "The Psycho-Sexual Reading of 'The Fall of the House of Usher,'" *Poe Studies*, V (June 1972), 8–9.

Massa, Ann. *American Literature in Context, IV: 1900–1920* (London, 1982), pp. 48–54.

Martindale, Colin. "Archetype and Reality in 'The Fall of the House of Usher,'" *Poe Studies*, V (June 1972), 9–11.

Mautner, Renata R. "The Self, the Mirror, the Other: 'The Fall of the House of Usher,'" *Poe Studies*, X (December 1977), 33–35.

May, Charles E. *Edgar Allan Poe: A Study of the Short Stories* (New York, 1991), pp. 103–107, 107–172.

May, Leila S. "'Sympathies of a Scarcely Intelligible Nature': The Brother-Sister Bond in Poe's 'Fall of the House of Usher,'" *Studies in Short Fiction*, XXX (Summer 1993), 387–396.

Mengeling, Marvin and Frances. "From Fancy to Failure: A Study of the Narrators in the Tales of E. A. Poe," *University Review*, XXXIV (Autumn 1967), 34–36.

Meyers, Jeffrey. *Edgar Allan Poe: His Life and Legacy* (New York, 1992), pp. 110–113.

Moffett, Harold Young. "Applied Tactics in Teaching Literature, 'The Fall of the House of Usher,'" *English Journal*, XVII (September 1928), 556–559.

Mollinger, Robert N. *Psychoanalysis and Literature: An Introduction* (Chicago, 1981), pp. 73–84.

Morse, David. *American Romanticism* (Totowa, N.J., 1987), pp. 109–113.

Nigro, August J. *The Diagonal Line: Separation and Reparation in American Literature* (Cranbury, N.J., 1984), pp. 62–65.

Obucchowski, Peter. "Unity of Effect in Poe's 'The Fall of the House of Usher,'" *Studies in Short Fiction*, XII (Fall 1975), 407–412.

Olson, Bruce. "Poe's Strategy in 'The Fall of the House of Usher,'" *Modern Language Notes,* LXXV (November 1960), 556–559.

Pahl, Dennis. *Architects of The Abyss: The Indeterminate Fictions of Poe, Hawthorne, and Melville* (Columbia, Mo., 1989), pp. 3–24.

Person, Leland S., Jr. *Aesthetic Headaches: Woman and Masculine Poetics in Poe, Melville and Hawthorne* (Athens, Ga., 1988), pp. 34–41.

Phillips, H. Wells. "Poe's Usher: Precursor of Abstract Art," *Poe Studies,* V (June 1972) 14–16.

Phillips, William L. "Poe's 'The Fall of the House of Usher,'" *Explicator,* IX (February 1951), Item 29.

Pittman, Diana. "'The Fall of the House of Usher,'" *Southern Literary Messenger* III (November 1941), 502–509.

Pollin, Burton R. *Discoveries in Poe* (Notre Dame, Ind., 1970), pp. 84–86, 206–208.

———. "Poe's Pen of Iron," *American Transcendental Quarterly,* II (Second Quarter 1969), 16–18.

Priestman, Martin. *Detective Fiction and Literature: The Figure on the Carpet* (New York, 1991), pp. 37–42.

Punter, David. *The Literature of Terror: A History of Gothic Fictions from 1765 to the Present Day* (London, 1980), pp. 203–206.

Quinn, Patrick F. *The French Face of Edgar Allan Poe* (Carbondale, Ill., 1957), pp. 237–246.

———. "A Misreading of Poe's 'The Fall of the House of Usher,'" *Ruined Eden of the Present: Hawthorne, Melville, and Poe,* G. R. Thompson and Virgil L. Lockke, eds. (West Lafayette, Ind., 1981), pp. 303–312.

———. "'Usher' Again: Trust the Teller!" *Idem.,* pp. 341–353.

Railton, Stephen. *Authorship and Audience: Literary Performance in the American Renaissance* (Princeton, 1991), pp. 143–146.

Ramsey, Paul J. "Poe and Modern Art," *College Art Journal,* XVIII (Spring 1959), 210–215.

Rashkin, Esther. *Family Secrets and the Psychoanalysis of Narrative* (Princeton, 1992), pp. 123–155.

Ravvin, Norman. "An Irruption of the Archaic: Poe and the Grotesque," *Mosaic,* XXV, No. 4 (1992), 12–15.

Rein, David M. *Edgar A. Poe: The Inner Pattern* (New York, 1960), pp. 74–78.

Richard, Claude. "Edgar A. Poe et l'esthetique du double," *Visages de l'angoisse,* Christian La Cassagnere, ed. (Clermont-Ferrand, France, 1989), pp. 277–286.

Riddel, Joseph N. "The 'Crypt' of Edgar Poe," *Boundary 2,* VII (Spring 1979), 117–144.

Ringe, Donald A. *American Gothic: Imagination and Realism in Nineteenth-Century Fiction* (Lexington, Ky., 1982), pp. 146–148.

Robinson, E. Arthur. "Order and Sentence in 'The Fall of the House of Usher,'" *Publications of the Modern Language Association,* LXXXVI (March 1961), 68–81.

Rountree, Thomas J. "Poe's Universe: The House of Usher and the Narrator," *Tulane Studies in English,* XX (1972), 123–134.

Rovit, Earl. "Melville and the Discovery of America," *Sewanee Review,* C (1992), 587–589.

St. Armand, Barton Levi. "The Mysteries of Edgar Allan Poe: The Quest for a Monomyth in Gothic Literature," *The Gothic Imagination: Essays in Dark Romanticism,* G. R. Thompson, ed. (Pullman, Wash., 1974), pp. 65–93.

———. "Poe's Landscape of the Soul: Association Theory and 'The Fall of the House of Usher,'" *Modern Language Studies,* VII (Fall 1977), 32–41.

———. "Usher Unveiled: Poe and the Metaphysic of Gnosticism," *Poe Studies,* V (June 1972), I–8.

Saliba, David R. *A Psychology of Fear: The Nightmare Formula of Edgar Allan Poe* (New York, 1986), pp. 162–190.

Samuels, Charles T. "Usher's Fall: Poe's Rise," *Georgia Review,* XVIII (Summer 1964), 208–216.

Schneider, Kirk J. *Horror and the Holy: Wisdom-Teaching and the Monster Tale* (Chicago, 1993), pp. 50–54.

Schwaber, Paul. "On Reading Poe," *Literature and Psychology*, XXI, No. 2 (1971), 83–86.

Shackleford, Lynne P. "Poe's 'The Fall of the House of Usher,'" *Explicator*, XLV (Fall 1986), 18–19.

Seelye, John, "Edgar Allan Poe: *Tales of the Grotesque and Arabesque*," *Landmarks of American Writing*, Hennig Cohen, ed. (New York, 1969), pp. 107–110.

Seronsy, Cecil C. "Poe and 'Kubla Khan,'" *Notes and Queries*, CCII (Summer 1957), 219–220.

Silverman, Kenneth, *Edgar A. Poe: Mournful and Never-Ending Remembrance* (New York, 1991), 150–152.

Simpson, Lewis. *The Dispossessed Garden: Pastoral and History in Southern Literature* (Athens, Ga., 1975), pp. 67–69.

Sinclair, David. *Edgar Allan Poe* (Totowa, N.J., 1977), pp. 173–176.

Sharp, Roberta. "Usher and Rosicrucianism: A Speculation," *Poe Studies*, XII (1979), 34–35.

Smith, Allan Gardner. "Edgar Allan Poe, the Will, and Horror Fiction," *American Fiction: New Readings*, Richard Gray, ed. (London, 1983), pp. 53–63. (G)

Smith, Herbert F. "Is Roderick Usher a Caricature?" *Poe Studies*, VI (December 1973), 49–50.

———. "Usher's Madness and Poe's Organicism: A Source," *American Literature*, XXXIX (November 1967), 379–389.

Spaulding, Kenneth A. "The Fall of the House of Usher," *Explicator*, X (June 1952), Item 52.

Spitzer, Leo. "A Reinterpretation of 'The Fall of the House of Usher,'" *Comparative Literature*, IV (Fall 1952), 351–363.

Stahlberg, Lawrence. "The Source of Ushers Fear," *Interpretations*, XIII (Fall 1981), 10–17.

Steele, Jeffrey. *The Representation of the Self in American Literature* (Chapel Hill, 1987), pp. 142–144.

Stein, William Bysshe. "The Twin Motif in 'The Fall of the House of Usher,'" *Modern Language Notes*, LXXV (February 1960), 109–111.

Stone, Edward. "Usher, Poquelin and Miss Emily: Progress of the Southern Gothic," *Georgia Review*, XIV (Winter 1960), 433–443.

Strandberg, Victor. "The Fall of the House of Usher," *Reference Guide to Short Fiction*, Noelle Watson, ed. (Detroit, 1994), pp. 704–705.

Symons, Julian. *The Tell-Tale Heart: The Life and Works of Edgar Allan Poe* (New York, 1978), pp. 235–238.

Tallack, Douglas. *The Nineteenth–Century American Short Story: Language, Form and Ideology* (London, 1993), pp. 45–46, 48–60.

Tate, Allen. "Our Cousin, Mr. Poe," *Partisan Review*, XVI (December 1949), 1212–1214.

———. "Three Commentaries: Poe, James, and Joyce," *Sewanee Review*, LVIII (Winter 1950), 1–5.

Thompson, G. R. "The Face in the Pool: Reflections on the Doppelgänger Motif in 'The Fall of the House of Usher,'" *Poe Studies*, V (June 1972), 16–21.

———. "Locke, Kant, and Gothic Fiction: A Further Word on the Indeterminism of Poe's 'Usher,'" *Studies in Short Fiction*, XXVI (Fall 1989), 547–550.

———. *Poe's Fiction: Romantic Irony in the Gothic Tales* (Madison, Wis., 1973), pp. 87–98.

———. "Poe and the Paradox of Terror: Structures of Heightened Consciousness in 'The Fall of the House of Usher,'" *Ruined Eden of the Present: Hawthorne, Melville, and Poe*, G. R. Thompson and Virgil L. Lockke, eds, (West Lafayette, Ind., 1981), pp. 315–340.

Tombleson, Gary E. "An Error in 'Usher,'" *Poe Studies*, XIV (June 1981), 8.

Uba, George R. "Malady and Motive: History and 'The Fall of the House of Usher,'" *South Atlantic Quarterly*, LXXXV (Winter 1986), 10–22.

Voloshin, Beverly R. "Explanation in 'The Fall of the House of Usher,'" *Studies in Short Fiction*, XXIII (Fall 1986), 419–428.

―――. "The Fall of the House of Usher," *Explicator*, XLVI (Spring 1988), 13–15.

―――. "Transcendence Downward: An Essay of 'Usher' and 'Ligeia,'" *Modern Language Studies*, XVIII (Summer 1988), 18–29.

Walker, I. M. "The 'Legitimate Sources' of Terror in 'The Fall of the House of Usher," *Modern Language Review*, LXI (October 1966), 585–592.

Warfel, Harry R. "Poe's Dr. Percival: A Note on 'The Fall of the House of Usher,'" *Modern Language Notes*, LIV (February 1939), 129–131.

Weaver, Mike. "Edgar Allan Poe and the Early Avant-Garde Film," *Essays and Studies by Members of the English Association*, XXX (1977), 73–85.

Weber, Jean-Paul. "Edgar Allan Poe or The Theme of the Clock," *La Nouvelle Revue Française*, IV (August–September 1958), 309–311.

Wilbur, Richard. "The House of Poe," *Poe: A Collection of Critical Essays*, Robert Regan, ed. (Englewood Cliffs, N.J., 1967), pp. 104–111.

Wilcox, Earl J. "Poe's Usher and Usher's Chronology," *Poe Newsletter*, I (October 1968), 31.

Woodson, Thomas, ed. *Twentieth-Century Interpretations of "The Fall of the House of Usher"* (Englewood Cliffs, N.J., 1969).

Wright, Nathalia. "Roderick Usher: Poe's Turn-of-the-Century Artist," *Artful Thunder: Visions of the Romantic Tradition in American Literature in Honor of Howard P. Vincent*, Robert J. Demott and Sanford E. Morovitz, eds. (Kent, Ohio, 1975), pp. 55–67.

Wuletich-Brinberg, Sybil. *Poe: The Rationale of the Uncanny* (New York, 1988), pp. 143–148.

Zeydel, Edwin H. "Edgar Allan Poe's Contacts with German as Seen in His Relations with Ludwig Tieck," *Studies in German Literature of the Nineteenth and Twentieth Centuries: Festschrift for Frederic E. Coenen*, Siegfried Mews, ed. (Chapel Hill, 1971), pp. 47–54.

EDGAR ALLAN POE, "The Purloined Letter"

Atkinson, Michael. *The Secret Marriage of Sherlock Holmes and Other Eccentric Readings* (Ann Arbor, 1996), pp. 52–63.

Aydelotte, William O. "The Detective Story as a Historical Source," *The Mystery Writer's Art*, Francis M. Nevis, Jr., ed. (Bowling Green, Ohio, 1970), pp. 306–325. (G)

Babender, Liahna K. "The Shadow's Shadow: The Motif of the Double in Edgar Allan Poe's 'The Purloined Letter,'" *Mystery and Detection Annual*, Donald Adams, ed. (Pasadena, 1972), pp. 21–32.

Beegel, Susan F. "The Literary Histrio as Detective," *Massachusetts Studies in English*, VIII, No. 3 (1983), 1–8. (G)

Bellei, Sergio. L. P. "'The Purloined Letter': A Theory of Perception," *Poe Studies*, IX (December 1976), 40–42.

Bennett, Maurice J. "The Detective Fiction of Poe and Borges," *Comparative Literature*, XXXV (Summer 1983), 262–275.

Blythe, Hal and Charlie Sweet. "The Reader as Poe's Ultimate Dupe in 'The Purloined Letter,'" *Studies in Short Fiction*, XXVI (Summer 1989), 311–315.

Brady, W. T. "Who Was Monsieur Dupin?" *Publications of the Modern Language Association*, LXXIX (September 1964), 509–510.

Brand, Dana. "Reconstructing the 'Flaneur': Poe's Invention of the Detective Story," *Genre*, XVIII (Spring 1985), pp. 35–56. (G)

Cawelti, John G. *Adventure, Mystery, and Romance: Formula Stories as Art and Popular Culture* (Chicago, 1976), pp. 80–97. (G)

Chambers, Ross. "Narrational Authority and 'The Purloined Letter,'" *Story and Situation: Narrative Seduction and the Power of Fiction* (Minneapolis, 1984), pp. 50–72.

Christopher, J. R. "Poe and the Detective Story," *Armchair Detective*, II (1968), 49–61. (G)

———. "Poe and the Tradition of the Detective Story," *The Mystery Writer's Art*, Francis M. Nevins, Jr., ed. (Bowling Green, Ohio, 1970), pp. 19–35. (G)

Crisman, William. "Poe's Dupin as Professional: The Dupin Stories as Serial Text," *Studies in American Fiction*, XXIII (Autumn 1995), 215–230.

Dameron, J. Lasley. "The Presidential Address: Poe's C. Auguste Dupin," *Tennessee Philological Bulletin*, XVII (1980), 5–15.

Daniel, Robert. "Poe's Detective God," *Furioso*, VI (Summer 1951),45–54, (G)

Fletcher, Richard M. *The Stylistic Development of Edgar Allan Poe* (The Hague, 1973), pp. 138–142.

Giddings, Robert. "Was the Chevalier Left-Handed? Poe's Dupin Stories," *Edgar Allan Poe: The Design of Order*, A. Robert Lee, ed. (Totowa, N.J., 1987), pp. 88–111.

Gilbert, Elliot L. "The Detective as Metaphor in the Nineteenth Century," *Journal of Popular Culture*, I (Winter 1967), 256–262. (G)

Grella, George. "Poe's Tangled Web," *Armchair Detective*, XXI (Summer 1998), 268–275. (G)

Grossvogel, David I. "'The Purloined Letter': The Mystery of the Text," *Mystery and Its Fictions: From Oedipus to Agatha Christie* (Baltimore, 1979), p. 93–107.

Halliburton, David. *Edgar Allan Poe: A Phenomenological View* (Princeton, 1983), pp. 237–245.

Hammond, J. R. *An Edgar Allan Poe Companion* (Totowa, N.J., 1981), pp. 95—97.

Harrison, Michael. "Dupin: The Reality Behind the Fictions," *The Exploits of the Chevalier Dupin* (Sauk City, WI, 1968), pp. 3–14. (G)

Haycraft, Howard. "Murder for Pleasure," *The Art of the Mystery Story*, Howard Haycraft, ed. (New York, 1946), pp. 158–177.

Hipolito, Terrence. "On the Two Poes," *The Mystery and Detective Annual 1972* (Item 16), pp. 15–20. (G)

Hoffman, Daniel. *Poe Poe Poe Poe Poe Poe Poe* (New York, 1972), pp. 119–125, 132–136.

Holland, Norman N. "Re-covering 'The Purloined Letter': Reading as Personal Transaction," *The Reader in the Text: Essays on Audience and Interpretation*, S. Suleiman and I. Crosman, eds. (Princeton, 1980), pp. 350–370.

Hull, Richard. "'The Purloined Letter': Poe's Detective Story Versus Panoptic Foucauldian Theory," *Style*, XXIV (Spring 1990). 201–214.

Irwin, John T. "A Clew to Clue: Locked Rooms and Labyrinths in Poe and Borges," *Raritan*, X, iv (1991), 42, 46–50.

———. "Mysteries We Reread: Mysteries of Rereading: Poe, Borges, and the Analytic Detective Story," *Modern Language Notes*, CI (1986), 1170–1198.

———. *The Mystery to a Solution: Poe, Borges, and the Analytic Detective Story* (Baltimore, 1994), pp. 22–29.

Jay, Gregory S. *America the Scrivener: Deconstruction and the Subject of Literary History* (Ithaca, 1990), 198–204.

Johnson, Barbara. "The Frame of Reference: Poe, Lacan, Derrida," *Yale French Studies*, LV/LVI (1977), 457–505.

———. *Psychoanalysis and the Question of the Text*, Geoffrey Hartman, ed. (Baltimore, 1978), pp.149–171.

Jones, Buford and Kent Linquist. "Monsieur Dupin: Further Details on the Reality Behind the Legend," *Southern Literary Journal*, IX (Fall 1976), 70–77. (G)

Kennedy, J. Gerald, "The Limits of Reason: Poe's Deluded Detectives," *American Literature*, XLVII (May 1975), 184–196. (G)

Knight, Stephen. *Form and Ideology in Crime Fiction* (Bloomington, Ind., 1981), pp. 58–65.

Kronick, Joseph G. "Edgar Allan Poe: The Error of Reading and the Reading of Error," *Literature and Psychology*, XXXV, No. 3 (1989), 22–42.

Kushigian, Julia A. "The Detective Genre in Poe and Borges," *Latin American Literary Review*, XI (Spring–Summer 1983), 27–39.

Lacan, Jacques. "Seminar on 'The Purloined Letter,'" *The Poetics of Murder: Detective Fiction and Literary Theory*, Glenn W. Most and William W. Stowe, eds. (New York, 1983), pp. 21–54.

Levine, Stuart. *Edgar Poe: Seer and Craftsman* (Deland, Fla., 1972), pp. 162–168.

Lewis, Ffrangcon C. "Unravelling a Web: Writer *versus* Reader in Edgar Allan Poe's Tales of Detection," *Watching the Detective: Essays on Crime Fiction* (Houndsmills, Eng., 1990), pp. 97–116.

Limon, John. *The Place of Fiction in the Time of Science: A Disciplinary History of American Writing* (Cambridge, England, 1990), pp. 101–104.

Lowdes, Robert A. W. "The Contribution of Edgar Allan Poe," *The Mystery Writer's Art*, Francis M. Nevins, Jr,, ed. (Bowling Green, Ohio, 1970), pp. 1–18. (G)

Major, Rene. "The Parable of the Purloined Letter: The Direction of the Cure and Its Telling," John Forrester, trans., *Stanford Literary Review*, VIII (Spring-Fall, 1991), 67–102.

Matthews, Brander. "Poe and the Detective Story," *Scribner's Magazine*, XLII (September 1907), 287–293, (G)

May, Charles E. *Edgar Allan Poe: A Study of the Short Stories* (New York, 1991), pp. 90–92.

Michael, J. S. *A World of Words: Language and Displacement in the Fiction of Edgar Allan Poe* (Durham, 1988), pp. 141–146.

Morse, David, *American Romanticism I: From Cooper to Hawthorne* (Totowa, N.J., 1987), pp. 101–103.

———. "Negation in 'The Purloined Letter': Hegel, Poe, and Lacan," *The Purloined Letter*, John P. Muller and William J. Richardson, eds. (Baltimore, 1988), pp. 343–368.

Muller, John P. and William J. Richardson. *The Purloined Poe: Lacan, Derrida and Psychoanalytic Reading* (Baltimore, 1988).

Murch, A. E. *The Development of the Detective Novel* (New York, 1958), pp. 67–83. (G)

Ohoka, Shohei. "On 'The Purloined Letter,'" *Gunzo*, XLIII (January 1988), 306–310.

Orel, Harold. "The American Detective Hero," *Journal of Popular Culture*, II (Winter 1968), 395–403. (G)

Palmer, Jerry. *Thrillers: Genesis and Structure of a Popular Genre* (New York, 1979), pp. 107–114. (G)

Panek, LeRoy L. "Play and Games: An Approach to Poe's Detective Tales," *Poe Studies*, X (December 1977), 39–41.

Pease, Donald. "Marginal Politics and 'The Purloined Letter': A Review Essay," *Poe Studies*, XVI (June 1983), 18–23.

Peraldi, Francois. "A Note on Time in 'The Purloined Letter,'" *The Purloined Letter*, John P. Muller and William J. Richardson, eds. (Baltimore, 1988), pp. 335–343.

Porter, Dennis. "Of Poets, Politicians, Policemen, and the Power of Analysis," *New Literary History*, XIX (Spring 1988), 501–519.

Priestman, Martin. *Detective Fiction and Literature: The Figure on the Carpet* (New York, 1991), pp. 53–57.

Rabkin, Eric S. *The Fantastic in Literature* (Princeton, 1976), pp. 60–67.

Rollason, Christopher. "The Detective Myth in Edgar Allan Poe's Trilogy," *American Crime Fiction: Studies in Genre*, Brian Docherty, ed. (New York, 1988), pp. 4–22.

Rosenheim, Shawn. "The King of 'Secret Readers': Edgar Poe, Cryptographer, and the Origins of the Detective Story," *ELH*, LVI (1989), 386–387.

Roth, Martin. "The Poet's Purloined Letter," *The Mystery and Detection Annual, 1973* (Beverly Hills, Calif., 1974), pp. 113–127.

Sandler, S. Gerald. "Poe's Indebtedness to Locke's *An Essay Concerning Human Understanding*," *Boston University Studies in English*, V (Spring 1961), 107–121.

Schweizer, Harold. "Nothing and Narrative 'Twitching' in 'The Purloined Letter,'" *Literature and Psychology* XXXVII, No. 4 (1991), 63–69.

Sippel, Erich W. "Bolting the Whole Shebang Together: Poe's Predicament," *Criticism*, XV (1973), 289–308. (G)

Stein, Aaron More. "The Mystery Story in Cultural Perspective," *The Mystery Story* (Del Mar, Calif., 1976), pp. 29–55.

Symons, Julian. *Bloody Murder: From the Detective Story to the Crime Novel: A History* (New York, 1985), pp. 34–41. (G)

———. *Mortal Consequences: A History—From the Detective Story to the Crime Novel* (New York, 1972), pp. 27–35, (G)

Van Dover, J. K. *You Know My Method: The Science of the Detective* (Bowling Green, Ohio, 1994), pp. 29–47. (G)

Van Leer, David. "Detecting Truth: The World of the Dupin Tales," *New Essays on Poe's Major Tales*, Kenneth Silverman, ed. (Cambridge, England, 1993), pp. 65–91.

Varnado, S. L. "The Case of the Sublime Purloin; or Burke's Inquiry as the Source of an Anecdote in 'The Purloined Letter,'" *Poe Newsletter*, I (October 1968), 27.

Voss, Arthur. *The American Short Story: A Critical Survey* (Norman, Okla., 1973), pp. 61–65.

Weiner, Bruce I. "'That Metaphysical Art': Mystery and Detection in Poe," *Poe and Our Times: Influences and Affinities*, Benjamin Franklin Fisher, ed. (Baltimore, 1986), pp. 32–48. (G)

Whalen, Terence. "Edgar Allan Poe and the Horrid Laws of Political Economy," *American Quarterly*, XLIV (1992), 405, 406–408.

Wilbur, Richard. *Major Writers of America*, Perry Miller, ed. (New York, 1962), pp. 378–380.

Williams, Michael J. S. *The World of Words: Language and Displacement in the Fiction of Edgar Allan Poe* (Durham, 1988), pp. 141–146.

Woodward, Servanne. "Lacan and Derrida on 'The Purloined Letter,'" *Comparative Literature Studies*, XXVI, i (1989), 39–49.

Wuletich-Brinberg, Sybil. *Poe: The Rationale of the Uncanny* (New York, 1988), pp. 158–174.

KATHERINE ANNE PORTER, "The Grave"

Baldeshwiler, Eileen. "Structural Patterns in Katherine Anne Porter's Fiction," *South Dakota Review*, XI (Summer 1973), 45–53. (G)

Bell, Vereen M. "'The Grave' Revisited," *Studies in Short Fiction*, III (Fall 1965), 39–45.

Brinkmeyer, Robert H., Jr. *Katherine Anne Porter's Artistic Development* (Baton Rouge, 1993), pp.179–181.

Brooks, Cleanth. "On 'The Grave,'" *Yale Review*, LV (December 1965), 275–279.

Cheatham, George. "Death and Repetition in Porter's Miranda Stories," *American Literature*, LXI (December 1999), 610–624.

———. "Literary Criticism, Katherine Anne Porter's Consciousness, and the Silver Dove," *Studies in Short Fiction*, XXV (Spring 1988), 109–115.

Curley, Daniel. "Treasure in 'The Grave,'" *Modern Fiction Studies*, IX (Winter 1963–1964), 377–384.

DeMouy, Jane Krause. *Katherine Anne Porter's Women: The Eye of Her Fiction* (Austin, Tex., 1993), pp. 139–144.

Emmons, Winifred S. *Katherine Anne Porter: The Regional Stories* (Austin, Tex., 1967), pp. 23–26.

Erdim, Esim. "The Ring or the Dove: the New Woman in Katherine Anne Porter's Fiction," *Women and War: The Changing Status of American Women from the 1930s to the 1950s*, Maria Diedrich and Dorothy F. Hornung, eds. (New York, 1990), pp. 58–61.

Gardiner, Judith Kegan. "'The Grave,'" 'On Not Shooting Sitting Birds,' and the Female Esthetic," *Studies in Short Fiction*, XX (Fall 1983), 265–270.

Givner, Joan. *Katherine Anne Porter: A Life* (New York, 1982), pp. 68–71.

Hardy, John Edward, *Katherine Anne Porter* (New York, 1973), pp. 20–24.

Hartley, Lodwick and George Core, eds. *Katherine Anne Porter: A Symposium* (Athens, Ga., 1969), pp. 81–92, 93–94, 115–119.

Hendrick, George. *Katherine Anne Porter* (New York, 1965), pp. 68–71.

Joselyn, Sister M. "'The Grave' as Lyrical Short Story," *Studies in Short Fiction*, I (Spring 1964), 216–221.

Kramer, Dale. "Notes on Lyricism and Symbols in 'The Grave,'" *Studies in Short Fiction*, II (Summer 1965), 331–336.

Mooney, Harry John, Jr., *The Fiction and Criticism of Katherine Anne Porter* (Pittsburgh, 1962), pp. 16–33.

Nance, William L. *Katherine Anne Porter and the Art of Rejection* (Chapel Hill, 1964), pp. 102–107.

Poss, S. H. "Variation on a Theme in Four Stories of Katherine Anne Porter," *Twentieth-Century Literature*, IV (April–July 1958), 21–29.

Prater, William. "'The Grave': Form and Symbol," *Studies in Short Fiction*, VI (Spring 1969), 336–338.

Rooke, Constance and Bruce Wallis. "Myth and Epiphany in Porter's 'The Grave,'" *Studies in Short Fiction*, XV (Summer 1978), 269–273.

Schwartz, Edward Greenfield. "The Fictions of Memory," *Southwest Review*, XLV (Summer 1960), 204–215.

Tanner, James T. F. *The Texas Legacy of Katherine Anne Porter* (Denton, Tex., 1990), pp. 80–84.

Titus, Mary. "'Mingled Sweetness and Corruption': Katherine Anne Porter's 'The Fig Tree' and 'The Grave,'" *South Atlantic Review*, LIII (May 1988), 111–125.

Unrue, Darlene Harbour. *Truth and Vision in Katherine Anne Porter's Fiction* (Athens, Ga., 1985), pp. 48–53.

———. *Understanding Katherine Anne Porter* (Columbia, S.C., 1988), pp. 58–61.

Walsh, Thomas F. "From Texas to Mexico," *Katherine Anne Porter and Texas: An Uneasy Relationship*, Clinton Machann and William Bedford Clark, eds. (College Station, Tex., 1990), pp. 76–78.

Warren, Robert Penn. "Irony with a Center: Katherine Anne Porter," *Selected Essays* (New York, 1958), pp. 156–170. (G)

Welty, Eudora. "My Introduction to Katherine Anne Porter," *Georgia Review*, XLIX (Spring/Summer 1990), 13–27. (G)

West, Ray B. "Katherine Anne Porter and 'Historic Memory,'" *Hopkins Review*, VI (Fall 1952), 16–27.

Yaeger, Patricia. "The Poetics of Birth," *Discourses of Sexuality: From Aristotle to Aids* (Ann Arbor, 1992), pp. 27–279.

IRWIN SHAW, "The Girls in Their Summer Dresses"

Baird, Joe L. and Ralph Grajeda. "A Shaw Story and Brooks and Warren," *CEA Critic*, XXVIII (February 1966), 1–4.

Berke, Jacqueline. "Further Observations on 'A Shaw Story and Brooks and Warren'", *CEA Critic*, XXIII (November 1970), 28–29.

Brooks, Cleanth and Robert Penn Warren. *Understanding Fiction* (New York, 1959), 88–90.

Gerlach, John. *Toward the End: Closure and Structure in the American Short Story* (University. Ala., 1985), pp. 124–125.

Giles, James R. *Irwin Shaw* (Boston, 1983), pp. 35–36.

Orvis, Mary. *The Art of Writing Fiction* (New York, 1948), pp. 70–73.

Shnayerson, Michael. *Irwin Shaw: A Biography* (New York, 1989), pp. 88–90.

LESLIE SILKO, "Yellow Woman"

Allen, Paula Gunn. "Kochinnenako in Academe: Three Approaches to Interpreting a Keres Indian Tale," *Leslie Marmon Silko, "Yellow Woman,"* Melody Graulich, ed. (New Brunswick, N.J., 1993), pp. 83–111.

———. "Whirlwind Man Steals Yellow Woman," *Leslie Marmon Silko, "Yellow Woman."* Melody Graulich, ed. (New Brunswick, N.J., 1993), pp. 113–114.

Beidler, Peter. "Silko's Originality in 'Yellow Woman,'" *Studies in American Indian Literature,* 8, No. 2 (1996), 61–84.

Blicksilver, Edith. "Traditional vs. Modernity: Leslie Silko on American Indian Women," *Southwest Review,* LXIV (Spring 1979), 149–160. (G)

Evers, Lawrence J. and Dennis W. Carr, eds. "A Conversation with Leslie Marmon Silko," *Sun Tracks,* III (Fall 1976), 28–33. (G)

Fisher, Dexter. "Stories and Their Tellers—A Conversation with Leslie Marmon Silko," *The Third Woman: Minority Women Writers of the United States,* Dexter Fisher, ed. (Boston, 1980), pp. 18–23. (G)

Graulich, Melody, ed. *Leslie Marmon Silko, "Yellow Woman"* (New Brunswick, N.J., 1993).

Hirsch, Bernard A. "'The Telling Which Continues': Oral Tradition and the Written Word in Leslie Marmon Silko's *Storyteller," Leslie Marmon Silko, "Yellow Woman,"* Melody Graulich, ed. (New Brunswick, N.J., 1993), pp. 151–183.

Jaskoski, Helen. "From the Time Immemorial: Native American Traditions in Contemporary Short Fiction," *Since Flannery O'Connor: Essays on the Contemporary American Short Story,* Loren Logsdon and Charles W. Mayer, eds. (Macomb, Ill., 1987), pp. 54–71. (G)

Larson, Charles R. *American Indian Fiction* (Albuquerque, 1978), pp. 150–151.

Lincoln, Kenneth. "Grandmother Storyteller: Leslie Silko," *Native American Renaissance* (Berkeley, 1983), pp. 222–250, (G)

Lucero, Ambrose. "For the People: Leslie Silko's Storyteller," *Minority Voices,* V (Spring–Fall 1981), 1–10. (G)

Ramsey, Jarold. "The Teacher of Modern American Indian Writing as Ethnographer and Critic," *College English,* XLI (October 1979), 163–169. (G)

Ruoff, A. LaVonne. "Ritual and Renewal: Keres Traditions in the Short Fiction of Leslie Silko," *MELUS,* IV (Winter 1978), 2–17. (G)

Ruppert, Jim. "Story Telling: The Fiction of Leslie Silko," *Journal of Ethnic Studies,* IX (Spring 1981), 53–58. (G)

Seyersted, Per. *Leslie Marmon Silko* (Boise, Idaho, 1980). (G)

———. "Two Interviews with Leslie Marmon Silko," *American Studies in Scandinavia,* XIII (1981), 17–33. (G)

Schweninger, Lee. "Writing Nature: Silko and Native Americans as Nature Writers," *MELUS,* XVIII (Summer 1993), 47–60. (G)

Smith, Patricia Clark, and Paula Gunn Allen. "Earthy Relations, Carnal Knowledge: Southwestern American Indian Women Writers and Landscape," *Leslie Marmon Silko, "Yellow Woman,"* Melody Graulich, ed. (New Brunswick, N.J., 1993), pp. 115–150.

ISAAC BASHEVIS SINGER, "Gimpel the Fool"

Alexander, Edward. *Isaac Bashevis Singer* (Boston, 1980), pp. 143–146.

———. *Isaac Bashevis Singer: A Study of the Short Fiction* (Boston, 1990), pp. 50–52, 108–109.

Beacham, Walton. "Isaac Bashevis Singer," *Critical Survey of Short Fiction,* Frank N. Magill, ed. (Englewood Cliffs, N.J., 1981), VI, 2242–2243.

Bezanker, Abraham. "I.B. Singer's Crisis of Identity," *Critique,* XIV, No. 2 (1972), 70–88. (G)

Buchen, Irving H. "Isaac Bashevis Singer and the Eternal Past," *Critique*, VIII (1966), 5–18. (G)

Eisenberg, J. A. "Isaac Bashevis Singer: Passionate Primitive or Pious Puritan?" *Critical Views of Isaac Bashevis Singer*, Irving Malin, ed. (New York, 1969), pp. 48–67. (G)

Fraustino, Daniel V. "'Gimpel the Fool': Singer's Debt to the Romantics," *Studies in Short Fiction*, XXII (Spring 1985), 228–231.

Friedman, Lawrence S. *Understanding Isaac Bashevis Singer* (Columbia, S.C., 1988), pp. 189–192.

Gittleman, Sol. *From Shtetl to Suburbia: The Family in Jewish Literary Imagination* (Boston, 1978), pp. 103–107.

Goonetilleke, D. C. R. A. "Gimpel the Fool," *Reference Guide to Short Fiction*, Noelle Watson, ed. (Detroit, 1994), pp. 717–718.

Hennings, Thomas. "Singer's 'Gimpel the Fool' and *The Book of Hosea*," *Journal of Narrative Technique*, XIII (Winter 1983), 11–19.

Kazan, Alfred. *Contemporaries* (Boston, 1962), pp. 283–288.

Kresh, Paul. *Isaac Bashevis Singer: The Magician of West 86th Street* (New York, 1979), pp. 203–204.

Lee, Grace Farrell. *From Exile to Redemption: The Fiction of Isaac Bashevis Singer* (Carbondale, Ill., 1997), pp. 15–24.

———. "'Gimpel the Fool': The Kabbalic Basis of Singer's Secular Vision," *Essays in Literature*, XIII (Spring 1986), 157–166.

Malin, Irving. *Isaac Bashevis Singer* (New York, 1972), pp. 70–72.

Morrow, Lance. "The Spirited World of I. B . Singer," *Atlantic Monthly*, CCXLIII (January 1979), 39–43.

Pinsker, Sanford. "The Fictive Worlds of I. B. Singer," *Critique*, XI, No. 2 (1969), 26–39.

———. *The Schlemiel as Metaphor: Studies in the Yiddish and American Jewish Novel* (Carbondale, Ill., 1971), pp. 62–70.

Siegel, Ben. "Sacred and Profane: Isaac Bashevis Singer's Embattled Spirits," *Critique*, VI (Spring 1964), 30–32.

Siegel, Paul N. "Gimpel and the Archetype of the Wise Fool," *The Achievement of Isaac Bashevis Singer*, Marcia Allentuck, ed. (Carbondale and Edwardsville, Ill., 1969), pp. 159–173.

Waxman, Barbara Frey. "Isaac Bashevis Singer's Spirit of Play: Games and Tricks in Some of Singer's Short Stories," *Studies in American Jewish Literature*, N.S. I (1981), 3–13.

Wisse, Ruth R. *The Schlemiel as Modern Hero* (Chicago, 1971), pp. 60–65.

JOHN STEINBECK, "The Chrysanthemums"

Barbour, Brian. "Steinbeck as a Short Story Writer," *A Study Guide to Steinbeck's The Long Valley*, Tetsumaro Hayashi, ed. (Ann Arbor, 1976), 113–128. (G)

Beach, Joseph Warren. *American Fiction, 1920–1940* (New York, 1960), pp. 311–314.

Daniels, Sandy, "Analysis of John Steinbeck's 'The Chrysanthemums,'" *Linguistics in Literature*, V (Spring/Summer 1980), 141–149.

Davison, Richard A. "Hemingway, Steinbeck, and the Art of the Short Story," *Steinbeck Quarterly*, XXI (Summer–Fall 1988), 73–84. (G)

Ditsky, John M. "A Kind of Play: Dramatic Elements in John Steinbeck's 'The Chrysanthemums,'" *Wascana Review*, XXXI (Spring 1986), 62–72.

Fontenrose, Joseph. *John Steinbeck: An Introduction and Interpretation* (New York, 1963), pp. 61–62.

Gullason, Thomas A. "Revelation and Evolution: A Neglected Dimension of the Short Story," *Studies in Short Fiction*, X (Fall 1973), 352–355.

Higdon, David Leon. "The Chrysanthemums," *Reference Guide to Short Fiction*, Noelle Watson, ed. (Detroit, 1994), pp. 667–668.

———. "Dionysian Madness in Steinbeck's 'The Chrysanthemums,'" *Classical and Modern Literature*, XI (Fall 1990). 59–65.

Hughes, R. S. *Beyond the Red Pony: A Reader's Companion to Steinbeck's Complete Short Stories* (Metuchen, N.J., 1987), pp. 58–62.

———. *John Steinbeck: A Study of the Short Fiction* (Boston, 1989), pp. 21–27, 154–165.

McMahan, Elizabeth E. "'The Chrysanthemums': Study of a Woman's Sexuality," *Modern Fiction Studies*, XIV (Winter 1968–1969), 453–458.

Male, Roy B. *Enter, Mysterious Stranger: American Cloistral Fiction* (Norman, Okla., 1979), pp. 66–68.

Marcus, Mordecai. "The Lost Dream of Sex and Children in 'The Chrysanthemums,'" *Modern Fiction Studies*, XI (Spring 1965), 54–58.

Matsumoto, Fusae. "Steinbeck's Women in *The Long Valley*," *John Steinbeck: East and West*, Tetsumaro Hayashi, Yasuo Hashiguchi, and Richard F. Peterson, eds. *Steinbeck Monograph Series*, No. 8 (1978), pp. 50–52.

Mellard, James M. *Four Modes: A Rhetoric of Modern Fiction* (New York, 1973), pp. 272–277.

Miller, William V. "Sexual and Spiritual Ambiguity in 'The Chrysanthemums,'" *Steinbeck Quarterly*, V (Summer–Fall 1972), 68–75.

Mitchell, Marilyn. "Steinbeck's Strong Women: Feminine Identity in the Short Stories," *Southwest Review*, LXI (Summer 1976), 304–325.

Noonan, Gerald. "A Note on 'The Chrysanthemums,'" *Modern Fiction Studies*, XV (Winter 1969–1970), 542.

Osborne, William. "The Education of Elisa Allen: Another Reading of John Steinbeck's 'The Chrysanthemums,'" *Interpretations*, VIII (1976), 10–15.

———. "The Texts of Steinbeck's 'The Chrysanthemums,'" *Modern Fiction Studies*, XII (Winter 1966–1967), 479–484.

Owens, Louis, *John Steinbeck's Re-vision of America* (Athens, Ga., 1985), pp. 108–113.

Pellow, C. Kenneth. "'The Chrysanthemums' Revisited," *Steinbeck Quarterly*, XXII (Winter–Spring 1989), 8–16.

Renner, Stanley. "The Real Woman Inside the Fence in 'The Chrysanthemums,'" *Modern Fiction Studies*, XXXI (Summer 1985), 305–317.

Rohrberger, Mary. "The Questions of Regionalism: Limitation and Transcendence," *The American Short Story, 1900–1945*, Philip Stevick, ed. (Boston, 1984), pp. 179–180.

Shillinglaw, Susan. "'The Chrysanthemums': Steinbeck's *Pygmalion*," *Steinbeck's Short Stories in "The Long Valley": Essays in Criticism*, Tetsumaro Hayashi ed. (Muncie, Ind., 1991), pp. 1–9.

Simmonds, Roy S. "The Original Manuscripts of Steinbeck's 'The Chrysanthemums,'" *Steinbeck Quarterly*, VII (Summer–Fall 1974), 102–111.

Sullivan, Ernest W., II. "The Cur in 'The Chrysanthemums,'" *Studies in Short Fiction*, XVI (Summer 1979), 215–217.

Sweet, Charles. "Ms. Elisa Allen and Steinbeck's 'The Chrysanthemums,'" *Modern Fiction Studies* XX (Summer 1974), 210–214.

Thomas, Leroy. "Steinbeck's 'The Chrysanthemums,'" *Explicator*, XLV (Spring 1987), 50–51.

Timmerman, John T. *The Dramatic Landscape of Steinbeck's Short Stories* (Norman, Okla., 1990), pp. 169–177.

———. *John Steinbeck's Fiction: The Aesthetics of the Road Taken* (Norman, Okla., 1986), pp. 63–68.

Watt, F. W. *John Steinbeck* (New York, 1962), pp. 42–44.

West, Ray B. *The Short Story in America, 1900–1950* (Chicago, 1952), pp. 48–50.

Wyatt, David. *The Fall Into Eden: Landscape and Imagination in California* (Cambridge, England, 1986), pp. 138–141.

Yano, Shigeharu. "Psychological Interpretations of Steinbeck's Women in *The Long Valley*," *John Steinbeck: East and West*, Tetsumaro Hayashi, Yasuo Hashiguchi, and Richard F. Peterson, eds., Steinbeck Monograph Series, No. 8 (1978), pp. 54–60. (G)

ELIZABETH TALLENT, "No One's a Mystery"

Hornby, Nick. *Contemporary American Fiction* (London, 1992), pp. 7–29. (G)

AMY TAN, "Young Girl's Wish"

Shear, Walter. "Generational Differences and the Diaspora in *The Joy Luck Club*," *Critique*, XXXIV (Spring 1993), 193–199. (G)

LEO TOLSTOY, "The Death of Ivan Ilych "

Bartell, James. "The Trauma of Birth in 'The Death of Ivan Ilych': A Therapeutic Reading," *Psychocultural Review*, II (Spring 1978), 97–117.

Beaty, James. *The Norton Introduction to the Short Novel* (New York, 1982), pp. 88–91.

Cain, T. G. S. *Tolstoy*, (London, 1977), pp. 159–164.

Cate, Hollis L. "On Death and Dying in Tolstoy's 'The Death of Ivan Ilych,'" *Hartford Studies in Literature*, VII (1975), 195–205.

Christian, R. F. *Tolstoy: A Critical Introduction* (Cambridge, England, 1969), pp. 236–238.

Comstock, Gary. "Face to Face with *It*: The Naive Reader's Moral Response to 'Ivan Ilych,'" *Neophilologus*, LXX (1986), 321–333.

Costa, Richard Hauer. "Maugham's 'Partial Self': The 'Unexpected View' on the Way to 'The Death of Ivan Ilych,'" *CEA Critic*, XLIII (May 1981), 3 –7.

Dayananda, Y. J. "'The Death of Ivan Ilych': A Psychological Study 'On Death and Dying,'" *Literature and Psychology*, XXII, No. 4 (1972), 191–197.

Donnelly, John. "Death and Ivan Ilych," *Language, Metaphysics, and Death*, John Donnelly ed. (New York, 1978), pp. 116–130.

Eng, Jan van der. "'The Death of Ivan Ilych': The Construction of the Theme; Some Aspects of Language and Time," *Russian Literature*, VII (March 1979), 159–189.

Engleberg, Edward. *Elegiac Fictions: The Motif of the Unlived Life* (University Park, Pa., 1989), pp. 87–96.

Glicksberg, Charles L. "Tolstoy and 'The Death of Ivan Ilych,'" *The Ironic Vision in Modern Literature* (The Hague, 1969), pp. 81–86.

Greenwood, E. B. *Tolstoy: The Comprehensive Vision* (New York, 1975), pp. 120–125.

Gustafson, Richard F. *Leo Tolstoy: Resident and Stranger* (Princeton, 1981), pp. 155–160.

Gutsche, George J. *Moral Appostasy in Russian Literature* (De Kalb, Ill., 1986), pp. 70–98.

Halperin, Irving. "The Structural Integrity of 'The Death of Ivan Ilych,'" *Slavic and East European Journal*, V (Winter 1961), 334–360.

Harder, Worth T. "Granny and Ivan: Katherine Anne Porter's Mirror for Tolstoy," *Renascence*, XLII (Spring 1990), 149–156.

Hirschberg, W. R., "Tolstoy's 'The Death of Ivan Ilych,'" *Explicator*, XXCIII (December 1969), Item 26.

Howe, Irving. *Classics of Modern Fiction: Ten Short Novels* (New York, 1972), pp. 113–121.

Jahn, Gary R. *"The Death of Ivan Ilych": An Interpretation* (New York, 1993).

————. "The Role of the Ending in Leo Tolstoy's 'The Death of Ivan Il'ich,'" *Canadian Slavic Papers*, XXIV (1982), 229–234.

Jarrell, Randall. *Third Book of Criticism* (New York, 1965), pp. 254–267.

Lisker, Sheldon A. "Literature and the Dying Patient," *Pennsylvania English*, XII, i (1985), 5–9.

McEwen, Fred B. "Count Leo Tolstoy," *Critical Survey of Short Fiction*, Frank N. Magill, ed. (Englewood Cliffs, N.J., 1981), VI, 2335–2337.

Meyers, Jeffrey. *Disease and the Novel, 1880–1960* (New York, 1985), pp. 19–29.

Napier, James L. "The Stages of Dying in 'The Death of Ivan Ilych,'" *College Literature*, X (1993), 147–157.

Olney, James. "Experience, Metaphor, and Meaning: 'The Death of Ivan Ilych,'" *Journal of Aesthetics and Art Criticism*, XXXI (1972), 101–114.

Pachmuss, Temira. "The Theme of Love and Death in Tolstoy's 'The Death of Ivan Ilych,'" *American Slavic and East European Review*, XX (1961), 72–83.

Parr, Susan B. *The Moral of the Story: Literature, Values, and American Education* (New York, 1982), pp. 53–60.

Parthe, Kathleen. "The Metamorphosis of Death in Tolstoy," *Language Sciences*, XVIII (1985), 205–214.

Rahv, Philip. "The Death of Ivan Ilych and Joseph K.," *Southern Review*, V (Summer 1939), 174–185.

Reeve, F. D. *The Russian Novel* (New York, 1966), pp. 262–266.

Russell, Robert. "From Individual to Universal: 'Smert Ivana Il'icha,'" *Modern Language Review*, LXXVI (1981), 629–642.

Salys, Rima. "Signs of the Road of Life: 'The Death of Ivan Il'ic,'" *Slavic and East European Journal*, XXX (1986), 19–28.

Schaarschmidt, Gunter. "Time and Discourse Structure in 'The Death of Ivan Il'ich,'" *Canadian Slavonic Papers*, XXI (September 1979), 356–366.

Simmons, Ernest J. *Introduction of Tolstoy's Writings* (Chicago, 1968), pp. 148–150.

Smyrniw, Walter. "Tolstoy's Depiction of Death in the Context of Recent Studies of the 'Experience of Dying,'" *Canadian Slavonic Papers*, XXI (1979), 367–379.

Sorokin, Boris. "Ivan Ilych as Jonah: A Cruel Joke," *Canadian Slavic Studies*, V (Winter 1971), 487–507.

Spanos, William V. "Leo Tolstoy's 'The Death of Ivan Ilych': A Temporal Interpretation," *De-Structing the Novel: Essays in Applied Postmodern Hermeneutics*, Leonard Orr, ed. (Troy, N.Y., 1982), pp. 1–64.

Speirs, Logan. *Tolstoy and Chekhov* (Cambridge, England, 1971), pp. 141–147.

Spence, G. W. *Tolstoy the Ascetic* (New York, 1968), pp. 63–68.

Trilling, Lionel. *Prefaces to the Experience of Literature* (New York, 1979), pp. 84–88.

Turner, C. J. G. "The Language of Fiction: Word Clusters in Tolstoy's 'The Death of Ivan Ilych,'" *Modern Language Review*, LXV (January 1970), 116–121.

Vannata, Dennis. "The Death of Ivan Ilych," *Reference Guide to Short Fiction*, Noelle Watson, ed. (Detroit, 1994), pp. 686–687.

Votteler, Thomas, ed. *Short Story Criticism: Excerpts from Criticism of the Works of Short Fiction Writers*, IX (Detroit, 1992), 362–408. (G)

Wasiolek, Edward. "Tolstoy's 'The Death of Ivan Ilych' and Jamesian Fictional Imperatives," *Modern Fiction Studies*, VI (Winter 1960–1961), 314–324.

————. *Tolstoy: The Major Fiction* (Chicago, 1979), pp. 165–179.

Wexelblatt, Robert. "The Higher Parody: Ivan Ilych's Metamorphosis and the Death of Gregor Samsa," *Massachusetts Review*, XXI (Fall 1980), 601–628.

Williams, Michael V. "Tolstoy's 'The Death of Ivan Ilych': After the Fall," *Studies in Short Fiction*, XXI (Summer 1984), 229–234.

Wiltshire, John. "The Argument of Ivan Ilych's Death," *Critical Review*, XXIV (1982), 46–54.

Winn, Harbour. "Hemingway's African Stories in Tolstoy's Ivan,'" *Studies in Short Fiction*, XVIII (Fall 1981), 451–453.

Zimmerman, Eugenia N. "Death and Transfiguration in Proust and Tolstoy," *Mosaic*, VI (Winter 1983), 161–172.

IVAN TURGENEV, "The Country Doctor"

Lainoff, Seymour. "The Country Doctors of Kafka and Turgenev," *Symposium*, XV, (Summer 1962), 130–135.

Masing-Delia, Irene. "Philosophy, Myth, and Art in Turgenev's Notes of a Hunter," *Russian Review*, L (1991), 441–443.

Seeley, Frank F. *Turgenev: A Reading of His Fiction* (Cambridge, Eng., 1991), pp. 104–105.

Struc, Roman S. "The Doctor's Predicament: A Note on Turgenev and Kafka," *Slavic and East European Journal*, IX (Summer 1965), 174–180.

JOHN UPDIKE, "A&P"

Burchea, Rachael C. "The Short Stories," *John Updike: Yea Sayings* (Carbondale, Ill., 1971), pp. 133–159. (G)

Dessner, Lawrence J. "Irony and Innocence in John Updike's 'A&P,'" *Studies in Short Fiction*, XXV (Summer 1988), 315–317.

Detweiler, Robert. *John Updike* (New York, 1972), pp. 67–69.

Doyle, Paul A. "Updike's Fiction: Motifs and Techniques," *Catholic World*, CIC (September 1964), 356–362, (G)

Emmett, Paul J. "A Slip That Shows Updike's 'A&P,'" *Notes on Contemporary Literature*, XV (March 1985), 9–11.

Fisher, Richard E. "John Updike: Theme and Form in the Garden of Epiphanies," *Moderna Språk*, LVI (1962), 255–260.

Fleischauer, John F. "John Updike's Prose Style: Definition at the Periphery of Meaning," *Critique*, XXX (Summer 1989), 277–290.

Flynn, Elizabeth A. "Composing Responses to Literary Texts: A Process Approach," *College Composition and Communication*, XXXIV (October 1983), 342–348.

Gilbert, Porter A. "John Updike's 'A&P': The Establishment and an Emersonian Cashier," *English Journal*, LXI (November 1972), 1155–1158.

Gingher, Robert S. "Has John Updike Anything to Say?" *Modern Fiction Studies*, XX (Spring 1974), 97–105.

Greiner, Donald J. *The Other John Updike: Poems, Short Stories, Prose, Plays* (Athens, Ohio, 1981), pp. 117–119.

Gross, Marjorie Hill. "Widening Perceptions in Updike's 'A&P,'" *Notes on Contemporary Literature*, XIV (November 1984), 8–9.

Hurley, C. Harold. "Updike's 'A&P': An 'Initial Response,'" *Notes on Contemporary Literature*," XX (May 1990), 12.

Jacoby, Jay. "Authority in English 102: Whose Text Is It Anyway.?" *CEA Critic*, LII (Fall 1989–Winter 1990), 2–12.

Kellner, Bruce. "A&P," *Reference Guide to Short Fiction*, Noelle Watson, ed. (Detroit, 1994), pp. 617–618.

Lucking, Robert A. "Updike and the Concerned Reader," *Arizona English Bulletin*, XVI (April 1974), 111–117. (G)

Luscher, Robert M. *John Updike: A Study of the Short Fiction* (New York, 1993), pp. 35–37.

McFarland, Ronald E. "Updike and the Critics: Reflections on 'A&P,'" *Studies in Short Fiction*, XX (Spring–Summer 1983), 95–100.

Muradian, Thaddeus. "The World of John Updike," *English Journal*, LIV (October 1965), 577–584. (G)

Oates, Joyce Carol. "Updike's American Comedies," *Modern Fiction Studies*, XXI (1975), 459–472.(G)

Overmeyer, Janet. "Courtly Love in the A&P," *Notes on Contemporary Literature*, II (May 1972), 4–5.

Peden, William. *The American Short Story: Continuity and Change, 1940–1975* (Boston, 1975), pp. 47–53. (G)

Petry, Alice H. "The Dress Code in Updike's 'A&P,'" *Notes on Contemporary Literature*, XVI, I (1986), 8–10.

Rupp, Richard H. "John Updike: Style in Search of a Center ," *Sewanee Review*, LXXV (Autumn 1967), 693–709. (G)

Schiff, James A. *John Updike Revisited* (New York, 1998), pp. 114–117.

Shaw, Patrick W. "Checking Out Faith and Lust: Hawthorne's 'Young Goodman Brown' and Updike's 'A&P,'" *Studies in Short Fiction*, XXIII (Summer 1996), 321–323.

Uphaus, Suzanne. *John Updike* (New York, 1980), pp. 124–127.

Waxman, Robert E. "Invitations to Dread: John Updike's Metaphysical Quest," *Renascence*, XXIX (Summer 1977), 201–210.

Wells, Walter. "John Updike's 'A&P': A Return to Araby," *Studies in Short Fiction*, XXX (Spring 1993), 127–133.

JOHN UPDIKE, "Here Come the Maples"

Detweiler, Robert. *John Updike* (Boston, 1984), pp. 170–171.

Uphaus, Suzanne. *John Updike* (New York, 1980), pp. 129–130.

Wilhelm, Albert E. "The Trail-of-the-Bread-Crumbs Motif in Updike's Maples Stories," *Studies in Short Fiction*, 25 (Winter 1988), 71–73.

JOHN UPDIKE, "Separating"

Luscher, Robert M. *John Updike: A Study of the Short Fiction* (New York, 1993), pp. 117–118.

Schiff, James A. *John Updike Revisited* (New York, 1998), pp. 121–126.

Segal, David, ed. *Short Story Criticism: Excerpts from Criticism of the Works of Short Fiction Writers*, XIII (Detroit, 1993), p. 387.

Uphaus, Suzanne. *John Updike* (New York, 1980), pp. 127–130. (G)

Wilhelm, Albert E. "Rebecca Cune: Updike's Wedge Between the Maples," *Notes on Modern American Literature*, VII (Fall 1983), 5–7.

ALICE WALKER, "To Hell with Dying"

Byerman, Keith E. *Fingering the Jagged Grain: Tradition and Form in Recent Black Fiction* (Athens, Ga., 1985), pp. 128–170. (G)

Christian, Barbara. *Black Feminist Criticism: Perspectives on Black Women Writers* (New York, 1985), pp. 31–46, 81–101. (G)

Cooke, Michael G. *Afro-American Literature in the Twentieth Century: The Achievement of Intimacy* (New Haven, 1984), pp. 157–176. (G)

Erickson, Peter. "Cast Out Alone/To Heal/and Recreate/Ourselves: Family Based Identity in the Work of Alice Walker," *CLA Journal*, XXIII (September 1979), 71–94. (G)

Hollister, Michael. "Tradition in Alice Walker's 'To Hell with Dying,'" *Studies in Short Fiction*, XXVI (Winter 1989), 90–94.

Hubbard, Dolan. "Society and Self in Alice Walker's *In Love and Trouble*," *American Woman Short Story Writers: A Collection of Critical Essays* (New York, 1995), pp. 211–213.

Jarrett, Mary. "The Idea of Audience in the Short Stories of Zora Neale Hurston and Alice Walker," *Journal of the Short Story in English*, XII (Spring 1989), 37–38.

Mickelson, Anne Z. *Reaching Out: Sensitivity and Order in Recent American Fiction by Women* (Metuchen, N.J., 1979), pp. 154–174. (G)

Petry, Alice Hall. "Alice Walker: The Achievement of the Short Fiction," *Modern Language Studies*, XIX (Winter 1989), 12–27. (G)

Snyder, Phillip A. "To Hell with Dying," *Reference Guide to Short Fiction*, Noelle Watson, ed. (Detroit, 1994), pp. 933–934.

Wade-Gayles, Gloria. "Black, Southern, Womanist: The Genius of Alice Walker," *Southern Women Writers: The New Generation*, Tonette Bond Inge, ed. (Tuscaloosa, Ala., 1990), pp. 301–323. (G)

Washington, J. Charles. "Positive Black Male Images in Alice Walker's Fiction," *Obsidian: Black Literature in Review*, III (Spring 1988), 23–48.

EUDORA WELTY, "Why I Live at the P.O."

Appel, Alfred, Jr. *A Season of Dreams: The Fiction of Eudora Welty* (Baton Rouge, 1963), pp.46–51.

Binding, Paul. *The Still Moment: Eudora Welty, Portrait of a Writer* (London, 1994), pp. 216–218.

Blackwell, Louise, "Eudora Welty and the Rubber Fence Family," *Kansas Magazine* (1965), 73–76.

Bryant, J. A. *Eudora Welty* (Minneapolis, 1968), pp. 8–9.

Buswell, Mary Catherine. "The Love Relationships of Women in the Fiction of Eudora Welty," *West Virginia University Bulletin: Philological Papers*, 13 (1961), 94–106.

Champion, Laurie. ed. *The Critical Response to Eudora Welty's Fiction* (Westport, Conn., 1994), pp. 43–48.

Daniel, Robert W. "Eudora Welty: The Sense of Place," *South: Modern Literature in Its Cultural Setting*, Louis D. Rubin and Robert D. Jacobs, eds. (Garden City, N.Y., 1961), pp. 276–286. (G)

Drake, Robert Y., Jr. "Comments on Two Eudora Welty Stories," *Mississippi Quarterly*, XIII (Summer 1960), 126–131.

DuPriest, Travis. "'Why I Live at the P.O.': Eudora Welty's Epic Question," *Christianity & Literature* XXXI, iv (1982), 45–54.

Eisenger, Chester E. "Traditionalism and Modernism in Eudora Welty," *Eudora Welty: Critical Essays*, Peggy Prenshaw, ed. (Jackson, Miss., 1979), pp. 3–25.

Ferris, Bill. "A Visit with Eudora Welty," *Images of the South: Visits With Eudora Welty and Walker Percy*, Bill Ferris, ed. (Memphis, 1977), pp. 11–26.

Glenn, Eunice. "Fantasy in the Fiction of Eudora Welty," *Critique and Essays on Modern Fiction*, John W. Aldridge, ed. (New York, 1992), pp. 606–517. (G)

Graves, Nora Calhoun. "Shirley-T. in Eudora Welty's 'Why I Live at the P.O.,'" *Notes on Contemporary Literature*, VII (March 1977). 6–7.

Gretlund, Jan Norby. *Eudora Welty's Aesthetics of Place* (Newark, Del., 1994), pp. 118–121.

Herrscher, Walter. "Is Sister Really Insane? Another Look at 'Why I Live at the P.O.,'" *Notes on Contemporary Literature* V (January 1975), 5–7.

Howard, Maureen. "The Collected Stories of Eudora Welty," *New York Times Book Review* (November 1, 1980), 1, 31–32. (G)

Isaac, Neil D. *Eudora Welty* (Austin, Tx., 1969). (G)

Johnston, Carol Ann. *Eudora Welty: A Study of the Short Stories* (New York, 1997), pp. 16–19.

Jones, Alun R. "The World of Love: The Fiction of Eudora Welty," *The Creative Present: Notes on Contemporary American Fiction*, Nona Balakian and Charles Simmons, eds. (New York, 1963), pp. 273–192. (G)

Jones, Anne Goodwyn. "The Incredible Shrinking You-Know-What: Southern Women's Humor," *Southern Cultures*, I (Summer 1995), 467–472. (G)

Jones, William M. "Name and Symbol in the Prose of Eudora Welty," *Southern Folklore Quarterly*, XXII (June 1958), 178–179.

Lewis, T. N. "Textual Variants in 'Why I Live at the P.O.,'" *Eudora Welty Newsletter*, XII (Summer 1988), 1–6.

Loe, Thomas. "Why I Live at the P. O.," *Reference Guide to Short Fiction*, Noelle Watson ed. (Detroit, 1994), p. 973.

Maclay, Joanna. "A Conversation with Eudora Welty," *Conversations with Eudora Welty*, Peggy Prenshaw, ed. (Jackson, Miss., 1984), pp. 258–277.

May, Charles, E. "Why Sister Lives at the P.O.," *Southern Humanities Review*, XII (Summer 1978), 243–249.

Murphy, Christina. *Critical Survey of Short Fiction*, Frank Magill, ed. (Englewood Cliffs, NJ, 1981), VI, 2415–2416.

Nissen, Axel. "Occasional Travelers in China Grove: Welty's 'Why I Live at the P. O.' Reconsidered," *Southern Quarterly*, XXXII, 1 (1993), 72–79.

Pickett, Nell Ann. "Colloquialism as Style in the First-Person-Narrator Fiction of Eudora Welty," *Mississippi Quarterly*, XXVI (Fall 1973), 572–576.

Pingatore, Diana R. *A Reader's Guide to the Short Stories of Eudora Welty* (New York, 1996), pp. 69–79.

Reesman, Jeanne Campbell. "Women, Language and the Grotesque in Flannery O'Connor and Eudora Welty," *Flannery O'Connor: New Perspectives*, Sura P. Rath and Mary Neff, eds. (Athens, Ga., 1996), pp. 38–56. (G)

Romines, Ann. "How Not to Tell a Story: Eudora Welty's First-Person Tales," *Eudora Welty: Eye of the Storyteller*, Dawn Trouard, ed. (Kent, Ohio, 1989), pp. 94–100.

Schmidt, Peter. *The Heart of the Story: Eudora Welty's Short Fiction* (Jackson, Miss., 1991), pp. 112–120.

Semel, Jay M. "Eudora Welty's Freak Show: A Pattern in 'Why I Live at the P.O.,'" *Notes on Contemporary Literature*, III (May 1973), 2–3.

Shaw, Valerie. *The Short Story: A Critical Introduction* (London, 1983), pp. 107–109.

Skaggs, Merrill Maguire. *The Folk of Southern Fiction* (Athens, Ga., 1972), pp. 243–244.

Tarbox, Raymond. "Eudora Welty's Fiction: The Salvation Theme," *American Imago*, 29 (Spring 1972), 70–91.

Vande Kieft, Ruth M. *Eudora Welty* (New York, 1963), pp. 67–69.

Wages, Jack D. "Names in Eudora Welty's Fiction: An Onomatological Prolegomenon," *Love and Wresting: Butch and O.K.*, Fred Tarplay, ed. (Commerce, Tx., 1973), pp. 65–70.

Warren, Robert Penn. *Selected Essays* (New York, 1958), pp. 156–169. (G)

Welty, Eudora. *Conversations with Eudora Welty*, Peggy Whitman Prenshaw, ed. (Jackson, Miss., 1984), pp. 19–20, 25, 160–161, 330–331.

Whitaker, Elaine E. "Welty's 'Why I Live at the P.O.,'" *Explicator*, L (Winter 1992), 115–117.

JOY WILLIAMS, "Taking Care"

Hornby, Nick. *Contemporary American Fiction* (London, 1992), pp. 124–132. (G)

WILLIAM CARLOS WILLIAMS, "The Use of Force"

Breman, Brian A. *William Carlos Williams and the Diagnostics of Culture* (Oxford., Eng., 1993), pp. 87, 98–102.

Coles, Robert. *William Carlos Williams: The Knack of Survival in America* (New Brunswick, N.J., 1975), pp. 58–59.

Dietrich, R. F. "Connotations of Rape in 'The Use of Force,'" *Studies in Short Fiction*, 3 (Summer 1966), 446–450.

Slate, J. E. "William Carlos Williams and the Modern Short Story," *Southern Review*, 4 (1968), 647–664.

Wagner, Linda. "Williams' 'The Use of Force': An Expansion," *Studies in Short Fiction*, 4 (Summer 1967), 351–353.

Watson, James G. "The American Short Story: 1930–1945," *The American Short Story*, Philip Stevick, ed. (Boston, 1984), pp. 120–121.